ALSO BY BEN MARCUS

The Age of Wire and String

Notable American Women

The Father Costume

The Anchor Book of New American Short Stories (editor)

The Flame Alphabet

Leaving the Sea

BEN MARCUS

≡ NEW AMERICAN STORIES ≡

Ben Marcus is the author of four books of fiction, *The Age of Wire and String*, *Notable American Women*, *The Flame Alphabet*, and *Leaving the
Sea*, and he is the editor of *The Anchor Book of
New American Short Stories*. His stories have
appeared in *Harper's*, *The New Yorker*, *Granta*, *The
Paris Review*, *McSweeney's*, *Tin House*, and *Con-
junctions*. Among his awards are the Berlin Prize,
a Guggenheim Fellowship, and a Whiting Writers'
Award. He lives in New York, where he is on the
faculty at Columbia University.

www.benmarcus.com

NEW AMERICAN STORIES

NEW
AMERICAN
STORIES

Edited by Ben Marcus

VINTAGE CONTEMPORARIES
Vintage Books
A Division of Penguin Random House LLC
New York

A VINTAGE CONTEMPORARIES ORIGINAL, JULY 2015

The Library of Congress Cataloging-in-Publication Data
New American stories / Ben Marcus.
pages cm.—(Vintage contemporaries original)
1. Short stories, American—21st century.   2. Short stories, American—20th century.
3. American fiction—21st century.   4. American fiction—20th century.
I. Marcus, Ben, 1967– editor.   II. Title.
PS648.S5N37 2015   813'.010806—dc23   2014048489

Vintage Books Trade Paperback ISBN: 978-0-8041-7354-4
eBook ISBN: 978-0-8041-7355-1

Book design by Stephanie Moss

www.vintagebooks.com

Printed in the United States of America
10 9 8 7 6 5 4 3 2 1

CONTENTS

INTRODUCTION

There is a game I play with my young son. He shuts his eyes while I sneak to the shadows with my weapon. On the dark side of a bookcase, concealed by a doorway, I stand and wait. I stifle my breathing, and the game begins.

My son does his best to avoid capture, even though he circles my hideout, risking the worst. He cannot yet play this game silently. He advertises his location with badly muffled squeals. He sprints through rooms, taking the corners too fast. He'll stumble, wipe out, right himself, and charge again. I always hear him coming. Maybe he wants to be captured just as much as he dreads it, but you can hear the conflict thumping inside him. He produces frightening sounds, a pure bullet of feeling. How does one body hold so much? What will I do when he grows up and learns to conceal this feeling, or, worse, when the feeling stops rising up so strongly in the first place?

My son can't be sure where or when the ambush is coming. But it always does. When he tears past me I roar from his blind spot, ensnaring him in a blanket. Down he goes, kicking and laughing, a thrashing little figure under cloth. I close the bundle, cinch it in my fist, and drag it from room to room.

My son is five now, as easy to lift as a pillow. I hoist him over my head, teeter on one leg for suspense, then plunge him onto the couch. He bounces high, still tucked inside the blanket. I hold on tight and swing until we're spinning. His little voice drifts up from far away. Inside his trap he is in heaven, or so it sounds. I swing him and drag him and toss him until I'm ready to collapse. When I let him go he is red and sweaty and wild. Usually he glares at me. Why did I stop? What is wrong with me? He begs, begs, for us to play again. It's all he wants to do. He promises not to peek, and I steal off to hide again.

My son would not put it this way, because he knows better than to try to dissect his own pleasure. But he is asking to be amazed and afraid in this situation we've contrived. He cannot really come to harm—the boy is so small that it is child's play to keep him safe—but by surrendering control, submitting himself to the darkness, to the fast passage inside a careening world, he can take himself to the bursting point. He is looking to suddenly feel a great many things, and to feel them intensely, inside this fictional crisis. And I can't blame him, because, more and more, I would like that very same thing.

When I want to be ambushed, captured, thrust into a strange and vivid world, and tossed aloft until I cannot stand it, until everything is at stake and life feels almost unbearably vivid, I do something simple. I read short stories. When I was young I read fiction because nothing much happened to me. As a reader I could fight a war, lose a father, be pushed from a bridge with a noose over my neck. I could grow up and grow old, turn angry and sad. I could love and hate and harm and get away with it. In stories I had children of my own, got divorced, worried, wondered, rode shotgun inside intellects far swifter than mine. My earliest reading was not just a romance with what was possible, but a romance with what was not. If something was never likely to happen in real life, I was doubly committed to live it in fiction. I think back to when I have had the most intense feelings, and most often those moments resulted not from cruising through a so-called real world of bodies and things, collecting actual experiences. Those feelings arose out of something invisible yet strangely more powerful: the language of others. Language has made some of the most durable feeling this world has seen. Not the functional kind of language we bleat at each other out in the world when we want something, or need to declare or deny something. Not the quotidian language that showers down everywhere around us to block us from our true thoughts. I'm thinking of the much more unusual and spell-like language of fiction, which generally does not occur out loud: razored, miraculously placed, set like stones into staggeringly complex patterns so that, somehow, life, or something more distilled and intense, more consistently moving, gets made.

I have been reading stories for forty-two years and I still find it astonishing that, by staring at skeletal marks on paper or a screen, we can invite such cyclones of feeling into our bodies. It is a kind of miracle. Our skin is never pierced and yet stories break the barrier and infect us regardless. We study these marks, move our finger along them, and they transmit worlds. If we could paint what happens between the page and our face, the signal channel saturated with color and shape, the imagery would be so tangled that the picture would blacken into pure noise, a dark architecture of everything that matters.

A story is simply a sequence of language that produces a chemical reaction in our bodies. When it's done well, it causes sorrow, elation, awe, fascination. It makes us believe in what's not there, but it also pours color over what is, so that we can feel and see the world anew. It fashions people, makes us care for them, then ladles them with conflict and disap-

pointment. It erects towns, then razes them. A story switches
on some unfathomably sophisticated machine inside us and
we see, gloriously, what is not possible.

And yet language is a prickly delivery system. It requires
attention, effort. It does not produce reliable results across
the population. The same text that makes one person weep
makes another blink with indifference or spit with contempt. By reading more, and more variously, we decimate
our immunity, increase our vulnerability to this substance,
but our private wiring does something profoundly subjective
to this material that would seem unique from body to body.
Language turns out to be the most unruly of medicines, the
most unknowable, and yet, provided we collaborate with it,
still among the most powerful.

Language is a drug, but a short story cannot be smoked.
You can't inject it. Stories don't come bottled as a cream.
You cannot have a story massaged into you by a bearish
old man. You have to stare down a story until it wobbles,
yields, then catapults into your face. But as squirrely as they
are to capture, stories are the ideal deranger. If they are
well made, and you submit to them, they go in clean. Stories
deliver their chemical disruption without the ashy hangover,
the blacking out, the poison. They trigger pleasure, fear, fascination, love, confusion, desire, repulsion. Drugs get flushed
from our systems, but not the best stories. Once they take hold,
you couldn't scrape them out with a knife. While working
on this book, I started to think of it as a medicine chest, filled
with beguiling, volatile material, designed by the most gifted
technicians. The potent story writers, to me, are the ones
who deploy language as a kind of contraband, pumping it
into us until we collapse on the floor, writhing, overwhelmed
with feeling.

Imagine trying to assert the importance of water. Food.

Love. The company of others. Shelter. There are some things
that we need so innately that it feels awkward and difficult
to explain why. To this list of crucial things, without which
we might perish, I would add stories. A short story works to
remind us that if we are not sometimes baffled and amazed
and undone by the world around us, rendered speechless and
stunned, perhaps we are not paying close enough attention.

In high school I made mix tapes for girls. The term for this
now would be playlist. You can create one with a few clicks,
and no one much cares. Back then a mix tape was an act of
love, a plea, a Hail Mary, an aphrodisiac. In other words, it
was an anthology, published in a limited edition of one copy.
Then it was surrendered to an audience of one, a girl not even
guaranteed to listen to it, because sometimes it must have
seemed like it was made by a stalker, a creep, a card-carrying
freak. To make a mix tape, before computers, you needed a
mule cart, a bag of hair, and a padded suit. It seemed to take
a whole year to produce, and I wasn't even one of those kids
who decorated the case with snakeskin and neon markers. I
just dumped songs from one tape to another, pulling from the
vast catalog of seventeen albums and twenty-four cassettes
that I owned. And when I handed it off to some poor girl, she
might regard it as a grim example of my biology, dropping it
like medical waste into her bag. The tape needed to perform
the charm and seduction that, with my own body and words,
I could not. Not that I didn't try. I wrote plenty of poetry in
a literary tradition that never took off: the wrong words in
the wrong order. And even though I hoped some handcrafted
poems would reveal me as a person worth shucking one's
clothing for, my verse was embarrassing, far too easy to understand. I had yet to realize how easy it is to dismiss what comes

to us with no thought, no struggle. If there is nothing left to think about, we stop thinking. I did not understand that my poetry needed to at least seem eligible for further reflection. It had no time-release feature, as do the stories in this anthology, to crack open in the body days later, bleeding out inside us until we start to glow. Obviousness was a clear turnoff. My poetry shut people down, maybe invited death into the home. I'm sure my fondness for rhyme didn't help, either.

I also made a classic mistake. I confused the description of feelings with the creation of them. I wanted to cause feeling in others, but all I did was assert, somewhat grandiosely, that I had feelings myself. This is an unpleasant thing to announce. I had a lot to learn.

So I retreated from creation to curation. As with the stories in this anthology, I chose music that somehow, in ways I could not understand, came spring-loaded with insights about me, a youth from nowhere who knew no one, who had said and done precisely nothing that mattered. The songs I liked already intuited what I thought and felt, deep within my well-guarded interior. No doubt this wasn't particularly difficult, because I had not thought or felt all that much yet. But this feeling—of being known, understood, seen, accounted for—seemed in urgent need of passing along. The songs, as fiction would later, worked a kind of excavation, breaking down resistance to reveal a territory that I otherwise did not have access to, fears and desires and mixed or half-formed feelings that had been hidden. When a song surfaced this stuff, I felt destroyed and remade, gifted with a new body, a weapon, a helmet. We don't just have our feelings. Our feelings have us, and change us, and the endorphins triggered by this kind of change became compulsory. If a piece of noise, or later a string of words, could perform this kind of archaeology, I hoped to undergo such a procedure as often as I could, and I looked for others who could enter the very same operating room. Life without it no longer seemed like life. To listen was to grow one's inner self, to become more of a person, to see and feel more possibility. A sweet medication for solitude? Sounds as ointment for some impossible sorrow? Maybe, but those were the minor spoils up against the feeling of purifying one's oxygen and sharpening the very air so that all I saw and felt leapt to a nearly unbearable resolution. It's one reason we read, listen, and look at things made with exquisite skill. I'm sure I also thought that I would somehow get credit for these stirring songs—the sad and introspective ones, the punchy and danceable ones, the oddball ones that came out of nowhere with beeps and glitches and clicks. Certainly I thought that I'd be seen differently after the girl had listened to the tape. If she liked these songs, and if she felt similarly discovered by them, she would, if not disrobe, at least see I was no caveman. Or, more likely, she'd copy the tape and pass it on to whomever she wanted to impress, whoever was, for her, someone she wanted to show her true self to.

This anthology aims to present the range of what American short-story writers have been capable of in the previous ten years or so, not as a museum piece but as a sampler of behaviors and feelings we can very nearly have only through reading. A sourcebook of compulsory emotions. For months I collected books, stories, links, and names. I asked writers, readers, editors, friends, and strangers to alert me to strong stories, favorite writers. Who should I read? Who am I missing out on? What is the most memorable story you've read in the last ten years? What story has shaken you?

The range of work I encountered was staggering. I have

sometimes wished for a bookstore organized not by genre but by feeling. You could shop by mood, by emotional complexity, by the amount of energy and attention that might be required. There'd be a special section for the kind of literature that holds your face to the fire. Until there is such a bookstore, we have anthologies.

Had I worked strictly from my passions, collecting the most intense and beautiful and memorable works I could find, stories exhibiting the highest degree of artistic mastery, this book would have grown so huge that you would have needed to carry it in a wagon.

I sought stylistic and formal variety in the stories not to be fair but because there seem to be endless ways, in fiction, to make the world come alive, to reckon with our time, to fearlessly reveal what's in front of us. To look to the past, to posit the future. To lean on language and bend and try to break it. To preserve and refine tradition, or to struggle otherwise. If writers can't genuinely make it new, they probably can't convincingly make it old, either. They are helpless but to make it now. But who we are now is impossible to fix, and impossible to generalize about. The minor labels that would scar our writers—*realist* and *experimentalist* would be the obvious ones—seem like someone else's nicknames, sounds we use to call off a dog. We say these words out loud and we feel the instant shame of having told a lie in a language we hardly even speak.

The idea was to put together a book that shows just what the short story can do. Had I chosen thirty-two stories that showcase the exact same methods and make love to the same traditions, that would be too many hammer blows to the face, when a single one will do. Each story here is a different weapon, built to custom specifications. Let's get bloodied and killed in thirty-two different ways.

Inside this book you'll find language smooth and seamless, jagged and mean. The kind of language you use and hear every day, and the kind you never thought possible. If these stories were paintings, one might depict the human figure in angry detail while another might puncture the figure until it spills over its frame, leaking color down the wall.

Therefore there are stories of the past. Stories of the future. Stories set in some gummy mixture of the two. Stories rocketing inside a character's head. Stories casting out into the world. Stories that burn out inside a few seconds. Stories that blanket a lifetime. Stories set here, stories set abroad. Stories set in some unsettling elsewhere. Speaking of which: stories that could happen, stories that couldn't, stories that did, stories that didn't. Stories that confirm our beliefs or assault them. Stories that hurt the mind. Stories that ate a poem. Stories that refute the dictionary. Stories pretty, strange, or plain. Stories so monstrously intimate I was often scared to reread them.

What resulted started to feel like a kind of *Whole Earth Catalog*. Not of things and goods, but of the strategies, in language, to attack our tendency—my own, anyway—to feel too little. I wanted to bring together stories I would not care to live without, a kind of atlas, or chemical pathway, to the sort of language-induced feelings that, to me, are no longer optional. The names of the moods and states and spirits these stories provoke, like the names of animals, or the names of people, are woefully inadequate.

When I could not shake a story, was kept up at night by it, and days or weeks later began to confuse the story with my own life, there was a sign that the story had taken seed. As I read, the stories I sided with were the ones that began to own me. They wouldn't relax their hold, and the more I read them, the more this arrangement seems secure. I kept the stories that won't unhand me. If I could forget a story then I suppose I did. And yet even then, the stories I forgot formed their own pile, where I revisited them each at least once, believing the defect to be mine.

In my reading I found stories that help us ignore our troubles, and stories that rub our faces in them. The first kind of story relieves us of the burden of some basic truths: We are made of flesh, it often hurts to be alive, and we are in a constant state of decay. If we lived in relentless contemplation of these facts, we would burst. Some of us already have. Pleasure arises when we forget our fears. Relief, an illusory break from time. A break from ourselves. Such stories provided entertainment but left no residue. When I examined myself for evidence of them days or weeks later, I could find none. A respite from some basic emotional reality—the central predicament of being a finite, feeling thing—came to seem too much like a vacation I hadn't earned. And didn't really want.

A deeper pleasure arguably comes when our fears are admitted, revealed in full color, enlarged and even strengthened, in the world of language. It was this kind of story I favored, a story not in flight from something elemental and inescapable—we are going away soon. Meanwhile, what is worth noticing, what is crucial to feel and think before we do? Why is it pleasurable, deeply so, to read sorrowful, dark, often difficult stories? What need is being satisfied? It's challenging to answer this without sounding like a glutton for end-times entertainment. When a story achieves a degree of moral honesty, not in its specific plot or its claims, not in its subject matter, necessarily, but in some of its deeper materials, its methods, language, style, and mood, in the emotional space it carves out within us, the result is eerily comforting, like being wrapped in a blanket and hurtled through space.

In the end it is far more disturbing when our entertainment denies our fears, our mounting suspicions, estranging us from a version of the world that is too safe and easy to be real. A story seemed to find its place here when it did not look away from what was coming.

—*Ben Marcus*

NEW AMERICAN STORIES

PARANOIA

Saïd Sayrafiezadeh

When April arrived, it started to get warm and everyone said that the war was definitely going to happen soon and there was nothing anybody could do to stop it. The diplomats were flying home, the flags were coming out, and the call-ups were about to begin. Walking across the bridge, I would sometimes see freight trains lumbering by, loaded top to bottom with tanks or jeeps, once even the wings of airplanes, heading out west or down south. Some line had been crossed, something said or done, something irrevocable on our side or on the enemy's, from which there was no longer any possibility of turning back. I hadn't been following matters that closely, so I had missed exactly when things had taken a turn. Nevertheless, everyone was saying that the war was going to happen soon and so I said it too.

Then May came and it got hot and Roberto broke his nose and asked me if I would come visit him in the hospital. "Blood everywhere," he told me over the phone. Apparently he had been lifting weights at the gym when one of his buddies, in order to emphasize some conversational point he was making, feinted like a boxer and swung at Roberto's face. The buddy had meant merely to pantomime the punch, but with his arms heavy-light from having just bench-pressed three hundred pounds, he had lost the ability to gauge distance, strength, or speed, and he cracked Roberto right in the nose.

I wanted to question the details of the story because Roberto was subject to hyperbole, and also because I was selfish and didn't want to make the trip across town, but I was the closest thing to family that Roberto had, and on the telephone he did sound like he had a sock stuffed down his throat and up his nose.

To make matters worse, my car happened to be in the shop, and according to the bus map, I had to catch three buses I'd never heard of. So what should have taken me twenty minutes was going to take an hour and a half. Sitting in the back of the J-23B with the air-conditioning barely working, I stared out the window as we crawled through residential neighborhoods whose houses were all hung with flags. There was no breeze, and the flags hung limply. Some of the homes displayed the MIA and POW flags from bygone wars, and every so often there'd be a sign stuck in a window that said PEACE or NO WAR or something to that effect, but those were few and far between, and for the most part everyone was on the same page. Ten minutes into the ride, I was sweating heavily; rivulets ran from my armpits down my sides and collected in the elastic of my underwear. This is what it must feel like for soldiers on the transport heading to battle, I thought. I was wearing shorts and my thighs adhered to the bus seat so that whenever I shifted, my skin peeled away from the plastic. The other passengers were old hands and obviously knew what was in store for them because they'd come equipped with things to fan themselves with, things like newspapers and magazines and even a flattened cereal box. Out of the corner of my eye, the rapid motion resembled birds alighting. Twenty-five minutes into the ride, I retrieved a discarded supermarket circular from under the seat in front of me and tried to use it as a fan, but the paper was too thin and kept flopping over and I wasn't able to gen-

erate any current. I folded it four times and then gave up and
tossed it back under the seat where I'd found it. A woman
looked at me with disapproval. She was waving a book in
front of her face.

"It was already on the floor," I said. I smiled. She shrugged.
She didn't care.

At every corner, the bus hit a red light, and we'd have
to sit idling for sixty seconds, stewing in the pot, and then
once the light turned green and the bus made it through the
intersection, it would stop again to let passengers on and off,
elderly people who took forever, fat people who took forever,
a man in a wheelchair who took five minutes, and by the time
we arrived at the end of the next block, the light would be
turning red again and we'd have to stop and idle and do the
whole thing all over. It was abysmal urban planning, humiliating and crushing. I kept urging the bus forward by tensing
and twisting and leaning forward like a bowler who imagines
his body language can influence the trajectory of the ball once
it's left his hand. My skin peeled. I blamed everyone: the bus,
the driver, the passengers. I blamed Roberto for breaking his
nose. Then I blamed myself for blaming Roberto. It wasn't
his fault. Nothing was his fault. His nose was just another
symptom of his vulnerability, his desperation, a strange man
in a strange land, hoping one day to magically transform into
an American and have a real life. "I'm already an American,"
he'd say indignantly, haughtily, in a clipped and formal way
that was supposed to emphasize the fact that he had lost,
through extreme effort, all traces of an accent. "I'm an American just like you!" But he wasn't just like me. He was dark—
dark-skinned, dark-haired, black-eyed, from some village that
nobody had ever heard of and which he'd left twelve years
earlier when his father was awarded a scholarship to study
architecture at our university, all expenses paid.

I had discovered him in the park one afternoon about two weeks after he arrived, thirteen years old, skinny and solitary, unable to speak a word of English, tossing a baseball up in the air. *"¿Te gusta jugar al béisbol?"* I'd said, because I'd been taking Spanish for two years, though the teacher, despite providing us with an extensive vocabulary and showing us how to conjugate every verb backward and forward, had neglected to teach us how to construct a complete sentence save one: "Do you like to play baseball?" Roberto had gazed at me in confusion, almost terror, until finally he responded, *"Sí, me gusta jugar al béisbol."* Four years later, his father graduated with honors and the family's visa expired, effective immediately. It was time to go back. But Roberto had no interest in going back. So they went back without him, leaving him with eight months of high school to go, alone and illegal, in an apartment that had been emptied of almost everything, including the furniture. I was there the day after they left. It looked like it had been ransacked. He had his bed and his clothes, but that was about it. The closets were open and empty, and the curtains were gone. Standing in the void of a three-bedroom apartment he couldn't pay for, he tried to act chipper about his prospects at age seventeen. In his newfound independence, he had taken the opportunity to cut out pictures of Arnold Schwarzenegger at various stages of his career and paste them on the wall like wallpaper. There was nothing in the refrigerator except a jar of mayonnaise and a can of tuna fish, but it didn't matter, because he didn't have any dishes.

A few blocks from the infamous Maple Tree Heights, I had to transfer to the K-4AB. It was just pulling away when I arrived. I chased after it as it sailed down the street. Some elderly black women passed me pushing shopping carts, and one said, "That's a shame, honey," and another said, "That's how they do you up here." At the end of the street was a hill with a sharp ascent, and a billboard that read, WELCOME TO MAPLE TREE HEIGHTS. The billboard looked brand-new except for the fact that someone had crawled up and spray-painted, "Don't come on in here." Every week there was a report on the news of some unfortunate event, many involving white people who had lost their way and wound up wandering through Maple Tree Heights, where they were set upon and beaten for sport. Most recently a mathematics professor had been whipped with a snakeskin belt. I reflected on how the scrawled message could be interpreted less as implied threat and more as honest warning. It also seemed possible that the message was not being directed outward at all but inward, at those who already lived in Maple Tree Heights and might be contemplating moving to some other part of the city.

It was ten o'clock in the morning and already muggy, slushy, the air slow-moving. "Hitting ninety today, folks," the weatherman had said. Everyone was saying that if it was ninety in May, what was it going to be in August. The sky was cloudless, and I could feel the undiluted sun beating straight down on the top of my head. There were various empty buildings surrounding me, and I had the sensation that I was being watched by someone somewhere. I felt exposed in my shorts, my whiteness made manifest by the paleness of my legs. Directly across the street was an Arby's with an American flag draped across its giant cowboy hat. I should go inside to wait for the bus, I thought. I'll be safe there. But as soon as I thought this, three black guys about my age came out of the restaurant with their roast-beef-sandwich bags and big boots and baseball caps and stood underneath the hat, smoking and staring at me. I put my hands in my pockets casually and looked up the street as if I were fixated on what was coming. Nothing was coming. The empty air wobbled in the heat. When I glanced back, the guys were still smoking and saying things to one another, low things, conspiratorial things. They had expertly tilted their baseball caps down so that I couldn't see where precisely they were looking, but I knew they were looking at me. I thought about running, but running implied terror. Or capitulation. For a moment I had a clear picture of myself disoriented, panting, turning in error up into Maple Tree Heights.

Then I heard my name being called. "Dean!" I heard. "Goddamn, Dean!"

When I looked back at the three guys, I saw that they were smiling and that I knew them, two of them; we had played together on the football team in high school. And here they came from underneath the Arby's hat, laughing, yelling, their bags of roast-beef sandwiches in one hand, their cigarettes in the other. "Goddamn, Dean," they said. "How long's it been?" There was some initial awkwardness as we tried to coordinate the hand slapping and the hugging and the sandwiches and the cigarettes, but eventually we managed to greet one another properly.

I introduced myself to the one I didn't know. "What's up, my man?" he said. He looked skeptical.

"We thought you were the police," Quincy said.

This made everyone laugh. The man I didn't know laughed bitterly, and I laughed out of relief at this fortunate turn of events. Troy blew smoke out of his nose, and Quincy blew it out of his mouth, and I wanted to ask for a cigarette, because I was eager to fortify our bond and because I only smoke when I can smoke for free. The man I didn't know removed a handkerchief and wiped his forehead. Then he took out his sandwich and bit into it, and I could smell the roast beef, which in the heat made me queasy.

"What are you doing all the way out here, Dean?" Quincy wanted to know. "This here is no-man's-land."

"I'm waiting for the bus," I said. "I'm on my way to see Robbie."

"Robbie?"

"Robbie Díaz?"

"Spanish Robbie?"

"Goddamn, man!"

"How's Robbie?"

"He broke his nose."

"That ain't cool."

"Tell him I said what's up."

"Bus?" said the man I didn't know. "There ain't no bus here."

I pointed to the sign above my head.

"There ain't no bus here," he repeated. He was the kind of person who offered the minimum amount of information possible.

"Bus stop is over there," Quincy said. He pointed up the street to an abandoned building with broken windows and a sign that said TEXTILES Something-or-other, INC. The words had eroded.

"Hey, Troy," I said. "How about letting me have one of those cigarettes?"

Troy aimed his pack in my direction, and out popped a cigarette halfway. A surge of nostalgia and tenderness coursed through me for our old football games. I put the cigarette to my lips with great anticipation, but Troy's matches were moist or stale, and each time I struck one, it would flare up for a second and then fizzle out. After the third miss, I asked the man I didn't know if I could use his lighter. He handed it to me grudgingly. It had a picture of an American flag on it. When I flicked the lighter, the flag fluttered as if waving in the wind.

"Let me see that," Quincy said, and we passed the lighter around, flicking it on and off, marveling at the trick, until the man I didn't know said not to waste any more fluid.

"I was just thinking about getting me a tattoo like that," Troy announced. "Right here." He pulled up his shirt to reveal a saggy and swollen stomach. "Here to here." He outlined the image like a teacher standing at a chalkboard. "Here's where the flagpole goes." He indicated his belly button.

"That would look good," I said, but I didn't think it would look good. I was dismayed by what had become of his body. He was round and spongy, as if he had rolled in a pan of chocolate dough. So was Quincy. The man I didn't know was the opposite, tall and stringy, with ropy muscles and long fingers and protruding knuckles. He was thin but sweating the most. Sweat streamed down from under his baseball cap, and he dabbed at it with his handkerchief. He was oddly genteel about this. Then he cracked his knuckles loudly, aggressively, and it made a sound like tree branches snapping. Troy pulled his shirt back down, and I had a vivid recollection of him standing in front of the locker-room mirror after one of our games, completely naked except for his socks, flexing and preening. At fifteen, he already had a man's body—shoulders, chest, and cock. He'd scored three touchdowns that game and knocked the opposing team's star player unconscious. Coach Slippo had given him the game ball. He had five game balls. "I've got some cuts in here for you," Troy had told the equipment manager, running his fingers through the creases of his stomach muscles and down to the edge of his pelvis. Everyone had laughed. The equipment manager had blushed.

Troy thought he was going to make the NFL. All of the guys thought they were going to make the NFL. They didn't even make college.

I sucked the smoke in and blew it out, and as I did, it felt like my mouth was a furnace door that I was opening. The smoke was hotter than the air, and it made my face fiery and my eyes water. I felt light-headed, and the smell of the roast beef was sickening. There was a thrumming in my eardrums. I feared I might puke on the sidewalk.

"You okay, Dean?" I heard Troy say. "You good?" His voice was far away. I wasn't sure if he was asking whether my life in general was good.

"It's hot out here," I said. It was all I could do to maintain my balance.

"This ain't hot," said the man I didn't know. "If you think this is hot, wait till August."

I was happy to engage in weather talk. "It's probably going to be a hundred degrees in August," I offered.

"A hundred degrees?" The man I didn't know was incredulous. "A hundred degrees?" He was outraged. He looked at me hard. "If it's ninety degrees in May, how's it going to be a hundred degrees in August? I'm telling you, my man, it's going to be hundred and *twenty-five* degrees in August."

Against my better judgment, I took another drag off the cigarette, and it had a surprisingly calming effect. The smoke came out white and round and hovered around my head in the still, heavy air.

"Hey, Dean," Quincy said suddenly, "you looking for a job?"

Troy said, "Dean don't need no job."

"They're hiring," Quincy said. He nodded to the textiles building down the street.

"Who's hiring?" I said.

"Mainframes, man," Quincy said.

"Chemicals and whatnot," Troy said.

"I don't ask no questions about what they make," said the man I didn't know.

"You watch," Quincy said. "Once the war starts, they'll be opening factories all up and down this street. There's going to be an industrial revolution right here in the ghetto." This broke them up. They slapped one another's hands, stinging slaps. I smiled but I didn't slap.

"Where you working at now, Dean?" Troy said. I told him.

"Damn."

"Damn."

"That's a good job."

"How'd you get that?"

"That's the kind of gig I want."

"Damn."

"That's what I'm going to get me," said the man I didn't know. He said this more to himself. Then he said to the rest of us, "I'm going to get one of those *essential* jobs, so that when the draft comes, they pass me up."

"There's not going to be any draft," I said. It was my turn to state something as fact.

The man looked at me in astonishment. He cocked his head. Then he guffawed and wiped his handkerchief over his entire face in one swift motion. "How'd you figure that one out, my man?"

"It's going to be a quick war," I said. "Marines are going to take the peninsula first thing." I drew in the air as if I was standing in front of a map. "Here's the bay . . . here's the peninsula . . . you'll see."

The guys got quiet as they pondered this.

"Anyway," I said cheerfully, "even if it's a long war, there'll still be plenty of people willing to join up."

"Plenty of *people*?" The man I didn't know snorted. "This here's the guy"—he turned to Troy and Quincy—"who thinks it's only going to be a hundred degrees in August."

At the hospital, the air-conditioning was going full blast and the sweat froze on my skin. It was almost twelve o'clock and I was exhausted and parched. I was also hungry. I went back to blaming Roberto for everything. People with all sorts of ailments came and went in the waiting room, and I thought about how this must be what it's like when soldiers get back from battle. I wasn't sure if Roberto had checked in under a false name. He was nervous about not being a citizen and was always going out of his way to cover his tracks. He had no driver's license, no bank account, no telephone, and his new apartment still had the name of the previous tenant, Cynthia Abernathy, on the mailbox even though she hadn't lived there for two years. Every so often he'd get a package for her, and he'd tell the delivery guy some elaborate and unnecessary story about how Cynthia was his wife but she was out of town because her mother was dying and he didn't know when she'd be back but he'd let her know that a package had come for her when he talked to her next but he wasn't sure when that would be because her mother was dying. It was always the same story. He was positive that the INS was tracking him and the delivery guy was an agent. In the meantime, he'd accumulated several mail-order kitchen gadgets, including an electric eggbeater.

"Don't you think they're going to start wondering why your mother-in-law never dies?" I'd ask him.

He never liked this. "You're going to be *penitent* one day," he'd say, dropping in one of those words he'd learned specifically for the SAT. "You're going to be *penitent* when they come for me. They're going to lock me up somewhere, like they did those apple pickers, and you're never going to hear from me again."

"I'm looking for Roberto Díaz," I told the hospital receptionist.

She checked the computer. No, she said, there was no Roberto Díaz listed.

"Then I'm looking for Rob Days," I said.

No, sorry.

"How about Bob Hays?" I was trying to recall all the various permutations he had used over the years.

No.

"I'm looking for Tyler McCoy," I said, because this was the name of the main character in his favorite gangster film.

The receptionist punched in Tyler McCoy, and I could tell by the way she slowly struck the keys that she was getting suspicious or impatient. "You sure do have a lot of friends," she said.

"I sure do," I said. And Tyler McCoy was in Room 831.

He was asleep when I got there, lying on his back with his mouth wide open like a drowning man trying to suck oxygen. He had bandages running ear to ear, and his nose, always prominent, seemed gigantic under the bandages, as if he had an anvil for a nose. His eyes were swollen, his hair was matted, and a *Reader's Digest* rested on his stomach, rising and falling with his haggard breath. Across the room a window faced out onto the roof of an adjacent wing of the hospital. The roof was white, and if you didn't know it was ninety degrees outside, you could mistake the whiteness for snow.

I pulled up a chair next to his bed and took a seat. He didn't stir. I thought about turning on the television and then, when he woke, apologizing for having disturbed him. From my vantage point, he looked to be all torso, as if he were lying

in bed after having had his legs amputated. This was a result
of having spent ten years lifting weights constantly and incorrectly. I'd experienced him straining, screaming, staggering,
a terrifying sight to behold as he attempted to hoist more
than was humanly possible, and the second the summit was
attained, not one second more, he would discard the barbell
midair so that it would drop and crash and bounce in explosive vanity. His chest was colossal and so were his shoulders
and his arms, and he had a thick blue vein in his neck that
was permanently engorged as it piped gallons of blood to his
muscles twenty-four hours a day. But his legs were thin, the
legs of a teenage girl or an insect, and they looked nonexistent beneath the pale blue hospital sheet. "Why don't you
try doing some cardio every once in a while?" I'd counsel.
He either didn't care or didn't notice that his proportions
bordered on the freakish. His physique had provided him
with those coveted manual-labor jobs—mover, deliverer,
unloader—and that was how he had survived all these years
without any aid or assistance except what he got from me.
Businesses needed men like him and were happy to pay him
under the table. He'd carried bricks, drywall, bales of hay.
"I've got a special job for Robbie," my mother once said. He'd
come over for dinner and wound up spending half an hour
lugging a tree trunk from our backyard to the curb. She'd
given him ten dollars. I'd yelled at her later for what I saw as
an example of her condescension, but my father intervened,
coming into the living room in his bare feet and no glasses
and uttering one of his platitudes, "Every man has to make
his own way in this world."

The way Roberto was making his own way in this world
now was through relatively sedentary employment as an
assistant to a cobbler who also happened to be his landlord
and who cut him a break on the rent in addition to giving him

shoes if they were left in the shop past sixty days. Roberto would be turning twenty-five soon, and he'd come up with a fairly reasonable plan that involved learning a trade, saving money, going to college, opening a business, starting a family. The cobbler paid him in cash twice a month, so twice a month he had an enormous roll of money that he liked to caress as if it were a puppy. The roll was generally in fives and tens and added up to no more than a couple hundred dollars, but it made him look and feel rich. "Like Tyler McCoy," he'd say, and he'd reenact in pitch-perfect detail the scene where Tyler McCoy is trying to get one guy to go in with another guy on the heist that turned out to be a double cross. "Me. You. Now. Together." When Roberto had satisfied himself with fondling the roll, we would walk to the post office, where he would buy all the money orders he needed to pay all the bills that were under assumed names. We'd wait in a long line of poor people and illegal immigrants and that occasional unfortunate American citizen who had just come in to buy a book of stamps. When we emerged from the post office an hour later, Roberto would be broke.

The mass of flesh suddenly shifted like an animal beneath forest leaves, and his swollen eyes opened. They were bloodshot and bleary, and it took a moment for him to orient himself. "Oh, shit," he said when he understood who I was and where we were. "You came. My man." His voice was thick and stuffy like air in a cellar, and I was surprised to hear the slightest trace of the accent he had rid himself of years ago. It could have been an earlier version of him rising from the dead. *Oh, shee. You came. My main.*

"Of course I came," I said, wounded, as if I had never contemplated otherwise. And because I knew it would make him happy and endear me to him, I added, "Of course I came, *Tyler.*"

He grinned, and the bandages pulled tight across his face, and the grin evaporated as he cried out in agony. I stood in alarm, but the pain subsided quickly. He struggled out of bed, throwing the sheet back with determination, bringing both feet to the floor and forcing himself upright so that he could face me.

"This is the best guy," he said with the utmost sincerity, as if introducing me to an audience. "This is the greatest guy in the whole world." This was an example of Roberto's hyperbole.

His trunklike arms came around my shoulders and squeezed me hard, until I felt like a child, even though I was taller than he was. I feared he would lift me off the ground and swing me. Instead, he laid his head against my chest, so that he was the one who seemed transformed into a boy, hugging his father the day before he left for good.

In June, the marines were put on high alert, the temperature reached one hundred degrees, and the bill from the hospital arrived. It was three thousand dollars.

I loaned Roberto two hundred to cover the minimum, and a few days later he called me from the cobbler's phone to invite me over to his apartment to see his "special surprise."

"What special surprise is that?" I said, but he refused to tell me. He had to get back to work.

So the following Saturday, which also turned out to be the hottest day of the year so far, I pulled up to his apartment building. It was early evening, but it seemed to be getting hotter, as if the setting sun were drawing nearer. Roberto lived in one of those neighborhoods that were either up-and-coming or on the way out, an equal mix of aluminum siding, college students, and small shops—one of which was the cobbler's shop, whose awning I now stood beneath, waiting desperately for Roberto to come downstairs and let me in. His doorbell never worked but I had been forbidden by the cobbler to yell up at the window. Instead, I had to arrive at our mutually agreed-upon time and stand on the sidewalk patiently and quietly until Roberto opened the door. If I showed up early, I'd have to wait; if I showed up late, Roberto would have to wait. Today I showed up right on time, but there was no Roberto. Every few minutes, behind the window, the cobbler would rise from his shoe machine and eye me mercilessly, as if he'd never seen me before and suspected I was up to no good. He hated me, and I hated him. He was fat, and he smoked constantly, and he had a thick head of black hair. I had a theory that he colored it with shoe polish. He was Italian or Greek or Armenian—we could never figure out which—and he had been in America for fifty years but could hardly speak English. Even Roberto made fun of him. "'I can no find a-black-a shoelazes . . .'" I'd gotten off to a bad start with him the first time I visited Roberto and screamed up at the window at eleven o'clock in the morning, *"Robbie!"*

"You no come here act like hoodlum," the cobbler had demanded. "Like nigger."

"Hey!"

"Hey!"

"That word's not called for!"

"I call police!"

"Fix the doorbell!"

"I fix you!"

"Fuck off!"

"That word not called for!"

"He's my window of opportunity," Roberto had shrieked when I told him what happened. So I went back downstairs, hat in hand, and apologized.

"My customers good customers" was all he said.

Fifteen minutes after I had arrived, Roberto still hadn't come down to open the door. This wasn't like him at all, and a subtle unease began to creep over me. I recalled the apple pickers who had been rounded up by the INS in the middle of the night, and I was on the verge of panicking when Roberto appeared from around the corner, carrying a big blue box that said DVD PLAYER. He was grinning freely, despite his nose being covered with bandages that made it look as if he had a small pillow in the middle of his face.

"What's in the box?" I said, though it was obvious what was in the box.

"Robbie!" said the cobbler, waving. "You buy me DVD player?"

Roberto laughed, and so did the cobbler. The cobbler's laugh was intended to make me the odd man out.

In his apartment Roberto sat cross-legged on the floor, tearing open the box as if it were Christmas Day. Styrofoam peanuts went everywhere, and when he removed the thin silver DVD player, it gleamed sharply in the evening light. He smiled at it lovingly. I sat on the sofa and fumed, dripping with sweat. His apartment was even hotter than outside. It was one square room with a kitchenette, a saggy sofa bed, and three folding chairs; the bathroom was down the hall and shared with six other tenants. All Roberto's furniture belonged to the cobbler, and so did the television and dishes. The wall of his kitchenette had been covered meticulously with those pictures of Arnold Schwarzenegger, the most prominent of which was him in a suit and tie with his arms and thighs pressing hard against the fabric. The apartment felt like a boiler room in a subsubbasement. It even sounded like a boiler room, with the constant low-frequency vibration coming from the cobbler's shoe machine. Roberto seemed wholly unaffected by the heat. He was always unaffected by the heat. I had never seen him sweat.

"Can't you open a window?" I asked.

With one gigantic arm, he swung open the window and then got back to fitting inputs into outputs. Immediately a fly came in through the window, but no breeze. I watched the fly settle on a plate and crawl around. Then a second fly came in. Roberto turned on the television to a game show that was nearing its climax. A woman had to pick the right color if she wanted to win fifty thousand dollars. The audience was screaming at her, and she was flustered.

"What will you do with *all that money?*" the host asked.

"I—I—I—I don't know."

"Pay back the greatest guy," I answered for her.

"What?" Roberto said. His pillow face swung in my direction.

"Pay back the greatest guy in the whole world," I said.

He stood up straight. In his small apartment, his size was immense, his camel legs notwithstanding, and as he loomed over me on the couch, I felt a twinge of vulnerability.

"I told you, I'm going to pay you every penny!" he said. His face twitched and the pillow-bandage bobbed, and from his pocket he withdrew a slip of paper on which was printed the company logo of Dr. Scholl's. Beneath this he had written in very precise handwriting, "I O Dean $200.00." He had dated it "June 14th" and added his initials, as if it were an official document he was endorsing. The gesture was surprisingly touching, and I felt remorseful, even guilty, as if I were the one who owed money.

Out loud I said, "What the hell am I supposed to do with this? Get it notarized?"

"Motorized?" he asked.

He shrugged. He folded the paper and put it in his pocket

and got back to work on the DVD player. The woman was just about to pick the color yellow when the game show was interrupted by breaking news: every branch of the military had been ordered to join the marines on high alert—the navy, the army, the air force, the coast guard, and branches I'd never heard of. There were maps with arrows, and the peninsula was highlighted. The experts were all in agreement; even the experts who used to disagree now agreed. Everything made sense. There was a sexy reporter interviewing soldiers at their base.

"We could be attacked without warning," she said. "Right here and now." Her eyes were dewy, her lips were thick. She wore a flak jacket and a helmet from under which flowed long brown hair.

"Do you miss your family?" she asked one of the soldiers.

"Yes, I do, ma'am," the soldier said.

Roberto came and sat beside me on the sofa.

"But I have to do what I have to do," the soldier said. He had blond hair, blue eyes, an upturned nose. If not for his twang, he could have been a California surfer. Night-vision goggles were propped on his forehead.

"Are you afraid of dying?"

"No, ma'am."

"Any day now," the reporter said, turning to us.

"Any day now," Roberto repeated. The sentiment seemed poignant. I draped my arm around his enormous shoulders. I was in a forgiving mood.

"Let's go get a DVD," I said.

Outside, the cobbler was closing up for the night. He was trying to pull the grate down over the shopwindow but was having trouble because he was old and fat. Roberto ran to his aid as if rescuing a child from the water's edge. "Wait! Wait! Stop! Stop!" He reached up with wide forearms, and in an instant the gate came crashing down onto the boiling sidewalk.

"Ah, you good man," the cobbler said.

At the video store we browsed the titles. We agreed, finally, on one of those funny buddy road movies. Then Roberto picked a porno that he said he was going to watch alone. And then he picked his favorite gangster movie with Tyler McCoy.

I paid for all three.

Back at the apartment, there were about forty flies walking over everything, including the dishes.

"Maybe you should close the window," I suggested.

He complied, trapping the heat and trapping the flies. Then he went to the refrigerator and took out some bread and cheese and tuna fish and put them on the counter where the flies were. He took out a jar of mayonnaise, and while his back was turned, the flies landed on the bread and cheese and tuna fish. When he was done making the sandwiches, he put one on a plate where the flies had been and handed it to me.

He sat down on the sofa bed and pressed play. The trailers ran and the sofa sagged. After that, the movie with Tyler McCoy began. I pressed pause.

"I thought we were going to watch the other one," I said. "The buddy one."

"Let's watch this one first."

"I've seen it three times," I said.

"So what," he said. "I've seen it three *hundred* times." This was no exaggeration.

He pressed play, and so began Tyler McCoy's rags-to-riches story through violent and immoral means. When the characters spoke, Roberto spoke, every word, soundlessly mouthing in perfect unison.

He pressed pause. "Why aren't you eating your sand-wich?" he asked.

"I think I saw a fly land on it," I admitted.

With irritation he said, "You are *opulent*," and he took the sandwich from me and bit into it, a huge, obvious bite so that I could see the food in his mouth. "And I am *indigent*."

Which was true. I'd had a DVD player for ten years.

On the Fourth of July, Roberto and I drove downtown to see the parade. There was nowhere to park, and we had to walk twenty minutes up a hill in 105-degree heat. The turn-out was extraordinary. The largest ever, people were saying. Other people were saying that each year the turnout should be the largest ever and that people shouldn't wait for a war to become patriots. "I keep my flag out year-round," one man said. "And you can pass by my house anytime to see if I'm telling the truth." The fountain was going, though we were supposed to be conserving water, and the parks people had somehow managed to get it to rise and fall in alternating colors of red, white, and blue. Up and down it went, hypnotically. Roberto and I stood shoulder to shoulder, transfixed by the spectacle. Children played along the edge, and parents screamed at them not to drink the water because it was poisonous.

The sun was straight overhead, but the heat felt as if it were coming from down below, from the asphalt, emanating up through my shoes and legs and out through my scalp. I had brought along a container of sunblock, SPF 45, which I kept applying to my face and neck every few minutes. Roberto looked at me in fascination and amusement. His nose was almost healed except for a small red mark that ran along the bridge and which he kept rubbing because he was self-conscious.

"Does my nose look big?" he asked.

"Not at all," I lied.

"Ladies and gentlemen," the emcee said, and a band started up, all trumpets and drums and tubas playing "My Country, 'Tis of Thee." People swayed and sang, and Roberto used the heartfelt moment as an opportunity to make his first payment. "To the best friend," he announced, holding a pile of crumpled bills. "To the greatest friend in the whole world." He handed over the fistful of dollars like he was pouring gold coins into my hands. "Count," he said.

I counted twenty dollars.

He displayed the sheet of paper with the Dr. Scholl's logo and his now updated balance sheet. He had crossed out "I O Dean $200.00" and replaced it with "I O Dean $180.00, RD," dated "July 4th."

I used some of the money to treat us to two foot-longs, and I was about to treat us to two more when an altercation broke out near the fountain. People pushed to get to the action, and Roberto and I pushed too, and the emcee said not to push. The crowd surged forward, and when the wall of people opened, I could see parade-goers shouting and pointing at a small ragtag group of protesters holding signs that said WAR IS NOT THE ANSWER and things of that nature.

We jeered at them, and they jeered back. "You're all fools," they screamed.

"It's the Fourth of July, for crying out loud," a woman next to me yelled back. Her face was pink, possibly burning, and she looked close to tears. "Isn't anything sacred to you people?"

Roberto cupped his hands around his mouth and bellowed, "Faggots!"

People laughed.

"Hey," I hissed at Roberto. "That word's not called for!"

Some of the parade-goers began splashing the protesters with blue water from the fountain, and soon the police
arrived to separate everyone and escort the protesters to a
special section at the other end of the park. The band struck
up the national anthem. We put our hands over our hearts
as veterans from previous wars began marching past, starting
with World War II. There were only a few of these, and they
ambled by slowly, looking confused and displaced, their uniforms baggy like diapers and draped with medals that glinted
in the sun. Their children and grandchildren and maybe
great-grandchildren helped them along and did the waving
for them. People applauded, but the applause seemed to dis-
orient the veterans. "Thank you," Roberto called, "thank you
for all you've done!"

As the wars progressed, the soldiers got younger, until
we arrived at the youngest, the new recruits. By the time
they appeared, I was exhausted from the heat and the clap-
ping. I felt like I was being immersed in boiling water, and
I was sure I had a terrible burn on the back of my neck.
Still, I mustered the energy and pounded my hands harder
than I had up to that point. This was bon voyage for the new
recruits—they were marching from the parade straight to the
train depot. "Last stop, the peninsula," the emcee said. The
crowd went wild. Roberto and I clapped harder yet. The soldiers came marching down in lines of twenty. Line after line.
Ten minutes of lines. A mass of bodies larger than the crowd
watching. They were decked out in the latest gear, everything
streamlined and advanced: goggles and helmets, tool belts
and boots, lights and antennas. They resembled astronauts
with automatic weapons.

"To the moon!" I yelled. It had a nice ring to it.

"To the moon!" Roberto yelled.

And then I saw a familiar face. I couldn't place the face,

but I knew that I knew it. I knew it vaguely. The man was tall and frail, and the helmet looked too large for his head, more like a bonnet than a helmet, and with each step it bobbled and appeared in danger of slipping off. He fumbled with the strap, trying to tighten it and keep pace at the same time. Sweat poured down his face as if he'd just climbed out of a swimming pool. He seemed on the verge of collapse.

"I know that man," I said.

"Thank you," Roberto shouted.

The man reached into one of the many pockets on his jacket and withdrew a handkerchief. In one clean motion, he brought the handkerchief down across his dripping face. Then he turned and looked at me. *The man I didn't know.*

"Hey," I called. I smiled and waved.

He squinted. He seemed to be looking at me and then beyond me. The attitude of haughty disdain that he'd had that day at the bus stop had been replaced by a look of fatigue and befuddlement. I wondered if Quincy and Troy were with him, and I scrutinized the lines of marching soldiers. An instant later, the man I didn't know had passed, and all I could see was his back, with his enormous pack weighed down by the essentials and an antenna sticking out.

I cried out after him, "I told you there wasn't going to be a draft!"

In August something strange happened: it got cold. In one day, it plummeted from a record high of 107 to 95 degrees. This felt like relief. But after that the temperature kept dropping, until by the middle of the month it was fifty-three. In the beginning of the cold snap, everyone was happy, and then everyone was scared. Everyone was saying that if it was fifty degrees in August, what was it going to be in December.

Things got busy at work and I didn't see Roberto for a
while. We made plans and I canceled plans, and then we made
plans again. He said he really wanted to watch that funny
buddy road movie we never got to watch. He said he had
my money. All of it. Or almost all of it. I wanted to tell him
not to worry about it, that it didn't matter, but it did matter,
and I rationalized that paying me back would help teach him
something about responsible American citizenship.

We finally arranged to meet on Saturday morning at ten
o'clock.

The night before, I was lying in bed, watching the news
about some bad things that had happened in Maple Tree
Heights, when it was interrupted by a special report: the
war had begun. The invasion was being broadcast live, lots of
lights and flashes and little bursts of smoke from afar. *Rat-a-
tat-tat.* Instead of troops landing on the peninsula, as we had
been led to believe, they were coming down over the mountains. The peninsula strategy had all been a deft misdirection
to fool the enemy. Ten thousand feet high, the mountains
were. Up one side and down the other, a hundred thousand
troops on the move. It was going to take them a week to
make the crossing. What was it like, I wondered, to reach the
summit?

I stayed up late, flipping back and forth between channels. The channels all showed the same footage, and all the
experts agreed: "Resistance is futile."

"Ladies and gentlemen," the newscaster said, "blink and
you might miss this war."

In the morning my car was broken again, it wouldn't start,
and I had to walk to Roberto's. It was freezing. It might as
well have been winter. The sun was hidden and the wind
blew hard, whipping the flags around. People drove past me
and honked in unity.

When I got to Roberto's apartment, I was numb. My nose was running and I had to pee. The gate to the cobbler's was up, but the shop looked unattended. I pounded my hands together and stomped my feet to get the blood going. Five minutes into waiting, I began to suspect that Roberto was about to come around the corner and "surprise" me with another box of electronics. Five minutes after that, I took my chances and shouted up to the window. *"Robbie!"*

Immediately the cobbler came out. He looked at me and sucked in the sides of his cheeks.

"The doorbell doesn't seem to be working," I said sarcastically.

He shook his head. "No talk here," he said. His eyes were tense and bloodshot, and he puffed hard on his cigarette. Smoke billowed out from all the orifices of his face. Beneath his apron, his stomach protruded, firm and round. "Come in store," he said. "No good talk out here."

I followed him inside. He put his cigarette in the ashtray and sat down at his machine as if he were about to get back to work. I leaned on the counter like a customer.

"Yesterday," he said as he rubbed his dirty hands over his face. "Yesterday they come." He wasn't looking at me as he spoke. Somehow his dirty hands hadn't made his face dirty.

"Who come?" I said.

"Oh, no," he said. He put his black palms up in defense. "I don't ask question."

"Who come?" I demanded.

He looked at me with trepidation. Slowly, stumblingly, full of error, he told me that yesterday they come for Roberto, yesterday, middle of day, four car, four car, no warning, all pull up same time, right outside, happen fast, take him way, take him. What I can do? I can do nothing. I am one man. They have law. Hurt me as much as hurt him.

He hunched his shoulders and he looked aggrieved. He was sorry, he said. "I pray for him now."

I believed him.

"He was nice boy," he said. "Hard worker. Hurt me too. Oh, boy." He ran his dirty fingers through his thick hair.

Then some people came in with their shoes, and he stood up to help them. His pack of cigarettes was on the counter, and I took one and stuck it in my mouth and lit it. He didn't notice. He didn't care. My boldness surprised me.

I took the long way home. I walked fast and hard. I smoked the cigarette, and the second I exhaled, the cold wind took the smoke. People drove past honking. I came down the hill and over the bridge. At the train tracks I stopped and tried to get my breath. I was wheezing. A small dot appeared way down the line. After a while it became a train. I could hear the rumble. When it drew closer, I could see that it was loaded with long tubular objects, missiles no doubt, twenty feet long, thirty feet, covered with canvas and strapped down with canvas belts. As the train approached, I saw the engineer hanging his head and arm out the window, and I motioned for him to pull the horn as I would have back when I was a kid. A moment later I heard the blast, *braaaaaammmmm*; it was louder than I had remembered, longer too, and then the train passed under the bridge as it headed out west or down south.

SLATLAND

Rebecca Lee

I went to Professor Pine for help twice in my life, once as a child and once as an adult. The first time, I was eleven and had fallen into an inexplicable depression. This happened in the spring of 1967, seemingly overnight, and for no reason. Any happiness in me just flew away, like birds up and out of a tree.

Until then I had been a normal, healthy child. My parents had never damaged me in any way. They had given me a dusty, simple childhood on the flatlands of Saskatchewan. I had two best friends—large, unselfish girls who were already gearing up for adolescence, sometimes laughing until they collapsed. I had a dog named Chest, who late at night brought me half-alive things in his teeth—bats with human faces, fluttering birds, speckled, choking mice.

My parents couldn't help noticing my sadness. They looked at me as if they were afraid of me. Sometimes at the dinner table the silence would be so deep that I felt compelled to reassure them. But when I tried to say that I was all right, my voice would crack and I would feel my face distorting, caving in. I would close my eyes then, and cry.

One night my parents came into my bedroom and sat down on my bed. "Honey," my father said, "your mother and I have been thinking about you a lot lately. We were thinking that maybe you would consider talking to somebody—you know, a therapist—about what is the matter." My father was an earnest, cheerful man, a geologist with a brush cut and a big heart. I couldn't imagine that a therapist would solve my problems, but my father looked hopeful, his large hand tracing a ruffle around my bedspread.

Three days later we were standing outside an office on the fourth floor of the Humanities Building. My appointment was not with a true therapist but rather with a professor of child psychology at the university where my father taught.

We knocked, and a voice called from behind the door in a bit of a singsong, "Come in, you, come in, you." Of course he was expecting us, but this still seemed odd, as if he knew us very well or as if my father and I were both little children—or elves. The man sitting behind the desk when we entered was wearing a denim shirt, his blond hair slicked back like a rodent's. He looked surprised—a look that turned out to be permanent. He didn't stand up, just waved at us. From a cage in the corner three birds squawked. My father approached the desk and stuck out his hand. "Peter Bergen," my father said.

"Professor Roland Boland Pine," the man said, and then looked at me. "Hello, girlie."

Despite this, my father left me alone with him. Perhaps he just thought, as I did, that Professor Pine talked like this, in occasional baby words, because he wanted children to respond as if to other children. I sat in a black leather chair. The professor and I just stared at each other for a while. I didn't know what to say, and he wasn't speaking either. It was easy to stare at him. As if I were staring at an animal, I felt no embarrassment.

"Well," he said at last, "your name is Margit?"

I nodded.

"How are you today, Margit?"

"I'm okay."

"Do you feel okay?"

"Yes. I feel okay."

"Do you go to school, Margit?"

"Yes."

"Do you like your teacher?"

"Not really."

"Do you hate him?"

"It's a her."

"Do you hate her?"

"No."

"Why are you here, Margit?"

"I don't know."

"Is everything okay at home?"

"Yes."

"Do you love your father?"

"Yes."

"Do you love your mother?" A long tic broke on his face, from the outer corner of his left eye all the way down to his neck.

"Yes."

"Is she a lumpy mother?"

"Pardon me?"

"Pardon me, Margit. I meant does your mother love you?"

"Yes."

"Does she love your father?"

I paused. "Yes."

"And does he love her?"

"I guess so."

"Margit, what is the matter?"

"Nothing. I just don't see why we're talking about my parents so much."

"Why don't they love each other?"

"They do—I said they do."

"Why can't you talk about this?"

"Because there's nothing to talk about."

"You can tell me the truth. Do they hurt each other? Lots of girls' parents hurt each other."

"No, they don't."

"Is one of them having an affair, maybe?"

I didn't say anything. "Maybe?" he repeated.

"Maybe," I said.

"Which one, Margit? Which one of the babyfaces?"

I stared at him. Another tic passed over his face. "Pardon me, Margit. I meant which one of your parents is having the affair?"

"My dad. But I don't think he's actually having it. I just heard him tell my mom a few months ago that he was considering it."

"And do you think he is?"

"I don't know. A few weeks ago I picked up the phone and a woman was talking to my dad. She told him that she had to have her breasts removed and asked if that would make a difference."

"How difficult for you. How sad for the girlie-whirl." Another tic, like a fault line shifting. "Margit, may I tell you something from my own childhood?"

This worried me, but I said yes.

"When I was young, I loved my mother. She was a real lumper. Then one day, kerpow, she was dead." He held his forefinger to his head as if it were the barrel of a gun and stared at me for a few seconds without speaking. "It wasn't actually her, you see, but a woman of about her age who happened to be walking toward me on the sidewalk. A man came running and shot her. I was so devastated that I fell right on top of her. I didn't care if he shot me, too. I was only ten at the time, and my mother's death could have scarred me for life. But it didn't. And do you know how I got from that moment to this one—how I got from there to here, to sitting behind this desk now, talking to you?"

I shook my head. "How?"

"I rose above the situation. Literally I did. I felt my mind lift out of my body, and I stared down at myself leaning over the bleeding woman. I said to myself, very calmly, There is little Roland from New Orleans, the little erky-terk, realizing that someday his mother will die."

He was looking at me so intently, and his birds were flapping in their cage with such fervor, that I felt I had to say something. "Wow," I said.

"I suggest you try it, Margit. For every situation there is a proper distance. Growing up is just a matter of gaining perspective. Sometimes you just need to jump up for a moment, a foot above the earth. And sometimes you need to jump very far. It is as if there are thin slats, footholds, from here to the sun, Margit, for the babyfaces to step on. Do you understand?"

"Yes," I said.

"Slatland, flatland, mapland."

"Pardon me?"

"Pardon me, Margit. I know so many languages that sometimes I say words out of place."

At the end of the session I asked him when I should return. He told me that another visit wouldn't be necessary, that usually his therapy worked the first time.

I didn't in fact understand what he had said to me, but his theory seemed to help anyway, as if it were a medication that worked whether you understood it or not. That very evening I was having dinner with my parents. It started as the usual dinner—me staring at my plate, my parents staring at me as

if I were about to break in two. But about halfway through
the meal I started feeling lightheaded. Nothing frightening
happened, but I did manage to lift slightly out of myself. I
looked down at our tiny family. I saw my father from above,
the deep map of his face. I understood in an instant that of
course he was having an affair, and that he was torn between
my mother and this other, distant woman. I saw my beautiful mother from above, and I could see how she must hate
this other woman, yet sympathize as well, because this other
woman was very ill. I understood how complicated it was to
be an adult, and how haunting, and how lovely. I longed to be
back in my body then, to be breathing and eating, straining
toward maturity. And when I returned, one split second later,
I hugged my parents, one after the other, with a spontaneity
that a depressed person could never muster.

In the twenty years that passed between my first visit to Professor Pine and my second, from 1967 to 1987, I remained
in the same city. I graduated from Massey and then from
LeBoldus High and then from the University of Saskatchewan, with a degree in biology. As an adult, I worked as a soil
consultant, traveling around the province to small satellite
towns in a flatbed truck that I could sleep in, if necessary, on
warm nights.

Bouts of the depression did return, but they never overwhelmed me. Perhaps my life was not the most rigorous testing ground for Professor Pine's technique, because my life
was relatively free of tragedy. Most of my depression erupted
out of nowhere. I'd be in the fields in the midst of a bright day,
and a dreariness would mysteriously descend. I'd sink into it
for a few minutes, but the lift would always come. I would
take a step up, or two or three, and recognize how good life

in fact was. From above, my job appeared to me excellent and strange. There I was, under a blazing sun, kneeling in a yellow expanse, weighing samples of earth. And later, with instruments as tiny and beautiful as jewelry, testing the dirt for traces of nitrogen and phosphorus, the gleam of potash.

One night, in the middle of the year 1985, I made the mistake of describing this technique to my fiancé, Rezvan Balescu, the Romanian liar. We had known each other for only two months at this point, but we were already engaged. We were standing on a small balcony outside our apartment. He was smoking, wearing pajamas under a down-filled jacket, and he was in the midst of one of his tirades on North America, which he loved and hated. "This place is so strange to me, so childish. You have so many problems that are not real, and you are so careful and serious about them. People discuss their feelings as if they were great works of art or literature that need to be analyzed and examined and passed on and on. In my country people love or they hate. They know that a human being is mysterious, and they live with that. The problems they have are real problems. If you do not eat, that's a problem. If you have no leg, that's a problem. If you are unhappy, that is not a problem to talk about."

"I think it is," I said.

"Exactly. That is because you are an American. For you, big things are small, and small things are big." Rezvan was always making these large declarations about North Americans in a loud voice from our balcony.

"I bet you one million in money," Rezvan said as he blew out smoke, "that the number of hours Americans spend per week in these—what do you call them?—therapy offices is exactly the same number of hours Romanians spend in line for bread. And for what? Nothing. To make their problems bigger. They talk about them all day so at night they are even bigger."

"I don't agree. The reason why people talk about their problems is to get over them, get rid of them. I went to a therapist once and he was very helpful."

"You?" He lifted an eyebrow, took a drag.

"Yes, when I was eleven."

"Eleven? What could be the problem at eleven?"

"I was just sad. My parents were getting divorced, and I guess I could tell that my dad was about to leave."

"But isn't that the correct emotion—sadness—when a father leaves? Can a therapist do anything to bring your father home?"

"No, but he gave me a way to deal with it."

"And what is that way? I would like to know."

"Well, just a way to separate from the situation."

"How do you separate from your own life?"

"Well, you rise above it. You gain some objectivity and perspective."

"But is this proper? If you have a real problem, should you rise above it? When a father leaves a child, the child feels sad. This seems right to me. This rising above, that is the problem. In fact, that is the problem of America. I cannot tell my family back home that if they are hungry or cold, they should just rise above it. I cannot say, 'Don't worry, go to the movies, go shop, here is ten dollars in money, go buy some candy. Rise above your situation.'"

"That's not what I mean. I mean you literally rise above it. Your mind hovers over your body, and you understand the situation from a higher perspective." I knew that if he pushed me far enough, this would end up sounding insane.

"So this is what your man, your eleven-year-old therapist, teaches you: to separate your mind from your body, to become unhinged. This does not teach you to solve the problem; this teaches you to be a crazy person."

But already I was drifting up until I was watching us from the level of the roof. There she is, I thought, Margit Bergen, twenty-nine years old, in love with Rezvan of Romania, a defector who escaped political hardship to arrive in a refugee camp in Austria and a year later in Regina, Saskatchewan, where he now stands on a balcony in the moonlight, hassling her about America, as if she contained all of it inside her.

I had met Rezvan in my father's lab at the university. Rezvan was a geologist, like my father. Technically, for grant reasons, he was a graduate student, but my father considered him a peer, because Rezvan had already worked for years as a geologist for the Romanian government.

Originally he had been a supporter of Ceauşescu. In fact, his father, Andrei, had been a friend of Ceauşescu's right up until the time Andrei died, in 1985. Rezvan, by his own account, stood by his father's deathbed as he died and held his father's hand, but both father and son refused to speak, because Rezvan had by then ceased to be loyal to Ceauşescu.

In the two years that Rezvan and I lived together, I would often rise from sleep to find him hunched over his desk, the arm of his lamp reaching over him. He wrote long letters into the night, some in English and some in Romanian. The English ones, he said, were to various government officials, asking for help in getting his family over to Canada. The ones in Romanian were to his family, an assortment of aunts and uncles and cousins. He wrote quickly, as in a fever, and if I crept up on him and touched his back, he would jump and turn over his letters immediately before looking up at me in astonishment. At the time, I thought this was simply an old habit of fear, left over from living for so long in a police state.

Sometimes he said he could not forgive his country for keeping his family captive. He told what he called jokes—dark, labyrinthine stories that always ended with some cartoonish, undignified death for Ceauşescu: his head in a toilet, his body flattened by a steamroller. Other times he spoke about his country with such longing—the wet mist of Transylvania, the dark tunnels beneath the streets of his town, the bookstores lined with propaganda that opened into small, dusty rooms in back filled with real books.

In this same way Rezvan loved and hated America. He would rant about it from the balcony, but then we would return to our bed and sit side by side, our backs to the wall, and watch the local and then the national news, where almost every night somebody would criticize the prime minister, Brian Mulroney. Rezvan could never get over this: men appearing on television to insult their leader night after night and never getting pulled off the air. Sometimes we would turn to the news from the United States, which we received through a cable channel from Detroit. This was a real treat for Rezvan during the period of Reagan-bashing. "I love that man," he said to me one night.

"Reagan? You don't like Reagan."

"I know, but look at him now." They were showing a clip of Reagan waving. His face did look kind. His eyes were veering off, looking skyward. He looked like somebody's benevolent, faintly crazy grandfather.

"All day long people insult him and he doesn't kill any of them."

Rezvan sometimes skipped work and came with me to the fields. He'd ride in the back of the truck, standing up, so that his head was above the cab, the wind pouring over him.

He wanted to know all the details of my job. He became better than I was at some things. He could spot poor field drainage from far away. He loved to point out the signs of it—the mint, the rushes, the wire grass, the willows.

For lunch we stopped in the towns along the way at small, fragrant home-style diners. Almost all of them were run by Ukrainian women. Each one adored Rezvan. He would kiss their hands and speak in his strange accent—part British, part Romanian—and they would serve him free platefuls of food, one after another, hovering over him as if he were a long-lost son from the old country.

One afternoon, while we were driving back to the city from a little town called Yellow Grass, I fell asleep at the wheel. I woke up after the crash to see Rezvan crumpled against the passenger door. I felt myself rising then, far above the car, far above even the tree line. From there I watched myself crawl out of the wreck and drag Rezvan out onto the grassy shoulder. And then, instead of watching my own body run down the long charcoal highway, I stayed above Rezvan. I watched the trees bow in the wind toward his body, listening for his heartbeat.

Later that night, when I entered his hospital room for the first time, I expected him to refuse to speak to me. Rezvan smiled, though. "In my country," he said, "you could work for Ceauşescu. He has been trying to do this to me for years." I started apologizing then, over and over. Rezvan just motioned me toward the bed and then put his arms around me. "It's okay, it's okay," he said. "Don't cry. This is America. This is what is supposed to happen. I will sue you, and your insurance will give us money, and we will go on a trip. To California, a vacation. I am so happy."

I wiped my eyes and looked at him. His head was cocked to the side. A thin white bandage was wrapped around his

forehead, and blood was still matted in the black curls of
his hair. One side of his face was torn apart. His leg was suspended in a sling. Still, he looked at me incredulously, wondering how I could be crying when this was such a stroke
of luck.

For the next few months he had a cane, which he loved.
He liked to point at things with it. The scars settled into faint
but permanent tracks down the left side of his face. He liked
that, too. We saw the movie *Scarface* over and over again.
When he discarded the cane, he still walked with a slight
limp, which gave his gait an easy rocking motion that seemed
strangely to suit him. He never once blamed me; I don't think
it ever crossed his mind.

Rezvan and I stayed engaged for two years. He seemed to
think of engagement as an alternative to marriage rather than
as a lead-up to it. I didn't mind, actually. I just wanted to be
with him. Life with Rezvan had a sort of gloss to it always.
He passed quickly from emotion to emotion, from sadness to
gratitude to arrogance, but he never fell into depression, ever.

Perhaps because I was so happy with Rezvan, I did not
notice what may have been obvious signs. But, oddly enough,
the signs indicating that a man is in love with another woman
are often similar to the signs of an immigrant in a new country, his heart torn in two. He wrote long letters home; he
hesitated to talk about the future; during lonely nights he
seemed to be murmuring as he fell asleep, but not to me.

Nearly a year passed before I even noticed anything, or
admitted to myself that I noticed anything. Then one day
Rezvan received a phone call at four in the morning. I didn't
understand a word of it, since it was in Romanian, but in
my half sleep I could hear him mutter the word *rila* again

and again, sometimes insistently. And when he hung up, after about an hour and a half, he just sat there in the living room like a paralyzed man, the light slowly rising across his body. I asked him, "Rezvan, what does *rila* mean?" He told me that it meant "well lit," as in a room.

Two days later, as I walked up our driveway in my house-coat, the mail in my hand, I glanced through the letters and noticed a thick letter from Rilia Balescu. Rila was Rilia, a person, a relative. When I walked in the door, Rezvan was standing in his striped pajamas drinking coffee, smoking, scratching his head. As I handed him the letter, I tried to read his face, but saw nothing. So I said, "Who is Rilia?"

"She is my sister, my baby sister. Gavrilia."

Does an extra beat pass before one tells a lie? This is what I had always believed, but Rezvan answered immediately. Perhaps he had been waiting for the question.

"I didn't know you had a sister."

"I don't like to talk about her. We disowned each other long ago. She follows Ceauşescu still; she has pictures of him and his son on her wall as if they were rock stars. I am trying to bring her over, but she is stubborn. She would rather go to the Black Sea and vacation with her boys than come here and live with me."

"So why have you never told me about her?"

"Because it is not wise to speak aloud the one thing you want more than anything. You know that."

"No, I don't know that."

"It's true. Romanians have a word for it: *ghinion*. It means don't speak aloud what you want most. Otherwise it will not happen. You must have a word for this in English?"

"Jinx."

"Okay. I did not tell you about my sister because of jinx."

"Why did you tell me her name meant 'well lit'?"

"Pardon?"

"The other day I asked you, and you said that 'Rilia' was the word for 'well lit.'"

"No, no. *Rila* is the word for 'well lit.' Rilia is my sister." He smiled and kissed my face. "We will have to work on your accent."

Over the next month we settled into a routine. When Rezvan finished writing his letters in the night, he padded down the driveway, set the letters in the mailbox, and lifted the tiny, stiff red flag so that our mailman would stop in the morning. And then, after Rezvan was asleep, I would rise out of bed and go to the mailbox myself, pick out the ones to Rilia, and slip them into the pocket of my housecoat. I did the same thing with the letters she sent him. I collected those in the morning.

At first it didn't feel like a strategy. I was desperate to know if Rilia really was his sister or his wife—as if her handwriting would tell me. Rezvan left for work an hour before I did, and I opened the letters then. I sat on our bed, laying the pages in front of me, cross-referencing. Some of her passages were blacked out by censors. I found many names, but mostly two, Gheorghe and Florian, again and again. Gheorghe and Florian, Gheorghe and Florian, Gheorghe and Florian. I began to realize, very slowly, that these were probably their children.

On one of these mornings my mother showed up at my door to drop off a skirt she had sewed for me. "Good," she said, bustling in, "you're home. I wanted to drop this off." Already, as she said this, she was rapidly moving through the rooms of our apartment. My mother liked to do this, to catch me off guard and check all my rooms immediately for anything I might hide if given the time. "What is this?" she said, reaching the bedroom, where all the pages were strewn across the bed.

"Oh, that's just some stuff I'm reading for Rezvan. Proofreading."

She picked up a sheet. "Oh, so now you proofread in Romanian?"

I smiled weakly. She didn't pry, but for once I wished she would. What I wanted to do was tell her that this was my life spread across the bed, thin as paper, written in a language I could not understand, dotted with four names—Rezvan, Gavrilia, Gheorghe, Florian—but never my own. I wanted to ask her how she felt when my father was having an affair. And I wanted to ask what happened to the other woman. My father never married her, even after he and my mother split. Where had she drifted off to? Did she ever lose her breasts? Did she get well again? Was she happy somewhere now?

I didn't tell my mother anything, but when she left that day, she gestured toward the bedroom. "You know that you can find people at the university who will translate that for you."

I nodded and stared at my feet.

"Maybe you don't really need them translated? Maybe you already know what they say?" She ducked her face under, so that she could look at my face. "It'll be okay," she said, "either way."

I stockpiled the letters for two months. I didn't intend to be malicious; I was just sitting on them until I could figure out what to do. Every night as I drove home from the fields, I thought, I will tell Rezvan tonight; I will say I know everything and I am leaving. But when dinner came, I could hardly speak. It was as if I were eleven all over again.

Even Rezvan was getting depressed. He said that his letters

were turning out to be all in vain. Perhaps, he said, he would quit writing them altogether. One night he said, "Nothing gets through those bastards. Perhaps I will never see Rilia again." Then he limped to the sink, rocking back and forth, and filled his glass with water. He turned to me and said, "Why would they want to keep us apart, anyway?" His head was tilted to the side, and he looked like a child. He stared at me as if he really expected me to answer.

"I don't know," I said. "I don't know about that stuff."

But of course I did. At the other end, across the ocean, men in uniforms were collecting letters and censoring them, blacking out whatever threatened them, and at this end I in my housecoat was doing the same thing.

I tried to rise above the situation, but that strategy didn't work at all. I was increasingly distressed at what I saw. I'd fly up and look down. There she is, I'd say, Margit Bergen of Saskatchewan. Who would have thought she'd grow up so crooked, crouched on her bed, obstructing love, hoarding it, tearing it apart with her own hands.

Until this point in my life I had always thought of myself as an open-minded person, able to step into another's shoes. But I could not picture this Rilia. Her face, and the faces of her children, were blank for me. I hoped that this inability, or unwillingness, to imagine another's face was not hatred, but I was deeply ashamed that it might be.

Finally, one windy night in November, as I cut into a roast, I said, "Rezvan, is Rilia your wife?"

"What do you know of Rilia? Has she called? Has she sent a letter?"

"No, not at all. I was just wondering."

"Tell me what you know."

"I don't know anything. I was just asking."

"Have you spoken to her on the phone?"

"No, I have not." I enunciated this very clearly. "Is she your wife, Rezvan?"

"I am not a liar," he said. "I will marry you to prove this. We will go to British Columbia and get married in the trees. Whenever you want. Tomorrow, if you like."

The next morning I put the letters in a bag and drove straight to the administrative offices at the university. A woman disappeared and reappeared with a list of professors who could translate Romanian for me. I had my choice of four. I glanced down the list and there, at number three, was Professor Roland Pine.

I found him in the same office. He had aged well, his hair now ash instead of blond, a few extra lines across his face. When he stood up to greet me, I saw that I had grown to be about half a foot taller than he was. His tic was still there, flashing across his face every fifteen seconds or so. As I shook his hand, I marveled that it had continued like this since the last time I'd seen him, keeping time as faithfully as a clock.

"My name is Margit Bergen. I came to you once as a child."

"Hello, Margit. It's nice to see you again. Was I helpful?"

"Yes, very. I've always been grateful."

"What was the problem in those days?"

"Just childhood depression, I guess. My parents were splitting up."

He squinted at me, and turned his face slightly to the side. "Oh, yes," he said. "That's right. Of course. Little Margit. You were such a girlie-whirl. So sad. What did you become?"

"You mean in my life?"

"In your life. What did you become?"

"A soil consultant."

"What a good job for you." He gestured toward the black leather chair. His birds fought in their high cages, their wings tearing at each other. "Mortalhead. You be nice to Eagerheart." He turned to me. "The kids love funny names, you know. Mortalhead, Eagerheart, Quickeye."

I smiled and sat down in the chair, pulling a stack of letters from my bag. "Professor Pine," I said.

"Call me Roland," he said. He leaned back. His face cracked in a tic. "Roland Boland. Just think: little Roland and little Margit, the professor and the soil consultant, back again, sitting in a warm office surrounded by bird-people." He rolled his eyes and grinned, almost girlishly.

I didn't know what to say. "Yes, it's nice," I eventually said. "Actually, Roland, I was wondering if you could help me out with a problem I have."

"I thought I solved all your problems." He looked disappointed.

"You did. I mean, for twenty years you did."

"What could be the problem now?"

"I need you to translate these letters for me, from Romanian."

"Romanian?" He took the stack of letters from me, and began to leaf through them. "Is your name Rezvan?" he said.

"He's a friend of mine."

"Then you should not read his letters." He smiled.

"Professor Pine, I really need you to do this for me."

"Who is Rilia?"

"I don't know. Look, you don't even need to read them to me. Just read them to yourself and tell me if the people writing them are married."

"Why do you want to know?"

"That doesn't matter. I just do."

"Why?"

I didn't say anything.

"Are you being a dirty-girlie?" He smiled—and then a tic, as forked as lightning.

I sighed and looked over at his birds, who were cawing loudly. One was green with black wings, and it was flapping furiously, staring at the letters fluttering in Professor Pine's hand.

"Fine, Professor Pine. If you don't want to read them, I'll take them to somebody else." I reached for the letters.

He pulled them back, toward his chest. "Okay, okay, girlie," he said. "You are so stubborn, Margit."

He read softly, in a lilting voice, as if he were reading me a bedtime story. "Rilia says, 'Remember how tiny Florian was at his birth? Now he is forty-five kilos, the same as his brother.' Rilia says, 'Remember the Black Sea, it is as blue as the first time we went to it.' Rilia says that Rezvan must be lying when he says there is so much food that sometimes he tosses rotten fruit from the window."

I interrupted. "Do you think they are married?"

"Well, they are both Balescus."

"They could be brother and sister?"

He frowned, and leafed through the letters again. "But here she calls him darling. Darling, barling, starling."

He looked up then. "Oh, no," he said, "don't cry. Please don't cry." He jumped up, came around the side of the desk, and crouched beside my chair. He looked up at me. His face was close, and the next tic was like slow motion. I saw the path that it followed, curving and winding like a river down his face.

He sat back on the edge of his desk. "It's going to be okay," he said. "We just have to figure out what the girlie wants. If you want Rezvan, the liar face, you can have him. Is that what you want?"

"No, I don't think so. I mean, I do, but I can't. He has kids and everything."

"Then it sounds like you've made up your mind already."

"Not really," I said.

"Margit, you need some perspective."

"Perspective?"

"You know"—he rolled his eyes upward—"Slatland."

Slatland—I remembered that that was what he'd called it, the drifting up and looking down.

"I've tried Slatland. It didn't work," I said.

"Slatland always works. Just close your eyes, all right, girlie?"

I started to stand up. "Thanks for your help, Professor Pine. I really have to go now." But then I felt it, the lift, and my mind started rising, until the caws of Mortalhead and Eagerheart and Quickeye were far below me. I could see the yellow fields surrounding my town, and then even those went out of focus. I hurtled faster and faster until I finally stopped, what seemed like minutes later.

So this is Slatland, I thought. I looked down, and to my left I saw North America, large and jagged, flanked by oceans. Its face was beautiful—craggy, broken, lined with rivers. I found my part of the continent, a flat gold rectangle in the upper middle. I saw what my daily life looked like from this distance: my truck beetling through the prairies, dust rising off its wheels the way desire must rise, thousands of fragments of stone lifting off the earth. And when the truck stopped and I stepped out into the bright, empty fields, my loneliness looked extreme. I could almost see it, my longing and desire for Rezvan rising out of me the way a tree rises out of its trunk. I perceived, in an instant, exactly what I should do to keep him. I saw how simple it all would be, just to keep collecting the letters every morning, one by one, in order that what was between Rezvan and his wife would die slowly and easily and naturally, and what was between him and me would grow in exactly the same proportion.

If I had been able to climb down then, to drop out of Slatland at that moment, everything would have remained simple, and probably Rezvan and I would still be together. But Slatland seemed to have a will of its own. It would not let me go until I looked down to my right. If I was willing to see the simplicity, the purity, of my own desire, then I also had to see the entire landscape—the way desire rises from every corner and intersects, creates a wilderness over the earth.

I stood on Slatland a long time before I looked down to my right. There it was, Eastern Europe, floating above the Mediterranean. I traced with my finger the outline of Romania. I squinted, down through the mist and mountains, down through the thick moss of trees, until I found her. She stood in a long line of people, her forty-five-kilo children hanging on her skirts. She bent to them and broke for them some bread as hard as stone. I hovered a few feet above her and watched. Even so, I might still have been able to return to my own life, my own province, unchanged if she hadn't turned her face upward right then, as if she had felt some rain, and looked directly at me.

This all happened very fast, in a blink of my eyes. When I opened them, Professor Pine was sitting on his desk, watching me. "You're a real erky-terk," he said, with a tic so extreme that it looked like it might swallow his face. He walked me to the door and handed me the letters, which later that night I would give to Rezvan. We would be standing on the balcony in the semidarkness of the moon, and I would be surprised at how easily they passed through my hands, as easily as water.

The birds shrieked. "Birdmen!" Professor Pine said. "Sometimes I feel like saluting them," he said to me. He shook my hand. "Good luck, girlie-whirl." Then he went up on his tiptoes and kissed me good-bye.

THE EARLY DEATHS OF LUBECK, BRENNAN, HARP, AND CARR

Jesse Ball

THE FIRST

Four of them were on one side of a dim room.

—I'm going to try it, said the first.

The girl watched herself in the mirror as the young man approached.

—I wonder, he said. I thought perhaps . . .

He stopped mid-sentence, for tears had begun to well up in the girl's eyes. She began to cry.

—Please, she said, just leave me alone.

She wore a straight brown dress, buttoned all up the side, and a long tweed coat. Her hair was braided into itself.

—Are you all right? he asked. Can I help you?

—You know, you can't just speak to people. That's not how things are anymore. No one wants to just be spoken to.

She rubbed her eyes.

—It's rather silly of you. Already you look a bit like a fool.

The barkeeper, standing just across the bar, nodded.

—There are rules, he said.

And indeed, on the wall, a list of rules.

—I'm sorry. I didn't know.

—That's no excuse.

The girl stood up as if to go.

—I'll take care of this, Myrna, said the bartender. You stay where you are. He came around the bar toward Harp. He was a big man, with thick forearms like a steelworker.

—It's time for you to go, lad. The others too.

—Come on, said Harp, taking a step back. The place is empty. I'll just go back to the table. We'll mind our own business.

—Hey, Barton! the man called to the back. Another man appeared.

—Get out.

Harp's friends had come over.

—What's the problem? said Lubeck.

—The lot of you, said the barkeeper. Get out.

—We didn't do anything, said Carr. Why should we leave? Our money's good.

The girl spoke up.

—He told me if I didn't go into the back with him he'd hit me. He said he was going to take me off somewhere and tear me in half. Wouldn't think nothing of it, he said. Just like that.

Her face was fierce and covered in tears.

—What? I didn't . . .

The barkeeper and the man called Barton looked at each other.

Barton grabbed Harp and lifted him from the ground. At a half run, he went for the door and heaved him through.

The barkeeper took Brennan's shoulder. Brennan wrenched away and ran out past Barton. It was a general flight.

—If I ever see you in here again, said the barkeeper.

......

Harp's face was bruised and cut from the street where he'd
been thrown. They dusted him off and continued on.

—What was that?

—Why did she say that?

—Who was that girl?

They soon came to another place and began again. Lubeck
was talking to two dressed like matchstick girls.

—Can you believe it?

—That's ridiculous, said the first girl. She must have a
score to settle, and she can't settle it.

—I don't know, said the second girl. Maybe you deserved
it. I don't know.

Lubeck spoke up.

—But Harp didn't say anything like that. The girl just
invented it. She made it all up.

—Well it had to come from somewhere, didn't it, said the
second matchstick girl. It had to come from somewhere.

—That's right, said the first matchstick girl. Even if she
was making it up.

—But it's not fair, said Carr. She made the whole thing
up. It wasn't true.

—Well, I guess you're right then, said the second matchstick girl. But any way you look at it, you lost. If she wasn't
lying, well then, your friend deserved what he got, and it was
her speaking up that caused him to get punished, in which
case she won, and if she *was* lying, then she managed to trick
those guys into throwing you out, in which case she still won.
She won and you lost, and it was the four of you against just
her. That's pretty good.

The matchstick girls agreed: the girl in the brown dress
had won. An hour or two went by.

It was thus late in the evening when one of the match-stick girls yelped.

—Hey, isn't that the girl. Isn't that her out the window?

—That's her, said Harp. Damned if it isn't her. Let's go.

—What'll we do? asked Carr.

—I don't know, said Harp. Let's go.

The party poured out into the street, with the four young men ahead of the others. Indeed, the long tweed coat and brown dress of the girl could be made out just up ahead. It had snowed the day before, and drifts and piles lined the street. The girl walked there in the company of an older man.

—Let's pelt them, said Harp.

He forced the brown gritty snow into a ball as the others did the same. Then with a shout, they ran forward, throwing the snowballs as hard as they could.

The first missed the man's shoulder by an arm's length. But the second struck him. He turned, face lit up with anger. The girl stopped too, and turned, and just at that moment, a snowball struck her hard in the face. In the moment before it struck a fact became plain to all of them: it was not the girl, but someone else, a woman of perhaps forty.

She tumbled down, falling heavily onto her back with a cry. The man started after them. What was there to do? They ran. Down the first alley, onto the next street, a right turn, a left, onto another street, onto another alley. They were young and in good health, so they made it safely away.

THE SECOND

Carr woke to banging on the door to his flat. He pulled on a pair of pants and went to see what it was.

It was Harp.

—You've got to come with me. It's bad. Come to Lubeck's place.

Lubeck and Brennan, two of the four young men, lived near the river in a big house owned by Lubeck's mother.

—Give me a second, said Carr.

He finished dressing and then the two were walking in the street.

—What is it?

—Lubeck got a letter. You'll see. More than that, Harp wouldn't say.

It was Lubeck's mother let Carr in. Brennan came to the door too. Lubeck was sitting in a chair by the window.

—What is it? asked Carr. What happened?

Brennan took a letter off a side table and handed it to Carr.

—Read it for yourself, he said.

Dear J. Lubeck,

It is my understanding that you and three others, L. Carr, F. Brennan, and J. Harp, were on Sycamore Street last night where I went walking with my wife. You must understand that we were at the hospital much of the night. My wife has been caused to have a miscarriage. While I might take this matter up with the police, I prefer, as a gentleman, to meet with you and decide the matter by force. Your family has long lived in this town, so I believe you will honor your commitment. Come then, tomorrow morning, that is, December 5, to the racing track out past

Elridge Green no later than six a.m. Bring a second,
as I shall.

> *Most sincerely,*
> *Judge Allen Henry*

Lubeck's mother called to Lubeck from across the room.

—You won't fail us, will you, John?

—There's nothing to do, said Lubeck, standing up, still looking out the window. There's nothing to do.

—That's right, said his mother. It's the only thing.

She looked at them one by one—Brennan, Carr, Harp—full in the face.

—A thing like that, she said. It's awful. There's no choice in the matter. You've got to have it out or we can't live in this town.

Lubeck's brothers and sisters had come into the room. There were eight of them of various ages. Lubeck's step-father also had come in.

—A bad business, a bad business, he said, and pulled at his mustache. Seems to me you deserve what you get.

—That's right, said Lubeck's mother.

—These days, what with automobiles and propeller air-planes, the power of man is getting stronger and stronger, said Lubeck's stepfather. If he doesn't learn some moral strength, it'll all be as unjointed as a scarecrow.

—I don't even know what you're saying, said Lubeck.

—Suit yourself, said Lubeck's stepfather.

—This is a very very bad thing, said Brennan.

—It's a very bad thing, all right, said Lubeck's mother.

......

The next morning, Carr went with Lubeck. Brennan had refused, and though Harp had wanted to come, Lubeck wouldn't have it.

—You've got to come along, Lubeck had told Carr. Just you.

They took Lubeck's stepfather's automobile and drove out from the town. The morning light where the snow still held was strong in their eyes, and they squinted as they came.

Soon they reached the track. A car could be seen through the bare trees and a few figures beside it.

Lubeck pulled in and stopped the engine.

—The pistols are there, the man said.

He was as old as the Judge. Both wore overcoats over dark suits. Both wore hats and thin leather gloves. They had laid a soft cloth over a portion of the car's hood. On the cloth were two revolvers. The scene was very dignified. One would want, as a child, to be old enough to take part in such a thing, to be there in the heaving coldness of morning, in the careful grace of winter, though of course, the true penalty of death cannot be considered in its depth by such a little fool as a child. No, no.

—Either, said the Judge.

—What?

—You can take either.

The Judge's second walked out and drew two lines in the earth of the cinder track, about twenty feet apart. He called Carr over.

—The way this thing is going to get done, well, this is it. Lubeck and Judge Henry will wait, each some yards behind their line. At our word, each approaches his line. When the line is reached, they begin to fire.

—How many shots can they . . . ?

—Eight in each revolver. If they both run out, we start again. He looked at Carr with disgust.

—You were with him, weren't you? You're one of them?

—I, well . . .

The man turned his back on Carr and approached the place where the Judge was waiting.

—All set, he said.

Judge Henry motioned to Lubeck to take a pistol from the hood. Lubeck hesitated, then chose, lifting the gun uncertainly.

Carr was at his side. They took a few steps together away from the others.

—You can leave. You don't have to do this, he said quietly. Leave the town. Leave the country.

Lubeck looked at him and then away.

—Tell them I'm ready.

—To your posts, said the Judge's second.

The Judge and Lubeck stepped out onto the track.

Carr felt as if someone were squeezing all the air out of his body. Things became slow and strained. He heard the man call "Now!" and watched as Lubeck and the Judge advanced, step by step. Near the lines, they raised their pistols. They pointed their pistols at each other. Carr couldn't breathe. He was held there, without breath, as the shots began. Lubeck fired and fired. The Judge fired, fired again. Both continued advancing. The noise was incredible. He felt he had never heard anything so loud. Lubeck fired and the Judge flinched, and then they were just walking at each other. The Judge let out three shots in a row. The shots poured from his revolver. Lubeck was not firing. His face was turned away. The first shot came. The second shot came. The third shot came, and Lubeck was backward off his feet.

Carr ran out onto the track. He slowed his pace as he drew closer. The bullet had taken Lubeck high in the cheek and gone straight through his head. The face was a bloody wreck. He was no longer there.

Carr realized he had started to breathe again. He turned. The Judge and his second were conferring. The second came over, passed Carr, knelt by Lubeck's body. He was taking the pistol back. He removed the pistol from Lubeck's hand, opened it, dropped the spent shells on the ground, and walked away.

Then he paused.

—You, the second said. Give this to Brennan. It was a letter.

Across the length of track, the Judge was looking straight into Carr's eye. His face was carved like a mask of a face.

THE THIRD

Carr drove very gently along the road. He had found soft leather driving gloves on the dash and he had put them on and now he was driving gently. He negotiated one turn, then another. He was bringing Lubeck's mother her son's body. Such a thing he had never done, but he felt it was within him to do it.

Lubeck was stretched out in the backseat. Carr had wrapped his head in a sack. Other than that, he might have been asleep. One often, however, can take the sign of a bag over a person's head to mean that something bad has either happened or will happen. So anyone observing the scene would not have to wonder for very long at the difficulties that were assailing young Carr as he drove gently on the twisting road back into town.

Over a small bridge and down by the harbor. Along an alley and stopped beside a huge oak. Then, to the door.

—*Come out*, he said. *Come out.*

They came out, many of them, a crowd of them, all down to the road where Lubeck was. Carr went gently away.

Do you know the surface of the stream? Do you know its depth? Do you see as fish see, that water is not one but many, that there are paths through it, just as through land, and that to pass along a stream is a matter well beyond the powers of any human being?

Carr was reading from a thin book. He was still near the harbor, on a bench. He felt that he could not leave without giving Brennan the letter. But he did not want to.

A little girl was there with a cygnet on a narrow leather leash. She drew near and looked at Carr. Carr looked at her.

—When it grows up, it will do its best to hurt you, he said. I know that much.

—Her name is Absinthe, said the girl. And I'm Jane Charon.

—Nice to meet you, Jane.

—Not so nice for me, said Jane stoutly. You say such horrible things.

—I saw a swan maul a child once, said Carr. The child had to be removed. To the hospital, I mean. The swan was beaten to death with a stick.

Jane covered the cygnet's ears. You'll have to imagine for yourself what that looked like. I don't really know where a bird's ears are.

—But, said Jane. If you were there, why didn't you help the child?

—Sometimes, when you see something awful about to happen, although you are a good person and mean everything for the best, you hope still that the bad thing will happen. You watch and hope that the awful thing will happen and that you will see it. Then when it happens you are surprised and shocked and pretend that you didn't want it to happen. But really you did. It was that way with me and the swan.

—So you were on the swan's side? asked Jane.

—I guess so. Yes, that's right.

—Well, that's even worse. It's all right for a person to pick a side, but once he's on that side he should stay there. You ought to have helped the swan escape. You should have stopped them from killing it and helped it away. Or even helped it to maul the child, if you were really the swan's friend. How could anyone ever trust you?

Jane gave Carr a stern look and continued on down the path. The cygnet nipped at him as it passed, but its beak got fouled up in Carr's coat, and it missed.

—You can't own a swan, anyway, Carr yelled. The Queen of England owns them all already.

And it was true. The Queen of England is the owner of all swans. It was decided a long time ago, and so it has always been.

The letter was in a cream-colored envelope. Francis Brennan, it said on the outside.

Carr gave the envelope to Brennan. He was standing on the stairs. Then he was handing the envelope to Brennan.

—What is this? said Brennan.

—They gave it to me. This morning, they gave it to me, for you. Brennan took the envelope reluctantly. He turned it over in his hand.

—Tell me how it happened, he said.

—He shot Lubeck, and then they gave me the envelope. That's it.

—That's it, said Brennan. He opened the envelope.

The floor of the room was wooden, and the boards ran for a very long way. Carr saw the board all the way to the wall and then back.

Brennan handed the opened letter back to Carr.

—What's there to do? said Brennan.

He was a man of some principle, Brennan. He was studying for a doctorate in philosophy and believed in maintaining a certain decorum in one's manner of life. Nevertheless, he had refused to go with Lubeck that morning, and now he was to go himself.

—You'll go with me, won't you? he said to Carr.

—I will, said Carr, feeling the massive unbowed hand of fate upon his shoulder.

A long pause, then:

—Was he a very good shot? asked Brennan.

—Rather not. They were pretty close, and firing and firing. He must have missed Lubeck six or seven times.

He did not say anything about how Lubeck had stopped firing. He felt it might make matters worse.

—Six or seven times, said Brennan to himself. Six or seven times. At how many paces?

—Paces? I don't know about paces. It was about twenty feet, though closer when he shot him.

Brennan nodded.

—Twenty feet.

It mustn't have seemed to Brennan that the Judge was a very good pistoleer. However, the fact of the matter is, it is not so easy to shoot someone with a gun, even when you want to. In the Great War, for instance, people were always shooting their guns in the air instead of at the enemy.

—I'm going to just be here, said Brennan.

—All right.

—I'll just be here, all right?

—All right. And I'll meet you here.

—Here's fine.

So Carr left. Outside it was already dark and quite cold. Certain patches of air were colder than others, for there was no wind at all, none. He walked through these various patches and thought all the while of the soft cloth on which the pistols had been laid.

At that exact moment, the cloth was wrapped about both pistols in an intricate way so that the pistols were both protected from each other and from outside objects. The pistols had been taken apart, cleaned and oiled, and put back together. Now they sat in the trunk of the Judge's automobile. The automobile was in the drive before the Judge's house. The Judge was inside, sitting with his wife. She was pleading with him.

THE FOURTH

Carr could not sleep. He tried to read, but couldn't make sense of anything. Then he thought, Perhaps if I sit at the table, which is bare, I will be able to think of something that will put me in a position to sleep.

Often, I think, when one can't sleep it is because one is of a sudden required to come to a certain conclusion or think through a certain idea, and one is unable to do it. Only by sheer exhaustion, deception, or pharmaceuticals can one pass by.

He sat at the table.

The ancient Egyptians believed that there was a traveler, a god who was a traveler, who would come sometimes to your table. You would never know him. He would just come knocking at your door, begging a meal, and if you let him in and fed him, if you gave him a place to stay, and kindness, he would reward you by teaching you the language that cats speak, so that when you were dead you could listen and learn from them the passage to paradise.

Lubeck was never kind, thought Carr. If anyone ever came begging at his door, he did not let that person in.

Brennan was waiting on the steps when Carr arrived. Lubeck's stepfather came out. He gave Brennan a key.

—There's not much to know anyway, he said. It all just continues. Brennan stood up.

—Let's go, he said.

Carr nodded to Lubeck's stepfather. Then away.

It was the same automobile. The sack had not stopped all the blood from coming out of the head the day before, and the backseat was stained.

—I'll drive, said Carr.

Brennan was singing beneath his breath. Carr could not make out what it was. They passed along the streets, over the bridge, out of the town, through fields on the raised road, and again there loomed up the specter of the track, the car through the bare trees, the waiting men beside it.

—How did this happen, said Brennan quietly.

—It's happening, said Carr.

—What's right? said Brennan. If I kill him, then his wife will have lost her husband and her child.

—You can't think about that, said Carr.

—Maybe I'll shoot him in the leg, said Brennan. Then it'll stop.

The pistols were laid out on the hood again, on the same cloth.

—Which one did Lubeck take? whispered Brennan.

—I don't remember, said Carr. They look the same.

—They are the same, said the Judge's second.

—They are not the same, said Brennan. One worked yesterday and the other didn't.

—Are you suggesting—

—No, no. I'm sure both revolvers fired, and accurately. That's not what I'm saying. But one *worked*. Which one was it?

The Judge heard the argument and came over.

—What's the trouble? he asked.

—He wants to know which gun was yours.

The Judge pointed to the left one. Brennan took it.

The marks were still on the track from the day before, but the Judge's second redrew them anyway, with a broken stick. He smoothed over the place where Lubeck fell. He motioned to Carr.

—This goes the same way.

—I've explained it to him, said Carr.

—Right.

Carr nodded to Brennan, who was holding the pistol in both his hands with the barrel pointed down. Brennan walked slowly to the line.

—No, said Carr. You have to be back a bit.

—Oh, said Brennan. I'm sorry, I forgot. His hands were shaking.

The Judge stood well behind his line. He nodded to his second. His second nodded to Carr.

—Ready? Carr asked Brennan.

Brennan's face was curled up. He shook it a little, enough for a nod.

—Now.

The Judge advanced to his line. Brennan stayed where he was.

The Judge raised the revolver and pointed it at Brennan. Brennan raised his pistol. He was still holding it with both hands. The gun shook uncontrollably.

—Come forward to the line, shouted the Judge's second. He turned to Carr. He's got to come forward.

—Brennan, go to the line, said Carr. Brennan looked around uncertainly.

—To the line.

He started to walk forward, his pistol held out before him.

The Judge's gun was pointed at Brennan. He held it carefully and squeezed. The sound came and was gone. It seemed to pass along over the ground, to catch at Brennan and throw him down, and then disperse.

Brennan was coughing and holding his chest. Blood was all on his mouth. He kept wiping it away, but the mouth stayed bloody. There was always more blood and more blood on the mouth.

—Leon, he said. Leon.

Carr knelt by him. The bullet had entered Brennan's chest and pierced his lung. His mouth was full of blood. Blood was on his face and neck, on his hands. He was still holding the pistol. Carr took it from him and put it on the ground.

—Frank, he said. Frank, you're all right.

—I'm all right, said Brennan.

—Just hold it together. We'll get you to a hospital.

—No one's getting to a hospital, said the Judge's second. Carr stood up.

—He's had a bullet through his chest. Isn't that enough for you? I'm taking him to a hospital, and you won't stop me.

—I certainly will, said the Judge's second. He took the pistol up off the ground and held it very seriously in his hand.

A minute passed. Then another. Brennan's coughing was quieter now. Carr started toward the car.

—I'm going to get help. I don't care what you say.

—It's useless to talk about it, said the Judge, approaching. He's dead already.

And indeed Brennan's chest had stopped moving.

—This, for you, said the second, handing Carr an envelope. James Harp, it read.

All around them the morning squatted unwelcoming with long trails of foiling distance.

The Judge and his second were standing together and speaking quietly.

What could they possibly be saying?

THE FIFTH

—James, he said. *James*, he said again, louder, banging on the door.

He could hear the sound of someone moving around inside.

—Harp, you bastard, open the door.

The door opened. Harp stood there in a dressing gown. He was a mess. His face was still swollen up.

—What do you want? he said.

—They're both dead.

—You think I don't know that?

Carr stood there. He couldn't say anything. He tried to, but he couldn't. He was just standing there, holding the envelope. He refused to look at it. He was not holding an envelope. He would not look at it.

He looked down at the envelope.

—What's that? said Harp.

—What?

—What are you holding? Carr, what's that in your hand?

Carr was standing there with the envelope after all. He handed it to Harp.

—It has my name on it. What, you were just standing there with an envelope with my name on it and not saying anything? You got it from them, didn't you? They send you along each day, their messenger. What is that? If you were my friend, you'd have thrown it away. Now I have to see it. Now I have to do something.

—Well, do something, said Carr.

Harp tore open the envelope. A girl came out from his room.

—What's that? she said.

—Nothing, said Harp.

—Give me that, she said. Give it to me.

She tried to take the envelope from Harp. He twisted away. She tore it out of his hands and ran back into the room.

—Come back here!

Harp ran after. Carr followed.

There was a fireplace in the far corner. The girl was standing in front of it. The letter was gone.

—It doesn't make a difference, Alice.

—What do you mean? she said. Harp said nothing.

—What does he mean?

—I don't know.

—You know, damn you. Tell me what he means.

—He means he knows what the letter said, even if he
didn't read it. There's nothing to be done.

She shrieked and started pounding on Harp's chest and
face with her hands.

—No! You're not going. You're not going.

Harp looked over her at Carr. His features had composed
themselves.

—Tomorrow morning? he said. Carr nodded.

Out on the street there was a dandy parade in progress. Little
boys were dressed up in bright blue soldier suits and carrying
little guns and swords and such. Others were with trumpets
and bugles, some with drums. It was quite a clatter. There
were adults too, in adult versions of the ridiculous child uniforms, walking at the front. There was a banner too, but the
banner was already gone up ahead, and Carr could not read
what it said.

The parade was going in the direction that Carr needed to
go. Should I join the parade? he wondered.

That's always the decision one is pressed to make. Do I
join the parade or not? In certain cases the decision is easy,
in others not so.

Now there was a mule with a very small child on it dressed
up also like a mule. Or rather like a monk in a hair shirt.

A hair shirt, thought Carr. I haven't seen one of those in a long time. Yes, these and other thoughts of guilt.

After the mule came four dancers bent up and twisted onto each other to look like an elephant. They were very successful in this. I imagine they were the best ones in the world at being in a parade and looking like an elephant. Even if everyone were to try to do it, they would still be the best, that's how good they were. I wouldn't want you to think that just because no one ever bothers trying to look like an elephant with other people together in a parade that these people being the best didn't mean much because certainly it did. They were pleasant to look at, dragging their way along the street. One had an arm to be the trunk, and it was painted gray like a trunk, and all the hair had been shaved from it. It moved back and forth the way an elephant trunk moves, always seeming like it was about to investigate some smell or shape. The people who made up this elephant were determined. It must have hurt a great deal to go all the way through the town on the hard pavement.

And that was that about the elephant. Already it was gone.

Next came a group of little girls with pigeons on their shoulders. These were the kind that send messages. Apparently there is a society of girls that does this all the time. Although I have never seen them in action, I believe it to be true. Carr saw the society pass there and immediately thought of a message he should like to send by pigeon. But, of course, the society was not accepting messages at that time.

When Carr finally got back to his house it was mid-afternoon. He sat on the floor and looked at the books piled up there.

In the evening, he told himself, I will go to a nice café and I will read straight through from beginning to end *Gargantua* in French. Then, someone will approach, a lovely girl most likely, and say, Oh, do you like Rabelais, and I will say, Well, sometimes, but just for light reading, and then I will take out a copy of Locke and pretend that I am a much more serious and orderly person than I actually am. Won't that go well for me.

In fact, at the café he read some Robert Louis Stevenson, who is not just for children, and this was very rousing, and he looked about himself with a bright strong gaze.

It did not seem possible to him that anything that was happening had actually happened or even could actually happen.

Is there to be a funeral, he wondered. Will their funerals be together? He said these things quietly to himself in such a way that they were not really questions. For he himself wondered if it was true that he was the fourth and that he would be the fourth. What, he wondered, would happen then?

Someone did approach him. It was a Prussian bandleader.

—Is there, said the man, some problem?

—No, said Leon Carr.

—Why have you been staring at me then?

—I'm sorry, said Carr. I have been thinking hard about something.

—Ah, said the man. Well, I suppose it's all right then. All the same, I would rather you stop doing it. Will you stop?

—I'll try, said Carr. But it's a bit difficult, you see. You're sitting across from me. If I'm thinking, and looking in that direction, then you might feel I'm looking at you, even if I'm not.

The Prussian bandleader thought about this.

—This is why, he said, in Prussia, we don't allow people to sit opposite one another. It makes for fewer offenses.

—One can't believe a word you say, said Carr.

—There's not much courtesy in you, is there? said the Prussian. Good night.

He doffed his hat to Carr and went back to his seat. From time to time Carr was mindful of staring at the man, and at those times he looked away.

Carr was thinking of how he had imagined for himself a house with a long porch set on a small elevation above a street in a seashore town. He had joined a daydreaming league in the days when those things were popular, and when they would all lie together daydreaming, he would dream of this house. The particulars of each room were clear in his head. He would have bookshelves lining the staircases in the house. There would be many staircases, at least one for every room. Bathrooms would be reached via staircases, rooms would never be on the same elevation. In fact, the house would be a bit of a conundrum for the architect and engineer. He had often imagined explaining his creation. What an argument that would be. He had imagined his reply. *Spare no expense, my boys, spare no expense. I am prepared to pay handsomely.* And then everyone would be smiling and understanding each other.

THE SIXTH

It was freezing cold when he woke. He'd left the window open the night before. He limped across the floor, still draped in blankets, shut the window, and returned to bed. The sky outside was lightening.

I won't go, he thought to himself. I can just stay here. Or, I can get all my things together and leave. I'll go to another town. That wouldn't be so bad. Nothing keeps me here, really. There's no one for me here. I can go.

But Carr most of all felt the guilt of what they'd done, and Carr, of them all, was the last one who would ever run away.

I will run away, he thought.

He packed his things up hastily into a large suitcase. Then he stood looking down into it.

If I don't go now, I'll never be in time to meet Harp.

The door shut. The suitcase was still open on the floor, and Carr, coat in hand, ran down the stairs and out into the day.

He drew his hand back to knock, and the door opened. Harp was standing there, very neatly dressed. He looked quite determined. The girl Carr had seen the day before was there as well, to watch them go. She was not as wild as the day before.

—Good-bye, she said.

—Good-bye.

Harp shut the door.

—The car's in the side alley, he said.

Out the back way and into the alley. There was the car. Out the alley into the street. Along the street to the bridge. Across the bridge to the roads beyond. All down all down to the track, where, through bare trees, one could see a stopped car and figures waiting.

—Whatever happens, don't worry, said Harp. It'll all work out.

—What do you mean?

—Don't worry about what I mean. Don't worry about anything. Just keep clear.

—All right, said Carr.

They got out. Again the Judge was standing with his second. Again the cloth was spread on the hood with the revolvers.

They approached.

The track was a long arc laid out to the side between craggy fists of trees and rising of hills. There were stands in the distance, and stables beyond the stands. Above the stands the sky seemed farther than it ought to be. What was the distance of the sky? Did it change from place to place? People thought once that heaven was somewhere beyond the moon. Everything was divided up that way. Some things were beneath the moon, others above. It meant something to be able to go beyond the moon.

The Judge's second was explaining about how Harp might use either of the revolvers. Harp was staring at the revolvers. He wasn't saying anything, just staring.

—Harp. Harp. Hey, Harp, said Carr. He felt that something was wrong.

—Harp!

Harp looked up suddenly. He was standing with his back to Carr. The Judge and his second were frozen.

—What's the meaning of this?

—I'm not going to die, not today, said Harp.

—What are you doing? shouted Carr.

There was an automatic pistol in Harp's hand.

—There's nothing else to do, said Harp. This is how it is.

—Think of what we did, said Carr. We can't fix that.

The Judge and his second were eyeing Harp warily. Harp seemed to waver for a second. He half lowered the pistol. Suddenly, the second dived at the car. He snatched one of the revolvers from the hood.

Harp turned his arm. He pointed his arm at the Judge's second and shot him in the back. The man sprawled out on the ground.

Harp turned the gun back to the Judge. The shooting had given him some strength. He spoke now with determination. The thing had started.

—You killed Lubeck, and you killed Brennan. Now it's up. It's up. He pointed the pistol at the Judge's head.

—No!

Carr dove at Harp. He didn't think, he just did it. It wasn't fair what they'd done to the Judge and his wife. It wasn't honorable. They had a debt to make good. They had to give the Judge a chance to even things.

He struck Harp from the side. Harp fell beneath him, his pistol going off harmlessly. Harp was underneath him, breathing hard.

Carr struggled to his feet. Harp was cursing and getting up. Then a shot came from behind him. Harp fell down again. The Judge was behind them. He put a bullet into Harp on the ground. Harp was writhing. The Judge put another bullet into him, and another.

—Stop it, shouted Carr.

He started for the Judge. But the Judge turned the pistol on him.

—Keep still.

Carr backed away.

—Stop it, he said.

The Judge knelt beside Harp. Harp was crying.

Another bullet came then into Harp's head and there was just a mess on the ground where Harp had been.

—Can you see it otherwise? the Judge asked. He straightened his coat.

Carr looked over at the Judge's second. The man was still alive, against the car, clutching at a hole in his chest.

The Judge put two fingers in his mouth and whistled. Out of the trees on the far side of the track came two cars. They pulled up. Out of one came a man with a black bag, a doctor. He knelt by the Judge's second and began to administer to him.

The Judge was quietly observing Carr.

—Why did you do that? he said.

—I don't know, said Carr. It was the wrong thing. I should have let him shoot you.

—But you didn't, said the Judge.

He moved as if to pat Carr on the shoulder. Carr pulled away.

—As you will, said the Judge.

He pointed to the cloth on the hood.

—Do you know what that cloth is for?

—No.

—It's for infants. Infants get wrapped in it when you take them home from the hospital. My wife bought it when she knew she was pregnant. Feel how soft it is.

He took the cloth and held it out to Carr. Reluctantly, Carr touched the cloth. It was very soft indeed.

The Judge threw it back onto the hood. He took an envelope from his coat.

—This one, he said, is for you. Good day.

THE SEVENTH

Carr went straight home, and though it was early afternoon, shuttered the windows, lay down, and was soon asleep.

A loud knocking at the door: the wife of the Judge was standing in the hall.

—Leon Carr?

She was wearing a thin wool dress with the same open tweed coat. Her cheeks were gaunt. Carr had never expected to see her. He had not arranged in his head any policy for how he would speak or act.

—I'm so sorry, said Carr. I'm sorry, I . . .

She took his hand in hers and looked patiently into his face. Carr felt almost like crying, so kindly did she treat him.

—I'm sorry, he said again. Come in and sit down.

Then it occurred to him that perhaps she might not want to come in.

—Is that all right? he asked. Would you rather stay out there?

—No, no, she said. Here.

She came into Carr's room. She took off her coat and sat on the bed. She was staring at him and staring at him. Her dress was very thin, and he felt very much for her then. He felt he should not, but he did and he looked at her, there, seated on his bed.

—I don't know what to say.

He tried to think of something kind to say. He felt that because Lubeck and Brennan and Harp were dead the guilt had not gone away but was concentrated all on him.

But she drew him down to the bed beside her and took

his hand. She slid it along her side and up onto her breast. She leaned in.

Her face was along his neck. She kissed him softly.

—It's all right, she murmured. It's all right.

His hand was along her and on her. In a moment, she had pulled her dress off over her head. She was pulling on his pants. She was on top of him. Her hair shrouded the room, and her lips were at the corner of his mouth.

They lay together there, in the bed, smoking.

—I suppose I should tell you, she said. There was no miscarriage.

She got out of the bed and put her dress back on. Carr was sitting with his eyes closed.

—What did you say? asked Carr.

—There was no miscarriage. It was just a reason for my husband to fight you. He felt the honor of young men isn't what it used to be, and if there weren't some serious reason, you wouldn't bear up.

She put on her coat.

—I'm just telling you, she said, because I feel bad about the whole thing. If you like, you don't have to fight him. You can just go. Don't feel guilty, that's all I'm saying.

—This is . . . completely . . . why didn't you come sooner? Do you just let your husband . . . ?

Carr jumped up out of the bed and began to pace back and forth. She was by the door.

—Anyway, she said. Thanks for the good time. The whole situation made this rather intimate.

Carr looked at her helplessly.

—My friends are dead, he said.

—I'm sorry about that.

She opened the door and went out, leaving it open. He went to the door.

—My friends are dead!

But the hallway was empty. Her footsteps sounded away down the stairs.

Now he was in the hall and she was gone.

They say that in a heavy storm one shouldn't be beneath trees for fear of lightning. Also they say don't go into an open field. This is very confusing, as, when I have on occasion been in a place of fields and trees during heavy rain and lightning, I become completely confused. At what point do I stay away from the trees? At what point from the fields? Do I dig a hole in the ground? Do I need to keep a little shovel with me for rainstorms? In such a hole wouldn't the rain collect and drown me? That's not so much better, and in fact would be much the same because I have heard that the bodies of people killed by lightning are bloated in a similar way to those found after a drowning.

Yes, Carr could not fix his mind particularly on anything. How senseless! What should Carr do? He felt very surely that he should go and shoot the Judge. Why had the Judge won the other duels? Because the others had felt guilty. They had let themselves die.

Except for Harp, who was treacherous. Yes, he had been treacherous, because he had thought they had killed the Judge's child, and yet he had still gone on as if they were in the right. What if I were to go to the Judge's house and kill him in the night? Would that be the right thing? And now he had slept with the Judge's wife. Ordinarily a rather bad business, it seemed not to count for anything now.

He would confront the Judge. He would go to the Judge's house, confront him, and then tomorrow morning shoot him to death at the duel.

He felt very good about this resolution. He dressed, put on his coat, and called for a cab to take him to the Judge's house.

The judge's house was, as you might suppose, quite a fine affair. Already the cab was there. He hadn't even remembered getting in. And then he got out.

He felt immediately dwarfed by the house. This is one of the techniques of the very wealthy. They make anyone who comes to visit them feel by virtue of architecture that he or she is a supplicant. I am not a supplicant, thought Carr. I am the aggrieved. I accuse.

He went up the steps. A man was standing at the top wearing a very comprehensive servant costume. Perhaps the man was a servant.

—I'm here to see the Judge.

—He doesn't know it, said the man.

—All the same, said Carr. I'll have my way. I have to see him.

—What you must do and what will happen: they're not the same thing, said the man. It's my job to see the Judge isn't disturbed. All kinds of people come here after the Judge decides criminal cases. They feel they have been dealt with unfairly.

He pursed his lips, then continued.

—Unfairly, fairly. Who's to say that? Why, the Judge. That's why he's a Judge. So, whatever it is that you're here about, why don't you just run along.

He returned to his initial pose.

—Listen, said Carr. I want to see the Judge. I'm going in through the door one way or another.

—Well, said the man. If you are going to go, I won't stop you. But I assure you, there are others more determined than I who are waiting inside.

Carr walked past the man and through the front doors of the house. Inside was a long entrance hall. A coatroom was on one side, with a man standing behind a counter. Before the doors that opened into the house, another man waited. Both wore the same servant costume as the first man.

—Coat, said the first man.

Carr gave the man his coat. He felt like not doing it, but he did it anyway. In giving in to even one of these people's demands, he felt he was giving up some initiative. Nonetheless, he gave up his coat.

—Hold on a second, said Carr.

The man brought the coat back and held it out to him.

Carr reached into one of the pockets and took something out.

The man smiled encouragingly at him in a rather nasty way. Carr sneered in return, but then thought better of it. He didn't want his coat mistreated.

—I'll be back for that.

—If you're not, said the man, we'll throw it away.

He held the coat mincingly in his fingers as though he preferred not to touch it.

Carr turned and walked to the next door.

—Not so fast, said the doorman, smirking meanwhile at the coatroom attendant.

—Not so fast, he said again. Both broke into laughter.

—I need to see the Judge, said Carr.

—Don't let me stop you, said the doorman.

Carr went to go through the door. He tried to turn the handle. The door was locked.

—The door is locked, he said.

Both men broke into fits of giggling.

—Do you have a key? he asked the doorman.

—Do I have a key? the doorman asked the coatroom attendant.

—Yes, of course he has a key. He's the doorman. Both continued their giggling.

—Listen, said Carr. I need to get through that door.

He grabbed the doorman roughly and started to shake him. The man was very weak and small and was hauled nearly off his feet.

—All right, all right, said the man. Here's the key. He gave the key to Carr.

Carr put the key into the lock and turned it. The doorman, loosed from Carr's grip, ran down the hall.

—You'll get it for this, he said.

Carr remembered his coat. He started back for it.

No, he thought. They'll think I'm weak if all I'm worried about is my coat. And also, he thought, that man is a coatroom attendant. They must have some sort of code by which they never let anything bad happen to coats. Otherwise, on what might their pride be based? He decided to rely upon this coatroom attendant's code, and he went on through the door.

On the other side was a broad curving interior staircase. To the left a broad hall that passed by him and went off a ways to the right, just past a wide fireplace.

Where to go? thought Carr.

A girl in a maid's uniform was carrying folded sheets.

—Oh my, she said.

—Where is the Judge?

—I couldn't say, she said. But no one can go around unaccompanied in this house.

She dropped the sheets and ran to the wall. There was a
bellpull there. Carr caught her just in time, pulling her back.
He had caught the back of her dress and it tore open. She
lunged again for the bellpull and it tore the rest of the way.
He was forced to grab her about the waist.

Laughter came then from the stairs.

Carr spun around, still holding the girl, who now clung to
him just in her underwear and torn-off dress.

On the stairs stood the Judge's wife and also three servant men.

—You have quite an appetite, said the Judge's wife.

Carr let the girl go. She clung to him now all the same.

—What are you doing? he said. Get off me.

—First you assault me, she said, and now that you've
ruined my virtue you want to get rid of me. I won't have it.

She held on tight. The girl was a bit too much for Carr.

—Get off me, he said, and shook her off.

—That's no way to treat her, said one of the servants.

—What's the big idea? said another.

—I just came to speak to the Judge. Everyone began to
laugh.

—A fellow like you, speak to the Judge!

A more ridiculous statement they had never heard.

—What's the idea in coming here? said the Judge's wife.
To the servants, then:

—Throw him out.

She turned and went back up the stairs. The servants
came down toward him.

Carr picked up a poker from the fireplace. The servants
eyed him warily.

—I'm going up. You can't stop me.

And then his arms were caught up from behind. Some-one had snuck up on him. The servants came up and took the poker from his hand. One slugged him in the stomach. He keeled over. They struck him a few more times and he blacked out. Then he was lifted hand and foot and taken back out the front, where they threw him unceremoniously on the ground.

Yes, that's where he was, mouth all full of dirt.

The servants had gone back inside.

Carr ran up the steps and into the house. He ran past the coatroom attendant and into the house proper. He ran up the front stairs and searched through the rooms on the upper floor. There were many rooms of every size and description. People were in some, and they shrieked and made horrified noises as he burst in and out. He ran and ran down the hall, which went on for perhaps one or two miles. He was con-tinually forced to stop, heaving and gasping for air, before running on again. Behind him, in the distance, he could make out pursuit.

I must look quite a horror, he thought, covered in dirt and running about. At the end of the hall was another stair. Up that stair he went and found himself in the countryside. It was a broad glad day and there was birdsong in the air. A party of young men was coming along the crest of a hill. He went to meet them.

—We've just come back from the war, they said.

—The war is over, they said.

—Come and sit with us.

There were proud young women with them, and all were

wrapped up in chains of flowers and summer grasses. Over
and over they kept saying it, it gave them such joy on their
mouths to say it, *the war is over, the war is over.*

Carr lay on his back and it was then he remembered
about his coat. He had forgotten it. He was on his way to, on
his way . . .

He was standing again outside the mansion. The door was
locked.

A cab pulled up. A slot in the house's front door slid open.
The coatroom attendant stuck his head through.

—That's your cab, he said. Best to leave now. Here's
your coat.

He stuffed the coat through the narrow slot. Carr took
it. It was not the same coat at all. This was a coat he had lost
once when changing trains, at least ten years before. This coat
was far too small for him.

—Thank you, said Carr.

—Don't thank me, said the coatroom attendant. I'm not
your friend. The slot slid shut.

Was he outside Lubeck's house? Lubeck's mother was there,
shepherding her children about. He could see her through
the window. Then she saw him.

He was inside, and looking at her.

—Oh, this won't do, she said. You're such a mess. Come,
children.

So all the children took Carr to a great cast-iron bathtub
and together they all bathed him and washed him, and when
he got out a fresh set of Lubeck's clothing was sitting there
waiting for him. He put the clothing on. It was a rather nice
pinstripe suit. The children gamboled and danced around him.

—Now you are clean and we shall talk, said Lubeck's mother. Lubeck's stepfather was also present.

—It's much better to gather yourself before important conversations, he said. It just won't do for you to go about like a filthy animal. We don't live in caves, you know. Not anymore.

Carr explained what had happened to him.

Both were horrified. Around them danced and sang the uncomprehending little children.

—The man must be shot! resolved Lubeck's stepfather. I will go and be your second tomorrow.

—Thank you, said Carr.

—But this business at the house, said Lubeck's mother. And this business with the Judge's wife. Why did you take her up to your room and have-to-do with her?

Carr shifted uncomfortably.

—I just felt so guilty, he said. I didn't know what to do.

—Is that what you do when you don't know what to do? Lubeck's mother and stepfather exchanged a look.

—What about this servant girl? asked Lubeck's stepfather. What did she look like with her clothes off?

—Stop it, you, said Lubeck's mother. That's about enough of that.

They walked Carr to the door, patting him on the shoulder and back and commiserating with him. They all felt very keenly the loss of Lubeck and Brennan. To be fair, they were not so sad about Harp.

—Treacherous cur, said Lubeck's stepfather. We should never have let him in the house.

The funeral was to be the following Tuesday.

—I hope to see you there, said Lubeck's mother. Brennan's family is going to travel the whole way, which will take from now until then, and they will stay here for a few days and then return. You are welcome to come and stay here if you like. It is better in such times as these to be around other people.

Tonight, Carr told them, he thought he would rather be alone.

—That's all very well, said Lubeck's stepfather. We are all alone in the face of uncomprehending death.

Lubeck's folks smiled encouragingly at Carr as he went away in the clothes of their murdered son.

Then the dream shuddered, and he woke.

He was lying in bed, in his room. He went to the window and opened it. It was dark out. He'd slept the whole afternoon. The dream was muddled in his head and sat with unconscionable weight. What was true?

He thought and thought.

The Judge's wife, he thought. She didn't come here. Then it was on him again. There was no lie. There had been a miscarriage. He sank to the ground beside the window and sat back, curled against the wall. They were guilty. They *had* done it.

There was a knock at the door.

Carr went toward the knocking. Lubeck's stepfather was standing in the corridor.

—Thought we'd check on you. Everything all right?

Carr shook his head.

—Tomorrow, eh?

Carr indicated that the man should come in.

—No, no, I'm not staying. Just stopped by for a moment.

A thought struck Carr:

—What is the Judge's house like? Have you ever seen it?

—It's a small place, near the mill. A stand of birch trees, and a red house left of the curve.

—I know it, said Carr. So that's the house. It's a small house.

—Yes, said Lubeck's stepfather. A small house. Are you going there?

—Not me.

Carr related the events of the morning.

—So, tomorrow. The track?

—Yes, said Carr. I don't see a way out.

—I'll go with you, said Lubeck's stepfather.

—You don't have to.

—I know I don't have to.

—All right.

—Tomorrow then, I'll come here.

—Tomorrow.

Carr shut the door. The dream had now gone from him completely. He could no longer remember having felt betrayed by the Judge and his wife. His anger at the Judge was vanished in every extremity. In every direction, he could see only what they had done, he, Brennan, Lubeck, and Harp, and how it could not be fixed.

No one explains this to you, he thought. That there are so many things without solution.

He lay down again, and lay for some time, with a blankness in his eyes before sleep drew him on like an ill-shaped coat.

Another dream, and Carr found himself sitting on the lawn of a great landed estate. He could not turn around. He did not know why. Behind him, someone was speaking. A man was speaking about the construction of a cemetery of black granite, of the need for the services of a particular sort of stonemason, of the rationale for a certain wind direction and distance from the sea. Carr drifted deeper into sleep and was gone even from his own dream.

THE EIGHTH

He lay in bed. He could smell the morning where it was around him. A dog was barking somewhere in the building. A wind was blowing, and the house creaked. Doors locked shut strained to be wall, but they might never be. In a moment he had risen and passed out of the room. He did not permit himself to look at it before he left.

Carr was early. He was outside. It was cold. It was early to have gone outside. There were trees that lined the street. Each had been allotted an area of stoned-in earth. More than a hundred years ago, it must have been, for now the trees' roots up and down the avenue stretched and crouched and broke at the surrounding stone. The trees rose to make a tunnel of the street in summer. In winter the fingers met in the air all along, winding about each other. He felt the permanence of the street, of the town, the permanence of the trees. The wind came up again and turned him, pushed him a half step. He looked away from the wind. The sky was brightening. The wind blew harder and harder. He turned up his collar and sheltered against the house.

When he looked back, the automobile was waiting. He got in.

Lubeck's stepfather squinted when he looked at him, put the car in gear, and pulled out into the road.

Carr looked down at his clothing. He was wearing his

best, a three-piece suit, an overcoat. Why? He himself could not say.

The car wound here and there. Lubeck's stepfather was taking a different route. Somehow this was a vague hope. He had never thought of driving in a different way to the track. Might that change things?

But soon enough, the ways came together, and it was over the bridge, through the curling country, and then up ahead they saw distinctly through the starkness a car and two figures waiting.

Lubeck's stepfather pulled to the side of the road.

—I'm sorry, Leon, he said. I can't stay.

Carr nodded. He patted the man's shoulder and got out. He could see through the trees the Judge's profile. The second figure was a woman.

Up to them went Carr.

He nodded to the Judge. He looked then clearly on the Judge's wife. She did not look like she had in his dream. This woman had been quite ill. What must it have been like? he wondered.

—I'm sorry.

The cloth was laid on the hood. The pistols were there.

The Judge had turned away. He was staring off into the trees. Carr touched his shoulder.

—I want to say, said Carr. I want to say I'm sorry to you both. We didn't know what we were doing. It's strange how luck can be so large and small. One turn, and everything goes. I mean . . .

The Judge looked at him wordlessly. The Judge's wife's face was drawn and pale. Her hand twitched.

Carr continued.

—I don't know what this is for you, what your life was, what it would have been. But this, it was something that happened in a street. There are streets and things that happen in them, and no one knows how or why. I want, I mean . . .

He looked around him. The day was now come completely and the track stretched away. The trees rose up. The drive curved into the road that ran on and on into the town that he knew, and beyond. Birds sailed effortlessly between cold branches.

—I mean, he said. I mean . . .

The Judge's wife moved. She put her hand on the Judge's arm.

—Allen, she said. It's time. Let's be done with it.

He turned toward her, and his back was to Carr. Her eyes came over the Judge's shoulder. They were dark and small. There was nothing in them, nothing at all.

—Love, said the Judge quietly, he stopped the other yesterday. Hasn't it been enough?

Carr could not hear her reply, but the Judge spoke again, and then she spoke. She spoke on and on, her voice rising. The Judge turned back then, and his face was grieving.

—Take one, he said. Take a gun. Let's be done with it.

Carr took the pistol closest to him. It felt strange in his hands, smooth and heavy.

The Judge took the other revolver and went out onto the track. Carr followed.

The lines were still there where they had been drawn. A sickness was in Carr's belly. He felt himself thin and weak. He was walking and he was not. He felt that he was watching himself walk to where he would begin.

The Judge was where he would be. Carr heard the Judge's wife call out the signal.

Then they were walking toward each other. Carr held the pistol out in front of him. He pointed it like a stick and pulled at it with his fingers. He pulled with all his fingers and it went off. It went off again. The Judge was still there. They were at the lines. The Judge fired. He fired again. Carr felt his chest was hurting. He felt his legs hurt. He was firing, and the air was very clear. There was a hole in his chest. He could see it there. When had it happened? This was another thing that could not be fixed. Panic and his face white, and he was on the ground with his hands.

He could not see the Judge. He could not see the Judge's wife. The cinders of the track were in his hair. He could feel the track beneath him, and stretching out in every direction above there was a depth to the clouds that seemed very far and good. But then he saw that it was shallow. He felt very much that the sky was shallow, not a trick but something worse, absent all human ambitions. He thought that there were clouds and then clouds behind clouds, and then just air. Where is there that's far enough?

Then shapes took their places. Men were looking down at him. The Judge, the doctor. There was blood on the Judge's coat. The doctor was saying something. He was moving his hands in a gesture. What did it mean? Carr felt if only he knew what the gesture meant, then there would have been something, some one thing to salvage from all of this. But the figures had become very small. One couldn't see them at all, no matter how hard one looked.

SOME OTHER, BETTER OTTO

Deborah Eisenberg

"I don't know why I committed us to any of those things," Otto said. "I'd much prefer to be working or reading, and you'll want all the time you can get this week to practice."

"It's fine with me," William said. "I always like to see Sharon. And we'll survive the evening with your—"

Otto winced.

"Well, we will," William said. "And don't you want to see Naomi and Margaret and the baby as soon as they get back?"

"Everyone always says, 'Don't you want to see the baby, don't you want to see the baby,' but if I did want to see a fat, bald, confused person, obviously I'd have only to look in the mirror."

"I was reading a remarkable article in the paper this morning about holiday depression," William said. "Should I clip it for you? The statistics were amazing."

"The statistics cannot have been amazing, the article cannot have been remarkable, and I am not 'depressed.' I just happen to be bored sick by these inane—Waving our little antennae, joining our little paws in indication of—Oh, what is the point? Why did I agree to any of this?"

"Well," William said. "I mean, this is what we do."

·······

Hmm. Well, true. And the further truth was, Otto saw, that he himself wanted, in some way, to see Sharon; he himself wanted, in some way, to see Naomi and Margaret and the baby as soon as possible. And it was even he himself who had agreed to join his family for Thanksgiving. It would be straining some concept—possibly the concept of "wanted," possibly the concept of "self"—to say that he himself had wanted to join them, and yet there clearly must have been an implicit alternative to joining them that was even less desirable, or he would not, after all, have agreed to it.

It had taken him—how long?—years and years to establish a viable, if not pristine, degree of estrangement from his family. Which was no doubt why, he once explained to William, he had tended, over the decades, to be so irascible and easily exhausted. The sustained effort, the subliminal concentration that was required to detach the stubborn prehensile hold was enough to wear a person right out and keep him from ever getting down to anything of real substance.

Weddings had lapsed entirely, birthdays were a phone call at the most, and at Christmas, Otto and William sent lavish gifts of out-of-season fruits, in the wake of which would arrive recriminatory little thank-you notes. From mid-December to mid-January they would absent themselves, not merely from the perilous vicinity of Otto's family, but from the entire country, to frolic in blue water under sunny skies.

When his mother died, Otto experienced an exhilarating melancholy; most of the painful encounters and obligations would now be a thing of the past. Life, with its humorous theatricality, had bestowed and revoked with one gesture, and there he abruptly was, in the position he felt he'd been born for: he was alone in the world.

Or alone in the world, anyway, with William. Marching ahead of his sisters and brother—Corinne, Martin, and

Sharon—Otto was in the front ranks now, death's cannon fodder and so on; he had become old overnight, and free.

Old and free! Old and free . . .

Still, he made himself available to provide legal advice or to arrange a summer internship for some child or nephew. He saw Sharon from time to time. From time to time there were calls: "Of course you're too busy, but . . ." "Of course you're not interested, but . . ." was how they began. This was the one thing Corinne and her husband and Martin and whichever wife were always all in accord about—that Otto seemed to feel he was too good for the rest of them, despite the obvious indications to the contrary.

Who was too good for whom? It often came down to a show of force. When Corinne had called a week or so earlier about Thanksgiving, Otto, addled by alarm, said, "We're having people ourselves, I'm afraid."

Corinne's silence was like a mirror, flashing his tiny, harmless lie back to him in huge magnification, all covered with sticky hairs and microbes.

"Well, I'll see what I can do," he said.

"Please try," Corinne said. The phrase had the unassailable authority of a road sign appearing suddenly around the bend: FALLING ROCK. "Otto, the children are growing up."

"Children! What children? Your children grew up years ago, Corinne. Your children are old now, like us."

"I meant, of course, Martin's. The new ones. Martin and Laurie's. And there's Portia."

Portia? Oh, yes. The little girl. The sole, thank heavens, issue of Martin's marriage to that crazy Viola.

"I'll see what I can do," Otto said again, this time less cravenly. It was Corinne's own fault. A person of finer sensibilities would have written a note, or used e-mail—or would face-savingly have left a message at his office, giving him time to prepare some well-crafted deterrent rather than whatever makeshift explosive he would obviously be forced to lob back at her under direct attack.

"Wesley and I are having it in the city this year," Corinne was saying. "No need to come all the way out to the nasty country. A few hours and it will all be over with. Seriously, Otto, you're an integral element. We're keeping it simple this year."

"'This year'? Corinne, there have been no other years. You do not observe Thanksgiving."

"In fact, Otto, we do. And we all used to."

"Who?"

"All of us."

"Never. When? Can you imagine Mother being thankful for anything?"

"We always celebrated Thanksgiving when Father was alive."

"I remember no such thing."

"I do. I remember, and so does Martin."

"Martin was four when Father died!"

"Well, you were little, too."

"I was twice Martin's age."

"Oh, Otto—I just feel sad, sometimes, to tell you the truth, don't you? It's all going so fast! I'd like to see everyone in the same room once a century or so. I want to see everybody well and happy. I mean, you and Martin and Sharon were my brothers and sister. What was *that* all about? Don't you remember? Playing together all the time?"

"I just remember Martin throwing up all the time."

"You'll be nice to him, won't you, Otto? He's still very sensitive. He won't want to talk about the lawsuit."

"Have you spoken to Sharon?"

"Well, that's something I wanted to talk to you about,

actually. I'm afraid I might have offended her. I stressed the fact that it was only to be us this year. No aunts or uncles, no cousins, no friends. Just us. And husbands or wives. Husband. And wife. Or whatever. And children, naturally, but she became very hostile."

"Assuming William to be 'whatever,'" Otto said, "why shouldn't Sharon bring a friend if she wants to?"

"William is *family*. And surely you remember when she brought that person to Christmas! The person with the feet? I wish you'd go by and talk to her in the next few days. She seems to listen to you."

Otto fished up a magazine from the floor—one of the popular science magazines William always left lying around—and idly opened it.

"Wesley and I reach out to her," Corinne was saying. "And so does Martin, but she doesn't respond. I know it can be hard for her to be with people, but we're not people—we're family."

"I'm sure she understands that, Corinne."

"I hope you do, too, Otto."

How clearly he could see, through the phone line, this little sister of his—in her fifties now—the six-year-old's expression of aggrieved anxiety long etched decisively on her face.

"In any case," she said, "I've called."

And yet there was something to what Corinne had said; they had been one another's environs as children. The distance between them had been as great, in any important way, as it was now, but there had been no other beings close by, no other beings through whom they could probe or illumine the mystifying chasms and absences and yearnings within themselves. They had been born into the arid clutter of one another's behavior, good and bad, their measles, skinned knees, report cards . . .

A barren landscape dotted with clutter. Perhaps the life of the last dinosaurs, as they ranged, puzzled and sorrowful, across the comet-singed planet, was similar to childhood. It hadn't been a pleasant time, surely, and yet one did have an impulse to acknowledge one's antecedents, now and again. Hello, that was us, it still is, good-bye.

"I don't know," William said. "It doesn't seem fair to put any pressure on Sharon."

"Heaven forfend. But I did promise Corinne I'd speak with Sharon. And, after all, I haven't actually seen her for some time."

"We could just go have a plain old visit, though. I don't know. Urging her to go to Corinne's—I'm not really comfortable with that."

"Oof, William, phrase, please, jargon."

"Why is that jargon?"

"Why? How should I know why? Because it is. You can say, 'I'm uncomfortable *about* that,' or 'That makes me uncomfortable.' But 'I'm uncomfortable *with* that' is simply jargon." He picked up a book sitting next to him on the table and opened it. *Relativity for Dummies.* "Good heavens," he said, snapping the book shut. "*Obviously* Martin doesn't want to talk about the lawsuit. Why bother to mention that to me? Does she think I'm going to ask Martin whether it's true that he's been misrepresenting the value of his client's stock? Am I likely to talk about it? I'm perfectly happy to read about it in the *Times* every day, like everyone else."

"You know," William said, "we could go away early this year. We could just pick up and leave on Wednesday, if you'd like."

"I would not like. I would like you to play in your concert, as always."

William took the book from Otto and held Otto's hand between his own. "They're not really so bad, you know, your family," he said.

Sometimes William's consolations were oddly like provocations. "Easy for you to say," Otto said.

"Not that easy."

"I'm sorry," Otto said. "I know."

Just like William to suggest going away early for Otto's sake, when he looked forward so much to his concert! The little orchestra played publicly only once a year, the Sunday after Thanksgiving. Otto endured the grating preparatory practicing, not exactly with equanimity, it had to be admitted, but with relative forbearance, just for the pleasure of seeing William's radiant face on the occasion. William in his suit, William fussing over the programs, William busily arranging tickets for friends. Otto's sunny, his patient, his deeply good William. Toward the end of every year, when the city lights glimmered through the fuzzy winter dark, on the Sunday after Thanksgiving, William with his glowing violin, urging the good-natured, timid audience into passionate explorations of the unseen world. And every year now, from the audience, Otto felt William's impress stamped on the planet, more legible and valuable by one year; all the more legible and valuable for the one year's diminution in William's beauty.

How spectacular he had been the first time Otto brought him to a family event, that gladiatorial Christmas thirty-odd years earlier. How had Otto ever marshaled the nerve to do it?

Oh, one could say till one was blue in the face that Christmas was a day like any other, what difference would it make if he and William were to spend that particular day apart, and so on. And yet.

Yes, the occasion forced the issue, didn't it. Either he and William would both attend, or Otto would attend alone, or they would not attend together. But whatever it was that one decided to do, it would be a declaration—to the family, and to the other. And, the fact was, to oneself.

Steeled by new love, in giddy defiance, Otto had arrived at the house with William, to all intents and purposes, on his arm.

A tidal wave of nervous prurience had practically blown the door out from inside the instant he and William ascended the front step. And all evening aunts, uncles, cousins, mother, and siblings had stared at William beadily, as if a little bunny had loped out into a clearing in front of them.

William's beauty, and the fact that he was scarcely twenty, had embarrassed Otto on other occasions, but never so searingly. "How *intelligent* he is!" Otto's relatives kept whispering to one another loudly, meaning, apparently, that it was a marvel he could speak. Unlike, the further implication was, the men they'd evidently been imagining all these years.

Otto had brought someone to a family event only once before—also on a Christmas, with everyone in attendance: Diandra Fetlin, a feverishly brilliant colleague, far less beautiful than William. During the turkey, she thumped Otto on the arm whenever he made a good point in the argument he was having with Wesley, and continued to eat with solemn assiduity. Then, while the others applied themselves to dessert, a stuccolike fantasy requiring vigilance, Diandra had delivered an explication of one of the firm's recent cases that was worth three semesters of law school. No one commented on *her* intelligence. And no one had been in the least deceived by Otto's tepid display of interest in her.

"So," Corinne had said in a loud and artificially genial tone as if she were speaking to an armed high-school student, "where did you and William meet, Otto?"

The table fell silent; Otto looked out at the wolfish ring of faces. "On Third Avenue," he said distinctly, and returned to his meal.

"Sorry," he said, as he and William climbed into the car afterward. "Sorry to have embarrassed you. Sorry to have shocked them. Sorry, sorry, sorry. But what was I supposed to say? All that completely fraudulent *interest*. The *solicitude*. The truth is, they've *never* sanctioned my way of life. Or, alternately, they've always *sanctioned* it. Oh, what on earth good is it to have a word that means only itself and its opposite!"

Driving back to the city, through the assaultively scenic and demographically uniform little towns, they were silent. William had witnessed; his power over Otto had been substantially increased by the preceding several hours, and yet he was exhibiting no signs of triumph. On the contrary, his habitual chipper mood was—where? Simply eclipsed. Otto glanced at him; no glance was returned.

Back in the apartment, they sat for a while in the dark. Tears stung Otto's eyes and nose. He would miss William terribly. "It was a mistake," he said.

William gestured absently. "Well, we had to do it sooner or later."

We? We did? It was as if snow had begun to fall in the apartment—a gentle, chiming, twinkling snow. And sitting there, looking at one another silently, it became apparent that what each was facing was his future.

......

Marvelous to watch William out in the garden, now with the late chrysanthemums. It was a flower Otto had never liked until William instructed him to look again. Well, all right, so it wasn't a merry flower. But flowers could comfortably embrace a range of qualities, it seemed. And now, how Otto loved the imperial colors, the tensely arched blossoms, the cleansing scent that seemed dipped up from the pure well of winter, nature's ceremony of end and beginning.

The flat little disk of autumn sun was retreating, high up over the neighbors' buildings. As Otto gazed out the window, William straightened, shaded his eyes, waved, and bent back to work. Late in the year, William in the garden . . .

Otto bought the brownstone when he and William had decided to truly move in together. Over twenty-five years ago, that was. The place was in disrepair and cost compara- tively little at the time. While Otto hacked his way through the barbed thickets of intellectual property rights issues that had begun to spring up everywhere, struggling to disentangle tiny shoots of weak, drab good from vibrant, hardy evil, Wil- liam worked in the garden and on the house. And to earn, as he insisted on doing, a modest living of his own, he proofread for a small company that published books about music. Even- tually they rented out the top story of the brownstone, for a purely nominal sum, to Naomi, whom they'd met around the neighborhood and liked. It was nice to come home late and see her light on, to run into her on the stairs.

She'd been just a girl when she'd moved in, really, nod- ding and smiling and ducking her head when she encountered them at the door or on the way up with intractable brown paper bags, bulging as if they were full of cats but tufted with peculiar groceries—vegetables sprouting globular appendages and sloshing cartons of mysterious liquids. Then, farther along in the distant past, Margaret had appeared.·

Where there had been one in the market, at the corner bar, on the stairs, now there were two. Naomi, short and lively, given to boots and charming cowgirl skirts; tall, arrestingly bony Margaret with arched eyebrows and bright red hair. Now there were lines around Naomi's eyes; she had widened and settled downward. One rarely recalled Margaret's early, sylvan loveliness.

So long ago! Though it felt that way only at moments— when Otto passed by a mirror unprepared, or when he bothered to register the probable ages (in comparison with his own) of people whom—so recently!—he would have taken for contemporaries, or when he caught a glimpse of a middle-aged person coming toward him on the street who turned into William. Or sometimes when he thought of Sharon.

And right this moment, Naomi and Margaret were on their way back from China with their baby. The adoption went through! Naomi's recent, ecstatic e-mail had announced. Adoption. Had the girls upstairs failed to notice that they had slid into their late forties?

Sharon's apartment looked, as always, as if it had been sealed up in some innocent period against approaching catastrophes. There were several blond wood chairs, and a sofa, all slipcovered in a nubby, unexceptionable fabric that suggested nuns' sleepwear, and a plastic hassock. The simple, undemanding shapes of the furnishings portrayed the humility of daily life—or at least, Otto thought, of Sharon's daily life. The Formica counter was blankly unstained, and in the cupboards there was a set of heavy, functional, white dishes.

It was just possible, if you craned, and scrunched yourself properly, to glimpse through the window a corner of
Sharon's beloved planetarium, where she spent many of her
waking hours; the light that made its way to the window
around the encircling buildings was pale and tender, an elegy
from a distant sun. Sharon herself sometimes seemed to Otto
like an apparition from the past. As the rest of them aged,
her small frame continued to look like a young girl's; her hair
remained an infantine flaxen. To hold it back she wore bright,
plastic barrettes.

A large computer, a gift from Otto, sat in the living room,
its screen permanently alive. Charts of the constellations
were pinned to one of the bedroom walls, and on the facing wall were topographical maps. Peeking into the room,
one felt as if one were traveling with Sharon in some zone
between earth and sky; yes, down there, so far away—that
was our planet.

Why did he need so many things in his life, Otto wondered; why did all these things have to be so special? Special,
beautiful plates; special, beautiful furniture; special, beautiful everything. And all that specialness, it occurred to him,
intended only to ensure that no one—especially himself—
could possibly underestimate his value. Yet it actually served
to illustrate how corroded he was, how threadbare his native
resources, how impoverished his discourse with everything
that lived and was human.

Sharon filled a teakettle with water and lit one of the
stove burners. The kettle was dented, but oddly bright, as if
she'd just scrubbed it. "I'm thinking of buying a sculpture,"
she said. "Nothing big. Sit down, Otto, if you'd like. With
some pleasant vertical bits."

"Good plan," Otto said. "Where did you find it?"

"Find it?" she said. "Oh. It's a theoretical sculpture. Abstract in that sense, at least. Because I realized you were right."

About what? Well, it was certainly plausible that he had once idly said something about a sculpture, possibly when he'd helped her find the place and move in, decades earlier. She remembered encyclopedically her years of education, pages of print, apparently arbitrary details of their histories. And some trivial incident or phrase from their childhood might at any time fetch up from her mind and flop down in front of her, alive and thrashing.

No, but it couldn't be called "remembering" at all, really, could it? That simply wasn't what people meant by "remembering." No act of mind or the psyche was needed for Sharon to reclaim anything, because nothing in her brain ever sifted down out of precedence. The passage of time failed to distance, blur, or diminish her experiences. The nacreous layers that formed around the events in one's history to smooth, distinguish, and beautify them never materialized around Sharon's; her history skittered here and there in its original sharp grains on a depthless plane that resembled neither calendar nor clock.

"I just had the most intense episode of déjà vu," William said, as if Otto's thoughts had sideswiped him. "We were all sitting here—"

"We *are* all sitting here," Otto said.

"But that's what I mean," William said. "It's supposed to be some kind of synaptic glitch, isn't it? So you feel as if you've already had the experience just as you're having it?"

"In the view of many neurologists," Sharon said. "But our understanding of time is dim. It's patchy. We really don't know to what degree time is linear, and under what circumstances. Is it actually, in fact, manifold? Or pleated? Is it frilly? And what is our relationship to it? Our relationship to it is extremely problematical."

"I think it's a fine idea for you to have a sculpture," Otto said. "But I don't consider it a necessity."

Her face was as transparent as a child's. Or at least as hers had been as a child, reflecting every passing cloud, rippling at the tiniest disturbance. And her smile! The sheer wattage—no one over eleven smiled like that. "We're using the tea-bag-in-the-cup method," she said. "Greater scope for the exercise of free will, streamlined technology . . ."

"Oh, goody," William said. "Darjeeling."

Otto stared morosely at his immersed bag and the dark halo spreading from it. How long would Sharon need them to stay? When would she want them to go? It was tricky, weaving a course between what might cause her to feel rejected and what might cause her to feel embattled . . . Actually, though, how did these things work? Did bits of water escort bits of tea from the bag, or what? "How is flavor disseminated?" he said.

"It has to do with oils," Sharon said.

Strange, you really couldn't tell, half the time, whether someone was knowledgeable or insane. At school Sharon had shown an astounding talent for the sciences—for everything. For mathematics, especially. Her mind was so rarefied, so crystalline, so adventurous, that none of the rest of them could begin to follow. She soared into graduate school, practically still a child; she was one of the few blessed people, it seemed, whose destiny was clear.

Her professors were astonished by her leaps of thought, by the finesse and elegance of her insights. She arrived at hypotheses by sheer intuition and with what eventually one of her mentors described as an almost alarming speed; she was like a dancer, he said, out in the cosmos springing weight-lessly from star to star. Drones, merely brilliant, crawled along behind with laborious proofs that supported her assertions.

A tremendous capacity for metaphor, Otto assumed it was; a tremendous sensitivity to the deep structures of the universe. Uncanny. It seemed no more likely that there would be human beings thus equipped than human beings born with satellite dishes growing out of their heads.

He himself was so literal minded he couldn't understand the simplest scientific or mathematical formulation. Plain old electricity, for example, with its amps and volts and charges and conductivity! Metaphors, presumably—metaphors to describe some ectoplasmic tiger in the walls just spoiling to shoot through the wires the instant the cage door was opened and out into the bulb. And molecules! What on earth were people talking about? If the table was actually just a bunch of swarming motes, bound to one another by nothing more than some amicable commonality of form, then why didn't your teacup go crashing through it?

But from the time she was tiny, Sharon seemed to be in kindly, lighthearted communion with the occult substances that lay far within and far beyond the human body. It was all as easy for her as reading was for him. She was a creature of the universe. As were they all, come to think of it, though so few were privileged to feel it. And how hospitable and correct she'd made the universe seem when she spoke of even its most rococo and farfetched attributes!

The only truly pleasurable moments at the family dinner table were those rare occasions when Sharon would talk. He remembered one evening—she would have been in grade school. She was wearing a red sweater; pink barrettes held back her hair. She was speaking of holes in space—holes in nothing! No, not in nothing, Sharon explained patiently—

in space. And the others, older and larger, laid down their speared meat and listened, uncomprehending and entranced, as though to distant, wordless singing.

Perhaps, Otto sometimes consoled himself, they could be forgiven for failing to identify the beginnings. How could the rest of them, with their ordinary intellects, have followed Sharon's rapid and arcane speculations, her penetrating apperceptions, closely enough to identify with any certainty the odd associations and disjunctures that seemed to be showing up in her conversation? In any case, at a certain point as she wandered out among the galaxies, among the whirling particles and ineffable numbers, something leaked in her mind, smudging the text of the cosmos, and she was lost.

Or perhaps, like a lightbulb, she was helplessly receptive to an overwhelming influx. She was so physically delicate, and yet the person to whom she was talking might take a step back. And she, in turn, could be crushed by the slightest shift in someone's expression or tone. It was as if the chemistry of her personality burned off the cushion of air between herself and others. Then one night she called, very late, to alert Otto to a newspaper article about the sorting of lettuces; if he were to give each letter its numerological value . . . The phone cord thrummed with her panic.

When their taxi approached the hospital on that first occasion, Sharon was dank and electric with terror; her skin looked like wet plaster. Otto felt like an assassin as he led her in, and then she was ushered away somewhere. The others joined him in the waiting room, and after several hours had the opportunity to browbeat various doctors into hangdog temporizing. Many people got better, didn't they, had only one episode, didn't they, led fully functioning lives? Why wouldn't Sharon be part of that statistic—she, who was so able, so lively, so sweet—so, in a word, healthy? When would she be all right?

That depended on what they meant by "all right," one of the doctors replied. "We mean by 'all right' what you mean by 'all right,' you squirrelly bastard," Wesley had shouted, empurpling. Martin paced, sizzling and clicking through his teeth, while Otto sat with his head in his hands, but the fateful, brutal, meaningless diagnosis had already been handed down.

"I got a cake," Sharon said. She glanced at Otto. "Oh. Was that appropriate?"

"Utterly," William said.

Appropriate? What if the cake turned out to be decorated with invisible portents and symbols? What if it revealed itself to be invested with power? To be part of the arsenal of small objects—nail scissors, postage stamps, wrapped candies— that lay about in camouflage to fool the credulous doofus like himself just as they were winking their malevolent signals to Sharon?

Or what if the cake was, after all, only an inert teatime treat? A cake required thought, effort, expenditure—all that on a negligible scale for most people, but in Sharon's stripped and cautious life, nothing was negligible. A cake. Wasn't that enough to bring one to one's knees? "Very appropriate," Otto concurred.

"Do you miss the fish?" Sharon said, lifting the cake from its box.

Fish? Otto's heart flipped up, pounding. Oh, the box, fish, nothing.

"We brought them home from the dime store in little cardboard boxes," she explained to William, passing the cake on its plate and a large knife over to him.

"I had a hamster," William said. The cake bulged resiliently around the knife.

"Did it have to rush around on one of those things?" Sharon asked.

"I think it liked to," William said, surprised.

"Let us hope so," Otto said. "Of course it did."

"I loved the castles and the colored sand," Sharon said. "But it was no life for a fish. We had to flush them down the toilet."

William, normally so fastidious about food, appeared to be happily eating his cake, which tasted, to Otto, like landfill. And William had brought Sharon flowers, which it never would have occurred to Otto to do.

Why had lovely William stayed with disagreeable old him for all this time? What could possibly explain his appeal for William? Otto wondered. Certainly not his appearance, nor his musical sensitivity—middling at best—nor, clearly, his temperament. Others might have been swayed by the money that he made so easily, but not William. William cared as little about that as did Otto himself. And yet, through all these years, William had cleaved to him. Or at least, usually. Most of the uncleavings, in fact, had been Otto's—brief, preposterous seizures having to do with God knows what. Well, actually he himself would be the one to know what, wouldn't he, Otto thought. Having to do with—who *did* know what? Oh, with fear, with flight, the usual. A bit of glitter, a mirage, a chimera . . . . A lot of commotion just for a glimpse into his own life, the real one—a life more vivid, more truly his, than the one that was daily at hand.

"Was there something you wanted to see me about?" Sharon asked.

"Well, I just . . ." Powerful beams of misery intersected in Otto's heart; was it true? Did he always have a reason when he called Sharon? Did he never drop in just to say hello? Not that anyone ought to "drop in" on Sharon. Or on anyone, actually. How barbarous.

"Your brother's here in an ambassadorial capacity," William said. "I'm just here for the cake."

"Ambassadorial?" Sharon looked alarmed.

"Oh, it's only Thanksgiving," Otto said. "Corinne was hoping—I was hoping—"

"Otto, I can't. I just can't. I don't want to sit there being an exhibit of robust good health, or noncontaminatingness, or the triumph of the human spirit, or whatever it is that Corinne needs me to illustrate. Just tell them everything is okay."

He looked at his cake. William was right. This was terribly unfair. "Well, I don't blame you," he said. "I wouldn't go myself, if I could get out of it."

"If you had a good enough excuse."

"I only—" But of course it was exactly what he had meant; he had meant that Sharon had a good enough excuse. "I'm—"

"Tell Corinne I'm all right."

Otto started to speak again, but stopped.

"Otto, please." Sharon looked at her hands, folded in her lap. "It's all right."

"I've sometimes wondered if it might not be possible, in theory, to remember something that you—I mean the aspect of yourself that you're aware of—haven't experienced yet," William said later. "I mean, we really *don't* know whether time is linear, so—"

"Would you stop that?" Otto said. "*You're* not insane."

"I'm merely speaking theoretically."

"Well, don't! And your memory has nothing to do with whether time is 'really,' whatever you mean by that, linear. It's plenty linear for us! Cradle to grave? Over the hill? It's a one-way street, my dear. My hair is not sometimes there and sometimes not there; we're *not* getting any younger."

At moments it occurred to Otto that what explained his appeal for William was the fact that they lived in the same apartment. That William was idiotically accepting, idiotically pliant. Perhaps William was so deficient in subtlety, so insensitive to nuance, that he simply couldn't tell the difference between Otto and anyone else. "And, William—I wish you'd get back to your tennis."

"It's a bore. Besides, you didn't want me playing with Jason, as I remember."

"Well, I was out of my mind. And at this point it's your arteries I worry about."

"You know," William said, and put his graceful hand on Otto's arm, "I don't think she's any more unhappy than the rest of us, really, most of the time. That smile! I mean, that smile can't come out of nowhere."

There actually were no children to speak of. Corinne and Wesley's "boys" put in a brief, unnerving appearance. When last seen, they had been surly, furtive, persecuted-looking, snickering, hulking, hairy adolescents, and now here they were, having undergone the miraculous transformation. How gratified Wesley must be! They had shed their egalitarian denim chrysalis and had risen up in the crisp, mean mantle of their class.

The older one even had a wife, whom Corinne treated with a stricken, fluttery deference as if she were a suitcase full of weapons-grade plutonium. The younger one was rest-

lessly on his own. When, early in the evening, the three stood
and announced to Corinne with thuggish placidity that they
were about to leave ("I'm afraid we've got to shove off now,
Ma"), Otto jumped to his feet. As he allowed his hand to be
crushed, he felt the relief of a mayor watching an occupying
power depart his city.

Martin's first squadron of children (Maureen's) weren't
even mentioned. Who knew what army of relatives, step-
relatives, half-relatives they were reinforcing by now. But
there were—Otto shuddered faintly—Martin's two newest
(Laurie's). Yes, just as Corinne had said, they, too, were growing up. Previously indistinguishable wads of self-interest, they
had developed perceptible features—maybe even character-
istics; it appeared reasonable, after all, that they had been
given names.

What on earth was it that William did to get children to
converse? Whenever Otto tried to have a civilized encounter
with a child, the child just stood there with its finger in its
nose. But Martin's two boys were chattering away, showing
off to William their whole heap of tiresome electronics.

William was frowning with interest. He poked at a keyboard, which sent up a shower of festive little beeps, and the
boys flung themselves at him, cheering, while Laurie smiled
meltingly. How times had changed. Not so many years earlier, such a tableau would have had handcuffs rattling in the
wings.

The only other representative of "the children," to whom
Corinne had referred with such pathos, was Martin's daughter, Portia (Viola's). She'd been hardly more than a toddler
at last sight, though she now appeared to be about—what?
Well, anyhow, a little girl. "What are the domestic arrangements?" Otto asked. "Is she living with Martin and Laurie
these days, or is she with her mother?"

"That crazy Viola has gone back to England, thank God; Martin has de facto custody."

"Speaking of Martin, where is he?"

"I don't ask," Corinne said.

Otto waited.

"I don't ask," Corinne said again. "And if Laurie wants to share, she'll tell you herself."

"Is Martin in the pokey already?" Otto asked.

"This is not a joke, Otto. I'm sorry to tell you that Martin has been having an affair with some girl."

"Again?"

Corinne stalled, elaborately adjusting her bracelet. "I'm sorry to tell you she's his trainer."

"His *trainer*? How can Martin have a trainer? If Martin has a trainer, what can explain Martin's body?"

"Otto, it's not funny," Corinne said with ominous primness. "The fact is, Martin has been looking very good, lately. But of course you wouldn't have seen him."

All those wives—and a trainer! How? Why would any woman put up with Martin? Martin, who always used to eat his dessert so slowly that the rest of them had been made to wait, squirming at the table, watching as he took his voluptuous, showy bites of chocolate cake or floating island long after they'd finished their own.

"I'm afraid it's having consequences for Portia. Do you see what she's doing?"

"She's—" Otto squinted over at Portia. "What is she doing?"

"Portia, come here, darling," Corinne called.

Portia looked at them for a moment, then wandered sedately over. "And now we'll have a word with Aunt Corinne," she said to her fist as she approached. "Hello, Aunt Corinne."

"Portia," Corinne said, "do you remember Uncle Otto?"

"And Uncle Otto," Portia added to her fist. She regarded him with a clear, even gaze. In its glade of light and silence they encountered one another serenely. She held out her fist to him. "Would you tell our listeners what you do when you go to work, Uncle Otto?"

"Well," Otto said, to Portia's fist, "first I take the elevator up to the twentieth floor, and then I sit down at my desk, and then I send Bryan out for coffee and a bagel—"

"Otto," Corinne said, "Portia is trying to learn what it is you *do*. Something I'm sure we'd all like to know."

"Oh," Otto said. "Well, I'm a lawyer, dear. Do you know what that is?"

"Otto," Corinne said wearily, "Portia's father is a lawyer."

"Portia's father is a global-money mouthpiece!" Otto said.

"Aunt Corinne is annoyed," Portia commented to her fist. "Now Uncle Otto and Aunt Corinne are looking at your correspondent. Now they're not."

"Tell me, Portia," Otto said; the question had sprung insistently into his mind, "what are you going to be when you grow up?"

Her gaze was strangely relaxing. "You know, Uncle Otto," she said pensively to her fist, "people used to ask me that a lot."

Huh! Yes, that was probably something people asked only very small children, when speculation would be exclusively a matter of amusing fantasy. "Well, I was only just mulling it over," Otto said.

"Portia, darling," Corinne said, "why don't you run into the kitchen and do a cooking segment with Bea and Cleveland?"

"It's incredible," Otto said when Portia disappeared, "she looks exactly like Sharon did at that age."

"Ridiculous," Corinne said. "She takes after her father."

Martin? Stuffy, venal Martin, with his nervous eyes and

scoopy nose, and squashy head balanced on his shirt collar? Portia's large, gray eyes, the flaxen hair, the slightly oversized ears and fragile neck recapitulated absolutely Sharon's appearance in this child who probably wouldn't remember ever having seen Sharon. "Her *father*?"

"Her father," Corinne said. "Martin. Portia's father."

"I know Martin is her father. I just can't divine the resemblance."

"Well, there's certainly no resemblance to— Wesley—" Corinne called over to him. "Must you read the newspaper? This is a social occasion. Otto, will you listen, please? I'm trying to tell you something. The truth is, we're all quite worried about Portia."

Amazing how fast one's body reacted. Fear had vacuumed the blood right through his extremities. One's body, the primeval parts of one's brain—how fast they were! Much faster than that recent part with the words and thoughts and so on, what was it? The cortex, was that it? He'd have to ask William, he thought, his blood settling back down. That sort of wrinkly stuff on top that looked like crumpled wrapping paper.

"Laurie is worried sick. The truth is, that's one reason I was so anxious for you to join us today. I wanted your opinion on the matter."

"On what matter?" Otto said. "I have no idea what this is about. She's fine. She seems fine. She's just playing."

"I know she's just playing, Otto. It's *what* she's playing that concerns me."

"What she's playing? What is she playing? She's playing radio, or something! Is that so sinister? The little boys seem to be playing something called Hammer Her Flat."

"I'm sure not. Oh, gracious. You and Sharon were both so right not to have children."

"Excuse me?" Otto said incredulously.

"It's not the radio aspect per se that I'm talking about, it's what that represents. The child is an observer. She sees herself as an outsider. As alienated."

"There's nothing wrong with being observant. Other members of this family could benefit from a little of that quality."

"She can't relate directly to people."

"Who can?" Otto said.

"Half the time Viola doesn't even remember the child is alive! You watch. She won't send Portia a Christmas present. She probably won't even call. Otto, listen. We've always said that Viola is 'unstable,' but, frankly, Viola is *psychotic.* Do you understand what I'm saying to you? Portia's *mother,* Otto. It's just as you were saying, *there's a geneti*—"

"I was saying *what*? I was saying nothing! I was only saying—"

"Oh, dear!" Laurie exclaimed. She had an arm around Portia, who was crying.

"What in hell is going on now?" Wesley demanded, slamming down his newspaper.

"I'm afraid Bea and Cleveland may have said something to her," Laurie said, apologetically.

"Oh, terrific," Wesley said. "Now I know what I'm paying them for."

"It's all right, sweetie," Laurie said. "It all happened a long time ago."

"But why are we celebrating that we killed them?" Portia asked, and started crying afresh.

"We're not celebrating because we killed the Indians, darling," Laurie said. "We're celebrating because we ate dinner with them."

"Portia still believes in Indians!" one of the little boys exclaimed.

"So do we all, Josh," Wesley said. "They live at the North Pole and make toys for good little—"

"Wesley, please!" Corinne said.

"Listener poll," Portia said to her fist. "Did we eat dinner with the Indians, or did we kill them?" She strode over to Otto and held out her fist.

"We ate dinner with them and *then* we killed them," Otto realized, out loud, to his surprise.

"Who are you to slag off Thanksgiving, old boy?" Wesley said. "You're wearing a fucking bow tie."

"So are you, for that matter," Otto said, awkwardly embracing Portia, who was crying again.

"And *I* stand behind my tie," Wesley said, rippling upward from his chair.

"It was Portia's birthday last week!" Laurie interrupted loudly, and Wesley sank back down. "Wasn't it!"

Portia nodded, gulping, and wiped at her tears.

"How old are you now, Portia?" William asked.

"Nine," Portia said.

"That's great," William said. "Get any good stuff?"

Portia nodded again.

"And Portia's mommy sent a terrific present, didn't she," Laurie said.

"Oh, what was it, sweetie?" Corinne said.

Laurie turned pink and her head seemed to flare out slightly in various directions. "You don't have to say, darling, if you don't like."

Portia held on to the arm of Otto's chair and swung her leg aimlessly back and forth. "My mother gave me two tickets to go to Glyndebourne on my eighteenth birthday," she said in a tiny voice.

Wesley snorted. "Got your frock all picked out, Portia?"

"I won't be going to Glyndebourne, Uncle Wesley," Portia said with dignity.

There was a sudden silence in the room.

"Why not, dear?" Otto asked. He was trembling, he noticed.

Portia looked out at all of them. Tears still clung to her face. "Because." She raised her fist to her mouth again. "Factoid: According to the Mayan calendar, the world is going to end in the year 2012, the year before this reporter's eighteenth birthday."

"All right," Corinne whispered to Otto. "Now do you see?"

"You're right, as always," Otto said, in the taxi later, "they're no worse than anyone else's. They're all awful. I really don't see the point in it. Just think! Garden garden garden garden garden, two happy people, and it could have gone on forever! They knew, they'd been told, but they ate it anyway, and from there on out, *family*! Shame, fear, jobs, mortality, envy, murder . . ."

"Well," William said brightly, "and sex."

"There's that," Otto conceded.

"In fact, you could look at both family and mortality simply as by-products of sexual reproduction."

"I don't really see the point of sexual reproduction, either," Otto said. "*I* wouldn't stoop to it."

"Actually, that's very interesting, you know; they think that the purpose of sexual reproduction is to purge the genome of harmful mutations. Of course, they also seem to think it isn't working."

"Then why not scrap it?" Otto said. "Why not let us divide again, like our dignified and immortal forebear, the amoeba."

William frowned. "I'm not really sure that—"

"Joke," Otto said.

"Oh, yes. Well, but I suppose sexual reproduction is fairly entrenched by now—people aren't going to give it up without a struggle. And besides, family confers certain advantages as a social unit, doesn't it."

"No. What advantages?"

"Oh, rudimentary education. Protection."

"'Education'! Ha! 'Protection'! Ha!"

"Besides," William said. "It's broadening. You meet people in your family you'd never happen to run into otherwise. And anyhow, obviously the desire for children is hardwired."

"'Hardwired.' You know, that's a term I've really come to loathe! It explains nothing, it justifies anything; you might as well say, 'Humans have children because the Great Moth in the Sky wants them to.' Or, 'Humans have children because humans have children.' 'Hardwired,' please! It's lazy, it's specious, it's perfunctory, and it's utterly without depth."

"Why does it have to have depth?" William said. "It *refers* to depth. It's good, clean science."

"It's not science at all, it's a cliché. It's a redundancy."

"Otto, why do you always scoff at me when I raise a scientific point?"

"I don't! I don't scoff at you. I certainly don't mean to. It's just that this particular phrase, used in this particular way, isn't very interesting. I mean, you're telling me that something is biologically *inherent* in human experience, but you're not telling me anything *about* human experience."

"I wasn't intending to," William said. "I wasn't trying to. If you want to talk about human experience, then let's talk about it."

"All right," Otto said. It was painful, of course, to see William irritated, but almost a relief to know that it could actually happen. "Let's, then. By all means."

"So?"

"Well?"

"Any particular issues?" William said. "Any questions?"

Any! *Billions.* But that was always just the problem: how to disentangle one; how to pluck it up and clothe it in presentable words? Otto stared, concentrating. Questions were roiling in the pit of his mind like serpents, now a head rising up from the seething mass, now a rattling tail . . . He closed his eyes. If only he could get his brain to relax . . . Relax, relax . . . Relax, relax, relax . . . "Oh, you know, William—is there anything at home to eat? Believe it or not, I'm starving again."

There was absolutely no reason to fear that Portia would have anything other than an adequately happy, adequately fruitful life. No reason at all. Oh, how prudent of Sharon not to have come yesterday. Though in any case, she had been as present to the rest of them as if she had been sitting on the sofa. And the rest of them had probably been as present to her as she had been to them.

When one contemplated Portia, when one contemplated Sharon, when one contemplated one's own apparently pointless, utterly trivial being, the questions hung all around one, as urgent as knives at the throat. But the instant one tried to grasp one of them and turn it to one's own purpose and pierce through the murk, it became as blunt and useless as a piece of cardboard.

All one could dredge up were platitudes: one comes into the world alone, snore snore; one, snore snore, departs the world alone . . .

What would William have to say? Well, it was a wonderful thing to live with an inquiring and mentally active person; no one could quarrel with that. William was immaculate in his intentions, unflagging in his efforts. But what drove one simply insane was the vagueness. Or, really, the banality. Not that it was William's job to explicate the foggy assumptions of one's culture, but one's own ineptitude was galling enough; one hardly needed to consult a vacuity expert!

And how could one think at all, or even just casually ruminate, with William practicing, as he had been doing since they'd awakened. Otto had forgotten what a strain it all was—even without any exasperating social nonsense—those few days preceding the concert; you couldn't think, you couldn't concentrate on the newspaper. You couldn't even really hear the phone, which seemed to be ringing now—

Nor could you make any sense of what the person on the other end of it might be saying. "What?" Otto shouted into it. "You what?"

Could he—the phone cackled into the lush sheaves of William's arpeggios—*bribery, sordid out*—

"William!" Otto yelled. "Excuse me? Could I what?"

The phone cackled some more. "Excuse me," Otto said. *"William!"*

The violin went quiet. "Excuse me?" Otto said again into the phone, which was continuing to emit gibberish. "Sort *what* out? Took her *where* from the library?"

"I'm trying to explain, sir," the phone said. "I'm calling from the hospital."

"She was *taken* from the library *by force?*"

"Unfortunately, sir, as I've tried to explain, she was understood to be homeless."

"And so she was taken away? By force? That could be construed as kidnapping, you know."

"I'm only reporting what the records indicate, sir. The records do not indicate that your sister was kidnapped."

"I don't understand. Is it a crime to be homeless?"

"Apparently your sister did not claim to be homeless. Apparently your sister claimed to rent an apartment. Is this not the case? Is your sister in fact homeless?"

"My sister is not homeless! My sister rents an apartment! Is that a crime? What does this have to do with why my sister was taken away, by force, from the library?"

"Sir, I'm calling from the hospital."

"I'm a taxpayer!" Otto shouted. William was standing in the doorway, violin in one hand, bow in the other, watching gravely. "I'm a lawyer! Why is information being withheld from me?"

"Information is not being withheld from you, sir, please! I understand that you are experiencing concern, and I'm trying to explain this situation in a way that you will understand what has occurred. It is a policy that homeless people tend to congregate in the library, using the restrooms, and some of these people may be removed, if, for example, these people exhibit behaviors that are perceived to present a potential danger."

"Are you *reading* this from something? Is it a crime to use a *public bathroom?*"

"When people who do not appear to have homes to go to, appear to be confused and disoriented—"

"Is it a *crime* to be *confused?*"

"Please calm *down*, sir. The evaluation was not ours. What I'm trying to tell you is that according to the report, your sister became obstreperous when she was brought to the homeless shelter. She appeared to be disoriented. She did not appear to understand why she was being taken to the homeless shelter."

......

"Shall I go with you?" William said, when Otto put down the phone.

"No," Otto said. "Stay, please. Practice."

So, once again. Waiting in the dingy whiteness, the fearsome whiteness no doubt of heaven, heaven's sensible shoes, overtaxed heaven's obtuse smiles and ruthless tranquillity, heaven's asphyxiating clouds dropped over the screams bleeding faintly from behind closed doors. He waited in a room with others too dazed even to note the television that hissed and bristled in front of them or to turn the pages of the sticky, dog-eared magazines they held, from which they could have learned how to be happy, wealthy, and sexually appealing; they waited, like Otto, to learn instead what it was that destiny had already handed down: bad, not that bad, very, very bad.

The doctor, to whom Otto was eventually conducted through the elderly bowels of the hospital, looked like an epic hero—shining, arrogant, supple. "She'll be fine, now," he said. "You'll be fine now, won't you?"

Sharon's smile, the sudden birth of a little sun, and the doctor's own brilliant smile met, and ignited for an instant. Otto felt as though a missile had exploded in his chest.

"Don't try biting any of those guys from the city again," the doctor said, giving Sharon's childishly rounded, childishly humble shoulder a companionable pat. "They're poisonous."

"Bite them!" Otto exclaimed, admiration leaping up in him like a dog at a chain link fence, on the other side of which a team of uniformed men rushed at his defenseless sister with clubs.

"I did?" Sharon cast a repentant, sidelong glance at the doctor.

The doctor shrugged and flipped back his blue-black hair, dislodging sparkles of handsomeness. "The file certainly painted an unflattering portrait of your behavior. 'Menaced dentally,' it says, or something of the sort. Now, listen. Take care of yourself. Follow Dr. Shiga's instructions. Because I don't want to be seeing you around here, okay?"

He and Sharon looked at each other for a moment, then traded a little, level, intimate smile. "It's okay with me," she said.

Otto took Sharon to a coffee shop near her apartment and bought her two portions of macaroni and cheese.

"How was it?" she said. "How was everyone?"

"Thanksgiving? Oh. You didn't miss much."

She put down her fork. "Aren't you going to have anything, Otto?"

"I'll have something later with William," he said.

"Oh," she said. She sat very still. "Of course."

He was a monster. Well, no one was perfect. But in any case, her attention returned to her macaroni. Not surprising that she was ravenous. How long had her adventures lasted? Her clothing was rumpled and filthy.

"I didn't know you liked the library," he said.

"Don't think I'm not grateful for the computer," she said. "It was down."

He nodded, and didn't press her.

There was a bottle of wine breathing on the table, and William had managed to maneuver dinner out of the mysterious little containers and the limp bits of organic matter from the fridge, which Otto had inspected earlier in a doleful search for lunch. "Bad?" William asked.

"Fairly," Otto said.

"Want to tell me?" William said.

Otto gestured impatiently. "Oh, what's the point."

"Okay," William said. "Mustard with that? It's good."

"I can't stand it that she has to live like this!" Otto said.

William shook his head. "Everyone is so alone," he said.
Otto yelped.

"What?" William said. "What did I do?"

"Nothing," Otto said. He stood, trying to control his trembling. "I'm going to my study. You go on upstairs when you get tired."

"Otto?"

"Just—please."

He sat downstairs in his study with a book in his hand, listening while William rinsed the dishes and put them in the dishwasher, and went, finally, upstairs. For some time, footsteps persisted oppressively in the bedroom overhead. When they ceased, Otto exhaled with relief.

A pale tincture spread into the study window; the pinched little winter sun was rising over the earth, above the neighbors' buildings. Otto listened while William came down and made himself breakfast, then returned upstairs to practice once again.

The day loomed heavily in front of Otto, like an opponent judging the moment to strike. How awful everything was. How awful he was. How bestial he had been to William; William, who deserved only kindness, only gratitude.

And yet the very thought of glimpsing that innocent face was intolerable. It had been a vastly unpleasant night in the chair, and it would be hours, he knew, before he'd be able to manage an apology without more denunciations leaping from his treacherous mouth.

Hours seemed to be passing, in fact. Or maybe it was minutes. The clock said seven, said ten, said twelve, said twelve, said twelve, seemed to be delirious. Fortunately there were leftovers in the fridge.

Well, if time was the multiplicity Sharon and William seemed to believe it was, maybe it contained multiple Sharons, perhaps some existing in happier conditions, before the tracks diverged, one set leading up into the stars, the other down to the hospital. Otto's mind wandered here and there amid the dimensions, catching glimpses of her skirt, her hair, her hand, as she slipped through the mirrors. Did things have to proceed for each of the Sharons in just exactly the same way?

Did each one grieve for the Olympian destiny that ought to have been hers? Did each grieve for an ordinary life—a life full of ordinary pleasures and troubles—children, jobs, lovers?

Everyone is so alone. For this, all the precious Sharons had to flounder through their loops and tucks of eternity; for this, the shutters were drawn on their aerial and light-filled minds. Each and every Sharon, thrashing through the razor-edged days only in order to be absorbed by this spongy platitude: *everyone is so alone!* Great God, how could it be endured? All the Sharons, forever and ever, discarded in a phrase.

And those Ottos, sprinkled through the zones of actuality—what were the others doing now? The goldfish gliding, gliding, within the severe perimeter of water; William pausing to introduce himself . . .

Yes, so of course one felt incomplete; of course one felt obstructed and blind. And perhaps every creature on earth, on all the earths, was straining at the obdurate membranes to reunite as its own original entity, the spark of unique consciousness allocated to each being, only then to be irreconcilably refracted through world after world by the prism of time. No wonder one tended to feel so fragile. It was infuriating enough just trying to have contact with a few other people, let alone with all of one's selves!

To think there could be an infinitude of selves, and not an iota of latitude for any of them! An infinitude of Ottos, lugging around that personality, those circumstances, that appearance. Not only once dreary and pointless, but infinitely so.

Oh, was there no escape? Perhaps if one could only concentrate hard enough they could be collected, all those errant, enslaved selves. And in the triumphant instant of their reunification, purified to an unmarked essence, the suffocating Otto-costumes dissolving, a true freedom at last. Oh, how tired he was! But why not make the monumental effort?

Because Naomi and Margaret were arriving at nine to show off this baby of theirs, that was why not.

But anyhow, what on earth was he thinking?

Still, at least he could apologize to William. He was himself, but at least he could go fling that inadequate self at William's feet!

No. At the *very* least he could let poor, deserving William practice undisturbed. He'd wait—patiently, patiently—and when William was finished, William would come downstairs. Then Otto could apologize abjectly, spread every bit of his worthless being at William's feet, comfort him and be comforted, reassure him and be reassured . . .

At a few minutes before nine, William appeared, whistling.

Whistling! "Good practice session?" Otto said. His voice came out cracked, as if it had been hurled against the high prison walls of himself.

"Terrific," William said, and kissed him lightly on the forehead.

Otto opened his mouth. "You know—" he said.

"Oh, listen—" William said. "There really is a baby!" And faintly interspersed among Naomi and Margaret's familiar creakings and bumpings in the hall Otto heard little chirps and gurgles.

"Hello, hello!" William cried, flinging open the door. "Look, isn't she fabulous?"

"We think so," Naomi said, her smile renewing and renewing itself. "Well, she is."

"I can't see if you do that," Margaret said, disengaging the earpiece of her glasses and a clump of her red, crimpy hair from the baby's fist as she attempted to transfer the baby over to William.

"Here." Naomi held out a bottle of champagne. "Take this, too. Well, but you can't keep the baby. Wow, look, she's fascinated by Margaret's hair. I mean, who isn't?"

Otto wasn't, despite his strong feelings about hair in general. "Should we open this up and drink it?" he said, his voice a mechanical voice, his hand a mechanical hand accepting the bottle.

"That was the idea," Naomi said. She blinked up at Otto, smiling hopefully, and rocking slightly from heel to toe.

"Sit. Sit, everyone," William said. "Oh, she's sensational!"

Otto turned away to open the champagne and pour it into the lovely glasses somebody or another had given to them some time or another.

"Well, cheers," William said. "Congratulations. And here's to—"

"Molly," Margaret said. "We decided to keep it simple."

"We figured she's got so much working against her already," Naomi said, "including a couple of geriatric moms with a different ethnicity, and God only knows what infant memories, or whatever you call that stuff you don't remember. We figured we'd name her something nice, that didn't set up all kinds of expectations. Just a nice, friendly, pretty name. And she can take it from there."

"She'll be taking it from there in any case," Otto said, grimly.

The others looked at him.

"I love Maggie," Naomi said. "I always wanted a Maggie, but Margaret said—"

"Well." Margaret shrugged. "I mean—"

"No, I know," Naomi said. "But."

Margaret rolled a little white quilt out on the rug. Plunked down on it, the baby sat, wobbling, with an expression of surprise.

"Look at her!" William said.

"Here's hoping," Margaret said, raising her glass.

So, marvelous. Humans were born, they lived. They glued themselves together in little clumps, and then they died. It was no more, as William had once cheerfully explained, than a way for genes to perpetuate themselves. "The selfish gene," he'd said, quoting, probably detrimentally, someone; you were put on earth to fight for your DNA.

Let the organisms chat. Let them talk. Their voices were as empty as the tinklings of a player piano. Let the organisms talk about this and that; it was what (as William had so trenchantly pointed out) this particular carbon-based life-form did, just as its cousin (according to William) the roundworm romped ecstatically beneath the surface of the planet.

He tried to intercept the baby's glossy, blurry stare. The baby was actually attractive, for a baby, and not bald at all, as it happened. Hello, Otto thought to it, let's you and I communicate in some manner far superior to the verbal one.

The baby ignored him. Whatever she was making of the blanket, the table legs, the shod sets of feet, she wasn't about to let on to Otto. Well, see if he cared.

William was looking at him. So, what was he supposed to do? Oh, all right, he'd contribute. Despite his current clarity of mind.

"And how was China?" he asked. "Was the food as bad as they say?"

Naomi looked at him blankly. "Well, I don't know, actually," she said. "Honey, how was the food?"

"The food," Margaret said. "Not memorable, apparently."

"The things people have to do in order to have children," Otto said.

"We toyed with the idea of giving birth," Margaret said. "That is, Naomi toyed with it."

"At first," Naomi said, "I thought, what a shame to miss an experience that nature intended for us. And, I mean, there was this guy at work, or of course there's always— But then I thought, what, am I an idiot? I mean, just because you've got arms and legs, it doesn't mean you have to—"

"No," William said. "But still. I can understand how you felt."

"Have to what?" Margaret said.

"I can't," Otto said.

"Have to what?" Margaret said.

"I *can't* understand it," Otto said. "I've just never envied the capacity. Others are awestruck, not I. I've never even remotely wished I were able to give birth, and, in fact, I've never wanted a baby. Of course it's inhuman not to want one, but I'm just not human. I'm not a human being. William is a human being. Maybe William wanted a baby. I never thought to ask. Was that what you were trying to tell me the other day, William? Were you trying to tell me that I've ruined your life? *Did* you want a baby? *Have* I ruined your life? Well, it's too bad. I'm sorry. I was too selfish ever to ask if you wanted one, and I'm too selfish to want one myself. I'm more selfish

than my own genes. I'm not fighting *for* my DNA, I'm fighting against it!"

"I'm happy as I am," William said. He sat, his arms
wrapped tightly around himself, looking at the floor. The
baby coughed. "Who needs more champagne?"

"You see?" Otto said into the tundra of silence William
left behind him as he retreated into the kitchen. "I really am
a monster."

Miles away, Naomi sat blushing, her hands clasped in her
lap. Then she scooped up the baby. "There, there," she said.

But Margaret sat back, eyebrows raised in semicircles,
contemplating something that seemed to be hanging a few
feet under the ceiling. "Oh, I don't know," she said, and the
room shuttled back into proportion. "I suppose you could
say it's human to want a child, in the sense that it's biologically mandated. But I mean, you could say that, or you could
say it's simply unimaginative. Or you could say it's unselfish
or you could say it's selfish, or you could say pretty much
anything about it at all. Or you could just say, well, I want
one. But when you get right down to it, really, one what?
Because, actually—I mean, well, look at Molly. I mean, actually, they're awfully specific."

"I suppose I meant, like, crawl around on all fours, or something," Naomi said. "I mean, just because you've got— But look,
there they already are, all these babies, so many of them, just
waiting, waiting, waiting on the shelves for someone to take
care of them. We could have gone to Romania, we could have
gone to Guatemala, we could have gone almost anywhere—
just, for various reasons, we decided to go to China."

"And we both really liked the idea," Margaret said, "that
you could go as far away as you could possibly get, and there
would be your child."

"Uh-huh." Naomi nodded, soberly. "How crazy is that?"

......

"I abase myself," Otto told William as they washed and dried the champagne glasses. "I don't need to tell you how deeply I'll regret having embarrassed you in front of Naomi and Margaret." He clasped the limp dishtowel to his heart. "How deeply I'll regret having been insufficiently mawkish about the miracle of life. I don't need to tell you how ashamed I'll feel the minute I calm down. How deeply I'll regret having trampled your life, and how deeply I'll regret being what I am. Well, that last part I regret already. I profoundly regret every tiny crumb of myself. I don't need to go into it all once again, I'm sure. Just send back the form, pertinent boxes checked: 'I intend to accept your forthcoming apology for—' "

"Please stop," William said.

"Oh, how awful to have ruined the life of such a marvelous man! Have I ruined your life? You can tell me; we're friends."

"Otto, I'm going upstairs now. I didn't sleep well last night, and I'm tired."

"Yes, go upstairs."

"Good night," William said.

"Yes, go to sleep, why not?" Oh, it was like trying to pick a fight with a dog toy! "Just you go on off to sleep."

"Otto, listen to me. My concert is tomorrow. I want to be able to play adequately. I don't know why you're unhappy. You do interesting work, you're admired, we live in a wonderful place, we have wonderful friends. We have everything we need and most of the things we want. We have excellent lives by anyone's standard. I'm happy, and I wish you were. I know that you've been upset these last few days, I asked if you wanted to talk, and you said you didn't. Now you do, but this happens to be the one night of the year when I most need my sleep. Can it wait till tomorrow? I'm very tired, and you're obviously very tired, as well. Try and get some sleep, please."

" 'Try *and* get some sleep'? 'Try *and* get some sleep'? This is unbearable! I've spent the best years of my life with a man who doesn't know how to use the word 'and'! 'And' is not part of the infinitive! 'And' means *'in addition to.'* It's not 'Try *and* get some sleep,' it's 'Try *to* get some sleep.' *To! To! To! To! To! To! To! Please try to get some sleep!*"

Otto sat down heavily at the kitchen table and began to sob.

How arbitrary it all was, and cruel. This identity, that identity: Otto, William, Portia, Molly, the doctor . . .

She'd be up now, sitting at her own kitchen table, the white enamel table with a cup of tea, thinking about something, about numbers streaming past in stately sequences, about remote astral pageants . . . The doctor had rested his hand kindly on her shoulder. And what she must have felt then! Oh, to convert that weight of the world's compassion into something worthwhile—the taste, if only she could have lifted his hand and kissed it, the living satin feel of his skin . . . Everyone had to put things aside, to put things aside for good.

The way they had smiled at one another, she and that doctor! What can you do, their smiles had said. The handsome doctor in his handsome-doctor suit and Sharon in her disheveled-lunatic suit; what a charade. In this life, Sharon's little spark of consciousness would be costumed inescapably as a waif at the margins of mental organization and the doctor's would be costumed inescapably as a flashing exemplar of supreme competence; in this life (and, frankly, there would be no other) the hospital was where they would meet.

"Otto—"

A hand was resting on Otto's shoulder.

"William," Otto said. It was William. They were in the clean, dim kitchen. The full moon had risen high over the neighbors' buildings, where the lights were almost all out. Had he been asleep? He blinked up at William, whose face, shadowed against the light of the night sky, was as inflected, as ample in mystery as the face in the moon. "It's late, my darling," Otto said. "I'm tired. What are we doing down here?"

THE DEEP

Anthony Doerr

Tom is born in 1914 in Detroit, a quarter mile from Inter-national Salt. His father is offstage, unaccounted for. His mother operates a six-room, underinsulated boardinghouse populated with locked doors, behind which drowse the grim possessions of itinerant salt workers: coats the colors of mice, tattered mucking boots, aquatints of undressed women, their breasts faded orange. Every six months a miner is laid off, gets drafted, or dies, and is replaced by another, so that very early in his life Tom comes to see how the world continually drains itself of young men, leaving behind only objects—empty tobacco pouches, bladeless jackknives, salt-caked trousers—mute, incapable of memory.

Tom is four when he starts fainting. He'll be rounding a corner, breathing hard, and the lights will go out. Mother will carry him indoors, set him on the armchair, and send some-one for the doctor.

Atrial septal defect. Hole in the heart. The doctor says blood sloshes from the left side to the right side. His heart will have to do three times the work. Life-span of sixteen. Eighteen if he's lucky. Best if he doesn't get excited.

Mother trains her voice into a whisper. *Here you go, there you are, sweet little Tomcat.* She moves Tom's cot into an upstairs closet—no bright lights, no loud noises. Mornings she serves him a glass of buttermilk, then points him to the brooms or steel wool. *Go slow,* she'll murmur. He scrubs the coal stove, sweeps the marble stoop. Every so often he peers up from his work and watches the face of the oldest boarder, Mr. Weems, as he troops downstairs, a fifty-year-old man hooded against the cold, off to descend in an elevator a thousand feet underground. Tom imagines his descent, sporadic and dim lights passing and receding, cables rattling, a half dozen other miners squeezed into the cage beside him, each thinking his own thoughts, men's thoughts, sinking down into that city beneath the city where mules stand waiting and oil lamps burn in the walls and glittering rooms of salt recede into vast arcades beyond the farthest reaches of the light.

Sixteen, thinks Tom. *Eighteen if I'm lucky.*

School is a three-room shed aswarm with the offspring of salt workers, coal workers, ironworkers. Irish kids, Polish kids, Armenian kids. To Mother the school yard seems a thousand acres of sizzling pandemonium. *Don't run, don't fight,* she whispers. *No games.* His first day, she pulls him out of class after an hour. *Shhh,* she says, and wraps her arms around his like ropes.

Tom seesaws in and out of the early grades. Sometimes she keeps him out of school for whole weeks at a time. By the time he's ten, he's in remedial everything. *I'm trying,* he stammers, but letters spin off pages and dash against the windows like snow. *Dunce,* the other boys declare, and to Tom that seems about right.

Tom sweeps, scrubs, scours the stoop with pumice one square inch at a time. *Slow as molasses in January,* says Mr. Weems, but he winks at Tom when he says it.

Every day, all day, the salt finds its way in. It encrusts washbasins, settles on the rims of baseboards. It spills out of the boarders, too: from ears, boots, handkerchiefs. Furrows of glitter gather in the bedsheets: a daily lesson in insidiousness.

Start at the edges, then scrub out the center. Linens on Thursdays. Toilets on Fridays.

He's twelve when Ms. Fredericks asks the children to give reports. Ruby Hornaday goes sixth. Ruby has flames for hair, Christmas for a birthday, and a drunk for a daddy. She's one of two girls to make it to fourth grade.

She reads from notes in controlled terror. *If you think the lake is big you should see the sea. It's three-quarters of Earth. And that's just the surface.* Someone throws a pencil. The creases on Ruby's forehead sharpen. *Land animals live on ground or in trees rats and worms and gulls and such. But sea animals they live everywhere they live in the waves and they live in mid water and they live in canyons six and a half miles down.*

She passes around a red book. Inside are blocks of text and full-color photographic plates that make Tom's heart boom in his ears. A blizzard of toothy minnows. A kingdom of purple corals. Five orange starfish cemented to a rock.

Ruby says, *Detroit used to have palm trees and corals and seashells. Detroit used to be a sea three miles deep.*

Ms. Fredericks asks, *Ruby, where did you get that book?* but by then Tom is hardly breathing. See-through flowers with poison tentacles and fields of clams and pink spheres with a thousand needles on their backs. He tries to ask, *Are these real?* but quicksilver bubbles rise from his mouth and float up to the ceiling. When he goes over, the desk goes over with him.

The doctor says it's best if Tom stays out of school and Mother agrees. *Keep indoors,* the doctor says. *If you get excited, think of something blue.* Mother lets him come downstairs for meals and chores only. Otherwise he's to stay in his closet. *We have to be more careful, Tomcat,* she whispers, and sets her palm on his forehead.

Tom spends long hours on the floor beside his cot, assembling and reassembling the same jigsaw puzzle: a Swiss village. Five hundred pieces, nine of them missing. Sometimes Mr. Weems reads to Tom from adventure novels. They're blasting a new vein down in the mines and in the lulls between Mr. Weems's words, Tom can feel explosions reverberate up through a thousand feet of rock and shake the fragile pump in his chest.

He misses school. He misses the sky. He misses everything. When Mr. Weems is in the mine and Mother is downstairs, Tom often slips to the end of the hall and lifts aside the curtains and presses his forehead to the glass. Children run the snowy lanes and lights glow in the foundry windows and train cars trundle beneath elevated conduits. First-shift miners emerge from the mouth of the hauling elevator in groups of six and bring out cigarette cases from their overalls and strike matches and spill like little salt-dusted insects out into the night, while the darker figures of the second-shift miners stamp their feet in the cold, waiting outside the cages for their turn in the pit.

In dreams he sees waving sea fans and milling schools of grouper and underwater shafts of light. He sees Ruby Hornaday push open the door of his closet. She's wearing a copper diving helmet; she leans over his cot and puts the window of her helmet an inch from his face.

He wakes with a shock. Heat pools in his groin. He thinks, *Blue, blue, blue.*

......

One drizzly Saturday, the bell rings. When Tom opens the door, Ruby Hornaday is standing on the stoop in the rain.

Hello. Tom blinks a dozen times. Raindrops set a thousand intersecting circles upon the puddles in the road. Ruby holds up a jar: six black tadpoles squirm in an inch of water.

Seemed like you might be interested in water creatures.

Tom tries to answer, but the whole sky is rushing through the open door into his mouth.

You're not going to faint again, are you?

Mr. Weems stumps into the foyer. *Jesus, boy, she's damp as a church, you got to invite a lady in.*

Ruby stands on the tiles and drips. Mr. Weems grins. Tom mumbles, *My heart.*

Ruby holds out the jar. *Keep 'em if you want. They'll be frogs before long.* Drops shine in her eyelashes. Rain glues her shirt to her clavicles. *Well, that's something,* says Mr. Weems. He nudges Tom in the back. *Isn't it, Tom?*

Tom is opening his mouth. He's saying, *Maybe I could—* when Mother comes down the stairs in her big, black shoes. *Trouble,* hisses Mr. Weems.

Mother dumps the tadpoles in a ditch. Her face says she's composing herself but her eyes say she's going to wipe all this away. Mr. Weems leans over the dominoes and whispers, *Mother's as hard as a cobblestone but we'll crack her, Tom, you wait.*

Tom whispers, *Ruby Hornaday,* into the space above his cot. *Ruby Hornaday. Ruby Hornaday.* A strange and uncontainable joy inflates dangerously in his chest.

Mr. Weems initiates long conversations with Mother in the kitchen. Tom overhears scraps: *Boy needs to move his legs. Boy should get some air.*

Mother's voice is a whip. *He's sick.*

He's alive! What're you saving him for?

Mother consents to let Tom retrieve coal from the depot and tinned goods from the commissary. Tuesdays he'll be allowed to walk to the butcher's in Dearborn. *Careful, Tomcat, don't hurry.*

Tom moves through the colony that first Tuesday with something close to rapture in his veins. Down the long gravel lanes, past pit cottages and surface mountains of blue and white salt, the warehouses like dark cathedrals, the hauling machines like demonic armatures. All around him the monumental industry of Detroit pounds and clangs. The boy tells himself he is a treasure hunter, a hero from one of Mr. Weems's adventure stories, a knight on important errands, a spy behind enemy lines. He keeps his hands in his pockets and his head down and his gait slow, but his soul charges ahead, weightless, jubilant, sparking through the gloom.

In May of that year, 1929, fourteen-year-old Tom is walking along the lane thinking spring happens whether you're paying attention or not; it happens beneath the snow, beyond the walls—spring happens in the dark while you dream—when Ruby Hornaday steps out of the weeds. She has a shriveled rubber hose coiled over her shoulder and a swim mask in one hand and a tire pump in the other. *Need your help.* Tom's pulse soars.

I got to go to the butcher's.

Your choice. Ruby turns to go. But really there is no choice at all.

She leads him west, away from the mine, through mounds of rusting machines. They hop a fence, cross a field gone to seed, and walk a quarter mile through pitch pines to a marsh where cattle egrets stand in the cattails like white flowers.

In my mouth, she says, and starts picking up rocks. *Out my nose. You pump, Tom. Understand?* In the green water two feet down Tom can make out the dim shapes of a few fish gliding through weedy enclaves.

Ruby pitches the far end of the hose into the water. With waxed cord she binds the other end to the pump. Then she fills her pockets with rocks. She wades out, looks back, says, *You pump*, and puts the hose into her mouth. The swim mask goes over her eyes; her face goes into the water.

The marsh closes over Ruby's back, and the hose trends away from the bank. Tom begins to pump. The sky slides along overhead. Loops of garden hose float under the light out there, shifting now and then. Occasional bubbles rise, moving gradually farther out.

One minute, two minutes. Tom pumps. His heart does its fragile work. He should not be here. He should not be here while this skinny, spellbinding girl drowns herself in a marsh. If that's what she's doing. One of Mr. Weems's similes comes to him: *You're trembling like a needle to the pole.*

After four or five minutes underwater, Ruby comes up. A neon mat of algae clings to her hair, and her bare feet are great boots of mud. She pushes through the cattails. Strings of saliva hang off her chin. Her lips are blue. Tom feels dizzy. The sky turns to liquid.

Incredible, pants Ruby. *Fucking incredible.* She holds up her wet, rock-filled trousers with both hands, and looks at Tom through the wavy lens of her swim mask. His blood storms through its lightless tunnels.

He has to trot to make the butcher's and get back home by noon. It is the first time Tom can remember permitting himself to run, and his legs feel like glass. At the end of the lane, a hundred yards from home, he stops and pants with the basket of meat in his arms and spits a pat of blood into the dandelions. Sweat soaks his shirt. Dragonflies dart and hover. Swallows inscribe letters across the sky. The street seems to ripple and fold and straighten itself out again.

Just a hundred yards more. He forces his heart to settle. *Everything,* Tom thinks, *follows a path worn by those who have gone before: egrets, clouds, tadpoles. Everything everything everything.*

The following Tuesday Ruby meets him at the end of the lane. And the Tuesday after that. They hop the fence, cross the field; she leads him places he's never dreamed existed. Places where the structures of the saltworks become white mirages on the horizon, places where sunlight washes through groves of maples and makes the ground quiver with leaf-shadow. They peer into a foundry where men in masks pour molten iron from one vat into another; they climb a tailings pile where a lone sapling grows like a single hand thrust up from the underworld. Tom knows he's risking everything—his freedom, Mother's trust, even his life—but how can he stop? How can he say no? To say no to Ruby Hornaday would be to say no to the world.

Some Tuesdays Ruby brings along her red book with its images of corals and jellies and underwater volcanoes. She tells him that when she grows up she'll go to parties where hostesses row guests offshore and everyone puts on special helmets to go for strolls along the sea bottom. She tells him she'll be a diver who sinks herself a half mile into the sea in a steel ball with one window. In the basement of the ocean, she says, she'll find a separate universe, a place made of lights: schools of fish glowing green, living galaxies wheeling through the black.

In the ocean, says Ruby, *half the rocks are alive. Half the plants are animals.*

They hold hands; they chew Indian gum. She stuffs his mind full of kelp forests and seascapes and dolphins. *When I grow up*, says Ruby. *When I grow up . . .*

Four more times Ruby walks around beneath the surface of a Rouge River marsh while Tom stands on the bank working the pump. Four more times he watches her rise back out like a fever. *Amphibian*. She laughs. *It means two lives.*

Then Tom runs to the butcher's and runs home, and his heart races, and spots spread like inkblots in front of his eyes. Sometimes in the afternoons, when he stands up from his chores, his vision slides away in violet streaks. He sees the glowing white of the salt tunnels, the red of Ruby's book, the orange of her hair—he imagines her all grown up, standing on the bow of a ship, and feels a core of lemon yellow light flaring brighter and brighter within him. It spills from the slats between his ribs, from between his teeth, from the pupils of his eyes. He thinks: *It is so much! So much!*

So now you're fifteen. And the doctor says sixteen?

Eighteen if I'm lucky.

Ruby turns her book over in her hands. *What's it like? To know you won't get all the years you should?*

I don't feel so shortchanged when I'm with you, he wants to say, but his voice breaks at *short-* and the sentence fractures.

They kiss only that one time. It is clumsy. He shuts his eyes and leans in, but something shifts and Ruby is not where he expects her to be. Their teeth clash. When he opens his eyes, she is looking off to her left, smiling slightly, smelling of mud, and the thousand tiny blond hairs on her upper lip catch the light.

......

The second-to-last time Tom and Ruby are together, on the last Tuesday of October 1929, everything is strange. The hose leaks, Ruby is upset, a curtain has fallen somehow between them.

Go back, Ruby says. *It's probably noon already. You'll be late.* But she sounds as if she's speaking to him through a tunnel. Freckles flow and bloom across her face. The light goes out of the marsh.

On the long path through the pitch pines it begins to rain. Tom makes it to the butcher's and back home with the basket and the ground veal, but when he opens the door to Mother's parlor the curtains blow inward. The chairs leave their places and come scraping toward him. The daylight thins to a pair of beams, waving back and forth, and Mr. Weems passes in front of his eyes, but Tom hears no footsteps, no voices: only an internal rushing and the wet metronome of his exhalations. Suddenly he's a diver staring through a thick, foggy window into a world of immense pressure. He's walking around on the bottom of the sea. Mother's lips say, *Haven't I given enough? Lord God, haven't I tried?* Then she's gone.

In something deeper than a dream Tom walks the salt roads a thousand feet beneath the house. At first it's all darkness, but after what might be a minute or a day or a year, he sees little flashes of green light out there in distant galleries, hundreds of feet away. Each flash initiates a chain reaction of further flashes beyond it, so that when he turns in a slow circle he can perceive great flowing signals of light in all directions, tunnels of green arcing out into the blackness— each flash glowing for only a moment before fading, but in that moment repeating everything that came before, everything that will come next.

......

He wakes to a deflated world. The newspapers are full of
suicides; the price of gas has tripled. The miners whisper that
the saltworks are in trouble.

Quart milk bottles sell for a dollar apiece. There's no butter, hardly any meat. Fruit becomes a memory. Most nights
Mother serves only cabbage and soda bread. And salt.

No more trips to the butcher; the butcher closes anyway.
By November, Mother's boarders are vanishing. Mr. Beeson
goes first, then Mr. Fackler. Tom waits for Ruby to come
to the door but she doesn't show. Images of her climb the
undersides of his eyelids, and he rubs them away. Each morning he clambers out of his closet and carries his traitorous
heart down to the kitchen like an egg.

The world is swallowing people like candy, boy, says Mr. Weems.
No one is leaving addresses.

Mr. Hanson goes next, then Mr. Heathcock. By April the
saltworks is operating only two days a week, and Mr. Weems,
Mother, and Tom are alone at supper.

Sixteen. Eighteen if he's lucky. Tom moves his few things
into one of the empty boarders' rooms on the first floor, and
Mother doesn't say a word. He thinks of Ruby Hornaday:
her pale blue eyes, her loose flames of hair. *Is she out there in
the city, somewhere, right now? Or is she three thousand miles
away?* Then he sets his questions aside.

Mother catches a fever in 1932. It eats her from the inside.
She still puts on her high-waisted dresses, ties on her apron.

She still cooks every meal and presses Mr. Weems's suit every Sunday. But within a month she has become somebody else, an empty demon in Mother's clothes—perfectly upright at the table, eyes smoldering, nothing on her plate.

She has a way of putting her hand on Tom's forehead while he works. Tom will be hauling coal or mending a pipe or sweeping the parlor, the sun cold and white behind the curtains, and Mother will appear from nowhere and put her icy palm over his eyebrows, and he'll close his eyes and feel his heart tear just a little more.

Amphibian. It means two lives.

Mr. Weems is let go. He puts on his suit, packs up his dominoes, and leaves an address downtown.

I thought no one was leaving addresses.

You're true as a map, Tom. True as the magnet to the iron. And tears spill from the old miner's eyes.

One blue morning not long after that, for the first time in Tom's memory, Mother is not at the stove when he enters the kitchen. He finds her upstairs sitting on her bed, fully dressed in her coat and shoes and with her rosary clutched to her chest. The room is spotless, the house wadded with silence.

Payments are due on the fifteenth. Her voice is ash. *The flashing on the roof needs replacing. There's ninety-one dollars in the dresser.*

Mother.

Shhh, Tomcat, she hisses. *Don't get yourself worked up.*

Tom manages two more payments. Then the bank comes for the house. He walks in a daze through blowing sleet to the end of the lane and turns right and staggers through the dry weeds till he finds the old path and walks beneath the creaking pitch pines to Ruby's marsh. Ice has interlocked in the shallows, but the water in the center is as dark as molten pewter.

He stands there a long time. Into the gathering darkness he says, *I'm still here, but where are you?* His blood sloshes to and fro, and snow gathers in his eyelashes, and three ducks come spiraling out of the night and land silently on the water.

The next morning he walks past the padlocked gate of International Salt with fourteen dollars in his pocket. He rides the trackless trolley downtown for a nickel and gets off on Washington Boulevard. Between the buildings the sun comes up the color of steel, and Tom raises his face to it but feels no warmth at all. He passes catatonic drunks squatting on upturned crates, motionless as statues, and storefront after storefront of empty windows. In a diner a goitrous waitress brings him a cup of coffee with little shining disks of fat floating on top.

The streets are filled with faces, dull and wan, lean and hungry; none belong to Ruby. He drinks a second cup of coffee and eats a plate of eggs and toast. A woman emerges from a doorway and flings a pan of wash water out onto the sidewalk, and the water flashes in the light a moment before falling. In an alley a mule lies on its side, asleep or dead. Eventually the waitress says, *You moving in?* and Tom goes out. He walks slowly toward the address he's copied and recopied onto a sheet of Mother's writing paper. Frozen furrows of plowed snow are shored up against the buildings, and the little golden windows high above seem miles away.

It's a boardinghouse. Mr. Weems is at a lopsided table playing dominoes by himself. He looks up, says, *Holy shit sure as gravity,* and spills his tea.

......

By a miracle Mr. Weems has a grandniece who manages the owl shift in the maternity ward at City General. Maternity is on the fourth floor. In the elevator Tom cannot tell if he is ascending or descending. The niece looks him up and down and checks his eyes and tongue for fever and hires him on the spot. *World goes to Hades but babies still get born*, she says, and issues him white coveralls.

Ten hours a night, six nights a week, Tom roves the halls with carts of laundry, taking soiled blankets and diapers down to the cellar, bringing clean blankets and diapers up. He brings up meals, brings down trays. Rainy nights are the busiest. Full moons and holidays are tied for second. God forbid a rainy holiday with a full moon.

Doctors walk the rows of beds injecting expecting mothers with morphine and something called scopolamine that makes them forget. Sometimes there are screams. Sometimes Tom's heart pounds for no reason he can identify. In the delivery rooms there's always new blood on the tiles to replace the old blood Tom has just mopped away.

The halls are bright at every hour, but out the windows the darkness presses very close, and in the leanest hours of those nights Tom gets a sensation like the hospital is deep underwater, the floor rocking gently, the lights of neighboring buildings like glimmering schools of fish, the pressure of the sea all around.

He turns eighteen. Then nineteen. All the listless figures he sees: children humped around the hospital entrance, their eyes vacant with hunger; farmers pouring into the parks; families sleeping without cover—people for whom nothing left on earth could be surprising. There are so many of them, as if somewhere out in the countryside great farms pump out thousands of ruined men every minute, as if the ones shuffling down the sidewalks are but fractions of the multitudes behind them.

And yet is there not goodness, too? Are people not helping one another in these derelict places? Tom splits his wages with Mr. Weems. He brings home discarded newspapers and wrestles his way through the words on the funny pages. He turns twenty, and Mr. Weems bakes a mushy pound cake full of eggshells and sets twenty matchsticks in it, and Tom blows them all out.

He faints at work: once in the elevator, twice in the big, pulsing laundry room in the basement. Mostly he's able to hide it. But one night he faints in the hall outside the waiting room. A nurse named Fran hauls him into a closet. *Can't let them see you like that*, she says, and wipes his face and he washes back into himself.

The closet is more than a closet. The air is warm, steamy; it smells like soap. On one wall is a two-basin sink; heat lamps are bolted to the undersides of the cabinets. Set in the opposite wall are two little doors.

Tom returns to the same chair in the corner of Fran's room whenever he starts to feel dizzy. Three, four, occasionally ten times a night, he watches a nurse carry an utterly newborn baby through the little door on the left and deposit it on the counter in front of Fran.

She plucks off little knit caps and unwraps blankets. Their bodies are scarlet or imperial purple; they have tiny, bright red fingers, no eyebrows, no kneecaps, no expression except a constant, bewildered wince. Her voice is a whisper: *Why here she is, there he goes, OK now, baby, just lift you here.* Their wrists are the circumference of Tom's pinkie.

Fran takes a new washcloth from a stack, dips it in warm water, and wipes every inch of the creature—ears, armpits, eyelids—washing away bits of placenta, dried blood, all the milky fluids that accompanied it into this world. Meanwhile the child stares up at her with blank, memorizing eyes, peering into the newness of all things. Knowing what? Only light and dark, only mother, only fluid.

Fran dries the baby and splays her fingers beneath its head and diapers it and tugs its hat back on. She whispers, *Here you are, see what a good girl you are, down you go,* and with one free hand lays out two new, crisp blankets, and binds the baby—wrap, wrap, turn—and sets her in a rolling bassinet for Tom to wheel into the nursery, where she'll wait with the others beneath the lights like loaves of bread.

In a magazine Tom finds a color photograph of a three-hundred-year-old skeleton of a bowhead whale, stranded on a coastal plain in a place called Finland. He tears it out, studies it in the lamplight. *See,* he murmurs to Mr. Weems, *how the flowers closest to it are brightest? See how the closest leaves are the darkest green?*

Tom is twenty-one and fainting three times a week when, one Wednesday in January, he sees, among the drugged, dazed mothers in their rows of beds, the unmistakable face of Ruby Hornaday. Flaming orange hair, freckles sprayed across her cheeks, hands folded in her lap, and a thin gold wedding ring on her finger. The material of the ward ripples. Tom leans on the handle of his cart to keep from falling.

Blue, he whispers. *Blue, blue, blue.*

He retreats to his chair in the corner of Fran's washing room and tries to suppress his heart. *Any minute,* he thinks, *her baby will come through the door.*

Two hours later, he pushes his cart into the post-delivery room, and Ruby is gone. Tom's shift ends; he rides the elevator down. Outside, rain settles lightly on the city. The streetlights glow yellow. The early morning avenues are empty except for the occasional automobile, passing with a damp sigh. Tom steadies himself with a hand against the bricks and closes his eyes.

A police officer helps him home. All that day Tom lies on his stomach in his rented bed and recopies the letter until little suns burst behind his eyes. *Deer Ruby, I saw you in the hospital and I saw your baby to. His eyes are viry prety. Fran sez later they will probly get blue. Mother is gone and I am lonely as the arctic see.*

That night at the hospital Fran finds the address. Tom includes the photo of the whale skeleton from the magazine and sticks on an extra stamp for luck. He thinks: *See how the flowers closest to it are brightest. See how the closest leaves are the darkest green.*

He sleeps, pays his rent, walks the thirty-one blocks to work. He checks the mail every day. And winter pales and spring strengthens and Tom loses a little bit of hope.

One morning over breakfast, Mr. Weems looks at him and says, *You ain't even here, Tom. You got one foot across the river. You got to pull back to our side.*

But that very day, it comes. *Dear Tom, I liked hearing from you. It hasn't been ten years but it feels like a thousand. I'm married, you probably guessed that. The baby is Arthur. Maybe his eyes will turn blue. They just might.*

A bald president is on the stamp. The paper smells like paper, nothing more. Tom runs a finger beneath every word, sounding them out. Making sure he hasn't missed anything.

......

*I know your married and I dont want anything but happyness
for you but maybe I can see you one time? We could meet at the
acquareyem. If you dont rite back thats okay I no why.*

Two more weeks. *Dear Tom, I don't want anything but
happiness for you, too. How about next Tuesday? I'll bring the
baby, okay?*

The next Tuesday, the first one in May, Tom leaves the hospital after his shift. His vision flickers at the edges, and he hears
Mother's voice: *Be careful, Tomcat. It's not worth the risk.* He
walks slowly to the end of the block and catches the first trolley to Belle Isle, where he steps off into a golden dawn.

There are few cars about, all parked, one a Ford with a
huge present wrapped in yellow ribbon on the backseat. An
old man with a crumpled face rakes the gravel paths. The
sunlight hits the dew and sets the lawns aflame.

The face of the aquarium is Gothic and wrapped in vines.
Tom finds a bench outside and waits for his pulse to steady.
The reticulated glass roofs of the flower conservatory reflect
a passing cloud. Eventually a man in overalls opens the gate,
and Tom buys two tickets, then thinks about the baby and
buys a third. He returns to the bench with the three tickets
in his trembling fingers.

By eleven the sky is filled with a platinum haze and the
island is busy. Men on bicycles crackle along the paths. A girl
flies a yellow kite.

Tom?

Ruby Hornaday materializes before him—shoulders erect,
hair newly short, pushing a chrome-and-canvas baby buggy. He
stands quickly, and the park bleeds away and then restores itself.

Sorry I'm late, she says.

She's dignified, slim. Two quick strokes for eyebrows, the same narrow nose. No makeup. No jewelry. Those pale blue eyes and that hair.

She cocks her head slightly. *Look at you. All grown up.*

I got tickets, he says.

How's Mr. Weems?

Oh, he's made of salt, he'll live forever.

They start down the path between the rows of benches and the shining trees. Occasionally she takes his arm to steady him, though her touch only disorients him more.

I thought maybe you were far away, he says. *I thought maybe you went to sea.*

Ruby parks the buggy and lifts the baby to her chest—he's wrapped in a blue afghan—and then they're through the turnstile.

The aquarium is dim and damp and lined on both sides with glass-fronted tanks. Ferns hang from the ceiling, and little boys lean across the brass railings and press their noses to the glass. *I think he likes it*, Ruby says. *Don't you, baby?* The boy's eyes are wide open. Fish swim slow ellipses behind the glass.

They see translucent squid with corkscrew tails, sparkling pink octopi like floating lanterns, cowfish in blue and violet and gold. Iridescent green tiles gleam on the domed ceiling and throw wavering patterns of light across the floor.

In a circular pool at the very center of the building, dark shapes race back and forth in coordination. *Jacks*, Ruby murmurs. *Aren't they?*

Tom blinks.

You're pale, she says.

Tom shakes his head.

She helps him back out into the daylight, beneath the

sky and the trees. The baby lies in the buggy sucking his fist, examining the clouds with great intensity, and Ruby guides Tom to a bench.

Cars and trucks and a white limousine pass slowly along the white bridge, high over the river. The city glitters in the distance.

Thank you, says Tom.

For what?

For this.

How old are you now, Tom?

Twenty-one. Same as you. A breeze stirs the trees, and the leaves vibrate with light. Everything is radiant.

World goes to Hades but babies still get born, whispers Tom.

Ruby peers into the buggy and adjusts something, and for a moment the back of her neck shows between her hair and collar. The sight of those two knobs of vertebrae, sheathed in her pale skin, fills Tom with a longing that cracks the lawns open. For a moment it seems Ruby is being slowly dragged away from him, as if he is a swimmer caught in a rip, and with every stroke the back of her neck recedes farther into the distance. Then she sits back, and the park heals over, and he can feel the bench become solid beneath him once more.

I used to think, Tom says, *that I had to be careful with how much I lived. As if life was a pocketful of coins. You only got so much and you didn't want to spend it all in one place.*

Ruby looks at him. Her eyelashes whisk up and down.

But now I know life is the one thing in the world that never runs out. I might run out of mine, and you might run out of yours, but the world will never run out of life. And we're all very lucky to be part of something like that.

She holds his gaze. *Some deserve more luck than they've gotten.*

Tom shakes his head. He closes his eyes. *I've been lucky, too. I've been absolutely lucky.*

The baby begins to fuss, a whine building to a cry. Ruby says, *Hungry.*

A trapdoor opens in the gravel between Tom's feet, black as a keyhole, and he glances down.

You'll be OK?

I'll be OK.

Good-bye, Tom. She touches his forearm once, and then goes, pushing the buggy through the crowds. He watches her disappear in pieces: first her legs, then her hips, then her shoulders, and finally the back of her bright head.

And then Tom sits, hands in his lap, alive for one more day.

A MAN LIKE HIM

Yiyun Li

The girl, unlike most people photographed for fashion magazines, was not beautiful. Moreover, she had no desire to appear beautiful, as anyone looking at her could tell, and for that reason Teacher Fei stopped turning the pages and studied her. She had short, unruly hair and wide-set eyes that glared at the camera in a close-up shot. In another photo, she stood in front of a bedroom door, her back to the camera, her hand pushing the door ajar. A bed and its pink sheet were artfully blurred. Her black T-shirt, in sharp focus, displayed a line of white printed characters: MY FATHER IS LESS OF A CREATURE THAN A PIG OR A DOG BECAUSE HE IS AN ADULTERER.

The girl was nineteen, Teacher Fei learned from the article. Her parents had divorced three years earlier, and she suspected that another woman, a second cousin of her father's, had seduced him. On her eighteenth birthday, the first day permitted by law, the daughter had filed a lawsuit against him. As she explained to the reporter, he was a member of the Communist Party, and he should be punished for abandoning his family, and for the immoral act of having taken a mistress in the first place. When the effort to imprison her father failed, the girl started a blog and called it A Declaration of War on Unfaithful Husbands.

"What is it that this crazy girl wants?" Teacher Fei asked out loud before reaching the girl's answer. She wanted her father to lose his job, she told the reporter, along with his social status, his freedom, if possible, and his mistress for sure; she wanted him to beg her and her mother to take him back. She would support him for the rest of his life as the most filial daughter, but he had to repent—and, before that, to suffer as much as she and her mother had.

What malice, Teacher Fei thought. He flung the magazine across the room, knocking a picture frame from the bookcase and surprising himself with this sudden burst of anger. At sixty-six, Teacher Fei had seen enough of the world to consider himself beyond the trap of pointless emotions. Was it the milkman, his mother asked from the living room. Milkmen had long ago ceased to exist in Beijing, milk being sold abundantly in stores now; still, approaching ninety, she was snatched from time to time by the old fear that a neighbor or a passerby would swipe their two rationed bottles. Remember how they had twice been fined for lost bottles, she asked as Teacher Fei entered the living room, where she sat in the old armchair that had been his father's favorite spot in his last years. Teacher Fei hadn't listened closely, but it was a question he knew by heart, and he said yes, he had remembered to pick up the bottles the moment they were delivered. Be sure to leave them in a basin of cold water so the milk does not turn, she urged. He stood before her and patted her hands, folded in her lap, and reassured her that there was no need to worry. She grabbed him then, curling her thin fingers around his. "I have nothing to say about this world," she said slowly.

"I know," Teacher Fei said. He bent down and placed her hands back in her lap. "Should I warm some milk?" he asked, though he could see that already she was slipping away into her usual reverie, one that would momentarily wash her mind clean. Sometimes he made an effort, coaxing her to walk with baby steps to exercise her shrinking muscles. A few years ago, the limit of her world had been the park two blocks down the street, and later the stone bench across the street from their flat; now it was their fifth-floor balcony. Teacher Fei knew that in time he would let his mother die in peace in this flat. She disliked strangers, and he couldn't imagine her in a cold bed in a crowded hospital ward.

Teacher Fei withdrew to the study, which had been his father's domain until his death. His mother had long ago stopped visiting this room, so Teacher Fei was the one who took care of the books on the shelves, airing the yellowing pages twice a year on the balcony, but inevitably some of the books had become too old to rescue, making way for the fashion magazines that Teacher Fei now purchased.

The black-clad girl taunted him from the magazine lying open on the floor. He picked her up and carefully set her on the desk, then fumbled in the drawer for an inkpot. Much of the ink in the bottle had evaporated from lack of use, and few of the brushes in the bamboo container were in good shape now. Still, with a fine brush pen and just enough ink on the tip, he was able to sketch, in the margin of the page, a scorpion, its pincers stabbing toward the girl's eyes. It had been six years since he retired as an art teacher, nearly forty since he last painted out of free will. Teacher Fei looked at the drawing. His hand was far from a shaking old man's. He could have made the scorpion an arthropod version of the girl, but such an act would have been beneath his standards. Teacher Fei had never cursed at a woman, either in words or in any other form of expression, and he certainly did not want to begin with a young girl.

......

Later, when Mrs. Luo, a neighbor in her late forties who had been laid off by the local electronics factory, came to sit with Teacher Fei's mother, he went to a nearby Internet café. It was a little after two, a slow time for the business, and the manager was dozing off in the warm sunshine. A few middle school students, not much older than twelve or thirteen, were gathered around a computer, talking in tones of hushed excitement, periodically breaking into giggles. Teacher Fei knew these types of kids. They pooled their pocket money in order to spend a few truant hours in a chat room, impersonating people much older than themselves and carrying on affairs with other human beings who could be equally fraudulent. In his school days, Teacher Fei had skipped his share of classes to frolic with friends in the spring meadow or to take long walks in the autumn woods, and he wondered if, in fifty years, the children around the computer would have to base their nostalgia on a fabricated world that existed only in a machine. But who could blame them for paying little attention to the beautiful April afternoon? Teacher Fei had originally hired Mrs. Luo for an hour a day so that he could take a walk; ever since he had discovered the Internet, Mrs. Luo's hours had been increased. Most days now she spent three hours in the afternoon taking care of Teacher Fei's mother and cooking a meal for both of them. The manager of the Internet café had once suggested that Teacher Fei purchase a computer of his own; the man had even volunteered to set it up, saying that he would be happy to see a good customer save money, even if it meant that he would lose some business. Teacher Fei rejected the generous offer—despite his mother's increasing loss of her grip on reality, he could not bring himself to perform any act of dishonesty in her presence.

Teacher Fei located the girl's blog without a problem. There were more pictures of her there, some with her mother. Anyone could see the older woman's unease in front of the camera. In her prime she would have been more attractive than her daughter was now, but perhaps it was the diffidence in her face that had softened some of the features that in her daughter's case were accentuated by rage. Under the heading "Happier Time," Teacher Fei found a black-and-white photo of the family. The girl, age three or four, sat on a high stool, and her parents stood on either side. On the wall behind them was a garden, painted by someone without much artistic taste, Teacher Fei could tell right away. The girl laughed with a mouthful of teeth, and the mother smiled demurely, as befitting a married woman in front of a photographer. The father was handsome, with perfectly shaped cheekbones and deep-set eyes not often found in a Chinese face, but the strain in his smile and the tiredness in those eyes seemed to indicate little of the happiness the daughter believed had existed in her parents' marriage.

Teacher Fei shook his head and scribbled on a scrap of paper the man's name and address and home phone number, as well as the address and number of his work unit, which were all listed by the girl. A scanned image of his resident's ID was displayed, too. Teacher Fei calculated the man's age, forty-six, and noted that on the paper. When he went to the message board on the girl's website, Teacher Fei read a few of the most recent posts, left by sympathetic women claiming to have been similarly hurt by unfaithful husbands or absent fathers. "Dearest Child," one message started, from a woman calling herself "Another Betrayed Wife," who praised the young girl as an angel of justice and courage. Teacher Fei imagined these women dialing the father's number at night, or showing up in front of his work unit to brandish cardboard

signs covered with words of condemnation. "To all who support this young woman's mission," he typed in the box at the
bottom of the Web page, "the world will be a better place
when one learns to see through to the truth instead of making hasty and unfounded accusations."

"A Concerned Man," Teacher Fei signed his message. A
different opinion was not what these women would want
to hear, but any man with a brain had to accept his responsibility to make the truth known. A girl among the group
of middle schoolers glanced at Teacher Fei and then whispered to a companion, who looked up at him with a snicker
before letting herself be absorbed again by the screen. An
old man with wrinkles and without hair. Teacher Fei assessed
himself through the girls' eyes: bored and boring, no doubt
undesirable in any sense, but who could guarantee the girls
that the flirtatious young man online who made their hearts
speed was not being impersonated by an equally disgraceful
old man?

Later that evening, when Teacher Fei had wrung a warm
towel to the perfect stage of moistness and passed it to his
mother, who sat on another towel on her bed, a curtain separating her partly undressed body from him, he thought about
the two girls and their youthful indifference. One day, if they
were fortunate enough to survive all the disappointments life
had in store for them, they would have to settle into their
no-longer-young bodies.

"Do you remember Carpenter Chang?" Teacher Fei's
mother asked from the other side of the curtain. Three times
a week, Mrs. Luo bathed Teacher Fei's mother, and on the
other evenings Teacher Fei and his mother had to make do
with the curtain as he assisted her with her sponge bath and

listened to her reminisce about men and women long dead. Half an hour, and sometimes an hour, would pass, his mother washing and talking on one side of the curtain, him listening and sometimes pressing for details on the other side. This was the time of day they talked the most, when Teacher Fei knew that although his mother's body was frail and her mind tangled by memories, she was still the same graceful woman who, with her unhurried storytelling, knew how to take the awkwardness out of a situation in which she had to be cared for by a grown son who had remained a bachelor all his life.

Having his mother as his only companion in old age was not how Teacher Fei had envisioned his life, but he had accepted this with little grievance. He enjoyed conversations with her, for whom things long forgotten by the world were as present as the air she shallowly breathed: two apprentices pulling a giant paper fan back and forth in a barbershop to refresh the sweating customers, the younger one winking at her while her grandfather snored on the bench, waiting for his daily shave; the machine her father had installed in the front hall of their house, operated by a pedaling servant, which cut a long tube of warm, soft toffee into small neat cubes that, once hardened, were wrapped in squares of cellophane by her and her four sisters; the cousins and second cousins who had once been playmates, fed and clothed and schooled alongside her and her sisters when they were young, but who later claimed to have been exploited as child laborers by her capitalist father; her wedding to Teacher Fei's father, attended by the best-known scholars of the day and lamented by most of her relatives, her mother included, as a bad match.

Teacher Fei's father had been the oldest and poorest of his mother's suitors. Twenty years her senior, he had worked as a part-time teacher in the elite high school that she and her sisters attended, and when she rejected him a renowned scholar wrote to her on his behalf, assuring the sixteen-year-old girl of what was beyond her understanding at the time: that Teacher Fei's father would become one of the most important philosophers in the nation and, more than that, would be a devoted husband who would love her till death parted them.

Teacher Fei had always suspected that his mother had agreed to see his father only to appease the scholar, but within a year the two had married, and afterward, before Teacher Fei's father found a university position, his mother used her dowry to help her husband support his parents and siblings in the countryside. Unable to become pregnant, she adopted a boy—Teacher Fei—from the long line of nephews and nieces who lived in close quarters in her husband's family compound, which had been built and rebuilt in the course of four generations. She had never hidden this fact from Teacher Fei, and he remembered being saddened after a holiday in his father's home village when he was eight and finally understood that he alone had been plucked from his siblings and cousins. His relatives, birth parents included, treated him with respect and even awe. It was his good fortune, his mother had said, comforting him, to have two pairs of parents and two worlds.

Poor man, she said now, and for a moment, lost in his reverie, Teacher Fei wondered if he had told her about the avenging daughter. Then he realized that his mother was still talking about the carpenter, who had once carved five coffins for his children, all killed by typhoid within a week. The carpenter's wife, who had been hired as a wet nurse for Teacher Fei when he first left his birth mother, had returned to the house years later with the news. Even as a ten-year-old, Teacher Fei could see that the woman had been driven out of her mind and would go on telling the story to any willing ears until her death.

It's the innocent ones who are often preyed upon by life's cruelty, Teacher Fei replied, and when his mother did not speak he recounted the girl's story from the magazine. He paused as his mother, dressed in her pajamas, pulled the curtain aside. All set for the dreamland, she said. He did not know if she had heard him, but when he tucked her in she looked up. "You should not feel upset by the girl," she said.

He was not, Teacher Fei replied; it was just that he found the girl's hatred extraordinary. His mother shook her head slightly on the pillow, looking past his face at the ceiling, as if she did not want to embarrass him by confronting his lie. "The weak-minded choose to hate," she said. "It's the least painful thing to do, isn't it?"

She closed her eyes as if exhausted. Rarely did she stay in a conversation with him with such clarity these days, and he wondered whether she had chosen to neglect the world simply because it no longer interested her. He waited, and when she did not open her eyes he wished her a night of good sleep and clicked off the bedside lamp.

"The weak-minded choose to hate," Teacher Fei wrote in his journal later that night. For years, he'd had the habit of taking notes of his mother's words. "I have nothing to say about this world," he wrote, the line most often repeated in the journal. Twenty-five years ago, his father, after a long day of musing in his armchair, had said the same thing, his final verdict before he swallowed a bottle's worth of sleeping pills. Teacher Fei's mother had not sounded out of sorts when she had called him that evening to report his father's words, nor had she cried the following morning on the phone with the news of his father's death. Teacher Fei suspected that if his mother had not been an active accomplice, she had, at the least, been informed of the suicide plan; either way it made no difference, for the border between husband and wife had long been obscured in his parents' marriage. What surprised Teacher Fei was his mother's willingness to live on. He visited her daily after his father's death and, within a year, moved in with her. He recorded and analyzed every meaningful sentence of hers, looking for hints that the words were her farewell to the world. He was intentionally careless about his pills, and hers, too, as he believed she must have been in his father's final days—they had always been a family of insomniacs—but by the fifth anniversary of his father's death, Teacher Fei stopped waiting. She had nothing to say about the world, his mother told him that day, more out of amusement than resignation, and he knew then that she would not choose to end her life.

The message that Teacher Fei had left on the girl's website was not there when he checked the next day at the Internet café. Why was he surprised? Still, his hands shook as he composed another message, calling the girl "a manipulative liar." A young couple, seventeen or eighteen at most, cast disapproving glances at Teacher Fei from another computer, seemingly alarmed by his vehement treatment of the keyboard.

The chat rooms he normally frequented held little attraction for him today. He was leaving on a business trip abroad, he told a friend in one chat room who called herself "Perfume Beauty," and then repeated the news to similarly named women in other chat rooms, knowing that they would find other idling men to flirt with. The night before, he had imagined the reaction of the girl and her female allies to his message, and had composed an eloquent retort to throw at these petty-minded women. But no doubt the girl would again erase his comment, and he could not stop her, nor could he expose her dishonesty. Teacher Fei logged off the computer and watched the boy sneak a hand under the girl's sweater and wiggle it around, perhaps trying to unhook her troublesome bra. The girl looked at the screen with a straight face, but her body, moving slightly in cooperation, betrayed her enjoyment.

The girl noticed Teacher Fei's attention first and signaled to her boyfriend to stop. Without withdrawing his hand, he mouthed a threat at Teacher Fei, who lifted his arms as if surrendering and stood up to leave. When he walked past the couple, he raised a thumb and gave the boy a smile, as though they were conspiring comrades; the boy, caught off guard, grinned disarmingly before turning his face away.

Teacher Fei had never cupped his hands around a woman's breasts, and for an instant he wished that he possessed the magic to make the boy disappear and take his place next to the girl. What stupidity, Teacher Fei chided himself, after he had gulped down a can of ice-cold soda water at a roadside stand. It was that angry girl and her fraudulence— that was what was depriving him of his peace. He wished that he had been his mother's birth son, that he had her noble and calm blood running through his veins, guarding him against the ugliness of the world.

The good fortune that his mother had once assured him of had not lasted long. At eighteen, he had been an ambitious art student about to enter the nation's top art institute, but within a year, his father, an exemplary member of the reactionary intellectuals, was demoted from professor to toilet cleaner, and Teacher Fei's education was terminated. For the next twenty years, Teacher Fei's mother accompanied his father from building to building, one hand carrying a bucket of cleaning tools and the other holding her husband's arm, as if they were on their way to a banquet. Yet, in the end, even she could not save her husband from despair. Teacher Fei's father had killed himself two years after he was restored to his position at the university.

The next day, Teacher Fei saw that his second message to the girl had also been confiscated by the cyberworld. A different message, left by a woman who hailed the girl as a guardian of the morality of modern China, taunted Teacher Fei in bold type.

He hastily composed another post, and then spent twenty minutes rephrasing it in a calmer tone, but a day later, when that message had also been deleted, his rage erupted. He called her "a scorpion girl" in a new message, saying that he hoped no man would make the mistake of his life by marrying her and succumbing to her poison; he took great pity on her father, since an evil daughter like her would make any father live in a hell.

Her father . . . Teacher Fei paused in his typing as the man's unhappy face in the photo came back to him. He decided to call the man's work unit, an institute affiliated with the Ministry of Propaganda, from a phone booth in the street. A woman answered, and when Teacher Fei asked for the man by name she inquired about the nature of his business. An old school friend who had lost touch, he said, apologizing that he did not have another number for him and so had to make the initial contact through the work unit.

The woman hesitated and then told him to wait. When the phone was picked up again, Teacher Fei was surprised by the voice, which sounded as though it belonged to a much older man. It didn't matter what his name was, Teacher Fei replied when the girl's father asked for it; he was merely calling as a man who was sympathetic to a fellow man's situation.

He then asked if there was a chance that they could meet in person. The line clicked dead while he was in mid-sentence.

When Mrs. Luo came the next day, Teacher Fei begged her to stay till later in the evening. He would pay her double for the extra hours, he said, and Mrs. Luo, after complaining about the inconvenience, agreed, adding that a man like Teacher Fei indeed deserved an occasional break from caring for an elderly woman. Mrs. Luo had not lowered her voice, and Teacher Fei glanced at his mother, who sat in the armchair with her eyes fixed on a square of afternoon sunshine on the floor. She was obedient and quiet in front of Mrs. Luo, who, like everybody else, believed that Teacher Fei's mother had long been lost in her own world of dementia.

A man like him. In the street, Teacher Fei pondered Mrs. Luo's words. What did that mean—a man like him—a bachelor without a son to carry on his blood, a retired art teacher whose name most of his students had forgotten the moment they graduated from elementary school, a disgraceful old man who purchased fashion magazines at the newsstand and wasted his afternoons alongside teenagers in a cyberworld, making up names and stories and sending out romantic lies? What did he deserve but this aimless walk in a world where the only reason for him to live was so that his mother could die in her own bed? There must be places for a man like him to go, inexpensive foot-massage shops where, behind an unwashed curtain, a jaded young woman from the countryside would run her hands where he directed her while she chatted with a companion behind another curtain. Or, if he was willing to spend more—and he could, for he had few expenditures beyond his magazines and the Internet café, and had long ago stopped buying expensive brushes and paper and pretending to be an artist—one of the bathing palaces would welcome him into its warmth, with a private room and a woman of his choice to wait on him.

It was a few minutes after five when Teacher Fei arrived at the institute, betting that the girl's father was not the type to leave work early, since there would be little reason for him to hurry home. While Teacher Fei waited for a guard to inform the man of his arrival, he studied the plaque at the entrance to the institute. THE ASSOCIATION OF MARXIST DIALECTICAL MATERIALISM, it said, and it occurred to Teacher Fei that had his father been alive he would have said that it was the parasites in these institutes who had ended hope for Chinese philosophers.

"Please don't get me wrong. I am a serious man," Teacher Fei said to the girl's father when he appeared. "A man most sympathetic to your situation."

"I don't know you," the man said. Had Teacher Fei not known his age, he would have guessed him to be older than sixty; his hair was more gray than black, and his back was stooped with timidity. A man closer to death than most men his age, Teacher Fei thought. But perhaps he would have more peace to look forward to in death.

A stranger could be one's best friend just as one's wife and daughter could be one's deadly enemies, Teacher Fei replied, and he suggested that they go out for tea or a quick drink. A small group of workers, on their way from the institute to the bus stop across the street, passed the pair of men; two women looked back at them and then talked in whispers to the group. The girl's father recoiled, and Teacher Fei wondered if the daughter knew that her father already lived in a prison cell, its bars invisible to the people in the street.

They could go to the man's office for a chat, Teacher Fei offered, knowing that this was the last thing he would want. The father hurriedly agreed to go to a nearby diner instead. He was the kind of man who was easily bullied by the world, Teacher Fei thought, realizing with satisfaction that he had not sought out the wrong person.

At the diner the girl's father chose a table in the corner farthest from the entrance, and in the dim light he squinted at the bench, wiping off some grease before he sat down. When the waitress came, Teacher Fei asked for a bottle of rice liquor and a plate of assorted cold cuts. He was not a drinker, nor had he ever touched marinated pig liver or tongue, but he imagined that a friendship between two men should start over harsh liquor and variety meats.

Neither spoke for a moment. When their order arrived, Teacher Fei poured some liquor for the girl's father. A good drink wipes out all pain for a man, Teacher Fei said, and then poured a glass for himself, but it soon became clear that neither of them would touch the drink or the meat, the man apparently feeling as out of place in the dingy diner as Teacher Fei did.

"What are you going to do?" Teacher Fei asked when the silence between them began to attract prying glances from the diner's middle-aged proprietress, who sat behind the counter and studied the few occupied tables.

The man shook his head. "I don't understand the question," he said.

"I think you should sue your daughter," Teacher Fei said, and immediately saw the man freeze with hostility. Perhaps someone had approached him with a similar proposition already. Or perhaps that was why the young girl had sued her father in the first place, egged on by an attorney, a manipulative man using her rage for his own gain.

Not that he could offer any legal help, Teacher Fei explained. He had been an art teacher in an elementary school before his retirement. He was in no position to do anything to hurt the girl's father, nor did he have the power to help him in his situation. It was only that he had followed his daughter's story in the media, and when he had seen the family picture he had known that he needed to do something for the girl's father. "'How many people in this world would understand this man's pain?' I asked myself when I saw your picture."

The girl's father flinched. "I am not the kind of man you think I am," he said.

"What?" Teacher Fei asked, failing to understand his meaning. He was not into other men, the girl's father said, so could Teacher Fei please stop this talk of friendship? The proprietress, who had been loitering around the nearby tables checking on the soy sauce bottles, perked up despite the man's hushed voice.

It took Teacher Fei a moment to grasp what the man was hinting at. Nor am I who you think I am, he thought of protesting, but why should he, when he had long ago made the decision not to defend himself against this ridiculous world?

The proprietress approached the table and asked about the quality of the food and drink. When the man did not reply, Teacher Fei said that they were very fine. The woman chatted for a moment about the weather and returned to her counter. Only then did the man insist that it was time for him to go home.

"Who is waiting at home?" Teacher Fei asked, and the man, taken aback, stood up and said he really needed to leave.

"Please," Teacher Fei said, looking up at the man. "Could you stay for just a minute?" If he sounded pathetic, he did not care. "You and I . . . ," he said slowly, glancing over at the entrance to the diner, where a pair of college students, a girl and a boy, were studying the menu on the wall. "We are the kind of men who would not kick our feet or flail our arms if someone came to strangle us to death. Most people would assume that we must be guilty if we don't fight back. A few would think us crazy or stupid. A very few would perhaps consider us men with dignity. But you and I alone know that they are all wrong, don't we?"

The man, who was about to leave some money on the table, tightened his fingers around the bills. Teacher Fei watched the college students take window seats, the boy covering the girl's hands with his own on the table. When the man sat back down, Teacher Fei nodded gratefully. He did not want to look up, for fear that the man would see his moist eyes. "When I was twenty-four, I was accused of falling in love with a girl student," he said. "Pedophile" had been the word used in the file at the school, the crime insinuated in the conversations taking place behind his back. The girl was ten and a half, an ordinary student, neither excelling among her classmates nor falling behind; one often encountered children like her in teaching, faces that blended into one another, names mis-recalled from time to time, but there was something in the girl's face, a quietness that did not originate from shyness or absentmindedness, as it usually did in children of her age, that intrigued Teacher Fei. He envisioned her at different ages—fifteen, twenty, thirty—but there was little desire in that imagining other than the desire to understand a face that had moved him as no other face had. "No, don't ask any questions, just as I won't ask whether you indeed kept a mistress while being married to your wife. It doesn't matter what happened between your cousin and you, or my girl student and me. You see, these accusations exist for the sake of those who feel the need to accuse. If it wasn't your cousin, there would have been another woman to account for your not loving your wife enough, no?"

The man took a sip from his glass, spilling the liquor when he put it down. He apologized for his clumsiness.

"My mother used to say that people in this country were very good at inventing crimes, but, better still, we were good at inventing punishments to go with them," Teacher Fei said.

When he and his cousin were young, they had vowed to marry each other, the man said; a children's game mostly, for when the time came they had drifted apart. She was widowed when they met again, and he tried to help her find a job in the city, but she was never his mistress.

"You don't have to explain these things to me," Teacher Fei said. "Had I not known to trust you, I would not have looked for you." The man could say a thousand things to defend himself, but people, his own daughter among them, would just laugh in his face and call him a liar. The crime that Teacher Fei had been accused of amounted to nothing more than a few moments of gazing, but one of the other students, a precocious eleven-year-old, had told her parents of the inappropriate attention the young teacher had paid to her classmate; later, when other girls were questioned, they seemed to be caught easily in the contagious imagining. He had just been curious, Teacher Fei said when he was approached by the principal. About what, he was pressed, but he could not explain how a face could contain so many mysteries visible only to those who knew what to look for. His reticence, more than anything, caused fury among the parents and his fellow teachers. In the end, he chose to be called the name that had been put in the file: A man's dirty desire was all his accusers could grasp.

"One should never hope for the unseeing to see the truth," Teacher Fei said now. "I could've denied all the accusations, but what difference would it have made?"

"So there was no . . . proof of any kind?" the man said, looking interested for the first time.

"Nothing to put me in jail for," Teacher Fei said.

"And someone just reported you?"

"We can't blame a young girl's imagination, can we?" Teacher Fei said.

The man met Teacher Fei's eyes. It was just the kind of thing his daughter would have done, the man said. "She'd have made sure you lost your job," he added with a bitter smile, surprising Teacher Fei with his humor. "Count yourself a lucky person."

Teacher Fei nodded. He had won the district mural contest for the school every year, his ambition and training in art making him a craftsman in the end, but shouldn't he consider it good fortune that his ability to paint the best portrait of Chairman Mao in the district had saved him from losing his job? The time to think about marriage had come and then gone, his reputation such that no matchmaker wanted to bet a girl's future on him. Still, his parents had treated him with gentle respect, never once questioning him. But as cleaners of public toilets they could do little to comfort him other than to leave him undisturbed in his solitude. Indeed, he was a lucky man, Teacher Fei said now; he had never married, so no one could accuse him of being an unfaithful husband or a bad father.

"Unwise of me to start a family, wasn't it?" the girl's father said. "Before my divorce, my daughter said there were three things she would do. First, she would sue me and put me in prison. If that failed, she would find a way to let the whole world know my crime. And if that didn't make me go back to her mother she would come with rat poison. Let me tell you—now that she has done the first two things, I am waiting every day for her to fulfill her promise, and I count it as my good fortune to have little suspense left in my life."

Teacher Fei looked at the college students paying at the counter, the boy counting money for the proprietress and the girl scanning the restaurant, her eyes passing over Teacher Fei and his companion without seeing them. "I have nothing to say about this world," Teacher Fei said.

Neither did he, the man replied, and they sat for a long time in silence till the proprietress approached again and asked if they needed more food. Both men brought out their wallets. "Let me," Teacher Fei said, and though the man hesitated for a moment, he did not argue.

In the dusk, a thin mist hung in the air. The two men shook hands as they parted. There was little more for them to say to each other, and Teacher Fei watched the man walk down the street, knowing that nothing would be changed by their brief meeting. He thought about his mother, who would be eager to see him return, though she would not show her anxiety to Mrs. Luo. He thought about his girl student: Fifty-two she would be now, no doubt a wife and mother herself, and he hoped that he had not been mistaken and she had grown into a woman like his mother. She—the girl student, whom he had never seen again—would outlive him, just as his mother had outlived his father, their beauty and wisdom the saving grace for a man like him, a man like his father. But for the other man, who would be watching the night fall around the orange halo of the streetlamps with neither longing nor dread, what did the future offer but the comfort of knowing that he would, when it was time for his daughter to carry out her plan of revenge, cooperate with a gentle willingness?

HOME

George Saunders

1.

Like in the old days, I came out of the dry creek behind the house and did my little tap on the kitchen window.

"Get in here, you," Ma said.

Inside were piles of newspaper on the stove and piles of magazines on the stairs and a big wad of hangers sticking out of the broken oven. All of that was as usual. New was: a water stain the shape of a cat head above the fridge and the old orange rug rolled up halfway.

"Still ain't no beeping cleaning lady," Ma said.

I looked at her funny.

"'Beeping'?" I said.

"Beep you," she said. "They been on my case at work."

It was true Ma had a pretty good potty mouth. And was working at a church now, so.

We stood there looking at each other.

Then some guy came tromping down the stairs: older than Ma even, in just boxers and hiking boots and a winter cap, long ponytail hanging out the back.

"Who's this?" he said.

"My son," Ma said shyly. "Mikey, this is Harris."

"What's your worst thing you ever did over there?" Harris said.

"What happened to Alberto?" I said.

"Alberto flew the coop," Ma said.

"Alberto showed his ass," Harris said.

"I hold nothing against that beeper," Ma said.

"I hold a lot against that fucker," Harris said. "Including he owes me ten bucks."

"Harris ain't dealing with his potty mouth," Ma said.

"She's only doing it because of work," Harris explained.

"Harris don't work," Ma said.

"Well, if I did work, it wouldn't be at a place that tells me how I can talk," Harris said. "It would be at a place that lets me talk how I like. A place that accepts me for who I am. That's the kind of place I'd be willing to work."

"There ain't many of that kind of place," Ma said.

"Places that let me talk how I want?" Harris said. "Or places that accept me for who I am?"

"Places you'd be willing to work," Ma said.

"How long's he staying?" Harris said.

"Long as he wants," Ma said.

"My house is your house," Harris said to me.

"It ain't your house," Ma said.

"Give the kid some food at least," Harris said.

"I will but it ain't your idea," Ma said, and shooed us out of the kitchen.

"Great lady," Harris said. "Had my eyes on her for years. Then Alberto split. That I don't get. You got a great lady in your life, the lady gets sick, you split?"

"Ma's sick?" I said.

"She didn't tell you?" he said.

He grimaced, made his hand into a fist, put it upside his head.

"Lump," he said. "But you didn't hear it from me."

Ma was singing now in the kitchen.

"I hope you're at least making bacon," Harris called out. "A kid comes home deserves some frigging bacon."

"Why not stay out of it?" Ma called back. "You just met him."

"I love him like my own son," Harris said.

"What a ridiculous statement," Ma said. "You hate your son."

"I hate both my sons," Harris said.

"And you'd hate your daughter if you ever meet her," Ma said.

Harris beamed, as if touched that Ma knew him well enough to know he would inevitably hate any child he fathered.

Ma came in with some bacon and eggs on a saucer.

"Might be a hair in it," she said. "Lately it's like I'm beeping shedding."

"You are certainly welcome," Harris said.

"You didn't beeping do nothing!" Ma said. "Don't take credit. Go in there and do the dishes. That would help."

"I can't do dishes and you know that," Harris said. "On account of my rash."

"He gets a rash from water," Ma said. "Ask him why he can't dry."

"On account of my back," Harris said.

"He's the King of If," Ma said. "What he ain't is King of Actually Do."

"Soon as he leaves I'll show you what I'm king of," Harris said.

"Oh, Harris, that is too much, that is truly disgusting," Ma said.

Harris raised both hands over his head like: Winner and still champ.

"We'll put you in your old room," Ma said.

2.

On my bed was a hunting bow and a purple Halloween cape with built-in ghost face.

"That's Harris's beep," Ma said.

"Ma," I said. "Harris told me."

I made my hand into a fist, put it upside my head.

She gave me a blank look.

"Or maybe I didn't understand him right," I said. "Lump? He said you've got a—"

"Or maybe he's a big beeping liar," she said. "He makes up crazy beep about me all the time. It's like his hobby. He told the mailman I had a fake leg. He told Eileen at the deli one of my eyes was glass. He told the guy at the hardware I get fainting dealies and froth at the mouth whenever I get mad. Now that guy's always rushing me outta there."

To show how fine she was, Ma did a jumping jack.

Harris was clomping upstairs.

"I won't tell you told about the lump," Ma said. "You don't tell I told about him being a liar."

Now this was starting to seem like the old days.

"Ma," I said, "where are Renee and Ryan living?"

"Uh," Ma said.

"They got a sweet place over there," Harris said. "Rolling in the dough."

"I'm not sure that's the best idea," Ma said.

"Your ma thinks Ryan's a hitter," Harris said.

"Ryan is a hitter," Ma said. "I can always tell a hitter."

"He hits?" I said. "He hits Renee?"

"You didn't hear it from me," Ma said.

"He better not start hitting that baby," Harris said. "Sweet little Martney. Kid's super-cute."

"Although what the beep kinda name is that?" Ma said. "I told Renee that. I said that."

"Is that a boy or a girl name?" Harris said.

"What the beep you talking about?" Ma said. "You seen it. You held it."

"Looks like a elf," Harris said.

"But girl or boy elf?" Ma said. "Watch. He really don't know."

"Well, it was wearing green," Harris said. "So that don't help me."

"Think," Ma said. "What did we buy it?"

"You'd think I'd know boy or girl," Harris said. "It being my freaking grandkid."

"It ain't your grandkid," Ma said. "We bought it a boat."

"A boat could be for boys or girls," Harris said. "Don't be prejudice. A girl can love a boat. Just like a boy can love a doll. Or a bra."

"Well, we didn't buy it a doll or a bra," Ma said. "We bought it a boat."

I went downstairs, got the phone book. Renee and Ryan lived over on Lincoln. 27 Lincoln.

3.

27 Lincoln was in the good part of downtown.

I couldn't believe the house. Couldn't believe the turrets. The back gate was redwood and opened so smooth, like the hinge was hydraulic.

Couldn't believe the yard.

I squatted in some bushes by the screened-in porch. Inside, some people were talking: Renee, Ryan, Ryan's parents, sounded like. Ryan's parents had sonorous/confident voices that seemed to have been fabricated out of previous, less sonorous/confident voices by means of sudden money.

"Say what you will about Lon Brewster," Ryan's dad said. "But Lon came out and retrieved me from Feldspar that time I had a flat."

"In that ridiculous broiling heat," said Ryan's mom.

"And not a word of complaint," said Ryan's dad. "A completely charming person."

"Almost as charming—or so you told me—as the Flemings," she said.

"And the Flemings are awfully charming," he said.

"And the good they do!" she said. "They flew a planeload of babies over here."

"Russian babies," he said. "With harelips."

"Soon as the babies arrived, they were whisked into various operating rooms all around the country," she said. "And who paid?"

"The Flemings," he said.

"Didn't they also set aside some money for college?" she said. "For the Russians?"

"Those kids went from being disabled in a collapsing nation to being set for life in the greatest country in the world," he said. "And who did this? A corporation? The government?"

"One private couple," she said.

"A truly visionary pair of folks," he said.

There was a long admiring pause.

"Although you'd never know it by how harshly he speaks to her," she said.

"Well, she can be awfully harsh with him as well," he said.

"Sometimes it's just him being harsh with her and her being harsh right back," she said.

"It's like the chicken or the egg," he said.

"Only with harshness," she said.

"Still, you can't help but love the Flemings," he said.

"We should be so wonderful," she said. "When was the last time we rescued a Russian baby?"

"Well, we do all right," he said. "We can't afford to fly a bunch of Russian babies over here, but I think, in our own limited way, we do just fine."

"We can't even fly over one Russian," she said. "Even a Canadian baby with a harelip would be beyond our means."

"We could probably drive up there and pick one up," he said. "But then what? We can't afford the surgery and can't afford the college. So the baby's just sitting here, in America instead of Canada, still with the lip issue."

"Did we tell you kids?" she said. "We're adding five shops. Five shops around the tri-city area. Each with a fountain."

"That's great, Mom," Ryan said.

"That is so great," Renee said.

"And maybe, if those five shops do well, we can open another three or four shops and, at that time, revisit this whole Russian-harelip issue," Ryan's father said.

"You guys continue to amaze," Ryan said.

Renee stepped out with the baby.

"I'm going to step out with the baby," she said.

4.

The baby had taken its toll. Renee seemed wider, less peppy. Also paler, like someone had run a color-leaching beam over her face and hair.

The baby did look like an elf.

The elf-baby looked at a bird, pointed at the bird.

"Bird," said Renee.

The elf-baby looked at their insane pool.

"For swimming," said Renee. "But not yet. Not yet, right?"

The elf-baby looked at the sky.

"Clouds," Renee said. "Clouds make rain."

It was like the baby was demanding, with its eyes: Hurry up, tell me what all this shit is, so I can master it, open a few shops.

The baby looked at me.

Renee nearly dropped the baby.

"Mike, Mikey, holy shit," she said.

Then she seemed to remember something and hustled back to the porch door.

"Rye?" she called. "Rye-King? Can you come get the Mart-Heart?"

Ryan took the baby.

"Love you," I heard him say.

"Love you more," she said.

Then she came back, no baby.

"I call him Rye-King," she said, blushing.

"I heard that," I said.

"Mikey," she said. "Did you do it?"

"Can I come in?" I said.

"Not today," she said. "Tomorrow. No, Thursday. His folks leave Wednesday. Come over Thursday, we'll hash it all out."

"Hash what out?" I said.

"Whether you can come in," she said.

"I didn't realize that was a question," I said.

"Did you?" she said. "Do it?"

"Ryan seems nice," I said.

"Oh God," she said. "Literally the nicest human being I have ever known."

"Except when he's hitting," I said.

"When what?" she said.

"Ma told me," I said.

"Told you what?" she said. "That Ryan hits? Hits me? Ma said that?"

"Don't tell her I told," I said, a little panicked, as of old.

"Ma's deranged," she said. "Ma's out of her frigging mind. Ma *would* say that. You know who's gonna get hit? Ma. By me."

"Why didn't you write me about Ma?" I said.

"What about her?" she said suspiciously.

"She's sick?" I said.

"She told you?" she said.

I made a fist and held it upside my head.

"What's that?" she said.

"A lump?" I said.

"Ma doesn't have a lump," she said. "She's got a fucked-up heart. Who told you she's got a lump?"

"Harris," I said.

"Oh, Harris, perfect," she said.

Inside the house, the baby started crying.

"Go," Renee said. "We'll talk Thursday. But first."

She took my face in her hands and turned my head so I was looking in the window at Ryan, who was heating a bottle at the kitchen sink.

"Does that look like a hitter?" she said.

"No," I said.

And it didn't. Not at all.

"Jesus," I said. "Does anybody tell the truth around here?"

"I do," she said. "You do."

I looked at her and for a minute she was eight and I was ten and we were hiding in the doghouse while Ma and Dad and Aunt Toni, on mushrooms, trashed the patio.

"Mikey," she said. "I need to know. Did you do it?"

I jerked my face out of her hands, turned, went.

"Go see your own wife, doofus!" she shouted after me. "Go see your own babies."

5.

Ma was on the front lawn, screaming at this low-slung fat guy. Harris was looming in the background, now and then hitting or kicking something to show how scary he could get when enraged.

"This is my son!" Ma said. "Who served. Who just came home. And this is how you do us?"

"I'm grateful for your service," the man said to me.

Harris kicked the metal garbage can.

"Will you please tell him to stop doing that?" the man said.

"He has no control over me when I'm mad," Harris said. "No one does."

"Do you think I like this?" the man said. "She hasn't paid rent in four months."

"Three," Ma said.

"This is how you treat the family of a hero?" Harris said. "He's over there fighting and you're over here abusing his mother?"

"Friend, excuse me, I'm not abusing," the man said. "This is evicting. If she'd paid her rent and I was evicting, that would be abusing."

"And here I work for a beeping church!" Ma shouted.

The man, though low-slung and fat, was admirably bold. He went inside the house and came out carrying the TV with a bored look on his face, like it was his TV and he preferred it in the yard.

"No," I said.

"I appreciate your service," he said.

I took him by the shirt. I was, by this time, good at taking people by their shirts, looking them in the eye, speaking directly.

"Whose house is this?" I said.

"Mine," he said.

I put my foot behind him, dropped him on the grass.

"Go easy," Harris said.

"That was easy," I said, and carried the TV back inside.

6.

That night the sheriff arrived with some movers, who emptied the house onto the lawn.

I saw them coming and went out the back door and watched it all from High Street, sitting in the deer stand behind the Nestons'.

Ma was out there, head in hands, weaving in and out of her heaped-up crap. It was both melodramatic and not. I mean, when Ma feels something deeply, that's what she does: melodrama. Which makes it, I guess, not melodrama?

Something had been happening to me lately where a plan would start flowing directly down to my hands and feet. When that happened, I knew to trust it. My face would get hot and I'd feel sort of like, Go, go, go.

It had served me well, mostly.

Now the plan flowing down was: grab Ma, push her inside, make her sit, round up Harris, make him sit, torch the place, or at least make the first motions of torching the place, to get their attention, make them act their age.

I flew down the hill, pushed Ma inside, sat her on the stairs, grabbed Harris by the shirt, put my foot behind him, dropped him to the floor. Then held a match to the carpet on the stairs and, once it started burning, raised a finger, like, Quiet, through me runs the power of recent dark experience.

They were both so scared they weren't talking at all, which made me feel the kind of shame you know you're not going to cure by saying sorry, and where the only thing to do is: go out, get more shame.

I stomped the carpet fire out and went over to Gleason Street, where Joy and the babies were living with Asshole.

7.

What a kick in the head: their place was even nicer than Renee's.

The house was dark. There were three cars in the driveway. Which meant that they were all home and in bed.

I stood thinking about that a bit.

Then walked back downtown and into a store. I guess it was a store. Although I couldn't tell what they were selling. On yellow counters lit from within were these heavy blue-plastic tags. I picked one up. On it was the word "MiiVOXMAX."

"What is it?" I said.

"It's more like what's it for, is how I'd say it," this kid said.

"What's it for?" I said.

"Actually," he said, "this is probably more the one for you."

He handed me an identical tag but with the word "MiiVOXMIN" on it.

Another kid came over with espresso and cookies.

I put down the MiiVOXMIN tag and picked up the MiiVOXMAX tag.

"How much?" I said.

"You mean money?" he said.

"What does it do?" I said.

"Well, if you're asking is it data repository or information-hierarchy domain?" he said. "The answer to that would be: yes and no."

They were sweet. Not a line on their faces. When I say they were kids, I mean they were about my age.

"I've been away a long time," I said.

"Welcome back," the first kid said.

"Where were you?" the second one said.

"At the war?" I said, in the most insulting voice I could muster. "Maybe you've heard of it?"

"I have," the first one said respectfully. "Thank you for your service."

"Which one?" the second one said. "Aren't there two?"

"Didn't they just call one off?" the first one said.

"My cousin's there," the second said. "At one of them. At least I think he is. I know he was supposed to go. We were never that close."

"Anyway, thanks," the first one said, and put out his hand, and I shook it.

"I wasn't for it," the second one said. "But I know it wasn't your deal."

"Well," I said. "It kind of was."

"You *weren't* for it or *aren't* for it?" the first said to the second.

"Both," the second one said. "Although is it still going?"

"Which one?" the first one said.

"Is the one you were at still going?" the second one asked me.

"Yes," I said.

"Better or worse, do you think?" the first one said. "Like, in your view, are we winning? Oh, what am I doing? I don't actually care, that's what's so funny about it!"

"Anyway," the second one said, and held out his hand, and I shook it.

They were so nice and accepting and unsuspicious—they were so *for* me—that I walked out smiling and was about a

block away before I realized I was still holding MiiVOXMAX.
I got under a streetlight and had a look. It seemed like just
a plastic tag. Like, if you wanted MiiVOXMAX, you handed
in that tag, and someone went and got MiiVOXMAX for you,
whatever it was.

8.

Asshole answered the door.

His actual name was Evan. We'd gone to school together.
I had a vague memory of him in an Indian headdress, racing
down a hallway.

"Mike," he said.

"Can I come in?" I said.

"I think I have to say no to that," he said.

"I'd like to see the kids," I said.

"Past midnight," he said.

I had a pretty good idea he was lying. Were stores open
past midnight? Still, the moon was high and there was something moist and sad in the air that seemed to be saying, Well,
it's not *early*.

"Tomorrow?" I said.

"Would that be okay for you?" he said. "After I get home
from work?"

I saw we'd agreed to play it reasonable. One way we were
playing it reasonable was saying everything like a question.

"Around six?" I said.

"Does six work for you?" he said.

The weird part was I'd never actually seen the two of
them together. The wife back there in his bed could have
been someone else entirely.

"I know this isn't easy," he said.

"You fucked me," I said.

"I would respectfully disagree with that," he said.

"No doubt," I said.

"I didn't fuck you and she didn't," he said. "It was a challenging circumstance for all involved."

"More challenging for some than for others," I said. "Would you give me that much?"

"Are we being honest?" he said. "Or tiptoeing around conflict?"

"Honest," I said, and his face did this thing that, for a minute, made me like him again.

"It was hard for me because I felt like a shit," he said. "It was hard for her because she felt like a shit. It was hard for us because while feeling like shits we were also feeling all the other things we were feeling, which, I assure you, were and are as real as anything, a total blessing, if I can say it that way."

At that point, I started feeling like a chump, like I was being held down by a bunch of guys so another guy could come over and put his New Age fist up my ass while explaining that having his fist up my ass was far from his first choice and was actually making him feel conflicted.

"Six o'clock," I said.

"Six o'clock's perfect," he said. "Luckily, I'm on flextime."

"You don't need to be here," I said.

"If you were me and I was you, would you maybe feel you might somewhat need to be here?" he said.

One car was a Saab and one an Escalade and the third a newer Saab, with two baby seats in it and a stuffed clown I was not familiar with.

Three cars for two grown-ups, I thought. What a country. What a couple selfish dicks my wife and her new husband were. I could see that, over the years, my babies would slowly transform into selfish-dick babies, then selfish-dick toddlers, kids, teenagers, and adults, with me all that time skulking around like some unclean suspect uncle.

That part of town was full of castles. Inside one was a couple embracing. Inside another a woman had like nine million little Christmas houses out on a table, like she was taking inventory. Across the river the castles got smaller. By our part of town, the houses were like peasant huts. Inside one peasant hut were five kids standing perfectly still on the back of a couch. Then they all leapt off at once and their dogs went crazy.

9.

Ma's house was empty. Ma and Harris were sitting on the floor in the living room, making phone calls, trying to find somewhere to go.

"What time is it?" I said.

Ma looked up at where the clock used to be.

"The clock's on the sidewalk," she said.

I went out. The clock was under a coat. It was ten. Evan had fucked me. I considered going back, demanding to see the kids, but by the time I got there it would be eleven and he'd still have a decent point re the lateness of the hour.

The sheriff walked in.

"Don't get up," he said to Ma.

Ma got up.

"Get up," he said to me.

I stayed sitting.

"You the one who threw down Mr. Klees?" the sheriff said.

"He's just back from the war," Ma said.

"Thank you for your service," the sheriff said. "Might I ask you to refrain from throwing people down in the future?"

"He also threw me down," Harris said.

"My thing is I don't want to go around arresting veterans," the sheriff said. "I myself am a veteran. So if you help me, by not throwing anyone else down, I'll help you. By not arresting you. Deal?"

"He was also going to burn the house down," Ma said.

"I wouldn't recommend burning anything down," the sheriff said.

"He ain't himself," Ma said. "I mean, look at him."

The sheriff had never seen me before, but it was like admitting he had no basis for assessing how I looked would have been a professional embarrassment.

"He does look tired," the sheriff said.

"Plenty strong, though," Harris said. "Threw me right down."

"Where are you folks off to tomorrow?" the sheriff said.

"Suggestions?" Ma said.

"A friend, a family member?" the sheriff said.

"Renee's," I said.

"Failing that, the shelter on Fristen?" the sheriff said.

"One thing I am not doing is going to Renee's," Ma said. "Everyone in that house is too high and mighty. They already think of us as low."

"Well, we are low," said Harris. "Compared to them."

"The other thing I'm not doing is going to any beeping shelter," Ma said. "They got crabs at shelters."

"When we first started dating I had crabs from that shelter," Harris said helpfully.

"I'm sorry this is happening," the sheriff said. "Everything's backward and inverted."

"I'll say," Ma said. "Here I work for a church and my son's a hero. With a Silver Star. Dragged a marine out by the beeping foot. We got the letter. And where am I? Out on the street."

The sheriff had switched off and was waiting to make his break for the door and get back to whatever was real to him.

"Find someplace to live, folks," he advised genially as he left.

Harris and I dragged two mattresses back in. They still had the sheets and blankets on and all. But the sheet on their mattress had grass stains on one edge and the pillows smelled like mud.

Then we spent a long night in the bare house.

10.

In the morning Ma called some ladies she'd known as a young mother, but one had a disk out and another had cancer and a third had twins who'd both just been diagnosed manic-depressive.

In the light of day Harris braved up again.

"So this court-martial thing," he said. "Was that the worst thing you ever did? Or was there worse things, which you did but just didn't get caught?"

"They cleared him of that," Ma said tersely.

"Well, they cleared me of breaking and entering that time," Harris said.

"Anyways, how is this any of your business?" Ma said.

"Probably he wants to talk," Harris said. "Get some air in there. Good for the soul."

"Look at his face, Har," Ma said.

Harris looked at my face.

"Sorry I mentioned it," he said.

Then the sheriff was back. He made me and Harris drag the mattresses out. On the porch we watched him padlock the door.

"Eighteen years you have been my dear home," Ma said, possibly imitating some Sioux from a movie.

"You're going to want to get a van over here," the sheriff said.

"My son served in the war," Ma said. "And look how you're doing me."

"I'm the same guy that was here yesterday," the sheriff said, and for some reason framed his face with his hands. "Remember me? You told me that already. I thanked him for his service. Call a van. Or your shit's going to the dump."

"See how they treat a lady works at a church," Ma said.

Ma and Harris picked through their crap, found a suitcase, filled the suitcase with clothes.

Then we drove to Renee's.

My feeling was, Oh, this will be funny.

11.

Although yes and no. That was just one of my feelings.

Another was, Oh, Ma, I remember when you were young and wore your hair in braids and I would have died to see you sink so low.

Another was, You crazy old broad, you narced me out last night. What was up with that?

Another was, Mom, Mommy, let me kneel at your feet and tell you what me and Smelton and Ricky G. did at Al-Raz, and then you stroke my hair and tell me anybody would've done the exact same thing.

As we crossed the Roll Creek Bridge I could see that Ma was feeling, Just let that Renee deny me, I will hand that little beep her beeping beep on a platter.

But then, bango, by the time we got to the far side and the air had gone from river-cool to regular again, her face had changed to: Oh, God, if Renee denies me in front of Ryan's parents and they once again find me trash, I will die, I will simply die.

12.

Renee did deny her in front of Ryan's parents, who did find her trash.

But she didn't die.

You should have seen their faces as we walked in.

Renee looked stricken. Ryan looked stricken. Ryan's mom and dad were trying so hard not to look stricken that they kept knocking things over. A vase went down as Ryan's dad blundered forward trying to look chipper/welcoming. Ryan's mom lurched into a painting and ended up holding it in her crossed red-sweatered arms.

"Is this the baby?" I said.

Ma turned on me again.

"What do you think it is?" she said. "A midget that can't talk?"

"This is Martney, yes," Renee said, holding the baby out to me.

Ryan cleared his throat, shot Renee a look like, I thought we'd discussed this, Love Muffin.

Renee changed the baby's course, swerved it up, like if she held it high enough, that would negate the need for me to hold it, it being so close to the overhead light and all.

Which hurt.

"Fuck it," I said. "What do you think I'm going to do?"

"Please don't say 'fuck' in our home," Ryan said.

"Please don't tell my son what the beep he can beeping say," Ma said. "Him being in the war and all."

"Thank you for your service," Ryan's dad said.

"We can easily go to a hotel," Ryan's mom said.

"You are not going to any hotel, Mom," Ryan said. "They can go to a hotel."

"We're not going to a hotel," Ma said.

"You can easily go to a hotel, Mother. You love a good hotel," Renee said. "Especially when we're paying."

Even Harris was nervous.

"A hotel sounds lovely," he said. "It's been many a day since I reclined in a nice place of that nature as a hotel."

"You'd send your own mother, who works for a church, along with your brother, a Silver Star hero just home from the war, to some fleabag?" Ma said.

"Yes," Renee said.

"Can I at least hold the baby?" I said.

"Not on my watch," Ryan said.

"Jane and I would like you to know how much we supported, and still do support, your mission," Ryan's father said.

"A lot of people don't know how many schools you fellows built over there," Ryan's mother said.

"People tend to focus on the negative," Ryan's dad said.

"What's that proverb?" Ryan's mother said. "To make something or other, you first have to break a lot of something or other?"

"I think he could hold the baby," said Renee. "I mean, we're standing right here."

Ryan winced, shook his head.

The baby writhed, like it too believed its fate was being decided.

Having all these people think I was going to hurt the baby

made me imagine hurting the baby. Did imagining hurting the baby mean that I *would* hurt the baby? Did I *want* to hurt the baby? No, Jesus. But: Did the fact that I had no intention of hurting the baby mean that I wouldn't, when push came to shove, hurt the baby? Had I, in the recent past, had the experience of having no intention of doing Activity A, then suddenly finding myself right in the middle of doing Activity A?

"I don't want to hold the baby," I said.

"I appreciate that," Ryan said. "That's cool of you."

"I want to hold this pitcher," I said, and picked up a pitcher and held it like a baby, with the lemonade spilling out of it, and, once the lemonade was pooling nicely on the hardwood floor, spiked the pitcher down.

"You really hurt my feelings!" I said.

Then was out on the sidewalk, walking fast.

13.

Then was back in that store.

Two different guys were there, younger than the earlier two. They might have been high schoolers. I handed over the MiiVOXMAX tag.

"Oh shit, snap!" the one guy said. "We were wondering where that was."

"We were about to call it in," the other guy said, bringing over espresso and cookies.

"Is it valuable?" I said.

"Ha, oh, boy," the first one said, and got some kind of special cloth from under the counter and dusted the tag off and put it back on display.

"What is it?" I said.

"It's more like what's it for, is how I'd say it," the first guy said.

"What's it for?" I said.

"This might be more in your line," he said, and handed me the MiiVOXMIN tag.

"I've been away a long time," I said.

"Us, too," the second kid said.

"We just got out of the army," the first kid said.

Then we all took turns saying where we'd been.

Turned out me and the first guy had been in basically the same place.

"Wait, so were you at Al-Raz?" I said.

"I was totally at Al-Raz," the first guy said.

"I was never in the shit, I admit it," the second guy said. "Although I did once run over a dog with a forklift."

I asked the first guy if he remembered the baby goat, the pocked wall, the crying toddler, the dark arched doorway, the doves that suddenly exploded out from under that peeling gray cave.

"I wasn't over by that," he said. "I was more over by the river and the upside-down boat and that little family all in red that kept turning up everywhere you looked?"

I knew exactly where he'd been. It was unbelievable how many times, pre- and post–exploding doves, I'd caught sight, on the horizon, down by the river, of some imploring or crouching or fleeing figure in red.

"It ended up cool with that dog, though," the second guy said. "He lived and all. By the time I left, he'd be like riding right up alongside me in the forklift."

A family of nine Indian-Americans came in, and the second guy went over to them with the espresso and cookies.

"Al-Raz, wow," I said, in an exploratory way.

"For me?" the first guy said. "Al-Raz was the worst day of the whole deal."

"Yes, me too, exactly," I said.

"I fucked up big-time at Al-Raz," he said.

Suddenly I found I couldn't breathe.

"My boy Melvin?" he said. "Got a chunk of shrapnel right in the groin. Because of me. I waited too long to call it in. There was this like lady party going on right nearby? About fifteen gals in this corner store. And kids with them. So I waited. Too bad for Melvin. For Melvin's groin."

Now he was waiting for me to tell the fucked-up thing I'd done.

I put down the MiiVOXMIN, picked it up, put it down.

"Melvin's okay, though," he said, and did a little two-finger tap on his own groin. "He's home, you know, in grad school. He's fucking, apparently."

"Glad to hear it," I said. "Probably he even sometimes rides up alongside you in the forklift."

"Sorry?" he said.

I looked at the clock on the wall. It didn't seem to have any hands. It was just a moving pattern of yellow and white.

"Do you know what time it is?" I said.

The guy looked up at the clock.

"Six," he said.

14.

Out on the street I found a pay phone and called Renee.

"I'm sorry," I said. "Sorry about that pitcher."

"Yeah, well," she said in her non-fancy voice. "You're gonna buy me a new one."

I could hear she was trying to make up.

"No," I said. "I won't be doing that."

"Where are you, Mikey?" she said.

"Nowhere," I said.

"Where are you going?" she said.

"Home," I said, and hung up.

15.

Coming up Gleason, I had that feeling. My hands and feet didn't know exactly what they wanted, but they were trending toward: push past whatever/whoever blocks you, get inside, start wrecking shit by throwing it around, shout out whatever's in your mind, see what happens.

I was on a like, shame slide. You know what I mean? Once, back in high school, this guy paid me to clean some gunk out of his pond. You snagged the gunk with a rake, then rake-hurled it. At one point, the top of my rake flew into the gunk pile. When I went to retrieve it, there were like a million tadpoles, dead and dying, at whatever age they are when they've got those swollen bellies like little pregnant ladies. What the dead and dying had in common was: their tender white underbellies had been torn open by the gunk suddenly crashing down on them from on high. The difference was: the dying were the ones doing the mad fear gesticulating.

I tried to save a few, but they were so tender all I did by handling them was torture them worse.

Maybe someone could've said to the guy who'd hired me, "Uh, I have to stop now, I feel bad for killing so many tadpoles." But I couldn't. So I kept on rake-hurling.

With each rake hurl I thought, I'm making more bloody bellies.

The fact that I kept rake-hurling started making me mad at the frogs.

It was like either: (A) I was a terrible guy who was knowingly doing this rotten thing over and over, or (B) it wasn't so rotten, really, just normal, and the way to confirm it was normal was to keep doing it, over and over.

Years later, at Al-Raz, it was a familiar feeling.

Here was the house.

Here was the house where they cooked, laughed, fucked. Here was the house that, in the future, when my name came up, would get all hushed, and Joy would be like, "Although Evan is no, not your real daddy, me and Daddy Evan feel you don't need to be around Daddy Mike all that much, because what me and Daddy Evan really care about is you two growing up strong and healthy, and sometimes mommies and daddies need to make a special atmosphere in which that can happen."

I looked for the three cars in the driveway. Three cars meant: all home. Did I want all home? I did. I wanted all, even the babies, to see and participate and be sorry for what had happened to me.

But instead of three cars in the driveway there were five.

Evan was on the porch, as expected. Also on the porch were: Joy, plus two strollers. Plus Ma.

Plus Harris.

Plus Ryan.

Renee was trotting all awkward up the driveway, trailed by Ryan's mom, pressing a handkerchief to her forehead, and Ryan's dad, bringing up the rear due to a limp I hadn't noticed before.

You? I thought. You jokers? You nutty fuckers are all God sent to stop me? That is a riot. That is so fucking funny. What are you going to stop me with? Your girth? Your good intentions? Your Target jeans? Your years of living off the fat of the land? Your belief that anything and everything can be fixed with talk, talk, endless yapping, hopeful talk?

The contours of the coming disaster expanded to include the deaths of all present.

My face got hot and I thought, Go, go, go.

Ma tried and failed to rise from the porch swing. Ryan helped her up by the elbow all courtly.

Then suddenly something softened in me, maybe at the sight of Ma so weak, and I dropped my head and waded all docile into that crowd of know-nothings, thinking: Okay, okay, you sent me, now bring me back. Find some way to bring me back, you fuckers, or you are the sorriest bunch of bastards the world has ever known.

SHHHH

NoViolet Bulawayo

Father comes home after many years of forgetting us, of not sending us money, of not loving us, not visiting us, not anything us, and parks in the shack, unable to move, unable to talk properly, unable to anything, vomiting and vomiting, Jesus, just vomiting and defecating on himself, and it smelling like something dead in there, dead and rotting, his body a black, terrible stick; I come in from playing Find bin Laden and he is there.

Just there. Parked. In the corner. On Mother's bed. So thin, like he eats pins and wire, so thin at first I don't even see him under the blankets. I am getting on the bed to get the skipping rope for playing Andy-over when F—when he lifts his head and I see him for the first time. He is just length and bones. He is rough skin. He is crocodile teeth and egg-white eyes, lying there, drowning on the bed.

I don't even know it's Father at the time so I run outside, screaming and screaming. Mother meets me with a slap and says, Shhhh, and points me back to the shack. I go, one hand covering my pain, the other folded in a fist in my mouth. By the time we are at the door I know without Mother saying anything. I know it's Father. Back. Back after all those years of forgetting us.

His voice sounds like something burned and seared his throat. My son. My boy, he says. Listening to him is painful;

I want to put my hands on my ears. He is like a monster up close and I think of running again but Mother is standing there in a red dress looking dangerous. My boy, he keeps saying, but I don't tell him that I'm a girl, I don't tell him to leave me alone.

Then he lifts his bones and pushes a claw toward me and I don't want to touch it but Mother is there looking. Looking like Jesus looks at you from Mother of Bones's calendar so you don't sin. I remain standing until Mother pushes me by the back of my neck, then I stagger forward and almost fall onto the terrible bones. The claw is hard and sweaty in my hand and I withdraw it fast. Like I've touched fire. Later, I don't want to touch myself with that hand, I don't want to eat with it or do nothing with it, I even wish I could throw the hand away and get another.

My boy, he says again. I do not turn to look at him because I don't even want to look at him. He keeps saying, My boy, my boy, until I finally say, *I'm not a boy, are you crazy? Go back, get away from our bed and go back to where you come from with your ugly bones, go back and leave us alone,* but I'm saying it all inside my head. Before I have finished saying all I'm trying to say he has shat himself and it feels like we're inside a toilet.

Mother had not wanted Father to leave for South Africa to begin with, but it was at that time when everybody was going to South Africa and other countries, some near, some far, some very, very far. They were leaving, just leaving in droves, and Father wanted to leave with everybody and he was going to leave and nothing would stop him.

Look at how things are falling apart, Felistus, he said one day, untying his shoes. We were sitting outside the shack and

Mother was cooking. Father was coming from somewhere, I don't know where, and he was angry. He was always angry those days; it was like the kind and funny man with the unending laugh and the many stories, the man who had been my father all those years, had gone and left an angry stranger behind. And little by little I was getting afraid of him, the angry stranger who was supposed to be my father.

Mother kept on stirring the pot on the fire, choosing to ignore him. Those days, you knew when and when not to talk to Father from the tone in his voice, that tone that could switch on and off like the lights. The tone he was using at that moment was switched to on.

We should have left. We should have left this wretched country when all this started, when Mgcini offered to take us across.

Things will get better, Mother said, finally. There is no night so long that doesn't end with dawn. It won't stay like this, will it? And besides, we can't all abandon our country now.

Yes the wife is right it will get better my son and the Lord God is here he will not forsake us he will not for he is a lov-ing God, Mother of Bones said, rubbing her hands together like she was washing them, like she was apologizing for some-thing, like it was cold outside. Mother of Bones said *God* like she knew God personally, like God was not even something bigger than the sky but a small, beautiful boy with spaced hair you could count and missing buttons on his Harvard shirt, who spoke with a stammer and played Find bin Laden with us. That's how it felt, the way Mother of Bones said *God*.

Then Father laughed, but it wasn't a laughing-laughing laugh.

You all don't get it, do you? Is this what I went to univer-sity for? Is this what we got independence for? Does it make sense that we are living like this? Tell me! Father said.

All I know is that I'm certainly not clamoring to go across the borders to live where I'm called a kwerekwere. Wasn't Nqobile here from that Hillbrow just two days ago telling us the truth of how it is over there? Mother said. She stirred more mealie-meal into the pot.

And besides, all my family is here. What about my aging parents? What about your mother? And you, get away, imbecile, go and play with your friends before I chop off those big ears, what are you listening for? she said to me, like she always did every time there was adult talk or they argued, and they argued a lot those days.

Father left not too long after that. And later, when the pictures and letters and money and clothes and things he had promised didn't come, I tried not to forget him by looking for him in the faces of the Paradise men, in the faces of my friends' fathers. I would watch the men closely, wondering which of their gestures my father would be likely to make, which voice he would use, which laugh. How much hair would cover his arms and face.

Shhhh—you must not tell anyone, and I mean *an-y-one*, you hear me? Mother says, looking at me like she is going to eat me. That your father is back and that he is sick. When Mother says this I just look at her. I don't say yes or nod, I don't anything. Because I have to watch Father now, like he is a baby and I am his mother, it means that when Mother and Mother of Bones are not there, I cannot play with my friends, so I have to lie to them about why.

In the beginning, when they come over to our shack to get me, I stand outside the door and yawn as wide as I can and tell them I am tired. Then I tell them I am having the headaches that won't go away. Then I tell them I am having the flu. Then diarrhea. It's not the lying itself that makes me feel bad but the fact that I'm here lying to my friends. I don't like not playing with them and I don't like lying to them because they are the most important thing to me and when I'm not with them I feel like I'm not even me.

One day I'm standing at the door with just my head out and I'm telling them I have measles. I don't know why I think it, but the word is suddenly there, on my tongue, speaking itself. *Measles.*

Is it painful? Sbho says. She is looking at me with her head tilted-like, the way a mother is supposed to do when you tell her about anything serious.

Yes, it is, I say. And then I add, It itches. Soon, it will become wounds and then I won't be able to come out to play for a while, I say. I cannot read the look on Stina's face but Godknows is looking at me with his mouth open. Bastard is just narrowing his eyes, watching me like I'm stealing something, and Sbho's face is twisted, as if she's sick with measles herself. Chipo is sitting down, drawing patterns with a stick on the ground.

What about the World Cup? Godknows says. You are not playing in the World Cup? We even found a real leather ball in Budapest because somebody forgot it outside.

Maybe my measles will be gone by the time it's World Cup, then I can come and be Drogba, I say, scratching my neck to make like it's itching.

True? Godknows says.

Yes, cross my heart and hope to die, I say.

Good, but you can't be Drogba, can't you see I'm already Drogba? Godknows says.

Liar, you're lying, Bastard says. You don't have measles and you're not sick and you haven't been sick. He is standing on one leg like a cock and chewing a blade of grass. He looks me in the eye and I know he wants me to say something back so he can say something worse. We are all standing there, everybody waiting for me to say something to Bastard, but I know I'm not opening my mouth.

We remain like that, and the silence is big and fat between us like it's something you can touch when the coughing starts. It is loud and raw and terrible and at first it takes me by surprise. I start, but then I quickly remember that he is in the shack. By now it's too late for me to do anything to hide it, and everybody is looking me in the eye, looking and waiting for me to say something, to explain.

I can't think what to say so I just stand there, sweating and listening to the cough pounding the walls, pounding and pounding and pounding, and I'm saying in my head, *Stop, please stop, stop stop stop stop please,* but he keeps pounding and pounding and pounding until I just turn around and slam the door shut, behind me a voice saying, Wait!

What you got in there? What you got?

I hear Bastard's voice close to the door, like he is going to maybe turn the handle and come in. I pull the latch and listen to him saying things and telling me to open and making jokes. When, finally, he goes quiet I sink down to the floor and just sit there, feeling tired. I look to the corner and he is looking at me with those eyes, wild, like he is some kind of animal caught in the glare of light on Mzilikazi Road, looking at me with his shrunken head, with his pinking lips, with his stench of sickness.

He coughs some more and I listen to the awful sound tearing the air. His body folds and rocks with each cough but I don't even feel for him because I'm thinking, *I hate you for this, I hate you for going to that South Africa and coming back sick and all bones, I hate you for making me stop playing with my friends.* When the coughing finally ceases he is sweating and breathing like somebody chased him all the way from Budapest and up and down Fambeki, and when he says, Water, in that tattered voice, I make like I don't even hear him because I'm hating him for making me stop my life like this. In my head I'm thinking, *Die. Die now so I can go play with my friends, die now because this is not fair. Die die die. Die.*

Father cannot climb Fambeki since he is sick, so Mother of Bones asks Prophet Revelations Bitchington Mborro to come and pray for him in the shack. We sit in a corner, me and Mother and Mother of Bones, watching. Prophet Revelations Bitchington Mborro sprinkles Father with holy water and then lights four candles: one red, maybe for the Father; one white, maybe for the Son; one yellow, maybe for the Holy Spirit; and one black, I don't know for what, maybe for the black majority, which is what the black of our flag stands for. Prophet Revelations Bitchington Mborro is crouching and humming to himself as he does all this, and finally, when he is done, he spreads a white cloth on the floor, kneels on it with a Bible at his side, and thunders.

At first my eyes are closed just like they are supposed to be when somebody is praying but then I get tired of closing them because Prophet Revelations Bitchington Mborro just keeps thundering and thundering. To make the time go I count to one hundred and when I finish he is still going on and on. On and on and on and on and on and on and on and on and on on on on on on on on on on on on on on on: I warn you in the name of Jesus, demon—cleanse him, Father—you mighty lion and healer of the sick—I lay myself before you, Jehovah Jaira, what-what. I just sit there, biting the insides of my mouth till I taste blood.

Father's eyes are open and the look inside them is that

of waiting, like waiting for a miracle. I look to the side and
Mother of Bones has her eyes closed and is praying fervently,
a vein popped on her forehead. Mother's eyes are open. She
doesn't give me a look that says she will kill me for keeping
my eyes open during prayer, so I just stay like that, watching.

Mother's eyes are tired and her face is tired; ever since
Father came she has been busy doing things for him—
watching him and cooking for him and feeding him and
changing him and worrying over him. I think of praying for
her so that her tiredness goes away but then I remind myself
I have decided that praying to God is a waste of time. You
pray and pray and pray and nothing changes, like for example
I prayed for a real house and good clothes and a bicycle and
things for a long, long time, and none of it has happened, not
even one little thing, which is how I know that all this praying for Father is just people playing.

I've thought about it properly, this whole praying thing, I
mean really thought about it, and what I think is that maybe
people are doing it wrong; that instead of asking God nicely,
people should be demanding and questioning and threatening to stop worshipping him. Maybe that way, he would
think differently and try to make things right, like he is supposed to; even that verse in the Bible says ask for anything
and you shall receive and, I mean, whose words are those?

After the longest time, Prophet Revelations Bitchington
Mborro finally says Amen, and opens his eyes. He wipes his
dripping face and head with the back of his sleeve as he tells
Mother of Bones that God showed him that my grandfather's
spirit, which has been in me all along, has left. When I hear
this I smile; even though I never felt like there was something
in me, it had still bothered me to hear Prophet Revelations
Bitchington Mborro say there was to begin with.

He goes on to tell Mother of Bones that it doesn't mean the spirit is gone because it has now got into Father and is devouring his blood and body, making him all bony and sick and taking his strength away. In order to avenge the spirit and heal Father, Prophet Revelations Bitchington Mborro says, we need to find two fat white virgin goats to be brought up the mountain for sacrifice, and that Father has to be bathed in the goats' blood. In addition, Prophet Revelations Bitchington Mborro says he will need five hundred U.S. dollars as payment, and if there are no U.S. dollars, euros will do. When he says this, Mother gets up angry-like and boils out of the shack, slamming the door behind her.

God also told me that the wife is possessed too, by three demons. One causes her to be unhappy all the time, one is the spirit of the dog, and the last one gives her a bad temper, rendering her a dangerous woman. But for now we have to deal with the husband, seeing how he is the most urgent case, Prophet Revelations Bitchington Mborro says, pointing his stick at Father.

They are huddling outside the shack when I open the door. Mother has gone to the border to sell and Mother of Bones is on Fambeki praying because she is fasting for Father's health. She cannot afford the two virgin goats and the five hundred U.S. dollars that Prophet Revelations Bitchington Mborro said to get and there are no doctors or nurses at the hospital because they are always on strike, so that's what Mother of Bones must do for now, fast and get on Fambeki and pray and pray and pray even though God will just ignore her.

It's your father in there. He has the Sickness, we know, Godknows says.

It's no use hiding AIDS, Stina says. When he mentions the Sickness by name, I feel a shortness of breath. I look around to see if there are other people within earshot.

It's like hiding a thing with horns in a sack. One day the horns will start boring through the sack and come out in the open for everybody to see, Stina says.

Where did he get it, South Africa? He wasn't sick when he left, was he? Godknows says.

Who told you all this? I say, looking from face to face. In my head I'm thinking just how much I hate him again, but now it's for a different reason. It's for putting me in this position where I have to explain to my friends and I don't know how anymore because I'm tired of all the lying.

Everybody knows, you ugly, Bastard says. We want to come in and see for ourselves.

There is nothing to see, I say. There is nobody in here. I realize that I am whispering, like I'm just talking to myself.

We saw your mother leave and we know your grandmother is on that kaka mountain wasting her time, so why don't you let us come in and see, Bastard says. He is already opening the door and letting himself in like he lives here. They all pile in, and I follow them like it's their shack and I'm just visiting.

We kneel around the bed, around Father, who is perched there like a disappearing king. This is the first time I am coming this close to him without Mother making me. I keep expecting for somebody to laugh at Father's bones but nobody makes a sound; it is all quiet like we are maybe at church and Jesus just entered and coughed twice. I am careful not to look anyone in the face because I don't want them to see the shame in my eyes, and I also don't want to see the laughter in theirs.

We don't speak. We just peer in the tired light at the long bundle of bones, at the shrunken head, at the wavy hair, most of it fallen off, at the face that is all points and edges from bones jutting out, the pinkish-reddish lips, the ugly sores, the skin sticking to the bone like somebody ironed it on, the hands and feet like claws. I know then that what really makes a person's face is the meat; once that melts away, you are left with something nobody can even recognize.

Bastard picks up the stick-like hand lying there beside Father as if somebody left it behind on the way to play. He cradles it in his like it's an egg and says, How are you, Mr. Darling's father? I have never heard Bastard sound like this, all careful and gentle like his words are made of feathers. We all lean forward and watch the thin lips move, the mouth struggling to mumble something and giving up because the words are stunning themselves on the carpet of sores around the inner lips, the tongue so swollen it fills the mouth. We watch him stop struggling to speak and I think about how it would feel to not be able to do a simple thing like open my mouth and speak, the voice drowning inside me. It's a terrifying feeling.

Where do you think he is going to go? Sbho says.

Can't you see he is stuck here and he is never getting out? Chipo says.

I mean when he dies, Sbho says.

I turn to look at her and she shrugs. I know Father is sick but the thought of him dead and gone-gone scares me. It's not like he'll be in South Africa, for example, where it is possible to tell yourself and other people that since that's where he went then maybe one day he will return. Death is not like that, it is final, like that girl hanging in a tree because as we later found out from the letter in her pockets, she had the

Sickness and thought it was better to just get it over with and kill herself. Now she is dead and gone, and Mavava, her mother, will never ever see her again.

To heaven. My father is going to heaven, I say, even if I don't really think there is a heaven; I just don't like the thought of him not going anywhere. I hear myself saying *my* like he is maybe my favorite thing, like he is mine, like I own him. He is looking like a child, just lying there, unable to do anything, and then I'm wishing I were big and strong so I could scoop him up and rock him in my arms.

Is that why Mother of Bones is always on that mountain praying? Is she praying for God to let him into heaven? Sbho says.

I don't know, maybe, I say.

Heaven is boring. Didn't you see, in that picture book back when we used to go to school? It's just plain and white and there is not even any color and it's too orderly. Like there will be crazy prefects telling you all the time: Do this, don't do that, where are your shoes, tuck in your shirt, shhh, God doesn't like it and will punish you, keep your voice low you'll wake the angels, go and wash, you are dirty, Bastard says.

Me, when I die I want to go where there's lots of food and music and a party that never ends and we're singing that Jobho song, Godknows says.

When Godknows starts singing Jobho, Sbho joins in and we listen to them sing it for a while and then we're all scratching our bodies and singing it because Jobho is a song that leaves you with no choice but to scratch your body the way that sick man Job did in the Bible, lying there scratching his itching wounds when God was busy torturing him just to play with him to see if he had faith. Jobho makes you call out to heaven even though you know God is occupied with better things and will not even look your way. Jobho makes you point your forefinger to the sky and sing at the top of your voice. We itch and we scratch and we point and we itch again and we fill the shack with song.

Then Stina reaches and takes Father's hand and starts moving it to the song, and Bastard moves the other hand. I reach out and touch him too because I have never really touched him ever since he came and this is what I must do now because how will it look when everybody is touching him and I'm not? We all look at one another and smile-sing because we are touching him, just touching him all over like he is a beautiful plaything we have just rescued from a rubbish bin in Budapest. He feels like dry wood in my hands, but there is a strange light in his sunken eyes, like he has swallowed the sun.

SPECIAL ECONOMICS

Maureen McHugh

"What are you doing?" a guy asked her.

"I am divorced," she said. She had always thought of herself as a person who would one day be divorced, so it didn't seem like a big stretch to claim it. Staying married to one person was boring. She figured she was too complicated for that. Interesting people had complicated lives. "I'm looking for a job. But I do hip-hop, too," she explained.

"Hip-hop?" He was a middle-aged man with stubble on his chin who looked as if he wasn't looking for a job but should be.

"Not like Shanghai," she said. "Not like Hi-Bomb. They do gangsta stuff, which I don't like. Old-fashioned. Like M.I.A.," she said. "Except not political, of course." She gave a big smile. This was all way beyond the guy. Jieling started the boom box. M.I.A. was Maya Arulpragasam, a Sri Lankan hip-hop artist who had started all on her own years ago. She had sung, she had danced, she had done her own videos. Of course M.I.A. lived in London, which made it easier to do hip-hop and become famous.

Jieling had no illusions about being a hip-hop singer, but it had been a good way to make some cash up north in Baoding where she came from. Set up in a plague-trash market and dance for yuan.

Jieling did her opening, her own hip-hop moves, a little

like Maya and a little like some things she had seen on MTV, but not too sexy, because Chinese people did not throw you money if you were too sexy. Only April, and it was already hot and humid.

> Ge *down, ge down,*
> *lang-a-lang-a-lang-a.*
> Ge *down, ge down,*
> *lang-a-lang-a-lang-a.*

She had borrowed the English. It sounded very fresh. Very criminal.

The guy said, "How old are you?"

"Twenty-two," she said, adding three years to her age, still dancing and singing.

Maybe she should have told him she was a widow? Or an orphan? But there were too many orphans and widows after so many people died in the bird flu plague. There was no margin in that. Better to be divorced. He didn't throw any money at her, just flicked open his cell phone to check listings from the market for plague trash. This plague-trash market was so big it was easier to check online, even if you were standing right in the middle of it. She needed a new cell phone. Hers had finally fallen apart right before she headed south.

Shenzhen people were apparently too jaded for hip-hop. She made fifty-two yuan, which would pay for one night in a bad hotel where country people washed cabbage in the communal sink.

The market was full of secondhand stuff. When over a quarter of a billion people died in four years, there was a lot of secondhand stuff. But there was still a part of the market for new stuff and street food, and that's where Jieling found the cell phone seller. He had a cart with stacks of flat plastic cell phone kits printed with circuits and scored. She flipped through; tiger-striped, peonies (old lady phones), metallics (old man phones), anime characters, moon phones, expensive lantern phones. "Where is your printer?" she asked.

"At home," he said. "I print them up at home, bring them here. No electricity here." Up north in Baoding she'd always bought them in a store where they let you pick your pattern online and then printed them there. More to pick from.

On the other hand, he had a whole box full of ones that hadn't sold that he would let go for cheap. In the stack she found a purple one with kittens that wasn't too bad. Very Japanese, which was also very fresh this year. And only one hundred yuan for the phone and three hundred minutes.

He took the flat plastic sheet from her and dropped it in a pot of boiling water big enough to make dumplings. The hinges embedded in the sheet were made of plastic with molecular memory and when they got hot, they bent, and the plastic folded into a rough cell phone shape. He fished the phone out of the water with tongs, let it sit for a moment, and then pushed all the seams together so they snapped. "Wait about an hour for it to dry before you use it," he said, and handed her the warm phone.

"An *hour*," she said. "I need it now. I need a job."

He shrugged. "Probably okay in half an hour," he said.

She bought a newspaper and scallion pancake from a street food vendor, sat on a curb, and ate while her phone dried. The paper had some job listings, but it also had a lot of listings from recruiters. ONE MONTH BONUS PAY! BEST JOBS! and NUMBER ONE JOBS! START BONUS! People scowled at her for sitting on the curb. She looked like a farmer, but what else was she supposed to do? She checked listings on her new cell phone. Online there were a lot more listings than in the paper. It was a good sign. She picked one at random and called.

The woman at the recruiting office was a flat-faced southerner with buckteeth. Watermelon-picking teeth. But she had a manicure and a very nice red suit. The office was not so nice. It was small, and the furniture was old. Jieling was groggy from a night spent at a hotel on the edge of the city. It had been cheap but very loud.

The woman was very sharp in the way she talked and had a strong accent that made it hard to understand her. Maybe Fujian, but Jieling wasn't sure. The recruiter had Jieling fill out an application.

"Why did you leave home?" the recruiter asked.

"To get a good job," Jieling said.

"What about your family? Are they alive?"

"My mother is alive. She is remarried," Jieling said. "I wrote it down."

The recruiter pursed her lips. "I can get you an interview on Friday," she said.

"Friday!" Jieling said. It was Tuesday. She had only three hundred yuan left out of the money she had brought. "But I need a job!"

The recruiter looked sideways at her. "You have made a big gamble to come to Shenzhen."

"I can go to another recruiter," Jieling said.

The recruiter tapped her lacquered nails. "They will tell you the same thing," she said.

Jieling reached down to pick up her bag.

"Wait," the recruiter said. "I do know of a job. But they only want girls of very good character."

Jieling put her bag down and looked at the floor. Her

character was fine. She was not a loose girl, whatever this woman with her big front teeth thought.

"Your Mandarin is very good. You say you graduated with high marks from high school," the recruiter said.

"I liked school," Jieling said, which was only partly not true. Everybody here had terrible Mandarin. They all had thick southern accents. Lots of people spoke Cantonese in the street.

"Okay. I will send you to ShinChi for an interview. I cannot get you an interview before tomorrow. But you come here at eight a.m. and I will take you over there."

ShinChi. New Life. It sounded very promising. "Thank you," Jieling said. "Thank you very much."

But outside in the heat, she counted her money and felt a creeping fear. She called her mother.

Her stepfather answered, *"Wei."*

"Is Ma there?" she asked.

"Jieling!" he said. "Where are you!"

"I'm in Shenzhen," she said, instantly impatient with him. "I have a job here."

"A job! When are you coming home?"

He was always nice to her. He meant well. But he drove her nuts. "Let me talk to Ma," she said.

"She's not here," her stepfather said. "I have her phone at work. But she's not home, either. She went to Beijing last weekend, and she's shopping for fabric now."

Her mother had a little tailoring business. She went to Beijing every few months and looked at clothes in all the good stores. She didn't buy in Beijing; she just remembered. Then she came home, bought fabric, and sewed copies. Jieling's stepfather had been born in Beijing and she thought that was part of the reason her mother had married him. He was more like her mother than her father had been. There was nothing in particular wrong with him. He just set her teeth on edge.

"I'll call back later," Jieling said.

"Wait, your number is blocked," her stepfather said. "Give me your number."

"I don't even know it yet," Jieling said, and hung up.

The New Life company was a huge, modern-looking building with a lot of windows. Inside it was full of reflective surfaces and very clean. Sounds echoed in the lobby. A man in a very smart gray suit met Jieling and the recruiter, and the recruiter's red suit looked cheaper, her glossy fingernails too red, her buckteeth exceedingly large. The man in the smart gray suit was short and slim and very southern looking. Very city.

Jieling took some tests on her math and her written characters and got good scores.

To the recruiter, the human resources man said, "Thank you, we will send you your fee." To Jieling he said, "We can start you on Monday."

"Monday?" Jieling said. "But I need a job now!" He looked grave. "I . . . I came from Baoding, in Hebei," Jieling explained. "I'm staying in a hotel, but I don't have much money."

The human resources man nodded. "We can put you up in our guesthouse," he said. "We can deduct the money from your wages when you start. It's very nice. It has television and air-conditioning, and you can eat in the restaurant."

It was very nice. There were two beds. Jieling put her backpack on the one nearest the door. There was carpeting, and the windows were covered in gold drapes with a pattern of cranes flying across them. The television got stations from Hong Kong. Jieling didn't understand the Cantonese, but there was a button on the remote for subtitles. The movies had lots of violence and more sex than mainland movies did—like the bootleg American movies for sale in the market. She wondered how much this room was. Two hundred yuan? Three hundred yuan?

Jieling watched movies the whole first day, one right after another.

On Monday she began orientation. She was given two pale green uniforms, smocks and pants like medical people wore, and little caps and two pairs of white shoes. In the uniform she looked a little like a model worker—which is to say that the clothes were not sexy and made her look fat. There were two other girls in their green uniforms. They all watched a DVD about the company.

New Life did biotechnology. At other plants they made influenza vaccine (on the screen were banks and banks of chicken eggs), but at this plant they were developing breakthrough technologies in tissue culture. It showed many men in suits. Then it showed a big American store and explained how they were forging new exportation ties with the biggest American corporation for selling goods, Wal-Mart. It also showed a little bit of an American movie about Wal-Mart. Subtitles explained how Wal-Mart was working with companies around the world to improve living standards, decrease CO_2 emissions, and give people low prices. The voice narrating the DVD never really explained the breakthrough technologies.

One of the girls was from way up north; she had a strong northern way of talking.

"How long are you going to work here?" the northern girl

asked. She looked as if she might even have some Russian in her.

"How long?" Jieling said.

"I'm getting married," the northern girl confided. "As soon as I make enough money, I'm going home. If I haven't made enough money in a year," the northern girl explained, "I'm going home anyway."

Jieling hadn't really thought she would work here long. She didn't know exactly what she would do, but she figured that a big city like Shenzhen was a good place to find out. This girl's plans seemed very . . . country. No wonder southern Chinese thought northerners had to wipe the pig shit off their feet before they got on the train.

"Are you Russian?" Jieling asked.

"No," said the girl. "I'm Manchu."

"Ah," Jieling said. Manchu like Manchurian. Ethnic Minority. Jieling had gone to school with a boy who was classified as Manchu, which meant that he was allowed to have two children when he got married. But he had looked Han Chinese like everyone else. This girl had the hook nose and the dark skin of a Manchu. Manchu used to rule China until the Communist Revolution (there was something in between with Sun Yat-Sen, but Jieling's history teachers had bored her to tears). Imperial and countrified.

Then a man came in from human resources.

"There are many kinds of stealing," he began. "There is stealing of money or food. And there is stealing of ideas. Here at New Life, our ideas are like gold, and we guard against having them stolen. But you will learn many secrets, about what we are doing, about how we do things. This is necessary as you do your work. If you tell our secrets, that is theft. And we will find out." He paused here and looked at them in what was clearly intended to be a very frightening way.

Jieling looked down at the ground because it was like watching someone overact. It was embarrassing. Her new shoes were very white and clean.

Then he outlined the prison terms for industrial espionage. Ten, twenty years in prison. "China must take its place as an innovator on the world stage and so must respect the laws of intellectual property," he intoned. It was part of the modernization of China, where technology was a new future— Jieling put on her "I am a good girl" face. It was like politics class. Four modernizations. Six goals. Sometimes when she was a little girl, and she was riding behind her father on his bike to school, he would pass a billboard with a saying about traffic safety and begin to recite quotes from Mao. *The force at the core of the revolution is the people!* He would tuck his chin in when he did this and use a very serious voice, like a movie or like opera. *Western experience for Chinese uses.* Some of them she had learned from him. *All reactionaries are paper tigers!* she would chant with him, trying to make her voice deep. *Be resolute, fear no sacrifice, and surmount every difficulty to win victory!* And then she would start giggling and he would glance over his shoulder and grin at her. He had been a Red Guard when he was young, but other than this, he never talked about it.

After the lecture, they were taken to be paired with workers who would train them. At least she didn't have to go with the Manchu girl, who was led off to shipping.

She was paired with a very small girl in one of the culture rooms. "I am Baiyue," the girl said. Baiyue was so tiny, only up to Jieling's shoulder, that her green scrubs swamped her. She had pigtails. The room where they worked was filled with rows and rows of what looked like wide drawers. Down the center of the room was a long table with petri dishes and trays and lab equipment. Jieling didn't know what some of it was, and that was a little nerve-racking. All up and down the room, pairs of girls in green worked at either the drawers or the table.

"We're going to start cultures," Baiyue said. "Take a tray and fill it with those." She pointed to a stack of petri dishes. The bottom of each dish was filled with gelatin. Jieling took a tray and did what Baiyue did. Baiyue was serious but not at all sharp or superior. She explained that what they were doing was seeding the petri dishes with cells.

"Cells?" Jieling asked.

"Nerve cells from the electric ray. It's a fish."

They took swabs, and Baiyue showed her how to put the cells on in a zigzag motion so that most of the gel was covered. They did six trays full of petri dishes. They didn't smell fishy. Then they used pipettes to put in feeding solution. It was all pleasantly scientific without being very difficult.

At one point everybody left for lunch, but Baiyue said they couldn't go until they got the cultures finished or the batch would be ruined. Women shuffled by them, and Jieling's stomach growled. But when the lab was empty, Baiyue smiled and said, "Where are you from?"

Baiyue was from Fujian. "If you ruin a batch," she explained, "you have to pay out of your paycheck. I'm almost out of debt, and when I get clear"—she glanced around and dropped her voice a little—"I can quit."

"Why are you in debt?" Jieling asked. Maybe this was harder than she thought; maybe Baiyue had screwed up in the past.

"Everyone is in debt," Baiyue said. "It's just the way they run things. Let's get the trays in the warmers."

The drawers along the walls opened out, and inside, the

temperature was kept blood warm. They loaded the trays into the drawers, one back and one front, going down the row until they had the morning's trays all in.

"Okay," Baiyue said, "that's good. We'll check trays this afternoon. I've got a set for transfer to the tissue room, but we'll have time after we eat."

Jieling had never eaten in the employee cafeteria, only in the guesthouse restaurant, and only the first night, because it was expensive. Since then she had been living on ramen noodles, and she was starved for a good meal. She smelled garlic and pork. First thing on the food line was a pan of steamed pork buns, fluffy white. But Baiyue headed off to a place at the back where there was a huge pot of congee—rice porridge—kept hot. "It's the cheapest thing in the cafeteria," Baiyue explained, "and you can eat all you want." She dished up a big bowl of it—a lot of congee for a girl her size—and added some salt vegetables and boiled peanuts. "It's pretty good, although usually by lunch it's been sitting a little while. It gets a little gluey."

Jieling hesitated. Baiyue had said she was in debt. Maybe she had to eat this stuff. But Jieling wasn't going to have old rice porridge for lunch. "I'm going to get some rice and vegetables," she said.

Baiyue nodded. "Sometimes I get that. It isn't too bad. But stay away from anything with shrimp in it. Soooo expensive."

Jieling got rice and vegetables and a big pork bun. There were two fish dishes and a pork dish with monkeybrain mushrooms, but she decided she could maybe have the pork for dinner. There was no cost written on anything. She gave her *danwei* card to the woman at the end of the line, who swiped it and handed it back.

"How much?" Jieling asked.

The woman shrugged. "It comes out of your food allowance."

Jieling started to argue, but across the cafeteria, Baiyue was waving her arm in the sea of green scrubs to get Jieling's attention. Baiyue called from a table. "Jieling! Over here!"

Baiyue's eyes got very big when Jieling sat down. "A pork bun."

"Are they really expensive?" Jieling asked.

Baiyue nodded. "Like gold. And so good."

Jieling looked around at other tables. Other people were eating the pork and steamed buns and everything else.

"Why are you in debt?" Jieling asked.

Baiyue shrugged. "Everyone is in debt," she said. "Just most people have given up. Everything costs here. Your food, your dormitory, your uniforms. They always make sure that you never earn anything."

"They can't do that!" Jieling said.

Baiyue said, "My granddad says it's like the old days, when you weren't allowed to quit your job. He says I should shut up and be happy. That they take good care of me. Iron rice bowl."

"But, but, but"—Jieling dredged the word up from some long-forgotten class—"that's *feudal*!"

Baiyue nodded. "Well, that's my granddad. He used to make my brother and me kowtow to him and my grandmother at Spring Festival." She frowned and wrinkled her nose. Country customs. Nobody in the city made their children kowtow at New Year's. "But you're lucky," Baiyue said to Jieling. "You'll have your uniform debt and dormitory fees, but you haven't started on food debt or anything."

Jieling felt sick. "I stayed in the guesthouse for four days," she said. "They said they would charge it against my wages."

"Oh." Baiyue covered her mouth with her hand. After a moment, she said, "Don't worry, we'll figure something out." Jieling felt more frightened by that than anything else.

Instead of going back to the lab they went upstairs and across a connecting bridge to the dormitories. Naps? Did they get naps?

"Do you know what room you're in?" Baiyue asked.

Jieling didn't. Baiyue took her to ask the floor auntie, who looked up Jieling's name and gave her a key and some sheets and a blanket. Back down the hall and around the corner. The room was spare but really nice. Two bunk beds and two chests of drawers, a concrete floor. It had a window. All of the beds were taken except one of the top ones. By the window under the desk were three black boxes hooked to the wall. They were a little bigger than a shoe box. Baiyue flipped open the front of each one. They had names written on them. "Here's a space where we can put your battery." She pointed to an electrical extension.

"What are they?" Jieling said.

"They're the battery boxes. It's what we make. I'll get you one that failed inspection. A lot of them work fine," Baiyue said. "Inside there are electric ray cells to make electricity, and symbiotic bacteria. The bacteria breaks down garbage to feed the ray cells. Garbage turned into electricity. Anti–global warming. No greenhouse gas. You have to feed it scraps from the cafeteria a couple of times a week or it will die, but it does best if you feed it a little bit every day."

"It's alive?!" Jieling said.

Baiyue shrugged. "Yeah. Sort of. Supposedly if it does really well, you get credits for the electricity it generates. They charge us for our electricity use, so this helps hold down debt."

The three boxes just sat there looking less alive than a boom box.

"Can you see the cells?" Jieling asked.

Baiyue shook her head. "No, the feed mechanism doesn't let you. They're just like the ones we grow, though, only they've been worked on in the tissue room. They added bacteria."

"Can it make you sick?"

"No, the bacteria can't live in people," Baiyue said. "Can't live anywhere except in the box."

"And it makes electricity."

Baiyue nodded.

"And people can buy it?"

She nodded again. "We've just started selling them. They say they're going to sell them in China, but really, they're too expensive. Americans like them, you know, because of the no-global-warming. Of course, Americans buy anything."

The boxes were on the wall between the beds, under the window, pretty near where the pillows were on the bottom bunks. She hadn't minded the cells in the lab, but this whole thing was too creepy.

Jieling's first paycheck was startling. She owed 1,974 RMB. Almost four months' salary if she never ate or bought anything and if she didn't have a dorm room. She went back to her room and climbed into her bunk and looked at the figures. Money deducted for uniforms and shoes, food, her time in the guesthouse.

Her roommates came chattering in a group. Jieling's roommates all worked in packaging. They were nice enough, but they had been friends before Jieling moved in.

"Hey," called Taohua. Then, seeing what Jieling had, "Oh, first paycheck."

Jieling nodded. It was like getting a jail sentence.

"Let's see. Oh, not so bad. I owe three times that," Taohua said. She passed the statement on to the other girls. All the girls owed huge amounts. More than a year.

"Don't you care?" Jieling said.

"You mean like little Miss Lei Feng?" Taohua asked. Everyone laughed and Jieling laughed, too, although her face heated up. Miss Lei Feng was what they called Baiyue. Little Miss Goody-goody. Lei Feng, the famous do-gooder soldier who darned his friend's socks on the Long March. He was nobody when he was alive, but when he died, his diary listed all the anonymous good deeds he had done, and then he became a Hero. Lei Feng posters hung in elementary schools. He wanted to be "a revolutionary screw that never rusts." It was the kind of thing everybody's grandparents had believed in.

"Does Baiyue have a boyfriend?" Taohua asked, suddenly serious.

"No, no!" Jieling said. It was against the rules to have a boyfriend, and Baiyue was always getting in trouble for breaking rules. Things like not having her trays stacked by 5:00 p.m., although nobody else got in trouble for that.

"If she had a boyfriend," Taohua said, "I could see why she would want to quit. You can't get married if you're in debt. It would be too hard."

"Aren't you worried about your debt?" Jieling asked.

Taohua laughed. "I don't have a boyfriend. And besides, I just got a promotion, so soon I'll pay off my debt."

"You'll have to stop buying clothes," one of the other girls said. The company store did have a nice catalog you could order clothes from, but they were expensive. There was debt limit, based on your salary. If you were promoted, your debt limit would go up.

"Or I'll go to special projects," Taohua said. Everyone

knew what special projects was, even though it was supposed to be a big company secret. They were computers made of bacteria. They looked a lot like the boxes in the dormitory rooms. "I've been studying computers," Taohua explained. "Bacterial computers are special. They do many things. They can detect chemicals. They are *massively* parallel."

"What does that mean?" Jieling asked.

"It is hard to explain," Taohua said evasively.

Taohua opened her battery and poured in scraps. It was interesting that Taohua claimed not to care about her debt but kept feeding her battery. Jieling had a battery now, too. It was a reject—the back had broken so that the metal things that sent the electricity back out were exposed, and if you touched it wrong, it could give you a shock. No problem, since Jieling had plugged it into the wall and didn't plan to touch it again.

"Besides," Taohua said, "I like it here a lot better than at home."

Better than home. In some ways, yes, in some ways, no. What would it be like to just give up and belong to the company? Nice things, nice food. Never rich. But never poor, either. Medical care. Maybe it wasn't the worst thing. Maybe Baiyue was a little . . . obsessive.

"I don't care about my debt," Taohua said serenely. "With one more promotion, I'll move to cadres housing."

Jieling reported the conversation to Baiyue. They were getting incubated cells ready to move to the tissue room. In the tissue room they'd be transferred to the protein and collagen grid that would guide their growth—line up the cells to approximate an electricity-generating system. The tissue room had a weird, yeasty smell.

"She's fooling herself," Baiyue said. "Line girls never get to be cadres. She might get onto special projects, but that's even worse than regular line work, because you're never allowed to leave the compound." Baiyue picked up a dish, stuck a little volt reader into the gel, and rapped the dish smartly against the lab table.

The needle on the volt gauge swung to indicate the cells had discharged electricity. That was the way they tested to see if the cells were generating electricity. A shock made them discharge, and the easiest way was to knock them against the table.

Baiyue could sound very bitter about New Life. Jieling didn't like the debt; it scared her a little. But, really, Baiyue saw only one side of everything. "I thought you got a pay raise to go to special projects," Jieling said.

Baiyue rolled her eyes. "And more reasons to go in debt, I'll bet."

"How much is your debt?" Jieling asked.

"Still seven hundred," Baiyue said. "Because they told me I had to have new uniforms." She sighed.

"I am so sick of congee," Jieling said. "They're never going to let us get out of debt."

Baiyue's way was doomed. She was trying to play by the company's rules and still win. That wasn't Jieling's way. "We have to make money somewhere else," Jieling said.

"Right," Baiyue said. "We work six days a week." And Baiyue often stayed after shift to try to make sure she didn't lose wages on failed cultures. "Out of spec," she'd say, and put it aside. She had taught Jieling to keep the out-of-specs for a day. Sometimes they improved and could be shipped on. It wasn't the way the supervisor, Ms. Wang, explained the job to Jieling, but it cut down on the number of rejects, and that, in turn, cut down on paycheck deductions.

"That leaves us Sundays," Jieling said.

"I can't leave the compound this Sunday."

"And if you do, what are they going to do, fire you?" Jieling said.

"I don't think we're supposed to earn money outside the compound," Baiyue said.

"You are too much of a good girl," Jieling said. "Remember, *it doesn't matter if the cat is black or white, as long as it catches mice.*"

"Is that Mao?" Baiyue asked, frowning.

"No," Jieling said, "Deng Xiaoping, the one after Mao."

"Well, he's dead, too," Baiyue said. She rapped a dish against the counter, and the needle on the volt meter jumped.

Jieling had been working just over four weeks when they were all called to the cafeteria for a meeting. Mr. Cao from human resources was there. He was wearing a dark suit and standing at the white screen. Other cadres sat in chairs along the back of the stage, looking very stern.

"We are here to discuss a very serious matter," he said. "Many of you know this girl."

There was a laptop hooked up and a very nervous-looking boy running it. Jieling looked carefully at the laptop, but it didn't appear to be a special projects computer. In fact, it was made in Korea. He did something, and an ID picture of a girl flashed on the screen.

Jieling didn't know her. But around her she heard noises of shock, someone sucking air through their teeth. Someone else breathed softly, *"Ai-yah."*

"This girl ran away, leaving her debt with New Life. She ate our food, wore our clothes, slept in our beds. And then, like a thief, she ran away." The human resources man nodded his head. The boy at the computer changed the image on the big projector screen.

Now it was a picture of the same girl with her head bowed and two policemen holding her arms.

"She was picked up in Guangdong," the human resources man said. "She is in jail there."

The cafeteria was very quiet.

The human resources man said, "Her life is ruined, which is what should happen to all thieves."

Then he dismissed them. That afternoon, the picture of the girl with the two policemen appeared on the bulletin boards of every floor of the dormitory.

On Sunday, Baiyue announced, "I'm not going."

She was not supposed to leave the compound, but one of her roommates had female problems—bad cramps—and planned to spend the day in bed drinking tea and reading magazines. Baiyue was going to use her ID to leave.

"You have to," Jieling said. "You want to grow old here? Die a serf to New Life?"

"It's crazy. We can't make money dancing in the plague-trash market."

"I've done it before," Jieling said. "You're scared."

"It's just not a good idea," Baiyue said.

"Because of the girl they caught in Guangdong. We're not skipping out on our debt. We're paying it off."

"We're not supposed to work for someone else when we work here," Baiyue said.

"Oh, come on," Jieling said. "You are always making things sound worse than they are. I think you like staying here being little Miss Lei Feng."

"Don't call me that," Baiyue snapped.

"Well, don't act like it. New Life is not being fair. We don't have to be fair. What are they going to do to you if they catch you?"

"Fine me," Baiyue said. "Add to my debt!"

"So what? They're going to find a way to add to your debt no matter what. You are a serf. They are the landlord."

"But if—"

"No *but if,*" Jieling said. "You like being a martyr. I don't."

"What do you care," Baiyue said. "You like it here. If you stay you can eat pork buns every night."

"And you can eat congee for the rest of your life. I'm going to try to do something." Jieling slammed out of the dorm room. She had never said harsh things to Baiyue before. Yes, she had thought about staying here. But was that so bad? Better than being like Baiyue, who would stay here and have a miserable life. Jieling was not going to have a miserable life, no matter where she stayed or what she did. That was why she had come to Shenzhen in the first place.

She heard the door open behind her, and Baiyue ran down the hall. "Okay," she said breathlessly. "I'll try it. Just this once."

The streets of Shanghai were incredibly loud after weeks in the compound. In a shop window, she and Baiyue stopped and watched a news segment on how the fashion in Shanghai was for sarongs. Jieling would have to tell her mother. Of course, her mother had a TV and probably already knew. Jieling thought about calling, but not now. Not now. She didn't want to explain about New Life. The next news segment was about the success of the People's Army in Tajikistan. Jieling pulled Baiyue to come on.

They took one bus and then had to transfer. On Sundays,

unless you were lucky, it took forever to transfer because fewer buses ran. They waited almost an hour for the second bus. That bus was almost empty when they got on. They sat down a few seats back from the driver. Baiyue rolled her eyes. "Did you see the guy in the back?" she asked. "Party functionary."

Jieling glanced over her shoulder and saw him. She couldn't miss him, in his careful polo shirt. He had that stiff party-member look.

Baiyue sighed. "My uncle is just like that. So *boring.*"

Jieling thought that, to be honest, Baiyue would have made a good revolutionary, back in the day. Baiyue liked that kind of revolutionary purity. But she nodded.

The plague-trash market was full on a Sunday. There was a toy seller making tiny little clay figures on sticks. He waved a stick at the girls as they passed. "Cute things!" he called. "I'll make whatever you want!" The stick had a little Donald Duck on it.

"I can't do this," Baiyue said. "There's too many people."

"It's not so bad," Jieling said. She found a place for the boom box. Jieling had brought them to where all the food vendors were. "Stay here and watch this," she said. She hunted through the food stalls and bought a bottle of local beer, counting out from the little hoard of money she had left from when she had come. She took the beer back to Baiyue. "Drink this," she said. "It will help you be brave."

"I hate beer," Baiyue said.

"Beer or debt," Jieling said.

While Baiyue drank the beer, Jieling started the boom box and did her routine. People smiled at her, but no one put any money in her cash box. Shenzhen people were so cheap. Baiyue sat on the curb, nursing her beer, not looking at Jieling or at anyone until finally Jieling couldn't stand it any longer.

"C'mon, *meimei*," she said.

Baiyue seemed a bit surprised to be called little sister, but she put the beer down and got up. They had practiced a routine to an M.I.A. song, singing and dancing. It would be a hit, Jieling was sure.

"I can't," Baiyue whispered.

"Yes you can," Jieling said. "You do good."

A couple of people stopped to watch them arguing, so Jieling started the music.

"I feel sick," Baiyue whimpered.

But the beat started, and there was nothing to do but dance and sing. Baiyue was so nervous, she forgot at first, but then she got the hang of it. She kept her head down, and her face was bright red.

Jieling started making up a rap. She'd never done it before, and she hadn't gotten very far before she was laughing and then Baiyue was laughing, too.

> *Wode meimei hen haixiude*
> *Mei ta shi xuli*
> *tai hen xiuqi—*
>
> *My little sister is so shy*
> *But she's pretty*
> *Far too delicate—*

They almost stopped because they were giggling, but they kept dancing, and Jieling went back to the lyrics from the song they had practiced.

When they had finished, people clapped, and they'd made thirty-two yuan.

They didn't make as much for any single song after that, but in a few hours they had collected 187 yuan. It was early evening, and night entertainers were showing up—a couple of people who sang opera, acrobats, and a clown with a wig of hair so red it looked on fire, stepping stork-legged on stilts waving a rubber Kalashnikov in his hand. He was all dressed in white. Uncle Death, from cartoons during the plague. Some of the day vendors had shut down, and new people were showing up who put out a board and some chairs and served sorghum liquor; clear, white, and 150 proof. The crowd was starting to change, too. It was rowdier. Packs of young men dressed in weird combinations of clothes from plague markets—vintage Mao suit jackets and suit pants and peasant shoes. And others, veterans from the Tajikistan conflict, one with an empty trouser leg.

Jieling picked up the boom box, and Baiyue took the cash box. Outside of the market, it wasn't yet dark.

"You are amazing," Baiyue kept saying. "You are such a special girl!"

"You did great," Jieling said. "When I was by myself, I didn't make anything! Everyone likes you because you are little and cute!"

"Look at this! I'll be out of debt before autumn!"

Maybe it was just the feeling that she was responsible for Baiyue, but Jieling said, "You keep it all."

"I can't! I can't! We split it!" Baiyue said.

"Sure," Jieling said. "Then after you get away, you can help me. Just think, if we do this for three more Sundays, you'll pay off your debt."

"Oh, Jieling," Baiyue said. "You really are like my big sister!"

Jieling was sorry she had ever called Baiyue "little sister." It was such a country thing to do. She had always suspected that Baiyue wasn't a city girl. Jieling hated the countryside. Grain spread to dry in the road and mother's-elder-sister and father's-younger-brother bringing all the cousins over on the day off. Jieling didn't even know all those country ways to say aunt and uncle. It wasn't Baiyue's fault. And Baiyue had been good to her. She was rotten to be thinking this way.

"Excuse me," said a man. He wasn't like the packs of young men with their long hair and plague clothes. Jieling couldn't place him, but he seemed familiar. "I saw you in the market. You were very fun. Very lively."

Baiyue took hold of Jieling's arm. For a moment Jieling wondered if maybe he was from New Life, but she told herself that that was crazy. "Thank you," she said. She thought she remembered him putting ten yuan in the box. No, she thought, he was on the bus. The party functionary. The party was checking up on them. Now *that* was funny. She wondered if he would lecture them on Western ways.

"Are you in the music business?" Baiyue asked. She glanced at Jieling, who couldn't help laughing, snorting through her nose.

The man took them very seriously, though. "No," he said. "I can't help you there. But I like your act. You seem like girls of good character."

"Thank you," Baiyue said. She didn't look at Jieling again, which was good, because Jieling knew she wouldn't be able to keep a straight face.

"I am Wei Rongyi. Maybe I can buy you some dinner?" the man asked. He held up his hands, "Nothing romantic. You are so young, it is like you could be daughters."

"You have a daughter?" Jieling asked.

He shook his head. "Not anymore," he said.

Jieling understood. His daughter had died of the bird flu. She felt embarrassed for having laughed at him. Her soft heart saw instantly that he was treating them like the daughter he had lost.

He took them to a dumpling place on the edge of the market and ordered half a kilo of crescent-shaped pork dumplings and a kilo of square beef dumplings. He was a cadre, a middle manager. His wife had lived in Changsha for a couple of years now, where her family was from. He was from the older generation, people who did not get divorced. All around them, the restaurant was filling up mostly with men stopping after work for dumplings and drinks. They were a little island surrounded by truck drivers and men who worked in the factories in the outer city—tough, grimy places.

"What do you do? Are you secretaries?" Wei Rongyi asked.

Baiyue laughed. "As if!" she said.

"We are factory girls," Jieling said. She dunked a dumpling in vinegar. They were so good! Not congee!

"Factory girls!" he said. "I am so surprised!"

Baiyue nodded. "We work for New Life," she explained. "This is our day off, so we wanted to earn a little extra money."

He rubbed his head, looking off into the distance. "New Life," he said, trying to place the name. "New Life . . ."

"Out past the zoo," Baiyue said.

Jieling thought they shouldn't say so much.

"Ah, in the city. A good place? What do they make?" he asked. He had a way of blinking very quickly that was disconcerting.

"Batteries," Jieling said. She didn't say bio-batteries.

"I thought they made computers," he said.

"Oh, yes," Baiyue said. "Special projects."

Jieling glared at Baiyue. If this guy gave them trouble at New Life, they'd have a huge problem getting out of the compound.

Baiyue blushed.

Wei laughed. "You are special project girls, then. Well, see, I knew you were not just average factory girls."

He didn't press the issue. Jieling kept waiting for him to make some sort of move on them. Offer to buy them beer. But he didn't, and when they had finished their dumplings, he gave them the leftovers to take back to their dormitories and then stood at the bus stop until they were safely on their bus.

"Are you sure you will be all right?" he asked them when the bus came.

"You can see my window from the bus stop," Jieling promised. "We will be fine."

"Shenzhen can be a dangerous city. You be careful!"

Out the window, they could see him in the glow of the streetlight, waving as the bus pulled away.

"He was so nice," Baiyue sighed. "Poor man."

"Didn't you think he was a little strange?" Jieling asked.

"Everybody is strange nowadays," Baiyue said. "After the plague. Not like when we were growing up."

It was true. Her mother was strange. Lots of people were crazy from so many people dying.

Jieling held up the leftover dumplings. "Well, anyway. I am not feeding this to my battery," she said. They both tried to smile.

"Our whole generation is crazy," Baiyue said.

"We know everybody dies," Jieling said. Outside the bus window, the streets were full of young people, out trying to live while they could.

They made all their bus connections as smooth as silk. So quick, they were home in forty-five minutes. Sunday night was movie night, and all of Jieling's roommates were at the movie, so she and Baiyue could sort the money in Jieling's room. She used her key card, and the door clicked open.

Mr. Wei was kneeling by the battery boxes in their room. He started and hissed, "Close the door!"

Jieling was so surprised, she did.

"Mr. Wei!" Baiyue said.

He was dressed like an army man on a secret mission, all in black. He showed them a little black gun. Jieling blinked in surprise. "Mr. Wei!" she said. It was hard to take him seriously. Even all in black, he was still weird Mr. Wei, blinking rapidly behind his glasses.

"Lock the door," he said. "And be quiet."

"The door locks by itself," Jieling explained. "And my roommates will be back soon."

"Put a chair in front of the door," he said, and shoved the desk chair toward them. Baiyue pushed it under the door handle. The window was open, and Jieling could see where he had climbed on the desk and left a footprint on Taohua's fashion magazine. Taohua was going to be pissed. And what was Jieling going to say? If anyone found out there had been a man in her room, she was going to be in very big trouble.

"How did you get in?" she asked. "What about the cameras?" There were security cameras.

He showed them a little spray can. "Special paint. It just makes things look foggy and dim. Security guards are so lazy now, no one ever checks things out." He paused a moment, clearly disgusted with the lax morality of the day. "Miss Jieling," he said. "Take that screwdriver and finish unscrewing that computer from the wall."

Computer? She realized he meant the battery boxes.

Baiyue's eyes got very big. "Mr. Wei! You're a thief!"

Jieling shook her head. "A corporate spy."

"I am a patriot," he said. "But you young people wouldn't understand that. Sit on the bed." He waved the gun at Baiyue.

The gun was so little it looked like a toy, and it was difficult to be afraid, but still Jieling thought it was good that Baiyue sat.

Jieling knelt. It was her box that Mr. Wei had been disconnecting. It was all the way to the right, so he had started with it. She had come to feel a little bit attached to it, thinking of it sitting there, occasionally zapping electricity back into the grid, reducing her electricity costs and her debt. She sighed and unscrewed it. Mr. Wei watched.

She jimmied it off the wall, careful not to touch the contacts. The cells built up a charge, and when they were ready, a switch tapped a membrane and they discharged. It was all automatic, and there was no knowing when it was going to happen. Mr. Wei was going to be very upset when he realized that this wasn't a computer.

"Put it on the desk," he said.

She did.

"Now sit with your friend."

Jieling sat down next to Baiyue. Keeping a wary eye on them, he sidled over to the bio-battery. He opened the hatch where they dumped garbage in them, and he tried to look in as well as look at them. "Where are the controls?" he asked. He picked it up, his palm flat against the broken back end where the contacts were exposed.

"Tap it against the desk," Jieling said. "Sometimes the door sticks." There wasn't actually a door. But it had just come into her head. She hoped that the cells hadn't discharged in a while.

Mr. Wei frowned and tapped the box smartly against the desktop.

Torpedinidae, the electric ray, can generate a current of

two hundred volts for approximately a minute. The power output is close to one kilowatt over the course of the discharge, and while this won't kill the average person, it is a powerful shock. Mr. Wei stiffened and fell, clutching the box and spasming wildly. One . . . two . . . three . . . four . . . Mr. Wei was still spasming. Jieling and Baiyue looked at each other. Gingerly, Jieling stepped around Mr. Wei. He had dropped the little gun. Jieling picked it up. Mr. Wei was still spasming. Jieling wondered if he was going to die. Or if he was already dead and the electricity was just making him jump. She didn't want him to die. She looked at the little gun, and it made her feel even sicker, so she threw it out the window.

Finally, Mr. Wei dropped the box.

Baiyue said, "Is he dead?"

Jieling was afraid to touch him. She couldn't tell if he was breathing. Then he groaned, and both girls jumped.

"He's not dead," Jieling said.

"What should we do?" Baiyue asked.

"Tie him up," Jieling said. Although she wasn't sure what they'd do with him then.

Jieling used the cord to her boom box to tie his wrists. When she grabbed his hands, he gasped and struggled feebly. Then she took her pillowcase and cut along the blind end, a space just wide enough that his head would fit through.

"Sit him up," she said to Baiyue.

"You sit him up," Baiyue said. Baiyue didn't want to touch him.

Jieling pulled Mr. Wei into a sitting position. "Put the pillowcase over his head," she said. The pillowcase was like a shirt with no armholes, so when Baiyue pulled it over his head and shoulders, it pinned his arms against his sides and worked something like a straitjacket.

Jieling took his wallet and identification papers out of his pocket. "Why would someone carry their wallet to a break-in?" she asked. "He has six ID papers. One says he is Mr. Wei."

"Wow," Baiyue said. "Let me see. Also Mr. Ma. Mr. Zhang. Two Mr. Lius and a Mr. Cui."

Mr. Wei blinked, his eyes watering.

"Do you think he has a weak heart?" Baiyue asked.

"I don't know," Jieling said. "Wouldn't he be dead if he did?"

Baiyue considered this.

"Baiyue! Look at all this yuan!" Jieling emptied the wallet, counting. Almost eight thousand yuan!

"Let me go," Mr. Wei said weakly.

Jieling was glad he was talking. She was glad he seemed like he might be all right. She didn't know what they would do if he died. They would never be able to explain a dead person. They would end up in deep debt. And probably go to jail for something. "Should we call the floor auntie and tell her that he broke in?" Jieling asked.

"We could," Baiyue said.

"Do not!" Mr. Wei said, sounding stronger. "You don't understand! I'm from Beijing!"

"So is my stepfather," Jieling said. "Me, I'm from Baoding. It's about an hour south of Beijing."

Mr. Wei said, "I'm from the government! That money is government money!"

"I don't believe you," Jieling said. "Why did you come in through the window?" Jieling asked.

"Secret agents always come in through the window?" Baiyue said, and started to giggle.

"Because this place is counterrevolutionary!" Mr. Wei said.

Baiyue covered her mouth with her hand. Jieling felt

embarrassed, too. No one said things like "counterrevolution-ary" anymore.

"This place! It is making things that could make China strong!" he said.

"Isn't that good?" Baiyue asked.

"But they don't care about China! Only about money. Instead of using it for China, they sell it to America!" he said. Spittle was gathering at the corner of his mouth. He was starting to look deranged. "Look at this place! Officials are all concerned about *guanxi*!" Connections. Kickbacks. *Guanxi* ran China, everybody knew that.

"So, maybe you have an anticorruption investigation?" Jieling said. There were lots of anticorruption investigations. Jieling's stepfather said that they usually meant someone powerful was mad at their brother-in-law or something, so they accused them of corruption.

Mr. Wei groaned. "There is no one to investigate them."

Baiyue and Jieling looked at each other.

Mr. Wei explained, "In my office, the Guangdong office, there used to be twenty people. Special operatives. Now there is only me and Ms. Yang."

Jieling said, "Did they all die of bird flu?"

Mr. Wei shook his head. "No, they all went to work on contract for Saudi Arabia. You can make a lot of money in the Middle East. A lot more than in China."

"Why don't you and Ms. Yang go work in Saudi Arabia?" Baiyue asked.

Jieling thought Mr. Wei would give some revolutionary speech. But he just hung his head. "She is the secretary. I am the bookkeeper." And then, in a smaller voice, "She is going to Kuwait to work for Mr. Liu."

They probably did not need bookkeepers in the Middle

East. Poor Mr. Wei. No wonder he was such a terrible secret agent.

"The spirit of the revolution is gone," he said, and there were real, honest-to-goodness tears in his eyes. "Did you know that Tiananmen Square was built by volunteers? People would come after their regular jobs and lay the paving of the square. Today people look to Hong Kong."

"Nobody cares about a bunch of old men in Beijing," Baiyue said.

"Exactly! We used to have a strong military! But now the military is too worried about their own factories and farms! They want us to pull out of Tajikistan because it is ruining their profits!"

This sounded like a good idea to Jieling, but she had to admit, she hated the news, so she wasn't sure why they were fighting in Tajikistan anyway. Something about Muslim terrorists. All she knew about Muslims was that they made great street food.

"Don't you want to be patriots?" Mr. Wei said.

"You broke into my room and tried to steal my— you know that's not a computer, don't you?" Jieling said. "It's a bio-battery. They're selling them to the Americans. Wal-Mart."

Mr. Wei groaned.

"We don't work in special projects," Baiyue said.

"You said you did," he protested.

"We did not," Jieling said. "You just thought that. How did you know this was my room?"

"The company lists all its workers in a directory," he said wearily. "And it's movie night, everyone is either out or goes to the movies. I've had the building under surveillance for weeks. I followed you to the market today. Last week it was a girl named Pingli, who blabbed about everything, but she wasn't in special projects.

"I put you on the bus; I've timed the route three times. I should have had an hour and fifteen minutes to drive over here and get the box and get out."

"We made all our connections," Baiyue explained.

Mr. Wei was so dispirited he didn't even respond.

Jieling said, "I thought the government was supposed to help workers. If we get caught, we'll be fined, and we'll be deeper in debt." She was just talking. Talking, talking, talking too much. This was too strange. Like when someone was dying. Something extraordinary was happening, like your father dying in the next room, and yet the ordinary things went on, too. You made tea, your mother opened the shop the next day and sewed clothes while she cried. People came in and pretended not to notice. This was like that. Mr. Wei had a gun, and they were explaining about New Life.

"Debt?" Mr. Wei said.

"To the company," she said. "We are all in debt. The company hires us and says they are going to pay us, but then they charge us for our food and our clothes and our dorm, and it always costs more than we earn. That's why we were doing rap today. To make money to be able to quit." Mr. Wei's glasses had tape holding the arm on. Why hadn't she noticed that in the restaurant? Maybe because when you are afraid, you notice things. When your father is dying of the plague, you notice the way the covers on your mother's chairs need to be washed. You wonder if you will have to do it, or if you will die before you have to do chores.

"The Pingli girl," he said, "she said the same thing. That's illegal."

"Sure," Baiyue said. "Like anybody cares."

"Could you expose corruption?" Jieling asked.

Mr. Wei shrugged, at least as much as he could in the pillowcase. "Maybe. But they would just pay bribes to locals, and it would all go away."

All three of them sighed.

"Except," Mr. Wei said, sitting up a little straighter, "the Americans. They are always getting upset about that sort of thing. Last year there was a corporation, the Shanghai Six. The Americans did a documentary on them, and then Western companies would not do business. If they got information from us about what New Life is doing . . ."

"Who else is going to buy bio-batteries?" Baiyue said. "The company would be in big trouble!"

"Beijing can threaten a big exposé, tell the *New York Times* newspaper!" Mr. Wei said, getting excited. "My Beijing supervisor will love that! He loves media!"

"Then you can have a big show trial," Jieling said.

Mr. Wei was nodding.

"But what is in it for us?" Baiyue said.

"When there's a trial, they'll have to cancel your debt!" Mr. Wei said. "Even pay you a big fine!"

"If I call the floor auntie and say I caught a corporate spy, they'll give me a big bonus," Baiyue said.

"Don't you care about the other workers?" Mr. Wei asked.

Jieling and Baiyue looked at each other and shrugged. Did they? "What are they going to do to you, anyway?" Jieling said. "You can still do a big exposé. But that way we don't have to wait."

"Look," he said, "you let me go, and I'll let you keep my money."

Someone rattled the door handle.

"Please," Mr. Wei whispered. "You can be heroes for your fellow workers, even though they'll never know it."

Jieling stuck the money in her pocket. Then she took the papers, too.

"You can't take those," he said.

"Yes I can," she said. "If after six months, there is no big corruption scandal? We can let everyone know how a government secret agent was outsmarted by two factory girls."

"Six months!" he said. "That's not long enough!"

"It better be," Jieling said.

Outside the door, Taohua called, "Jieling? Are you in there? Something is wrong with the door!"

"Just a minute," Jieling called. "I had trouble with it when I came home." To Mr. Wei she whispered sternly, "Don't you try anything. If you do, we'll scream our heads off, and everybody will come running." She and Baiyue shimmied the pillowcase off of Mr. Wei's head. He started to stand up and jerked the boom box, which clattered across the floor. "Wait!" she hissed, and untied him.

Taohua called through the door, "What's that?"

"Hold on!" Jieling called.

Baiyue helped Mr. Wei stand up. Mr. Wei climbed onto the desk and then grabbed a line hanging outside. He stopped a moment as if trying to think of something to say.

"'A revolution is not a dinner party, or writing an essay, or painting a picture, or doing embroidery,'" Jieling said. It had been her father's favorite quote from Chairman Mao. "'. . . It cannot be so refined, so leisurely and gentle, so temperate, kind, courteous, restrained, and magnanimous. A revolution is an insurrection, an act by which one class overthrows another.'"

Mr. Wei looked as if he might cry, and not because he was moved by patriotism. He stepped back and disappeared. Jieling and Baiyue looked out the window. He did go down the wall just like a secret agent from a movie, but it was only

two stories. There was still the big footprint in the middle of
Taohua's magazine, and the room looked as if it had been hit
by a storm.

"They're going to think you had a boyfriend," Baiyue
whispered to Jieling.

"Yeah," Jieling said, pulling the chair out from under the
door handle. "And they're going to think he's rich."

It was Sunday, and Jieling and Baiyue were sitting on the
beach. Jieling's cell phone rang, a little chime of M.I.A. hip-
hop. Even though it was Sunday, it was one of the girls from
New Life. Sunday should be a day off, but she took the call
anyway.

"Jieling? This is Xia Meili? From packaging. Taohua told
me about your business? Maybe you could help me?"

Jieling said, "Sure. What is your debt, Meili?"

"Thirty-eight hundred RMB," Meili said. "I know it's a lot."

Jieling said, "Not so bad. We have a lot of people who
already have loans, though, and it will probably be a few
weeks before I can make you a loan."

With Mr. Wei's capital, Jieling and Baiyue had opened a
bank account. They had bought themselves out, and then
started a little loan business where they bought people out
of New Life. Then people had to pay them back with a little
extra. They had each had jobs—Jieling worked for a company that made toys. She sat each day at a table where she
put a piece of specially shaped plastic over the body of a little
doll, an action figure. The plastic fit right over the figure and
had cut-outs. Jieling sprayed the whole thing with red paint,
and when the piece of plastic was lifted, the action figure had
a red shirt. It was boring, but at the end of the week, she got
paid instead of owing the company money.

She and Baiyue used all their extra money on loans to get girls out of New Life. More and more loans, and more and more payments. Now New Life had sent them a threatening letter saying that what they were doing was illegal. But Mr. Wei said not to worry. Two officials had come and talked to them and had showed them legal documents and had them explain everything about what had happened. Soon, the officials promised, they would take New Life to court.

Jieling wasn't so sure about the officials. After all, Mr. Wei was an official. But a foreign newspaperman had called them. He was from a newspaper called the *Wall Street Journal,* and he said that he was writing a story about labor shortages in China after the bird flu. He said that in some places in the West there were reports of slavery. His Chinese was very good. His story was going to come out in the United States tomorrow. Then she figured officials would have to do something or lose face.

Jieling told Meili to call her back in two weeks—although hopefully in two weeks no one would need help to get away from New Life—and wrote a note to herself in her little notebook.

Baiyue was sitting looking at the water. "This is the first time I've been to the beach," she said.

"The ocean is so big, isn't it."

Baiyue nodded, scuffing at the white sand. "People always say that, but you don't know until you see it."

Jieling said, "Yeah." Funny, she had lived here for months. Baiyue had lived here more than a year. And they had never come to the beach. The beach was beautiful.

"I feel sorry for Mr. Wei," Baiyue said.

"You do?" Jieling said. "Do you think he really had a daughter who died?"

"Maybe," Baiyue said. "A lot of people died."

"My father died," Jieling said.

Baiyue looked at her, a quick little sideways look, then back out at the ocean. "My mother died," she said.

Jieling was surprised. She had never known that Baiyue's mother was dead. They had talked about so much, but never about that. She put her arm around Baiyue's waist, and they sat for a while.

"I feel bad in a way," Baiyue said.

"How come?" Jieling said.

"Because we had to steal capital to fight New Life. That makes us capitalists."

Jieling shrugged.

"I wish it was like when they fought the revolution," Baiyue said. "Things were a lot more simple."

"Yeah," Jieling said, "and they were poor and a lot of them died."

"I know," Baiyue sighed.

Jieling knew what she meant. It would be nice to . . . to be sure what was right and what was wrong. Although not if it made you like Mr. Wei.

Poor Mr. Wei. Had his daughter really died?

"Hey," Jieling said, "I've got to make a call. Wait right here." She walked a little down the beach. It was windy and she turned her back to protect the cell phone, like someone lighting a match. "Hello," she said, "hello, Mama, it's me. Jieling."

THIS APPOINTMENT
OCCURS IN THE PAST

Sam Lipsyte

Davis called, told me he was dying.

He said his case was—here was the essence of Davis—time sensitive.

"Come visit," he said. "Bid farewell to the ragged rider."

"You?" I said. "The cigarette hater? That's just wrongness."

"Nonetheless, brother, come."

"Who was that?" said Ondine, my ex-mother-in-law. I kissed her cream-goldened shoulder, slid out of bed.

"A sick friend. I've known him twenty years, more, since college. I might have to leave town for a while."

"No," said Ondine. "You're leaving town for good. The occupation ends today. It's been calamity for us, for the region. Go to your friend."

"He's not really my friend."

"All the more reason to go to him," said Ondine. "Jesus would be in Pennsylvania by now."

Ypsilanti was easy to leave. I wasn't from there. I'd just landed there. The Michigan Eviscerations had begun in Manhattan. Martha was a junior at NYU, heiress to a fuel-injection fortune. I was the cheeky barista who kept penciling my phone number on her latte's heat sleeve. Cheeky and, I should add, quite hairy. Martha finally dialed the smudged figures on the corrugated cuff, cavorted in my belly fur. The woman never exhibited any qualms about our economic divide. After all, she'd remind me, I was a Jew. One day I'd just quit mucking around with burlap sacks of Guatemalan Sunrise and start brewing moolah.

"You can't help it," she said. "It's a genetic thing. You weren't allowed to own land in the Middle Ages."

I wasn't allowed to own land in Michigan either. We got married, but her folks bought the Ann Arbor house in her name. Martha enrolled for a master's degree at the university. She demanded that I concoct a passion she could bankroll, a "doable dream." What would it be? Poetry journal? Microlabel for the new jam rock? Nanobatch raki boutique? I mulled over these and other notions but mostly focused on my favored pursuit: grilling premium meats. I grilled grass-fed beef, saddles of rabbit, bison, organic elk. My mulled projects moldered. I'd always pictured myself the genius *in* the journal, *on* the label, not running the damn things. Moreover, wasn't there bookkeeping involved, basic math? No matter what Martha believed about my inherited numerical wizardry honed on the twisty streets of Antwerp, or maybe Münster, I could barely count.

I grilled until the grilling season ended. Around the time the first shipment of Danish birch arrived for my new curing shed, Martha kicked me to what in this municipality wasn't quite a curb. She'd met an equally hirsute Scot from the engineering school. His name happened to be Scott, and his people had the twisty brain too. Besides, our sex life was a wreck. We were down to those resentful tugs and frigs. She said the stench of burnt meat put her off. I figured it was also the weight I'd put on, the perpetual slick of cook grease on my chest beneath my loose kimono.

Ondine, an old beauty with hair the color of metallic marmalade, was historically attuned to her daughter's fecklessness. She took pity, rented me a unit in a shingle-stripped Victorian she owned in Ypsilanti, let me slide on the rent until I found a job. I never did, but she seemed satisfied to visit a few times a week for my attentions. She called my style of lovemaking "poignant."

Still, even before Davis called, I could tell she was getting bored.

"I'm getting bored," she said.

It came to her suddenly, unbidden, the way it might strike you that you hadn't gone candlepin bowling or eaten smoked oysters in years.

"You bore the piss out of me," she said.

I stood, started to dress.

Ondine reached out, pinched my ass fuzz.

"Ouch."

"Don't be so sensitive. Lots of things bore me. Things I love. My husband. My house. My daughter. My Native American pottery collection. It's not an insult."

But if not an insult, it was a signal. Now, weeks later, I headed east in one of Ondine's several Mazdas, a parting gift, along with a generous cash severance and a few keepsake snapshots of her in aspects of the huntress.

The dashboard robot in the Mazda goaded. Beneath its officious tones I sensed confusion, a geopositional wound. Had some caustic robot daddy made it feel directionless? Meanwhile, the comics on the satellite radio joked about their dainty white cocks. Such candor was supposed to prevent the race war.

My neck ached, and I bought an ice pack, wedged it up against my headrest. My tongue was a mess. I still tasted Ondine. Deep in Pennsylvania I ate a coq au vin quesadilla. It's what Jesus would have ordered, and it was delicious.

I had to drive fast, before I ate too much road food.

The ragged rider, Davis had called himself, but I couldn't parse the phrase. I was naturally undetective.

Clues clenched me up.

I'd booked a tiny room in the Hudson Lux in New York City, high up and hushed, a loneliness box of polished walnut and chrome. You could picture yourself dead of a hanging jackoff in such a room, your necktie living up to its name, your lubricated fingers curled stiff near your hips. I stretched out on the narrow bed, decided not to picture this. It wasn't the kind of thing I figured I'd ever try. Aficionados cited the bliss spasm caused by air loss, but I wondered if most got orgasmic on the gamble. Anyway, everything in my life was a gamble, a wager that somebody would see to my needs. Was I secretly here because I thought Davis would somehow fit the bill even though he was sick? If so, who was sicker?

Now I shut my eyes, and Davis loped into view. He stood in an orchard of pomegranates, his legs greaved in a low, personal mist. Tall, homely Davis, with his hamster-fluff hair and granny specs.

We used to sip espressos in the campus café. Davis would read from his critical works: "In truth, of which there can be no certainty, the Peter Frampton phallus must be unfurled from the constrictive denim of manufactured desire's sweatshop."

I loved his papers, these phrases that seemed to trickle out of a plastic port under his shirt or hiss from slits in his hands. I wasn't one of those narcissists who thought I had to understand something for it to be important. Besides, he wasn't wrong about whatever the hell he meant.

He wasn't wrong about much. I rarely went to lectures. Davis tutored me.

We drank beer in the old sailors' bar and Davis would whisper about the Russians—Pushkin, in particular, whose story "The Shot" he so admired.

"Pushkin invented Russian literature as we know it," he said.

"But I don't know it," I said.

Davis studied Latin, computers, knew some physics, dabbled in questions that plagued those he sneeringly called the string-cheese-theory people. He taught me to marvel at the elegance of Nagle's law and the Peck conjecture, though maybe they had other names. Even words associated with counting undid me.

We slurped whiskey in our basement apartment with our friends and possible friends. Davis was the savior. I was his handsome disciple. Eventually Davis would get huffy about the cigarette smoke and stomp around the piles of books and laundry, the stray Stratocaster, the tripod with the liquid swivel. We were making an experimental video for our band, the Interpellations, but who wasn't?

"How can you breathe in corporate death like that!" Davis shouted one night. "Smoke the kind, like me."

"We're not hippies," said Caldwell, neobeat goblin. "I'll take the bourbon of my fathers."

"But this is the one thing the hippies got right!" Davis said, held aloft his cinnamon-scented bong. "Maybe they sold out the working class, but they grooved! Anyway, there are

too many of them. So few of us. They will rule our lives forever. They will never pass the torch."

"Do we deserve it?" I said. I guess I'd gotten tired of being
his disciple.

"I do," said Davis.

"So what kind of ruling-class motherfucker, are you," I
said, "to be talking about the torch?"

I knew this would bother him. He'd been born into citrus money. We'd get crates of tangelos delivered to our door.
Also, his girlfriend, the Brilliant Brianna, which was her official nickname, had made some late-night sojourns to my ashy
mattress. Davis starred in the Invention of Monogamy semi-
nar, so his hands were tied, so to speak, but I could tell he
seethed.

"Be nice," Brianna mouthed now, but I plowed on, foolishly, for her, I imagine. I was not yet heart literate.

"Davis," I said. "Davis."

"What is it, Sasha, my brother?"

"My name isn't Sasha."

"Is it something?"

"Davis," I said. "You've grown clownish. I'm sure you're
right about the cigarettes. But you're not our father."

"I don't believe in fathers," said the goblin Caldwell.
"Except my bourbon fathers. Listen to Sasha."

"Davis sucks," called a girl near the stereo. "Sasha, or whatever, is our hero. Ask Brianna."

Brianna ducked her head, but Davis caught her eye. He
threw her an evil glance as he departed. We stayed, drank,
smoked, forgot bad things. We laughed. We stood up and
sat down. We impersonated each other standing up and sitting down. We told tedious stories about our childhoods,
feigned enthrallment. That part of the evening arrived when
people sat closer together on the carpet. One groupuscule,

a reedy boy and two brawny women, groped and giggled, mashed their faces for a trilateral smooch. Brianna and I fell entwined into the couch.

"What makes you think you're smart enough to talk to him like that?" she whispered, tongued my ear. "You're just a dumb piece of gash. We like you for your innocent enthusiasm. Remember that."

"I will."

"No, you won't."

That's when Davis returned with his velvet-lined mahogany pistol case. A brace of Berettas gleamed from their notches: compacts, pearl handled, gold flecked. We broke our clinches as Davis called the room to attention.

"Big happenings, entertainment-wise, folks. Gather round for what will prove a violent and transformative highlight of your lives."

"Guns?" called a tall fellow with a can of dip. He was a theater jock from Texas, which meant he affected flasks and went bare chested under his pleather vest.

"Put those away," said Brianna. "Davis, this is not funny."

"It's just a game. They're not loaded."

"What game?" said Brianna.

"Come, Princess," he said to me. "I mean, Countess. Choose one."

"You're drunk," said Brianna.

"Somewhat. Also stoned. Why do we even say stoned? So brutal. So Levitical. Pick a pistol, dreamboy. We're going to play out that scene for our friends here. From the Pushkin."

"And then will you can it?" I said.

"Like Steinbeck."

"Goddamn ridiculous." I hardly looked at the pistols, drew one from the box, took a position near the stereo. The girl who stood there smirked.

"They're not loaded," I said.

"Bummer."

I shrugged, raised the pistol at Davis.

"Did I grant you first shot?" said Davis.

"I'm following the story. I'm the young, handsome soldier everyone has left your orbit to be near. You are the older, bitter officer who can't compete with my charisma."

"Funny," said Davis. "Not exactly as I saw it, but I admire your hustle. You framed the scene first. We'll go with your version."

"It all fits, Davis. You called for the duel. You're the crack shot. I've never even fired a gun."

"True. Well, on with it, then. You may have the first metaphorical shot, you upper-crust social usurper. Just flick that safety off."

"What about the tangelos?"

"My poor father has a little tree. Now take your shot."

Our audience, stymied in their lust, groaned at our stagecraft.

I grinned and pulled the trigger. Davis fell back with the bang. There was a neat hole in the drywall.

"Shitsnickers!" called the kid with the dip.

Brianna swayed in shock. The goblin squealed under the table, and the girl by the stereo clutched her ears.

Powder smoke hung in a clot. The room hummed with vanished noise. We stood there, grave and giddy.

I shook, and laid the pistol on the coffee table. My stomach cramped, and I wanted a cigarette. I wanted to see the body. I started to move, but Davis popped up, waved his Beretta.

Brianna swooped in and wrapped him in her arms.

"Baby," he cried. "Was that dramatic? Was it worthy?"

"Are you hurt?"

"Not a scratch! How did it look?"

"It was radically transgressive," she said. "Of something."

Davis nuzzled his lady, shoved her away.

"Now we must complete this man deed."

"No," said Brianna. "No, sweetie. The piece landed perfectly. Don't fiddle."

"It's okay," I said, lighting a Korean cigarette I'd mooched from a pack on the table.

"It is?" said the girl by the stereo.

"Davis'll put one in your frontal cortex," said the Texan.

"No, he won't," I said.

"You going to duck it like Davis?" said the goblin.

"Just watch."

Davis hocked a loogie and leveled his gun. The room got quiet. Davis winked, lowered the Beretta.

"No, no," he said with the quiet and cadence of a maestro. "I think I'll take my shot another day. I think I'll wait. Until our friend here is a little older. When he's lost his bunny-like nihilist strut. When he's discovered love. When he's struck a truce with feeling. When his every thought and action isn't guided by childish terror. When he's graduated from douchebaggery. When he truly understands all that he's about to lose. Let's forget these shenanigans for now. Just a little show. But you, buddy of my heart, you'd best watch the ridges and the roads. It could be years from now, but watch for the ragged rider's approach. He comes only for his shot."

"And . . . scene," I said. We'd taken some drama classes together. The others clapped hard for our skit, or the oratory, really. Davis, wasted in the right ratios, was a natural. We both took a bow.

......

I had one of those phones that did everything, but I could never master the simplest apps. Every time I tried to add to my schedule, these words would flash on the calendar display: "This appointment occurs in the past." I grew to rely on the feature. It granted me texture, a sense of rich history.

I was remarking on this to Davis in the midtown diner where we'd agreed to meet. I suppose you could call it a retro diner, but what diner isn't? They're all designed to make you think fried food won't kill you because it's the 1950s and nobody knows any better, and besides, there's a chance you haven't been born yet.

We dug into our bacon and cheddar chili burgers. I watched Davis chew.

He didn't look sick at all. He was still ugly but a good deal less so. Some men get handsome later. It's up to them to make it count. He'd replaced his granny glasses with modish steel frames. He looked scientific, artistic, somebody trained to talk to astronauts about their dreams. He eyed me over his drippy meat.

"That's funny," he said. "I could look at your phone, maybe fix it."

"No," I said. "I like it that way."

We were silent for a moment.

"So," I said. "The ragged rider."

"Indeed."

"You look fantastic. I thought you'd be much more winnowed."

"It's not that kind of disease."

"What kind is it?"

"We're still working on that. The doctors."

"I'm sorry. Whatever it is."

"It's in the blood. They know that. I'm sorry, too. But at least it's given me an excuse to gather my old friends."

"We haven't talked since—"

"Since graduation," said Davis.

"No," I said. "That other time."

We'd run into each other in a cocktail lounge in San Francisco several years after college. Davis wore a suit of disco white and toasted the would-be silicon barons at his table. I, assistant manager of this spacey blue sleazepit for the young and almost rich, sloshed Dom in their flutes. Davis slipped me some cash and a wink, but he flailed in a world beyond his code capacity. His group appeared composed of algorithmic gangsters, expert wielders of their petty and twisty Jewish, Welsh, Cambodian, Nubian, and Mayan brains. They hadn't spent their undergraduate years soused, brandishing pistols and theory. They'd been those morose, slightly chippy bots I'd noticed at the refectory whenever I rolled in for some transitional pancakes after a night of self-bludgeoning. They were churls with huge binders, and I'd always known they were my betters.

"Be honest," said Davis at the bar. "Are you gunning for maître d' or is this research for a screenplay?"

"I'm trying to pay my rent, sycophant."

"We were like brothers."

"Cain and the other one."

"That's true. So what's your life plan?"

"Drinking," I said. "One day at a time."

"These people here think I'm Swiss," said Davis. "They think I have PhDs in cognitive science and computer engineering. There's a serious tip involved if you help maintain my cover."

"What's the angle?"

"I need them to work for stock options. I've got a start-up. It's called the Buddy System Network. You become friends with people online, share your opinions, your stories, put up pictures. Only connect, right? What do you think?"

"I think you're a freaking crackpot. Your idea is ludicrous. People aren't machines."

"If you'd read more great literature, you'd know that machines are exactly what people are."

Now, as we sat in the diner, Davis—the new, dying, steely, reframed Davis—dragged a waffle fry through his chili burger sauce.

"So what have you been doing?" I said, thoughtless as usual.

"Right now I seem to be dying. Before that I was looking to break into your line of work. Sponging off wealthy women. My tangelo flow isn't what it used to be. The economy mugged the Davis dynasty. Come to my place tomorrow, will you? It would mean a lot to me."

That night, back in my shimmering crypt, I called Martha in Michigan.

"This is crazy," I said. "Let's patch it up."

"You turd, I'm married again."

"Oh, right," I said. "Scott. How well does he grill?"

"We're vegans now."

"No dairy?"

"Kills the sex drive."

"So that's what it was."

"No, honey, it was other things with us."

"How's your mom?"

"Let's not revisit that incident."

"Incident? Try era."

"I've got to go."

Down in the hotel bar, I thought of how much Davis and

I still had to discuss. Our friendship, for example, and how quickly we'd passed through each other, from fascinated strangers to loyal chums to relics of each other's worlds. We'd been pawns of proximity, choiceless as brothers. I'd always sort of hated him, really, his arrogance, his masks, his whispery fake ways with my mind. I'd been nothing to him, just his handsome stooge, a barker for his depraved tent.

Now, I could tell you my family history and you could do some amateur noodle prods, conclude I needed one such as Davis to salve my certain hurts. Was it the time my mother beat my hands with a serving spoon while I stood enchanted by the ripples in her gray rayon blouse? Or the occasion my father recited a limerick that began "There once was a dumb fucking boy / who was never his daddy's joy"? Yes, we could solve for why, but we could also eat another slice of coconut cake. *Why* won't save you, anyway. *Why* makes it worse. And Davis, I realized, he wasn't sick.

He was sick.

I took the train and then the bus to his place in Red Hook. He lived in a refurbished ink factory. I pushed through the iron doors and climbed the stairs until I saw a metal plate with Davis's name on it. This building, he'd told me at the diner, was owned by rich artists who rented cheap, unsafe spaces to poor artists. Davis had a good deal with these slumlord aesthetes.

His apartment, empty and unlocked, was a great cement room with high windows. Greasy carpets covered the floor. A pair of half-shredded cane chairs and a stained divan connoted a parlor. I recognized all the furniture from the old days. He'd added nothing. Even the stereo had survived.

Davis appeared in his doorway. "Everyone's up on the roof, kid. Follow me."

He led me up a narrow ladder to a nearly nautical hatch.

I popped through after him, my chin at tar level, surveyed the roof scene—so many pasty, dulled versions of the people I'd known, our old audience, and strangers, too. Caldwell the goblin had gone waxen and squinty. The Texan, dipless, had a tidy potbelly. He sported a polo shirt and unsevere trousers, golf philanthropical. The girl who once stood by the stereo was now a woman who hovered near a hooded grill. It resembled a Greek design I'd coveted from catalogs back in Ypsilanti. I could smell the seared tuna smoke, the zuke-juice vapors. Davis pulled me from the hatch, led me to the sawhorse bar. We had vistas of city and sea.

"My friend will have the rum punch," said Davis to the teen boy with the ladle.

"Okay, Dad."

Davis pounced on my surprise.

"You bet your life I have a magnificent son. This is Owney. Eugene Onegin Davis."

"A pleasure."

"You're doing the math, but I'll save you the trouble. Especially you. She drifted away from both of us that fateful night. But we crossed paths in Marfa years later."

"She?"

"She," said a voice. A dark, glitter-dusted hand brushed my shoulder: Brianna.

"So, you two are . . ."

"God, no," said Brianna. She still had the heart-threshing looks, the wicked corneal glint of a serious reader. "We still care for each other, and we both love Eugene, but our affections have relocated."

"Well phrased," said Davis.

"So," I said. "How are you dealing with the illness?"

Brianna looked baffled.

"Great news," said Davis. "I'm not terminal. That's you,

I'm afraid. I'm going to live forever. I've gotten my hands on some black market Super Resveratrol. I'll tell you, some of these scientists become dope slingers just to keep their three houses going. But no, I'm fine. How was I going to get you out here? For my shot?"

"Your what?"

"Please, you've already figured it out, I'm sure. Down deep"—he poked my chest bone—"you must have understood exactly what was going on."

"I don't have much of a deep down."

"But remember, this can't work unless you know what you will be missing."

"The future?" I said, and broke from his grip.

"What can't work?" said Brianna.

"Nothing, sweetie."

"Brilliant Brianna," I said. "Did you know I was married? The union didn't last. I couldn't forget you. I sexed it with the mother, though. That was tender."

"See, that song won't pass the audition," said Davis. "I have to know I'm ventilating a contented man. Otherwise it's a mercy job. So you've drifted a bit. Lived with uncertainty. You're a student of life. You're the eternal student. You should have lived centuries ago in Germany. Besides, you're a stud, my man. Women want to make love to your sunglasses. It's always been that way. You've pursued and overtaken happiness. Maybe you'll suddenly decide to make a ton of money, find a beauty to bear your children. This life, it's all so exalted, so tremendous and full of wonder, and also relaxing. Are you with me?"

"I've just been running from anything that resembled revelation. For twenty years I've been running."

"Nonsense," said Davis. "You have friends. You have health."

"I did quit the cowboy killers," I said. "And you and me, we had a ball, just hanging out, talking."

"I didn't like you," said Davis. "Go another way."

I stepped forward and stroked his lapels. He shucked me off.

"You condescended," said Davis. "Acted like you were killing time until a better life came along."

"You never cared for my ideas," I said, and snatched his hand, kissed his knuckles.

"What ideas?"

"Not ideas. Something. I've blocked most of it. Our whole friendship is a blur."

"I remember every microsecond," said Davis.

"It's really good to see you," I said.

"Fetch the party favor, Owney."

The boy reached under the bar for the mahogany box. Davis lifted out the Beretta.

"We'll just need one of these."

The new guests, who had gathered in for our sloppy matinee, gasped. The old hands, the repeat attendees, stood back.

"Not this homoerotic gunplay again," said the goblin.

"Homosocial," said Brianna. "Or, no, you're right."

"Shitesnickers," said the Texan, whom I'd overheard talking about his Irish roots.

"Just blanks," said the goblin. "They're old farts now. Wouldn't dare."

"It's a prank," a man with a gray-blond beard said to his date. "They all went to college together and it's like a sketch they do."

"Juvenile, entitled," said the date.

"It's like that Chekhov play," said another woman. "The one with the gun that must go off if you dare introduce it."

"No," the woman by the grill cried, wrapped herself around my waist. "Didn't you know it was me! Me all along!"

"Me who?" I said.

"Debbie!"

Brianna giggled, blew me a French kiss. It mattered that she'd never loved me, or ever saw me as anything but a pleasant face to mount. I'd always known this, but never understood how germane it was to what I'd begun calling, suddenly, inanely, my life narrative, which I assumed would culminate in our bright joining.

But here was Debbie instead.

"Debbie!" said Davis to me. "Yes! Of course. Your reason to live, pal! Debbie! The tragic element of your demise."

Davis pointed his oiled Lombardic hole puncher and took aim, as he had years before, when I had the soul of a laboratory coke mouse, craved only life's jolt, couldn't know wise joy.

"Debbie, honey," I whispered. "Move away. I'll be with you in a moment."

I raised my arms and tilted my head in the manner of the carpentered carpenter.

"And now, ladies and gentlemen, to complete a procedure begun many, many years ago, when I, Standish James Davis, having been fired upon by this knave during the latter days of Bush the Elder, take, as my duelist's right, the second and, fate willing, final shot of this contest. Furthermore—"

"Cap his monkey ass!" shouted Brianna.

Davis obliged.

Summertime, the neighbors come around to the backyard of the sweet rickety house Ondine sold us, watch me wheel up to the grills and baste the meats and flip them into Styrofoam boxes and thermal bags. We do only takeout, pork or beef, with biscuits and pop, and only on the weekend. We don't even have an official name, but I hear some people call our operation the Capo's, because a rumor floated that I was once some edge player in the North Jersey mob, got marked for a whack. Hence the wound, the wheelchair.

These are good people, but they watch too much television. Debbie, who works the register and is my wife, insists we do without one. We pass long evenings in our house drinking tea and talking about books and art and politics, or watching old movies on the computer, or having gentle, atrocious sex.

Sometimes Ondine comes over for poker or we all go out for chimichangas. Last time, after a few drinks, I asked Ondine about her daughter.

"Martha? She'll never be happy with anybody but herself."

"Lucky girl."

"You lucked out, too," said Ondine.

"I know," I said. "But life gets really murky sometimes."

"It's true, honey. Like a fish tank nobody cleans. Just fish shit and dead fish. But that's how you know it's life."

Debbie is a big deal over at the university, where she got a professorship as soon as I was healed enough to marry. We didn't plan on Ypsilanti, but Michigan happened to want her. Sometimes I read her presentations for typos, but I don't understand them. Turned out she was the brilliant one of our bunch.

I never charged Davis, and they ruled the shooting an accident. If I'd charged him, I could have taken him to civil court and gutted him, but he wasn't lying about the disappearance of his family fortune. Last I heard, he ran some kind of permanent luau up on that Red Hook roof, and also a break-dancing camp for private school kids. Brianna, somebody told me, makes films of women giving birth alone in public spaces. I never even knew she liked that sort of thing.

I'm not sure why Debbie stays with me. Her devotion must have fixed itself to the memory of my brief, illusory splendor, or else she has some plan of revenge for the years I missed her charms. I would deserve that, if only because I know in my heart that if she were the ruined one, I would not stay.

It turns out you can live, even prosper, with that kind of truth. Until, I presume, you cannot.

I still wonder why our reenactment of that Pushkin story meant so much to Davis. My real confession is that I never even read the thing. Davis just told it to me. And the way he did so, now that I recall his manner, makes me suspect he hadn't read it, either.

Typical, I guess. We were poseurs, but why do you think poseurs pose? Because they want to be invited to the dominion of the real, an almost magical zone of unselfed sensation, and they know their very desire for it disqualifies them. Consider that, the next time you cluck your tongue at some awful, grandiose fake.

Dude just wants to feel.

I did almost achieve that sensation, or a cheater's version of it, but it had not much to do with Davis, or the rest.

It happened the night before I went to Red Hook, while I sat at the bar in the Hudson Lux. A woman took the next stool. She wore a silk dress with pearls, ordered one of those something-tinis. We introduced ourselves, but she had a thick accent and I couldn't make out her name.

"You a hairy motherfucker," she said, caressed my forearm where I'd rolled my sleeve.

"You want to see all of it?" I said.

Her room was just like my room, with more moon in the window.

We were on the bed when she asked the big New York, or at least Hudson Lux, question.

"What do you do?"

"I'm a barista by training," I said. "Though I enjoy grilling. I've also been a schoolteacher and worked construction and run the night shift at a homeless shelter and interned at a men's magazine."

"You here on business?"

"Are you here on business?" I said.

"You mean right now?"

"Yes," I said.

"Yes," she said. "What do you want?"

"Well, part of me just wants to die, but the other part wants to live, to really live."

"Okay," she said.

I slipped my belt off slowly, slung it from a hook in the door, looped.

It all followed rather quickly after that, a surge of bliss, a great groinal shudder, a shell burst of froth and light. Then I got cold, fogged. I floated in a bitter-tasting cloud, but in that moment I also glimpsed everything that was good and sweet and fresh, and also incredibly refreshing and relaxing, and I saw how I could reach that place and remain there for a very long time. After that, I think, somebody clutched my legs, my knees, shoved me upward, and a bald man with an earpiece and a combat knife cut me down from the door.

MEN

Lydia Davis

There are also men in the world. Sometimes we forget, and think there are only women—endless hills and plains of unresisting women. We make little jokes and comfort each other and our lives pass quickly. But every now and then, it is true, a man rises unexpectedly in our midst like a pine tree, and looks savagely at us, and sends us hobbling away in great floods to hide in the caves and gullies until he is gone.

ANOTHER MANHATTAN

Donald Antrim

They had lied to each other so many times, over so many years, that deceptions between them had become commonplace, practically repertoire. Everyone knew this about them—it wasn't news among their friends. That night, they had dinner reservations with Elliot and Susan, who were accustomed to following the shifts in attitude and tone—Kate's theatrical sighs, for instance, in reaction to Jim's mournful looks across the table at her—brought on by the strain of living in an atmosphere of worry and betrayal. It was winter, and dark, and the air in their little apartment was dry and nauseatingly warm; and yet what they needed, it seemed to Jim, was not to flee their home for another night of exciting conversational pauses and sly four-way flirting. They needed to sit down together, no matter how stuffy it got in the living room, no matter how loudly the radiators hissed and banged, and take turns speaking their minds. They had to talk. But first he would stop at the florist's on his way home from the outpatient clinic. If he walked through the door carrying a bouquet, there was a chance that Kate might smile.

There was a chance also that it wouldn't look awkward or strange when, at the end of the evening—he didn't really believe that he and Kate would be staying in—he paired with Susan for the walk through the cold, from the restaurant to Elliot's car. It might look, in other words, as if he were not bothered by Kate's whispering to another man. (She had a way, with Elliot, of bowing her head and mumbling furiously through the strands of hair that fell across the side of her face, so that, in order to make out her words, Elliot was forced to stoop and lean into the fog of her breath.) Jim's own affair, his affair with Susan, had been over for almost five months, long enough, he thought, as he approached the florist's on the corner by his and Kate's building, for him to begin experimenting—later that same night, if the mood was right—with innocently putting his arm around Susan's shoulder while she and he and Kate and Elliot walked in two sets of two toward the parking garage.

Of course, he wanted to be careful not to punish Kate, or at least not to seem to punish her, for her success in adultery. Elliot made her laugh—in a sweet way. Anyone meeting them for the first time would think they were a new couple.

It was wrong to hate her.

He'd arrived at the florist's. Inside, he went straight over to the roses in their refrigerated case. Though it was a cold day, cold and very windy, and he'd come in chilled, the short walk across the heated space warmed him, and he could feel the frigid air hit him in the face when he yanked open the glass door. He leaned in and peered at the flowers. He asked the girl, "Do you have yellow roses that haven't already bloomed and, you know, opened?"

Yellow roses, signifying friendship more than eros, seemed right, given the complex potentials of the evening.

"We only have these."

"They're pretty, but they're not going to last."

She was pretty as well, the girl showing him roses. Had he seen her in here before and somehow not noticed? How old was she? Should he risk looking into her eyes? Was she wearing a ring? What about her ass? And what had he said to her just now? Blooming and opening meant the same thing in relation to flowers. He'd become inarticulate in her presence.

Kate, in the meantime, was upstairs in the apartment, talking on the phone to Elliot. The call had gone on for more than five hours. Kate had had to use all available phones: her cell phone and, before the cell, the apartment's two cheap cordless handsets, one in the kitchen and one in the bedroom. "Can you hear beeping? I've got to switch phones. Hang on," she'd exclaimed when the kitchen phone's battery began dying. Carrying that phone (her first of the call), she'd gone into the bedroom, picked up its brother from the night table, and said, into this new phone, "Are you there? Can you hear me? Hold on while I hang up the other phone," after which she'd taken both phones to the kitchen and dropped the dead one into its cradle on the wall. A small cabinet door beside this phone opened onto a narrow and dark airshaft that had once housed a dumbwaiter. Kate opened and closed this empty cabinet several times while explaining, on the bedroom phone, why Elliot's being married and her being married shouldn't necessarily be considered something they had in common. That they were both childless could stand as an area of emotional parity, she felt, considering the fact that they both remained unsure as to whether to have children, while their spouses frequently made it clear that, in their opinions—Susan's specifically regarding Elliot, Jim's specifically regarding Kate, and neither Susan nor Jim meaning to suggest a marital reconfiguration—they'd make "a great dad" or "a great mom."

Elliot interrupted: "Don't you get tired of hearing that?"

"It's beside the point," Kate answered, and went on, "Oh, Elliot, why is talking to you so damn fucking difficult?"

"Do you need an answer?"

"You know me, always curious." How stupid was that?

She'd been trying, not for the first time, to lovingly make clear to Elliot why she could no longer sleep with him. During the first hours of the conversation she'd been able to control the impulse to bait and flirt. But the business of swapping phones, the walking from room to room in the stuffy apartment, had, as it were, weakened her. It was as if, in losing that first phone, she'd lost a line of defense, however symbolic, against Elliot's desire. Or maybe, she thought as she stood in the kitchen, opening and closing the dumbwaiter door with one hand, the necessary act of sacrificing one phone for another could be read as a veiled enactment of the sort of ambivalence required for alternating between lovers in the first place. Or was that too absurd?

"Say that once more. I didn't hear what you were saying," she said to Elliot. The heating pipes banged; day was turning to dusk. She listened to the hiss of steam escaping from the radiator beneath the kitchen window. Elliot began again, "I was saying that I sometimes think that you think that because I'm a psychiatrist I can automatically see all the different sides of a situation. But I'm not that kind of psychiatrist."

"Please don't talk to me like I'm one of your postdocs," she said, and he took a long breath.

He said, "Kate, we're involved with each other, Kate."

"Jim's your friend."

"And so are you my friend."

"Your wife is my friend, too." She continued, "Fuck, I hate this. Now *this* motherfucking phone is beeping. Hold on. Elliot, can you hold on?" She swapped the bedroom phone for the insufficiently charged kitchen phone, went with that phone back into the bedroom, and sat on the edge of the bed.

"Kate, why are you bringing up Susan? I need to know what your point is. We agreed that we weren't going to talk about Susan. So where are you going with this? Kate? Are you there?"

He waited.

"Will you talk to me? Please, don't do this. Don't do this, Kate. All right, fuck this, fuck this, fuck—"

His phone was beeping. It wasn't the battery. It was another call. He said, "Kate, hang on a minute. Hang on, Kate."

He took the call. "Hello?"

"It's me," she said, and then told him in a miserable voice that both her home phones were dead, and that she was on her cell phone and just wanted to say that she didn't much enjoy dishonesty.

"You'll have to speak up," he said.

"Can you hear me? Tell me when the signal is clear." She pressed the cell phone against her ear and walked from the bedroom to the living room, then into the kitchen, then straight down the hall, passing the tiny second bathroom, with the broken, unusable toilet, to the apartment's minia-ture front foyer.

"Here?" she said. "Here?"

"I'm losing you," he said. And so she retraced her route, winding up back in the living room, where she turned on a lamp. The sky was dark. Everywhere on the city's horizon she saw other people's lit windows. Once again, Elliot had bul-lied her—or she'd *let* him bully her—into leaving open the question of their affair. What was the use in arguing, anyway? Jim would come home any minute, and, a little later, the two of them would go out and meet Elliot and Susan for dinner. How crazy was that? She still had to shower and dress. She conceded to Elliot, "All right, I'll think about it."

"Tomorrow, then?" Elliot said, and added, "I knew you'd come to your senses." He joked that if he didn't get out of his office in the next few minutes he'd be forced to show up at the restaurant in his white coat. They said goodbye, and she put down the phone and wept for a quarter of an hour.

Downstairs at the florist's, Jim's bouquet for Kate was growing and growing. It featured not only yellow roses but red and pink solitaires, along with sprigs of heather, freesia, and alstroemeria; green and white calla lilies; blue irises; mums; and some other things the girl had plucked from buckets and waved in the air for him to see and approve. "What else? What does she like?" she'd asked him, as she leaned into the refrigerator and reached for more.

"That looks so nice. I think she'll like just what you like," he said, and wondered whether it was okay for him to have said it. Was it provocative? There were no other customers in the shop. Staying close but keeping his distance, he followed the girl from one display case to another. He might as well have been buying lingerie, he felt; and, in fact, it seemed to him that the bouquet was somehow intended for the girl, as much as for Kate, who would've been, well, not exactly mortified to know that her husband was downstairs using a shopgirl as a proxy to get himself worked up for sex later that night.

"Baby's breath," the girl said to him.

"Excuse me?"

"I love baby's breath."

"In that case, we'll have to have a bunch," Jim said.

"Good."

She turned away, laid the unfinished bouquet on its side on the countertop beside the cash register, and, with her back to him, said, "We have a *lot* to work with here." She glanced back over her shoulder (did she want him to come closer?), then, quickly—what a great flirt, he thought—turned away again and set to work breaking down the bouquet and separating the flowers into groups, a variegated series of stacks that she arranged not by color or type (except in the case of the combined red, pink, and yellow roses) but, as became clear, by stem length. When she had her piles, she picked up clippers.

"This will take a minute," she said.

He watched her snip the stems. He said, "Take your time."

But there was a problem: What were these flowers going to cost? The bouquet as she assembled it—as it came to *be*, in her hands—was broader and taller by far than what he'd come into the florist's wanting. It was less a bouquet than a proper arrangement, a centerpiece, thanks in part to the leafy green branches the girl stuffed between blossoms, and the pale white baby's breath, which she didn't so much layer as clump into the globular mass.

"Can we take some out?" he asked, and wished he hadn't. What kind of man courts a woman by letting her make an enormous bouquet for his wife, then asks her to pare back?

"What would you like me to take out?" the girl asked. Was she annoyed? She had her back to him. Did she think less of him? Did she think he was a cheap bastard who cheats on his wife?

"It's just that I was hoping to use a particular Arts and Crafts vase on the mantel, which, in my opinion, these would look lovely in," he elaborately lied. (Actually, there was a vase on the mantel—but so what?) He went on, "What I mean to say is that the vase I have in mind isn't very big."

Did he need excuses? Did he need to bring up his home life?

He went into reverse. "Come to think of it, never mind about that vase on the mantel. It would be a shame to wreck such a nice bouquet."

"I'm not going to wreck anything."

Was she scolding him? Were things heating up between them? He waited for her next move.

"I can give you a bigger vase," she proposed, finally.

He held his breath. She had to be at least twenty years younger than he. But it wasn't their age difference, nor the fact that he was married, that made him feel uncertain of himself. The problem was his thought process: The lithium he was taking in small doses brought a slower speed to reality. It was the lithium or the antidepressant cocktail or all of it in concert. At times, when he spoke, he felt as if a kind of mental wind were blowing his thoughts back at him, forcing him to self-consciously order his syntax as he pushed words out.

"I just got—I just got out of the hospital!" he blurted.

He watched her as she turned to face him; in her hands she held white lilies and a red satin bow, and her eyes looked left, right, left.

"I shouldn't've said that! Forget I said that! I didn't mean to say that! Give me the vase. I want a vase."

"Oh!" she said, as if startled to realize that she was still clutching pieces of the bouquet. "Let me run in the back and get one."

While Jim and the girl sorted themselves out downstairs, Kate was marching around the apartment in her red heels, shoving things into her purse and looking in the usual places for her keys. She had to flee before Jim walked in. She could phone him from the street and tell him that she'd meet him at the restaurant. Going from Elliot to Jim to Elliot *and* Jim *and* Susan without a break was bullshit. But, seriously, where was she going to go? It was too cold out to sit on a bench. The bar next door to the restaurant was bleak and depressing, an old men's dive, and the bar inside the restaurant would be a mob scene of people pushing for tables. She could stand idly flipping through magazines at the newsstand across Broadway, but that would mean accommodating the line of men squeezing past her to look at porn at the rear of the store. She slammed the apartment door behind her and started down the five flights of stairs. Too often in winter she failed to leave the apartment before sunset. It worked hell on her mood.

Outside, the wind was blowing hard. She wasn't wearing a hat. She tightened her scarf around her neck, tugged up her coat collar, lowered her head, and walked toward Broadway with her fists punched down into her pockets and her purse clinched under her arm. If only it would snow. But when did it ever snow anymore? Hat or no hat, she wouldn't have minded a few snowflakes swirling down through the city light to settle on her head. When she'd been a girl, snow had lain on the ground all winter. That was what she remembered. Of course, she was thinking of the farm, of New England, not New York. So what was her point? These days, it rarely snowed the way it had back in the years before her parents died. The snowfalls she remembered from her childhood seemed lost to time and, she supposed, the changing climate.

She hurried along as quickly as she could in her high heels. At Broadway, she turned uptown and passed the florist's, where the pretty shop assistant had just come out from the back with the flowers—flowers for *her*, for Kate—in their vase.

"Here we are," the girl announced to Jim. She extended her arms and held the flowers out in front of her, presenting them. Before he could move to take them from her, however— it was the medication, warping his mind and delaying his reaction—she heaved the arrangement onto the counter and explained that she'd had to search high and low for an extra-heavy vase, one that was not only broad enough but also deep enough to properly anchor the bouquet.

Jim and the girl admired her creation. With its stalks vertical and free to fan out or droop down, the bouquet's real immensity became apparent. Roses with their thorns stuck out everywhere, and the lilies, whose columnar stalks the girl had bunched at the center, shot up through the top of the bouquet like, like, like—like insane trees towering above some insane world, he thought. He was light-headed when he spoke. "I love the way you've used ribbons and bows to tie the blossoms into clusters. It looks like a bouquet made of little bouquets! There's so much to see. I can smell the lilies. Don't you want to inhale that scent? Do you know the painter Fragonard? Do you know Boucher? Look at Boucher's flowers. They're practically obscene. There might be a Boucher hanging at the Frick."

He went for it. "Do you like museums?"

"When I have time."

"I could show you the Frick." He grinned widely and shrugged his shoulders and tipped his head, and she mirrored him, shrugging her own shoulders and making a funny face.

"You're very good at what you do," he added, and she said, "Thank you," then asked him, "How would you like to pay?"

He tried to imagine what he'd be forced to spend. Whatever the amount, it would be too great. The bills from his recent hospitalizations were mainly covered by Kate's insurance—the policy was hers; they'd gone ahead and got married in order for him to take advantage of it during this protracted (Kate's word, sometimes used sarcastically) time of crisis in his life—but there were nevertheless many outstanding fees, brand-new bills arriving every other week, plus

the only partly reimbursable expense of the aftercare program he attended across town, on the Upper East Side.

"Let's charge it." He handed the girl his debit card.

She swiped the card. "It's not going through," she said.
After passing the card through the machine a second time,
she apologized. "This doesn't automatically mean that there's
a problem with the account," she said. "You'll have to contact
your bank. Would you like to try another account?"

"I don't have another. Tell me the total?"

"Three hundred and forty-one dollars and sixty cents."

His anxiety spiked and he took a breath. How could a
bouquet of flowers be that much?

He put his hand in his pocket and felt around for cash,
but what was the point?

"Hold on a minute," he said.

What to do, what to do? He was going to have to call
his wife. Was he going to have to call her? He was going to
have to call her. He took out his phone and dialed—in that
moment he was glad that he had his meds on board—and
right away Kate picked up and hollered, "Where *are* you?
I'm at the restaurant with Susan! Elliot is out parking the car.
Did you go to your *therapy*?"

"Could you not shout, Kate?"

"It's goddamn packed in here!"

"I need to talk to you, privately," he said, and turned away
from the shopgirl. But there was no way, in the small space,
to keep the girl from overhearing, so he put his hand over the
phone, leaned toward her, and whispered, "I'll be right back,"
then stepped out of the shop, stood on the sidewalk in the
freezing wind, and slowly, deliberately humiliated himself,
saying to Kate, "I stopped on my way home and bought you
flowers, but the bank account isn't cooperating with my card

for some reason and now I'm stuck at the florist's because I don't have enough cash on me, and I think the problem is simply that—shit, I don't know what the problem is, I must not have kept my eye on the balance, and it's possible that we're overdrawn. I know we've talked about this. But it's not a serious problem, I promise."

"Oh, Jim. Are you *spending*? How much have you *spent*?" Kate cried, and he winced.

He said, "Is Susan there?"

"Do you not hear a word I say? She's right here! We're drinking Manhattans. Are you coming? We're waiting for you. Why do you want to talk to Susan? Jim, are you spending our money?"

"I don't want to talk to Susan. I'd just prefer that this conversation be private between the two of us."

"Please, Jim, as if everyone we know doesn't already know everything there is to know?"

"I'm not—I am not spending our money."

"You're agitated."

"Why are you diagnosing me? I'm not agitated. I wanted to surprise you with flowers. But clearly it was just another of my many mistakes. I'll think twice next time. Everything I do is unwanted."

"Stop it," Kate said to him then.

Through the phone he could hear sounds from the restaurant bar, voices and other noises in the after-work crush. Then the wind came up, and the only sound he heard was the phone's own static. The wind died, and Kate's voice was saying, "Elliot is here now, and Lorenzo is clearing us a table. Let me talk to someone about the flowers."

In this way he was forced to trudge back into the shop, hold the phone out, and say to the girl, "She wants to talk to you."

The girl hesitated, then reached out and let him pass the phone into her hand.

"Hello?" she said into his phone.

He retreated to a corner of the store. Joking aside, he didn't care to loiter about, smelling the flowers, while the girl wrote down his wife's American Express number. He would never learn the girl's name, not now, Kate would see to that, he told himself as he peered out from his hiding place behind a leafy potted tree. He saw the shop's buckets of flowers and the refrigerators in a row, and the door leading to the back, but where was the girl? He heard her laugh in response to some remark Kate must've made, and realized that she was standing behind the bouquet. "Oh, don't I just know that about men and their important purchases!" she exclaimed.

What was Kate saying to her? Was he being made fun of? Was she calling him bipolar?

He had a problem with anxiety and suicidality, and, as Kate had reminded him in their conversation a moment earlier, everyone knew about his previous autumn's sojourns on the Fifty-ninth Street Bridge and his games of chicken—no, not games, not at all, really—on the fire escape outside their bedroom window.

He didn't want to think about any of that. Yet it was the reason he was now crouched behind a ficus, eavesdropping while a girl he wanted to fuck got treated to an earful of Kate—on *his* phone! And what was the big problem, anyway, if a handful of times on his way home from day care, as he sometimes called his ongoing treatment, he'd got excited about life and jumped off the crosstown bus at Fifth Avenue and run into Bergdorf Goodman and ridden the elevator to the second floor and tried on clothes until closing? Was that unhealthy? His doctors didn't think he was manic-depressive;

in fact, they'd ruled it out. Kate had been reading the clinical literature, though, and felt autodidactically certain that the Payne Whitney professionals were minimizing something in plain sight: His death-trip history, considered alongside the "conspicuous" spending on coats, ties, shirts, and shoes, represented, at the least, she thought, a mixed-state depression. "Why don't they have you on olanzapine?" she'd got in the habit of asking him. He begged her not to interfere with his treatment, and suggested—thinking of her father's death and the forfeiture of the family farm in Massachusetts, when she was a teenager—that her consuming anxiety about bankruptcy, her emphasis on this as a potentially mortal trauma, might have less to do with his new handmade suits than with the ways in which his almost dying had reactivated an old mourning in her.

He peered from behind the ficus. He was wearing a ridiculous cashmere overcoat, and his suit today was a medium-gray flannel herringbone. It featured, on the jacket, minimal shoulder padding, dual vents, and a graceful, three-rolled-to-two-button stance (his current favorite lapel style), and, on the pants, single reverse pleats and one-and-a-quarter-inch-cuffed trouser legs. Why would a man ever not cuff his trousers? He kept a single jacket-sleeve button open on the left, another open on the right. He didn't look like blown credit. Did he?

Kate was going to kill him. She was mad enough to kill him. That was a fact. What was he doing, charging expensive flowers for no reason on an average night in the middle of the week when they were already committed to a crippling tab—it was sure to be a huge bar bill, by evening's close—for dinner with Elliot and Susan? But, Kate thought, as she sat with their friends, waiting for him at a tiny table near the back of the restaurant, this was how it went with her husband: He made the gestures; she absorbed the costs. "How awful this all is," she sighed. She was on the phone to the girl at the florist's. Kate hadn't meant to be audible, not to the girl, and certainly not to Elliot, who would take her vexation over Jim as a cue to call her up the next day and argue for more afternoons at the hotel.

She'd been going once or sometimes twice a week to the Upper East Side to meet Elliot at the Lowell Hotel, on Sixty-third Street between Madison and Park. She rode the bus. Typically, she arrived first. She got the room key, went up, and showered; if Elliot was delayed at the lab and the day was growing dark, she might unlock the minibar and make a Manhattan or an approximation of a Manhattan, then recline naked by the window and look north toward the East Nineties, Carnegie Hill, where her mother, an only child, like Kate, had lived before marrying her father and moving to the farm.

Manhattans had been her mother's drink. Unlike her mother, Kate tried to keep herself to three an evening. At Lorenzo's that night, she was ahead of pace, finishing her second before having eaten a bite. She held her glass in one hand and her phone in the other, listening hard through the restaurant noise as the girl at the florist's recited back her AmEx number. Elliot sat quietly beside her. He had his arms crossed, and his chair pushed back at an angle to make room for his legs. Susan had got up from the table; she'd announced to Kate—sounding well on the way to being tight—"Kate, you're my best friend, but I don't know how you drink such a strong drink." To Kate and Elliot together, she'd added, "Will you two do me a big giant favor? Will you snag Lorenzo and ask him to bring me a Cosmo?"

"Don't utter a word to me about my husband," Kate warned Elliot, once Susan had gone to the bathroom.

Into the phone, to the girl, she said, "I'm sorry, I didn't mean you. I was talking to somebody else."

Meanwhile, in the women's room, Susan was on her own phone, calling Jim's number from a stall.

It was the girl who answered, of course.

"Hello, can you hold?" the girl said. The line went briefly dead. After a pause, the girl came back and said, "May I ask who is calling?"

"May I ask who's answering?"

"Hold, please."

"Sir?" the girl called out to Jim. She looked this way and that for him. Where had he gone? The shop closed at eight. It was nearly closing time. "A woman is calling you!"

"I'm here! I'm right here!" he answered from behind his tree.

"He'll be with you in one second," he heard her promise into the phone. After that, there was a pause, before, in a businesslike tone, the girl resumed with Kate. "I'm sorry to have to ask you this again. Would you mind verifying the last five digits and the expiration date?"

Back when he was in the hospital—in the past six months, there had been three emergency-room visits and two locked-ward admissions—he had spent day after day lying on a mattress, crying. His doctors (along with the psychiatric nurses and the social workers who led the daily therapy groups) had encouraged him to uncurl himself from the fetal position and try, at least try, to watch television or play a board game with the other patients, but this had mostly proved too great a challenge. There had been times when, walking to or from the bathroom or the water fountain or the patients' common room, or standing in line to receive his medications at the nurses' station, or even simply sitting upright on the table in the examining room, he'd had the strong sensation that the air through which he moved was gathering around him and becoming—really, no word was sufficient to name it—substantive. Its weight pressed in on him. This hurt, it hurt terribly, yet when he tried to locate the source of the pain he could not: It came, as he knew, only from himself. On the mattress, shattered and sobbing over Kate and their messed-up love, he'd lain crushed.

"Sir?"

The girl's voice seemed to echo through the shop. He peeked up. When had she come out from behind the bouquet? He could see her standing on the other side of the tree. She was looking at him through the leaves.

"Are you all right, sir?"

"I maybe—I need a minute." His mouth was dry and his heart was beating fast. That could be his meds.

"There's someone who wants to talk to you. Do you think you can take the call? Would you like to try?" She held his phone out with one hand, reaching toward him through the branches.

He had to reach into the tree to meet her hand. He was sweating.

"Hello?" he said into the phone.

"What the hell, Jim?" Susan said to him from the women's-room toilet at Lorenzo's.

"Susan, how are you?" he said.

"I've been better."

"I'm sorry."

"We're all here, Jim. We're waiting and waiting for you."

"I'm doing my best to get there. Have you ordered yet? What are the specials? What looks good?"

"Kate is beside herself. She says the two of you are bankrupt. She says you've spent all the money."

"I haven't."

"Don't lie to me, Jim. Please, don't lie to me." She was sniffling, beginning to weep, lightly.

"Stop crying, stop crying, baby," he whispered into the phone. Then he laid his hand over the receiver and said to the girl, who was still peering down at him through the leaves of the tree, "You'll have to excuse me one more time." With a powerful effort of will, he stood upright and came out from behind the ficus. He didn't dare look at the girl, but he heard her telling him, as he pushed painfully past her toward the door, that it looked like his wife's American Express card wasn't working, either—and was there any way for him to pay for the flowers?

He waved his hand, motioning that he'd return. He stepped out into the cold on Broadway. He pulled up his overcoat's shawl collar. The door to the florist's closed behind him.

Back at their table for four, Kate and Elliot had hit a snag.

"Let me talk to him," Elliot said. He had his elbows on the table. He'd drunk almost none of his Scotch.

"That's not a good idea."

"Give me your phone." He held out his hand.

"I'm on hold."

"Kate," he said.

"Leave me alone."

"As you wish," he said, leaning back in his chair, and she burst out at him, "How can you act like this? You're a doctor. How can you be so unfeeling?"

He said, "What does my being a doctor have to do with my feelings?" (She rolled her eyes at this, but he didn't appear to notice.) He went on, "I may be a doctor, but I'm not your husband's doctor."

"His name is Jim, remember?"

"I think you're drunk. That's what I think."

He got up from the table, patted his pockets—checking

for his own phone—and said, "Goddamn it, I do research. I don't treat patients. He has excellent doctors. I'll call him myself."

When he'd gone and Kate was alone, Lorenzo arrived with Susan's Cosmopolitan.

"Everybody has gone away and left you," Lorenzo said, and Kate chirped back, "Everybody's gone!"

"Let me bring you another Manhattan." Lorenzo placed Susan's cocktail on the table and picked up Kate's empty glass. Kate managed a little smile. She held her phone to her ear. "Jim? Jim, are you there?" she whispered.

Six blocks downtown, Jim was on the line to Susan. "I'm here, I'm here with you, baby," he assured her. In fact, he wasn't thinking of sleeping with her again. Oh, he'd loved sleeping with Susan—that wasn't the problem. But that evening his body was compressing: The weight of the air was on him, flattening his libido and his trust in humankind.

"Susan," he said. "Susan."

"What is it?" she said. Her voice filled the stall. "What is happening? Is it happening? Is it happening to you now? I'm so scared. What do I *do*?"

"Susan," he said. "Susan."

He explained to her that in a few minutes he was going to calmly walk back inside the florist's and steal a mysterious and beautiful bouquet that he and an angel had made for Kate. He'd helped the angel, he pointed out. He was feeling honest. He acknowledged to Susan that he was speaking metaphorically when it came to angels—in order to seem aboveboard and keep her trust. He needed her to be cool when he entered the restaurant, he told her. Then he ended the call and switched over to Kate.

"I'm coming," he said.

"I'm glad," she said.

"I love you," he said.

"I love you, I love you," she said. She was alone at their table.

She said, "Have you talked to Elliot?"

He said, "I haven't heard from him."

Elliot, in the meantime, had been unable to get through, Jim's phone lines having been taken up by both their wives. He'd left two messages already, one saying, "Jim, call me, all right?"; the other, "Jim, will you call me?" His third attempt got through, but Jim didn't answer. He heard the beeping, plucked the phone away from his ear, glanced at it, saw who was calling, and said, to Kate, "It's him. There is no way that I want to speak to him right now."

"I understand," she said. Then she said, "Just get here, dear, and have dinner with us. We all need food. We need to eat."

He said, "Has he taken care with you, since I've been gone?"

"Gone?" she said.

"I don't know how else to put it."

She asked, "Will you stay where you are, until people come?"

"Don't send an ambulance," he said to her.

He put his phone in his pocket. He turned and faced the door to the flower shop. A few people swept past him on the windy avenue—or so it seemed; his thoughts were with the pain beneath his temple. He wanted to put it out. He could imagine different ways to do this. This was how it was when his mind turned to high open windows or unlocked rooftop fire doors or breaks in the chain-link fences lining bridge walkways.

He took a step forward. The door was made partly of glass, and he could see into the shop. It occurred to him that it would be easy to break the window with his fist and deliberately cut up the veins in his arms. Instead, he put his hand on the doorframe and pushed. He stuck his head inside. He was acting guiltily, though he knew there was no reason to, not at the florist's—he hadn't done anything yet. Still, he snuck in, ashamed.

The girl was nowhere in sight. The bouquet looked bigger than it had the last time he'd sized it up. How would he manage to get it up Broadway in his trembling hands? Beside it on the table—careful, he had to be careful—were the girl's pruning shears, as well as regular scissors and a small sharp knife.

He told himself to let those things lie.

Uptown at the restaurant, Lorenzo brought Kate her drink. She asked for bread, and apologized to him for taking so long to order dinner. "We'll all be here together soon," she sighed.

She was right about that. Elliot had given up trying to reach Jim, and the cold had driven him back inside. He was threading his way down the aisle to their table. Susan, too, would return, as soon as she had peed. Pride had made her unable to while on the phone.

And that left Jim, who had no desire to become a thief. Might he, instead, offer something in barter for the flowers? His wristwatch wasn't worth much. His overcoat was brand-new, and cost well more than the watch and the bouquet combined. He decided to leave an IOU, promising to come back another day with money, or if not with actual money, then with a clear idea of when one or another of his or his wife's credit cards might again be active and usable.

But when he tried to hold a pen in his hand, he could not; and when he tried to focus his eyes on the piece of paper lying beside the cash register—it was the scrap of a receipt on which the girl had penciled Kate's American Express information—he found that his mind was frantic. This was his disorder. This was the descent. He crumpled the receipt and shoved it into his pocket. He reached for the bouquet. The girl had put water in the vase.

Had you been walking downtown on Broadway that February night at a little past eight, you might have seen a man hurrying toward you with a great concrescence of blooms. You might have noticed that he did not even pause for traffic signals, but charged across streets against the lights; and so you might rightly have supposed that he could not see through the flowers that he held (doing what he could to keep clear of thorns) at arm's length before him. Whenever a siren sounded in the distance—and, once, beating helicopter blades in the night sky caused him to sprint up a side street—he dropped into a furtive, crouching gait. His balance was off; he was paranoid about police. Windblown flowers lashed at his head. Seen from a distance, he might have brought to mind an old, out-of-favor stereotype: the savage in a headdress. But as he came closer, you would have noticed his European clothes, his stylish haircut; and you might have asked yourself, "What's wrong with that man?"

Had you stepped to the side as he hurtled past, tightened your scarf securely around your neck, and continued on your way, you might next have encountered a young woman on a street corner, distraught and coatless. "Did you happen to see a man carrying a bouquet of flowers?" she might have asked in a startled voice, and you would have looked away from her bare, pale legs, pointed upwind, and told her, "He went that way." By then, the first snowflakes would have been swirling through the caverns between the apartment buildings, down onto the thoroughfare.

Jim looked up and saw the snow on his way into Lorenzo's. For an instant, he took it as an omen—of what, though? He pulled hard on the restaurant door, forcing it open, and stumbled with his tattered flowers into the dark realm between the door and the velvet drapes that had been hung to keep the cold from sweeping in over diners at the front of the room.

He parted the curtains. "Pardon me," he said to the people seated near the entrance. Long- and short-stemmed flowers alike had snagged on the drapes. Now a waiter approached— and here came Lorenzo, too, calling, in his soft, ristoratore's voice, "*Ciao*, James. *Ciao*. I cannot call you Jim, you know."

"Lorenzo, *ciao*," Jim said. The waiter was busy tugging on the curtains. Lorenzo lent a hand. "This way, try this way," Lorenzo instructed. Jim spun left then right, enshrouding himself—and the bouquet—within the folds of drapery fabric. There followed a flurry of petals. The rose thorns came loose; the bouquet's topmost stems sprung free. He tumbled out into the room.

"I'm good, I'm fine," he said, nodding reassuringly (he hoped) to Lorenzo, the waiter, the people who'd turned in their seats to stare.

"What has happened to you, James?" Lorenzo pulled his white silk pocket square from his breast pocket and reached around the yellow and pink and blue and white flowers to dab at Jim's forehead.

"I ran all the way here," Jim said.

"You're bleeding," Lorenzo told him. Jim saw the blood spotting Lorenzo's handkerchief.

Lorenzo said, "You have a lot of scratches. You look like you've been in a fight with some squirrels or something." He laughed, nicely.

"I've—I have been fighting, Lorenzo. Not with squirrels. Roses," Jim specified, and Lorenzo said, "Ah, of course. Let me take them."

He spoke to the waiter. "Paul, will you please take these

from James?" To Jim, he added, "We will bring them to your table."

"No, no," Jim said. He explained to Lorenzo that the flowers were a gift for Kate, and that he needed to present them himself. This was crucial, he informed Lorenzo. He clutched the vase. His pants were wet from water that had sloshed over the rim. Water stained his shoes. He could see tiny snags marking the sleeves of his overcoat and the front of his suit. How frustrating, after having labored so hard to avoid the thorns. His clothes would have to go to a reweaver, he thought. Then his thinking disintegrated into bitter resignation. Everything he touched was ruined. The flowers were almost destroyed.

Nonetheless, he bore them down the aisle. Here and there, people ducked forward in their chairs, or to the side, letting him through. As he progressed toward the back, the room quieted. People put down their silverware, their wineglasses; Jim felt eyes watching him.

"Eat! Live while you can!" he wanted to proclaim to the crowd. But what did he have to teach anyone? He was a thief, a common criminal—worse. He'd stolen a bouquet to give to the love of his life.

When she saw him, she was filled with happiness. She'd had a lot to drink—but, well, it wasn't that alone.

"Kate," he said. She stood, and he lurched toward her. Elliot and Susan stood as well. They flanked Kate, who came out from between them—not unlike Jim, she was unsteady on her feet—saying, "I'm sorry, excuse me," as she tacked her way through the sea of tables.

They met near the bathrooms. The bar was to their right. Kate raised her open hands to wipe the blood from his face. Blood had run down his neck, and stained the collar of his shirt. "These are for you," he told her.

She was quietly crying, whispering, "They're beautiful, beautiful." Then her crying began in force, and she wailed, "You made it, oh, you *made* it, we were all so scared, and I felt so lost."

"I'm here," he said, and his own tears started. He wanted to tell her that everything would be better, that *he* would be better, that one day soon he would work again, and start paying some bills, and take the burden off her shoulders; that they would be able, at last, to leave the little apartment with the busted plumbing. He wanted to tell her how much he needed her.

But he could see, out of the corner of his eye, his horrid reflection in the mirror behind the bar. He looked down at Kate's hands, the blood smeared across her palms. And he saw the restaurant-goers and the waiters and waitresses and busboys, who, not knowing what to make of the bleeding and the crying and the broken lilies arcing over Jim's and Kate's heads like some insane wedding canopy, had come from the kitchen or the bar to stand mutely around them. The pain in his body grew, and the words that spilled out of him were not words of love. Or they were. He spoke to his wife, as he spoke to the people gathered.

"Don't you see, Kate? Don't you *see?* It's time for me to go. I can't do this anymore. I have no place here. I don't belong. I hurt so. You can live and be happy. That will never be true for me."

"No, no, baby," she wept at him.

Someone touched his arm. It was Elliot, who'd come up behind him. He said to Jim, "Let's get in the car."

Lorenzo was there, too. Kate said to Jim, "Honey, let Lorenzo take the flowers. Just for now," and he did.

A moment later, Lorenzo came back with a wet cloth.

Kate used it to wipe her eyes and to clean Jim's face and her hands. She tied the belt around his overcoat. She said, "There."

They went out of the restaurant, the four of them. Susan let Jim lean on her, and Elliot steadied Kate. On the way out the door, they heard Lorenzo, behind them, telling his patrons, "Everything is all right. Our friend has had a bad time. Please, let me buy everyone a drink."

On Broadway, the wind had died, and the air seemed to have warmed. They walked out into new snow. And, wouldn't you know, Jim did wrap his arm around Susan's shoulders, and Elliot ducked down close to Kate, listening to her mumble whatever it was she had to say to him.

At the garage, Jim and Kate got into the back seat of Elliot's car. Susan sat beside Elliot. Elliot started the engine, turned on the headlights and the windshield wipers. *Thump, thump, thump.* He steered east. During the trip, Jim took his belt from around his waist. He gave Kate his scarf and his phone and his keys and all his money, which amounted to about thirty dollars.

Later, she would get on her knees on the emergency-room floor and extract the laces from his shoes. A nurse would come, then another, and a doctor promising sleeping pills.

By that time, after midnight, Elliot and Susan would have driven up the FDR Drive and out of Manhattan, through the Bronx, and into Westchester County.

"You can go home now, if you'd like," the doctor said to Kate. "We won't let anything happen to him."

He gave Kate a plastic garbage bag, into which she put Jim's overcoat and his suit jacket. She would use the last of his money for her crosstown taxi, and for milk and cereal at the Korean market near the apartment.

In the deep of the night, they came for him. A male nurse

helped him into a wheelchair, and then pushed him through the white labyrinth of hallways and waited for the elevator.

Margaret, one of the night nurses, met him on the ward. She said, "Hello, Mr. Davis. You're back with us again, I see." She asked, "Do you think you can walk?" She gave him Ativan and a paper cup of water, and watched while he swallowed. Then she showed him to a room of his own.

MEET THE PRESIDENT!

Zadie Smith

"What you got there, then?"

The boy didn't hear the question. He stood at the end of a ruined pier, believing himself quite alone.

But now he registered the presence at his back, and turned. "What you got there?"

A very old person, a woman, stood before him, gripping the narrow shoulder of a girl child. Both of them local, typically stunted, dim: they stared up at him stupidly. The boy turned again to the sea. All week long he had been hoping for a clear day to try out the new technology—not new to the world, but new to the boy—and now at last here was a break in the rain. Gray sky met gray sea. Not ideal, but sufficient. Ideally he would be standing on a cairn in Scotland or some other tropical spot, experiencing backlit clarity. Ideally he would be—

"Is it one of them what you see through?"

A hand, lousy with blue veins, reached out for the light encircling the boy's head, as if it were a substantial thing, to be grasped like the handle of a mug.

"Ooh, look at the green, Aggie. That shows you it's on."

The boy was ready to play. He touched the node on his finger to the node at his temple, raising the volume.

"Course, he'd have to be somebody, Aggs, cos they don't

give 'em to nobody"—the boy felt the shocking touch of a hand on his own flesh. "Are you somebody, then?"

She had shuffled around until she stood square in front of him, unavoidable. Hair as white as paper. A long, shapeless black dress, made of some kind of cloth, and what appeared to be a pair of actual glasses. Forty-nine years old, type O, a likelihood of ovarian cancer, some ancient debt infraction—nothing more. A blank, more or less. Same went for the girl: never left the country, 85 percent chance of macular degeneration, an uncle on the database, long ago located, eliminated. She would be nine in two days. Melinda Durham and Agatha Hanwell. They shared no more DNA than strangers.

"Can you see us?" The old woman let go of her charge and waved her hands wildly. The tips of her fingers barely reached the top of the boy's head. "Are we in it? What are we?"

The boy, unused to proximity, took a single step forward. Farther he could not go. Beyond was the ocean; above, a mess of weather, clouds closing in on blue wherever blue tried to assert itself. A dozen or so craft darted up and down, diving low like seabirds after a fish, and no bigger than seabirds, skimming the dirty foam, then returning to the heavens, directed by unseen hands. On his first day here the boy had trailed his father on an inspection tour to meet those hands: intent young men at their monitors, over whose shoulders the boy's father leaned, as he sometimes leaned over the boy to ensure he ate breakfast.

"What d'you call one of them there?"

The boy tucked his shirt in all round: "AG 12."

The old woman snorted as a mark of satisfaction, but did not leave.

He tried looking the females directly in their dull brown eyes. It was what his mother would have done, a kindly woman with a great mass of waist-length flame-colored hair, famed for her patience with locals. But his mother was long dead, he had never known her, he was losing what little light the day afforded. He blinked twice, said, "Hand to hand." Then, having a change of heart: "Weaponry." He looked down at his torso, to which he now attached a quantity of guns.

"You carry on, lad," the old woman said. "We won't get in your way. He can see it all, duck," she told the girl, who paid her no mind. "Got something in his hands—or thinks he does."

She took a packet of tobacco from a deep pocket in the front of her garment and began to roll a cigarette, using the girl as a shield from the wind.

"Them clouds, dark as bulls. Racing, racing. They always win." To illustrate, she tried turning Aggie's eyes to the sky, lifting the child's chin with a finger, but the girl would only gawk stubbornly at the woman's elbow. "They'll dump on us before we even get there. If you didn't have to, I wouldn't go, Aggie, no chance, not in this. It's for you I do it. I've been wet and wet and wet. All my life. And I bet he's looking at blazing suns and people in their what-have-yous and all togethers! Int yer? Course you are! And who'd blame you?" She laughed so loud the boy heard her. And then the child—who did not laugh, whose pale face, with its triangle chin and enormous, fair-lashed eyes, seemed capable only of astonishment—pulled at his actual leg, forcing him to mute for a moment and listen to her question.

"Well, I'm Bill Peek," he replied, and felt very silly, like somebody in an old movie.

"Bill Peek!" the old woman cried. "Oh, but we've had Peeks in Anglia a long time. You'll find a Peek or two or three down in Sutton Hoo. Bill Peek! You from round here, Bill Peek?"

His grandparents? Very possibly. Local and English—or his great-grandparents. His hair and eyes and skin and name suggested it. But it was not a topic likely to engage his father, and the boy himself had never felt any need or desire to pursue it. He was simply global, accompanying his father on his inspections, though usually to livelier spots than this. What a sodden dump it was! Just as everyone had warned him it would be. The only people left in England were the ones who couldn't leave.

"From round here, are you? Or maybe a Norfolk one? He looks like a Norfolk one, Aggs, wouldn't you say?"

Bill Peek raised his eyes to the encampment on the hill, pretending to follow with great interest those dozen circling, diving craft, as if he, uniquely, as the child of personnel, had nothing to fear from them. But the woman was occupied with her fag and the girl only sang "Bill Peek, Bill Peek, Bill Peek" to herself, and smiled sadly at her own turned-in feet. They were too local even to understand the implied threat. He jumped off the pier onto the deserted beach. It was low tide—it seemed you could walk to Holland. He focused upon the thousands of tiny spirals on the sand, like miniature turds stretching out to the horizon.

Felixstowe, England. A Norman village; later, briefly, a resort, made popular by the German royal family; much fishing, once upon a time. A hundred years earlier, almost to the very month, a quaint flood had killed only forty-eight people. Over the years, the place had been serially flooded, mostly abandoned. Now the sad little town had retreated three miles inland and up a hill. Pop.: 850. The boy blinked twice more; he did not care much for history. He narrowed his attention to a single turd. *Arenicola marina.* Sandworms. Lugworms. These were its coiled castings. Castings? But here he found his interest fading once again. He touched his temple and

said, "Blood Head 4." Then: "Washington." It was his first time
at this level. Another world began to construct itself around
Bill Peek, a shining city on a hill.

"Poor little thing," Melinda Durham said. She sat on the
pier, legs dangling, and pulled the girl into her lap. "Demented
with grief she is. We're going to a laying out. Aggie's sister is
laid out today. Her last and only relation. Course, the cold
truth is, Aggie's sister weren't much better than trash, and a
laying out's a sight too good for her—she'd be better off laid
out on this beach here and left for the gulls. But I ain't going
for *her*. I do it for Aggie. Aggie knows why. Aggie's been a
great help to me what with one thing and another."

While he waited, as incidental music played, the boy idly
checked a message from his father: at what time could he be
expected back at the encampment? *At what time could he be
expected.* This was a pleasing development, being an inquiry
rather than an order. He would be fifteen in May, almost a
man! A man who could let another man know when he could
be expected, and let him know in his own sweet time, when
he had the inclination. He performed some rudimentary
stretches and bounced up and down on the balls of his feet.

"Maud, that was her name. And she was born under the
same steeple she'll be buried under. Twelve years old. But so
whorish—" Melinda covered Aggie's ears, and the girl leaned
into the gesture, having mistaken it for affection. "So whorish she looked like a crone. If you lived round here, Bill Peek,
you'd've *known* Maud, if you understand me correctly. You
would've known Maud right up to the biblical and beyond.
Terrible. But Aggie's cut from quite different sod, thank
goodness!" Aggie was released and patted on the head. "And
she's no one left, so here I am, muggins here, taking her to
a laying out when I've a million other stones to be lifted off
the pile."

The boy placed a number of grenades about his person. In each chapter of the Pathways Global Institute (in Paris, New York, Shanghai, Nairobi, Jerusalem, Tokyo), the boy had enjoyed debating with friends the question of whether it was better to augment around the "facts on the ground," incorporating whatever was at hand ("flagging," it was called, the pleasure being the unpredictability), or to choose spots where there were barely any facts to work around. The boy was of the latter sensibility. He wanted to augment in clean, blank places, where he was free to fully extend, unhindered. He looked down the beach as the oil streaks in the sand were overlaid now with a gleaming pavement, lined on either side by the National Guard, saluting him. It was three miles to the White House. He picked out a large pair of breasts to wear, for reasons of his own, and a long, scaled tail, for purposes of strangulation.

"Oh, fuck a duck—you wouldn't do me an awful favor and keep an eye on Aggie just a minute, would you?—I've left my rosary! I can't go to no laying out without it. It's more than my soul's worth. Oh, Aggie, how did you ever let me leave without it? She's a good girl, but she's thoughtless sometimes—her sister were thoughtless, too. Bill Peek, you will keep an eye on her, won't you? I won't be a moment. We're shacked up just on that hill by the old Martello tower. Eight minutes I'll be. No more. Would you do that for me, Bill Peek?"

Bill Peek nodded his head, once rightward, twice leftward. Knives shot out of his wrists and splayed beautifully like the fronds of a fern.

It was perhaps twenty minutes later, as he approached the pile of rubble—pounded by enemy craft—that had once been the Monument, that young Bill Peek felt again a presence at his back and turned and found Aggie Hanwell with her fist in her mouth, tears streaming, jaw working up and down in an agonized fashion. He couldn't hear her over the explosions. Reluctantly, he paused.

"She ain't come back."

"Excuse me?"

"She went but she ain't come back!"

"Who?" he asked, but then scrolled back until he found it. "M. Durham?"

The girl gave him that same astonished look.

"My Melly," she said. "She promised to take me but she went and she ain't come back!"

The boy swiftly located M. Durham—as much an expedience as an act of charity—and experienced the novelty of sharing the information with the girl, in the only way she appeared able to receive it. "She's two miles away," he said, with his own mouth. "Heading north."

Aggie Hanwell sat down on her bum in the wet sand. She rolled something in her hand. The boy looked at it and learned that it was a periwinkle—a snail of the sea! He recoiled, disliking those things which crawled and slithered upon the earth. But this one proved broken, with only a pearlescent nothing inside it.

"So it was all a lie," Aggie said, throwing her head back dramatically to consider the sky. "Plus one of them's got my number. I've done nothing wrong but still Melly's gone and left me and one of them things's been following me, since the pier—even before that."

"If you've done nothing wrong," Bill Peek said, solemnly parroting his father, "you've nothing to worry about. It's a precise business." He had been raised to despair of the type of people who spread misinformation about the Program.

Yet along with his new maturity had come fresh insight into the complexities of his father's world. For didn't those with bad intent on occasion happen to stand beside the good, the innocent, or the underaged? And in those circumstances could precision be entirely guaranteed? "Anyway, they don't track children. Don't you understand anything?"

Hearing this, the girl laughed—a bitter and cynical cackle, at odds with her pale little face—and Bill Peek made the mistake of being, for a moment, rather impressed. But she was only imitating her elders, as he was imitating his.

"Go home," he said.

Instead she set about burrowing her feet into the wet sand.

"Everyone's got a good angel and a bad angel," she explained. "And if it's a bad angel that picks you out"—she pointed to a craft swooping low—"there's no escaping it. You're done for."

He listened in wonderment. Of course he'd always known there were people who thought in this way—there was a module you did on them in sixth grade—but he had never met anyone who really harbored what his anthro-soc teacher, Mr. Lin, called "animist beliefs."

The girl sighed, scooped up more handfuls of sand, and added them to the two mounds she had made on top of her feet, patting them down, encasing herself up to the ankles. Meanwhile all around her Bill Peek's scene of fabulous chaos was frozen—a Minotaur sat in the lap of stony Abe Lincoln and a dozen carefully planted IEDs awaited detonation. He was impatient to return.

"Must advance," he said, pointing down the long stretch of beach, but she held up her hands, she wanted pulling up. He pulled. Standing, she clung to him, hugging his knees. He felt her face damp against his leg.

"Oh, it's awful bad luck to miss a laying out! Melly's the

one knew where to go. She's got the whole town up here," she said, tapping her temple, making the boy smile. "Memoried. No one knows town like Melly. She'll say, 'This used to be here, but they knocked it down,' or, 'There was a pub here with a mark on the wall where the water rose.' She's memoried every corner. She's my friend."

"Some friend!" the boy remarked. He succeeded in unpeeling the girl from his body, and strode on down the beach, firefighting a gang of Russian commandoes as they parachuted into view. Alongside him a scurrying shape ran; sometimes a dog, sometimes a droid, sometimes a huddle of rats. Her voice rose out of it.

"Can I see?"

Bill Peek disemboweled a fawn to his left. "Do you have an Augmentor?"

"No."

"Do you have a complementary system?"

"No."

He knew he was being cruel—but she was ruining his concentration. He stopped running and split the visuals, the better to stare her down. "Any system?"

"No."

"Therefore no. No, you can't."

Her nose was pink, a drop of moisture hung from it. She had an innocence that practically begged to be corrupted. Bill Peek could think of more than a few Pathways boys of his acquaintance who wouldn't hesitate to take her under the next boardwalk and put a finger inside her. And the rest. As the son of personnel, however, Bill Peek was held to a different standard.

"Jimmy Kane had one—he was a fella of Maud's, her main fella. He flew in and then he flew out—you never knew when he'd be flying in again. He was a captain in the Army.

He had an old one of them . . . but said it still worked. He said it made her nicer to look at when they were doing it. He was from nowhere, too."

"Nowhere?"

"Like you."

Not for the first time the boy was struck by the great human mysteries of this world. He was almost fifteen, almost a man, and the great human mysteries of this world were striking him with satisfying regularity, as was correct for his stage of development. (From the Pathways Global Institute prospectus: "As our students reach tenth grade they begin to gain insight into the great human mysteries of this world, and a special sympathy for locals, the poor, ideologues, and all those who have chosen to limit their own human capital in ways that it can be difficult at times for us to comprehend.") From the age of six months, when he was first enrolled in the school, he had hit every mark that Pathways expected of its pupils—walking, talking, divesting, monetizing, programming, augmenting—and so it was all the more shocking to find himself face-to-face with an almost nine-year-old so absolutely blind, so lost, so developmentally debased.

"*This*"—he indicated Felixstowe, from the beach with its turd castings and broken piers, to the empty-shell buildings and useless flood walls, up to the hill where his father hoped to expect him—"is nowhere. If you can't move, you're no one from nowhere. 'Capital must flow.'" (This last was the motto of his school, though she needn't know that.) "Now, if you're asking me where I was born, the event of my birth occurred in Bangkok, but wherever I was born I would remain a member of the Incipio Security Group, which employs my father—and within which I have the highest clearance." He was surprised by the extent of the pleasure this final, outright lie gave him. It was like telling a story, but in a completely new way—a story that could not be verified or checked, and which only total innocence would accept. Only someone with no access of any kind. Never before had he met someone like this, who could move only in tiny local spirals, a turd on a beach.

Moved, the boy bent down suddenly and touched the girl gently on her face. As he did so he had a hunch that he probably looked like the first prophet of some monotheistic religion, bestowing his blessing on a recent convert, and, upon re-watching the moment and finding this was so, he sent it out, both to Mr. Lin and to his fellow Pathways boys, for peer review. It would surely count toward completion of Module 19, which emphasized empathy for the dispossessed.

"Where is it you want to go, my child?"

She lit up with gratitude, her little hand gripped his, the last of her tears rolling into her mouth and down her neck. "St. Jude's!" she cried. She kept talking as he replayed the moment to himself and added a small note of explanatory context for Mr. Lin, before he refocused on her stream of prattle: "And I'll say goodbye to her. And I'll kiss her on her face and nose. Whatever they said about her she was my own sister and I loved her and she's going to a better place—I don't care if she's stone cold in that church, I'll hold her!"

"Not a church," the boy corrected. "Fourteen Ware Street, built 1950, originally domestic property, situated on a floodplain, condemned for safety. Site of 'St. Jude's'—local, outlier congregation. Has no official status."

"St. Jude's is where she'll be laid out," she said, and squeezed his hand. "And I'll kiss her no matter how cold she is."

The boy shook his head and sighed.

"We're going in the same direction. Just follow me. No speaking." He put his finger to his lips, and she tucked her chin into her neck meekly, seeming to understand. Restarting, he flagged her effectively, transforming little Aggie Hanwell into his sidekick, his familiar, a sleek reddish fox. He was impressed by the perfect visual reconstruction of the original animal, apparently once common in this part of the world. Renamed Mystus, she provided cover for his left flank and mutely admired Bill Peek as he took the traitor vice president hostage and dragged him down the Mall with a knife to his neck.

After a spell they came to the end of the beach. Here the sand shaded into pebbles and then a rocky cove, and barnacles held on furiously where so much else had been washed away. Above their heads, the craft were finishing their sallies and had clustered like bees, moving as one back to the landing bay at the encampment. Bill Peek and his familiar were also nearing the end of their journey, moments away from kicking in the door to the Oval Office, where—if all went well—they would meet the president and be thanked for their efforts. But at the threshold, unaccountably, Bill Peek's mind began to wander. Despite the many friends around the world watching (there was a certain amount of kudos granted to any boy who successfully met the president in good, if not record, time, on his first run-through), he found himself pausing to stroke Mystus and worry about whether his father would revoke his AG after this trip. It had been a bribe and a sop in the first place—it was unregistered. Bill had wanted to stay on at the Tokyo campus for the whole summer, and then move to Norway, before tsunami season, for a pleasant fall. His father had wanted him by his side, here, in the damp, unlit graylands. An AG 12 was the compromise. But these later models were security risks, easily hacked, and the children of personnel were not meant to carry hackable devices. That's how much my father loves me, Bill Peek thought hopefully, that's how much he wants me around.

Previously the boy had believed that the greatest testament to love was the guarantee—which he had had all his life—of total personal security. He could count on one hand the amount of times he'd met a local; radicals were entirely unknown to him; he had never traveled by any mode of transport that held more than four people. But now, almost adult, he had a new thought, saw the matter from a fresh perspective, which he hoped would impress Mr. Lin with its age-appropriate intersectionality. He rested against the Oval Office door and sent his thought to the whole Pathways family: "Daring to risk personal security can be a sign of love, too." Feeling inspired, he split the visual in order to pause and once more appreciate the human mysteries of this world slash how far he'd come.

He found that he was resting on a slimy rock, his fingers tangled in the unclean hair follicles of Agatha Hanwell. She saw him looking at her. She said, "Are we there yet?" The full weight of her innocence emboldened him. They were five minutes from Ware Street. Wasn't that all the time he needed? No matter what lay beyond that door, it would be dispatched by Bill Peek, brutally, beautifully; he would step forward, into his destiny. He would meet the president! He would shake the president's hand.

"Follow me."

She was quick on the rocks, perhaps even a little quicker than he, moving on all fours like an animal. They took a right, a left, and Bill Peek slit many throats. The blood ran down the walls of the Oval Office and stained the presidential seal and at the open windows a crowd of cheering, anonymous well-wishers pressed in. At which point Mystus strayed from him and rubbed herself along their bodies, and was stroked and petted in turn.

"So many people come to see your Maud. Does the soul good."

"How are you, Aggie, love? Bearing up?"

"They took her from the sky. Boom! 'Public depravity.' I mean, I ask you!"

"Come here, Aggs, give us a hug."

"Who's that with her?"

"Look, that's the little sis. Saw it all. Poor little thing."

"She's in the back room, child. You go straight through. You've more right than anybody."

All Bill Peek knew is that many bodies were lying on the ground and a space was being made for him to approach. He stepped forward like a king. The president saluted him. The two men shook hands. But the light was failing, and then failed again; the celebrations were lost in infuriating darkness. . . . The boy touched his temple, hot with rage: a low-ceilinged parlor came into view, with its filthy window, further shaded by a ragged net curtain, the whole musty hovel lit by candles. He couldn't even extend an arm—there were people everywhere, local, offensive to the nose, to all other senses. He tried to locate Agatha Hanwell, but her precise coordinates were of no use here; she was packed deep into this crowd—he could no more get to her than to the moon. A fat man put a hand on his shoulder and asked, "You in the right place, boy?" A distressing female with few teeth said, "Leave him be." Bill Peek felt himself being pushed forward, deeper into the darkness. A song was being sung, by human voices, and though each individual sang softly, when placed side by side like this, like rows of wheat in the wind, they formed a weird unity, heavy and light at the same time. *"Because I do not hope to turn again . . . Because I do not hope . . ."* In one voice, like a great beast moaning. A single craft carrying the right hardware could take out the lot of them, but they seemed to have no fear of that. Swaying, singing.

Bill Peek touched his sweaty temple and tried to focus on a long message from his father—something about a successful inspection and Mexico in the morning—but he was being pushed by many hands, ever forward, until he reached the back wall where a long box, made of the kind of wood you saw washed up on the beach, sat on a simple table, with candles all around it. The singing grew ever louder. Still, as he passed through their number, it seemed that no man or woman among them sang above a whisper. Then, cutting across it all like a stick through the sand, a child's voice wailed, an acute, high-pitched sound, such as a small animal makes when, out of sheer boredom, you break its leg. Onward they pushed him; he saw it all perfectly clearly in the candlelight—the people in black, weeping, and Aggie on her knees by the table, and inside the driftwood box the lifeless body of a real girl, the first object of its kind that young Bill Peek had ever seen. Her hair was red and set in large, infantile curls, her skin very white, and her eyes wide open and green. A slight smile revealed the gaps in her teeth, and suggested secret knowledge, the kind of smile he had seen before on the successful sons of powerful men with full clearance—the boys who never lose. Yet none of it struck him quite as much as the sensation that there was someone or something else in that grim room, both unseen and present, and coming for him as much as for anybody.

THE LARGESSE OF THE SEA MAIDEN

Denis Johnson

SILENCES

After dinner, nobody went home right away. I think we'd enjoyed the meal so much we hoped Elaine would serve us the whole thing all over again. These were people we've gotten to know a little from Elaine's volunteer work—nobody from my work, nobody from the ad agency. We sat around in the living room describing the loudest sounds we'd ever heard. One said it was his wife's voice when she told him she didn't love him anymore and wanted a divorce. Another recalled the pounding of his heart when he suffered a coronary. Tia Jones had become a grandmother at the age of thirty-seven and hoped never again to hear anything so loud as her granddaughter crying in her sixteen-year-old daughter's arms. Her husband, Ralph, said it hurt his ears whenever his brother opened his mouth in public, because his brother had Tourette's syndrome and erupted with remarks like "I masturbate! Your penis smells good!" in front of perfect strangers on a bus or during a movie, or even in church.

Young Chris Case reversed the direction and introduced the topic of silences. He said the most silent thing he'd ever heard was the land mine taking off his right leg outside Kabul, Afghanistan.

As for other silences, nobody contributed. In fact, there came a silence now. Some of us hadn't realized that Chris had lost a leg. He limped, but only slightly. I hadn't even known he'd fought in Afghanistan. "A land mine?" I said.

"Yes, sir. A land mine."

"Can we see it?" Deirdre said.

"No, ma'am," Chris said. "I don't carry land mines around on my person."

"No! I mean your leg."

"It was blown off."

"I mean the part that's still there!"

"I'll show you," he said, "if you kiss it."

Shocked laughter. We started talking about the most ridiculous things we'd ever kissed. Nothing of interest. We'd all kissed only people, and only in the usual places. "All right, then," Chris told Deirdre. "Here's your chance for the conversation's most unique entry."

"No, I don't want to kiss your leg!"

Although none of us showed it, I think we all felt a little irritated with Deirdre. We all wanted to see.

Morton Sands was there, too, that night, and for the most part he'd managed to keep quiet. Now he said, "Jesus Christ, Deirdre."

"Oh, well. OK," she said.

Chris pulled up his right pant leg, bunching the cuff about halfway up his thigh, and detached his prosthesis, a device of chromium bars and plastic belts strapped to his knee, which was intact and swiveled upward horribly to present the puckered end of his leg. Deirdre got down on her bare knees before him, and he hitched forward in his seat—the couch; Ralph Jones was sitting beside him—to move the scarred stump within two inches of Deirdre's face. Now she started to cry. Now we were all embarrassed, a little ashamed.

For nearly a minute, we waited.

Then Ralph Jones said, "Chris, I remember when I saw you fight two guys at once outside the Aces Tavern. No kidding," Jones told the rest of us. "He went outside with these two guys and beat the crap out of both of them."

"I guess I could've given them a break," Chris said. "They were both pretty drunk."

"Chris, you sure kicked some ass that night."

In the pocket of my shirt I had a wonderful Cuban cigar. I wanted to step outside with it. The dinner had been one of our best, and I wanted to top off the experience with a satisfying smoke. But you want to see how this sort of thing turns out. How often will you witness a woman kissing an amputation? Jones, however, had ruined everything by talking. He'd broken the spell. Chris worked the prosthesis back into place and tightened the straps and rearranged his pant leg. Deirdre stood up and wiped her eyes and smoothed her skirt and took her seat, and that was that. The outcome of all this was that Chris and Deirdre, about six months later, down at the courthouse, in the presence of very nearly the same group of friends, were married by a magistrate. Yes, they're husband and wife. You and I know what goes on.

ACCOMPLICES

Another silence comes to mind. A couple of years ago, Elaine and I had dinner at the home of Miller Thomas, formerly the head of my agency in Manhattan. Right—he and his wife, Francesca, ended up out here, too, but considerably later than Elaine and I—once my boss, now a San Diego retiree.

We finished two bottles of wine with dinner, maybe three bottles. After dinner, we had brandy. Before dinner, we had cocktails. We didn't know one another particularly well, and maybe we used the liquor to rush past that fact. After the brandy, I started drinking Scotch, and Miller drank bourbon, and, although the weather was warm enough that the central air conditioner was running, he pronounced it a cold night and lit a fire in his fireplace. It took only a squirt of fluid and the pop of a match to get an armload of sticks crackling and blazing, and then he laid on a couple of large chunks that he said were good, seasoned oak. "The capitalist at his forge," Francesca said.

At one point we were standing in the light of the flames, I and Miller Thomas, seeing how many books each man could balance on his out-flung arms, Elaine and Francesca loading them onto our hands in a test of equilibrium that both of us failed repeatedly. It became a test of strength. I don't know who won. We called for more and more books, and our women piled them on until most of Miller's library lay around us on the floor. He had a small Marsden Hartley canvas mounted above the mantel, a crazy, mostly blue land-scape done in oil, and I said that perhaps that wasn't the place for a painting like this one, so near the smoke and heat, such an expensive painting. And the painting was masterful, too, from what I could see of it by dim lamps and firelight, amid books scattered all over the floor. . . . Miller took offense. He said he'd paid for this masterpiece, he owned it, he could put it where it suited him. He moved very near the flames and took down the painting and turned to us, holding it before him, and declared that he could even, if he wanted, throw it in the fire and leave it there. "Is it art? Sure. But listen," he said, "art doesn't own it. My name ain't Art." He held the canvas flat like a tray, landscape up, and tempted the flames with it, thrusting it in and out. . . . And the strange thing is that I'd heard a nearly identical story about Miller Thomas and his beloved Hartley landscape some years before, about an evening very similar to this one, the drinks and wine and brandy and more drinks, the rowdy conversation, the scattering of books, and, finally, Miller thrusting this painting toward the flames and calling it his own property, and threatening to burn it. On that previous night, his guests had talked him down from the heights, and he'd hung the painting back in its place, but on our night—why?—none of us found a way to object as he added his property to the fuel and turned his back and walked away. A black spot appeared on the canvas and spread out in a sort of smoking puddle that gave rise to tiny flames. Miller sat in a chair across the living room, by the flickering window, and observed from that distance with a drink in his hand. Not a word, not a move, from any of us. The wooden frame popped marvelously in the silence while the great painting cooked away, first black and twisted, soon gray and fluttering, and then the fire had it all.

ADMAN

This morning I was assailed by such sadness at the velocity of life—the distance I've traveled from my own youth, the persistence of the old regrets, the new regrets, the ability of failure to freshen itself in novel forms—that I almost crashed the car. Getting out at the place where I do the job I don't feel I'm very good at, I grabbed my briefcase too roughly and dumped half of its contents in my lap and half in the parking lot, and while gathering it all up I left my keys on the seat and locked the car manually—an old man's habit—and trapped them in the Rav. In the office, I asked Shylene to call a locksmith and then to get me an appointment with my back man.

In the upper right quadrant of my back I have a nerve that once in a while gets pinched. The T4 nerve. These nerves aren't frail little ink lines; they're cords, in fact, as thick as your pinkie finger. This one gets caught between tense muscles, and for days, even weeks, there's not much to be done but take aspirin and get massages and visit the chiropractor. Down my right arm I feel a tingling, a numbness, sometimes a dull, sort of muffled torment, or else a shapeless, confusing pain.

It's a signal: it happens when I'm anxious about something.

To my surprise, Shylene knew all about this something. Apparently, she finds time to be Googling her bosses, and she'd learned of an award I was about to receive in, of all places, New York—for an animated television commercial. The award goes to my old New York team, but I was the only one of us attending the ceremony, possibly the only one interested, so many years down the line. This little gesture of acknowledgment put the finishing touches on a depressing picture. The people on my team had gone on to other teams, fancier agencies, higher accomplishments. All I'd done in better than two decades was tread forward until I reached the limit of certain assumptions, and stepped off. Meanwhile, Shylene was oohing, gushing, like a proud nurse who expects you to marvel at all the horrible procedures the hospital has in store for you. I said to her, "Thanks, thanks."

When I entered the reception area, and throughout this transaction, Shylene was wearing a flashy sequined carnival mask. I didn't ask why.

Our office environment is part of the New Wave. The whole agency works under one gigantic big top, like a circus—not crowded, quite congenial, all of it surrounding a spacious break-time area, with pinball machines and a basketball hoop, and every Friday during the summer months we have a happy hour with free beer from a keg.

In New York, I made commercials. In San Diego, I write and design glossy brochures, mostly for a group of Western resorts where golf is played and horses take you along bridle paths. Don't get me wrong—California's full of beautiful spots; it's a pleasure to bring them to the attention of people who might enjoy them. Just, please, not with a badly pinched nerve.

When I can't stand it, I take the day off and visit the big art museum in Balboa Park. Today, after the locksmith got me back into my car, I drove to the museum and sat in on part of a lecture in one of its side rooms, a woman outsider artist raving, "Art is man and man is art!" I listened for five minutes, and what little of it she managed to make comprehensible didn't even merit being called shallow. Just the same, her paintings were slyly designed, intricately patterned, and coherent. I wandered from wall to wall, taking some of it in, not much. But looking at art for an hour or so always changes the way I see things afterward—this day, for instance, a group of mentally handicapped adults on a tour of the place, with their twisted, hovering hands and cocked heads, moving among the works like cheap cinema zombies, but good zombies, zombies with minds and souls and things to keep them interested. And outside, where they normally have a lot of large metal sculptures—the grounds were being dug up and reconstructed—a dragline shovel nosing the rubble monstrously, and a woman and a child watching, motionless, the little boy standing on a bench with his smile and sideways eyes and his mother beside him, holding his hand, both so still, like a photograph of American ruin.

Next, I had a session with a chiropractor dressed up as an elf.

It seemed the entire staff at the medical complex near my house were costumed for Halloween, and while I waited out front in the car for my appointment, the earliest one I could get that day, I saw a Swiss milkmaid coming back from lunch, then a witch with a green face, then a sunburst-orange superhero. Then I had the session with the chiropractor in his tights and drooping cap.

As for me? My usual guise. The masquerade continues.

FAREWELL

Elaine got a wall phone for the kitchen, a sleek blue one that wears its receiver like a hat, with a caller-ID readout on its face just below the keypad. While I eyeballed this instrument, having just come in from my visit with the chiropractor, a brisk, modest tone began, and the tiny screen showed ten digits I didn't recognize. My inclination was to scorn it, like any other unknown. But this was the first call, the inaugural message.

As soon as I touched the receiver I wondered if I'd regret this, if I was holding a mistake in my hand, if I was pulling this mistake to my head and saying "Hello" to it.

The caller was my first wife, Virginia, or Ginny, as I always called her. We were married long ago, in our early twenties, and put a stop to it after three crazy years. Since then, we hadn't spoken, we'd had no reason to, but now we had one. Ginny was dying.

Her voice came faintly. She told me the doctors had closed the book on her, she'd ordered her affairs, the good people from hospice were in attendance.

Before she ended this earthly transit, as she called it, Ginny wanted to shed any kind of bitterness against certain people, certain men, especially me. She said how much she'd been hurt, and how badly she wanted to forgive me, but she didn't know whether she could or not—she hoped she could—and I assured her, from the abyss of a broken heart, that I hoped so, too, that I hated my infidelities and my lies about the money, and the way I'd kept my boredom secret, and my secrets in general, and Ginny and I talked, after forty years of silence, about the many other ways I'd stolen her right to the truth.

In the middle of this, I began wondering, most uncomfortably, in fact with a dizzy, sweating anxiety, if I'd made a mistake—if this wasn't my first wife, Ginny, no, but rather my second wife, Jennifer, often called Jenny. Because of the weakness of her voice and my own humming shock at the news, also the situation around her as she tried to speak to me on this very important occasion—folks coming and going, and the sounds of a respirator, I supposed—now, fifteen minutes into this call, I couldn't remember if she'd actually said her name when I picked up the phone and I suddenly didn't know which set of crimes I was regretting, wasn't sure if this dying farewell clobbering me to my knees in true repentance beside the kitchen table was Virginia's, or Jennifer's.

"This is hard," I said. "Can I put the phone down a minute?" I heard her say OK.

The house felt empty. "Elaine?" I called. Nothing. I wiped my face with a dishrag and took off my blazer and hung it on a chair and called out Elaine's name one more time and then picked up the receiver again. There was nobody there.

Somewhere inside it, the phone had preserved the caller's number, of course, Ginny's number or Jenny's, but I didn't look for it. We'd had our talk, and Ginny or Jenny, whichever, had recognized herself in my frank apologies, and she'd been satisfied—because, after all, both sets of crimes had been the same.

I was tired. What a day. I called Elaine on her cell phone. We agreed she might as well stay at the Budget Inn on the East Side. She volunteered out there, teaching adults to read, and once in a while she got caught late and stayed over. Good. I could lock all three locks on the door and call it a day. I didn't mention the previous call. I turned in early.

I dreamed of a wild landscape—elephants, dinosaurs, bat caves, strange natives, and so on.

I woke, couldn't go back to sleep, put on a long terry-cloth robe over my p.j.'s, and slipped into my loafers and went walking. People in bathrobes stroll around here at all hours, but not often, I think, without a pet on a leash. Ours is a good neighborhood—a Catholic church and a Mormon one, and a posh town-house development with much open green space, and, on our side of the street, some pretty nice smaller homes.

I wonder if you're like me, if you collect and squirrel away in your soul certain odd moments when the Mystery winks at you, when you walk in your bathrobe and tasseled loafers, for instance, well out of your neighborhood and among a lot of closed shops, and you approach your very faint reflection in a window with words above it. The sign said "Sky and Celery." Closer, it read "Ski and Cyclery."

I headed home.

WIDOW

I was having lunch one day with my friend Tom Ellis, a journalist—just catching up. He said that he was writing a two-act drama based on interviews he'd taped while gathering material for an article on the death penalty, two interviews in particular.

First, he'd spent an afternoon with a death-row inmate in Virginia, the murderer William Donald Mason, a name not at all famous here in California, and I don't know why I remember it. Mason was scheduled to die the next day, twelve years after killing a guard he'd taken hostage during a bank robbery.

Other than his last meal, of steak, green beans, and a baked potato, which would be served to him the following noon, Mason knew of no future outcomes to worry about and seemed relaxed and content. Ellis quizzed him about his life before his arrest, his routine there at the prison, his views on the death penalty—Mason was against it—and his opinion as to an afterlife—Mason was for it.

The prisoner talked with admiration about his wife, whom he'd met and married some years after landing on death row. She was the cousin of a fellow inmate. She waited tables in a sports bar—great tips. She liked reading, and she'd introduced her murderer husband to the works of Charles Dickens and Mark Twain and Ernest Hemingway. She was studying for a Realtor's license.

Mason had already said goodbye to his wife. The couple had agreed to get it all out of the way a full week ahead of the execution, to spend several happy hours together and part company well out of the shadow of Mason's last day.

Ellis said that he'd felt a fierce, unexpected kinship with this man so close to the end, because, as Mason himself pointed out, this was the last time he'd be introduced to a stranger, except for the people who would arrange him on the gurney the next day and set him up for his injection. Tom Ellis was the last new person he'd meet, in other words, who wasn't about to kill him. And, in fact, everything proceeded according to the schedule, and about eighteen hours after Ellis talked with him, William Mason was dead.

A week later, Ellis interviewed the new widow, Mrs. Mason, and learned that much of what she'd told her husband was false.

Ellis located her in Norfolk, working not in any kind of sports bar but, instead, in a basement sex emporium near the waterfront, in a one-on-one peep show. In order to talk to her, Ellis had to pay twenty dollars and descend a narrow stairway, lit with purple bulbs, and sit in a chair before a curtained window. He was shocked when the curtain vanished upward to reveal the woman already completely nude, sitting on a stool in a padded booth. Then it was her turn to be shocked, when Ellis introduced himself as a man who'd shared an hour or two of her husband's last full day on earth. Together, they spoke of the prisoner's wishes and dreams, his happiest memories and his childhood grief, the kinds of things a man shares only with his wife. Her face, though severe, was pretty, and she displayed her parts to Tom unselfconsciously, yet without the protection of anonymity. She wept, she laughed, she shouted, she whispered all of this into a telephone handset that she held to her head, while her free hand gestured in the air or touched the glass between them.

As for having told so many lies to the man she'd married— that was one of the things she laughed about. She seemed to assume that anybody else would have done the same. In addition to her bogus employment and her imaginary studies in real estate, she'd endowed herself with a religious soul and joined a nonexistent church. Thanks to all her fabrications, William Donald Mason had died a proud and happy husband.

And, just as he'd been surprised by his sudden intimacy with the condemned killer, my friend felt very close to the widow, because they were talking to each other about life and death while she displayed her nakedness before him, sitting on the stool with her red spike-heeled pumps planted wide apart on the floor. I asked him if they'd ended up making love, and he said no, but he'd wanted to, he certainly had, and he was convinced that the naked widow had felt the same, though you weren't allowed to touch the girls in those places, and this dialogue, in fact both of them—the death-row interview and the interview with the naked widow—had taken place through glass partitions made to withstand any kind of passionate assault.

At the time, the idea of telling her what he wanted had seemed terrible. Now he regretted his shyness. In the play, as he described it for me, the second act would end differently.

Before long, we wandered into a discussion of the difference between repentance and regret. You repent the things you've done, and regret the chances you let get away. Then, as sometimes happens in a San Diego café—more often than you'd think—we were interrupted by a beautiful young woman selling roses.

ORPHAN

The lunch with Tom Ellis took place a couple of years ago. I don't suppose he ever wrote the play; it was just a notion he was telling me about. It came to mind today because this afternoon I attended the memorial service of an artist friend of mine, a painter named Tony Fido, who once told me about a similar experience.

Tony found a cell phone on the ground near his home in National City, just south of here. He told me about this the last time I saw him, a couple of months before he disappeared, or went out of communication. First he went out of communication, then he was deceased. But when he told me this story there was no hint of any of that.

Tony noticed the cell phone lying under an oleander bush as he walked around his neighborhood. He picked it up and continued his stroll, and before long felt it vibrating in his pocket. When he answered, he found himself talking to the wife of the owner—the owner's widow, actually, who explained that she'd been calling the number every thirty minutes or so since her husband's death, not twenty-four hours before.

Her husband had been killed the previous afternoon in an accident at the intersection where Tony had found the cell phone. An old woman in a Cadillac had run him down. At the moment of impact, the device had been torn from his hand.

The police said that they hadn't noticed any phone around the scene. It hadn't been among the belongings she'd collected at the morgue. "I knew he lost it right there," she told Tony, "because he was talking to me at the very second when it happened."

Tony offered to get in his car and deliver the phone to her personally, and she gave him her address in Lemon Grove, nine miles distant. When he got there he discovered that the woman was only twenty-two and quite attractive, and that she and her husband had been going through a divorce.

At this point in the telling, I think I knew where his story was headed.

"She came after me. I told her, 'You're either from Heaven or from Hell.' It turned out she was from Hell."

Whenever he talked, Tony kept his hands moving—grabbing and rearranging small things on the tabletop—while his head rocked from side to side and back and forth. Sometimes he referred to a "force of rhythm" in his paintings. He often spoke of "motion" in the work.

I didn't know much about Tony's background. He was in his late forties but seemed younger. I met him at the Balboa Park museum, where he appeared at my shoulder while I looked at an Edward Hopper painting of a Cape Cod gas station. He offered his critique, which was lengthy, meticulous, and scathing—and which was focused on technique, only on technique—and spoke of his contempt for all painters, and finished by saying, "I wish Picasso was alive. I'd challenge him—he could do one of mine and I could do one of his."

"You're a painter yourself."

"A better painter than this guy," he said of Edward Hopper.

"Well, whose work would you say is any good?"

"The only painter I admire is God. He's my biggest influence."

We began having coffee together two or three times a month, always, I have to admit, at Tony's initiation. Usually I drove to his lively, disheveled Hispanic neighborhood to see him, there in National City. I like primitive art, and I like folktales, so I enjoyed visiting his rambling old home, where he lived surrounded by his paintings, like an orphan king in a cluttered castle.

The house had been in his family since 1939. For a while, it was a boardinghouse—a dozen bedrooms, each with its own sink. "Damn place has a jinx or whammy: First, Spiro— Spiro watched it till he died. Mom watched it till she died. My sister watched it till she died. Now I'll be here till I die," he said, hosting me shirtless, his hairy torso dabbed all over with paint. Talking so fast I could rarely follow, he did seem deranged. But blessed, decidedly so, with a self-deprecating and self-orienting humor that the genuinely mad seem to have misplaced. What to make of somebody like that? "Richards in the *Washington Post*," he once said, "compared me to Melville." I have no idea who Richards was. Or who Spiro was.

Tony never tired of his voluble explanations, his self-exegesis—the works almost coded, as if to fool or distract the unworthy. They weren't the child drawings of your usual schizophrenic outsider artist, but efforts a little more skillful, on the order of tattoo art, oil on canvases around four by six feet in size, crowded with images but highly organized, all on biblical themes, mostly dire and apocalyptic, and all with the titles printed neatly right on them. One of his works, for instance—three panels depicting the end of the world and the advent of Heaven—was called "Mystery Babylon Mother of Harlots Revelation 17:1–7."

This period when I was seeing a bit of Tony Fido coincided with an era in the world of my unconscious, an era when I was troubled by the dreams I had at night. They were long and epic, detailed and violent and colorful. They were exhausting. I couldn't account for them. The only medication I took was something to bring down my blood pressure, and it wasn't new. I made sure I didn't take food just before going to bed. I avoided sleeping on my back, steered clear of disturbing novels and TV shows. For a month, maybe six weeks, I dreaded sleep. Once, I dreamed of Tony—I defended him against an angry mob, keeping the seething throng at bay with a butcher knife. Often, I woke up short of breath, shaking, my heartbeat rattling my ribs, and I cured my nerves with a solitary walk, no matter the hour. And once—maybe the night I dreamed about Tony, I don't remember—I went walking and had the kind of moment or visitation I treasure, when the flow of life twists and untwists, all in a blink—think of a taut ribbon flashing: I heard a young man's voice in the parking lot of the Mormon church in the dark night telling someone, "I didn't bark. That wasn't me. I didn't bark."

I never found out how things turned out between Tony and the freshly widowed twenty-two-year-old. I'm pretty sure it went no further, and there was no second encounter, certainly no ongoing affair—because he more than once complained, "I can't find a woman, none. I'm under some kind of a damn spell." He believed in spells and whammies and such, in angels and mermaids, omens, sorcery, wind-borne voices, in messages and patterns. All through his house were scattered twigs and feathers possessing a mysterious significance, rocks that had spoken to him, stumps of driftwood whose faces he recognized. And, in any direction, his canvases, like windows opening onto lightning and smoke, ranks of crimson demons and flying angels, gravestones on fire, and scrolls, chalices, torches, swords.

Last week, a woman named Rebecca Stamos, somebody I'd never heard of, called me to say that our mutual friend Tony Fido was no more. He'd killed himself. As she put it, "He took his life."

For two seconds, the phrase meant nothing to me. "Took it," I said. . . . Then, "Oh, my goodness."

"Yes, I'm afraid he committed suicide."

"I don't want to know how. Don't tell me how." Honestly, I can't imagine why I said that.

MEMORIAL

A week ago Friday—nine days ago—the eccentric religious painter Tony Fido stopped his car on Interstate 8, about sixty miles east of San Diego, on a bridge above a deep, deep ravine, and climbed over the railing and stepped into the air. He mailed a letter beforehand to Rebecca Stamos, not to explain himself but only to say goodbye and pass along the phone numbers of some friends.

Sunday I attended Tony's memorial service, for which Rebecca Stamos had reserved the band room of the middle school where she teaches. We sat in a circle, with cups and saucers on our laps, in a tiny grove of music stands, and volunteered, one by one, our memories of Tony Fido. There were only five of us: our hostess, Rebecca, plain and stout, in a sleeveless blouse and a skirt that reached down to her white tennis shoes; myself in the raiment of my order, the blue blazer, khaki chinos, tasseled loafers; two middle-aged women of the sort to own a couple of small obnoxious dogs—they called Tony "Anthony"; a chubby young man in a green jumpsuit—some kind of mechanic—sweating. Tony's neighbors? Family? None.

Only the pair of ladies who'd arrived together actually knew each other. None of the rest of us had ever met before. These were friendships, or acquaintances, that Tony had kept one by one. He'd met us all in the same way— he'd materialized beside us at an art museum, an outdoor market, a doctor's waiting room, and he'd begun to talk. I was the only one of us even aware he devoted all his time to painting canvases. The others thought he owned some kind of business—plumbing or exterminating or looking after private swimming pools. One believed he came from Greece; others assumed Mexico, but I'm sure his family was Armenian, long established in San Diego County. Rather than memorializing him, we found ourselves asking, "Who the hell was this guy?"

Rebecca had this much about him: while he was still in his teens, Tony's mother had killed herself. "He mentioned it more than once," Rebecca said. "It was always on his mind." To the rest of us this came as new information.

Of course, it troubled us to learn that his mother had taken her own life, too. Had she jumped? Tony hadn't told, and Rebecca hadn't asked.

With little to offer about Tony in the way of biography, I shared some remarks of his that had stuck in my thoughts. "I couldn't get into ritzy art schools," he told me once. "Best thing that ever happened to me. It's dangerous to be taught art." And he said, "On my twenty-sixth birthday, I quit signing my work. Anybody who can paint like that, have at it, and take the credit." He got a kick out of showing me a passage in his hefty black Bible—first book of Samuel, chapter 6?— where the idolatry of the Philistines earns them a plague of hemorrhoids. "Don't tell me God doesn't have a sense of humor."

And another of his insights, one he shared with me several times: "We live in a catastrophic universe—not a universe of gradualism."

That one had always gone right past me. Now it sounded ominous, prophetic. Had I missed a message? A warning?

The man in the green jumpsuit, the garage mechanic, reported that Tony had plunged from our nation's highest concrete-beam bridge down into Pine Valley Creek, a flight of four hundred and forty feet. The span, completed in 1974 and named the Nello Irwin Greer Memorial Bridge, was the first in the United States to be built using, according to the mechanic, "the cast-in-place segmental balanced cantilever method." I wrote it down on a memo pad. I can't recall the mechanic's name. His breast-tag said "Ted," but he introduced himself as someone else.

Anne and her friend, whose name also slipped past me— the pair of women—cornered me afterward. They seemed to think I should be the one to take final possession of a three-ring binder full of recipes that Tony had loaned them—the collected recipes of Tony's mother. I determined I would give it to Elaine. She's a wonderful cook, but not as a regular thing, because nobody likes to cook for two. Too much work and too many leftovers. I told them she'd be glad to get the book.

The binder was too big for any of my pockets. I thought of asking for a bag, but I failed to ask. I didn't know what to do with it but carry it home in my hands and deliver it to my wife.

Elaine was sitting at the kitchen table, before her a cup of black coffee and half a sandwich on a plate.

I set the notebook on the table next to her snack. She stared at it. "Oh," she said. "From your painter." She sat me down beside her and we went through the notebook page by page, side by side.

Elaine: she's petite, lithe, quite smart; short gray hair, no makeup. A good companion. At any moment—the very next second—she could be dead.

I want to depict this book carefully, so imagine holding it in your hands, a three-ring binder of bright-red plastic weighing about the same as a full dinner plate, and now setting it in front of you on the table. When you open it, you find a pink title page, "Recipes. Caesarina Fido," covering a two-inch thickness of white college-ruled three-hole paper, the first inch or so the usual—casseroles and pies and salad dressings, every aspect of breakfast, lunch, and supper, all written in blue ballpoint. Halfway through, Tony's mother introduces ink of other colors, mostly green, red, and purple, but also pink, and a yellow that's hard to make out; and, as these colors come along, her penmanship enters a kind of havoc, the letters swell and shrink, several pages big and loopy, leaning to the right, and then, for the next many pages, leaning to the left, then back the other way; and here, where these wars and changes begin, and for better than a hundred pages, all the way to the end, the recipes are only for cocktails. Every kind of cocktail.

Earlier that afternoon, as Anne handed the binder over to me at Tony's memorial, she made a curious remark. "Anthony spoke very highly of you. He said you were his best friend." I thought it was a joke, but Anne meant this seriously.

Tony's best friend? I was confused. I'm still confused. I hardly knew him.

CASANOVA

When I returned to New York City to pick up my prize at the American Advertisers Awards, I'm not sure I expected to enjoy myself. But on the second day, killing time before the ceremony, walking north through midtown in my dark ceremonial suit and trench coat, skirting the park, strolling south again, feeling the pulse and listening to the traffic noise rising among high buildings, I had a homecoming. The day was sunny, fine for walking, brisk, and getting brisker—and, in fact, as I cut a diagonal through a little plaza somewhere above Fortieth Street, the last autumn leaves were swept up from the pavement and thrown around my head, and a sudden misty quality in the atmosphere above seemed to solidify into a ceiling both dark and luminous, and the passersby hunched into their collars, and, two minutes later, the gusts settled into a wind, not hard but steady and cold, and my hands dove into my coat pockets. A bit of rain speckled the pavement. Random snowflakes spiraled in the air. All around me, people seemed to be evacuating the scene, while across the square a vendor shouted that he was closing his cart and you could have his wares for practically nothing, and for no reason I could have named I bought two of his rat dogs with everything and a cup of doubtful coffee and then learned the reason—they were wonderful. I nearly ate the napkin. New York!

Once, I lived here. Went to Columbia University, studying history first, then broadcast journalism. Worked for a couple of pointless years at the *Post*, and then for thirteen tough but prosperous years at Castle and Forbes on Fifty-Fourth, just off Madison Avenue. And then took my insomnia, my afternoon headaches, my doubts, and my antacid tablets to San Diego and lost them in the Pacific Ocean. New York and I didn't quite fit. I knew it the whole time. Some of my Columbia classmates came from faraway places like Iowa and Nevada, as I had come a shorter way from New Hampshire, and after graduation they'd been absorbed into Manhattan and had lived there ever since. I didn't last. I always say, "It was never my town."

Today it was all mine. Today I was its proprietor. With my overcoat wide open and the wind in my hair, I walked around and for an hour or so presided over the bits of litter in the air—so much less than thirty years ago!—and the citizens bent against the weather, and the light inside the restaurants, and the people at small tables looking at one another's faces and talking. The white flakes began to stick. By the time I entered Trump Tower, I'd had a long, hard, wet walk. I repaired myself in the restroom and found the right floor. At the ceremony, my table was near the front—round, clothed in burgundy, and surrounded by eight of us; the other seven much younger than I, a lively bunch, fun and full of wisecracks. And they seemed impressed to be sitting with me, and made sure I sat where I could see. All that was the good part.

Halfway through dessert, the nerve in my back began to act up, and by the time I heard my name and started toward the podium my right shoulder blade felt as if it were pressed against a hissing old New York steam-heat radiator. At the head of the vast room, I held the medallion in my hand—that's what it was, rather than a trophy; an inscribed medallion three inches in diameter, good for a paperweight—and thanked a list of names I'd memorized, omitted any other remarks, and got back to my table just as another pain seized me, this one in the region of my bowels, and now I repented my curbside lunch, my delicious New York hot dogs, especially the second one, and, without sitting down or even making an excuse, I let this bout of indigestion carry me out of the room and down the halls to the men's lavatory, where I hardly had time to fumble the medallion into my lapel pocket and get my jacket on the hook.

I'd sat down with my intestines in flames, first my body bearing this insult, and then my soul insulted, too, when someone came in and chose the stall next to mine. Our public toilets are just that—too public; the walls don't reach the floor. This other man and I could see each other's feet. Or, at any rate, our black shoes, and the cuffs of our dark trousers.

After a minute, his hand laid on the floor between us, there at the border between his space and mine, a square of toilet paper with an obscene proposition written on it, in words large and plain enough that I could read them whether I wanted to or not. In pain, I laughed. Not out loud.

I heard a small sigh from the next stall.

By hunching down into my own embrace and staring hard at my feet, I tried to make myself go away. I didn't acknowledge his overture, and he didn't leave. He must have taken it that I had him under consideration. As long as I stayed, he had reason to hope. And I couldn't leave yet. My bowels churned and smoldered. Renegade signals from my spinal nerve hammered my shoulder and the full length of my right arm, down to the marrow.

The awards ceremony seemed to have ended. The men's room came to life—the door whooshing open, the run of voices coming in. Throats and faucets and footfalls. The spin of the paper towel dispenser.

Somewhere in here, a hand descended to the note on the floor, fingers touched it, raised it away. Soon after that the man, the toilet Casanova, was no longer beside me.

I stayed as I was, for how long I couldn't say. There were echoes. Silence. The urinals flushing themselves.

I raised myself upright, pulled my clothing together, made my way to the sinks.

One other man remained in the place. He stood at the sink beside mine as our faucets ran. I washed my hands. He washed his hands.

He was tall, with a distinctive head—wispy colorless hair like a baby's, and a skeletal face with thick red lips. I'd have known him anywhere.

"Carl Zane!"

He smiled in a small way. "Wrong. I'm Marshall Zane. I'm Carl's son."

"Sure, of course—he would have aged, too!" This encounter had me going in circles. I'd finished washing my hands, and now I started washing them again. I forgot to introduce myself. "You look just like your dad," I said. "Only twenty-five years ago. Are you here for the awards night?"

He nodded. "I'm with the Sextant Group."

"You followed in his footsteps."

"I did. I even worked for Castle and Forbes for a couple of years."

"How do you like that? And how's Carl doing? Is he here tonight?"

"He passed away three years ago. Went to sleep one night and never woke up."

"Oh. Oh, no." I had a moment—I have them sometimes—when the surroundings seemed bereft of any facts, and not even the smallest physical gesture felt possible. After the moment had passed, I said, "I'm sorry to hear that. He was a nice guy."

"At least it was painless," the son of Carl Zane said. "And, as far as anyone knows, he went to bed happy that night." We were talking to each other's reflection in the broad mirror. I made sure I didn't look elsewhere—at his trousers, his shoes. But, for this occasion, we men, every one of us, had dressed in dark trousers and black shoes. "Well . . . enjoy your evening," the young man said.

I thanked him and said good night, and, as he tossed a wadded paper towel at the receptacle and disappeared out the door, I'm afraid I added, "Tell your father I said hello."

MERMAID

As I trudged up Fifth Avenue after this miserable interlude, I carried my shoulder like a bushel-bag of burning kindling and could hardly stay upright the three blocks to my hotel. It was really snowing now, and it was Saturday night, the sidewalk was crowded, people came at me, forcing themselves against the weather, their shoulders hunched, their coats pinched shut, flakes battering their faces, and though the faces were dark I felt I saw into their eyes.

I came awake in the unfamiliar room I didn't know how much later, and, if this makes sense, it wasn't the pain in my shoulder that woke me but its departure. The episode had passed. I lay bathed in relief.

Beyond my window, a thick layer of snow covered the ledge. I became aware of a hush of anticipation, a tremendous surrounding absence. I got out of bed, dressed in my clothes, and went out to look at the city.

It was, I think, around one a.m. Snow six inches deep had fallen. Park Avenue looked smooth and soft—not one vehicle had disturbed its surface. The city was almost completely stopped, its very few sounds muffled yet perfectly distinct from one another: a rumbling snowplow somewhere, a car's horn, a man on another street shouting several faint syllables. I tried counting up the years since I'd seen snow. Eleven or twelve—Denver, and it had been exactly the same, exactly like this. One lone taxi glided up Park Avenue through the virgin white, and I hailed it and asked the driver to find any restaurant open for business. I looked out the back window at the brilliant silences falling from the street lamps, and at our fresh black tracks disappearing into the infinite—the only proof of Park Avenue; I'm not sure how the cabbie kept to the road. He took me to a small diner off Union Square, where I had a wonderful breakfast among a handful of miscellaneous wanderers like myself, New Yorkers with their large, historic faces, every one of whom, delivered here without an explanation, seemed invaluable. I paid and left and set out walking back toward midtown. I'd bought a pair of weatherproof dress shoes just before leaving San Diego, and I was glad. I looked for places where I was the first to walk and kicked at the powdery snow. A piano playing a Latin tune drew me through a doorway into an atmosphere of sadness: a dim tavern, a stale smell, the piano's weary melody, and a single customer, an ample, attractive woman with abundant blond hair. She wore an evening gown. A light shawl covered her shoulders. She seemed poised and self-possessed, though it was possible, also, that she was weeping.

I let the door close behind me. The bartender, a small old black man, raised his eyebrows, and I said, "Scotch rocks, Red Label." Talking, I felt discourteous. The piano played in the gloom of the farthest corner. I recognized the melody as a Mexican traditional called "Maria Elena." I couldn't see the musician at all. In front of the piano a big tenor saxophone rested upright on a stand. With no one around to play it, it seemed like just another of the personalities here: the invisible pianist, the disenchanted old bartender, the big glamorous blonde, the shipwrecked, solitary saxophone. And the man who'd walked here through the snow . . . And as soon as the name of the song popped into my head I thought I heard a voice say, "Her name is Maria Elena." The scene had a moonlit, black-and-white quality. Ten feet away, at her table, the blond woman waited, her shoulders back, her face raised. She lifted one hand and beckoned me with her fingers. She was weeping. The lines of her tears sparkled on her cheeks. "I am a prisoner here," she said. I took the chair across from her and watched her cry. I sat upright, one hand on the table's surface and the other around my drink. I felt the ecstasy of a dancer, but I kept still.

WHIT

My name would mean nothing to you, but there's a very good chance you're familiar with my work. Among the many TV ads I wrote and directed, you'll remember one in particular.

In this animated thirty-second spot, you see a brown bear chasing a gray rabbit. They come one after the other over a hill toward the view—the rabbit is cornered, he's crying, the bear comes to him—the rabbit reaches into his waistcoat pocket and pulls out a dollar bill and gives it to the bear. The bear looks at this gift, sits down, stares into space. The music stops, there's no sound, nothing is said, and, right there, the little narrative ends, on a note of complete uncertainty. It's an advertisement for a banking chain. It sounds ridiculous, I know, but that's only if you haven't seen it. If you've seen it, the way it was rendered, then you know that it was a very unusual advertisement. Because it referred, really, to nothing at all, and yet it was actually very moving.

Advertisements don't try to get you to fork over your dough by tugging irrelevantly at your heartstrings, not as a rule. But this one broke the rules, and it worked. It brought the bank many new customers. And it excited a lot of commentary and won several awards—every award I ever won, in fact, I won for that ad. It ran in both halves of the twenty-second Super Bowl, and people still remember it.

You don't get awards personally. They go to the team. To the agency. But your name attaches to the project as a matter of workplace lore—"Whit did that one." (And that would be me, Bill Whitman.) "Yes, the one with the rabbit and the bear was Whit's."

Credit goes first of all to the banking firm who let this strange message go out to potential customers, who sought to start a relationship with a gesture so cryptic. It was better than cryptic—mysterious, untranslatable. I think it pointed to orderly financial exchange as the basis of harmony. Money tames the beast. Money is peace. Money is civilization. The end of the story is money.

I won't·mention the name of the bank. If you don't remember the name, then it wasn't such a good ad after all.

If you watched any prime-time television in the 1980s, you've almost certainly seen several other ads I wrote or directed or both. I crawled out of my twenties leaving behind a couple of short, unhappy marriages, and then I found Elaine. Twenty-five years last June, and two daughters. Have I loved my wife? We've gotten along. We've never felt like congratulating ourselves.

I'm just shy of sixty-three. Elaine's fifty-two but seems older. Not in her looks but in her attitude of complacency. She lacks fire. Seems interested mainly in our two girls. She keeps in close contact with them. They're both grown. They're harmless citizens. They aren't beautiful or clever.

Before the girls started grade school, we left New York and headed west in stages, a year in Denver (too much winter), another in Phoenix (too hot), and finally San Diego. San Diego. What a wonderful city. It's a bit more crowded each year, but still. Completely wonderful. Never regretted coming here, not for an instant. And financially it all worked out. If we'd stayed in New York I'd have made a lot more money, but we'd have needed a lot more, too.

Last night Elaine and I lay in bed watching TV, and I asked her what she remembered. Not much. Less than I. We have a very small TV that sits on a dresser across the room. Keeping it going provides an excuse for lying awake in bed.

I note that I've lived longer in the past, now, than I can expect to live in the future. I have more to remember than I have to look forward to. Memory fades, not much of the past stays, and I wouldn't mind forgetting a lot more of it.

Once in a while, I lie there as the television runs, and I read something wild and ancient from one of several collections of folktales I own. Apples that summon sea maidens, eggs that fulfill any wish, and pears that make people grow long noses that fall off again. Then sometimes I get up and don my robe and go out into our quiet neighborhood looking for a magic thread, a magic sword, a magic horse.

THE COUNTRY

Joy Williams

I attend a meeting called Come and See! The group gathers weekly at the Episcopal church in one of the many, many rooms available there but in the way these things are it's wide open to everyone—atheists, Buddhists, addicts, depressives, everyone. The discussion that evening concerned the old reliable: Why Are We Here? And one woman, Jeanette it was, offered that she never knew what her purpose was until recently. She discovered her purpose was to be there with the dying in their final moments. Right there, in attendance. Strangers for the most part. No one she knew particularly well. She found that she loved this new role. It was wonderful, it was amazing to be present for that moment of transport. It was such an honor being there and she believed she provided reassurance. And she shared with us the story of this one old girl who was actively dying—that was her phrase, *actively dying*—and at one point the old girl looked at Jeanette and said, "Am I still here?" and when she was told yes, yes, she was, the dying woman said, "Darn."

"She was so cute," Jeanette said.

My fellow travelers in Come and See! listened to this with equanimity. Jeanette was as happy as I'd ever seen her— she doesn't come every week—and enthusiastic as she shared with us how positive and comforting it is to witness the final voyage. She's affiliated with the church somehow, she studied chaplaincy services or something, so she has a certain amount of access to these situations; that is, she's not doing this illegally or inappropriately or anything.

I sincerely cannot remember the circumstances that brought me to Come and See! for the first time and why I continue to attend. I seldom speak and never share. I sit erect but with my eyes downcast, focusing on a large paper clip that has rested in a groove between two tiles for months. Surely the chairs must be folded and stacked or rearranged for other functions and the floor swept or mopped on occasion, but the paper clip remains.

Beside me, Harold—he's sixty-three and the father of two-year-old triplets—says, "I believe we are here for the future, to build a better future," blandly cutting off any communal amplification of Jeanette's deathbed theme.

My eyes lowered, I stare at the paper clip. I dislike Harold. Triplets, for god's sakes. One day I will no longer come here and listen to these wretched things.

After Come and See! there is a brief social period when packaged cheese and crackers and cheap wine are provided. There is always difficulty in opening the cheese packets. Someone always manages to spill wine.

Jeanette appears before me. After some consideration, I smile.

She says, "I'm sorry, I've forgotten your name."

"That was my best wintery smile," I say.

"Yes, it was quite good."

I hope she thinks I would be a challenge, an insurmountable challenge.

Poor Pearl limps up. She has multiple sclerosis or something similarly awful and she begins talking about being with a number of her cats over the years as they died and it is not something she would wish on her vilest enemy and how she

never learns from this experience and how it never becomes
beautiful.

I leave the ladies to thrash this one out and exit through
the courtyard, which is being torn up for some reason of
regeneration. Or perhaps they're just going to pave it over
with commemorative bricks. Last year, Easter services were
held in this courtyard because the sanctuary had been van-
dalized. Worshippers arrived for the sunrise service and
found the sound system ripped out, flowers smashed, bal-
loons filled with green paint exploded everywhere. Teenagers
going through an initiation into some gang, probably. Several goats in some fellow's yard were beaten and harassed
that morning as well, the same group being responsible most
likely, although the authorities claim there are no gangs in
our town. No one was ever charged. The church would forgive them, that's the way the church works, but the man who
owns the goats is still upset. Perhaps the poor creatures were
meant to be scapegoats in the biblical sense, cast into the
wilderness of suffering with all the sins of the people upon
their heads.

There is such evil in the world, so much evil. I believe
Jeanette is evil, though maybe she's more like one of those
medically intuitive dogs they're developing or exploiting.
The dogs don't suffer from their knowledge. That is, empathy is beside the point here; they can just detect that illness
is present in a body before, sometimes long before, more
standardized inquiry and tests confirm it. In Jeanette's case,
though some groundwork is undoubtedly required, she's
honing her instinct of arrival, appearing just before another
is about to enter the incomprehensible refuge. She'll be writing a book about her experiences next.

I leave the courtyard and commence my walk home. It's
not particularly pleasant but there is no alternative route,

or, rather, the alternatives are equally dispiriting. Highways are being straightened and widened everywhere, with the attendant uprooted trees and porta-toilets for the workmen.

I navigate my passage across the first monstrous intersection, where a sign announces the imminent arrival of a dessert parlor named Better Than Sex. I would like to move to the country but the boy refuses. Besides, "the country" exists only in our fantasies anymore. When I was a child, the country was where overly exuberant family pets often found themselves. One of our dogs, Tank, who liked to wander and eat clothes and the dirt in flowerpots, was dispatched to the country, where he would have more room to run and play and do his mischief under the purview of a tolerant farmer. When I returned from school that afternoon, Tank was settling into his new home. My parents' explanations and assurances became so elaborate that I knew something terrible was being withheld from me.

Above me, billboards advertise gun shows, mobile-telephone plans and law firms that specialize in drunk-driving cases. I looked into renting a billboard recently but my application was rejected.

> THE GREATEST PROSPERITY COMES TO ITS END,
> DISSOLVING INTO EMPTINESS; THE MIGHTIEST
> EMPIRE IS OVERTAKEN BY STUPOR AMIDST
> THE FLICKER OF ITS FESTIVAL LIGHTS.
> —RABINDRANATH TAGORE

it would have said.

The billboard people told me they didn't know who Rabindranath Tagore was and could not verify anything he might have thought. He was certainly foreign and his sentiments insurrectionary. As well, what he was saying wasn't advertising anything. This night I see that space I tried to claim depicts black-and-white cows painting the words EAT MORE CHIKIN on the side of a barn.

I could far more easily drive to church and spare myself the discomfort of walking through this wasteland but I am in no hurry to reach home. I never know whom I will be coming home to, whether it will be mother, father, wife, or son. Often it is just my son, my boy, and matters are quite as they should be, but since the end of school things have become more volatile. We live alone, you understand, the child and I. He's nine, and the changes in this decade have been unfathomable. Indeed, it's a different civilization now. My parents, with whom we were very close, died last year. My wife left in the spring. She just couldn't feel anything for us anymore, she said, and was only trying to salvage the bit of life she could.

Dusty pickups speed by, gun racks prominent. Gun racks in vehicles have surged in popularity. Even expensive sedans display cradled weapons, visible through lightly tinted windows. People know their names and capabilities like they used to know those of baseball players. Not my boy, though. He doesn't know these things. He knows other things. For example, we planted a few trees in the yard after his mother left, fruit trees, citrus. The tree that bears the fruit is not the tree that was planted. He knows that, it goes without saying.

It's almost dark now as I turn down our street. It's garbage day tomorrow and my neighbors have rolled their vast receptacles to the curb. The bins are as tall as the boy and they contain God knows what, and over and over again.

The door is unlocked, the lights are on. "Hi, Daddy," Colson says. He's in the kitchen making sandwiches for supper. "Daddy," he says, "we have to eat soon because I want to go to bed." I'm not disappointed that he's himself tonight, though more and more, given the situation, that self seems imaginary. He likes to play the Diné prayer songs tape as we eat, particularly the "Happy Birthday, My Dear Child" track. The chants are unintelligible but then the words *Happy Birthday Happy Birthday to You* arise in this morose intonation and he never tires of it.

In the morning my wife is in the yard, cutting back the orange tree. We rush out and prevent her from doing more. Summer is not the time to prune anything of course and we just planted the trees, they haven't even adjusted to being in the soil yet with the freedom of their roots to wander. She dismisses our concerns but flings down the little saw, which I have never seen before, and leaves, though were you to ask if we actually saw her leave we would have to say no. The tree looks terrible and with small cries we gather up the broken buds and little branches. Still, it will survive. It has not been destroyed, we assure each other, at least not this day. There is no question of our planting a replacement. This would not be a useful lesson to learn.

Perhaps she is annoyed because, since her absence, Colson has seldom tried to invoke her except in the broadest terms. That is because, he explains, she is only gone from us, not from the world she still inhabits. I think her arrival this morning was a shock to him and I doubt she will visit us again.

I pick up the curved saw. It looks new but now blond crumbs of wood cling to its shiny serrated teeth.

"Should we keep this?" I ask Colson.

He frowns and shakes his head, then shrugs and returns to the house. He's through with her. I wonder if somehow I have caused this latest unpleasantness. I have never known how to talk about death or the loss of meaning or love. I seek but will never find, I think.

I toss the saw into the closest container at the very moment I hear the trash truck moving imperiously down the street. It's garbage day. Garbage day! The neighborhood prepares for it with joy. Some wish it would arrive more than once a week.

Later I bring up the possibility of moving. We could have an orchard and bike trails and dig a pond for swimming. We could have horses. "You can pick up horses these days for a song," I say.

"A song?" the boy says. "What kind of song?"

But I can't think of any. I gaze at him foolishly.

"Like the Diné prayer songs," he suggests.

"Yes, but we don't even have to pray for horses. We can just get them."

Immediately I realize I have spoken infelicitously, without grace. He doesn't say anything right away but then he says, "You have to be here to prepare for not being here."

The voice is familiar to me because it is my mother's voice, though I find it less familiar than it was. She's been in a grave for over a year now, my father with her. They'd been working at an animal sanctuary in their retirement and were returning home from a long day of caring for a variety of beasts. They had borrowed my car, as they were getting new tires for their own. I had planned to drive them home that night but the arrangement had been altered for some reason. We still don't know exactly what happened. A moment's inattention, possibly.

The sanctuary that was so important to them was controversial, as the animals were not native to this region, though the natives hardly enjoy grateful regard here, being considered either pests or game. It has since closed, the animals removed to what are referred to as other facilities, where some of them can still be visited. In fact, Colson and I went out to visit one of the elephants my father was particularly fond of. There were two in the original preserve—Carol and Lucy—but they were separated, which seemed to me a dreadful decision. We visited Carol, who is an hour closer. She has some disease of the trunk that makes it difficult for her to eat, but someone was obviously still taking care of her. It wasn't a good visit, not at all. We felt bad that we had come. Knowing what we now know would break my parents' hearts, I think, but when Colson talks on their behalf they do not speak of elephants, those extraordinary beings. They do not speak of extraordinary matters. Colson does not bring them back to perform feats of omniscience or magicians' tricks. I don't know why he brings them back. I tried to prevent him at first. I appealed to his reasonableness, though in truth he is not particularly reasonable. I threatened him with psychiatric counseling, hours of irrelevant questioning and quizzes. I told him his performances were futile and cruel. I teased him and even insulted him, saying that if he considered himself gifted or precocious he was sadly mistaken. Nothing availed.

When he enters these phases I become exhausted. Sometimes, I admit, I flee. He doesn't seem to need me to fulfill his conversations with the dead, if indeed they are conversations. They seem more like inhabitations. And they're harmless enough, if disorienting, though this morning's remark disturbs me, perhaps because his mother, my wife, had just made her unnecessary appearance. Really, why would she return only to hack wordlessly at our little tree? It seems so unlikely.

"Sorry?" I say.

"We are here to prepare for not being here," he says in my mother's soft, rather stroke-fuddled voice.

It's as though he is answering the very question posed at Come and See! I took him there once. Sometimes someone brings a child or grandchild, it's not unheard of. He listened

attentively. No one expected him to contribute and everyone found him adorable. "Don't ever take me into that stupid room again," he later instructed me.

He may be right that it is a stupid room and that of all
the great rooms he might or will enter, attentively and with
expectation, it will on conclusion be the stupidest.

I study Colson. My dear boy is skinny and needs a haircut.
He rubs his eyes the way my mother did. Don't rub your eyes
so! we'd all exclaim. But I say nothing.

Colson says, "Then you're in the other here, where the
funny thing is no one realizes you've arrived."

He sits down heavily at the kitchen table. "Would you like
a cup of tea?" I ask.

"That would be nice," he says in my mother's voice of
wonderment.

But I can't find the tea. We haven't had tea in the house
since they died. We'd keep it on hand just for them when
they visited.

"I'll go out and get some right now," I say.

But he says not to bother. He says, "Just sit with me, talk
with me."

I sit opposite my boy. I notice that the clock on the stove
reads 9:47 and the stovetop is dusty, as though no one has
cooked on it for a long time. I vow that I will cook a hot,
nourishing, and comforting dinner tonight. And I do, and we
talk quietly then as well, though nothing of import is being
decided or even said.

I find it easier to be with my father when Colson brings
him. Though he always seemed rather inscrutable to me he
now doesn't sadden me so. He would not accept an offer of
tea that he suspected was unlikely to be provided. He was
able to confer with the animals in a way my mother couldn't,
and felt that great advances would soon be made in appreciat-

ing and comprehending animal consciousness, though these advancements would coincide with the dramatic world-wide decline of our nonhuman brothers and sisters. Once, I'm ashamed to say, I maudlinly brought up the Tank of my childhood, and my father said he had been shot by a sheriff's deputy who thought he was a stray, and that the man had also shot a woman's horse in winter, making the same claim, and that he had been reprimanded but neither fined nor fired. Yes. And that they had lied to me, my mother and father. It was Colson who told me this in my father's voice, Colson, who had never known Tank or felt his "happy fur," as I called it as a child. Bad, happy Tank. He ate his dinner from my mother's Bundt pan. It slowed him down some, having to work around the pan. He always ate his food too fast.

But this was the only time a disclosure occurred, and I am more cautious now in conversation. I find I want neither the past nor the future illuminated. But my discomfort is growing that my boy will find access to other people, people we do not know, like the woman the next town over who died in a fire of her own setting, or even one of Jeanette's unfortunate customers. That I will come home one evening and that Colson will not be himself but a stranger whose death means little to me and that even so we will talk quietly and inconsequentially and with puzzled desperation.

The week passes. Colson has a tutor in mathematics for the summer who is oblivious to the situation and I have the office I'm obliged to occupy. Colson wants to be an engineer or an architect but he has difficulty with concepts of scale and measurability. The tutor claims he's progressing nicely but Colson never talks about these hours, only stubbornly reiterating his desire to create soaring nonutilitarian spaces.

At the end of the week I return to Come and See! My

passage through the construction zone is much the same. I suppose change will appear to come all at once. Suddenly there will be a smooth six-lane road with additional turning lanes and sidewalks with high baffle walls concealing a remaining landscape soon to be converted to housing. The walls will be decorated with abstract designs or sometimes the stylized images of birds. I've seen it before. Everyone's seen it before.

Jeanette is the only one there. I feel immediately uncomfortable and settle quickly into my customary chair. There is the paper clip, as annoying and meaningless a presence as ever.

"There's a flu going around," she says.

"The flu?" I say. "Everyone has the flu?"

"Or they're afraid of contracting the flu," she says. "The hospital is even restricting visitors. You haven't heard about the flu?"

"Only in the most general terms," I say. "I didn't think there was an epidemic."

"Pandemic, possibly a pandemic. We should all be in our homes, trying not to panic."

We wait but no one shows up. There's a large window in the room that looks out over the parking lot, but the lot is empty and continues to be empty. The sky is doing that strange thing it does, brightening fiercely before dark.

"Why don't we begin anyway?" she says. "'For where two are gathered in my name . . .' and so on. Or is it three?"

"Why would it be three?" I say. "I don't think it's three."

"You're right," she says.

She has a round pale face and small hands. Nothing about her is attractive, though she is agreeable, certainly, or trying to be.

"I'm not dying," I say. God only knows what possessed me.

"Of course not!" she exclaims, her round face growing pink. "Goodness!"

But then she says, "On Wednesday, Wednesday I think it was, it was certainly not Thursday, I was in this woman's room where the smell of flowers was overwhelming. You could hardly breathe and I knew her friends meant well, but I offered to remove the arrangements, there were more than a dozen of them, I'm surprised there wasn't some policy restricting their number, and she said, 'I'm not dying,' and then she died."

"You never know," I say.

"I hope they let me back soon."

"Why wouldn't they?"

"Thank you," she says quietly.

"I meant to say why would they?"

She stands up but then sits down again. "No," she says, "I'm not leaving."

"It's disgusting what you're doing, you're like the thief's accomplice," I say. "No one can be certain about these things."

Suddenly she appears not nervous or accommodating in the least.

We do not speak further, just sit there staring at each other until the sexton arrives and insists it's time to lock the place up.

At home, Colson is watching a television special on our dying oceans.

"Please turn that off," I say.

"Grandma wanted to watch it."

He has made popcorn and poured it into a large blue bowl that is utterly unfamiliar to me. It's a beautiful bowl of popcorn.

"You have another bowl like that?" I ask. "I want to make myself a drink."

He laughs like my wife might have when she still loved me, but then returns to watching the television.

"This is tragic," he says. "Can anything be done?"

"So much can be done," I say. "But everything would have to be different."

"Well," he sighs, "now Grandma and Poppa know. She wanted to watch it."

"Have you heard anything about a flu," I ask. "Does anyone you know have the flu?"

"Grandma died of the flu."

"No. They died in a car accident. You know that."

"Sometimes they get mixed up," he says.

Colson's the age I was when I was told about the country. Ten years later I'd be married. I married too young and unwisely, for sure.

"Do they sometimes tell you stories you don't believe?"

"Daddy," he says with no inflection, so I don't know what he means.

We finish the popcorn. He did a good job. Every kernel was popped. I take the bowl to the sink and rinse it out carefully, then I take a clean dish towel from a drawer and dry it. It really is an extraordinarily lovely bowl. I don't know where to put it because I don't know where it came from.

A few days later my father is back. He was a handsome man with handsome thick gray hair.

"Son," he says, "I don't know what to tell you."

"It's all right," I say.

"No, it's not all right. I wish I knew what to tell you."

"Colson, honey," I say. "Stop."

"That's no way to have an understanding," he says. "Your mother and I just wish it were otherwise."

"Me too," I say.

"We wish we could help but there's so much they haven't figured out. You'd think by now, but they haven't."

"Who's they," I ask reluctantly.

But Colson doesn't seem to have heard me. He runs his fingers through his shaggy hair, which looks damp and hot. My boy has always run hot. I wonder if he's bathing and brushing his teeth. My poor boy, I think, my poor dear boy. Someone should remind him.

The following afternoon when Colson is with his tutor, who, I think, is deceiving both of us, though to all appearances he is a forthright and sincere young man, I drive almost one hundred miles to see Lucy, the other elephant. She is being sponsored by two brothers who maintain the county's grave-yards, some sort of perpetual care operation, though to be responsible for an elephant is quite another matter, I would think. The brothers are extremely private and shun publicity. It was only after great effort that I learned anything about them at all or the actual whereabouts of Lucy. Someone—though neither of the brothers, a friend of the brothers is how I imagine him—agreed to show me around the grounds that she now occupies, but I find that once I reach the gate I cannot continue.

I turn back, ashamed, and more estranged from my situation than ever.

When I return home the tutor has left and Colson is put-ting his drawings in order, cataloging them by some method unknown to me. When my mother and father were taken from us so abruptly I knew that Colson was terribly bereaved. Still, he did not want my father's safari hat or his water-bottle holster. He did not want his watch or his magnetic travel backgammon. Nor did he want my mother's collection of ink pens, which I suggested would be ideal for his drawings. He wanted no mementos. Instead he went directly to communi-cation channels that are impossible to establish.

"Where were you, Daddy," Colson asks.

"Why, at work," I say quickly.

Surely I am back at my usual time. I seldom lie, indeed I cannot even remember the circumstances of my last falsehood. Why would he ask such a question? I kiss him and go into the kitchen to make myself a drink but then remember that I have stopped drinking.

"A lady came by today but I told her I didn't know where you were."

"What did she look like?" I ask, and of course he describes Jeanette to a T.

I am so weary I can hardly lift my hand to my head. I must make dinner for us but I think the simplest omelet is beyond my capabilities now. I suggest that we go out but he says he has already eaten with the tutor. They had tacos made and sold from a truck painted with flowers and sat at a picnic table chained to a linden tree. I have no idea what he's talking about. My rage at Jeanette is almost blinding and I gaze at him without seeing as he orders and then reorders his papers, some of which seem to be marked with only a single line. I feel staggeringly innocent. That is the unlikely word that comes to me. Colson puts away his papers and smiles, a smile so radiant that I close my eyes without at all wanting to, and then rather gently somehow it is day again and I am striding through the bustling wasteland to Come and See! The reflection concerns Gregory of Nyssa. He is a popular subject but I am forever having difficulty in recalling what I already know about him. Something about the Really Real and its ultimate importance to us, though the Really Real is inaccessible to our understanding. Food for thought indeed, and over and over again.

When the meeting concludes and we are dismissed I practically hurl myself on Jeanette, who has uncharacteristically contributed nothing to the conversation this night.

"Don't ever come to my house again," I say.

"Was I really there, then? I thought I had the wrong place. Was that your son? A fine little boy. He can certainly keep a secret, can't he."

"I'll call the police," I say.

"Goodness," she laughs. "The police."

It sounds absurd, I have to agree.

"I was concerned about you," she says. "You haven't been here for a while. You've been avoiding us."

"Don't ever again . . ." I say.

"A delightful little boy," she continues. "But you mustn't burden him with secrets."

". . . to my house." I couldn't be more insistent.

"Actually," she says, "no one would fault you if you stopped attending. How many times must we endure someone making a hash of Gregory of Nyssa? People are so tenacious when they should be free. Free!"

I begin to speak but find I have no need to speak. The room is more familiar to me than I would care to admit. Who was it whose last breath didn't bring him home?

Or am I the first?

A HAPPY RURAL SEAT
OF VARIOUS VIEW:
LUCINDA'S GARDEN

Christine Schutt

They met Gordon Brisk on a Friday the thirteenth at the Clam Box in Brooklin. They pooh-poohed the ominous signs. The milky stew they ate was cold—so what? They were happy. They were at sea; they were at the mess, corkskinned roughs in rummy spirits, dumb, loud, happy. And they really didn't have so much to say to each other. They were only a few months married and agreed on everything, and for the moment nearly everything they did—where and how they lived—was cheap or free. They expected gifts at every turn and got them.

So it was at the Clam Box on a Friday night—lime pits along the rim of the glass, Pie feeling puckered—when Gordon Brisk introduced himself as a friend of Aunt Lucinda's from a long time ago. Nick said he had seen Gordon's paintings, of course. And Gordon said, "Am I supposed to be surprised?"

Gordon told a story that included Aunt Lucinda when she was their age, young. There were matches in it and another young woman who almost died. Aunt Lucinda in the story was the same—all love, love, love and this time for Gordon—

and as for Gordon himself? He held up his hands. His hands
had been on fire. He said, "Just look at these fuckers," and
they did. They looked and looked. The hands should have
scared them, but they were drunk and sunburned and happy.
They were glad, they insisted, glad to have met him. "Our
first famous person," Pie said after the after-dinner drinks
when she and Nick were in the Crosley driving home. Pie
was driving, too fast; she was saying how she loved those
amber-colored, over-sweet drinks, the ones floated with an
orange slice and a cherry. She had had too many, so was it
any surprise she hit something? She hit what they thought
was a raccoon. It was definitely something large and dark,
but fatally hesitant. Pie was driving the Crosley, a gardener's
mini-car, which had no business on a public road, but Pie had
wanted to drive it. The Crosley was a toy, yet whatever Pie
hit hobbled into the woods, dragging its broken parts.

Home again and in their beds, Pie and Nick took aspirin
and turned away from each other and slept. Next morning—
frictive love—and then as usual in the garden, Aunt Lucinda's
garden, the famous one, a spilling-over, often photographed,
sea-coast garden. The garden was how they lived for free. They
were the caretakers in an estate called the Cottage. Some
cottage! Why would Aunt Lucinda leave this paradise they
asked, but she had told them. His name was Bruno and his
wealth exceeded hers. The villa he owned in Tuscany was
staffed. "Everything here is arranged for my pleasure," so
Aunt Lucinda said.

Gordon had said, "Scant pleasure." He had said, "I'll tell
you pleasure. The killing kind." And then to most everyone
at the Clam Box bar, he described his wife: shoe-black hair
and pointy parts. That cunt was the source of the fire, or so
he had said at the Clam Box. "I was fucking around" was
what Gordon had said, "but who wouldn't?"

They were untested, Pie and Nick. They were newly everything; and now here they were caretakers for a summer before the rest of life began, and on this morning, as on so many mornings, the cloudless sky grew blue, then bluer. White chips of birds passed fast overhead, and the water was bright; they looked too long at its ceaseless signals and at noon they zombied to it. They let the water assault them until, cold and helpless, they let the waves knock them back to shore and up the beach. Sand caught in all the cracked places, and it felt good to take off their suits and finger it out. They lay directly on the sand; they dozed, they woke, they brushed themselves off. They wanted nothing. They were dry and their suits were dry and, for a moment, warm against them, and they walked to the shore; Nick and Pie walked along the shore and then into the water and they knew the water all over again. So went the afternoon in light—no clouds—whereas indoors was dark. It was dark, but they ran through the mud room toward the phone. They ran, and then they missed it. Who cared? They had the late afternoon before them. They tended the garden. Nick and Pie, they watered the deep beds; they flourished arcs; they beaded hooded plants and cupped plants and frangible rues. They washed paths. The wet rock walls turned into gems. What a place this was! How could Aunt Lucinda's Bruno match it? Of course, the sunsets could be overlong if all they did was watch them, but they were distracted. The hot showers felt coarse against their sunburned skin and the lotion was cold. They put on pastel colors and saw their eyes in the mirror—another blue! Another summer dusk, stunned by the sun's garish setting, they stood close to the grill and the radio's news. They were in love and could listen, horrified but untouched, to whatever the newscaster had to say. But the flamboyant infanticide accomplished with duct tape was too much. Just north of them it had happened in the next and poorest county.

"Turn that off!" Nick said, and Pie did.

For them, nothing more serious than the dark they finally sat in with plates on their laps and at their feet melted drinks that looked dirty.

"Death: will it be sudden and will we be smiling? Will we know ourselves and the life we have lived?"

"Don't even think such things!"

But Pie did, and Nick did, too. He said, "Think of something else," and Pie came up with Gordon.

Gordon at the Clam Box. His high color and his scribbled hair. The way he startled whenever they had swayed closer. Was he afraid he might be touched? But there were all those women. An actress they had heard of. A lot of other men's wives. Aunt Lucinda. "A beauty," was what he said of her. Cornelia Shelbey had been a girlfriend, too, until the Count swooped down. A prick, the Count. Cornelia Shelbey was a cunt.

"What are we?" they had asked.

"Conceited!"

Nevertheless, Gordon called them. The picnic was his idea. Midmorning and already hot, the coast, a scoured metal, stung their eyes. Even as they drove against the wind, they felt the heat. There was no shade for a picnic. The tablecloth, cornered with rocks, blew away. The champagne was wavy. The food they ate was salty or dry; no tastes to speak of. Nick wanted peanut butter and jelly on pink, damp bread. Instead here were cresses and colored crisps. Then the champagne began. Pie swallowed too much of an egg too fast and it hurt her throat. Gordon said of Aunt Lucinda's Bruno, "The man's a fool. He knows nothing about art, but he lets people play with his money." Gordon picked at the knees of his loose khaki pants and what he found he flicked away in the sea grass. He asked, "How do you play with yours?"

They told him just how little they had.

"Too bad!" he said. "Poor you."

Pie washed her sticky hands in the cooler's melting ice. Gordon yawned. Then they all three pushed the picnic back into the basket, didn't bother to fold, drove home. A storm the next day; the power thunked out. Nick and Pie still had a headache from the picnic—too much champagne and whatever they had drunk after—so they took more aspirin. They napped; they looked at the sky; they shared a joint, and they knocked around in bed and felt rubbed and eased when they were finished. It was quiet in the Cottage except for the sound of the rain. They talked about money until they made themselves thirsty. Downstairs on the porch they saw Gordon in the garden under the tent of a golf umbrella. Gordon said he'd walked all the way from the village to them, walked in the rain to get sober. "Last night," he said sadly. He shut the umbrella and sat on the porch with his head in his ruined hands. So they lit the fat joint rolled against the threat of all-day rain, and Gordon was glad of it. "Yes," he said, and inhaled deeply and exhaled in a noisy way, seeming satisfied, which was how they felt, too. Forgotten were the woozy picnic and the problems of money. After all Nick and Pie were a handsome couple, young and loved. Aunt Lucinda was rich even if they weren't. Hundreds of people had come to their wedding, and now they were caretakers to a scenic estate called the Cottage. The Cottage on Morgan Bay. For them the sky cleared and the sun came out and the garden began to sizzle. Gordon stayed on. He watched the happy couple, swatted by the waves: how they exhausted themselves until he was exhausted, too, and he slept. They all slept. They slept through the white hours of afternoon when the light was less complex. When they woke, the sand was peachy colored, and the sky was pretty. Gordon said he wanted to do something, but what? Why didn't they have any money! They had the Crosley. "Fun," Pie said. "Some fun," Nick said. "You killed some kind of animal in that toy."

Pie said, "I could bike to Gary's and see if he has any clams. We could have a clambake."

"Down here? After five? It's damp and cold and there's not as much beach."

"You come up with something why don't you."

"The lotion's hot. It can't feel good," Gordon said, but Pie said he was wrong.

"I'm so sunburned anything against my skin feels cool," she said.

Gordon wiped his hands on her breasts. He said, "Lovely." He said, "Maybe you'll think of something to do. I'll call you."

A line they had heard before—had used themselves. I'll call you augured disappointment.

Nick's handsome face was crinkled. "What the fuck?" he said.

"What's this?" Pie asked.

"You're more ambitious" was what Nick finally said.

A cup of soup was dinner; the radio, left off.

"Find some music," Pie said, and left Nick to wander through the Cottage. She swiped at Aunt Lucinda's clothes until she found it: Valentino tap pants, and she tapped downstairs to nobody's music but her quavery own.

"The best you could do?" Pie asked.

"Look at you," he said.

On the beach, they agreed, their daydreaming was sometimes dangerous. The memory of Gordon's misanthropic breath against their faces came in gusts.

"Jesus," Pie said, remembering.

"What?"

The hollows of her body, especially at her hips, were exciting to them both, and they smiled to see the sand running out of Nick's hand and into the ditched place between her hips.

"Jesus," Pie said.

"I was thinking I would lick."

Back to the garden, to the doused and swabbed, every morning, afternoon. Nick staked the droopers and Pie cut back. The heavy-headed mock orange, now past, Pie hacked at and hacked until the shorn shrub looked embarrassed.

"Poor thing," Nick said.

And Pie laughed. "I've turned the grandpa of the front walk into a kid." Pie, a long girl, wobbly in heeled shoes, bow-legged, shifty—bored, perhaps—but friendly, quick to laugh, on any errand making an impression. Nick left her on the village green the next afternoon, a lean girl in a ruffled bib. What was she wearing exactly? Something skimpy, faded, pink. She wore braids (again) or that was how Nick remembered her when he described Elizabeth Lathem Day—Pie was her father's invention. A girl, a pretty speck, a part of summer and passing through it. She was. Pie was a white blonde, a blonde everywhere—it made Nick hard to think of her. She had close blond fur between her legs. He liked to comb it with his fingers, pull a little bit. Fuck.

"Where the hell is she?" Nick couldn't help himself.

Lucinda said there was no family precedent; no one was mad that she knew of.

"Don't think we weren't getting along. Quite the opposite."

Dogs snuffed in the woods off leashes. Heavy yellow and black dogs, their rheumy eyes mournful; their hard tails

always looked wet and swapped against the shrubs. Once
the dogs barked; Nick heard though they were out of sight.
Something they had found dead and offensive—not her, not
Pie—thank God! Although after the dogs, the reports, the
calls, the case grew fainter. Also, also Nick was drinking. He
was forgetting he had this job. He found himself standing in
front of open broom closets and cabinets, in front of the dishwasher and sinks. Sometimes his hands were wet.

Watering; he finished watering the wilted patches, then
sat on the porch and worried his roughed-up hands, cut and
dirty and uncared for, ugly as roots and clumsy. Hard even
to phone, to push the buttons accurately, but he did and to
his surprise Gordon Brisk answered, and said, "I'm only just
home but I've heard. I'm sorry."

And that was that.

What was this guy all about was what Nick wanted to
know.

"Tell me," Nick said to Lucinda. Addresses, historic dis-
tricts, the watch he wore, his antique truck, Gordon's conversation was an orange pricked with cloves—an aromatic
keepsake of Episcopal Christmases; so it came as a surprise
when she said he was a Jew. A Jew?

"You've not seen a lot of the world, Nick."

True, he hadn't. He had married young.

But Nick did not want to travel: he wanted to stay at the
Cottage at least until spring, maybe through another summer. Who knew? Pie might come back. Why would Gordon
say more? Nick and Pie hadn't seen him since—when? That
hot, flashy day Brisk discovered they only looked rich; they
had money enough to get by. But how much was that? How
much did it cost to get by pleasantly? They were young,
newly married. The most expensive things they bought were
medicinal, recreational.

"You have no idea how happy we have been here," Nick said. This was the truth uttered later, after whatever had passed for dinner, after the bath that made him sweat, the third or fourth Scotch. "We were really, really happy."

The mothers and fathers—on both sides—made visits. They remarked on the garden and the ocean; they said no one would leave such a place voluntarily. So Nick stayed on at the Cottage. He watched the seasons redden then blue then brittle and brown the plants. The decline could be beautiful, but Nick's hands, ungloved, grew grotesque. A fungus buckled and yellowed his thumbnail. His hands, all rose-nicks and dirt, reminded him of Gordon's hands. Gordon talking about something to do with love, saying they had no idea, speaking in his seer voice, the old, pocked, vacant voice, prophesying horrors they could not imagine.

Not us, Pie thought and Nick thought, too; weren't they always harmonious after Gordon left? They said, "We're lucky." Together: "We are."

"You have no idea," Gordon had said another day on the beach. He had said to Nick, "Someday your mouth will bleed in your sleep, and her cunt, too, will stain whatever it touches."

"Love?"

Gordon in the buff on the beach that time, pulling at the bunched part between his legs, lifting up a purse of excitable skin. The black-haired, peaky creature called his wife had been a cunt. Gordon had said, "I was on my way home when I saw the smoke. Up in smoke! My wife and some of my paintings." Gordon had asked, "You know what I tried to save, don't you?"

Nick had suspected it was not his wife.

But what was Nick doing to find his?

Why was it Gordon that Nick thought so much about

when Gordon had shut up his house and gone somewhere south, southwest?

Oh, the summer! The summer felt next door despite the cold. Nick talked to anybody. He shut the place up. He was there after last call, at the bar, saying his good-byes at the Clam Box, already shivering yet still polite. Likable boy.

It was a dry cold, a snowless night, and Nick, so exposed in the Crosley, hurt driving into it. The starless sky was friendly, and the moon, if there was one, was wide.

HAMMER AND SICKLE

Don DeLillo

We walked across the highway bridge, thirty-nine of us in jumpsuits and tennis sneakers, with guards front and back and at the flanks, six in all. Beneath us the cars were blasting by, nonstop, their speed magnified by our near vantage and by the sound they made passing under the low bridge. There's no word for it, that sound, pure urgency, sustained, incessant, northbound, southbound, and each time we walked across the overpass I wondered again who those people were, the drivers and passengers, so many cars, the pressing nature of their passage, the lives inside.

I had time to notice such things, time to reflect. It's a killing business, reflection, even in the lowest levels of security, where there are distractions, openings into the former world. The inmate soccer game at the abandoned high school field across the highway was a breezy departure from the daily binding and squeezing of meal lines, head counts, regulations, reflections. The players rode a bus, the spectators walked, the cars zoomed beneath the bridge.

I walked alongside a man named Sylvan Telfair, tall, bald, steeped in pathos, an international banker who'd dealt in rarefied instruments of offshore finance.

"You follow soccer?"

"I don't follow anything," he said.

"But it's worth watching under the circumstances, right? Which is exactly how I feel."

"I follow nothing," he said.

"My name's Jerold."

"Very good," he said.

The camp was not enclosed by stone walls or coiled razor wire. The only perimeter fencing was a scenic artifact now, a set of old wooden posts that supported sagging rails. There were four dormitories with bunk-bed cubicles, toilets and showers. There were several structures to accommodate inmate orientation, meals, medical care, TV viewing, gym work, visits from family and others. There were conjugal hours for those so yoked.

"You can call me Jerry," I said.

I knew that Sylvan Telfair had been denied a special detention suite with audiovisual systems, private bath, smoking privileges and a toaster oven. There were only four of these in the camp and the man seemed, in bearing alone, in his emotional distance and discreet pain, to be entitled to special consideration. Stuck in the dorms, I thought. This must have seemed a life sentence wedged into the nine years he'd brought with him from Switzerland or Liechtenstein or the Cayman Islands.

I wanted to know something about the man's methodology, the arc of his crimes, but I was reluctant to ask and he was certain not to answer. I'd been here only two months and was still trying to figure out who I wanted to be in this setting, how I ought to stand, sit, walk, talk. Sylvan Telfair knew who he was. He was a long-striding man in a well-pressed jumpsuit and spotless white sneakers, laces knotted oddly behind the ankles, a man formally absent from his slightest word or gesture.

The traffic noise was a ripple at the treetops by the time we reached the edge of the camp complex.

......

When I was in my early teens I came across the word *phantasm*. A great word, I thought, and I wanted to be phantasmal, someone who slips in and out of physical reality. Now here I am, a floating fever dream, but where's the rest of it, the dense surround, the thing with weight and heft? There's a man here who aspires to be a biblical scholar. His head is bent severely to one side, nearly resting on his left shoulder, the result of an unnamed affliction. I admire the man, I'd like to talk to him, tilting my head slightly, feeling secure in the depths of his scholarship, the languages, cultures, documents, rituals. And the head itself, is there anything here more real than this?

There's another man who runs everywhere, the Dumb Runner he's called, but he's doing something obsessive and true, outside the margins of our daily protocols. He has a heartbeat, a racing pulse. And then the gamblers, men betting surreptitiously on football, engaged all week in the crosstalk of point spreads, bunk to bunk, meal to meal, Eagles minus four, Rams getting eight and a half. Is this virtual money they're betting? Stand near them when they talk and it's real, touchable, and so are they, gesturing operatically, numbers flashing neon in the air.

We watched TV in one of the common rooms. There was a large flat screen, wall-mounted, certain channels blocked, programs selected by one of the veteran inmates, a different man each month. On this day only five places were occupied in the eighty or so folding chairs in the arched rows. I was here to see a particular program, an afternoon news broadcast, fifteen minutes, on a children's channel. One segment was a stock market report. Two girls, earnestly amateurish, reported on the day's market activity.

I was the only one watching the show. The other inmates sat half dazed, heads down. It was a matter of time of day, time of year, dusk nearly upon us, the depressive specter of last light stirring at the oblong windows high on one wall. The men sat distanced from each other, here to be alone. This was the call to self-examination, the second-guessing of a lost life, no less compelling than the believer's call to prayer.

I watched and listened. The girls were my daughters, Laurie and Kate, ten and twelve. Their mother had told me, curtly, over the phone, that the kids had been selected to appear on such a program. No details available, she said, at the present time, as if she were reporting, herself, from a desk in a studio humming with off-camera tensions.

I sat in the second row, alone, and there they were, sharing a table, speaking about fourth-quarter estimates, first one girl, then the other, a couple of sentences at a time, credit quality, credit demand, the tech sector, the budget deficit. The picture had the quality of online video, user-generated. I tried to detach myself, to see the girls as distant references to my daughters, in jittery black and white. I studied them. I observed. They read their lines from pages held in their hands, each looking up from the page as she yielded to the other reader.

Did it seem crazy, a market report for kids? There was nothing sweet or charming about the commentary. The girls were not playing at being adult. They were dutiful, blending occasional definitions and explanations into the news, and then Laurie's eyes showed fleeting panic in her remarks about the Nasdaq Composite—a mangled word, a missing sentence. I took the report to be a tentative segment of a barely noticed show on an obscure cable channel. It wasn't any crazier, probably, than most TV, and anyway who was watching?

My bunkmate wore socks to bed. He tucked his pajama legs into the socks and lay on his bunk, knees up and hands folded behind his head.

"I miss my walls," he said.

He had the lower bunk. This was a matter of some significance in the camp, top or bottom, who gets what, like every prison movie we'd ever seen. Norman was senior to me in age, experience, ego and time served and I had no reason to complain.

I thought of telling him that we all miss our walls, we miss our floors and ceilings. But I sat and waited for him to continue.

"I used to sit and look. One wall, then another. After a while I'd get up and walk around the apartment, slowly, looking, wall to wall. Sit and look, stand and look."

He seemed to be under a spell, reciting a bedtime story he'd heard as a child.

"You collected art, is that it?"

"That's it, past tense, collected. Major museum quality."

"You've never mentioned this," I said.

"I've been here how long? They're somebody else's walls now. The art is scattered."

"You had advisers, experts on the art market."

"People used to come and look at my walls. Europe, Los Angeles, a Japanese man from some foundation in Japan."

He sat quietly for a time, remembering. I found myself remembering with him. The Japanese man took on facial features, a certain size and shape, portly, it seemed, pale suit, dark tie.

"Collectors, curators, students. They came and looked," he said.

"Who advised you?"

"I had a woman on Fifty-seventh Street. There was a guy in London, Colin, knew everything about the Postimpressionists. A dear sweet man."

"You don't really mean that."

"It's something people say. One of those expressions that sound like someone else is talking. A dear sweet man."

"A loving wife and mother."

"I was happy to have them look. All of them," he said. "I used to look with them. We'd go picture to picture, room to room. I had a house in the Hudson Valley, more paintings, some sculpture. I went there in the autumn for the fall colors. But I barely looked out the windows."

"You had the walls."

"I couldn't take my eyes off the walls."

"And then you had to sell."

"All of it, every last piece. Pay fines, pay debts, pay legal fees, provide for family. Gave an etching to my daughter. A snowy night in Norway."

Norman missed his walls but he was not unhappy here. He was content, he said, unstuck, unbound, remote. He was free of the swollen needs and demands of others but mostly disentangled from his personal drives, his grabbiness, the life-long mandate to accrue, expand, construct himself, to buy a hotel chain, make a name. He was at peace here, he said.

I lay on the top bunk, eyes closed, listening. Throughout the building men in their cubicles, one talking, one listening, both silent, one sleeping, tax delinquents, alimony delinquents, insider traders, perjurers, hedge-fund felons, mail fraud, mortgage fraud, securities fraud, accounting fraud, obstruction of justice.

......

Word began to spread. By the third day most of the chairs in the common room were occupied and I had to settle for a place near the end of the fifth row. On screen the girls were reporting on a situation rapidly developing in the Arab Emirates.

"The word is Dubai."

"This is the word crossing continents and oceans at the shocking speed of light."

"Markets are sinking quickly."

"Paris, Frankfurt, London."

"Dubai has the worst debt per capita in the world," Kate said. "And now its building boom has crumbled and it can't pay the banks what it owes them."

"It owes them fifty-eight billion dollars," Laurie said.

"Give or take a few billion."

"The DAX index in Germany."

"Down more than three percent."

"The Royal Bank of Scotland."

"Down more than four percent."

"The word is Dubai."

"This debt-ridden city-state is asking banks to grant six months' freedom from debt repayments."

"Dubai," Laurie said.

"The cost of insuring Dubai's debt against default has increased one, two, three, four times."

"Do we know what that means?"

"It means the Dow Jones Industrial Average is down, down, down."

"Deutsche Bank."

"Down."

"London—the FTSE One Hundred Index."

"Down."

"Amsterdam—ING Group."

"Down."

"The Hang Seng in Hong Kong."

"Crude oil. Islamic bonds."

"Down, down, down."

"The word is Dubai."

"Say it."

"Dubai," Kate said.

The old life rewrites itself every minute. In four years I'll still be here, puddling horribly in this dim waste. The free future is hard to imagine. I have trouble enough tracing the shape of the knowable past. This is no steadfast element, no faith or truth except for the girls, being born, getting bigger, living.

Where was I when this was happening? I was acquiring meaningless degrees, teaching a freshman course in the dynamics of reality TV. I changed the spelling of my first name to Jerold. I used my index and middle fingers to place quote marks around certain ironic comments I made and sometimes used index fingers only, setting off a quotation within another quotation. It was that kind of life, self-mocking, and neither the marriage nor the business I briefly ran seems to have happened in any fixed consideration. I'm thirty-nine years old, a generation removed from some of the inmates here, and I don't remember knowing why I did what I did to put myself in this place. There was a time in early English law when a felony was punishable by removal of one of the felon's body parts. Would this be an incentive to modern memory?

I imagine myself being here forever, it's already forever, eating another meal with the political consultant who licks

his thumb to pick bread crumbs off the plate and stare at
them, or standing in line behind the investment banker who
talks to himself aloud in beginner's Mandarin. I think about
money. What did I know about it, how much did I need it,
what would I do when I got it? Then I think about Sylvan
Telfair, aloof in his craving, the billion-euro profit being sepa-
rable from the things it bought, money the coded impulse,
ideational, a kind of discreet erection known only to the man
whose pants are on fire.

"The fear continues to grow."

"Fear of numbers, fear of spreading losses."

"The fear is Dubai. The talk is Dubai. Dubai has the debt.
Is it fifty-eight billion dollars or eighty billion dollars?"

"Bankers are pacing marble floors."

"Or is it one hundred and twenty billion dollars?"

"Sheiks are gazing into hazy skies."

"Even the numbers are panicking."

"Think of the prominent investors. Hollywood stars.
Famous footballers."

"Think of islands shaped like palm trees. People skiing in
a shopping mall."

"The world's only seven-star hotel."

"The world's richest horse race."

"The world's tallest building."

"All this in Dubai."

"Taller than the Empire State Building and the Chrysler
Building combined."

"Combined."

"Swim in the pool on the seventy-sixth floor. Pray in the
mosque on the one hundred and fifty-eighth floor."

"But where is the oil?"

"Dubai has no oil. Dubai has debt. Dubai has a huge number of foreign workers with nowhere to work."

"Enormous office buildings stand empty. Apartment buildings unfinished in blowing sand. Think of the blowing sand. Dust storms concealing the landscape. Empty storefronts in every direction."

"But where is the oil?"

"The oil is in Abu Dhabi. Say the name."

"Abu Dhabi."

"Now let's say it together."

"Abu Dhabi," they said.

It was Feliks Zuber, the oldest inmate at the camp, who'd chosen the children's program for viewing. Feliks was here every day now, front row center, carrying with him a sentence of seven hundred and twenty years. He liked to turn and nod at those nearby, making occasional applause gestures without bringing his trembling hands into contact, a small crumpled man, looking nearly old enough to be on the verge of outliving his sentence, tinted glasses, purple jumpsuit, hair dyed death black.

The length of his sentence impressed the rest of us. It was a term handed down for his master manipulation of an investment scheme involving four countries and leading to the collapse of two governments and three corporations, with much of the money channeled in the direction of arms shipments to rebels in a breakaway enclave of the Caucasus.

The breadth of his crimes warranted a far more stringent environment than this one but he'd been sent here because he was riddled with disease, his future marked in weeks and days. Men were sometimes sent here to die, in easeful circumstances. We knew it from their faces, mainly, the attenuated range of vision, the sensory withdrawal, and from the stillness they brought with them, a cloistered manner, as if bound by vows. Feliks was not still. He smiled, waved, bounced and shook. He sat on the edge of his chair when the girls delivered news of falling markets and stunned economies. He was a man watching an ancient truism unfold on wide-screen TV. He would take the world with him when he died.

The soccer field was part of a haunted campus. A grade school and high school had been closed because the county did not have the resources to maintain them. The antiquated buildings were partly demolished now, a few wrecking machines still there, asquat in mud.

The inmates were glad to keep the field in playable condition, chalking the lines and arcs, planting corner flags, sinking the goals firmly in the ground. The games were an earnest pastime for the players, men mostly middle-aged, a few older, two or three younger, all in makeshift uniforms, running, standing, walking, crouching, often simply bending from the waist, breathless, hands on knees, looking into the scuffed turf where their lives were mired.

There were fewer spectators as the days grew colder, then fewer players. I kept showing up, blowing on my hands, beating my arms across my chest. The teams were coached by inmates, the games refereed by inmates, and those of us watching from the three rows of old broken bleacher seats were inmates. The guards stood around, here and there, watching and not.

The games became stranger. Rules were invented, broken and abridged, a fight started now and then, the game going on around it. I kept waiting for a player to be stricken, a heart attack, a convulsive collapse. The spectators rarely cheered or moaned. It began to feel like nowhere, men moving in the dreamy distance, linesmen sharing a cigarette. We walked across the bridge, watched the game, walked back across the bridge.

I thought about soccer in history, the inspiration for wars, truces, rampaging mobs. The game was a global passion, spherical ball, grass or turf, entire nations in spasms of elation or lament. But what kind of sport is it that disallows the use of players' hands, except for the goalkeeper? Hands are essential human tools, the things that grasp and hold, that make, take, carry, create. If soccer were an American invention, wouldn't some European intellectual maintain that our historically puritanical nature has compelled us to invent a game structured on anti-masturbatory principles?

This is one of the things I think about that I never had to think about before.

The notable thing about Norman Bloch, my bunkmate, was not the art that used to hang on his walls. What impressed me was the crime he'd committed. This was itself a kind of art, conceptual in nature, radical in scale, a deed so casual and yet so transgressive that Norman, here a year, would be spending six more years in the camp, the bunk, the clinic, the meal lines, in the squalling noise of the hand dryers in the toilets.

Norman did not pay taxes. He did not file quarterly reports or annual returns and he did not request extensions. He did not backdate documents, establish trusts or foundations, open secret accounts or utilize the ready mechanisms of offshore jurisdictions. He was not a political or religious protester. He was not a nihilist, rejecting all values and institutions. He was completely transparent. He just didn't pay.

It was a kind of lethargy, he said, the way people avoid doing the dishes or making the bed.

I brightened at that. Doing the dishes, making the bed. He said he didn't know exactly how long it was since he'd last paid taxes. When I asked about his financial advisers, his business associates, he shrugged, or so I imagined. I was in the top bunk, he was in the bottom, two men in pajamas, passing the time.

"Those girls. Pretty amazing," he said. "And the news, especially the bad news."

"You like the bad news."

"We all like the bad news. Even the girls like the bad news."

I thought of telling him that they were my daughters. No one here knew this and it was better that way. I didn't want the men in the dorm looking at me, talking to me, spreading the word throughout the camp. I was learning how to disappear. It suited me, it was my natural state, day by day, to be phantasmal again.

Best not to speak of the girls.

Then I spoke of them, quietly, in six or seven words. There was a long pause. He had a round face, Norman, with a squat nose, his bushy hair going gray.

"You never said this, Jerry."

"Just between us."

"You never say anything."

"Just to you. No one else. It's true," I said. "Kate and Laurie. I sit and watch them and it's hard to understand how any of this happened. What are they doing there, what am I doing here? Their mother writes the reports. She didn't tell me this but I know it's her. She's masterminding the whole thing."

"What's she like, their mother?"

"We're legally separated."

"What's she like?" he said.

"Fairly smart, like in a cutting-edge way. Sneaky sort of pretty. You have to pay attention to see it."

"You still love her? I don't think I ever loved my wife. Not in the original meaning of the word."

I didn't ask what he meant by that.

"Did your wife love you?"

"She loved my walls," he said.

"I love my kids."

"You love their mother too. I can sense it," he said.

"From where, the lower bunk? You can't even see my face."

"I've seen your face. What's to see?"

"We fell apart. We didn't drift apart, we fell apart."

"Don't tell me I'm not right. I sense things. I read into things," he said.

I looked into the ceiling. It had rained for several hours and I thought I could hear traffic noise on the wet highway, cars racing beneath the overpass, drivers leaning into the night, trying to read the road at every flex and bend.

"I'll tell you what it's like. It's like they're playing a game," he said. "All those names they're saying. The Hang Seng in Hong Kong. That's funny to a kid. And when kids say it, it's funny to us. And I'll make you a bet. Plenty of kids are watching that report and not because it's on a kids' channel. They're watching because it's funny. What the hell's the Hang Seng in Hong Kong? I don't know. Do you know?"

"Their mother knows."

"I'll bet she does. She also knows it's a game, all of it. And all of it's funny. You're lucky," he said. "Terrific kids."

Happy here, that was Norman. We're not in prison, he liked to say. We're at camp.

......

Over time the situation in the Gulf began to ease. Abu Dhabi
provided a ten-billion-dollar bailout and relative calm soon
moved into the Gulf and across the digital networks to markets everywhere. This brought on a letdown in the common
room. Even as the girls showed improvement in their delivery and signs of serious preparation, the men stopped coming
in large numbers and soon there was only a scatter of us, here
and there, sleepy and reflective.

We had TV but what had we lost, all of us, when we entered
the camp? We'd lost our appendages, our extensions, the data
systems that kept us fed and cleansed. Where was the world,
our world? The laptops were gone, the smartphones and light
sensors and megapixels. Our hands and eyes needed more
than we could give them now. The touch screens, the mobile
platforms, the gentle bell reminders of an appointment or a
flight time or a woman in a room somewhere. And the sense,
the tacit awareness, now lost, that something newer, smarter,
faster, ever faster, was just a bird's breath away. Also lost
was the techno-anxiety that these devices routinely carried with them. But we needed this no less than the devices
themselves, that inherent stress, those cautions and frustrations. Weren't these essential to our mind-set? The prospect
of failed signals and crashed systems, the memory that needs
recharging, the identity stolen in a series of clicks. Information, this was everything, coming in, going out. We were
always on, wanted to be on, needed to be on, but this was
history now, the shadow of another life.

Okay, we were grown-ups, not bug-eyed kids in tribal
bondage, and this was not an Internet rescue camp. We lived
in real space, unaddicted, free of deadly dependence. But
we were bereft. We were pulpy and slumped. It was a thing

we rarely talked about, a thing that was hard to shake. There were the small idle moments when we knew exactly what we were missing. We sat on the toilet, flushed and done, staring into empty hands.

I wanted to find myself in front of the TV set for the market report, weekdays, four in the afternoon, but could not always manage. I was part of a work detail that was bused on designated days to the adjacent Air Force base, where we sanded and painted, did general maintenance, hauled garbage and sometimes just stood and watched as a fighter jet roared down the runway and lifted into the low sun. It was a beautiful thing to see, aircraft climbing, wheels up, wings pivoting back, the light, the streaked sky, three or four of us, not a word spoken. Was this the time, more than a thousand other moments, when the measure of our ruin was brought to starkest awareness?

"All of Europe is looking south. What do they see?"

"They see Greece."

"They see fiscal instability, enormous debt burden, possible default."

"*Crisis* is a Greek word."

"Is Greece hiding its public debt?"

"Is the crisis spreading at lightning speed to the rest of the southern tier, to the euro zone in general, to emerging markets everywhere?"

"Does Greece need a bailout?"

"Will Greece abandon the euro?"

"Did Greece hide the nature of its debt?"

"What is Wall Street's role in this critical matter?"

"What is a credit default swap? What is a sovereign default? What is a special-purpose entity?"

"We don't know. Do you know? Do you care?"

"What is Wall Street? Who is Wall Street?"

Tense laughter from pockets in the audience.

"Greece, Portugal, Spain, Italy."

"Stocks plunge worldwide."

"The Dow, the Nasdaq, the euro, the pound."

"But where are the walkouts, the work stoppages, the job actions?"

"Look at Greece. Look in the streets."

"Riots, strikes, protests, pickets."

"All of Europe is looking at Greece."

"*Chaos* is a Greek word."

"Canceled flights, burning flags, stones flying this way, tear gas sailing that way."

"Workers are angry. Workers are marching."

"Blame the worker. Bury the worker."

"Freeze their pay. Increase their tax."

"Steal from the worker. Screw the worker."

"Any day now, wait and see."

"New flags, new banners."

"Hammer and sickle."

"Hammer and sickle."

Their mother had the girls delivering lines in a balanced flow, a cadence. They weren't just reading, they were acting, showing facial expression, having serious fun. Screw the worker, Kate had said. At least their mother had assigned the vulgar line to the older girl.

Was the daily market report becoming a performance piece?

......

All day long the story passed through the camp, building to building, man to man. It concerned a convict on death row in Texas or Missouri or Oklahoma and the last words he'd spoken before an individual authorized by the state injected the lethal substance or activated the electric current.

The words were, *Kick the tires and light the fire—I'm going home.*

Some of us felt a chill, hearing the story. Were we shamed by it? Did we think of that man on the honed edge of his last breath as more authentic than we were, a true outlaw, worthy of the state's most cruelly scrupulous attention? His end was officially sanctioned, an act welcomed by some, protested by some. If he'd spent half a lifetime in prison cells, in solitary confinement and finally on death row for one or two or multiple homicides, where were we and what had we done to be placed here? Did we even remember our crimes? Could we call them crimes? They were loopholes, evasions, wheedling half-ass felonies.

Some of us, less self-demeaning, simply nodded at the story, conveying simple credit to the man for the honor he'd brought to the moment, the back-country poetry of those words. By the third time I heard the story, or overheard it, the prison was located decisively in Texas. Forget the other places—the man, the story and the prison all belonged in Texas. We were somewhere else, watching a children's program on TV.

"What's this business about hammer and sickle?"

"Means nothing. Words," I said. "Like Abu Dhabi."

"The Hang Seng in Hong Kong."

"Exactly."

"The girls like saying it. Hammer and sickle."

"Hammer and sickle."

"Abu Dhabi."

"Abu Dhabi."

"Hang Seng."

"Hong Kong," I said.

We went on like that for a while. Norman was still murmuring the names when I shut my eyes and began the long turn toward sleep.

"But I think she means it. I think she's serious. Hammer and sickle," he said. "She's a serious woman with a point to make."

I stood watching from a distance. They passed through the metal detector, one by one, and moved toward the visitors' center, the wives and children, the loyal friends, the business partners, the lawyers who would sit and listen in a confidential setting as inmates stared at them through tight eyes and complained about the food, the job assignments, the scarcity of sentence reductions.

Everything seemed flat. The visitors on the footpath moved slowly and monochromatically. The sky was barely there, drained of light and weather. Families were bundled and wan but I didn't feel the cold. I was standing outside the dormitory but could have been anywhere. I imagined a woman walking among the others, slim and dark-haired, unaccompanied. I don't know where she came from, a photograph I'd once seen, or a movie, possibly French, set in Southeast Asia, sex beneath a ceiling fan. Here, she was wearing a long white tunic and loose trousers. She belonged to another setting, this was clear, but there was no need for me to wonder what she was doing here. She'd come up out of the drowsy mind or down from the flat sky.

There was a name for the outfit she was wearing and I nearly knew it, nearly had it, then it slipped away. But the woman was there, still, in pale sandals, the tunic slit on the sides, with a faint floral design front and back.

The ceiling fan turned slowly in the heavy heat, a thought I didn't want or need, but there it was, more thought than image, going back years.

Who was the man she was here to see? I was expecting no visitors, didn't want them, not even my daughters, not right for them to see me here. They were two thousand miles away in any case, and otherwise engaged. Could I place the woman in my immediate presence, face to face across a table in the large open space that would soon be filled with inmates, wives and kids, a guard at an elevated desk, keeping watch?

One thing I knew. The name of her outfit was two words, brief words, and it would make me feel the day was worthwhile, the full week, if I could remember those words. What else was there to do? What else could I think about that might yield a decent measure of completion?

Vietnamese—the words, the tunic, the trousers, the woman.

Then I thought of Sylvan Telfair. He was the inmate she was here to see, a man of worldwide address. They'd met in Paris or Bangkok. They'd stood on a terrace in the evening, sipping wine and speaking French. He was refined and assured and at the same time somewhat reticent, a man to whom she might be attracted, even if she was my idea, my secret silken vision.

I stood watching, thinking.

By the time the words came to me, much later in the day, *ao dai*, I'd lost all interest in the matter.

......

We were grouped, clustered, massed, paired, men everywhere, living in swarms, filling every space, arrayed across the
limits of vision. I liked to think of us as men in Maoist self-
correction, perfecting our social being through repetition.
We worked, ate and slept in mechanized routine, weekly,
daily, hourly, advancing from practice to knowledge. But
these were the musings of idle time. Maybe we were just tons
of assimilated meat, our collected flesh built into cubicles,
containered in dormitories and dining halls, zippered into
jumpsuits in five colors, classified, catalogued, this color for
that level of offense. The colors struck me as a kind of comic
pathos, always there, brightly clashing, jutting, crisscrossing.
I tried not to think of us as circus clowns who'd forgotten
their face paint.

"You consider her your enemy," Norman said. "You and
her, blood enemies."

"I don't think that's true."

"It's only natural. You think she's using the girls against
you. This is what you believe, down deep, whether you admit
it or not."

"I don't think that's the case."

"That has to be the case. She's attacking you for the mistakes you made in business. What was your business? How
did it get you here? I don't think you ever said."

"It's not interesting."

"We're not here to be interesting."

"I ran a company for a man who acquired companies.
Information got passed back and forth. Money changed hands.
Lawyers, traders, consultants, senior partners."

"Who was the man?"

"He was my father," I said.

"What's his name?"

"He died quietly before the fact."

"What fact?"

"The fact of my conviction."

"What's his name?"

"Walter Bradway."

"Do I know that name?"

"You know his brother's name. Howard Bradway."

"One of the hedge-fund musketeers," he said.

Norman was searching his memory for visual confirmation. I pictured what he was picturing. He was picturing my uncle Howie, a large ruddy man, bare-chested, in aviator glasses, with a miniature poodle huddled in the crook of his arm. A fairly famous image.

"A family tradition. Is that it?" he said. "Different companies, different cities, different time frames."

"They believed in right and wrong. The right and wrong of the markets, the portfolios, the insider information."

"Then it was your turn to join the business. Did you know what you were doing?"

"I was defining myself. That's what my father said. He said people who have to define themselves belong in the dictionary."

"Because you strike me as somebody who doesn't always know what he's doing."

"I pretty much knew. I definitely knew."

I could hear Norman unraveling the improvised cellophane wrap on his little jar of fig spread and then using his finger to rub the stuff across a saltine cracker. On visitors' days his lawyer smuggled a jar of Dalmatian fig spread into the camp, minus the metal cap. Norman said he liked the name, Dalmatia, Dalmatian, the Balkan history, the Adriatic, the large spotted dog. He liked the idea of having food of that particular name and place, all natural ingredients, and eating it on a standard cafeteria cracker, undercover, a couple of times a week.

He said that his lawyer was a woman and that she concealed the fig spread somewhere on her body. This was a throwaway line, delivered in a monotone and not intended to be believed.

"What's your philosophy of money?"

"I don't have one," I said.

"There was the year I made a shitpile of money. One year in particular. We could be talking, total, easy nine figures. I could feel it adding years to my life. Money makes you live longer. It seeps into the bloodstream, into the veins and capillaries. I talked to my primary-care physician about this. He said he had an inkling I could be right."

"What about the art on your walls? Make you live longer?"

"I don't know about the art. Good question, the art."

"People say great art is immortal. I say there's something mortal in it. It carries a glimpse of death."

"All those gorgeous paintings, the shapes and colors. All those dead painters. I don't know," he said.

He lifted his hand toward my bunk, up and around, with a splotch of fig preserves on half a cracker. I declined, but thanks. I heard him chewing the cracker and sinking into the sheets. Then I lay waiting for the final remarks of the day.

"She's talking directly to you. You realize this, using the girls."

"I don't think so, not even remotely."

"In other words this never occurred to you."

"Everything occurs to me. Some things I reject."

"What's her name?"

"Sara Massey."

"Good and direct. I see her as a strong woman with

roots going back a long way. Principles, convictions. Getting revenge for your illegal activities, for the fact you got caught, maybe for joining your father's business in the first place."

"How smart I am not to know this. What grief it spares me."

"This sneaky-pretty woman in your words. She's reminding you what you did. She's talking to you. Abu Dhabi, Abu Dhabi. Hang Seng, Hong Kong."

All around us, entombed in cubicles, suspended in time, reliably muted now, men with dental issues, medical issues, marital issues, dietary demands, psychic frailties, sleep-breathing men, the nightly drone of oil-tax schemes, tax-shelter schemes, corporate espionage, corporate bribery, false testimony, Medicare fraud, inheritance fraud, real estate fraud, wire fraud, fraud and conspiracy.

They started arriving early, men crowding the common room, some carrying extra folding chairs, snapping them open. There were others standing in the side aisles, a spillover of inmates, guards, kitchen staff, camp officials. I'd managed to squeeze into the fourth row, slightly off-center. The sense of event, news in high clamor, all the convergences of emotional global forces bringing us here in a wave of complex expectation.

A cluster of rain-swept blossoms was fixed to one of the high windows. Spring, more or less, late this year.

There were four common rooms, one for each dorm, and I was certain that all were packed, inmates and others collected in some odd harmonic, listening to children talk about economic collapse.

Here, as time approached, Feliks Zuber rose briefly from his seat up front, raising a weary hand to quiet the settling crowd.

I noticed at once that the girls wore matching jackets. This was new. The picture was sharper and steadier, in color. Then I realized they were seated at a long desk, a news desk, not an ordinary table. Finally the scripts—there were no scripts. They were using a teleprompter, delivering lines at fairly high speed with occasional tactical pauses, well placed.

"Greece is selling bonds, raising euros."

"Markets are calming."

"Greece is moving toward a new austerity."

"Immediate pressure is relieved."

"Greece and Germany are talking."

"Votes of confidence. Calls for patience."

"Greece is ready to restore trust."

"Aid package of forty billion dollars."

"How do they say thank you in Greek?"

"Efharisto."

"Say it again, slowly."

"F. Harry Stowe."

"F. Harry Stowe."

They exchanged a fist-bump, deadpan, without looking at each other.

"The worst may be over."

"Or the worst is yet to come."

"Do we know if the Greek bailout will do what it is designed to do?"

"Or will it do just the opposite?"

"What exactly is the opposite?"

"Think about markets elsewhere."

"Is anyone looking at Portugal?"

"Everyone's looking at Portugal."

"High debt, low growth."

"Borrow, borrow, borrow."

"Euro, euro, euro."

"Ireland has a problem. Iceland has a problem."

"Have we thought about the British pound?"

"The life and death of the British pound."

"The pound is not the euro."

"Britain is not Greece."

"But is the pound showing signs of cracking? Will the euro follow? Is the dollar far behind?"

"There is talk about China."

"Is there trouble in China?"

"Is there a bubble in China?"

"What is the Chinese currency called?"

"Latvia has the lat."

"Tonga has the ponga."

"China has the rebimbi."

"The rebimbo."

"China has the rebobo."

"The rebubu."

"What happens next?"

"It already happened."

"Does anyone remember?"

"Market plunges one thousand points in an eighth of a second."

"A tenth of a second."

"Faster and faster, lower and lower."

"A twentieth of a second."

"Screens glow and vibrate, phones jump off walls."

"A hundredth of a second. A thousandth of a second."

"Not real, unreal, surreal."

"Who is doing this? Where is it coming from? Where is it going?"

"It happened in Chicago."

"It happened in Kansas."

"It's a movie, it's a song."

I could feel the mood in the room, a pressing intensity, a need for something more, something stronger. I remained detached, watching the girls, wondering about their mother, what she had in mind, where she was leading us.

Laurie said softly, in a lilting voice: "Who do we trust? Where do we turn? How do we ever get to sleep?"

Kate said briskly, "Can computer technology keep up with computerized trading? Will long-term doubts yield to short-term doubts?"

"What is a fat-finger trade? What is a naked short sale?"

"How many trillions of dollars pledged to bleeding euro economies?"

"How many zeros is a trillion?"

"How many meetings deep in the night?"

"Why does the crisis keep getting worse?"

"Brazil, Korea, Japan, Wherever."

"What are they doing and where are they doing it?"

"They're on strike again in Greece."

"They're marching in the streets."

"They're burning banks in Greece."

"They're hanging banners from sacred temples."

"Peoples of Europe, rise up."

"Peoples of the world, unite."

"The tide is rising, the tide is turning."

"Which way? How fast?"

There was a long pause. We watched and waited. Then the news report reached its defining moment, do-or-die, the point of no return.

The girls recited together:

"Stalin Khrushchev Castro Mao."

"Lenin Brezhnev Engels—Pow!"

These names, that exclamation, delivered in rapid sing-song, roused the inmates to spontaneous noise. What kind of noise was it? What did it mean? I sat stone-faced, in the middle of it, trying to understand. The girls repeated the lines once, then again. The men yelled and clamored, these flabby white-collar felons, seeming to reject everything they'd believed all their lives.

"*Brezhnev Khrushchev Mao and Ho.*"

"*Lenin Stalin Castro Zhou.*"

The names kept coming. It resembled a school chant, the cry of leaping cheerleaders, and the men's response grew in volume and feeling. It was tremendous, totally, and it scared me. What did these names mean to the inmates? We were a long way from the funny place-names of earlier reports. These names were immense imprints on history. Did the inmates want to replace one doctrine, one system of government with another? We were the end products of the system, the logical outcome, slabs of burnt-out capital. We were also men with families and homes, whatever our present situation. We had beliefs, commitments. It went beyond systems, I thought. They were asserting that nothing mattered, that distinctions were dead. Let the markets crash and die. Let the banks, the brokerage firms, the groups, the funds, the trusts, the institutes all turn to dust.

"*Mao Zhou—Fidel Ho.*"

The aisles, meanwhile, were still and hushed—guards, doctors, camp administrators. I wanted it to be over. I wanted the girls to go home, do their homework, withdraw into their cell phones.

"*Marx Lenin Che—Hey!*"

Their mother was crazy, perverting the novelty of a children's stock market report. The inmates were confused, stirring themselves into mindless anarchy. Only Feliks Zuber made sense, pumping his fist, feebly, a man who was here for attempting to finance a revolution, able to hear trumpets and drums in that chorus of names. It took a while before the energy in the room began to recede, the girls' voices becoming calmer now.

"We're all waiting for an answer."

"Accordingly, analysts say."

"Eventually, investors maintain."

"Elsewhere, economists claim."

"Somewhere, officials insist."

"This could be bad," Kate said.

"How bad?"

"Very bad."

"How bad?"

"End-of-the-world bad."

They stared into the camera, finishing in a whisper.

"F. Harry Stowe."

"F. Harry Stowe."

The report was over but the girls remained on-screen. They sat looking, we sat looking. The moment became uneasy. Laurie glanced to the side and then slid off her chair and moved out of camera range. Kate stayed put. I watched a familiar look slide into her eyes and across her mouth and jaw. This was the look of noncompliance. Why should she submit to an embarrassing exit caused by some dumb technical blunder? She would stare us all down. Then she would tell us exactly how she felt about the matter, about the show itself and the news itself. This is what made me want to get up and leave, to slip unnoticed out of the row and along the wall and into the dusty light of late afternoon. But I stayed and looked and so did she. We were looking at each other. She leaned forward now, placing her elbows on the desk, hands folded at chin level like a fifth-grade teacher impatient with my snickering and fidgeting or just my stupidity. The tension in the room had mass and weight. This is what

I feared, that she would speak about the news, all news all
the time, and about how her father always said that the news
exists so it can disappear, this is the point of news, whatever
story, wherever it is happening. *We depend on the news to dis-*
appear, my father says. *Then my father became the news. Then*
he disappeared.

But she only sat and looked and soon the inmates began
to get restless. I realized that my hand was covering the lower
part of my face, in needless parental disguise. People, a few at
a time, then more, then groups, all leaving now, some crouching down as they moved between the rows. Maybe they were
being careful not to block the view of others but I thought
that most were slinking out, in guilt and shame. Either way,
the view stayed the same, Kate on camera, sitting there looking at me. I felt hollowed out but I couldn't leave while
she was still there. I waited for the screen to go blank and
finally, long minutes later, that's what happened, in streaks
and tremors.

The room had emptied out by the time a cartoon
appeared, a fat boy rolling down a bumpy hill. Feliks Zuber
was still in his seat up front, he and I in lone attendance now,
and I waited for him to turn and wave at me, or simply sit
there, dead.

I opened my eyes sometime before first light and the dream
was still there, hovering, nearly touchable. We can't do justice to our dreams, reworking them in memory. They seem
borrowed, part of another life, ours only maybe and only in
the farthest margins. A woman is standing beneath a ceiling fan in a tall shadowy room in Ho Chi Minh City, the
name of the city indelibly webbed within the dream, and
the woman, momentarily obscured, is stepping out of her

sandals and beginning to look familiar, and now I realize why this is so, because she is my wife, very weirdly, Sara Massey, slowly shedding her clothing, a tunic and loose trousers, an *ao dai*.

Was this meant to be erotic, or ironic, or just another random package of cranial debris? Thinking about it made me edgy and after a moment I lowered myself from the end of the top bunk, quietly. Norman lay still, wearing a black sleep mask. I dressed and left the cubicle and went across the floor and out into the predawn mist. The guardpost at the camp entrance was lighted, someone on duty to admit delivery vans that would be arriving with milk, eggs and headless chickens from local farms. I cut across to the old wooden fence and ducked between the rails, then stood awhile, staring into the dark, aware of my breathing, surprised by it, as if it were an event that only rarely and memorably takes place.

I felt my way slowly along a row of trees that lined one side of a dirt path. I moved toward the sound of traffic and reached the highway bridge in ten or twelve minutes. The bridge itself was closed to traffic, with repairwork in perennial progress. I stood at a point roughly midway across and watched the cars speed below me. There was a half moon hanging low and looking strangely submerged in the pale mist. Traffic was steady, coming and going, pickups, hatchbacks, vans, all carrying the question of who and where, this early hour, and splashing the unwordable sound of their passage under the bridge.

I watched and listened, unaware of passing time, thinking of the order and discipline of the traffic, taken for granted, drivers maintaining a distance, fallible men and women, cars ahead, behind, to the sides, night driving, thoughts drifting. Why weren't there accidents every few seconds on this one stretch of highway, even before morning rush? This is what

I thought from my position on the bridge, the surging noise and sheer speed, the proximity of vehicles, the fundamental differences among drivers, sex, age, language, temperament, personal history, cars like animatronic toys, but that's flesh and blood down there, steel and glass, and it seemed a wonder to me that they moved safely toward the mystery of their destinations.

This is civilization, I thought, the thrust of social and material advancement, people in motion, testing the limits of time and space. Never mind the festering stink of burnt fuel, the fouling of the planet. The danger may be real but it is simply the overlay, the unavoidable veneer. What I was seeing was also real but it had the impact of a vision, or maybe an ever-present event that flares in the observer's eye and mind as a burst of enlightenment. Look at them, whoever they are, acting in implicit accord, checking dials and numbers, showing judgment and skill, taking curves, braking gently, anticipating, watchful in three or four directions. I listened to the air blast as they passed beneath me, car after car, drivers making instantaneous decisions, news and weather on their radios, unknown worlds in their minds.

Why don't they crash all the time? The question seemed profound to me, with the first touch of dawn showing to the east. Why don't they get backended or sideswiped? It seemed inevitable from my elevated perspective—cars forced into the guardrails, nudged into lethal spins. But they just kept coming, seemingly out of nowhere, headlights, taillights, and they would be coming and going all through the budding day and into the following night.

I closed my eyes and listened. Soon I'd be going back to the camp, sinking into the everydayness of that life. Minimum security. It sounded childlike, a term of condescension and chagrin. I wanted to open my eyes to empty roads and blazing light, apocalypse, the thundering approach of something unimaginable. But minimum security was where I belonged, wasn't it? The least possible quantity, the lowest degree of restriction. Here I was, a truant, but one who would return. When I looked, finally, the mist was lifting, traffic heavier now, motorcycles, flatbeds, family cars, SUVs, drivers down there peering, the noise and rush, the compelling sense of necessity.

Who are they? Where are they going?

It occurred to me then that I was visible from the highway, a man on the bridge, at this hour, in silhouette, a man standing and watching, and it would be a natural response for the drivers, some of them, to glance up and wonder.

Who is he? What is he doing there?

He is Jerold Bradway, I thought, and he is breathing the fumes of free enterprise forever.

PLAY

Mathias Svalina

HIDE-&-GO-SEEK
(for 2 or more players)

Little children tend to disappear. Especially if there are large
trees, tall grass or white canvases nearby. One child is born It.
He covers his eyes with his palms & counts to 100. When he
uncovers his eyes he sings:

> *A bushel of wheat, a bushel of rye;*
> *If you're not ready,*
> *Close your eyes.*

The weakest children will close their eyes & return home
where they will never be allowed to open their eyes again.
The It child seeks out everything that has been hidden. He
digs in the earth, he combs through the clouds, he strips the
bark from the trees & he skins all the animals. When he finds
another child he shouts, "1-2-3-4 for _____," nam-
ing the one he has found.

He covers his eyes with his palms again & counts to 100.
When he wakes up the other children have grown up & are

driving their cars into the lakes, surrounded by millions of
fireflies.

DROP THE HANDKERCHIEF
(for 7 or more players)

Children must be taught not to play favorites. One child
is born It. The It-child carries a clean white handkerchief
with him wherever he goes. When he comes upon a circle
of children he runs around the circle & drops the handkerchief behind one of the children. That child must run in the
opposite direction around the circle of children. The children
hold hands & refuse to allow either the It-child or the chosen
child to stop running. These two continue running for the
rest of their lives.

There is one child who is born inside the circle, which is
called the mush pot. This child also has a clean white handkerchief & must take turns looking into the eyes of each of
the children while showing each the handkerchief. The handkerchief was left for the mush-pot-child by his father, whom
he has never met. His father drives a bright blue car & can be
seen working at the candle factory five nights a week.

CROSSING THE BROOK
(for 2 or more players)

If you draw two lines on the asphalt, about two feet apart,
then a brook will spring up between the lines. Children
will then run in groups & try to jump the brook. They will

scream as they are running. They will scream as they are jumping. If they land in the brook they must run home & change their stockings.

The successful jumpers are guided into a white bus & driven to wider & wider brooks. The last child to make a jump is the winner. Those that fall into the brooks must run home to change their stockings. But they are so far from home & the driver of the white bus will not speak to them. There is a light in the forest. Is that a distant fire or the buttery windows of a warm farmhouse? It is difficult to tell from here, where the sleet has just begun to fall.

ANIMAL CHASE
(for 5 or more players)

Two bases are marked off, at either end of America. Each child takes the name of an Animal. One child is It. He stands in the center of America & writes newspaper columns about the decline of America. He starts a radio show & becomes tremendously influential. He begins to see himself as no longer It but the voice of the people. When he goes to sleep at night his mother tucks him in & whispers, "Sweet dreams, voice of the people." When his father drops him off at school he calls out, "Have a great day, voice of the people."

The Animals lurk in the darkness of the forest & the shadows of the demolished factories. When stray children pass the shadows they pounce on them. Licking the blood from their claws & beaks they whisper to themselves, "I am Animal. I am Animal."

When the first game ends all children trade names & a new child becomes It.

BALL CHASE
(for 4 or more players)

For this game, a row of red caps may be set against a wall or a fence; a series of holes may be dug in the ground; a number of circles may be drawn; a line of hoops may be used; a line of fighter pilots may lead from the sacristy to the altar; a stack of books may catch fire in the basement; a circle of priests may cough up wet flags; a group of boys may hide in the coat closet; a set of cars may crash together in the middle of the intersection; a troupe of dancers may be sent in to rescue them; a flock of birds may dive-bomb the stained glass window; a pocketful of change may spill over the intersection; a child may drop her Popsicle in the middle of the sun-hot street.

There may be a red ball; there may be a bird you cannot see with an extraordinarily loud song; there may be a gown, blouse or shirt hanging from the iron gate; each child may be happy, morose or distracted; there may be many children circling a dry well; there may be one child at the top of a dead elm tree; there may be songs, lit candles in the elbows of the branches, or a pile of gasoline-soaked rags in the corner of the garage; there may be lines of sugar down the playground dirt; there may be piles of toy trucks in a freshly dug pit; there may be sunlight, so much sunlight every child must squint, must hold her hands up to the sun to block the light out, must step forward without being able to see.

MAKING JAM
(for 1 or more players)

Making jam is for the quietest boy in the class. One day he wears a white sack over his head & ties it tight at his throat. The students in his class all begin to notice him & smile.

The next day he paints his entire body the color of the walls. The students gather their plastic chairs around him & patiently watch.

The next day he removes his arms & legs & replaces them with abstract nouns. He hides his arms & legs in a mop closet where no one will find them. At this point he is no longer shy. The other students call him new names that they make up as they go along. The county government awards him an award that comes with a large silver medal.

The medal is so large that he must remove his torso & replace it with the medal. When the students look at him they are blinded by the shine of the medal. When birds fly by him they get confused.

After he is elected governor the boy remembers his arms &
legs, but when he opens the mop closet door he sees that
each arm & leg has grown into a full person. They all look
similar to him, but none of them look exactly like him.

JIGGLE THE HANDLE
(for 2 players)

One child is the hunter & one child is the knife. One child is
the ocean & one child is the sliver of metal stuck in the pad
of the thumb. One child screams with pleasure & one child
holds a heat-flaccid candle. One child bears the pain & one
child stares at the spinning rims on a shiny Toyota.

Why wash your hair? Why brush your teeth? Why do anything at all?

Bedtime approaches & bedtime passes & the elm tree
retains its moonlit silhouette. The taste of candy is sweeter
than a dream about Styrofoam. A black velvet bag could
contain anything, but you should never stick your hand
inside it.

IT LOOKS LIKE WAR
(for 16 or more players)

One child is taller than the other children. One child is the
smallest. The child with the darkest skin does not sit beside
the child with the shiniest shoes. The child with the longest

hair does not like the child with the longest name. The children gather in a circle & sing:

> *Weak man, poor man, blind man, wife*
> *There are no wounds when there is no knife*
> *Strong man, rich man, priest or king*
> *Every city looks sacred when it is burning.*

The light refracting through broken bifocals can start a fire in the scattered newspapers. The soldiers outside the gates drain blood from their horses & drink it with black pepper.

EVERYTHING COSTS $20
(for 6 or more players)

Everything costs $20. Everything breaks the moment after you buy it. Everything stacks in the corners. The blinds curl from your fingerprints. The rubber is hard. Six grapes beside the kitchen sink wrinkle. What amphitheater. What color of skin. The money rings & rings. The gunshots can be heard from blocks away.

Paper planes fall from the roof of the factory as the schoolchildren scamper this way & that. Microphones grow from the tips of the drought-dead trees. Each child picks a paper plane from a puddle.

Everything was broken before you bought it. Everything is listed on the window. Speak into the microphones so that the children can hear you. Give your ticket to the teacher to exit the classroom. The clock is fast. No, the clock is broken. The lights begin flashing. The children run from the alarms.

At home the children eat their suppers with the TV on. When their mothers ask, *How was school*, they say, *OK*.

BROKEN KATE
(for 6 or more players)

The only way to break a Kate is to attach a lockbox to its wrists & send it out to search for the lost sheep. The sheep wander all across America & they hide behind stumps & metal mailboxes. The sheep wander so far away from one another that they forget they are sheep & they begin to look at large stones & think the stones are televisions. They begin to look around for the remote, but instead only find the remote that dims the dining room lights. The only way to protect the sheep is to hold them in your arms as you would a fragile cuckoo clock.

There are so many ways to drown. There are so many bridges. One child backs another into a corner & stares. The teacher walks over with the lockboxes. Her shoes squeak on the linoleum. The fluorescent flutter of sweat & the scent of dry-erase boards. Teacher's earrings jingle. Teacher's shoes squeak. Oh, Kate, oh, Kate. I am so sorry.

TAIL END CHARLIE
(for 4 or more players)

The night before they go in behind enemy lines the children write their names on their chests with permanent markers. They write their names on their shoes with greasepaint. They carve hearts into the plaster beside their beds & cram them full of initials.

The children fall asleep repeating their names to themselves. They discover new names inside their names. The new names are the names their ghosts will have. They knot little nooses of dental floss around the names & tie them to their pinkies.

The machine gun bursts splashes in the sand, as if flaying it with whips. The sky is so blue that someone will have to give it a name like Tom or Beginning. One of the children finds that his gun is made of ice. Another child finds that his gun is made of dried dirt. A third child finds that he is the gun & he cannot stop killing. In Pittsburgh the children are burning the federal buildings tonight.

POP GOES THE WEASEL
(for 4 children & an audience of voters)

One child must come from a family that sleeps in the caves. One child must come from a family that sleeps underground. One child finds a hollow tree & fills it with the stuffed animals he steals from the supermarket trash bins. One child bites into a doughnut & breaks his front teeth on a piece of sea glass. The children decide which child is It & the It child must run for president.

The It child walks into crowds of thousands, shaking hands with all the men & kissing the cheeks of all the women & rubbing perfumed oils on the foreheads of the babies. He must appear on TV & pretend like there is no camera in the room. He says words & then some of the members of the audience of voters repeat the words. Other members of the audience of voters go home & rewire their radios.

When the It child is assassinated backstage after a speech the other children write books about the It child. They appear on radio talk shows & discuss the mystery of the It child. They drop a bucketful of pennies into the dryer & listen to them clatter.

MADMEN

Lucy Corin

The day I got my period, my mother and father took me to pick my madman. The whole time, my dad kept his hands in his pockets and my mom acted like it was her show. I hadn't let her in on how scared I was that I might be a freak born with endometrial tissue of steel. Apparently it didn't cross her mind that I might be worried, watching all my friends go through it and what was up with my body. I stopped digging, looked in my pants, and told her what was going on in there, and what she said was, "All right, but hurry and get back out here."

It was getting toward lunch and we were digging a drainage ditch from the shed down to the woods. With my lateness, our preparations had become elaborate. We thought of everything, and my madman was going to really like his situation, I felt sure. We had a couple chickens he could take care of or else eat. Some of the almond trees still dropped nuts, and who doesn't like nuts? We had a circle of rocks for a fire pit with a view of the creek and an iron pot handed down from my grandmother, the one that her madman used and her father's madman used before that. In the shed I'd hung the curtains from my room before I was old enough to make my own decisions. They had a tassel fringe that I thought looked like paper-chain dolls with their hands merged together.

So I ran inside and did my best to remember what she'd told me about tampons when I was like ten, and then I ran back out and we finished the ditch even though I felt heavy and gross. In the shed we freshened up the straw, and then I went back inside *again* to shower while my mom called my dad at work so he could meet us. A lot of people would consider my mother grim, but I could hear her on the phone, at least until I turned on the water, and she sounded excited about taking me for my big day.

In the shower, I thought about my madman. It was getting hotter, so there were going to be a lot to choose from. Over the weekend, at my friend Carrie's birthday, we'd told our fortunes with a questionnaire we found online. Her madman wouldn't come out but we'd heard the basics about him. For what kind of house I wanted I put *Treehouse, Houseboat, Malibu Mansion,* and for my risk choice, *Outhouse.* If you don't put a risk, it undermines the integrity. For what kind of job I put *Parachuter, Famous Scientist, Hang-Gliding Instructor,* and *World Peace*—which isn't a job, but it's the thought that counts. For who I was going to marry I put *Anthony, No One, A Lesbian,* and *Yo' Mama.* For pet I put *Yo' Mama, Giraffe, Ant Farm,* and *Crabs.* I was completely not being serious by the time I got to car because I know I'm never getting a car so I just put *Anything, Flying Saucer, Argh!!!,* and *Who cares my parents are never getting me a car* (though the window only had room for twenty characters, so it ended up *Who cares my parents*). But the point is I got serious with the madman question. Even kids who seem like they don't care about their madman are faking it. They care.

"How did you know which madman was yours?" I asked Carrie later, in private. She said she looked each of them in the eyes, even just for a fraction of a second with the fast ones, but then with her madman she got them to take her into his cell—he was in the far back corner and she'd almost thought the cell was empty. He was pale and "Seriously," she said, "I know it's hard to believe, but he *blended in.*" I wondered if he was an albino madman, which suddenly seemed exotic and perfect.

"Is that how you knew?" I asked.

"No," she said. All the other girls were asleep. It was dark and we were near the window, face to face with our legs over opposite arms of a giant overstuffed chair, with the black sky surrounding us and everyone's sleeping bags covering the living room floor. It was like we were in a rowboat, bobbing in a sea made of our sleeping friends. "I went in and he wouldn't look at me. I put my hand on his chin like this, you know, like when an older man wants to kiss you in the movies." She shrugged. It seemed like our boat rocked. "I know that sounds creepy, but it's not. I just felt older than him, and he kept turning his chin and not looking at me."

"Will he look at you now?" I asked.

"That's not the point," she said. "Plus none of your beeswax." She said she picked that phrase up from her madman.

I wanted one like my uncle had, who was an accomplished musician. Special. Or one time I was downtown, some girl was totally engrossed in window shopping, and her madman was sniffing around the sidewalk, lifting pebbles with his toes, humming very low, very soothing. I pretended like I was window shopping too, to get closer, and when I caught the tune, it didn't even seem to be coming from him. More like it was surrounding him, moving through him, something like religion, or wisdom. Some people would be surprised how important wisdom is to me. I try to remember what he hummed, but I was young and I can't remember. I mean, I know I'm still young. But your brain changes.

Deep in the night I woke up and it was just me in the

giant chair. Across the room, across the ocean of sleeping girls like waves, I saw Carrie and her madman in the doorway that went into the kitchen. They were silhouetted, standing forehead to forehead, passing a sandwich back and forth. Then the madman reached over and tugged on a handful of her hair. Like ringing a bell, but soft. Then Carrie reached over for a handful of his hair and tugged back.

Of course I don't remember my online fortune, that's never the part that sticks, and no one believes it anyhow. It's more about answering the questions plus what you're willing to tell people.

The shower went predictably. After my shower, I went right for the skirt and blouse I thought were a perfect balance of mature and still had hints of my personality. But once I put it on it was more like a combination of pretentious and someone who was not trustworthy. I started from scratch. I picked my underwear—serious underwear, but new. Carcrash undies. Then I picked footwear: dressy boots with square heels. Once you know the shoes, that narrows your options. Soon my mom was screaming for me. "It's not a beauty pageant!" I don't know why she has to scream, the house is not that big. I guess it doesn't matter what I was wearing. But it does to me.

All the way in the car I wished I had skipped the tampon and went with a pad. It must have been in crooked, but at the time I thought this must be what it's like. My mom, who is a bad driver and also incredibly opinionated about driving, was on her cell phone talking a hundred percent understandingly about someone in the hospital after an incident in the home, and then suddenly on another call, a hundred percent enthusiastically about someone's idea for self-catering a wedding in a schoolhouse on a cliff. She's not faking, either. Endless empathy, one person after another, all day long, like a buffet. I just wanted my madman.

Meanwhile I watched the world go by out the side window, comparing regular view versus including the mirror. I kept wondering if the world was going to look different after I had a madman, so I wanted to get a good "before" shot of it. To sum up, the world was: green, green, green, house, street, green, gas station, green, green, strip mall, green with brown, then hillier and hillier. Then, exactly as my mother was saying "schoolhouse" again, we went by this little white schoolhouse I'd never noticed before. It was as if her saying the word "schoolhouse" made it appear—I was so surprised I tried to point it out to her, but she shook her head not to interrupt, and by then she'd missed it. Or maybe it was a church.

It had its own velvet hill. It had a weathervane. A deer ate puffs of grass the mower had missed by its front steps. A motorcycle was parked nearby, tilted on its kickstand. It looked like it was thinking. The weathervane was spinning, so I couldn't tell what it was, a horse, a whale . . . It didn't seem windy out, but it's hard to tell. Being in the car was like another planet.

I know it sounds stupid, but this was a big day for me, and everything felt like it might be important at any second.

After a few more hills, the facility rose up in the middle of nowhere. Ours was a nice facility, known to be professional and well equipped, but in some counties it could be hard, even dangerous to go, and some kids brought their whole extended families for protection. In those counties some kids ended up with a madman who died almost immediately. That's meaningful to go through, but it's better if you have time for a broader perspective. The building looked like a normal white country inn, but closer up you could see it went on and on down the hill. We pulled into the parking lot and my mother stopped the car by as usual bumping into the curb. Maybe three other cars were spaced out in the lot, and two beat-up vans. My mother was still working on her phone call, though she did make some eye contact with me, meaning "just a minute." The person would never know, from her nodding and assenting noises, that she was in any way ready to get off the phone, which she never really is. It's the empathy. She loves to empathize. Sometimes I feel bad because maybe I don't. She dove her hand into her purse, which sat open on the seat beside her, the most crammed thing in history, and dragged out a length of crinkled toilet paper because she doesn't believe in Kleenex. My mother was admirable—for example, trying to teach me to be the last person on earth resisting the corporate identity takeover of personhood. It made me so angry at myself when I just wanted her to go away, which is not the same as wanting her to die, although she will never understand the difference. She blew her nose using one hand and pushed the toilet paper back into the purse.

Oh my god we were still in the parking lot. When I tapped her on the shoulder she looked about to smack me so I just sat there, probably the fastest route to her hanging up anyway. But I was resenting getting into a bad mood. My phone, for instance, was on vibrate for privacy on the occasion, and the last thing I needed was to be in a bad mood making a decision like this. She kept being herself on the phone. I got angrier and angrier. Then luckily my dad pulled into the spot next to us. I jumped out of the car to meet him, and he's such a huge dork, he never knows what to do, but then sometimes he does exactly the right thing, and this time he got out of his truck with a shopping bag with a bow stuck on it because he can't wrap boxes, although it's funny when he tries.

I hugged him and took the bag. "What have we *here*!" I said, and dug in. It was a harness for my madman, the best kind, made of real leather with quality hand-stitching and brass appointments. My mother came around the car, stuffing her phone into her purse, saying, "Poor Irene!" She was about to launch into recounting everything from the phone, and it's true that Irene's life is pretty shocking and worth hearing about, but all I thought was, *Isn't there a time and a place?* I handed her the gift bag for her to put in the car and catch the hint. She put her hand on my head and I could see her deciding whether to say something or not. For good reason she didn't know if expressing her opinion was the best idea when it came to getting me to feel what she wanted. Finally she just plunked my gift into the back of Dad's truck and said, "Here we go."

We stepped up to the giant double doors, the kind with wire netting between the panes, and I buzzed the buzzer. A plaque on a rock by the stoop read AN ATTACHMENT TO ONE-SELF IS THE FIRST SIGN OF MADNESS. It was riveted under an engraving of a Ship of Fools, a little hard to see but you could tell it was a really good artist. A woman's face appeared in the window, filling it with puffy red hair, and I thought I was making it up, but she had the kind of eyes a cat has—golden with black diamond-shaped slits instead of pupils. I grabbed my dad's hand in the midst of a flashback to *The Wizard of Oz* where I'm Dorothy and Oz is the doorman but you don't know it yet. My dad held my ID up to the window. She let us in. She wrote some stuff down from my ID and then gave it back to me. She was obviously really nice, but I couldn't look at her. She sat us in the waiting room with another family and left through another set of double doors. This family was one with a boy who must have been turning thirteen, which is when they get theirs. It's really unfair. They should have to go when they start splooging in the night or whatever. God, boys are known for being immature in general, but this one seemed especially short, making me feel extra freakish, that everyone has their madman already and here I am with this kid with a *cowlick*. But I went right over and plunked down next to him and asked, "What is up with her eyes?"

He said, "It's just a disease. My dad's a doctor. Dad, what's it again?"

His dad was reading a magazine about cars. "Coloboma of the iris," he said. His mother was sitting so close to his dad that their thighs touched all the way to the knee. Her magazine was called *Pet City*.

I whispered to the boy, "God, if I wasn't already crazy and she was my nurse, I think I'd go crazy." I could tell he thought I was making light of the situation, but I wasn't.

"She's nice," he said.

I said, "I know."

I was nervous, and I was going to remember this for the rest of my life.

There was a nurses' station, but when I went over no one was at it. I slid the window open and put my head through. All I saw was extra pamphlets and forms piled around a computer, but I still felt sneaky so I stopped looking. Soon enough the red-haired cat-eyed nurse returned and the boy went through the double doors into the back with his mom, dad, and cowlick. My mom took another call and the room echoed with her voice. My dad walked around inspecting things—looking into the nurses' station to see what I'd been looking at, squinting at a poster, pressing a thumb into the cushion on the chair like meat to test it for doneness, picking a stray bit of paint from the glass of the window that looked onto the parking lot. He was trying to find something to comment on. He picked up a pamphlet from a rack and started to say something but swallowed it and pretended to be chuckling to himself. There's no such thing as chuckling to yourself. You do it so someone will notice, even if you're by yourself and the person is imaginary. My parents are such a classic couple. They'll either get divorced or he'll get smaller and smaller and she'll get bigger and bigger until they die. Then the red-haired cat-eyed nurse came through the double doors with a smile like homemade pie and said, "Ready, sweetheart?"

"Remember," my mother said, "you, too, could grow up to be a madman."

Shut up, Mom. No one cares about this more than I do.

The gallery was white and clean, and everything—the bars on the cells, the bars on the beds in the cells, even the chamber pots—seemed thicker because of layers of white paint, the sheets fragile by comparison. How could Carrie have looked each one in the eyes? The hall was narrow and endless, like a mirror facing a mirror. You could never look into all those eyes. The space swam with light and occasional arms of madmen waved through the bars. The ceiling was so white it disappeared. Cells lined one side, and the other side was a vast blank wall to walk along. This meant that you could only look into one cell at a time, but if you stayed near the wall you could keep out of reach. I could hear, dimly, that there was an army, like millions of them, beyond the walls. It was the sound of madmen who were not ready. My mother gripped my elbow and adjusted the strap of her purse.

I know from case studies in our Health and Human Development book that when a madman is reeling with madness it's like his skin is ripped off, his consciousness is that naked. Just stepping from the entryway into view of the first cell I felt something—a wave—like there was empty space left where all these people had been so naked and now I was standing in it. The madman in there wasn't even looking at me and I felt it. In fact, he was facing the back wall. He was bare and yellowish, with the knobs of his spine poking out and a cloth tied around his waist. He might have been peeing, my first potential madman. But he might have just been standing there, looking at the wall. I was just standing there, looking at the bars, with my mom latched to my elbow. Hands deep in his pockets, my father approached the laminated information card at the first madman's cell and read it for our information in a low voice while I took in this prospect with my eyes.

He was a Melancholic madman. He glanced at us absently and then took a seat in a back corner of the cell on a three-legged stool, resting his chin on his fist.

"'Appearance: gloomy brow, shrunken head, lethargic, passive,'" my father read. "'Medical history: mad with grief after violating his word to his wife; shunned men and fled to the forest.'"

"I don't know, what do you think?" said my mother.

"I don't know," I said. I didn't know what to do—imagine my life as his, or imagine him in my life, or what. At some point the nurse had left, and I felt very alone.

"Let's look at another," my mother said, and I knew that meant he would be fine for another girl, but not for us. I'd settled on picturing him on his stool by the window in our shed with his gloomy brow, in his thinking position. Where was I in this picture? Was I stirring his pot? Was I pulling up a stool of my own to sit beside him? Was he starting to cry? We stepped to the next cell.

This madman paced and a broken chain from one arm dragged on the ground. He had heaping wads of wiry hair.

"'Appearance,'" read my father. My mother craned her neck over his shoulder at the card, to keep an eye on if he'd miss something. "'A bold, threatening mien, a hurried step, splayed gait, restless hands, violent breathing.'" In the madman's hair I could see a bird's nest and part of a blue eggshell. His eyes moved mechanically in his head, like they had little rollers behind them, but I could hear him making low animal noises of being alive. His sandals slapped the floor as he paced, making angrier slaps than I thought sandals could even make. Heat came off him like from a toaster. Then he whirled to face me, looked right at me, and said, "I heard that, pussy," and before I could even register this, my mother had yanked me to the next cell.

"Perverts are still madmen, but don't pick a pervert just to pick a pervert," she said.

The madman with the nest called, "I can fucking hear you!"

But it was interesting—as soon as we were no longer in front of his cell, it was as if we'd changed the channel. I could hear the dull white noise of whatever world tumbled down the hill behind the gallery, but it must have been something with the acoustics because I could no longer hear the madman at all—not his breathing or his sandals or his chain or anything he might have yelled—not once I was looking into the next cell. They'd really made things orderly. Or my brain had done it. But either way, I saw so many madmen that day: the whole world was made of one madman, and then it was made of the next.

The next was a Decadent Hedon, hunched under a burlap robe, but I could tell by the way the folds fell that he was leaning on a crook: "'Appearance'" (my mother reading this time), "'slothful, bloated, swarthy, indolent, irresolute, fair hair, eburnated protrusions, overall sour.'" His sleeve slipped and showed a hand, but immediately he shifted just enough for the cloth to cover it again. He had long nails. "'Medical history: succumbed to the folly of the idle rich. Discovered inebriated at a marina.'" My mother read it like a schoolchild, or a schoolteacher, that voice. Even though the Decadent Hedon ignored us, I felt embarrassed with my parents reading as if he wasn't there. I kept trying to look at him in a way that would let him know. Then I thought, *What, should we not read the information?* That's when I said, "Hello, I'm Alice." I didn't expect any one thing or another. On impulse I guess I thought he might appreciate it.

"Fantastico," said the madman, rolling his eyes either at me or because that's what madmen do. The tone, though, was pretty obviously "You know what I mean, you pawn/idiot/cracker/et cetera."

I thought of our shed and the curtains from my bedroom. I knew a madman like that wouldn't like me. He didn't say anything else, in fact he went right back to not acknowledging that we were there, just gazed, lazy-eyed, as if over a vast tabletop, through the wall behind me, through the waiting area beyond it, and out over the hills and valleys of whatever the hell he thought of the world.

I felt ashamed that I wanted so badly for my madman to like me. Like this was all about me. Which it was. I was the one coming of age.

I don't know how I got us to the next one. Oh, yes I do: my mother said, "Honey, have a look at this."

This one was Contemporary Bipolar. Like two for one. He was low, now, "sickly, peevish, having suffered a recent rejection of a manuscript he'd sent to an important publisher." I'm paraphrasing what my father read. They'd found him holding court in a city park, where everyone called him Professor, wearing round glasses with no glass in them. He had this enthusiastic teenage boy who'd follow him around with an apple crate to stand on. Mom observed that you could tell different doctors wrote up the information cards. She said this one had been in a creative mood. The conclusion of the medical history was that this madman was the son of a lowly cleaning lady and had never been to college. It marveled that he could be so erudite in his philosophies, though the doctor confessed he had not heard of many of the figures the mad-man liked to quote. He was not sure if this was a measure of his own ignorance, as he had only taken introductory courses in the classics, and although he had done very well in them, it had been a long time ago. My father attempted a knowing glance at my mother, which she rejected. He whispered to me, "Next thing you know, that doctor's gonna be eating a madeleine."

I said, "What are you talking about?" and then I felt bad.

Next there was a woman madman: "with monstrous breasts, contorted, black"—actually, the madmen were a vari-ety of races and racial mixtures, but this card pointed out *black* for some reason—"eyes bulging, head and arms thrown back, clothes discarded on the floor" (all noted on the card, as well as true to my observation), "with a madman's staff, clenching hands, found biting her own arm, broken out of chains, bold, brazen, brainless"; then a Cretin, with his wiener in a bottle, peeing, then holding the bottle up and looking in it with a monocle ("He's imitating his physician," my father interpreted, "monkey see monkey do"; to which my mother flashed him a look about insensitively using a monkey anal-ogy and he said, "I'm just explaining!"); a Cuckold wearing a Cuckold's horns, I don't know what they were made out of but they looked real; a Schizo-affective who on his card it said "mute" and explained that like so many, he'd latched on, in an early delusion, to where the Bible says, "If thine eye offend thee, pluck it out," a sentence which, gathering from my education, has resulted in madmen missing just about every body part you can think of, but this madman had cut his tongue out, and then, to cauterize it, stuffed a flaming torch down his throat. Mom: "*Cauterize* means seal up"; me: "I know," but I didn't. Then a Possessed guy with landscape tattoos. Then a short guy evolving into a divine being, officially Monomaniac, with sticks stuck into his hair like a crown, trying to look down on us. Next a Wildman dragging a club, with a face like a "panther or a goat," this heavy lumpy body, like he'd broken everything and healed back wrong; then a Phlegmatic, "sad, recumbent, forgetful, pale, eating the bread of the workers of iniquity . . . protruding eyes, weak chin, terror"; and next a rich girl whose secret lover had joined the army and died. Then Frenetic. Fevered delirium, "raving but seated, ready to be purged." Drawings on one wall of his cell showed a warden after a patient with a billy club and a doctor after a patient with a needle, and on another wall a drawing of being looked at by two tall people with a short one. The one with most detail I recognized from our textbook: an operation to remove the Stone of Folly. The doctor had given the madman the stone just cut from his head, and the madman held it in the air like a jewel. The drawing showed it glinting with light. The drawings were good, considering they'd been done with a stick and fingers and who knows what for paint.

I got dizzy on and off through the madmen, partly because all the iron in my body was rushing out between my legs but also because of the madness. After the Recumbent Frenetic was a pair of cells each containing a Fool, dancing, a man fool and next door to him a woman fool: one with a feather headdress, one with bells around the wrists and ankles. Light-hearted types, goiter on the neck of one, one with a pink balloon on a branch of a bifurcated stick, counterparts dancing like mirror images—how could they know through the wall? It didn't make sense to look at them individually, but I couldn't see both cells at once. The gallery was too narrow, I couldn't back up enough, so I looked from one to the other trying, but it made me feel seasick. I felt at odds with myself, that phrase came to me. Like I was related to whatever invisible puppet master was making them dance together when they couldn't even see each other. I think I spent less time with them than anyone, but the effect went straight to my body.

Plus there was the madman in the cell right after them.

This one had an information card that folded out like an accordion. "'At sixteen,'" my father read, "'she became insane over the favor her older sister received from a young man, her husband, so that she was institutionalized.'"

"Whose husband?" my mother asked. "Who lets these people write?" My mother had continued her commentary all through the gallery; I'd just tuned most of it out. But the point here is this madman's huge long history:

"Periodic manias, daily three to six in the afternoon. Much of the day she behaved normally, but from noon until three sank into the deepest melancholy. Following that she would become lively, and at exactly three in the afternoon she would get a fit of rage and smash everything, attack her attendants and drink enormous amounts of ice water. At six she would become calm again. Taken in by a family when she was seventeen, who, within a year, interrupted three suicide attempts with a silk cord." My mother, again concerned with grammar, wondered how the family might have used a silk cord thusly. But the story went that the girl was finally found so dead she was almost black (I hadn't known this about death), but they revived her, and while they were deciding what to do with her next, she disappeared. Turned out she wanted to be a dancer, which I used to want to be myself, and started working at strip clubs by night and taking dance classes by day and through her stripper and dance friends met up with a troupe of trapeze artists who went across the country and Europe, meeting up with circuses and innovative performing groups, putting on intense acts that, for certain invite-only audiences, were rumored to contain explicit sex with emotional and intellectual depth. A distinguished artist within this community, her prison record called it Live Queer Porn. "And yet," said the account, "such transgressions often bear the germs of healing in them."

Then something happened. The account said: "suddenly." Suddenly she quit the troupe, burned her costumes, wrapped herself in rags, took up a staff of madness decorated with shells, strung a crucifix around her neck, and joined a group of pilgrims on their way to Rome. They were a whole group of people who felt bad about themselves so they went to Rome, but when they got there, the girl threw her rags into the Tiber and wouldn't go into the cathedral. She slept in the Colosseum for months. Then something else happened which I forgot, and probably they skipped some stuff, and she ended up at a mission taking care of orphans even though she refused to wear the crucifix or explain what she was praying, which she was allowed to do because she'd impressed all the religious people, one of whom eventually fell in love with her, ruining his career, but she wasn't interested in him like that, and this whole episode seemed to wear her out, so she kissed her orphans goodbye one by one and then left on a boat in the night, which wrecked in a storm near Messina, where she washed up and was taken in by a group of shepherds—her feet were all cut up—until she could walk, by which time the local doctor had fallen for her and kept inventing medical problems so she'd stay. But once she figured that out, he just left everything and went with her through a junglelike landscape until one night they were accosted. She cut the thumbs off the assailant and escaped, but the doctor was killed. There was definitely some more religion, stone temples, shamans and stuff, Amazons, and a battle she helped win with poison she discovered in local sap, but she started drinking heavily and rather than admit her addiction to her tribe, she slunk into the jungle, where she lived on fruit and roots—that'll dry you out—and then something else and she ended up here, in godforsaken nowhere California, after an episode not far from my school actually, where she had been "excessively frightened by soldiers" is how the write-up put it, please note the air quotes which are so annoying but I'm serious because I believe I've heard about those assholes.

You'd think she'd look like a model but she didn't—she was plump and ordinary, with small features and a round, almost silly nose, her eyes and skin sort of pulled out of place a fraction. And you'd think to have done all those things she'd be old, but she seemed more like she could be my sister just done with college with a place of her own. My mother said the doctors were obviously believing her delusions, and she was going to ask the cat-eyed nurse if this was some kind of test, but god, Mom, can't you just have an interesting life? Or is it like everyone really does end up with one of four kinds of cars and one of four kinds of house and one of four kids you met in junior high?

Obviously, this is the madman I wanted. Obviously, my mother said no.

I'm paraphrasing.

This is my day, I told her. This is the one day that of all days is my day and it's not up to you. This decision is going to make me who I am. The woman madman, round and rosy, watched me yelling at my mother with a small smile on her face, looking somewhere between our yelling heads. I don't know what my father was doing. I was so angry. Sometimes when I get really angry, I get really articulate. I said exactly what I was thinking, exactly the way I would want to have said it. But it doesn't matter if you're right, if you made your case, and it doesn't matter if god, somewhere, is on your side. Whatever happens, happens anyway. My mother said obviously they were trying to pawn this madman off, otherwise why would her case history be ten times longer than anyone else's? I said I didn't care if it was all lies, I loved her. I said I felt inspired and connected, at which point the rosy woman looked at me like I was crazy, and her eyes went right into mine, and I could feel my feelings flaring behind my eyes, just as her feelings were flaring behind hers, lighting them up, so I knew we were both lit up, so I knew at least in that way I was right.

Well, that's what it was like at the time. I don't know. You get caught up in a moment.

It seemed real.

I said okay, whatever, I'll take the Dancing Fools. My mother was so mad her lips had disappeared. I still don't know where my father was. And I don't know what the madmen were thinking of all this yelling. They've seen it all, anyway. I could sort of hear some laughing, but who knows at what, and again the acoustics. Me and my mom having out this scene, and in front of a completely undeterminable audience, if that's even a word. When we were finally silent and I finally looked at her again, she was building up to say something and then swallowing it and then building up again. When she finally said it, she said it like it was the worst, meanest thing she could possibly say.

"You are on your own" is what she finally pronounced, and because she said it to be the meanest possible thing to say, it was.

As we learned in class, when madness comes, it comes up the spine and radiates. Madman after madman has described it this way through history, often saying they were touched by god. Of course that's not what I felt from my mother— boy, she would love that—but my point is it was very physical receiving her words, like being iced over and then cracked. I thought of madness while I felt it. Then she stormed away down the hall, which would have had more of the abrupt effect she was after except the hall was so long she kind of dissipated down it. Plus, after a couple minutes of me watch- ing her recede, still gasping from how mean she was, my father appeared from behind me and followed after her like a can trailing a car when you just got married. *Boom* went the double doors, way far away, or *whoosh* or something. I don't even remember, but it seemed to let noise out from behind the scenes, and even though I know the doors went to the waiting room, what came out was what you'd expect from those vast back rooms that spilled down the hill behind the asylum: babbling, screaming.

The whole idea is you take in a madman and that teaches you about Facing the Incomprehensible and Understanding Across Difference, and soon we are one big family. Without looking at her again, I left my place in front of the cell of the rosy woman I'd wanted and stared into the cell of the Imbe- cile who was next. What had he been doing through all that with his lumpy head and beaky honker? It felt like a betrayal to even stand there, to even try to imagine who he was, so I turned around.

Turning around meant I faced a white wall. It occurred to me that I was seeing exactly what all the madmen see, but without the bars. What's that developmental stage called when you can finally do abstract thinking? Algebra? Just kidding.

I didn't want to look at any more madmen. I sat down on the floor. I kept looking at the wall. It was so white.

Then the double doors swung open and smacked the walls with an echoing bang, and then *thump thump* came the cat-eyed nurse with her outward-reaching hair and rubber shoes making squeaks every few steps. Hands came waving through bars as she stomped toward me, though as she neared I could see she wasn't angry at all, or stomping, it was just the sound of moving down that unpredictable gallery. Some hands she slapped five or did twinkle fingers with, and quips went back and forth that I couldn't hear. She got to me and stood with her hands on her hips and gazed down at me mock-somethingly, which got me sheepish, as I'm sure she intended.

"You seriously want the Dancing Fools," she said.

"Yes."

"*That* I would not have predicted." She walked a little circle around me, shaking her red mane, and I pretended I wasn't freaked out to look at her, and after a few seconds of pretending, it was true. *I'm not freaked out by a cat*, I thought, *and I'm not freaked out by a nurse. So where's the problem?* That's where I was, emotionally. "Do you *dare* me to give you the Fools?" she asked.

"No, I don't *dare* you, it's just what I pick."

She stopped and crouched next to me. She was wearing orange tights with her white uniform and I hadn't even noticed it before. Now that the rest of her was normal, the tights could look crazy.

"Look, miss. I get 'rude' all day from people like *them*," she said. "Do you think I need 'rude' from *you*?" I could feel her looking at me, but no matter how much of a problem I didn't have with her I could not look directly into those fucked-up golden orbs of doom, and just like that, her life stretched before me: one endless gallery of madmen seen as if through a keyhole because of my catty eyes. I had one cat-eyed kid left from a litter lost tragically, and a husband always out on the prowl.

I'm kidding.

What happened is off I hopped from my high horse because she was nice, she was right about me, and I didn't need to understand her back.

She pulled a small spiral notebook from the front pocket of her skirt. There was a list of names in handwriting that looked like calligraphy: Bobo, Kai, Armand, Kelly. "These are all fine choices, and they all like you fine," she said. I hadn't seen any of them yet. They were farther down the gallery. Maybe there was an information card on me. The kingdom of the mad is inexhaustible, as they say. I knew a kid once whose parents were against the madman system, and he got out of it by spending summers building houses for the poor and taking a test on human rights history. I was glad my parents weren't around to interfere, but I still thought of that kid's parents, parents like one thing, like conjoined twins, but reverse: of two bodies and one mind.

Then suddenly I thought I felt blood spilling out of me and I stood up in a panic, like a rabbit on the highway, no idea which way to go. It was awful. Along with my boots, I was wearing brown pants that were plain but just cut really nice for my body, but I hadn't been thinking, when I put them on, about my period and all that could happen. I had no idea what would happen with this color pants if I leaked. The madman in the cell behind me, the imbecile with the head and the beak, who at some point had snuggled up with his sheet on his cot and was possibly sleeping, sat up with a jerk and said, in a voice that sounded not like an Imbecile talking back to a dream, not like an Imbecile at all: "No, please, not me. I'll do anything. I've got a bad feeling about you."

"You want to meet them?" said the nurse, still holding out her spiral notebook.

"I need to go to deal with my period," I said. "I'll take Armand."

Honestly, I know that in some cultures girls are supposed to feel shame over their period, and it's not like I feel anyone should be ashamed of what they are, but if you're like, "Oh, the flow of my blood, the essence of my womanhood," well, that is just stupid and disgusting. There I am with my responsible-looking pants on the handbag hook in the stall, standing in my socks and, oh yeah, my naked ass, at the counter wiping blood off my crash-appropriate underwear with a paper towel. What, then, is least disgusting: put your underwear back on all damp and horrific, put your underwear on inside out so the damp part rubs up on your favorite and nicest pants, put them back on and stuff them with toilet paper that might fall down your leg at any second, don't put them back on and hope you don't leak again until you can get more underwear and perhaps a *panty liner* which why didn't your mother fucking suggest this ever, and why have you never seen any panty liners in the house? Perhaps it is your mother that is disgusting. And even then where do you put your underwear, in your pocket or what? Because you left your bag in the car because you wanted your hands free for picking out your madman. Not to mention I thought this place was so well equipped, and hasn't anyone ever noticed that girls who are on the *first* day of their *first* period and don't know what they're doing come here all the time? So where's looking that in the eyes and understanding it? So also, as Carrie would say, none of your beeswax about what is least disgusting in my worldview.

Outside the bathroom the nurse was waiting for me, leaning on the wall like she was from the fifties.

"You okay?"

"Yes," I said.

"Armand, still? You sure?"

"Yes."

She smiled, then, a 100 percent genuine smile which there's no faking. I know, because I have watched myself in the mirror and tried.

So his name was Armand, and in that way my madman transformed from a madman to the name of a man, which is only a little different but counts at least some. The nurse pushed back through one set of double doors to go get him ready, and I pushed through another, into the waiting room with a pile of forms and my vacant parents, who were staring at posters on opposite ends as if they were looking out portholes in a ship. Where their heads weren't blocking, I could see that one poster was a phrenology diagram, and the other was a color-coded brain scan. Were they even looking at what they were looking at? Twinges in my belly were either anxiety or cramps or both. I didn't know anyone who'd just picked a name from a list on advice from a psychiatric/psychotic-looking nurse. But I know you can never pick exactly right. There'd be a whole other batch any other day. One day you could walk in and it's your old friend Bitsy from second grade wearing a rag and picking her butt and looking at you and the space next to you like it's the same thing. Which maybe it is. I didn't throw a dart, but the way I chose my madman had very little magic in it, and what should I learn from that?

Well, it had a little magic, like a pebble in a setting forged for a diamond.

Oh, Armand, I thought. *My own little pebble.* The phrase came back to me: *coloboma of the iris*, and it sounded like a lullaby.

Meanwhile, I handed some forms to my dad and we sat as if peacefully doing paperwork while all the weight in the room slid toward the black hole created by my mother as she ignored us both. I'd missed something, something between them, and probably something with the nurse, as well. I asked my dad, I guess to break the ice, "Why do so many of them have sticks?" because all I knew about my madman was, according to the nurse, he was not going to leave his behind and I should be okay with that. And his cloak.

"Staffs," my father said, considering. "Shepherds used to carry crooks. Madmen have traditions."

"What they have," my mother said, still focused on the phrenology poster, "is a brain disorder."

I pictured sheep like marbles, always wandering off, pictured a madman named Armand on a grassy hill, his marbles rolling away, trying to pull them back with his crook, useless. How far he must have traveled, hiking back roads and mountain trails, fording creeks with it, balancing with three legs. I pictured that. How he might have speared a fish with it, or clubbed a rabbit over the head to eat, or slain an enemy in the night. Or used it for a wand, to turn seawater potable, to ward off evil, to punish his tormentors. Or the stick was bifurcated. It split. In order to represent his brain.

"Okay, geniuses, perhaps it's not a brain disorder," my mother said, as if anyone had said anything. "He's been emasculated by his madness. In fact, it's a dick. Let him have it. It makes him feel better." Unsurprisingly, this seemed to hurt my father's feelings. It also appeared that while she was not yet talking to me, she wanted me to know she was there, so that was a good sign.

The nurse materialized in the nurses' station and I met her in the window. I gave her the paperwork and she gave me a SMTWTFS pillbox, a chart that showed how it was set up, and a bag of meds. She gave me the number of a psychopharmacologist named Dr. Sandy and said this is who to call for refills or if Armand seemed too down for too long, or too excited over nothing, or not sleeping, or having trouble talking or moving, or not making sense when he talked, or violent. She must have seen the look in my eyes because she said, "Just call the number if something doesn't seem right. Trust your instincts." It felt good for her to say that, although I wondered about the boy with the cowlick and if he should trust his instincts, too, if everyone, no matter how dumb, young, or crazy, should be trusting instincts. The rosy woman with her adventures, the nurse with her crazy eyes and her white uniform. There were instincts all over the place. I looked up to see my mother leaving the building. A length of toilet paper struggled to escape from her jacket pocket.

My dad said, "She sees you growing up and she's afraid of losing you."

"She said that?"

"Not exactly."

In the parking lot our car and truck were staring straight ahead like they weren't ready to talk, either. My mom's head was a rock hovering impossibly over her steering wheel. I decided to ride home with my dad because at least he was

normal. I felt bad for about three seconds, putting the madman in the back for our first ride, but I enjoyed horrifying my
mother by doing it. She glared at me from behind the window while she felt through her purse for her phone. Receipts,
her falling-apart checkbook, an extra ring of like forty keys
and I don't know if there's been forty things in her life that
had locks, a separate falling-apart wallet for pictures, open
dirty Life Savers and all kinds of crap that why doesn't she
just throw away, like a manual for our Mister Mixer, for god's
sake I've seen it in there, all these things I knew were bulging
out of her purse and spilling into the car and I'm sure slid
under the seat without her noticing because she was so busy
glaring at me. I just hopped into the back of the truck, and
my dad helped me fit my madman into his harness, which fit
perfectly from what I could tell with him enveloped in his
cloak. I clipped him to the tarp-ties and hopped into the cab.
By that time, her car was gone. And my bag was still in there,
too. I made peace with the possibility that I would sacrifice
my best pants to my big day.

At first, my madman didn't seem sure how to position
himself and he wouldn't put his staff down. I watched by
using the mirrors so he wouldn't feel self-conscious. He definitely wobbled while we were backing up but then sat leaning against the cab and held the staff in his lap. He'd been
quiet but helpful while we were fitting his harness on. I was
so distracted I wasn't taking it all in, and again, I felt bad about
that, but he was helping in this very gentle/unobtrusive way,
letting a hand creep out from his cloak and taking a strap and
then passing it back through the other side. He didn't say a
thing or make a sound. I should have just put her out of my
mind and really taken this opportunity, I mean it was our first
impression, and as soon as we got going I felt so bad I wanted
to cry for wasting it, but the thing about madmen is most of

their memories are fucked up, so you never know when anything you do or don't do will stick, and they've been through so much that you kind of can't go wrong anyway, as long as you're not overall abusive or evil. As a group, they really know how to let things go, or else they'd be dead already. The truck had one of those sliding panels in the back window, so I could poke my head out every so often and see the top of his head, still hidden in his cloak, and the fabric blowing around him like a ghost but in reverse, heavy and black instead of filmy white, but still moving around as if there wasn't anyone in there when of course there was.

Then I watched my dad's head bobbing along the strip of landscape. His cheek looked really soft, even with a not-great shaving job. The plan was we'd go home and let the madman just be by himself or rest in the shed while we had dinner as a family to celebrate. Then I would bring him his plate and I guess get to know him? That's the part I hadn't done so much imagining in anticipation. I was also having my doubts about being greeted at the house with any lasagna.

"Whatever happened to your madman, Dad?" I knew it was a woman madman, and I knew it made him nervous to talk about it, and I knew he felt like he hadn't always done the right thing. I'd heard all about my mother's madmen, how she'd had one and then another and they'd both been cured, and she had a box tied with ribbons that had letters from them in it, and a certificate of appreciation from California, and invitations to come work for boards of things. The landscape was blurry and peripheral because I was looking at my dad, and I thought of the schoolhouse with the spinning weathervane out of time with everything else, and tried to remember if we'd passed it already, but I felt turned around trying to anchor myself in the recollection, and immediately after that it seemed irrelevant. Things were different, weren't they? But for some reason my dad was still hesitating the way he always had about his experiences, and I just had this sudden image of him peeling back his face, revealing his own madness, and crying out: "I'll tell you what happened to my madman! I married her!"

Instead, he winced. He said, "Honey, it's private. And very sad. And this is your big day."

I know you don't show just anyone your madman, like sex, but even people who talk all the time about something that's supposedly private are covering for something else. The more I was part of the whole adult world, the more turned out as one secret after another. My madman was still just a cloak and a stick, and oh yeah, we call him Armand. But there was my dad, who I'd supposedly known all my life, and what was he?

If the world looked different so far, the difference was it didn't look so symbolic. That is not what a girl wants when she comes of age.

At the house, my mother's car was in the driveway with its daytime running lights still on and both doors flopped open. Eyes rolled back, limbs splayed.

"Take Armand to his shed," said my father.

He was terrified.

Back in the gallery of madmen, when my mother was yelling because of what I wanted, I looked at her eyes and tried to see them objectively. Their blueness, whiteness, redness. I tried to look at her eyeballs themselves—not the lids or brow or her crow's feet or the other muscles in her face. I wanted to know how emotion could come shooting from her eyes the way it did. Maybe I couldn't block out the rest of her face, maybe that was impossible, like pretending I wasn't her kid would be impossible. Maybe the feelings came from the situation and not her body. Maybe the situation and her body were the same thing or I will never understand because I don't have enough empathy.

She said I was romanticizing. She said I'd like anyone if I knew the whole story. She said being free is not being free if you are in pain. She said madness is pain.

I said, "I have pain."

She said, "It's different for them because it's more."

What do you want to be wearing when your father comes back from checking on your mother and you learn that this time your mother has actually killed herself? This is what I wondered, sitting in the cab of the truck in the driveway, looking at the familiar world, which had become so still. Sweatpants, I thought, because you can sleep in them and be in public in them. Cross-trainers because they have good grip and breathe. Layers on top: a long-sleeved shirt under a short-sleeved shirt because it's flexible and I've seen pictures of her wearing that when I was a baby, also a fleece vest because I might have to sleep in the hospital with air conditioning, or, I kept thinking, you might have to be outside at night. I kept picturing that. Looking for her in the woods behind the house. Which one time I did do. My father was out of town and she had been crying for so many hours, I'd tried being nice, I'd tried leaving her alone, and I threatened to call Dad and she said "Go ahead" in a way I took to mean if I called him, she'd finish herself off for sure. I even put my face up to hers and then screamed in a sudden burst like saying "boo!" but as loud and angry as possible and not funny. It freaked me out about myself when I screamed like that. Eventually it was like two in the morning and I was in my bed holding the phone, trying to decide what would be the moment I would call a hospital, trying to decide what the sign would be, and I heard the front door, and looked out the window, and saw her take off running into the woods. One time our cat had gone missing and years later I found her collar and her bones in the woods while I was walking, and then that night we all went into the woods to bury her, with candles, stones we'd chosen, and a baby tree, and it was beautiful. When my mother took off into the woods, I hesitated to follow her. I had this image of a beautiful candlelight thing and then just, I don't know, peace, being on my own.

But I did follow her into the woods. It was so dark but I found her curled up on the trail by a fallen mossy log. She was covered in dirt and not crying anymore. She came with me, which I don't know what I would have done if she hadn't, but for some reason I didn't even have to touch her, she just came with me. At the house she said, "Thank you for saving my life," and I let her take a bath, even though I was scared of what might happen in there, but I told myself to stop being dramatic, she was my mother and she could take a bath. Maybe I believed that I had saved her life, and that's what let me go to sleep and next day tell my father a version of it when he came home that was true but unemotional in a way that let him not make a big deal out of it and let me think it wasn't a big deal after all. But even then I knew it wasn't me that saved her life. It wasn't about me. I was just there while she was maybe going to die and maybe not, and then she just didn't.

I got out of the truck and stood in the driveway, unhooking Armand's harness. He scrambled to his feet under his cloak and used his staff of madness to steady himself on the ridged bed. I reached out my hand—the idea was he could take it and walk along to the tailgate—and there was a moment when he seemed to be deciding between dropping his stick to take my hand or not. It was impossible to know for sure with the cloak, but I had the distinct impression that he might have only one arm.

The sun was starting to set. The house was behind us. He didn't take my hand, just made his way to the end of the truck, and I lowered the tailgate, and then he sat on it. His legs dangled. I glanced to see if I could see his feet, if they would be in boots, or shoes, or sandals, or rags, or nothing. If he would have feet. But his cloak floated below them, and only the staff poked out. I hopped up onto the tailgate with him, careful not to touch him, and the truck rocked like a boat, and so, like a lookout at the prow of a ship of fools, I put my hand to my forehead and squinted toward the sun into the distance. I could spy with my little eye the roof of the shed, partway down the hill, and sparks like tiny fires in the low water in the creek, and the woods like a curtain with everything beyond darker than ever, sucking up the light. Soon the sun was setting enough that it was past the time when the pieces of the world are sharp and distinct from each other and on to when everything becomes one fuzzy mass. Our eyes saw and then didn't see the forms we knew were in there, and then saw again for a second, and then were just making it up. Okay, that's what *my* eyes were doing, anyhow. At some point I was going to have to say something to him, and if he had a voice he was probably going to say something back. Maybe something would change then. The sun was so close to set, but it hadn't set all the way. Instead of saying something, I thought about the weathervane, spinning, because I wanted the moment to last forever.

THE ARMS AND LEGS
OF THE LAKE

Mary Gaitskill

Jim Smith was riding the train to Syracuse, New York, to see his foster mother for Mother's Day. He felt good and he did not feel good. Near Penn Station, he'd gone to a bar with a green shamrock on it for good luck. Inside, it was dark and smelled like beer and rotten meat in a freezer—nasty but also good because of the closed-door feeling; Jim liked the closed-door feeling. A big white bartender slapped the bar with a rag and talked to a blobby-looking white customer with a wide red mouth. A television showed girl after girl. When Jim said he'd just gotten back from Iraq, the bartender poured him a free whiskey. "For your service," he'd said.

Jim looked out the train window at the water going by and thought about his white foster father, the good one. "You never hurt a little animal," his good foster had said. "That is the lowest, most chicken thing anybody can do, to hurt a little animal who can't fight back. If you do that, if you hurt a little animal, no one will ever respect you or even like you." There had been green grass all around, and a big tree with a striped cat in it. Down the street, ducks had walked through the wet grass. He'd thrown some rocks at them, and his foster father had gotten mad.

"For your service," said the bartender, and poured him

another one, dark and golden in its glass. Then he went down
to the other end and talked to the blob with the red mouth,
leaving Jim alone with the TV girls and their TV light flashing on the bar in staccato bursts. Sudden flashing on darkness; time to tune that out, thought Jim. Time to tune in to
humanity. He looked at Red Mouth Blob.

"He's a gentle guy," said Blob. "Measured. Not the kind
who flies off the handle. But when it comes down, he will
get down. He will get down there and he will bump with
you. He will bump with you, and if need be, he will bump
on you." The bartender laughed and hit the bar with his rag.

Bump *on* you. Bumpety-bump. The truck bumped along
the road. He was sitting next to Paulie, a young blondie from
Minnesota who wasn't wearing his old Vietnam-style vest.
Between low sand-colored buildings, white-hot sky swam in
the sweat dripping from his eyelashes. There was the smell of
garbage and shit. A river of sewage flowed in the street and
kids were jumping around in it. A woman looked up at him
from the street and he could feel the authority of her eyes as
far down as he could feel, in an eyeless, faceless place inside
him, where her look was the touch of an omnipotent hand.
"Did you see that woman?" he said to Paulie. "She look like
she should be wearing jewels and riding down the Tigris in
a gold boat." "That one?" said Paulie. "*Her?* She's just hajji
with pussy." And then the explosion threw them out of the
truck. There was Paulie, sitting up, with blood geysering out
his neck, until he fell over backward with no head on him.
Then darkness came, pouring over everything.

The bartender hit the bar with his rag and came back
down the bar to pour him another drink.

He looked around the car of the train. Right across from
him there was a man with thin lips and white finicky hands

drinking soda from a can. Just up front from that there was a thick-bodied woman, gray, like somebody drew her with a pencil, reading a book. Behind him was blond hair and a feminine forehead with fine eyebrows and half ovals of eyeglass visible over the frayed seat. Beyond that, more foreheads moved in postures of eating or typing or staring out the window. Out the window was the shining water, with trees and mountains gently stirring in it. She had looked at them and they had blown up. Where was she now?

"Excuse me." The man with thin lips was talking to him. "Excuse me," he said again.

"Excuse me," said Bill Groffman. "You just got back from Iraq?"

"How did you know?" the guy replied.

"I got back myself six months ago. I saw your jacket and shoes."

"All right," said the guy, like to express excitement, but with his voice flat and the punctuation wrong. He got up to shake Bill's hand, then got confused and went for a high five that he messed up. He was a little guy, tiny really, with the voice of a woman. Old, maybe forty, and obviously a total fuckup—who could mess up a high five?

"Where were you?" asked Bill.

"Baghdad," said the guy, blatting the word out this time. "Where they pulled down Saddam Hussein. They pulled—"

"What'd you do there?"

"Supply. Stocking the shelves, doin' the orders, you know. Went out on some convoys, be sure everything get where it supposed to go. You there?"

"Name it—Ramadi, Fallujah, up to Baquba, Balad. Down to Nasiriyah, Hillah. And Baghdad."

"They pulled down the statue . . . pulled it down. Everybody saw it on TV. Tell me, brother, can you—what is this body of water out the window here?"

"This is the Hudson River."

"It is? I thought it was the Great Lakes."

"No, my man. The Great Lakes is Michigan and Illinois. Unless you're in Canada."

"But see, I thought we *were* in Illinois." He weaved his head back and forth, back and forth. "But I was not good in geography. I was good in MATH." He blatted out the word *math* as if it were the same as *Baghdad*.

But he was not thinking about Baghdad now. He was tuned in to the blond forehead behind him, and it was tuned in to him; it was focused on Jim. He could feel it very clearly, though its focus was confused. He looked at its reflection in the window. The forehead was attached to a small pointy face with a tiny mouth and eyeglass eyes, a narrow chest with tits on it, and long hands that were turning a piece of paper like a page. She was looking down and turning the pages of something, but still, her blond forehead was coming at him. It did not have authority; it was looking to him for authority. It was harmless, vaguely interesting, nervous, and cute.

When Bill was gone, he realized that nobody at home would understand what was happening. He realized it, and he accepted it. You talk to a little boy in broken English and Arabic, make a joke about the chicken or the egg—you light up a car screaming through a checkpoint and blow out a little girl's brains. You saw it as a threat at the time—and maybe the next time it would be. People could understand this fact—but this was not a fact. What was it? The guy who put a gun in his mouth and shot himself in the portable shitter, buddies who lost hands and legs, little kids dancing around cars with rotting corpses inside, shouting, "Bush! God Is Great! Bush!"—anybody could understand these events as information. But these events were not information. What were they? He tried to think what they were and felt like a small thing with a big thing inside it, about to break the thing that held it. He looked out the window for relief. There was a marsh going by, with soft green plants growing out of black water, and a pink house showing between some trees. House stood for home, but home was no relief. Or not enough. When he came home, his wife told him that the dog he'd had since he was sixteen was missing. Jack had been missing for weeks and she hadn't told him. At least six times when they'd been on the phone and he'd asked, "How's Jack?" she'd said, "He's good."

"Hey," said the little guy. "You sure this a river?"

"Positive."

Positive. She said she didn't tell him about Jack because he had only a few weeks left and she wanted him to stay positive. Which was right. They both agreed it was important to stay positive. And so she'd said, "He's good," and she'd said it convincingly, naturally. He hadn't known she was such a good liar.

"The reason I'm asking is, it looks too big to be a river. A lake is always going to be bigger than a river. I remember that from school. The river leads to the lake; the river is the arms and legs of the lake. Only thing bigger than the lake is the ocean. Like it says in the Bible, you know what I'm saying?"

Bill didn't answer because the smell of shit and garbage was up in his nose. The feel of sand was on his skin, and he had to try not to scratch it, or rub it in public like this crazy ass would surely do. Funny: The crazy ass—he should have some idea of what it was like, even if he was just supply. But even if he did, Bill didn't want to discuss it with him. All the joy you felt to be going home; how once you got home you couldn't feel it anymore. Like his buddy whose forearm had been blown off, who still felt his missing arm twitch—except it was the reverse of that. The joy was there, almost like he could see it. But he couldn't feel it all the way. He could make love to his wife, but only if he turned her over. He could tell it bothered her, and he didn't know how to explain why it had to be that way. Even when they lay down to sleep, he could relax only if she turned with her back to him and stayed like that all night.

"But that don't look like the arm or the leg. That look like the lake. Know what I'm sayin'?"

Bill looked out the window and put on his headset. It was Ghostface Killah, and he turned up the volume—not to hear better, but to get his mind away from the smell and the feeling of sand.

Like it says in the Bible, you know what I'm sayin'? The white guy across the aisle laughed when he heard that, a thick, joyless chuckle. Puerile, thought Jennifer Marsh. Like a high school kid. Probably racist, too. Jennifer had marched against the war. She didn't know any soldiers; she had never talked to any. But she was moved to hear this guy, just back from war, talking so poetically about rivers and lakes. I should reach out to him, she thought. I should show support. I'll get up and go to the snack car for potato chips, and on the way back, I'll catch his eye.

The idea stirred Jennifer, and made her a little afraid. Afraid that he would look at her, a middle-aged white woman, and

instantly feel her to be weak, artificially delicate, a liar. But
I'm not weak, thought Jennifer. I've fought to get where I am.
I haven't lied much. Her gaze touched the narrow oval shape
of the soldier's close-cropped head, noticing the quick, reactive way it turned from aisle to window and back. Sensitive,
thought Jennifer; delicate, and naturally so. She felt moved
again; when the soldier had stood to shake hands with the
guy across the aisle, his body had been slim and wiry under
the ill-fitting clothes. He looked strong, but his strength was
wiry and tensile—the strength of a fragile person made to
be strong by circumstance. His voice was strange, and he
blurted out certain words with the harshness of a sensitive
person trying to survive the abrading force of the world.

See me comin' (blaow!) start runnin' and (blaow! blaow!) . . .
Phantom limb, phantom joy. Music from the past came up
behind Ghost's words; longing, hopeful music. *Many guys
have come to you* . . . His son, Scott, had been three when he
left; now he was nearly five, healthy, good-looking, smart,
everything you would want. He looked up at his father as if
he were somebody on TV, a hero, who could make everything right. Which would've been great if it were true. . . .
With a line that wasn't true . . . "Are you going to find Jack
tonight, Daddy?" asked Scott. "Can we go out and find him
tonight?" . . . *And you passed them by* . . .

"The lake is bigger—but wait. You talkin' 'bout the ocean?"
      Jennifer's indignation grew. The soldier's fellow across the
aisle was deliberately ignoring him and so, stoically adjusting
to being ignored, he was talking to himself, mimicking the
voice of a child talking to an adult, then the adult talking

back. "The ocean is bigger than the lake," said the adult. "The ocean is bigger than *anything.*"

He hadn't meant to look for Jack; the dog was getting old, and if he hadn't come back after two weeks, he must be dead or somewhere far away. But Wanda had done the right thing and put up xeroxed flyers all over their town, plus a town over in every direction. He saw Jack's big bony-headed face every time he went to the post office or the grocery store, to the gas station, pharmacy, smoke shop, office supply, department store, you name it. Even driving along back roads where people went for walks, he glimpsed Jack's torn, flapping face stapled to trees and telephone poles. Even though the pictures showed Jack as a mature dog, he kept seeing him the way he was when he got him for Christmas nine years before: a tiny little terrier, all snout and paws and will to chew shit up. He greeted Bill every day when he came home from school; he slept on his bed every night. When Scott was born, he slept in front of the crib, guarding it.

Jennifer tried to imagine what this man's life was like, what had led him to where he was now. Gray, grim pictures came half-formed to her mind: a little boy growing up in a concrete housing project with a blind face of malicious brick; the boy looking out the window, up at the night sky, kneeling before the television, mesmerized by visions of heroism, goodness, and triumph. The boy grown older, sitting in a metal chair in a shadowless room of pitiless light, waiting to sign something, talk to somebody, to become someone of value.

......

The first time he went out to find Jack, he let Scott go with him. But Scott didn't know how to be quiet, or listen to orders; he would suddenly yell something or dart off, and once Bill got so mad that he thought he'd knock the kid's head off. So he started going out alone—late, after Scott and Wanda were in bed. They lived on a road with only a few houses on it across from a stubbly field and a broken, deserted farm. There was no crime and everybody acted like there could never be any. But just to be sure, he took the Beretta Wanda had bought for protection. At first, he carried it in his pocket with the safety on. Then he carried it in his hand.

Jennifer grieved; she thought, I can't help. I can't understand. But I can show support. This man has been damaged by the war, but still he is profound. He will not scorn my support because I'm white. As if he had heard, the soldier turned around in his seat and smiled. Jennifer was startled by his face—hairy, with bleary eyes, his mouth sly and cynical with pain.

"My name's Jim," the soldier said. "Glad to meet you."

Jennifer shook his proffered hand.

"Where you headed today?" he asked.

"Syracuse. For work."

"Yeah?" He smiled. His smile was complicated—light on top, oily and dark below. "What kind of work?"

"I'm giving a talk at a journalism school—I edit a women's magazine."

"Yeah? An editor?"

His smile was mocking after all, but it was the sad mocking men do when the woman has something and they don't. There was no real force behind it.

"I heard you talk about being in Iraq," she said.

"Yeah, uh-huh." He nodded emphatically, then looked out the window as if distracted.

"What was it like?"

He looked out the window, paused, and began to recite: "They smile and they say you okay / Then they turn around and they bite / With the arrow that fly in the day / And the knife in the neck at night."

"Did you make that up? Just now?"

"Yes, I did." He smiled again, still mocking, but now complicitous, too.

"That's good. It's better than a lot of what I read."

Did you make that up? Just now? Stupid, stupid woman, stupider than the drunk nigger she was talking to. Carter Brown, the conductor, came down the aisle, wishing he had a stick to knock off some heads with, not that they were worth knocking off really. That kind of white woman—would she never cease to exist? You could predict it: Put her in a car full of people, including black people who were sober and sane, hell, black people with PhDs, and she would glue herself, big-eyed and serious, to the one pitiful fool in the bunch. He reached the squawk box and snatched up the mouthpiece.

"To whoever's been smoking in the lavatory, this message is for you," he said into it. "If you continue to smoke in the lavatory, we will, believe me, find out who you are, and when we do, we will put you off the train. We will put you off, where you will stand on the platform and smoke until the next train comes sometime tomorrow. Have a nice day."

Not that the sane and sober would talk to her, it being obvious what she was—another white jackass looking for the truth in other people's misery. He went back down the aisle, hoping against hope that she would be the smoker and that he would get to put her off the train.

"Did you talk to the Iraqis?" she asked.

"Sure. I talked to them. I talked mostly to kids. I'd tell 'em to get educated, become a teacher. Or a lawyer."

"You speak their language?"

"No, no, I don't. But I still could talk to 'em. They could understand."

"What were they like?"

"They were like people anywhere. Some of them good, some not."

"Did any of them seem angry?"

"Angry?" His eyes changed on that word, but she wasn't sure how.

"Angry at us. For tearing up the country and killing them."

She thinks she's the moral one, and she talks this way to a soldier back from hell?

Mr. Perkins, sitting behind, could hear the conversation, and it filled him with anger. Yes, the man was obviously not playing with a full deck. No, the war had not been conducted wisely, and, no, there were no WMD. But anyone, *anyone* who knew what war was should be respected by those who didn't. Perkins knew. It was long ago, but still he knew: The faces of the dead were before him. They were far away, but he had known them. He had put his hands on their corpses, taken their personal effects: Schmidt, Heinrich, PFC, 354th Fortress Artillery . . . *Zivilberuf: Oberlehrer.* He remembered that one because of those papers he'd kept. God knows where they were now, probably in a shoe box in the basement, mixed up with letters, random photos of forgotten people, bills and tax statements that never got thrown out. *Schmidt, Heinrich.* His first up-close kill. He'd thought the guy looked like a schoolteacher, and, by Christ, he had been. That's why he'd kept the papers—for luck.

Yes, he knew, and obviously this black man knew—and how could she know, this "editor" with her dainty, reedy voice? More anger came up in him, making him want to get up and chastise this fool woman for all to hear. But he was heavy with age and its complexity, and anyway, he knew she just didn't know better. As an educated professional, she ought to know better, but obviously she didn't. She talked and talked, just like his daughter used to do about Vietnam, when she was a seventeen-year-old *child.*

"Angry?" said the soldier. "No. Not like you."

She said, "What do you mean? I'm not angry."

The soldier wagged his finger slowly, as if admonishing a child. "The thing you need to know is, those people know war. They know war for a long time. So not angry, no. Not like you think about angry."

"But they didn't—"

The finger wagged again. "Correct. They don't want this war. But they know. . . . See. They make a life. The shepherd drives his animals with the convoy. The woman carries water while they shoot. Yes, some, they hate—that's the knife in the neck. But some smile. Some send down their good food. Some appreciate the work we do with the kids, the schools. . . ."

......

He could walk for hours, every now and then calling the dog and stopping to listen. He walked across the field and into the woods and finally into the deserted farm. When he walked, he didn't think of Iraq always. He thought of Jack when he was a pup, of wrestling with him, of giving him baths, of biking with the dog running alongside, long, glistening tongue hanging out. He thought of how patient Jack was when Scott was a baby, how he would let the child pull on his ears and grab his loose skin with tiny baby fists.

But the feeling of Iraq was always underneath, dark and liquid, and pressing up against the skin of every other thing, sometimes bursting through: a woman's screaming mouth so wide, it blotted her face; great piles of sheep heads, skinned, boiled, covered in flies; the Humvee so thick with flies, they got in your mouth; somebody he couldn't remember eating a piece of cake with fresh offal on his boot; his own booted foot poking out the doorless Humvee and traveling over endless gray ground. In the shadows of the field and the woods and the deserted farm, these things took up as much space as his wife and his child, the memories of his dog. Sometimes they took up more space. When that happened, he took the safety off the gun.

Like, an angry, cripple, man, don't push me! Ghost's voice and the old music ran parallel but never touched, even though Ghost tried to blend his voice with the old words. Sad to put them together, but somehow it made sense. Bill took off his headset and turned back toward the guy across from him, feeling bad for ignoring him. But he was busy talking to the older blonde behind him. And she seemed very interested to hear him.

......

"And the time I went out on the convoy? See, they got respect, at least those I rode with. 'Cause they didn't fire on people unless they know for a fact they shot at us. Not everybody over there was like that. Some of 'em ride along shooting out the window like at the buffalo."

"But how could you tell who was shooting?" asked Jennifer. "I hear you can't tell."

"We could observe. We could observe from a distance for however long it took, five, sometimes maybe even ten minutes. If it was a child, or somebody like that, we would hold fire. If it was an enemy . . ."

If it was an enemy, thought Bill Groffman, he would be splattered into pieces by ten people firing at once. If it was an enemy, he would be dropped with a single shot. If it was an enemy, she would be cut in half, her face gazing at the sky in shock, her arms spread in amazement as to where her legs might've gone. If it was an enemy, his or her body would be run over by trucks until they were dried skin with dried guts squashed out, scummed-over eyes staring up at the convoy driving by. *Oooh, that's gotta hurt!*

"Still," said Jennifer. "I don't see how they could not be mad about us being there."

Oooh, that's gotta hurt! Six months ago, he would not have been able to hold back. He would've gotten into it with this woman, shut her up, scared the shit out of her. The war was stupid, okay. It was probably for oil. But it was also something else. Something you could not say easily with words. There was enemy shooting at you and then there was the thing you could say with words. There was dead squashed enemy and there was the thing you could say with words. There was joking at squashed bodies and nothing else to be said.

"Here," said Jim. "Let me ask you something now."

"Okay," said Jennifer.

"Do you ever feel guilty?"

"What?"

"Do. You. Ever. Feel. Guilty." He smiled.

"Doesn't everybody?"

"I didn't ask about everybody. I asked 'bout you."

"Sometimes," she said. "Sometimes I feel guilty."

"Good. Because guilt is not a bad thing. Guilt can instruct you; you can learn from guilt. Know what I mean?"

"I think so." She felt something, but she didn't know if it was manipulated or real.

He smiled. "So here's what I want to say. Guilt, you can live with. But you can't live with regret. Can't learn from it, can't live with it. So don't ever feel regret."

The thing was, Perkins could not really understand this man, either. He didn't know if it was because he had forgotten, or because war was different now, or because the man was black, or because . . . Well, the man was not right, that was obvious. But you heard things about a lot of them that didn't seem right. You supported them, absolutely; you wanted to be proud; what happened after Vietnam should never be allowed to happen again—but then you read someplace that they didn't care about killing civilians, that it was like video games to them. Stuff about raping young girls, killing their families, doing sex-type things with prisoners, taking pictures of it—and then you'd read somebody sneering that "the Greatest Generation" couldn't even fire their guns, while these new guys, they *liked* to kill.

"Now I have another question. Is that okay?"

"Yeah."

"When you look out that window, what do you see?"

Jennifer looked and thought; even though he was crazy, she wanted to give a good answer. "Trees," she said. "Sky. Water. Plants, earth."

He smiled. "All of that *is* there. I see it, too. But that is not all I see."

"What do you see?"

In his head, Bill saw a horror movie. It was one he'd seen a long time ago. It was some kind of fight between good—or maybe it was just normalcy—and evil. Evil had gotten the upper hand, and good was going to lose. "We can't stop them now!" cried the scientist. But then by mistake the evil people woke up something deeper than evil. They woke things underground called *Mogred* or some shit, things who knew only destruction and didn't care who was destroyed; they made the earth come open and humanoid monsters without faces came out the crack. They weren't on anybody's side, but because evil had annoyed them by waking them up, they attacked evil.

Jim saw trees and shining water. He saw lake water, river water, sewage water. He saw the eyes of God in the water, and they were shining with love. In the eyes of God, even the sewage water in the street was shining. In the eyes of God, a woman came out on the street, moving very quick. She pulled up her robe and walked into the shining sewage and pulled a child out by the hand. She led the child and looked at Jim, and the mouth of God roared.

Outside the train window, the mouth of God was silent. It was silent and it was chewing—it was always chewing. That was okay; it needed to eat to keep the body going. And the eyes of God were always shining with love. And the nose of God—that was something you grabbed at on your way to the chewing mouth. Like those people in the old television movie climbing on the giant presidents.

The war was like the crack in the ground that let the Mogred out. The crack in the ground had nothing to do with arguments about smart or stupid, right or wrong. The crack in the ground was even sort of funny, like in the movie with shitty special effects, the monsters pouring out the hole like a football team.

Who told anybody they couldn't shoot their weapons? That's what Perkins wondered. If the American army couldn't shoot, who killed all those Germans and Japanese? True: Straight off the ramp, chest-deep in the ocean, fighting its sucking wet muscle toward the shore with machine-gun fire hammering down around you and shells slamming your eardrums, pushing on floating corpses as you got close—you couldn't see what to shoot at then. They hadn't been chasing a ragged Third World army with inferior weapons and they hadn't been wearing body armor. They came out of the ocean into roaring death, men exploding like bloody meat, and all of it sucked into the past before memory could grab on to it or the nerves had time to react. At least that must be why he could not recall most of it as anything but a blur.

The war was a crack in the ground, and the Iraqis were the Mogred, pouring out. Then somehow he and his buddies had become Mogred. Then it was nothing but Mogred all around, clawing and killing. Bill glanced at the guy sitting across from him; that was no Mogred. No way.

"I can't tell you what I see," said Jim. "And what I see you will never see. Because I have been touched by God." There was a wheel of colors spinning in his mind, gunfire and music playing. A little ragged boy ran down the street, a colored pinwheel in his hand. A ragged little boy tried to crawl away, and was stopped by a bullet. Laughter came out an open window. "You never hurt a little animal," his foster father said.

Unseeing and unhearing, she stared impassively in his face. "By Jesus, you mean?"

He felt himself smile. "Not by Jesus, no. Lots of people have been touched by Jesus. But I have been touched by God."

Unfeeling spread through her face like ice, stilling the warmth and movement of her skin. With unfeeling came her authority. "How'd you get to skip Jesus?" she asked.

"If I told you that, we would have to be talking all day and all night. And then you'd be like me." He smiled. Ugliness bled through his smile, the weak, heartbreaking ugliness of the mentally ill. Dear God, could they really have sent this man into combat?

When his daughter was a little girl, sometimes she would ask him to tell her a war story, her eyes soft and shining with trust, wanting to hear about men killing one another. But he never told her about killing. He told her about the time he was standing guard one night, when he thought he heard an enemy crawling through the brush to throw a grenade; just before he squeezed the trigger, a puppy came wiggling into the foxhole with him. He told her about the time in Italy, when he and his buddies saw a tiny woman carrying a great jug of water on her head, and he'd said, "Hell, I'm going to help that woman!" He'd stopped her and taken the jug off her head and almost collapsed, it was so heavy; his buddies had fallen about laughing. . . .

"Were you in the National Guard?" she asked. "Were you a reservist?"

"Naw," he said. "I was active duty."

"Well," she said. "I really appreciate talking to you. But I have to get back to my work now."

"All right." He extended his hand across the seat.

"And thank you for your service," she said. "Even if I don't agree with the cause."

This pitiful SOB had been in *Iraq*? That was one fucked-up piece of information, but it made all the sense in the world, thought Carter Brown as he took the ticket stub down off the overhead. They deliberately went out and got the dumbest, most desperate people for this war—them and kids like his nephew Isaiah who *were* in the National Guard so they could go to school. Isaiah, who got A report cards all through community college and who would be in a four-year school now if he wasn't busy being shot at. He tapped the spooky-looking white guy on the shoulder maybe a little too hard to let him know his stop was coming up and—hell, everybody on this train was nuts—the man just about jumped out of his seat.

Perkins was relieved to hear her finally become respect-ful. Even if the guy was half-wrapped. At least liberals had changed since Vietnam. Everyone had changed. His daugh-ter, who used to fight him so hard about Vietnam, supported this war less equivocally than he did. She told him about attending a dinner for a returning soldier who, when he got up to speak, said, "I'm not a hero. I'm a killer. But you need killers like me so that you can go on having all the nice things you have." Some of the people at the dinner had been dis-turbed, but not her. She'd thought it was great. She'd thought it was better than platitudes or ideals; she'd thought it was real.

He looked at his watch. When they got to the station, he'd go to the bathroom for another smoke.

One night when there was a full moon, out in the field across from the house where his wife and child slept, he remem-bered his first night in Iraq. He remembered how good he'd felt to be there. There had been a full moon then, too, and its light had made a luminous path on the desert, like something you could walk out of the world on. He remembered thinking, We are going to do something great here. We are going to turn these people's lives around.

"Your stop, comin' up."

Now there was the man across the aisle, talking to himself and nodding. Now there he was in the dark field, holding a loaded gun pointed at nothing. There were all the people criticizing him for not getting a job, for being cold to his wife, for yelling at his son, for spending so much time looking for a dead dog. He put away his iPod, shouldered his pack. They didn't get it, and he didn't blame them. But alone in the field or in the woods, looking for his dog, was when he could feel what had happened in Iraq and stand it.

The train was pulling into the station; people were getting up with their things; conductors were getting ready to work the doors. The silent soldier stood up with his pack and briefly clasped hands with the crazy soldier. Perkins fingered his packet of cigarettes.

He had been a returning hero; then people forgot the war had ever happened. Then war was evil and people who fought it were stupid grunts who went crazy when they came back. Then people suddenly went, "Hey, the Greatest Generation!" Then just as suddenly, they were the assholes who couldn't even shoot their weapons. No, not even assholes, just nice boys who didn't know what was real. These guys now—some people said they were killers, some said heroes, and some said both. What would they be in fifty years?

When people got off the train, Jim got up and wandered away, and for a moment Jennifer thought he'd gotten off. But then she saw him wandering toward the back of the car,

apparently talking to himself as well as to other people as he
went. She tried to pay attention to the short essay she had
been working on before her conversation with him. It was
by a novelist who was in love with a vegetarian and who
had gone to great lengths to pretend that he was even more
"vegan" than she was in order to impress her. It was light and
funny, and she felt too bitter now to appreciate those things.

Coming out of the bathroom, Perkins noticed the couple,
the woman first. She was black, and normally he didn't like
black, but she was beautiful and something else besides. Her
soft eyes and full presence evoked sex and tenderness equally,
and he could not help but hold her casual gaze. Or he would
have, if she hadn't been sitting next to a giant of a man with
quick, instinctive eyes.

Old white fool look away quick—good. Shouldn't have
looked at all, and wouldn't if they were anyplace else. Chris
put one hand on Lalia's arm and worked the game on his
laptop with the other. He wasn't mad; old man couldn't help
but look. Lalia was all beauty beside him, shining and real in
a world of polluted pale shit. He killed the dude crawling at
him in the street, then got the one coming out the window.
He moved down her arm and put his hand over hers; her
fingers responded as if linked to him. His feelings grew huge.
Dudes came rushing at him in the hallway; he capped 'em.
He was looking forward to tonight, to the hotel room he'd
reserved, the one that was supposed to have a mirror over
the bed and a little balcony where they'd drink champagne
with strawberries in chocolate. He killed dudes coming out
the door; he entered the secret chamber. He wanted it to be

something they would always remember. He wanted it to be the way it had been the first time with her.

It was humiliating to be old, to shrink before the glowering eyes of a stronger man. But just mildly. He understood the young gorilla—you'd have to protect that woman. He thought of Dody, when she was young, how it was to go out with her; he'd always had to be looking out for trouble, for some idiot wanting to start something. You always had to watch for that if you were with a good-looking female, and it could become automatic. Sometimes it had made him scared and sometimes angry, and the heat of his anger had gotten mixed up with the heat in her eyes, the curves of her small body, the heat she gave off without knowing it. That was all gone now, almost. They still kissed, but not with their tongues, just on the lips. Still, he remembered. . . .

It took a long time to get with her, years, but when it finally happened, it was like the song his aunt used to listen to when she sat by the window, her glass of Bacardi and juice tilted and the sunlight coming in, her knees opening her skirt—the song that made him run and hide in the closet the first time he heard it, because it was too much of something, something with no words, but somehow living in the singer's voice and words, high-voiced sweet-strong words that made him remember his mama, even though everybody said he was too young to remember. *If I ever saw a girl / That I needed in this world / You are the one for me* . . . The words were like the poems on cheap cards, like the poems nerds wrote to get A's in class—but the way this singer said them, they were deep and powerful, and they said things no words could say, things

his mama said with her hand, touching his face at night, or
his aunt, just brushing against him with her hip. . . . A trapdoor opened; the secret chamber was flooded with dudes
wearing masks.

Oh, my little love, yeah . . . He had her every way, with no
holding back, with his shirt over the light to make it soft. She
was a quiet lover, but the warm odor that came off her skin
was like a moan you could smell, and though she moved like
every other woman, she said things with her moves that no
other woman said. When they finished, she turned around
and pushed the hair off her dazed eyes, and—*oh, my little
love*—took his face in her hands. Nobody ever touched his
face, and the move surprised him so that he almost slapped
her away. Then he put his hands over hers and let her hold
his face.

He remembered that when the war ended, the Italians invited
the victorious Americans to come see a local company put on
an opera. They went for something to see, but it was mostly
boring, too hot, everybody smelling bad up in the little balcony, the orchestra looking half-asleep, flies swarming—but
then there was this one woman singing. He made his buddies
quit horsing around, and they did; they turned away from
their jokes and listened to the small figure on the stage below,
a dream of love given form by her voice and pouring from
her to fill the room. When he and his friend Bill Steed went
backstage to meet her, it turned out she was older than they'd
thought, and not pretty, with makeup covering a faded black
eye. But he still remembered her voice.

......

In the essay Jennifer was editing, the writer claimed that sometimes whom you pretend to be is who you really are. He said that sometimes faking was the realest thing you could do.

"Bitch! What you think you doin', bitch!"

Her heart jumped; she looked up, to see a huge black man looming over somebody in the seat behind him, yelling curses—oh no, it was him. He was yelling at Jim. A woman stood and grabbed the huge man's shoulder, saying, "Nuh, nuh, nuh," a beseeching half word, over and over. She meant no, don't, but the big man grabbed Jim, lifted him up, and shook him like a doll. The woman shrank back, but she said it more sharply, "Nuh, nuh!" Ignoring her, the man stormed down the aisle to where Jennifer sat, holding Jim up off the ground as if he were nothing. Jim was talking to the man, but words were nothing now. She felt the whole train, alert with fear but distant, some not even looking. She stood up. The man threw Jim, threw his whole body down the aisle of the train. She tried to speak. Jim leapt off the floor with animal speed and put his arms up as if to fight. She could not speak. Next to her, an old man stood. "Ima kill you!" shouted the big man, but he didn't. He just looked at the old man and said, "He touch my wife's breast! I look over and see his hand right on it!" Then he looked at her. He looked as if he'd waked suddenly from a dream and was surprised to see her there.

"It's all right," said the old man mildly. "You stopped him."

"It's not all right," said the young man, but quietly. "Nothin' all right." He turned and walked the other way. "You ruinin' my vacation," he said as he went. "Pervert!" He didn't look at his wife on his way out of the car.

The old man sat down. Jennifer looked at Jim. He was pacing back and forth in the aisle, talking to himself, his face a fierce inward blank.

......

There's no God, no face, you weak, lying—*you lying sack of shit!* There is just the woman and the roaring and the world and the pit. Jim fell into the pit, and as he fell, all the people in it screamed things at him. Teachers, foster parents, social workers, kids, parents, all the people he'd ever known standing on ledges in gray crowds, screaming at him as he fell past. He landed hard enough to break his bones. He was under an overpass, standing with his backpack and crying while his father drove away, with his mother yelling in the front seat and his sister crying in the back, looking out with her hands on the window. Paulie sat next to him with no head and blood pouring up. His uncle said, No, I cannot take those children. Paulie fell backward and blood ran from him. Dancing children lay in pieces; guns shot. The woman and the child ran, fell, ran, far away. His foster mother opened the door and let in the warm light of the living room; the bed creaked as she sat and sang to him. The trees shivered; the giant fist slammed the ground; they shivered. The long grass rippled in the machine-gun fire. The pit opened, but Jim stayed on the shivering ground. He did not fall again. His sister came to him and held him in her arms. *La la la la la la la la la means / I love you*. He closed his eyes and let his sister take him safely into darkness. She could do that because she was already dead. He didn't know it then. But she was.

The door between cars exploded open and they came rolling down the aisle, two conductors and a human bomb, the bomb saying, "And we on our honeymoon! In Niagara Falls! The only reason we even took the train is she's afraid to fly—and this happens?"

"I know just the one you mean." The black conductor sighed. "I know just the one."

"And she's pregnant!"

"Don't worry, we'll get him off," said the white conductor. "We'll have the cops come get him. He won't bother you no more."

Carter had no pleasure in putting the man off the train. He could barely look at his sad, weak-smiling face. He even felt sorry for the blond woman sitting there with her dry, pale eyes way back in her head, looking like she'd been slapped. He got the clanking door open, kicked down the metal steps, handed down the man's bag, and thought, Cheney should have to fight this war. Bush should have to fight it, Saddam Hussein and Osama bin Laden should fight it. They should be stripped naked on their hands and knees, placed within striking distance of one another, each with one foot chained to the floor. Then give them knives and let them go at it. Stick their damn flags up their asses so they can wave 'em while they fight. "Utica," he yelled, "this stop, Utica."

He didn't seem to mind being put off the train; he was even pretty cheerful about it. Jennifer looked out the window to see what happened to him once he got off, and saw him talking to two policemen who stood with folded arms, nodding politely at whatever it was he was saying. She heard the big guy up ahead of her, still going over it. "I heard him talking to you," he said to someone. "What was he saying?"

"Crazy stuff," replied a woman. "I was real quiet, hoping he'd go away, but he just kept on talking."

"Why did he *do* that?" asked the big man. "I don't usually do nobody like that, but he—"

"No, you were right," said the woman. "If you hadn't done something, the next person he grabbed might've been a little girl!"

"Yeah!" The big man's voice sounded relieved. Then he spoke to his wife, loudly enough for Jennifer to hear him several seats away. "Why didn't you *say* anything?" he asked.

Because he like my brother. I could feel it when he touch me. My brother grab a teacher's butt in the sixth grade; he do it for attention, it's not even about the butt. I can't talk about it here, Chris, with all these people listening; I can feel them, and this is too *private*. But my brother coulda turned out like this man here. Kids beat on him when he was like six, he had to be in the hospital, and for a long time after, he talked in this whisper voice that you can hardly hear, like he's talking to himself and to the world in general, talking like a radio with the dial just flipping around, giving out stories that don't make sense, but all about kicking and punching and killing people. He gets older and anything anybody says to him, he's like, "Ima punch him! An then do a double back-flip and kick him in the nuts! An then in the butt! An then—" It so annoying, and he still doing it when he gets older, only then he talks 'bout how somebody does this or that, he's gonna pull out a gun and shoot him. He talks like he a killah but he a *baby*, and everybody knows it. My brother now, he works as a security guard in a art museum, where he sits all day and reads his books and plays his games. But he coulda got hurt real bad—and looked at one way, he talk so stupid, he almost deserves it. But look the other way, Chris. You do that, you see he lives in Imagination, not the world; shit don't mean for him what it do for us. You see that and you wanna protect him even if he is a damn fool, and also I don't want you into any trouble over me; our baby is in me, and it is *our day*. I love you; that's why I don't say nothin, Chris—

She put her hand on his arm and felt him withdraw from her without moving. Her heart sank. She looked out the window; they were moving past people's yards. Two white kids, just babies, were standing in wet yards with their mouths open, looking at the train, one with his fat little legs bare, only wearing shoes and a hoodie. Her heart hurt. Please come back, she said with her hand. I love you. Don't let this take away our beautiful night.

Disgraceful all around, thought Perkins. That they would treat a vet like that, that a vet would act like that. He looked out the window at small homes set in overgrown backyards: broken pieces of machinery sitting in patches of weeds, a swing set, a tied-up dog barking at the train, barbed wire snarled around chain link. A long time ago, he would've gone home and told his wife about the guy being put off the train; they would've talked about it. Now he probably wouldn't even mention it to her. They used to talk about everything. Now silence and routine were where he felt her most. He looked out on marshy land, all rumpled mud and pools of brown water with long grasses and rushes standing up. His reflection in the glass floated over it, a silent, impassive face with heavy jowls and a thin, downward mouth. And there, with his face, also floated the face of Heinrich Schmidt, PFC.

He didn't touch that lady's breast; he touched her shoulder. Maybe the train rocked or something, made his hand move down, but he was just trying to talk to her. The conductor knew that—he told him so—but they'd had to take him off the train anyway. It wasn't good, but it wasn't that bad. The police said there would be another train, sometime. But there was no lake to look at here. Where you sat down here, there were just train tracks and an old train that didn't work any-more. He would sit for a while and look at them and then he would call his foster mother. He would tell her there'd been a problem he'd had to solve, a fight to be broken up, and he couldn't get back on the train. His foster mother had strong hands; she could break up fights, using the belt when she had to. She served food; she rubbed oil into his skin; she washed his back with a warm cloth. She led a horse out of the sta-ble, not her horse, the horse of some women down the road, the one that sometimes his sister, Cora, would ride. She was so scared to get up on it at first, but then she sat on it with her hands up in the air, not even holding on, and they took her picture.

They said Cora died of kidney failure and something that began with a *p*. They had the letter when he got back to the base. He read the letter and then he sat still a long time. Before he left for Iraq, she'd had her toes cut off, and she said she was going to get better. When she took him to the airport, she walked with a fancy cane that had some kind of silver bird head on it. He couldn't picture her dead. He could picture Paulie, but not Cora. When he came home, he still thought he might see her at the airport, standing there look-ing at him like he was an idiot, but still there, with her new cane. He thought he might see her up in Syracuse, riding her horse. Even though he knew he wouldn't. He thought he might see her on her horse.

Riding her horse across a meadow with flowers in it, rid-ing in a race and winning a prize, everybody cheering, not

believing she'd really won, cheering. Then they'd have a bar-
becue like they used to have, when the second foster father
was there, basting the meat with sauce and Jim helping out.
The cats walking around, music turned up loud so they could
hear it out the window, his foster singing him a dirty song to
the tune of "Turkey in the Straw." It was mostly a funny song,
so it wasn't dirty; and his foster always told him not to hurt
anything, so it wasn't bad. Or his other foster father did—he
wasn't sure. He'd tell his foster about lying on the ground
and feeling it shiver in terror, watching the grass and the trees
shiver. He might tell him about seeing a little boy trying to
crawl away and getting shot. Because his foster father had
known Jesus. But he did not know the face of God.

Or did he? Softly, Jim sang, *Way down south where the
trains run fast / A baboon stuck his finger up a monkey's ass. /
The baboon said, Well fuck my soul / Get your fucking finger
out of my asshole.* A family came down the stairs, little girls
running ahead of their mother. They wouldn't think his sister
would win the prize, but she would; she would race on her
horse ahead of everybody, her family cheering for her. Not
just her foster family, but her real family, Jim's real family.
Like the Iraqis had cheered when they first came into the
town. Before they had shot.

RAW WATER

Wells Tower

"Just let me out of here, man," said Cora Booth. "I'm sick. I'm dying."

"Of what?" asked Rodney, her husband, blinking at the wheel, scoliotic with exhaustion. He'd been sitting there for four days, steering the pickup down out of Boston, a trailer shimmying on the ball hitch, a mattress held to the roof of the camper shell with tie-downs that razzed like an attack of giant farting bees.

"Ford poisoning," Cora said. "Truckanosis, stage four. I want out. I'll walk from here."

Rodney told his wife that a hundred and twenty miles lay between them and the home they'd rented in the desert, sight unseen.

"Perfect," she said. "I'll see you in four days. You'll appreciate the benefits. I'll have a tan and my ass will be a huge wad of muscle. You can climb up on it and ride like a little monkey."

"I'm so tired. I'm sad and confused," said Rodney. "I'm in a thing where I see the road, I just don't comprehend it. I don't understand what it means."

Cora rolled down the window to photograph a balustrade of planted organ cactuses strobing past in rows.

"Need a favor, chum?" she said, toying with his zipper.

"What I need is to focus here," Rodney said. "The white lines keep swapping around."

"How about let's scoot up one of those little fire trails," Cora said. "You won't get dirty, I promise. We'll put the tailgate down and do some stunts on it."

The suggestion compounded Rodney's fatigue. It had been a half decade since he and Cora had made any kind of habitual love, and Rodney was fine with that. Even during his teenage hormone boom, he'd been a fairly unvenereal person. As he saw it, their marriage hit its best years once the erotic gunpowder burned off and it cooled to a more tough and precious alloy of long friendship and love from the deep heart. But Cora, who was forty-three, had lately emerged from menopause with large itches in her. Now she was hassling him for a session more days than not. After so many tranquil, sexless years, Rodney felt there was something unseemly, a mild whang of incest, in mounting his best friend. Plus she had turned rough and impersonal in her throes, like a cat on its post. She didn't look at him while they were striving. She went off somewhere by herself. Her eyes were always closed, her body arched, her jaw thrusting up from the curtains of her graying hair, mouth parted. Watching her, Rodney didn't feel at all like a proper husband in a love rite with his wife, more a bootleg hospice man bungling a euthanasia that did not spare much pain.

"Later. Got to dog traffic. I want to get the big stuff moved in while there's still light," said Rodney to Cora, though night was obviously far away, and they were making good time into the hills.

The truck crested the ridge into warm light and the big view occurred. "Brakes, right now," said Cora.

The westward face of the mountain sloped down to the vast brownness of the Anasazi Trough, a crater of rusty land in whose center lay sixty square miles of the world's newest inland ocean, the Anasazi Sea.

Rodney swung the truck onto the shoulder. Cora sprang to the trailer and fetched her big camera, eight by ten, an antique device whose leather bellows she massaged after each use with neat's-foot oil. She set up the tripod on the roadside promontory. Sounds of muffled cooing pleasure issued from her photographer's shroud.

Truly, it was a view to make a visual person moan. The sea's geometry was striking—a perfect rectangle, two miles wide and thirty miles long. But its water was a stupefying sight: livid red, a giant, tranquil plain the color of cranberry pulp.

The Anasazi was America's first foray into the new global fashion for do-it-yourself oceans—huge ponds of seawater, piped or channeled into desert depressions as an antidote to sea-level rise. The Libyans pioneered the practice with the great systematic flood of the Qattara Depression in the Cairo desert. The water made one species of fox extinct and thousands of humans rich. Evaporation from the artificial sea rained down on new olive plantations. Villages emerged. Fisherfolk raised families hauling tilefish and mackerel out of a former bowl of hot dirt. American investors were inspired. They organized the condemnation of the Anasazi Trough a hundred miles northwest of Phoenix and ran a huge pipe to the Gulf of Mexico. Six million gallons of seawater flowed in every day, to be boiled and filtered at the grandest desalination facility in the western hemisphere.

A land fever caught hold. The minor city of Port Miracle burgeoned somewhat on the sea's western shore. On the east coast sat Triton Estates, a gated sanctuary for golfers and owners of small planes. But before the yacht club had sold its last mooring, the young sea began to misbehave. The evaporation clouds were supposed to float eastward to the highlands and wring fresh rain from themselves. Instead, the clouds caught a thermal south, dumping their bounty on the far side of the Mexican border, nourishing a corn and strawberry bonanza in the dry land outside Juárez. With no cloud cover over the Anasazi, the sun went to work and started cooking the sea into a concentrated brine. Meanwhile, even as acreage spiraled toward Tahoe prices, the grid spread: toilets, lawns, and putting greens quietly embezzling the budget of desalinated water that should have been pumped back into the sea to keep salt levels at a healthy poise. By the sea's tenth birthday, it was fifteen times as saline as the Pacific, dense enough to float small stones. The desalination plant's reverse-osmosis filters, designed to last five years, started blowing out after six months on the job. The land boom on the Anasazi fell apart when water got so expensive that it was cheaper to flush the commode with half-and-half.

The grocery-store papers spread it around that the great pond wouldn't just take your money; it would kill you dead. Local news shows ran testimonies of citizens who said they'd seen the lake eat cows and elks and illegal Mexicans, shrieking as they boiled away. Science said the lake was not a man-eater, but the proof was in that gory water, so the stories stayed on prime time for a good number of years.

The real story of the redness was very dull. It was just a lot of ancient, red, one-celled creatures that thrived in high salt. The water authority tested and retested the water and declared the microbes no enemy to man. They were, however, hard on curb appeal. When the sea was only twelve years old, the coastal population had dwindled to ninety-three, a net loss of five thousand souls no longer keen on dwelling in a case of pinkeye inflamed to geologic scale.

The story delighted Cora Booth as meat for her art. She'd

long been at work on a group of paintings and photographs
about science's unintended consequences: victims of robot
nanoworms designed to eat cancer cells but which got hungry for other parts, lab mice in DNA-grafting experiments
who'd developed a crude sign language using the hands of
human infants growing from their backs. Once the tenants
had fled and the situation on the sea had tilted into flagrant
disaster, Cora banged out some grant proposals, withdrew
some savings, and leased a home in Triton Estates, a place
forsaken by God and movie stars.

Salvage vandals had long ago stolen the gates off the entrance
to the Booths' new neighborhood, but a pair of sandstone
obelisks topped with unlit gas lamps still stood there, and
they still spelled class. Their new home stood on a coastal
boulevard named Naiad Lane, a thin track of blond scree.
They drove slow past a couple dozen homes, most of them
squatly sprawling bunkerish jobs of off-white stucco, all of
them abandoned, windows broken or filmed with dust; others
half-built, showing lath, gray bones of sun-beaten framing,
pennants of torn Tyvek corrugating in the wind. Rodney
pulled the truck into the driveway at number thirty-three,
a six-bedroom cube with a fancy Spanish pediment on the
front. It looked like a crate with a tiara. But just over the
road lay the sea. Unruffled by the wind, its water lay still and
thick as house paint, and it cast an inviting pink glow on the
Booths' new home.

"I like it," said Cora, stepping from the truck. "Our personal Alamo."

"What's that smell?" said Rodney when they had stepped
inside. The house was light and airy, but the air bore a light
scent of wharf breath.

"It's the bricks," said Cora. "They made them from the thluk they take out of the water at the desal plant. Very clever stuff."

"It smells like, you know, groins."

"Learn to love it," Cora said.

When they had finished the tour, the sun was dying. On the far coast, the meager lights of Port Miracle were winking on. They'd only just started unloading the trailer when Cora's telephone bleated in her pocket. On the other end was Arn Nevis, the sole property agent in Triton Estates and occupant of one of the four still-inhabited homes in the neighborhood. Cora opened the phone. "Hi, terrific, okay, sure, hello?" she said, then looked at the receiver.

"Who was that?" asked Rodney, sitting on the front stair.

"Nevis, Arn Nevis, the rental turkey," said Cora. "He just sort of barfed up a dinner invitation—*Muhhouse, seven thirty*—and hung up on me. Said it's close, we don't need to take our truck. Now, how does he know we have a truck? You see somebody seeing us out here, Rod?"

They peered around and saw nothing. Close to land, a fish or something buckled in the red water, other than themselves the afternoon's sole sign of life.

But they drove the Ranger after all, because Rodney had bad ankles. He'd shattered them both in childhood, jumping from a crabapple tree, and even a quarter mile's stroll would cause him nauseas of pain. So the Booths rode slowly in the truck through a Pompeii of vanished home equity. The ride took fifteen minutes because Cora kept experiencing ecstasies at the photogenic ruin of Triton Estates, getting six angles on a warped basketball rim over a yawning garage, a hot tub brimming and splitting with gallons of dust.

Past the grid of small lots they rolled down a brief grade
to number three Naiad. The Nevis estate lay behind high
white walls, light spilling upward in a column, a bright little
citadel unto itself.

Rodney parked the truck alongside an aged yellow Mercedes. At a locked steel gate, the only breach in the tall wall,
he rang the doorbell and they loitered many minutes while
the day's heat fled the air. Finally a wide white girl appeared
at the gate. She paused a moment before opening it, appraising
them through the bars, studying the dusk beyond, as though
expecting unseen persons to spring out of the gloom. Then
she turned a latch and swung the door wide. She was sixteen or so, with a face like a left-handed sketch—small teeth,
one eye bigger than the other and a half-inch lower on her
cheek. Her outfit was a yellow towel, dark across the chest
and waist where a damp bathing suit had soaked through.
She said her name was Katherine.

"Sorry I'm all sopped," she said. "They made me quit
swimming and be butler. Anyway, they're out back. You were
late so they started stuffing themselves." Katherine set off for
the house, her hard summer heels rasping on the slate path.

The Nevis house was a three-wing structure, a staple shape
in bird's-eye view. In the interstice between the staple's legs
lay a small rectangular inlet of the sea, paved and studded
with underwater lights; it was serving as the family's personal
pool. At the lip of the swimming area, a trio sat at a patio set
having a meal of mussels. At one end of the table slouched
Arn Nevis, an old, vast man with a head of white curls, grown
long to mask their sparseness, and a great bay window of
stomach overhanging his belt. Despite his age and obesity,
he wasn't unattractive; his features bedded in a handsome

arrangement of knobs and ridges, nearly cartoonish in their prominence. Arn was in the middle of a contretemps with a thin young man beside him. The old man had his forearms braced on the tabletop, his shoulders hiked forward, as though ready to pounce on his smaller companion. On the far side of the table sat a middle-aged woman, her blouse hoisted discreetly to let an infant at her breast. She stroked and murmured to it, seemingly unaware of the stridency between the men.

"I didn't come here to get hot-boxed, Arn," the smaller man was saying, staring at his plate.

"Hut—hoorsh," stuttered Nevis.

"Excuse me?" the other man said.

Nevis took a long pull on his drink, swallowed, took a breath. "I said, I'm not hot-boxing anybody," said Nevis, enunciating carefully. "It's just you suffer from a disease, Kurt. That disease is caution, bad as cancer."

The woman raised her gaze and, seeing the Booths, smiled widely. She introduced herself as Phyllis Nevis. She was a pretty woman, though her slack jowls and creased dewlap put her close to sixty. If she noticed her visitors' amazement at seeing a woman of her age putting an infant to suck, she didn't show it. She smiled and let a blithe music of welcome flow from her mouth: Boy, the Nevises sure were glad to have some new neighbors here in Triton. They'd met Katherine, of course, and there was Arn. The baby having at her was little Nathan, and the other fellow was Kurt Hackberry, a business friend but a real friend, too. Would they like a vodka lemonade? She invited the Booths to knock themselves out on some mussels, tonged from the shallows just off the dock, though Cora noticed there was about a half a portion left. "So sorry we've already tucked in," Phyllis said. "But we always eat at seven thirty, rain or shine."

Katherine Nevis did not sit with the diners but went to the sea's paved edge. She dropped her towel and slipped into the glowing water without a splash.

"So you drove down from Boston?" Hackberry asked, plainly keen to quit the conversation with his host.

"We did," said Rodney. "Five days, actually not so bad once you get past—"

"Yeah, yeah, Boston—" Nevis interrupted with regal vehemence. "And now they're here, sight unseen, whole thing over the phone, not all this fiddlefucking around." Nevis coughed into his fist, then reached for a plastic jug of vodka and filled his glass nearly to the rim, a good half-pint of liquor. He drank a third of it at one pull, then turned to Cora, his head bobbing woozily on his dark neck. "Kurt is a Chicken Little. Listens to ninnies who think the Bureau of Land Management is going to choke us off and starve the pond."

"Why don't they?" Cora asked.

"Because we've got their nursh—their nuh—their nads in a noose is why," said Nevis. "Because every inch of shoreline they expose means alkali dust blowing down on the goddamned bocce pitches and Little League fields and citrus groves down in the Yuma Valley. They're all looking up the wrong end of a shotgun, and us right here? We're perched atop a seat favored by the famous bird, if you follow me."

Nevis drained his glass and filled it again. He looked at Cora and sucked his teeth. "Hot damn, you're a pretty woman, Cora. Son of a bitch, it's like somebody opened a window out here. If I'd known you were so goddamned lovely, I'd have jewed them down on the rent. But then, if I'd known you were hitched up with this joker I'd have charged you double, probably." He jerked a thumb and aimed a grin of long gray teeth at Rodney. Rodney looked away and pulled at a skin tab on the rim of his ear. "Don't you think, Phyllis?" said Nevis. "Great bones."

"Thank you," Cora said. "I plan to have them bronzed."

"Humor," Nevis said flatly, gazing at Cora with sinking red eyes. "It's that actress you resemble. Murf. Murvek. Urta. Fuck am I talking about? You know, Phyllis, from the god-damn dogsled picture."

"Drink a few more of those," said Cora. "I'll find you a cockroach who looks like Brigitte Bardot."

"Actually, I hate alcohol, but I get these migraines. They mess with my speech, but liquor helps some," Nevis said. Here, he sat forward in his chair, peering unabashedly at Cora's chest. "Good Christ, you got a figure, lady. All natural, am I right?"

Rodney took a breath to say a hard word to Nevis, but while he was trying to formulate the proper phrase Phyllis spoke to her husband in a gentle voice.

"Arny, I'm not sure Cora appreciates—"

"An appreciation of beauty, even if it is sexual beauty, is a great gift," said Nevis. "Anyone who thinks beauty is not sexual should picture tits on a man."

"I'm sure you're right, sweetie, but even so—"

Nevis flashed a brilliant crescent of teeth at his wife and bent to the table to kiss her hand. "Right here, the most won-derful woman on earth. The kindest and most beautiful and I married her." Nevis raised his glass to his lips. His gullet pumped three times while he drank.

"His headaches are horrible," said Phyllis.

"They are. Pills don't work but vodka does. Fortunately, it doesn't affect me. I've never been drunk in my life. Any-way, you two are lucky you showed up at this particular juncture," Nevis announced through a belch. "Got a petition for a water-rights deal on Birch Creek. Hundred thousand gallons a day. Fresh water. Pond'll be blue again this time next year."

This news alarmed Cora, whose immediate thought was that her work would lose its significance if the story of the Anasazi Sea ended happily. "I like the color," Cora said. "It's exciting."

Nevis refilled his glass. "You're an intelligent woman, Cora, and you don't believe the rumors and the paranoia peddlers on the goddamned news," he said. "Me, I'd hate to lose it, except you can't sell a fucking house with the lake how it is. Of course, nobody talks about the health benefits of that water. My daughter?" He jerked his thumb at Katherine, still splashing in the pool, and lowered his voice. "Before we moved in here, you wouldn't have believed her complexion. Like a lasagna, I'm serious. Look at her now! Kill for that skin. Looks like a marble statue. Hasn't had a zit in years, me or my wife neither, not one blackhead, nothing. Great for the bones, too. I've got old-timers who swim here three times a week, swear it's curing their arthritis. Of course, nobody puts that on the news. Anyway, what I'm saying is, buy now, because once this Birch Creek thing goes through, this place is going to be a destination. Gonna put the back nine on the golf course. Shopping district, too, as soon as Kurt and a few other moneymen stop sitting on their wallets like a bunch of broody hens."

Nevis clouted Hackberry on the upper arm with more force than was jolly. Hackberry looked lightly terrified and went into a fit of vague motions with his head, shaking and nodding, saying "Now, Kurt, now, Kurt" with the look of a panicked child wishing for the ground to open up beneath him.

......

When he had lapped the fluid from the final mussel shell, Arn Nevis was showing signs of being drunk, if he was to be taken at his word, for the first time in his life. He rose from the table and stood swaying. "Clothes off, people," he said, fumbling with his belt.

Phyllis smiled and kept her eyes on her guests. "We have tea, and we have coffee and homemade peanut brittle, too."

"Phyllis, shut your mouth," said Nevis. "Swim time. Cora, get up. Have a dip."

"I don't swim," said Cora.

"You can't?" said Nevis.

"No," said Cora, which was true.

"Dead man could swim in the water. Nathan can. Give me the baby, Phyllis." He lurched for his wife's breast, and with a sudden move, Phyllis clutched the baby to her and swiveled brusquely away from her husband's hand. "Touch him and I'll kill you," Phyllis hissed. Nathan awoke and began to mewl. Nevis shrugged and lumbered toward the water, shedding his shirt, then his pants, mercifully retaining the pair of yellowed briefs he wore. He dove messily but began swimming surprisingly brisk and powerful laps, his whalelike huffing loud and crisp in the silence of the night. But after three full circuits to the far end of the inlet and back, the din of his breathing stopped. Katherine Nevis, who'd been sulking under the pergola with a video game, began to shriek. The guests leaped up. Arn Nevis had sunk seven feet or so below the surface, suspended from a deeper fall by the hypersaline water. In the red depths' wavering lambency, Nevis seemed to be moving, though in fact he was perfectly still.

Rodney kicked off his shoes and jumped in. With much effort, he hauled the large man to the concrete steps ascending to the patio and, helped by Cora and Hackberry, heaved him into the cool air. Water poured from Rodney's pockets.

He put his palms to the broad saucer of Nevis's sternum and rammed hard. The drowned man sputtered.

"Wake up. Wake *up*," said Rodney. Nevis did not answer. Rodney slapped Nevis on the cheek, and Nevis opened his eyes to a grouchy squint.

"What day is it?" asked Rodney. By way of an answer, Nevis expelled lung water down his chin.

"Who's that?" Rodney pointed to Phyllis. "Tell me her name."

Nevis regarded his wife. "Big dummy," he said.

"What the hell does that mean?" Rodney said. "Who's that?" He pointed at Nevis's infant son.

Nevis pondered the question. "Little dummy," he said, and began to laugh, which everybody took to mean that he had returned, unharmed, to life.

Kurt Hackberry and Katherine led Arn inside while Phyllis poured forth weeping apologies and panting gratitude to the Booths. "No harm done. Thank God he's all right. I'm glad I was here to lend a hand," Rodney said, and was surprised to realize that he meant it. Despite the evening's calamities, his heart was warm and filled with an electric vigor of life. The electricity stayed with him all the way back to number thirty-three Naiad Lane, where, in the echoing kitchen, Rodney made zestful love to his wife for the first time in seven weeks.

Rodney woke before the sun was up. The maritime fetor of the house's salt walls and recollections of Arn Nevis's near death merged into a general unease that would not let him sleep. Cora stirred beside him. She peered out the window, yawned, and said that she wanted to photograph the breaking of the day. "I'll come with you," Rodney said, and felt childish to realize that he didn't want to be left in the house alone.

Cora was after large landscapes of the dawn hitting Triton Estates and the western valley, so the proper place to set up was on the east coast, in Port Miracle, with the sun behind the lens. After breakfast they loaded the Ford with Cora's equipment and made the ten-minute drive. They parked at the remnant of Port Miracle's public beach and removed their shoes. Most of the trucked-in sand had blown away, revealing a hard marsh of upthrust minerals, crystalline and translucent, like stepping on warm ice. Rodney lay on the blanket they had brought while Cora took some exposures of the dawn effects. The morning sky involved bands of iridescence, the lavender-into-blue-gray spectrum of a bull pigeon's throat. Cora made plates of the light's progress, falling in a thickening portion on the dark house-key profile of the western hills, then staining the white homes scattered along the shore. She yelled a little at the moment of dawn's sudden ignition when red hit red and the sea lit up, flooding the whole valley with so much immediate light you could almost hear the *whong!* of a ball field's vapor bulbs going on.

"Rodney, how about you go swimming for me?"

"I don't have a suit."

"Who cares? It's a ghost town."

"I don't want to get all sticky."

"Shit, Rodney, come on. Help me out."

Rodney stripped grudgingly and walked into the water. Even in the new hours of the day, the water was hot and alarmingly solid, like paddling through Crisco. It seared his pores and mucous parts, but his body had a thrilling buoyancy in the thick water. A single kick of the legs sent him gliding like a hockey puck. And despite its lukewarmth and viscosity, the water was wonderfully vivifying. His pulse surged. Rodney stroked and kicked until he heard his wife yelling for him to swim back into camera range. He turned around, gamboled for her camera some, and stepped into the morning, stripped clean by the water, with a feeling of having been peeled to new young flesh. Rodney did not bother to dress. He carried the blanket to the shade of a disused picnic awning. Cora lay there with him, and then they drowsed until the sun was well up in the sky.

Once the drab glare of the day set in, the Booths breakfasted together on granola bars and instant coffee from the plastic crate of food they'd packed for the ride from Massachusetts.

Cora wished to tour Port Miracle on foot. Rodney, with his bad ankles, said he would be happy to spend the morning in his sandy spot, taking in the late-summer sun with a Jack London paperback. So Cora went off with her camera, first to the RV lot, nearly full, the rows of large white vehicles like raw loaves of bread. She walked through a rear neighborhood of kit cottages, built of glass and grooved plywood and tin. She photographed shirtless children, Indian brown, kicking a ball in a dirt lot, and a leathery soul on a sunblasted Adirondack chair putting hot sauce into his beer. She went to the boat launch, where five pink women, all of manatee girth, were boarding a pontoon craft. Cora asked to take their picture but they giggled and shied behind their hands and Cora moved on.

At the far end of town stood the desalination facility, a cube of steel and concrete intubated with ducts and billowing steam jacks. Cora humped it for the plant, her tripod clacking on her shoulder. After calling into the intercom at the plant's steel door, Cora was greeted by a gray-haired, bearded man wearing something like a cellophane version of a fisherman's hard-weather kit. Plastic pants, shirt, hat, plus gloves and boot gaiters and a thick dust mask hanging around his neck. His beard looked like a cloudburst, though he'd carefully imprisoned it in a hairnet so as to tuck it coherently within his waterproof coat.

"Whoa," said Cora, taken aback. Recovering herself, she explained that she was new to the neighborhood and was hoping to find a manager or somebody who might give her a tour of the plant.

"I'm it!" the sheathed fellow told her, a tuneful courtliness in his voice. "Willard Kamp. And it would be my great pleasure to show you around."

Cora lingered on the threshold, taking in Kamp's protective gear. "Is it safe, though, if I'm just dressed like this?"

"That's what the experts would tell you," said Kamp, and laughed, leading Cora to a bank of screens showing the brine's progress through a filter-maze. Then he ushered her up a flight of stairs to a platform overlooking the concrete lagoons where the seawater poured in. He showed her the flocculating chambers where they added ferric chloride and sulfuric acid and chlorine and the traveling rakes that brought the big solids to the surface in a rumpled brown sludge. He showed her how the water traveled through sand filters, and then through diatomaceous earth capsules to further strain contaminants, before they hit the big reverse-osmosis trains that filtered the last of the impurities.

"Coming into here," Kamp said, slapping the side of a massive fiberglass storage tank, "is raw water. Nothing in here but pure H's and O's."

"Just the good stuff, huh?" Cora said.

"Well, not for our purposes," Kamp said. "It's no good for us in its pure form. We have to gentle it down with additives, acid salts, gypsum. Raw, it's very chemically aggressive. It's so hungry for minerals to bind with, it'll eat a copper pipe in a couple of weeks."

This idea appealed to Cora. "What happens if you drink it? Will it kill you? Burn your skin?"

Kamp laughed, a wheezing drone. "Not at all. It's an enemy to metal pipes and soap lather, but it's amiable to humankind."

"So what's with all the hazmat gear?" asked Cora, gesturing at Kamp's clothes.

Kamp laughed again. "I'm overfastidious, the preoccupation of a nervous mind."

"Nervous about what?"

His wiry brow furrowed and his lips pursed in half-comic consternation. "Well, it's a funny lake, isn't it, Cora? I am very interested in the archaebacteria, the little red gentlemen out there."

"But it's the same stuff in fall foliage and flamingos," Cora said, brandishing some knowledge she'd picked up from a magazine. "Harmless."

Kamp reached into his raincoat to scratch at something in his beard. "Probably so. Though they're also very old. Two billion years. They were swimming around before there was oxygen in the atmosphere, if you can picture that. You've heard, I guess, the notion that that stuff in our pond is pretty distinguished crud, possibly the source of all life on earth."

"I hadn't."

"Well, they say there's something to it," said Kamp. "Now, it's quite likely that I haven't got the sense God gave a monkey wrench, but it seems to me that a tadpole devious enough to put a couple of million species on the planet is one I'd rather keep on the outside of my person."

......

Of Port Miracle's eighty dwellers, nearly all were maroon ancients. They were unwealthy people, mainly, not far from death, so they found the dead city a congenial place to live the life of a lizard, moving slow and taking sun. But they were not community-center folk. Often there was public screaming on the boulevard, sometimes fights with brittle fists when someone got too close to someone else's wife or yard. Just the year before, in a further blow to the Anasazi's image in the press, a retired playwright, age eighty-one, levered open the door of a Winnebago parked on his lot and tortured a pair of tourists with some rough nylon rope and a soup-heating coil.

According to the rules of the Nevis household, young Katherine was not permitted past the sandstone obelisks at the neighborhood's mouth. But the morning after the dinner party her father was still abed with a pulsing brain, and would likely be that way all day. Knowing this, Katherine slipped through the gate after breakfast, wheeled her little 97 cc minibike out of earshot, and set a course to meet two pals of hers, Claude Hull and Denny Peebles, on the forbidden coast.

She found them by the public pier, and they greeted her with less commotion than she'd have liked. They were busy squabbling over some binoculars through which they were leering at the fat women out at sea on the pontoon barge.

"Let me look," Claude begged Denny, who had snatched the Bausch & Lombs, an unfair thing. The Bausch & Lombs belonged to Claude's father, who owned Port Miracle's little credit union and liked to look at birds.

Denny sucked his lips and watched the women, herded beneath the boat's canopy shade, their bikinis almost wholly swallowed by their hides. They took turns getting in the water via a scuba ladder that caused the boat to lurch comically when one of them put her bulk on it. The swimming lady would contort her face in agonies at the stinging water while her colleagues leaned over the gunwale, shouting encouragement, bellies asway. After a minute or two, the others would help the woman aboard and serve her something in a tall chilled glass and scrub at her with implements not legible through the Bausch & Lombs. The women were acting on a rumor that the sea's bacteria devoured extra flesh. It had the look of a cult.

"Big white witches," whispered Denny.

"Come on, let me hold 'em, let me look," said Claude, a lean, tweaky child whose widespread eyes and bulging forehead made it a mercy that he, like the other children who lived out here, attended ninth grade over the computer. Denny, the grocer's child, had shaggy black hair, a dark tan, and very long, very solid arms for a boy of fourteen. "Fuck off," said Denny, throwing an elbow. "Get Katherine to show you hers. You'll like 'em if you like it when a girl's titty looks like a carrot."

"I'm not showing Claude," said Katherine.

In the sand beside Denny lay a can of Scotchgard and a bespattered paper bag. Katherine reached for it.

"Mother may I?" Denny said.

"Bite my fur," said Katherine. She sprayed a quantity of the Scotchgard into the bag, then put it to her mouth and inhaled.

"Let me get some of that, Kathy," Claude said.

"Talk to Denny," said Katherine. "It's not my can."

"Next time I'm gonna hook up my camera to this thing, get these puddings on film," said Denny, who was lying on his stomach in the sand, the binoculars propped to his face. "Somebody scratch my back for me. Itches like a motherfucker."

"Sucks for you," said Katherine, whose skull now felt luminous and red and full of perfect blood.

"You scratch it for me, Claude," said Denny. "Backstroke, hot damn. Look at those pies. Turn this way, honey. Are you pretty in your face?"

Just last week, for no reason at all, Denny Peebles had wedged Claude Hull's large head between his knees and dragged him up and down Dock Street while old men laughed. Claude loved and feared Denny, so he reached out a hand and scratched at Denny's spine.

"Lower," Denny said, and Claude slid his hand down to the spot between Denny's sacral dimples, which were lightly downed with faint hair. "Little lower. Get in the crack, man. That's where the itch is at."

Claude laughed nervously. "You want me to scratch your *ass* for you?"

"It itches, I told you. Go ahead. It's clean."

"No way I'm doing that, man. You scratch it."

"I can't reach it. I'm using my hands right now," said Denny. "I'm trying to see these fatties."

Katherine sprayed another acrid cloud into the bag and sucked it in. Dust clung in an oval around her mouth, giving the effect of a chimpanzee's muzzle.

"Just do it, Claude," Katherine said. "He likes it. He said it's clean. You don't believe him?"

Denny took the glasses from his face to look at the smaller boy. "Yeah, you don't believe me, Claude? What, I'm a liar, Claude?"

"No, no, I do." And so Claude reached into Denny's pants and scratched, and this intimate grooming felt very good to Denny in a hardly sexual way, so to better concentrate on the sensation, he rested the binoculars and held his hand out for the can of Scotchgard and the paper bag.

......

After an hour on the beach, Rodney put a flat stone in his paperback, retrieved his pants, and got up to stretch his legs. He had the thought that strolling through the still water might cushion his ankles somewhat, so he waded in and set off up the cove. Forbidding as the water looked, it teemed with life. Carp fingerlings nibbled his shins. Twice, a crab scuttled over his bare toes. He strolled on until he reached the pier, a chocolate-colored structure built of creosoted wood. Rodney spied a clump of shells clinging to the pilings. These were major oysters, the size of cactus pads. He tried to yank one free, but it would not surrender to his hand. It was such a tempting prize that he waded all the way back to the truck and got the tire iron from under the seat. Knee-deep in the water, he worked open a shell. The flesh inside was pale gray and large as a goose egg. That much oyster meat would cost you thirty dollars in a Boston restaurant. The flesh showed no signs of dubious pinkness. He sniffed it—no bad aromas. He spilled it onto his tongue, chewing three times to get it down. The meat was clean and briny. He ate two more and felt renewed. Wading back to shore, a few smaller mollusks in hand, he peered under the wharf and spotted Katherine Nevis on the beach with her friends. The desolation of the town had cast a shadow on the morning, and it cheered Rodney to see those children out there enjoying the day. It would be unneighborly, Rodney thought, not to say hello.

When Rodney got within fifty yards, Denny and Claude looked up, panicked to see a shirtless fellow coming at them with a tire iron, an ugly limp in his gait. They took off in a kind of skulking lope and left Katherine on the beach. Obviously Rodney had caught them in the middle of some teenage mischief, and he chuckled to see the boys scamper.

Katherine cupped a hand over the beige matter on her face and looked at her toes as Rodney approached. He wondered about the grime, but instead asked after her dad. "I dunno," she said. "I'm sure he's doing awesome."

Rodney nudged the Scotchgard can with his foot. "Stain-proofing the beach?" he asked. Katherine said nothing. "Whatever happened to just raiding your parents' booze?"

"He has to drive all the way to Honerville to get it," she said. "He keeps it locked up, even from my mom."

Rodney put the tire iron in his belt and dropped his oysters. He took out his handkerchief and reached for her, thinking to swab her face. She shrank away from him. "Don't fucking touch me," she said. "Don't, I swear."

"Easy, easy, nobody's doing anything," Rodney said, though he could feel the color in his cheeks. "It's just you look like you need a shave."

Cautiously, a little shamefully, she took the handkerchief and daubed at her lips while he watched. The girl was conscious of being looked at, and she swabbed herself with small ladylike motions, making no headway on the filth.

"Here," said Rodney, very gently, taking the hanky from her damp hand. He sucked awhile at the bitter cloth, then he knelt and cradled the girl's jaw in his palm, rubbing at her mouth and chin. "Look out, you're gonna take off all my skin," she said, making a cranky child's grimace, though she didn't pull away. He heard her grunting lightly in her throat at the pleasure of being tended to. A smell was coming off her, a fragrance as warm and wholesome as rising bread. As he scrubbed the girl's dirty face, he put his nose close to her, breathing deeply and as quietly as he could. He had mostly purged the gum from Katherine's upper lip when she jerked away from him and hearkened anxiously to the sound of a slowing car. Arn Nevis's eggnog Mercedes pulled into the gravel lot. He got out and strode very quickly down the shingle.

"Hi, hi!" Nevis cried. His hair was in disarray, and his hands trembled in a Parkinsonian fashion. In the hard noon-day light, he looked antique and unwell. Rodney saw, too, that Nevis had a fresh pink scar running diagonally across his forehead, stitch pocks dotting its length. Rodney marveled a little that just the night before, he'd felt some trepidation in the big man's presence. "Kath—Kuh, Kutch." Nevis stopped, marshaled his breathing, and spoke. "Kuh, come here, sweetie. Been looking for you. Mom's mad. Come now, huk—honey. See if I can't talk your mom out of striping your behind."

In his shame, Arn did not look at Rodney, which at once amused and angered the younger man. "Feeling okay, there, Arn?"

"Oh, shuh-sure," Nevis said, staring at a point on Rodney's abdomen. "Thank God it's Friday."

"It's Thursday," Rodney said.

"Oysters," the old man said, looking at Rodney's haul where he'd dropped it on the ground. "Oh, they're nice."

Rodney crouched and held them out to Nevis in cupped hands. Nevis looked at the oysters and then at Rodney. His was the manner of a craven dog, wanting that food but fearing that he might get a smack if he went for it. "Go on," said Rodney.

With a quick move, Nevis grabbed a handful. His other hand seized Katherine's arm. "Alrighty, and we'll see you soon," said Nevis over his shoulder, striding to his car.

The days found an agreeable tempo in Cora and Rodney's new home. Each morning they rose with the sun. Each morning, Rodney swam far into the sea's broads, then returned to the house, where he would join Cora for a shower, then downstairs to cook and eat a breakfast of tremendous size. When the dishes were cleared, Cora would set off to gather pictures. Rodney would spend two hours on the computer to satisfy the advertising firm in Boston for which he still worked part-time, and then he'd do as he pleased. His was a life any sane person would envy, yet Rodney was not at ease. He felt bloated with a new energy. He had never been an ambitious person, but lately he had begun to feel that he was capable of resounding deeds. He had dreams in which he conquered famous wildernesses, and he would wake up with a lust for travel. Yet he was irritable on days when he had to leave the valley for provisions not sold in Port Miracle's pitiable grocery store. One day he told Cora that he might quit his job and start a company, though he grew angry when Cora forced him to admit that he had no idea what the company might produce. For the first time in his life, he resented Cora, begrudged the years he'd spent at her heel, and how he'd raised no fuss when she'd changed her mind after five years of marriage and said she didn't want children after all. His mind roved to other women, to the Nevis girl, a young thing with a working womb, someone who'd shut up when he talked.

When Cora left him the truck, he often went fishing off the wharf at Port Miracle, always coming home with several meals' worth of seafood iced down in his creel. He would wait until he got home to clean the catch so that Cora could photograph the haul intact.

"Ever seen one of these?" Cora asked him one night. She was sitting at the kitchen table with her laptop, whose screen showed a broad fish ablur with motion on the beach. "This thing was kind of creeping around in the mud down by that shed where the oldsters hang out."

"Huh," Rodney said, kissing Cora's neck and slipping a hand into her shirt. "Snakehead, probably. Or a mudskipper."

"It's not. It's flat, like a flounder," she said. "Quit a second. I wish I could have kept it, but this kid came along and bashed it and took off. Look."

She scrolled to a picture of Claude Hull braining the crawling fish with an aluminum bat.

"Mm," said Rodney, raising his wife's shirt and with the other hand going for her fly.

"Could you quit it?"

"Why?"

"For one thing, I'm trying to deal with my fucking work. For another, I'm kind of worn out. You've gotten me a little raw, going at me all the time."

Sulking, he broke off his advances and picked up his phone from the counter. "Tell you what," he said. "I'll call the neighbors. Get them over here to eat this stuff. We owe them a feed."

He stepped outdoors and called the Nevises, hoping to hear Katherine's hoarse little crow timbre on the other end. No one answered, so Rodney phoned two more times. He had watched the road carefully that morning and knew the family was home.

In fact, Katherine and her mother were out on a motorboat cruise while Arn Nevis paced his den, watching the telephone ring. He did not want to answer it. His trouble with words was worsening. Unless he loosened his tongue with considerable amounts of alcohol, the organ was lazy and intractable. In his mind, he could still formulate a phrase with perfect clarity, but his mouth no longer seemed interested in doing his mind's work and would utter a slurring of approximate sounds. When Nevis finally answered the telephone and heard Rodney's invitation, he paused to silently rehearse the words *I'm sorry, but Phyllis is feeling a bit under the weather.* But Nevis's tongue, the addled translator, wouldn't take the order. "Ilish feen urtha" and then a groan was what Rodney heard before the line went dead.

Until recently, the headaches Arn Nevis suffered had been slow pursuers. A stroll through the neighborhood would clear the bad blood from his temples and he'd have nearly a full day of peace. But lately, if he sat still for five minutes, the glow would commence behind his brow. He would almost drool thinking about a good thick augur to put a hole between his eyes and let the steam out of his head. After five minutes of that, if he didn't have a bottle around to kill it, white pain would bleach the vision from his eyes.

The pain was heating up again when he hung up on Rodney Booth, so he went out through the gate and strolled up to the dry tract slated to become nine new putting greens once the water lease on Birch Creek went through. He set about measuring and spray-painting orange hazard lines in the dirt where a ditcher would cut irrigation channels. Nevis owned most of this land himself, and he was tallying his potential profits when motion in the shadow of a yerba santa bush caught his eye. Scorpions, gathered in a ring, a tiny pocket mouse quaking at the center of them. The scenario was distasteful. He raised his boot heel and made to crush the things, but they nimbly skirted the fat shadow of his foot. The circle parted and the mouse shot out of sight.

He glanced at his watch. Four thirty. In half an hour, he had an appointment to show number eight Amphitrite Trail to a prospective buyer. The flawless sky and the light breeze were hopeful portents. Arn felt confident that on this day, he would make a good sale. To celebrate the prospect, Arn took the quart of peppermint schnapps from his knapsack, but then it occurred to him to save it, to drink it very quickly just before the client's arrival for maximum benefit to his difficult tongue.

Eight Amphitrite was a handsome structure, a three-thousand-square-foot Craftsman bungalow, the only one like it in the neighborhood. The plot was ideally situated, up on high ground at the end of the road with no houses behind it. Sitting there on the front steps, Nevis felt a particular comfort in the place, an enlargement of the safe feeling he experienced in restaurants when he found a spot with his back to the wall and a good view of the door. Nevis checked his watch. Ten of five. He opened the bottle and tipped it back. He stretched his tongue, whispering a silent catechism: "Radiant-heat floors, four-acre lot, build to suit."

Arn had just finished the last of the schnapps when a Swedish station wagon pulled into the drive. A young man got out, tall, with soft features, combed sandy hair, and a cornflower-blue shirt rolled to the elbows. He watched Arn Nevis pick himself up off the stairs and come toward him with his hand out. "Mr. Nevis?" the young man had to ask, for Arn did not much resemble the photograph on his website. His white shirt was badly wrinkled and yellowed with per-spiration stains, and his hair looked like a patch of trodden weeds. His left eye was badly bloodshot and freely weeping.

"Urt! Guh," Arn Nevis said, then paused in his tracks, opening and closing his mouth as though priming a dry pump. The client watched him, aghast, as though Nevis was some unhinged derelict impersonating the man he'd come to meet. "Guh—good day!" Nevis said at last, and having expelled that first plug of language, the rest flowed out of him easily. "Mister Mills? It's an absolute delight, and I'm so glad you could pay us a visit on this fabulous day."

"Daniel, please," the young man said, still looking guarded. But the anxiety slowly drained from Mills's features as Nevis rolled into a brisk and competent disquisition on eight Amphitrite's virtues. "That nice overlay on the foundation? That's not plastic, friend. It's hand-mortared fieldstone harvested out of this very land. Clapboards are engineered, and so's the roofing shake, so eat your heart out, termites, and fifteen years to go on the warranty on each."

Nevis was ushering Mills over the threshold when his pitch halted in mid-stream. Nevis gaped at the empty living room, his mouth open, his eyes stretched with wonder. "My gosh," he said.

"What?" asked Daniel Mills.

"My gosh, Ted, this is that same house, isn't it?" Nevis said, laughing. "From Columbus. When you and Rina were still married."

Mills looked at Arn a moment. "It's Daniel. I—I don't know any Rina."

Nevis's eyes moved in their sockets. He began to laugh. "Jesus Christ, what the hell am I saying?" he said. "My apologies. I've had this fever."

"Sure," said Mills, taking a step back.

"So over yonder is a galley kitchen," said Nevis, leading the way. "Poured concrete counters, and a built-in—"

"Excuse me, you've got something here," murmured Mills, indicating Nevis's upper lip. Nevis raised a finger to his face and felt the warm rush of blood pouring from his nose, dripping from his chin, landing in nickel-size droplets on the parquet floor.

By his sixth week in Triton Estates, an exuberant insomnia assailed Rodney Booth. While his wife snored beside him,

Rodney lay awake. His body quivered with unspent energy. His blood felt hot and incandescent. With each stroke of his potent heart, he saw the red traceries of his arteries filling with gleeful sap, bearing tidings of joy and vigor to his cells. His muscles quaked. His loins tittered, abloat with happy news. His stomach, too, disturbed his rest. Even after a dinner of crass size, Rodney would lie in bed, his gut groaning as though he hadn't eaten in days. He would rise and go downstairs, but he could not find foods to gratify his hunger. Whether cold noodles, or a plate of costly meats and cheeses, all the foods in his house had a dull, exhausted flavor, and he would eat in joyless frustration, as though forced to suffer conversation with a hideous bore.

Exercise was the only route to sleep for Rodney. His ankles plagued him less these days, and after dinner he would rove for hours in the warm autumn dark. Some nights he strolled the shore, soothed to hear the distant splashes of leaping night fish. Sometimes he went into the hills where the houses stopped. The land rose and fell before him, merging in the far distance with the darkness of the sky, unbroken by lights of civilization. A feeling of giddy affluence would overtake Rodney as he scrambled along. All that space, and nobody's but his! It was like the dream where you find a silver dollar on the sidewalk, then another, then another, until you look up to see a world strewn with free riches.

On these strolls, his thoughts often turned to Katherine Nevis, that fine, wretched girl imprisoned at the end of Naiad Lane behind the high white wall. He recalled the smell of her, her comely gruntings that day on the shore, the tender heft of her underjaw in his palm. One evening the memory of her became so intolerable that it stopped him in his tracks, and he paused between the dunes in an intimate little hollow where dust of surprising fineness gathered in plush drifts.

Rodney stooped to caress the soft soil, warm in his hand. "Listen, you and me are in a predicament here, Katherine," he explained to the dust. "Oh, you don't, huh? Fine. You stay right there. I'll get it myself."

With that, he unbuckled his pants and fell to zealously raping the dirt. The sensation was not pleasurable, and the fierceness of the act did not sit right with Rodney's notion of himself, but in the end he felt satisfied that he had completed a job of grim though necessary work.

Floured with earth, he made his way to the water and swam vigorously for twenty minutes. Then he crawled into bed beside his wife and slept until the sun rose, minding not at all the pricking of the soft sheets against his salty skin.

The following night Rodney ranged along the shore and back up into the hills, yet his step was sulky and his heart was low. As with the pantry foods he did not care to eat, that evening the great open land had become infected with a kindred dreariness. Squatting on a boulder, Rodney gazed at the column of clean light spilling from the enclosure of the Nevis home. A breathless yearning caught hold. The desert's wealth of joy and deliverance seemed to have slipped down the rills and drainages, slid past the dark houses, leached south along the hard pink berm, and concentrated in the glare above the one place in the Anasazi Basin where Rodney was not free to roam. He stood and walked.

Rodney told himself he would not enter the Nevis property. The notion was to loiter at the gate, have a glimpse of the courtyard, sport a little with the pull of the place, the fun of holding two magnets at slight bay. And perhaps Rodney would have kept his promise to himself had he not spotted, bolted to the top of a length of conduit bracketed to the wall, a fan of iron claws, put there to discourage shimmiers. The device offended Rodney as an emblem of arrogance and vanity. Who was Arn Nevis to make his home a thorny fort? The spikes were pitiful. A determined crone could have gotten past them. Rodney jumped and grasped in either hand the two outermost claws. With a strength and ease that surprised him, he vaulted himself over the hazard and onto the lip of the wall.

He dropped onto the flagstones and the agony in his ankles caused his lungs to briefly freeze with pain. Rodney held his breath, waiting to hear a barking dog or an alarm, but heard nothing. Beyond the batteries of floodlights, only a single window glowed in the far corner of the house. Rodney waited. Nothing stirred.

Crouched in the courtyard, a new oil seemed to rise in Rodney's joints. His body felt incapable of noisy or graceless moves. He removed the screen from an open window and found himself in the Nevises' living room. He paused at a grand piano and rested his fingers in a chord on the sheeny keys. The temptation to sound the notes was strong, so electrified was Rodney that the house was under his authority. The fragrance in the room was distasteful and exciting—an aroma of milk and cologne—and it provoked in him an unaccountable hunger. He padded to the Nevises' kitchen. In the cold light of the open refrigerator, Rodney unwrapped and ate a wedge of Gruyère cheese. Then he had a piece of unsweetened baking chocolate, which he washed down with a can of Arn's beer. Still, his stomach growled. Under a shroud of crumpled tinfoil, he found a mostly intact ham, and he gnawed the sugary crust and then went at it with his jaws and teeth, taking bites the size of tennis balls, glutting his throat and clearing the clog with a second, then a third can of his neighbor's beer.

When he had at last had all he wanted, Rodney's breathing had become labored. He was dewed in hot sweat. His bladder, too, was full, but his feeling of satiety there in the kitchen was so delicate and golden that he did not feel like shifting an inch to find a toilet. So he lowered his zipper and relished the sound of fluid hitting terracotta tiles, which mingled with the keen scent of his own urine in a most ideal way.

He had only just shut the refrigerator door when a white motion in the window caught his eye. Who was it but Katherine Nevis, the darling prisoner of the house? She plodded across the rear courtyard, on flat, large girl's feet, heading for the little inlet. She shed her robe, and Rodney was unhappy to see that even at that private hour of the evening, she still bothered to wear a bathing suit. She dove, and the water accepted her with the merest ripple. For many minutes, Rodney watched her sporting and glorying in the pool, diving and breaching, white, dolphinlike exposures of her skin bright against the dark red tide. When he could put it off no longer, Rodney stepped through the sliding door and went to her.

"Howdy!" he called, very jolly. She whirled in the water, only her head exposed. Rodney walked to the edge of the pool. "Hi there!" he said. She said nothing, but sank a little, gathering the water to her with sweeping arms, taking it into her mouth, pushing it gently over her chin, breathing it, nearly. She said nothing. Rodney put his fists on his hips and grinned at the surveillant moon. "Hell of a spotlight. Good to swim by, huh?"

Her eyes were dark but not fearful. "How'd you get in here?" the girl said wetly.

"Oh, I had some business with your dad," he said.

"My dad," she repeated, her face a suspicious little fist.

"Maybe I'll get in there with you," Rodney said, raising his shirt.

"Do what you like," the girl said. "I'm going inside."

He put a hand out. She took it and pulled herself into the night air. He picked up her robe. Draping it on her, he caught her sourdough aroma, unmasked by the sulfur smell of the sea. His heart was going, his temples on the bulge.

"Stay," he said. "Come on, the moon's making a serious effort here. It's a real once-in-a-month kind of moon."

She smiled, then stopped. She reached into the pocket of her robe and retrieved a cigarette. "Okay. By the way, if I yelled even a little bit, my mom would come out here. She's got serious radar. She listens to everything and never sleeps. Seriously, how'd you get through the gate?"

Rodney stretched his smile past his dogteeth. A red gas was coming into his eyes. "She's one great lady, your mom." He put a hand on the girl's hip. She pushed against it only slightly, then sat with her cigarette on a tin-and-rubber chaise longue to light it. He sat beside her and took the cigarette, holding it downwind so as to smell her more purely. He made some mouth sounds in her ear. She closed her eyes. "Gets dull out here, I bet," he said.

"Medium," she said. She took back the ocher short of her roll-your-own. He put his hand on her knee, nearly nauseated with an urge. The girl frowned at his fingers. "Be cool, hardcore," she said.

"Why don't you . . . how about let's . . . how about . . ."

"Use your words," she said.

He put his hand on the back of her head and tried to pull her to his grasping lips. She broke the clasp. "What makes you think I want to kiss your mouth?"

"Come on," he groaned, nearly weeping. "God*damn*, you're beautiful."

"Shit," the girl said.

"You are a beautiful woman," said Rodney.

"My legs are giant," she said. "I've got a crappy face."

"Come here," he said. He lipped some brine from her jaw.

"Don't," she said, panting some. "You don't love me yet."

Rodney murmured that he did love Katherine Nevis very much. He kissed her, and she didn't let him. He kissed her again and she did. Then he was on her and for a time the patio was silent save the sound of their breath and the crying of the chaise's rubber slats.

He'd gotten her bikini bottoms down around her knees when the girl went stiff. "Quit," she whispered harshly. He pretended not to hear her. "Shit, goddammit, stop!" She gave him a hard shove, and then Rodney saw the problem. Arn Nevis was over by the house, hunched and peering from the blue darkness of the eave. Nevis was perfectly still, his chin raised slightly, mouth parted in expectancy. His look changed when he realized he'd been spotted. From what Rodney could tell, it wasn't outrage on the old man's features, just mild sadness that things had stopped before they'd gotten good.

Three mornings later, Rodney Booth looked out his bedroom window to see a speeding ambulance dragging a curtain of dust all the way up Naiad Lane to the Nevis home. He watched some personnel in white tote a gurney through the gate. Then Rodney went downstairs and poured himself some cereal and turned the television on.

Later that afternoon, as Rodney was leaving for the wharf with his fishing pole and creel, Cora called to him. She'd just gotten off the phone with Phyllis Nevis, who'd shared the sad news that her husband was in the hospital, comatose with a ruptured aneurysm, not expected to recover. Rodney agreed that this was terrible. Then he shouldered his pole and set out for the wharf.

The day after the ambulance bore Arn Nevis away, Rodney began to suffer vague qualmings of the conscience relating to the Nevis family. He had trouble pinpointing the source of the unease. It was not sympathy for Nevis himself. There was nothing lamentable about an old man heading toward death in his sleep. And his only regret about his tender grapplings with the sick man's daughter was that they hadn't concluded properly. Really, the closest Rodney could come to what was bothering him was some discomfort over his behavior with Phyllis Nevis's ham. He pictured mealtime in her house, the near widow serving her grieving children the fridge's only bounty, a joint of meat, already hard used by unknown teeth. The vision made him tetchy and irritated with himself. He felt the guilt gather in his temples and coalesce into a bother-some headache.

That afternoon, Rodney harvested and shucked a pint or so of oysters. He packed in ice three pounds of fresh-caught croaker filets. He showered, shaved, daubed his throat and the line of hair on his stomach with lemon verbena eau de cologne. In the fridge he found a reasonably good bottle of Pouilly-Fuissé, and he set off up Naiad Lane.

Phyllis Nevis came to the gate and welcomed him in. "I brought you something," Rodney said. "It isn't much."

She looked into the bag with real interest. "Thank you," she said. "That's very, very kind."

"And the wine is cold," said Rodney. "Bet you could use a glass."

"I could," said Phyllis quietly.

Together they walked inside. Rodney put the fish in the refrigerator. He opened the bottle and poured two large glasses. Phyllis went upstairs and then returned with her baby, Nathan. She sat on the sofa, waiting for Rodney, giving the infant his lunch.

Rodney gave the woman a glass and sat close beside her.

"Thank you," said Phyllis, tears brightening her eyes. "One week, tops. That's what they said."

"I'm so, so sorry," Rodney said. He put his arm around her, and while she wept, she allowed herself to be drawn into the flushed hollow of Rodney's neck. The infant at her breast began to squeal, and the sound inflamed the pain in Rodney's temples, and he had an impulse to tear the baby from her and carry it out of the room. Instead, he swallowed his wine at a gulp. He poured himself a second glass and knocked it back, which seemed to dull the pain a little. Then he settled against the cushion and pressed Phyllis's tearful face into his neck. While she quaked on him, Rodney stroked the tender skin behind her ears and stared off through the picture window. Far above the eastern hills, a council of clouds shed a gray fringe of moisture. The promise of rain was a glad sight in the mournful scene, though in fact this was rain of a frail kind, turning to vapor a mile above the brown land, never to be of use to women and men on earth.

PEE ON WATER

Rachel B. Glaser

Though alien to the world's ancient past, young blood runs similar circles. All those bones are born from four grandparents. Baby teeth and baby teeth all down the line. Jackets didn't used to zip up. There wasn't a single door.

Earth is round and open, whole and beating in its early years. The stars are in a bright smear against the blackboard. A breath pulled so gradual the breath forgets. Winds run back and forth. Clouds idly shift their shapes. Stubborn ice blocks will not be niced down by the fat sun. Melted tears run, then freeze. Tiny cells slide into tiny cells. The wind learns to whistle. The sun starts setting in a colorful display. Ice melts into oceans, lakes, and ponds. Plants have their first batch of leaves. Guppies shiver in the lake. Shiver, have babies, babies shiver. Crawlers. Diggers. Stingers. The plants get bit and chewed. Leaves grow more intricate. Beings start dragging with them, little lives. Moments where they crawl on sand. Moments where they look behind them. They eat plants. They eat stomachs. Lick bones. They pee on grass. Pee on dirt. Pee on snow. Their skin is cut by teeth, by claws. Water fills their lungs. Blood cries itself in a blind pool. Blood dries on leaves. Blood browns on fur.

Creatures big as mountains stomp on top of mountains.

Then new ones. New ones. Feathers, spikes, hooves. Clouds crawl smugly. The air smells cool. Atoms bump and lump. Birds have sex. Bears have sex. The sun gets better at setting. Monkeys play with sticks. Monkeys eat ants. They get sexy about each other's butts. The monkeys fuck from behind. They sleep in leaves, in mud, in trees. They protect their babies and teach them. The sun glares in their eyes, making spots.

Ants amble on, self-consciously changing direction. Rain makes them flinch, makes them happy. The monkeys make faces. The monkeys get smart. Two monkeys look at each other with knowing eyes. The trees sway. The birds chat. The knowing eyes are locked in a gaze. They look away. They look back. They have sophisticated children. The new monkeys need less and less protective hair. They have babies. They fight, throw punches, show teeth and bite. They think each other are sexy. Raise their babies away from the others. The new female monkeys have vaginas more between their legs, less likely to snag on branches. Males try sex with females from the front. Boobs get bigger to remind males what butts felt like.

This is the nice time of early men and monkeys, before cigarette butts cozied fat into the grass. No plastics, no prayers. Wood isn't sliced into slats, it's still living it up in trees. The rain is surprising, usual. Men and monkeys leave their lives with their bodies. Early men paint, cry, stare into fire meditatively. Pee on grass. Pee on dirt. Wear furs, have babies, catch dogs. Fall in love with dogs. Pause at oceans and their rambling edges. Sticks complicate grass. Grass complicates sand. The ground and every thousand thing on top of it. Curves and lumps. Uneven clouds. But click the clock radio through a.m. to p.m., spin the equal sphere like a sonic hedgehog. The leaves live the leaves fall, the leaves live the leaves die.

......

Men ride horses, roam plains, live in trees, in caves, wipe the sleep out of their eyes. They dance to a beat, carve wood into arrows. Pleasure and fun plus boredom and loss. The fun of hands gliding on top of water. Of mud oozing between toes. Knotted hair is pulled back. Dirt gets comfortable on skin.

A band crouches in the bushes. Horses down, blood on ground. Blood on grass. Blood on brains. Legs are separated from bodies. Trees stand still, sway, stand still. The first restaurant opens. Families look alike. Caught dogs love man back. The middle of the night waits for people to run bravely through it. A toothbrush with bristles is invented. Dandelions lose petals, grow big fluffy heads.

Days of work. Hands on rakes. Hands on shovels. Hands on rocks. Hands in clay. Hands in water. Aches in bones, aches in muscles, aches in head. Night chases day. Seasons switch slow. People pee in bushes, in open trenches. There are jobs, schools, songs. There are moms and dads. Young and carrying their children haphazard down the street. Older and with their hands in dough. Men feel cool riding horses. Arrows are pulled on tight bows, yanked back near ears, released in wild flight. Blood dries in sand. Blood dries in hair.

The sun casts pyramid shadows on packed sand. A girl awakens to be seventeen. The heat is hot on the street. Sand in teeth. "Sister!" her boyfriend says. He gives her love poems written with the picture language. They are about bathing together in the river, touching and holding red fish. The girl laughs, "Brother, what fish?"

"The ones that feel right in hands." He nudges her. He hunts honey all day. He and others sacrifice an animal. Remove its lower entrails and fill the body with loaves and honey and spices. They offer it to a god. The boyfriend sneaks out to meet the seventeen-year-old girl. They get drunk, tongue on tongue, tongue on lips, tongue on cheeks. She puts honey and crocodile dung in her vagina to block out sperm. They sniff water lilies, get high, fall clumsily asleep.

Chairs are rare. They sit patiently in rooms. Mutton fat is boiled to make soap. Rocks are fired out of bamboo poles. Condoms are made from fish and animal intestines. Men feel cool playing the lute. They pee in private. Fish are caught with hooks. Held in rigid hands. Unhooked with fish eyes wide and watching, wishing for water, wishing for water. Diseases wriggle, latch on to cells, to genes, to skin. A bishop writes a book that recommends letting children have a childhood. He says babies should have their spirits stirred "by kisses and embraces," that "children should learn to play." Children say their jokes a few more times aloud. They balance their spoons on their noses. They lie in the flower field and hum.

A lake sits still and wet, creating dynamic calm. Girls no longer swim lakes. "Fish bite our thi-ighs!" A collective whine. The ducks don't give a fuck. "More for us." The ducks stick their face in their feathers. "You've chay-yanged!" They eye the girls: "You used to wear your hair in knots."

"Don't remind us." The girls watch the lake with the others, for the dynamic calm.

A rebellious inventor is sick of shit on the street. Of shit in bushes, of pee in puddles. He takes his evenings by himself, working hard on a necessary for his godmother, the Queen. His wife laughs. His friends laugh. He tinkers with pipes. Meanwhile, he shits in the outhouse. He smells pee on the sidewalk. He wants a machine that will whirl it all invisible. He succeeds in making a flush toilet. A plumbing wonder! He tries it out. Pees into the toilet. Each drop twinks. A pull of the flush and the toilet answers, a magic wave! The sewage system is not advanced enough to handle the water disposal. A smell creeps out of the pipes. The inventor's friends laugh. He never builds another, though he and the Queen both use theirs.

The first chocolate factory. First personal ad. Friends add on to long running jokes. Young Beethoven goes deaf from his father beating the shit out of him. Dogs get annoyed at having their ears inspected. Deadly fever epidemics kill thousands. A band of adventurers plot to overtake something. The year without summer. June snow comes down in sheets. The seventeen-year-old girl gets arrested for wearing pants. First safety pin. First saxophone. A pencil with an eraser attached. Two people say the same thing at the same time and laugh. Diamonds are discovered in Africa. Diaries discovered in underwear drawers. First White House Easter egg roll. First train robbery. Boxers start wearing gloves. Flush toilets work with new sewage systems. Everyone begins to pee on water.

At the World's Fair, someone rolls a waffle and scoops ice cream in it. Plastic is invented. Neon lights. One hundred twenty-seven kisses in a single movie. Fire department horses retire. Men feel cool driving cars. Chuck Berry fucks time into place, pulls it into beats and it hangs. It plays. Women use Lysol disinfectant in their vaginas to prevent pregnancy. Crowds of bodies are buried in the ground. Bombs are made with chemicals about to freak out. The seventeen-year-old girl looks into the toilet at the shape of shit that sits there, complete as one thing, a size similar to her boyfriend's penis. Not right, but close maybe, and she puts her hand above the water, widening her fingers to remember the length.

Cars come close to smashing. Flags paraded around, then stuck on the moon. A little sister orders her baseball card collection by cuteness. Wild animals have no more room. Land gets so full of buildings, when town girls and city boys escape into the open, "God" is waiting in the fields. Cars smash, glass in a crowd of shards. Huge ambivalent teen models lounge across highway billboards. Dust gathers between VCR remote buttons.

A bunch of fifth-grade girls hang out with fifth-grade boys and the boys start looking through the videotapes for something to show the girls. The girls don't know what but they giggle and try to sit up so their stomachs don't bunch but they bunch anyway. A boy sticks in the video and it's of a man raping a woman against a pinball machine. The fifth graders stare, leaving the potato chips alone in the bowl. A boy laughs. A girl tries it out, laughs a little too.

Dog walkers pick up after their dogs. Shit in plastic. Shit in trash. Shit on grass. Pee on grass. Pee on pavement. Pee on pee. Cars come close to smashing. Ketchup proudly won't leave bottle. Underwear inches up in butts. Bullets find their snug way into bodies. Moms and dads talk in whispers while children pretend to sleep in the backseat. Snow falls all night, everyone wakes to good moods. Guitars, bought optimistically, lean grandly forgotten against bedroom walls. Raindrops race on car windows.

Harper dribbles the ball down the court, guarded by Ward, head fakes right, passes left to Pippen. Pippen up against

Oakley, looks to see if Longley has posted, but Longley hasn't posted, Longley is tangled with Ewing. Longley's arms curl around Ewing while Longley's little eyes look to lock with Steve Javie's eyes, but Javie's eyes follow the ball. Pippen drives by Oakley, then passes to Kerr, who bounces it to Jordan. Jordan holds the ball, his eyes twinkle. He passes it back. Alone behind the three-point line, Kerr takes a breath, grimaces, shoots the ball into a spiraling three-point attempt, which hits the rim and sails out of bounds.

Someone is killed wearing a Mickey Mouse shirt. Blood on head. Blood on mouse. Blood on pavement. The mouse still smiles. The sun is in a rhythm. The sky stays put. Babies grow into sturdier shapes. The rocks stay. The paintings stay. The people leave. Blood slows and then sits. Tongues get hot and hurt in their mouths. The sitcoms play on. Newly dead bodies get put in wood. Spacemen invade space. Dog catchers catch dogs. Then the sound, dirt on wood.

Girls sit outside a mall in the cold. One girl is sure life stops at dirt on wood. Black like outer space. But the seventeen-year-old girl says firmly, "When you die, you watch movie remakes of your life." The girls smile, but the cold tells them it is dirt on wood. A boy rides loops in the parking lot, his butt high off his bike seat. Sperm bite eggs. Wet new eyes. Tongues on tongues, dirt on wood.

Cell phones are used as weak flashlights. City teenagers discover grass. People strap bombs under their outfits and enter buildings. Religions are dragged through time. A pet dog catches a rabbit, hears his name called, turns around, loses the rabbit.

The buildings get straighter, sturdier, simpler, shinier. On New Year's, everyone looks funny in their 2020 glasses, 2050 glasses, 2086 glasses. Every famous person born finds the time to die. The newspaper isn't on paper. Scientists are still trying to make pain less painful.

Wake to half thoughts and a dirty mouth. Remember your first name and last. Toothpaste on the toothbrush. The day cut into hours. Stream your pee onto water. Remember the fields of trees, the wayward grass? We couldn't help crowd everything with squares. Dictionaries, mattresses, apartment complexes. All buildings with flat faces, with rows and rows of square eyes. Pages, screens, tiles. The curves got covered with lines. The birds have sex. The bears eat trash. Life still runs enough years. Plenty more than before. Fur ruffles in the wind. Candles coy and shy their hot face. Many parts are still the same. The day is light and easy to see in. A soap bar slims down to a sliver.

LOVE IS A THING ON SALE FOR MORE MONEY THAN THERE EXISTS

Tao Lin

This was the month that people began to suspect that terrorists had infiltrated Middle America, set up underground tunnels in the rural areas, like gophers. During any moment, it was feared, a terrorist might tunnel up into your house and replace your dog with something that resembled your dog but was actually a bomb. This was a new era in terrorism. The terrorists were now quicker, wittier, and more streetwise. They spoke the vernacular, and claimed to be philosophically sound. They would whisper into the wind something mordant and culturally damning about McDonald's, Jesus, and America—and then, if they wanted to, if the situation eschatologically called for it, they would slice your face off with a KFC spork.

People began to quit their jobs. They saw that their lives were small and threatened, and so they tried to cherish more, to calm down and appreciate things for once. But in the end, bored in their homes, they just became depressed and susceptible to head colds. They filled their apartments with pets, but then neglected to name them. They became nauseous and unbelieving. They did not believe that they themselves were nauseous, but that it was someone else who was nauseous—that it was all, somehow, a trick. A fun joke. "Ha," they thought. Then they went and took a nap. Sometimes, late at night and in Tylenol-Cold hazes, crouched and blanket-hooded on their beds, they dared to squint out into their lives, and what they saw was a grass of bad things, miasmic and low to the ground, depraved, scratching, and furry—and squinting back! It was all their pets, and they wanted names. They just wanted to be named!

Life, people learned, was not easy. Life was not cake. Life was not a carrot cake. It was something else. A get-together on Easter Island. You, the botched clone of you, the Miami Dolphins, Cocoa Puffs, paper plates, a dwindling supply of clam juice. That was life.

The economy was up, though, and crime was down. The president brought out graphs on TV, pointed at them. He reminded the people that he was not an evil man, that he, of course, come on now—he just wanted everyone to be happy! In bed, he contemplated the abolition of both anger and unhappiness, the outlawing of them. Could he do that? Did he have the resources? Why hadn't he thought of this before? These days he felt that his thinking was off. Either that, or his thinking about his thinking was off. He began to take pills. Ginseng, Ginkoba. Tic Tacs. It was an election year, and the future was very uncertain. Leaders all over the globe began to go on TV with graphs, pie charts, and precariously long series of rhetorical questions.

This was also the month that Garret and Kristy stopped experimenting with caffeine. They had, in their year and a half together, tried all the coffees, cut back to tea, tried tea and coffee together—thinking that tea caffeine was different than coffee caffeine—tried snorting tea, swallowing coffee beans, tea cakes, and had then gone back to coffee.

Now they were using caffeine pills. One per day, like a vitamin—tacitly, with only a little shame.

They went to college in Manhattan and lived together in Brooklyn, where the sky was a bleeding-mushroom gray and the pollution seemed to rise directly off the surface of things—cars, buildings, the ground—like a foul heat, a kind of gaseous, urban mirage.

Garret would occasionally glimpse something black and fizzy moving diagonally across the reddening sky. He often suspected that The Future Was Now. Was the future now? Or was it coming up still? He had seen all the apocalypse movies of the nineties, and all the signs were here: the homeless people rising up and walking around, the businessmen entering the parks and sitting down, sitting there all day, leaving late at night—*why?*; the focus on escape—people always talking about escaping to California, Hawaii, Florida; and the stalled technology, how all that was promised—underwater houses, hover cars, domed cities on the moon, robots that would shampoo your hair and assure you that everything was going to be okay—was not here, and would probably never be here. They had lied. Someone had lied.

Garret's dreams were increasingly of normal things that, because of their utter messagelessness, had very natural-seeming undertones of foreboding and impending doom to them. In one dream, Garret was in the shower. He soaped himself, dropped the soap, picked up the soap, put it adjacent the shampoo, and read the shampoo bottle. "Pert Plus," it said.

"I'm thinking about taking a year off," Kristy said. She was graduating a year early due to summer classes and AP credits. "To figure out who I am. I'm not a basketball star. I'm not Jane Goodall. I'm not Mary Stuart Masterson."

It was a Friday morning and they were in bed.

"I always think Jane Goodall is the ape's name," Garret said. "But it's not. It's the name of the blonde lady."

Garret had a psychology lecture today. They decided to meet after, at four, at the deli place.

"The deli with the red thing," Garret said. "Four. Don't be late."

"I'll be there at three fifty."

"I know you're going to be late," Garret said. Then he left the apartment. Why was Kristy always late? It was winter and raining. The city seemed a place under siege, an undersea metropolis with a grade-school planetarium dome for a sky, newspapery and cheap, folding down like something soaked. The subway smelled of urine, and some of the streets had long pools of green radioactive sludge on them. Garret went and sat in the deli, which had a red awning. He disliked the word "awning." The complete, incomplete word of it. Yawning; they just took the Y off. What was happening? His view was of the sidewalk, a craggy area of Washington Square Park, and some scaffolding. He sat there for a long time, until the deli owner came out from in back to tell him that he couldn't just sit there all day.

Garret nodded and stood. "Sorry," he said.

"Move to Hawaii," said the deli owner. He patted Garret on the back. "Take a jet airplane to Hawaii and be happy."

"Okay," Garret said. He bought a pre-made salad, an orange drink, and a sugar cookie. He thought that he wouldn't go to class. Jesus loves you, he then thought. But Jesus isn't *in love* with you. He thought about that for a while. Awning, he thought. Gnawing. Woodpecker.

Kristy showed up around five. She ran in, her hair wet.

"I forgot you said four," she said. "I was thinking that I was supposed to *leave* at four."

They walked to Union Square, leaning against one another like weary, wounded people. It was not raining anymore, but the sky was still gray. Kristy asked how Garret's class went. Garret shrugged. They didn't speak anymore after that. They began to sweat, as it was a warm winter. Global warming had finally arrived, maybe. For a long time it was on its way, it was coming, it was imminent, Hollywood made a movie about it, and now it was probably here.

They went in all the stores, then for coffee, and then Garret started making halfhearted jokes about the terrorists. "What if the terrorists opened their own store . . . and sold bad things?" Garret said. "What would they sell?" he said.

It sometimes seemed to him that for love to work, it had to be fair, that he should tell only half the joke, and she the other half. Otherwise, it would not be love, but something completely else—pity or entertainment, or stand-up comedy. "Well? What they would sell?" Garret said. "I can't do everything in this relationship." Sometimes, recently, coffee would make him sleepy and unreasonable and begrudging. He began to remember all the times that Kristy was late, all the times she promised not to be late anymore.

"Yes you can," Kristy said. "You can do anything you want."

"I'm always trying to cheer you up," Garret said. "It seems like this. I'm always trying to make you laugh and you're always depressed."

"What if a terrorist kicked your ass?" Kristy said.

Some areas of the ground had steam coming out of them, and a gigantic truck was coming down the street, like some kind of municipal battering ram. There was always a gigantic truck coming down the street like some kind of municipal battering ram.

"I'm about to do something," Garret said. He bought two rainbow-sprinkled ice-cream cones from an ice-cream truck, and that was his dinner. "I wanted to, so I did it," he said to Kristy. He looked around to see if anyone was disapproving of this, of two rainbow-sprinkled ice-cream cones at once. He almost sneered. Kristy bought a large package of Twizzlers and a coffee the size of a canteen. They went back to Brooklyn, and lay on their bed. Turned off all the lights. And they held each other. "I love you," Kristy said. But she said it softly and Garret didn't hear over the noise of the air conditioner, which bulged out from high on the wall, like a hoary, machine growth, a false but vexing machination—the biscuit-brown plastic appliance *thing* of it, trembling, dripping, clanging, probably not even working.

The radio hit that year was "Sigh (Hole)," an R&B song by a pop-rock band:

> There-ere's a hole in you
> Gets emptier, ah-oh, each day
> But you don't needn't be blue
> Everything's-uh gonna be, yeah, okay

For the chorus, the band sighed, Caribbeanly, into their microphones. Except the rhythm guitarist, who had to sing-talk, "We are sighing, we are sighing," to let the people know. The music video had celebrities who looked into the camera—looked right at you! *faint!*—and sighed like they really, really, truly meant it. They were sighing at all the distress in the world, people said. Or else because of the ever-invasive paparazzi. There were arguments. Name-calling. People stood up in chain restaurants, pointed diagonally down, and said, "It's because of the paparazzi, you fool." Then they requested a booth table. At night, they sent out mass, illogical, spam e-mails. The celebrities themselves had no comment.

After a psychology lecture, Garret asked a classmate out for lunch. The classmate frowned a little. She had been poking Garret in his shoulder and smiling at him all semester. "Hmm," she said, "I don't think so."

Garret went into the park, where the trees were all leafless. Their petrified-gray branches clawed at the air, like rakes. There was a cemetery wind, dry and slow and slabbed as marble. Elephant graveyard, Garret thought. He sat on a bench and called Kristy. He asked if she wanted to see a movie tonight. She had just gotten out of class, but had another one. "I'll just meet you back at the apartment then," Garret said. He didn't want to see a movie anymore. "I have to study in the library anyway."

"I'll meet you at the library, then," Kristy said.

"I'll just meet you at the apartment. I have to study."

"I won't be late this time," Kristy said. "I'll just meet you at the library."

"No; that isn't it. I just have to study."

"What isn't it?" Kristy said.

"What?"

"Nothing," Kristy said. "Fine then; bye."

Garret went across the street to the library. There was a hole in the sidewalk the size of a bathtub. Construction was being done, was always being done. It was the journey that mattered, Garret thought woozily, the getting-there part. The mayor, and then the president, had begun saying that. "And where are we going?" the mayor had asked. "When will we get there? What will happen to us once we get there?" He really wanted to know.

A woman with a red bandana stepped in front of Garret and gave him a flyer for an anti-war meeting. It was vague to Garret these days what was happening in the rest of the world. He found it difficult to comprehend how large the world was, how many people there were. He would think of the Middle East, of strife and mortar, then suddenly of Australia, and then New Zealand, giant squid, tuna fish, and then of Japan, all the millions of people in Japan; and he'd get stuck there, on Japan—trying to imagine the life of one Japanese person, unable to, conjuring only an image of wasabi, minty and mounded, against a flag-white background.

Garret saw Kristy coming out of a building across the street. He turned, went behind a pillar, and looked. Kristy was with a taller man who had a tiny head. She laughed and the taller man smiled. They went together into another building.

At the anti-war meeting, they wanted to abolish the words "we," "us," and "them." Some others wanted to abolish the word "I." They were frustrated. "We this, we that; us this, them that; us vs. them, no wonder things are the way they are." They wanted semantic unity. They were going to make friends with the terrorists. That was their plan. An older man—a professor?—stood and made the case that the terrorists did not want any new friends, had enough friends already, too many, actually; that what they really wanted was romantic love. He was probably a graduate student. Another man stood and said, "Love is a thing on sale for more money than there exists." It seemed an inappropriately capitalist thing to say, or else much too cynical, and the man was ignored. Finally, it was settled: whatever happened, they would just make friends. There were sign-up sheets, and then a six-piece jazz-rock band played. The drummer had six cymbals, four of them tiny. People eyed him askance. Was six cymbals, four of them tiny, appropriate for wartime?

Garret walked out into the night, feeling very dry in the mouth, and with a headache.

He stood around for a while, and then called Kristy.

"Kristy's at her sister's apartment taking a nap. She's asleep now. I'm her sister."

"You're Kristy's sister?" Garret said.

"Okay. So Kristy's sleeping." She hung up.

One weekend they got out of classes and flew down to Florida, to Garret's mother's house, for a weeklong vacation.

They went to Red Lobster. Kristy ordered the house salad with crabmeat on top.

"I found out I have arthritis in my hands," said Garret's mother. She was taking piano lessons from a young person. Her husband was gone, had found a truer love and was gone, about which she was sometimes jealous, though mostly she felt just sleepy, which she usually interpreted as contentment. She had bought four gas masks, to protect against certain types of terrorism, had wept after she read the instruction manual cover-to-cover, alone, late one night after bathing the dogs.

"Four gas masks," she said. "I feel so stupid. I mean, why four? Why not five, then, or a thousand?" She started to laugh but then stopped and yawned. Kristy looked vertically down at her crabmeat salad. Garret's mother smiled at Kristy's forehead, then asked her son to consider transferring to a school in Florida.

Garret made a noise. He shrugged. He forked at his lobster, which looked mangled and too much like a large insect.

At home, the three of them together tried on the gas masks. They held their faces to the dogs, the two toy poodles, who turned away, went into separate rooms and barked at the walls. They were almost ninety in dog years.

"If I gained thirty pounds," Kristy said in bed, "would you still be with me?"

For love to work, Garret believed, you had to lie all the time, or you had to never lie at all. "I don't know," he said. You had to pick one and then let the other person know which you had picked. You had to be consistent, and sometimes a little stupid. "I can't tell the future," Garret said. "Obviously. Can you?"

A few minutes passed, and then Kristy got up, called the airline place, called a cab, and flew to New York. The next day, though, she flew back, and the rest of the week in Florida was very calm and sunny. They went canoeing, saw fish the size of legs through algae-gauzy water. Garret's mother made a cake. "To Garret and Kristy, with Love: Long and Happy Lives," said the cake. They watched a lot of TV, the three of them on the sofa. Terrorism, polls showed, was now believed to be the largest threat to human safety, ahead of cancer, heart disease, suburban gangs, piranhas, and swimming on a full stomach.

Back in Brooklyn, the new fear was that the terrorists could live inside walls, were maybe already living inside walls—cells of them, entire families, with flashlights, plotting and training, rappelling down the pipes.

Garret began to say things like, "Without coffee I am nothing," and "Terrorism Schmerrorism Berrorism Schlerorrism," which he said mostly for the torpidity of it, the easy mindlessness of it. He felt that the bones of his jaw and skull were growing, felt the fatty pout of his lips, the discomfort of bigger bones behind his mouth and face. He stopped going to classes, and applied for jobs in Chinatown. He tried not to

think. He tried just to love. Anything there was, he tried just
to love. It didn't work that way, though. It just didn't. Love,
after all, was not sold in bundles, by the pound. Love was not
ill-lit, enervated, Chinatown asparagus.

Though if love was an animal, Garret knew, it would
probably be the Loch Ness Monster. If it didn't exist, that
didn't matter. People made models of it, put it in the water,
and took photos. The hoax of it was good enough. The idea
of it. Though some people feared it, wished it would just go
away, had their lives insured against being eaten alive by it.

Late one night, Kristy got up to use the bathroom.

"What's this on it?" Garret said. "Kristy, why are you slamming the door?" He had just had a dream where he walked
to a deli and ordered a bagel with cream cheese, but instead
received a bagel with something else on it; he couldn't tell
what—and then the sound of a door closing.

"I had to use the bathroom," Kristy said.

"Please don't slam the door," Garret said. "Be more considerate." He shifted his head. His hair against the pillow made
a loud, prolonged noise—a noise that, before it stopped,
seemed as if it might go on forever.

They rarely made love anymore, and only in the mornings,
when one of them would wake up, knead against the other,
and then start grabbing in that direction. Their heads would
be floury and egg-beaten, operating on a kind of toasted, bakery lust, and they'd have sex like that—faces turned away,
mouths closed and puffy and hard, eyes scrunched shut.

Afterward, Garret would feel masturbatory and boneless.

He attended another anti-war meeting. There was another
war that was going to happen soon. People stood up and said
things. One person said, "People are going to seek happiness.
People need to understand that other people are going to do
what they think will make them happiest. So people need

to just back off, let this happen." She had a ring in her nose, like a bull. The ring was a pale piece of bone. "Revolution is from the inside out," she said. "It's over," someone else said, "the world is done for, doomed—and I say oh well, oh, well," then stood and walked briskly out of the room, jumping to slap the top of the doorway on the way out. There was a long moment of nothing, and then a heavyset, kind-faced man sitting adjacent Garret said loudly, at the ground, "Fuck war, *fuck, war.*" People gathered around and patted his back. Some of them, confused and tired, or else just lazy, patted Garret's back, patted anyone's back. There were, again, sign-up sheets against the wall. Garret signed up for three differ-ent things. He walked out into the city. Drunk people were moving slantly across the sidewalks and streets, though it was only Wednesday.

Garret thought that he might go back to Florida. Maybe get a job on a golf course. He once had a friend who drove one of those armored carts around, vacuuming up golf balls on golf ranges. Maybe he'd do that.

"Come home," Garret's mother said on the phone. "You can take a semester off. Kristy can too. Both of you can come live here and be safe." She said that the terrorists were plan-ning to take hostage the entire island of Manhattan. She had heard on talk radio. They were going to attach outboard motors to Manhattan and drive it like a barge into the Atlan-tic Ocean. No one knew what the terrorists would do after that, though. Maybe have a cruise around the world, a caller said. Low-key, with virgin piña coladas. Maybe start their own country, another caller said, to legitimize their terror-ism, make it humanitarian and moral and—

He was cut off there.

......

Kristy had an appointment made to remove her wisdom teeth. She asked Garret to accompany her, but Garret said he had a class that morning. He would meet her after, though.

Kristy's face became lumpy and hard after the operation. "I feel like a monster," she said. They went into an ice-cream store, and she began to weep. Garret thought about getting up to hug her, but then just put a hand on her head, across the table. "You look fine," he said. "It won't last, anyway."

Kristy went to her sister's place and Garret went back to Brooklyn.

They didn't talk for a week. Then Garret called her. She said she hadn't called because her face was swollen. She didn't want Garret to see. Garret said he didn't care. They agreed to meet for a movie that night at nine. She said that things would change from now on. She wouldn't be late anymore. They'd go ice-skating.

She came running up for the movie at 8:59. Her face was red and blue on one side; it looked a little bludgeoned, or else diseased.

Garret had the tickets ready and they went in. They watched the trailers and then Kristy reached onto Garret's lap and held his hand. Garret leaned over and whispered, "Come outside a minute, I have to tell you something."

Outside, Kristy smiled at him, and then Garret wasn't sure, but he said it anyway: "If a terrorist said to you that if you were late he'd kill you and your family, would you be one minute early? You wouldn't; you'd be half the fucking day early." He had rehearsed in his head.

"What the hell are you saying, Garret?" said Kristy. "Are you kidding me? Don't do this. You don't know what you're talking about."

But there were things that you had to worry about, Garret knew, that you had to care about. If he didn't say anything, then she would be twenty minutes late, then an hour, then she wouldn't show up at all. Or she'd show up and throw a pie in his face. You had to keep your life under control. Preempt it. You had to let it know that you were not happy. Though maybe you didn't. Maybe it was that you should let things go, be tolerant and easygoing and not ever worry. Ease yourself toward acceptance and quietude, toward, what though—death? No; that didn't seem right. You were supposed to resist death.

"Yeah I do," Garret said. "I'm talking about you shouldn't be late all the time. It's inconsiderate."

"Will you realize what you're saying right now? I was *early* this time."

"I know, but you *ran* here," Garret said. "You could have easily been late."

"So what? I was early."

They stood there for a long time. All the moody emptinesses inside of them swelled and joined, and then ensconced them, like bubbles, and there, inside, they floated—the qualmish, smoked-out bodies of them, stale and still and upsidedown. People around them drifted in and out of cars, into stores, across streets and over sidewalks.

"You should have been twenty minutes early," Garret finally said. "You should have thought, 'Hmm, I've been late so many times, maybe I should come much earlier this time, in case one of my excuses comes up to delay me.'"

"You should have been an hour early"—once he started, he knew, he had to keep going; the anger came from nowhere, it came and was here—"sitting and waiting, to make up for all the hundreds of hours you've been late before, to compensate, to *make sure*." The city lights overlapped in the air, became swimmy, blotchy, and brown. What was reasonable and what was required and what was just plain stupid? Should he apologize? All of life seemed just to be one thing—one slapdashed, stuffed turkey of a thing, flying out of the oven and into the night, into orbit; something once familiar and under control, but now just out there, unknown, by itself, charred and brainless and rarely glimpsed.

"That's it," Kristy said. "I'm going to your place right now to get my stuff."

They went back to Garret's apartment. They walked the entire way. Across the avenues and over the Brooklyn Bridge. She walked about twenty feet in front. He followed. The night was noisy and black, starless and warm. Maybe it was not winter at all, but summer.

At his apartment, Garret sat on his bed.

Kristy smashed her possessions into her piece of luggage. "You can keep these for your next girlfriend." She held up two mud-green three-pound weights.

"Can you be quiet a little? My suitemate is probably trying to sleep," Garret said. "Why are you so angry, anyway? You're leaving me, so calm down."

Kristy's mouth began to bleed, a slow seeping at the edge, like an early sign of mutation. Her cheek had been swollen for too long. There was maybe something wrong with the stitches. "Fuck," she said. "You didn't even come with me for my wisdom teeth." She wiped her mouth with one of Garret's shirts. "You had to go to class? You skip all your fucking classes!"

"That's my shirt," Garret said. "That's inconsiderate." Against the bureau was a stack of photos that they had taken together. "Take your photos," Garret said. Kristy kicked them across the floor. She threw her sandals against the wall. They lodged in the window blinds and dust went in the air.

"Why are you acting like this?" Garret said.

Kristy set her luggage upright, the wheels aimed at the door. "Why don't you install soundproof walls for your suitemate?" she said. "If you care about him so much, why don't you?"

"I will," Garret said. "That's considerate of you, finally." They looked at each other. Blood oozed again out of Kristy's mouth, and then out her nose, like a crushed thought. She went and grabbed her sandals from the blinds. She set her luggage outside the door, got in position to properly slam the door with both hands, and then slammed it. The door bounced off its frame without closing.

Kristy wheeled her luggage down the outside hall. It made squeaky noises, and train-track noises. Garret sat and listened. For a moment he felt sorry for her, for himself, for the whole wrecked and blighting world—it was hopeless, really—but then he felt okay, felt that things were not that bad; he felt friendly, and he felt that this moment of softness, of calm, though maybe it was just that he was tired, was good, was enough, that if there could be this feeling, then things would go on, month after month, one good and tiny feeling per; it was okay. And he wanted suddenly, badly, to share all this, and so he called out, "Have a good week." He stood and shouted, "Wait; I hope you can be happy now; I hope we can be friends still, really," and then Kristy was back, was looking, was saying, "You're a real shithead," was saying some other things, her face inflamed, and the door, then, slamming shut, making a loud noise.

THE TOAST

Rebecca Curtis

Last week I received, via Priority Mail, a card inviting me to a wedding that I'd very much like to attend. After eighteen years of partnership, the card said, Ms. Leala Kroger, Esq.—my older sister—and Mr. Mattathias Williams, Esq.—my older sister's boyfriend—were getting married on the island of Oahu. Two days after the card arrived, my sister called from her Colorado mountain home and said that she wanted to tell me herself that she and her partner-in-life, best friend, and the father of her six- and eight-year-old daughters were getting married in Hawaii in the second week of May 2014, and that in order to attend the wedding I would need to reserve a room *this week* using the code KROGERWILLIAMS2014, and I said, "Wonderful."

The wedding, my sister said, would not be fancy. However, there would be a hair-metal band, a five-course local organic vegan dinner, and a life-size fair-trade chocolate baby elephant. I'm afraid that my sister went on explaining details about the wedding, and I stopped listening; this is because I caught Lyme disease five years ago and have neurological damage that makes it difficult for me to listen when people talk, especially when what they're saying isn't interesting.

It was an eighty-degree November evening in Park Slope, Brooklyn, and I was sitting at my oak desk in my attic apartment. I had a nice apartment. One room, true, and in an attic; but cozy. The window looked over the owner's garden. I was fond of its wide orange floorboards and the mice that pattered out from beneath my futon whenever I ate buttered crackers. On my desk was the stack of student stories that I needed to read for the next day, and next to them was a letter from a collection agency.

"So you'll come?" my sister said.

I considered what to say. I knew that even if you're an unmarried forty-year-old woman who steals reams of paper from her workplace and collects unemployment compensation illegally, there are things that no one who's decent does, and I knew that skipping your sister's wedding was one of them.

Also, I wasn't *broke*. There was room on my Platinum MasterCard, and on my Capital One card. But I owed $1,200 in rent, $820 in credit card bills, $1,275 in overdue student-loan payments, and $13,756.46 to the collection agency.

So when my sister said, "You'll come?" I scratched my nose.

I figured a plane ticket to my sister's wedding in Hawaii would cost $2,000.

I could not tell her I was broke. Last year, when I quit my job as a creative-writing teacher at an Ivy League university, my sister said, in a disapproving way, "Why are you giving up your job?" When I explained that I'd enrolled in a program to earn a degree as a health coach and planned to help people *transform their lives* by helping them eat healthful diets, avoid toxins, and exercise, my sister said, in her attorney's voice, "You should keep your job." My sister also said, "Sonya, you used to be *a writer*. You used to talk to me about your *writing*. Now all you talk about is fluoride." She reminded me that it would take years to get enough clients to support myself as a health coach, and that once I *did* get clients, I'd be sued. She said my ideas about health were odd, and predicted that if I gave up my position at the university, before the year's end I'd be broke. I told my sister not to worry and that no matter what, I wouldn't ask her for a loan. But I'd failed, since graduating from the health-coach program, to get enough clients, even though I offered free consultations to all the fat, hormonally imbalanced women I met in local health-food stores and sent "You need a health coach" emails to all my former Ivy League colleagues. So now, after my sister announced her wedding and repeated in a sobby voice, "Please come," I told her, "I'll try." Then I said the only thing that, given the circumstances, I could: I said I'd won a fellowship to a writing colony. I'd won a "special fellowship prize" to "Yaddo," I told my sister, and I needed to "go there and write all next May." I'd try to change my dates, but the "Yaddo people" would not let me, I said, because it was impossible. Yaddo was a rare opportunity, I said, and there was no way any writer could pass it up.

In reality I would never go to a colony to write, because in my apartment I have a desk, and I have a pen and paper. I wouldn't go to Yaddo unless I wanted to have sex with some lousy-in-the-sack, fluoride-drinking writers. But I knew my sister would *believe* me if I said I was blowing off her wedding for a colony.

"I really want you at my wedding, but I know it's important for you to get writing done," she said, probably because I hadn't written anything in five years.

"Thanks," I said, and just as I was weighing health-coach-y things to say in return, like "I'm glad you're getting married in Hawaii, it sounds like that's an important thing for you to do," my older sister's voice got high like a girl's and she said, "Maybe you could write something."

And I said, "Eh," because recently she'd told me that the

book I published six years ago was "bad," "needed more plot," and made her sick.

"No," she said, "I don't mean *a story*, I mean a note for Matty, something we could read at the rehearsal dinner so it'd be like you're there. You know . . . ," she said, "a toast."

"Oh," I said.

She said, "It wouldn't have to be *good*."

"Oh," I said.

She said, "I *mean* it wouldn't have to be fancy. You don't have to spend more than ten minutes on it."

I stretched at my desk. Because I was still teaching one writing class as an adjunct professor at the Ivy League university, there were sixteen student stories on my desk that I needed to read and type praise about. Also, because I needed cash, I had resolved to log on to an online forum where women posted descriptions of their menstruation troubles and to write emails to all the women offering to make their menstruation troubles go away. So I had work to do. But it's hard to turn down a small request when one has just rejected a large one.

"Okay," I said.

My sister's throat cleared.

"Of course you know this," she said, "but the toast needs to be appropriate."

"Of course," I said.

Then she said, in a weighing-options-thoughtfully voice, "It's my *wedding*, so the toast should probably be funny and light."

"Yes," I said.

"Everyone will be making speeches," she said, "all my friends and Matty's friends and everyone I love."

She paused.

"I mean everyone I love besides *you*," she said.

I said, "All right."

She repeated, "I'm thinking 'light and funny,' some 'light and funny' anecdote would be nice."

I could tell that part of her was glad I wasn't coming to the wedding.

She said, "Maybe you could write about something funny that happened when we were kids. Something Matty hasn't heard." She paused. "But please don't lecture about the dangers of fluoride and mercury. For just once, I would like you not to be a health coach, and *just* to be my sister."

"Sure," I said.

"Because when you're a health coach," she said, "you can be annoying, and not everybody is interested in hearing about the effects of fluoride." I told her I supposed that was true. "You know," my sister said softly, "don't ever tell Matty I told you this, but he *thought* you wouldn't come to the wedding. He didn't know it was because of Yaddo. He thought you just wouldn't *care* about the wedding. He thinks you don't like him."

I tried not to think about which of my credit cards were about to accrue late-payment fees, and to think instead about my sister's future husband, who is an anti-immigration lawyer for the government. I said I liked him.

"That's why a toast from you to him would be really nice," my sister said. "To show you like him."

"Okay," I said.

"You know," my sister said, her voice knowing and pea-flavored, "in the eighteen years I've been with him, you and Matty have never talked much. I mean *really* talked. He'd love a note from you. He's a thoughtful person."

So I said I wanted to be closer to my sister's boyfriend, even though I've never met a man who is more of a walking pancake. Don't get me wrong, as a health coach I try to see people's inner strengths and auras, and I do, when I squint; my sister's boyfriend is a nice man, a better man than me, since I'm a woman. He's a smarter-than-average guy who's managed to be loyal to my sister for eighteen years and who will put up with anything, it seems, but that's not his fault, because he's an A blood-type. The A blood-types evolved when agriculture began, and they can digest grains, which is more than an O can say. They also have a strong mind–body connection, and I've noticed that a lot of them crave stinky cheese, even though it forms mucus in their gut and gives them allergies, and they also crave tomatoes, even though those give them arthritis, and they *think* they like steak, a lot of them, even though their intestines are too long to digest it in a timely fashion and it putrefies into impacted fecal matter in their colon. Worse, the whole crowd of A blood-types are followers, and when it's time to punch a man who needs to be punched, they'll just sit there and smile as if everything is all right. Truth be told, I felt bad for my sister's boyfriend. After college, when my sister told him they were moving in together, he said he did not want to, but my sister told him he was doing it, so he did. A year later, when they were attending the law school my sister selected for them, my sister said she wanted a dog, and her boyfriend said he didn't want one, so my sister bought two Great Danes, and whenever I visited her she'd yell, "Matty! Go pick up the poo in the yard!" Once my sister got pregnant, she told Matty that they should move all the way up to Boulder and commute an hour back to Denver for work, and he said he didn't want to do that, but they did it, and once my sister had two babies, she'd yell things like, "Matty! Someone needs to put the chains on the Subaru and drive over the Front Range to get the girls at playdate!" and he'd do it, or "Matty, I need you to make dinner!" and he'd make it; but then, my sister's bossiness was because my sister "saw" all the things that needed to be done around the house that her boyfriend didn't "see" because he was watching soccer on TV, and my sister did 80 percent of the things that needed to be done herself and merely forced her boyfriend to "see" the other 20 percent. I was ready to be friends with my sister's boyfriend, but he was boring. I had no animosity toward him but no interest in him; and he had never (as perhaps he had no reason to) shown any interest, not even of the fraternal kind, in me.

I'd heard him say to my littlest niece once, "Your aunt Sonya likes to say funny things. That's because she's a writer. Writers make stuff up, so we take her stories with a grain of salt." I'd also heard him say, to my other niece, "Your aunt Sonya went to school to be a health coach. We hope she gets some clients, so she doesn't have to come live with us."

I didn't have jack to say to my sister's boyfriend. So after I got off the phone with my sister, I wrote responses to two of my students' stories. One story was about a student who has angry feelings toward his old-maid writing teacher. The student says to the teacher, "How old are you? Your 40, I found you on Facebook. Your an old maid," and the teacher responds, "Yes, I have hair on my face. I'm not a good writer so I teach. Now my prime is done, I wish I were dead," and the student says, "Every dog has it's day," and pulls an automatic rifle out of his pocket and shoots the teacher in the head. I typed two pages of praise about the story's energetic language. Then on the manuscript I wrote, "Jacob, great story. Please avoid clichés such as 'Now my prime is done.' B." Then, in a fit of pique I knew would get me fired, I added a minus to the B. The second story was about a woman who marries her son. They are both the same age, twenty-three, because the woman dies after giving birth and is reborn.

After typing up a paragraph of praise, I scrawled on the manuscript, "How awesome that the protagonist's fiancée is his dead mother who died giving birth to him and was instantly reborn in the same town! Great plot. B." I tried to think of a topic that would interest my sister's boyfriend and provide a light, toast-appropriate anecdote about my sister.

Even though my sister is the person I'm most disappointed in in the world, I try to stay positive, and when I considered my sister's many feats, like the fact that at age seventeen she scored five goals to bring our high school's lacrosse team to an All New England Championship, and at eighteen won first place in a national debate competition even though she once had a lisp, and that unlike me she owns three SUVs, a Boulder mountain house, a small yacht, three dogs, one horse, and two daughters, it all—and by "it" I mean her accomplishments—came down to the fact that she's my *older* sister.

According to www.firstborns.com, firstborns are alike in that they're bastards, or more often, at least. Beyond that, they *achieve*, always within the framework of the orthodoxy. Even when they think they're "insurgents," they work within the system. I don't know how many times I explained to my sister that, though she defends wrongfully terminated chambermaids and textile workers when they get laid off, she's a cog in the corporate machine; she says, "No, I go *against* the system!" and I say, "Leala, without you the system *couldn't exist*." Lawyers like her "defending" workers, I explained, is what *makes* a system in which so many are wiretapped and underpaid seem acceptable, and if we didn't have token "defendants," we could see our democracy, I told her, for what it is: an ant farm in which humans are milked like aphids.

My sister, like all firstborns, is unable to question received ideas. For example, even though I've explained to her that the fluoride in America's water is a radioactive waste product of aluminum manufacturing that causes cancer, thyroid problems, wrinkles, and obesity, and that rather than protect teeth, it *makes them break*, she says, "But, Sonya, I still think it's good for me." She is unable to conceive that the world might be "upside down," so to speak, and *this* is because, despite the fact that she's not some grain-eating, crowd-following A, she's an oldest child, a firstborn, and got the shit beaten out of her at a very young age.

Oldest siblings, I learned on firstborns.com, disappoint their parents when they pop out from the vagina looking not-as-expected; soon, if they're not retarded, they sense their parents' disappointment, and in reaction they achieve. All the first American astronauts to fly into outer space were firstborns. Oldest children are disproportionately represented in law, medicine, banking, and engineering.

Two-thirds of all entrepreneurs are firstborns. Oldest kids average two points higher on IQ tests. Oldest children are more self-righteous, insecure, and self-deluded than any other kind of offspring. That wasn't on firstborns.com.

I jotted down the stats from the website. But after I did it, I realized that it was not good toast material. Also, I realized, my sister's boyfriend would have no interest in it, because he's a firstborn.

So I gave up. I had no interest in my sister's boyfriend or in his marrying—a stupid move—my sister. I recalled how when I was angry at her as a kid, I used to hit our dog, because I lost in our physical fights, because she was bigger, but if I hit our dog, a docile English sheepdog, she would let me have whatever I wanted, as long as I didn't hit the dog, and it became a tool of mine, when my sister was being obtuse I'd hit the dog's gray rear, and my sister would say, "Don't hit the dog," and her gray-green eyes would glisten and she'd grab my arm, but I kept pounding the dog's flat hind, the dog had hip dysplasia and a keen would emit from her black lips and I'd pound her rump until my sister said, "Okay, you win," and I remembered how when my parents killed the dog, my sister was ten, I was seven, and the dog was three, and my sister tried to construct a human blockade, she wanted me to stand in the front door of our house and hold hands with her so that our parents would be unable to drag the dog—to whom my mother had become allergic—through the door to the car to drive it to the pound. "Come on, Sonya," my sister said. "It will work, a human chain, we can stop them!" and I said, "They'll just use the other door, idiot," and went to read a book in my room. Fortunately, the death of Almond—oh, Almond, who licked my father's hand every time he stuck it forth even though once he threw a wrench at her head and knocked her flat—reminded me of a usable anecdote.

One time when I was three years old and my sister was six, our mother wanted to comb our hair, so first she combed my sister's hair, and then she chased me all around the house, saying, "Come here right now or you'll get a punishment," and, "As soon as your father comes home he's going to give you a punishment." Her best and only friend in the world, Haven, was coming over, and our mother wanted her friend, whom she hadn't seen in ten years, to think that her life was a good one, and she thought that Haven would not think this unless her girls had combed-out tresses.

We lived in Massachusetts then, of course, in the Colonial my parents built in the seventies, in a hay field midway up a pine-covered mountain in the Berkshires.

Now you, my future brother-in-law, are low-key, relaxed, and reasonable. But perhaps you know how it is to be anxious about a problem-scenario-upcoming, and to get fixated on the perfection of one detail, and to begin to believe that if it's tilted just so, at the right angle—which is infinitesimally different from all others and is correct—that its rightness will right the whole. My mother wanted to convey to her best and only friend that she, Jordan, the girl Haven had loved in junior high, was happy, safe, and living in a well-kept house.

My mother has trouble making friends. In all her life— during the thirty-three years I knew her, when she spoke to me—in all that time, when she spoke of friends, she spoke only of Haven. In my early years, there was no occasion to refer to friends, because her world was ours: she, my sister, and I lived together in the house on the hill through winter and summer. Sometimes our father was home and sometimes he was "on a trip"; speech was about him—*"when your father gets home"*—or else us: "You need a bath"; "I want you to play quietly"; "What do you want for lunch?" *"My friend Haven"* was reserved for the highest order of discussion when she was talking to us (Leala and me), although perhaps she was also talking to herself. Our mother did, from time to time, in an effort to relate to us, reveal facts from her childhood.

She told us—the most memorable story she told—about mean girls who made fun of her hair at recess, the leader one day approaching her, walking with the others to where she stood alone, and saying to the others, "Look at Jordan's hair."

She told us about the leader walking up to her hair. Touching it.

"Stay still, Jordan," the leader said. Our mother did. Our mother was short, dark, and had moles on her neck. Her hair was black, curly, thick, and dry.

"Jordan," the leader said, "where did you get your hair? Is it African?"

"Look at her hair," the leader said to the others—her hands were in it—"Jordan has Negro hair."

Then the leader yanked our mother's hair.

"Ow!" our mother said.

"I had to test," the leader said quietly to our mother, "to see if it's real."

"Watch out, girls!" the leader yelled. "Jordan's hair's got bugs in it!"

Then the girls walked away saying, "Bugs, bugs!" and after that no girl went near my mother if she could avoid it, and if by seating arrangement a girl was forced to she'd say, "Oh *no*, bugs!"

"After that day," our mother told us, "I went home and begged my mother to comb my hair. But she didn't always have time. So, many days I went around with my hair wild."

These stories were lessons. But occasionally, if she was in the best mood, our mother would say, "My friend Haven . . . ," and it was only ever a snippet, and I couldn't even tell you the stories, because they weren't memorable. Haven and she used to go to dances together in high school. They didn't like any of the other girls, so they would get ready together at Haven's house and go together as "dates" and even dance together too, if they felt like it. For a while, in high school, she and Haven double-dated. And Haven ended up marrying her high school sweetheart, although my mother did not marry hers. They went to a Catholic high school in Montpelier, Vermont, and there were nuns—not memorable ones—and Haven came from a lower-middle-class family, and her parents were divorced, and she lived with her mother. Haven had two older sisters and an older brother and my mother liked to spend time at her house.

You, my brother-to-be, will have heard the story of how our mother's mother died of cancer when our mother was ten and her father was put in a mental hospital. A boring story: when our mother was ten, her mother died, her dad went in the bin, and our mother and her sister were sent to the neighbors'. By the time my mother met Haven, she would have been living for two years with "Auntie Frances"— Frances who had four of her own girls and worked as a nurse and whom my mother has hardly spoken of since, not to me, not to Leala. She said, for example, of her childhood, "I spent most of my time at my friend Haven's house," not, "When I lived with Auntie Frances, I often spent the afternoon at my friend Haven's." There was no Frances.

She once said, "Haven's family didn't have much money, but their house was a fun place to be. It was always lively. They were always doing some project or other."

A statement full of clichés and generalities.

"It's because of Haven that I love crafts," my mother once told us. She was helping us make Christmas ornaments with her sewing machine. My sister and I designed the ornaments from old panty hose, which we cut with scissors into the shape of old ladies and stuffed with cotton; our mother sewed together what we made. She had gotten out the sewing machine for this.

"Haven was a very talented painter," she said. And Haven could sew, she even made her own clothes, beautiful clothes, *as good as the ones in the stores,* and knit scarves. Haven did pottery. Haven was very talented.

We thought our mother was talented. On occasion she would draw us a picture, if we begged—say, of a bunny rabbit—and her pictures were always better than ours. But more than that: her rabbits seemed *about to leap.*

"I'm not talented at all," our mother said. "I'm not good. You should see the things my friend Haven used to make." So we knew very little of Haven, who was now coming to visit, except that Haven was our mother's bosom buddy.

"We were inseparable," our mother said. "The mean girls at school used to say, 'Hey, what's wrong with you two, are you lesbians?'"

Eventually, we learned, Haven got a car, and she gave my mother rides to high school so she didn't have to walk two miles and take three buses; and when my mother turned sixteen and her auntie Frances finally said, "There is no room for you here. I'm sorry, but I've housed you this long. I have my own daughters and expenses—I've got your younger sister to take care of too, now, and that's all I can manage. You're sixteen, find a place, ask a friend if you can live with them," my mother knew immediately that she would ask Haven, and she did, and Haven threw her arms around my mother's sixteen-year-old body, horsey, I guess, fit but muscular, our mother didn't play sports but she walked a lot, she was only four feet eleven inches tall, and dark-eyed, tan, with that wild black hair, and Haven said, "That's a fabulous idea," and they planned girlishly how to persuade Haven's mother to take our mother into the house, and though there was no money and no room, somehow they did.

Everyone worked. Haven's mother worked as a secretary full-time and then she came home and made dinner; Haven's older sisters worked after school (her brother was already in college); Haven worked at a clothing boutique most weeknights; my mother bused tables at a lobster shack. The house was a house of girls and chaos and my mother lived in Haven's room with Haven.

"I always knew I could ask Haven and she'd say yes," our mother told us. "She was that kind of friend."

"And she was very beautiful, Haven was, and many boys

liked her, but Haven was tough and didn't wear dresses, she wore jeans and smoked cigarettes and ignored them all."

And then our mother went to college at the University of Vermont, and Haven went to college, too, but somewhere else, out of state, a liberal-arts college where she'd won a fellowship, and our mother met our father, and Haven married her high school sweetheart and moved with him to upstate New York and our mother never—or almost never—saw Haven again.

In her presentation to us of this matter, our mother and Haven were exactly as good friends now as they always had been. They exchanged Christmas cards each year, and about the many cards we received—that got taped, forming a decorative frame, to the door of our hall—our mother would not remark, except for the one from Haven. When it came, she would say, "I got a card from my friend Haven!" and we would have to come look at the card, and then she would tape it up.

"Oh, Haven!" our father would say, if he was home and had been made to view the card. "How's she doing? Hope she's well!" But he had met her only once.

Sometimes in a blue moon, our mother would say, "I got a letter from Haven, my friend Haven," and she'd be in an odd mood the rest of the day. She'd think of a craft project for us to do, Leala and me, and take a nap on the couch in the living room, with a heavy afghan pulled up to her neck.

"Haven loved Snickers bars," she once said.

At any rate, although they hadn't seen each other in ten years, my mother still spoke as if she and Haven were as close as ever. For example, if Leala referred to her best friend, Juliana, who sat next to her in second grade, my mother would respond, "*My* best friend is Haven."

All this—the existence of the apocryphal Haven—was the

reason that my middle name was Haven, and that "Haven," whoever she was, was Leala's godmother—twice gifts had arrived on Leala's birthday, from "Haven"—it was the reason our mother now chased me through the halls yelling, "Come here right now and let me spank you, don't you run from me"; she could not bear for Haven to arrive and see that her two daughters—Leala, skinny, big gray eyes, black hair, and myself—had uncombed hair.

Our mother lived alone most of the time. Our father often did six-day stints "on alert" at Pease Air National Guard Base, flew refuelers for bombers in the Falkland Islands, visited bases in Japan and Guam. Our mother got fat and became depressed. She protests when I (Leala will not) claim (or used to claim) that she was unhappy. "I'm very happy!" she says. "I was happy! I love my life!" But Leala and I remember days when she washed and ironed every curtain in the house. "The curtains were terrible," she told us, "so much dust." Every two weeks she washed, waxed, and buffed the wood floors of the kitchen, the dining room, and the lower halls inch by inch on her hands and knees. "Water is wood's worst enemy," she told us. "Wood *hates* water." She took an hour-long nap each day on the couch with the afghan pulled over her and said, "You girls play outside." Every week she made double batches of chocolate-chip cookies, and once they were laid out on paper towels on the kitchen counters we asked, "Aren't you going to have one?" and she'd say, "No, I'm on a diet," and later eat three.

But that morning she rose at six a.m., weeded the strawberry garden, dusted the house, and drove us to Shop 'n Save and bought a roaster, then drove to Dairy Queen and bought an ice-cream cake, even though we only had thirty dollars to last us until the end of the month, because our mother had remembered that Haven liked ice cream. Now our mother re-dusted the baseboards while Leala and I danced in the den and peered out the windows, squinting into the sunlight at the white disappearing end of our dirt road in anticipation of the car that would be Haven's.

This story is boring, I apologize. Leala was her first child, which is what I want to tell you, and responsible for everything. It was to Leala that our mother said, "I chose to stay home with you and be a mother to you, because I wanted you to feel you had a mother. And I don't regret my decision. But if I hadn't had you, I could have had a career.

"I would have gone to medical school," our mother said to Leala. "I was a biology major in college and I got all A's. I wanted to be a doctor, and I am still interested in medicine to this day."

Which is just to say that Leala was not the only, but she was the first and the cause. She accepted this. At five years old, Leala set the table for dinner. She'd walk down our half-mile-long driveway to get the mail and bring it back. She would dust all the windowsills, all the banisters and furniture, and then fold the laundry, and if my mother said, "It's time to comb your hair," Leala would sit and wait for it. Our mother would yank. She'd yank yank yank as she combed, and Leala would sit there with her legs crossed and tears streaming down her face but she wouldn't move, at most she'd say, "Ow," or, "Go softer, please," and my mother would say, "Sit *still*"; and by the time she was done, Leala might have said, "It really hurts!" but she'd still sit there, her face puffy and streaked.

Not me. The second I felt a yank I was up and running. She'd say, "It needs combing," and I'd say, "I don't care!" and she'd say that as soon as my father came home he would spank me, give me the spanking I deserved, and so forth; I didn't give a shit—though in the end she might catch me and spank me herself and I'd say I hated her, it was not untrue, and she'd say, "I'm not going to comb your hair, you don't deserve it," and in the end, if it ended my way, Leala would comb my hair.

I sat in the middle of the dining room, and Leala stood behind me and combed. If she caught a snarl she stopped, held the chunk of hair carefully, tight above the snarl, but loose from the head, and took the snarl out with a pick. I only ever wanted Leala to comb my hair, and this fact, which was mirrored in everything—if it was bath time, only Leala could bathe me; if it was night, only Leala could put me to bed—enraged our mother. Sometimes she gave in to it. "Fine, Leala can comb your hair."

Other times she'd say, "Leala's not your mother, *I'm* your mother, and *I'm* combing your hair."

Leala was the one who, when the house was a mess and our mother was on the couch with a headache, said to me, "Let's clean up the house before Dad comes home," and, "Mom's tired, let's make dinner."

She was also easy to take advantage of. I wanted nothing more than to play with her all day long. We had a wooden dollhouse, four feet tall, handmade and painted red, and we'd play Barbies. I'd take the two new Barbies that were hers and give her two old scruffies, I'd take Ken, and my Barbies would rape her Barbies. My Barbies got the Barbie car, the horses from the ranch—which they had sex with—and the gauzy pink gowns. When Leala got tired of Barbies I'd say, "No. More Barbies!" and she'd say, "Ohhh-kay," and my Barbies would rape her Barbies again.

Other days, we'd play Monopoly and I'd buy everything I landed on and lose money until Leala went upstairs to pee and I stole cash from the bank. If we played checkers, when I lost I'd point and yell, "Look out the window!" and when Leala looked out the window I'd move my pieces to better spots, and when she said, "Why'd you tell me to look out the window?" I'd tell her there'd been a deer outside but that she'd missed it.

She was the only one I allowed to comb my hair, which I've said.

But it occurs to me now that I've remembered wrong, or re-pasted another memory over this one, because Haven arrived, and both our hair was uncombed, and this was part of—if not all of—our mother's anger and shame.

"Their hair's not combed," our mother said. "They wouldn't let me."

"Oh," Haven said, "they're adorable," and "What's *your* name?" and "How old are *you*?" and so forth, which Leala answered politely, I grudgingly, and eventually Haven said, in a halting voice, "I'll comb their hair, if they'll let me."

"They would *love* for you to comb their hair," our mother said, "wouldn't you, Leala?" and Leala nodded.

(Who was this woman? Her godmother. She'd received gifts wrapped in glossy, thick paper. Atop them, slipped under velvet ribbon, there was a hearts-and-glitter-decked card, inside of which was written, "To Liora Leala, from your Godmother, Haven." "I want her to be *my* godmother," I said when the presents came. A doll with a white porcelain face and real black hair and a turquoise Spanish dress—the best doll either one of us had—sat on Leala's bed, and I wasn't allowed to touch it because it was from Haven.)

That morning, several hours later than expected, a tan sedan had made its way up our driveway—slowly, as if not sure it'd got the right house—and a tall, elegant woman with shoulder-length, silky brown hair that turned up at the ends stepped out. She wore a cream-colored suit: a narrow skirt and a tailored jacket that cut in at the waist and dashed out and bore a shiny band around its smallest part. The jacket had cloth-covered buttons.

Our mother wore a plaid skirt—which she'd made herself from a pattern and fabric bought at Fabric Mart—and a turtleneck.

Leala and I pressed our faces against the den's windows when the car came.

Our mother went down the path toward Haven and said, "You're here!" And Haven paused, threw her arms open as if to indicate the world—the empty field around the house, the forest—and said, "What a wonderful house!"

The two hugged, they came inside, tea was made. Haven made much of us, and Leala allowed Haven to comb her hair. I refused, and this was the worst thing that happened during the visit, it was the thing to which our mother later attributed its failure—"You were rude to my friend Haven," she said. "It's inexcusable." And I replied, "I didn't want her to comb my hair."

Haven, at the time, had said, "It's okay, I don't have to comb her hair . . . she doesn't know me, I'm a stranger." Haven was seated in our dining room. Her back was straight in the suit, her legs were elegantly crossed. Her tea sat unsipped beside her. She had not wanted ice-cream cake. Had they run out of things to say? I don't know. She'd been taken upstairs and shown the rooms—that took five minutes—and she had seen the strawberry garden. Leala sat at the dining-room table, having had her hair combed, and drew with crayons on paper, a tall, big-eyed woman with pretty hair who was probably Haven, and a short, fat one who was our mother. Our mother stood nearby and watched.

My mother yelled at me: "She wants to comb your hair, let her comb it!"

Her voice was very angry. I knew quite well that she was concerned about the impression her friend would have of the house, her rude daughters, a miserable failure, tangled daughters, messy house, plaid skirt. I knew how she wanted Haven to love her.

"No," I said.

Haven said, "It's okay, it's okay."

Our mother said, "If you don't let her comb your hair you are going to get a punishment when your father comes home."

I said, "I don't care."

Pause.

I said, "Leala can comb my hair."

"Really, it's fine," Haven said, "really."

Our mother said, "Leala's your *sister*, she's a child, let *Haven* comb your hair, she's an *adult*. Now go sit still so she can comb it. If you are rude to my friend Haven"—her head had lowered like a bull's—"I will take you up to your room and I will spank you so hard that you will be sorry."

Haven was handed the comb. I steeled my nerves. I cannot describe the pain of being a little girl and having your hair combed. Why it is so painful is a mystery. The fact of the pain invites disbelief and seems ludicrous.

Haven asked every ten seconds, "Does it hurt? Does it hurt?"

She combed and yanked. My hair was snarled with all the things I'd touched or eaten that day: bubble gum, pine pitch, Elmer's Glue, boogers.

"No," I whispered.

At length my sister and I were told to play outside, so our mother and Haven could reminisce. They reminisced for thirty minutes—I have no idea what was said—then we were called in to say goodbye to Haven, and we said goodbye with that child's feeling of knowing that someone is supposed to be important but that they are nothing, a dust mote about to disappear into the stratosphere—and our fat mother hugged Haven, and Haven stepped in her suit down the walk and got into her car, and the tan sedan rolled down the driveway, because she had a long trip ahead of her, after all, and had only stopped by our house on her way to the White Mountains, where she would see family. Our mother's references to Haven were fewer after that, but on the occasions she did refer to her, she'd add, "You met her."

Whenever our mother said, "You met her," Leala's eyes acquired a blank look. Noticing that Leala had put down her book, our mother would say, "You *loved* her," because of the gross thing Leala did as Haven left, to save the visit.

In the following years, Christmas cards still came from Haven, and occasionally our mother's voice would firm up and in reference to something she'd say, *"My best friend, Haven."* Soon Leala had a perm, the rage among ten-year-olds, but she still played with Barbie dolls because I demanded it, though often she'd say, "I don't want to, I'm too old," until I would come up to where she was lying on the couch reading a book and say, "I have an idea. Let's play the Mystery of Who Decapitated Barbie," and she'd say, "How do you play that?" and I'd hold up her decapitated Barbie.

Which is all just to say that it was only Leala to whom our mother said, when she was ten, "Why do you read books all day? Don't you have friends? Are you a loser? Why don't you get on your bike and ride it to a friend's?" although we lived on a lonely mountain road, such that any bike ride to a classmate's involved a steep, blind-curved ten-mile descent and a ride home uphill, but our mother cleverly placed the emphasis of her challenge in such a way that Leala responded with the only possible answer: "I have friends."

And our mother would say, "Then ride your bike to them."

And so Leala got on her bike and rode it to see her friends, except there were no bike paths and twice she got hit by cars and sent to the hospital.

And it was only Leala to whom our mother said, "You're gloomy, you pout, the reason that you have no friends is that you're unlikable," and, "You have bad posture," and, "Your teeth are yellow, you have yellow teeth."

And it was Leala who at ten years old cooked a thousand dinners and cleaned up afterward too, in hopes of making anyone happy, and who during each dinner was told by our father that she was not sitting correctly, *because she was hunching.* "Sit up straight," he'd say, and it was she who was told by him each night that she was "picking at her food" and told, "You're lying," when she claimed she felt sick.

She had worms, of course, from age six to fourteen, Leala, pinworms slipping through her intestines and colon all night, laying eggs and eating her blood and undigested food, and tapeworms, which was why she hunched in pain at the table, but she was too stupid to figure it out, too stupid until one day she looked back at her poop in the toilet and saw one lift its long white head and peer at her, and even then she had to go and ask our mother what it was.

Only Leala was criticized during dinner and only Leala was told she was sickly-looking, ungrateful for not finishing her meal, a loser.

I don't know what it is to be a firstborn. But I know that when my older sister fell ill, no one helped her. She had to go to five doctors to get a correct diagnosis for Lyme disease, to persuade a doctor to prescribe the one year of intravenous antibiotics she needed to recover, and she had to sue her insurance company to compel them to cover the cost of her medications. She did this while working full-time, and while very sick, by herself. After my sister recovered, she believed, for years, that other people with Lyme disease would want to use the legal documents she'd used to compel their insurance companies to cover treatment, but no one she offered the documents to ever wanted them, including me.

Oldest siblings. Stubborn, deluded, retarded in the cosmic sense.

It was 2006. At the time, I had just been hired for a prestigious full-time job teaching creative writing at the Ivy League university. I was putting the finishing touches on a story about a beautiful woman who is set up by her thoughtless older sister on a blind date, which goes badly because the date turns out to have acne. The story had been accepted for publication by a magazine, and the editor and I had decided that the bad blind date should not only have acne, he should be psychotic, and that the older sister should have chosen the psychotic date for the younger sister on purpose, because she is jealous of the younger's beauty.

"I have a question," my sister said on the phone, out of the blue.

"Yes?" I said.

"Well," my sister began, "I've been reading your stories." She meant the ones in my book, which had just come out.

"They're . . . good," my sister said, "I mean I enjoyed them, even though I don't understand literary fiction, but I noticed that a lot of the stories feature older sisters, and that the older sisters are always horrible."

"What do you mean?" I said. I paged through the galleys of the story about the bad blind date.

"Well," my sister said, "in one story, the older sister tries to murder the younger sister by feeding her to wolves. In another, she murders her by feeding her to monsters."

"Well," I said. "Monsters, that's silly. Monsters aren't real."

"In another," my sister continued, "the older sister kills some homeless men with a gun and then tries to kill her sister."

"What's your point?" I said.

"I don't mean to attack you," my sister said, "but why, in your stories, are the older sisters always horrible? Am I horrible?"

"Of course not," I said.

I immediately felt guilty. I had made the older sisters in my stories horrible. I was not sure why. To cover this, I launched into an explanation of how literary fiction works. I included a sub-lecture about the need for drama, the use of distortion, and the distinction between fiction and reality.

"Okay," my older sister said, "but in your stories, all the older sisters are evil. I could understand if it was one story, but *all* of them?"

I moved my galleys around and wondered whether the sexy bit where the psychotic blind date tries to titillate the protagonist's nipple through her sweater would be used as a pull quote.

"You don't understand," I said. "It's *fiction*. And"—I paused grandly—"some of those stories were *dreams*!"

"Okay," my sister said. "I know I don't understand fiction."

I examined my galleys, let my pen hover, and crossed out a line. The line was, "Oh please, don't. I'm not ready for that!" The protagonist says it when the psychotic date, a law student, gives her a shoulder rub while they stand in line to buy theater tickets. I looked at the line. I decided the protagonist should tease the psychotic law student. I changed it to, "Mmmm. Is it raining out? I think I'm wet!"

It was not the fault of literary authors, I said, that they wrote fiction, and fans—including relatives—should not confuse fiction and reality.

"My art is beyond my control," I said. There was a pause.

"Well, I would like it," my sister said, her voice smaller than usual, lower, "if it's not too much to ask—I mean I know you can't control inspiration—if just once, at some point, you could write a story in which an older sister is a good person."

I shifted my galley.

I added a line. "'You are incredibly beautiful,' the law student said, shifting the knife in his pocket. 'Falling asleep next to you would be a big big privilege.'"

I shrugged. "I'll try," I said.

"It's okay if it's dark," my sister said. "But not depressing, okay? I'm interested in female protagonists who overcome adversity, like in a fantasy novel, and maybe feel a little, you know, joy."

"Hmmm," I said.

That week, my sister put an ad in the Denver paper (titled LYME PATIENTS!) that offered, for a one-dollar postage cost, copies of her template legal letter to anyone with Lyme disease, so that they could use the documents to get insurance coverage for IV antibiotics.

No one responded.

So this is the dark but joyful part of the story. The time changes, and the characters do, too—that is, I'm still around, but I've disguised myself so cunningly that not even the cleverest reader will recognize me.

It was six in the evening in Park Slope, Brooklyn, a month after the stock-market crash of 2008. Creative Writing Professor X, lecturer status on the faculty of an Ivy League university, was in her room on the fourth floor of the brownstone in which she and some journalists in their twenties rented space. Professor X was seated at a messy writing table, rereading the fifth paragraph of a manuscript titled "Jenn's Day at the Mall," which she had already read three times. Professor X had Lyme disease, and although she had done two years of daily intravenous antibiotics, she was not getting better. She was wearing leggings, two pairs of sweatpants, two thermal shirts, a sweater, a sweatshirt, a wool hat, and three pairs of socks. All her clothes were dirty. The left sleeves of the sweater, thermal shirt, and sweatshirt were pulled up to her elbow so that she could reach the lock mechanism on the plastic tube attached to her PICC line, which was hooked up to an IV bag. She adjusted the lock mechanism every few minutes and the liquid in the bag hanging from the IV pole dripped faster or slower, and every time Professor X adjusted the tightness of the lock, she stared at the clock in front of her, wrote down the position of the second hand, counted the drops that fell from the IV-pole bag in one minute, wrote down the number of drops, and then wrote the time again. On the desk in front of her were several dusty, unopened parcels, two empty coffee cups, a stack of bills, a landline phone, and dozens of empty packets of nicotine gum.

Professor X reread the fifth paragraph a fourth time: "'Jenny, what a great sample sale,' Miranda said. 'All the samples are my size! I'm a two! I hope I'm not fat!'"

"Lively language here . . ." Professor X wrote in the margin. She paused, fighting back nausea. She took a sip of water, opened a bottle of prescription antifungals, and put five in her mouth.

X's cell phone rang. X looked at the phone and, feeling sly, saw that it was the man assigned to her by the collection company, and did not answer.

She peered out the window. In the yard below she could see her landlord, a short, heavyset Haitian woman pruning flowers in her garden. Above the treetops, at eye level, a flock of crows sailed into blue sky through white clouds and telephone lines.

Professor X read the manuscript for some time.

Eventually, Professor X wrote on the manuscript in front of her, "I wonder what the dresses at the sample sale look like? I wish I could see them. Except I am not a size 2, ha ha! Maybe we could see a physical description?" She made a smiley face on the manuscript. Then she realized that the smiley face was a frown face. Then she realized, with fright, that what she'd written was illegible. The liquid dripping into her PICC line had increased speed. Feeling nauseated, Professor X leaned forward and vomited. The vomit was the color of the green cucumber drink she had drunk that afternoon, according to her doctor's orders. Some vomit dripped down the desk's front onto the floor.

A knock came at the door. Professor X glanced at the tube in her left arm. "Wait," she said, but the door pushed open.

The landlord walked in.

The landlord was sixty-five years old, a single woman with two grown sons. She'd never married, worked for forty years in a factory, and saved enough money to buy a brownstone. The landlord was bipolar, sometimes bringing X fried plantains and chicken and sometimes entering her room without warning to yell at her. She reminded X of her mother.

. The landlord held up a yogurt container. "I found *this*. Look!" She stepped into the room and shook the container.

X recognized the brand of yogurt that her roommate Y, a culture journalist for the *Wall Street Journal*, ate at night while watching *Gossip Girl*.

"I happened to be looking over the trash, to make sure it was ready for the garbagemen, and sitting right on top of your trash I found a recycle, *again*, I *told* you, if they find recycles they'll fine!" She was yelling. "I don't *want* them finding recycles in the trash in front of my house once they find it in the trash in front of your house, *once* they *mark you*, I want my privacy, when your skin is like mine they already watch you, I don't want them in my—"

She looked at the girl, X. "Oh, you have your *thing* in." She stared at the IV bag. "How long are you doing that for? You've had it in a long time now, haven't you? When are you getting it out?"

"I don't know," Professor X said.

"Well, I hope you get it out soon, you—" The landlord stepped into X's room. She looked at X's unmade bed and messy desk. She saw the vomit. "What's *that*? Oh, you threw up. Are you sick? Why don't you clean it up? You need to clean it, you can't just *leave* it there. I just put on a *new* layer of varnish on those floors, *just* before you moved in—"

"I'm sorry," Professor X said. "Look, it just happened, I'll clean it, but look, I want to talk to you—"

"About *what*? Don't you get ornery with me. Are you going to be *rude* again?" The landlord stepped into the middle of X's room.

"I thought," Professor X said, looking at her PICC line and then the door, "I mean, we talked . . . This part of the house is my private space . . ."

"I knocked," the landlord said, taking five steps forward,

until she was two feet from X. "Don't you try that with me. This is *my* house, and I just happened to be going upstairs to the roof to investigate some noises I heard up there, and I knocked and you said, 'Come in.'"

X replied, as calmly as possible, that she had not said, "Come in."

The landlord lifted the yogurt container. "Don't tell me what I heard," the landlord yelled. "Are you calling me a liar? I heard you say—

"Oh my God." Her eyes shifted to the space heater on the floor. "Is that one of those *things*? You know better, it's in the lease, no space heaters! That will start a fire in my house! I know a woman who owned a house, one of her tenants used a space heater, her whole house burned down. That is what happens, I give you privacy and never go in your room and look what you do, I can't *trust* you!"

Professor X unplugged the space heater.

"I'm sorry," she said.

"What's *wrong* with you?" the landlord said. She crossed her arms over her bosoms. "Why are you dressed in so many clothes and a hat, like it's winter? Are you trying to make me feel bad about the thermostat?"

Professor X said she was not trying to make the landlord feel bad. She paused. "Do you mind . . . I'd like to talk later . . . I'm working now." She held up the student manuscript with her scrawlings on it. X realized that the paper was tinged with vomit. "I'm sorry about the recyclable," Professor X said.

The landlord stepped backward. She eyed X, the IV pole, and the vomit. She uncrossed her arms.

"I go to church every day, and the Lord keeps me well," she said softly. "My pastor says every illness is an illness of the mind. It may be physical, but it *starts*"—she tapped her head—"*here*. Cleanse the *mind* and tell your sins to *God* and he will make you *well*. You are not *ill* because you caught something, you are *ill* because you are *sick*. Any physical symptom we have is a manifestation of something we have done to make *God* displeased. When our mind is sick our body registers the problem, do you get me? Do you go to church? Do you *pray*? I will pray for you."

"Thank you," Professor X said.

"I need a rent check. Tomorrow. In the morning, before I go to the bank."

"Okay," Professor X said.

The landlord shut the door behind her with a click.

X's landline rang. X glanced at the caller ID and saw that it was Claude Valdenmorten, the man from the collection company. She did not pick up. But his voice clipped through the speaker. "This is Claude Valdenmorten. Professor X," Claude said, "I have called you eight times this week. You need to call me. This is *not* going to just go away, Professor X. You can't just pretend that it doesn't exist—"

Professor X hit "silent."

She unhooked her IV bag, walked to the bathroom down the hall, brushed her teeth, and drank tap water.

Her phone rang.

"It's Gail Jones, the nutritionist," the nutritionist said. "I got your blood work. You have aluminum poisoning." The nutritionist went on to say that X's alkaline phosphates were low and her BUN in the tanker. Didn't X feel cold? Was she having difficulty remembering words? Professor X asked the nutritionist how she could have gotten aluminum poisoning.

"Tap water."

"Tap water?"

"From the fluoride," the nutritionist said. "They put it in

tap water. It's very reactive. It combines with metals in water and carries them into your brain."

Usually, the nutritionist said, fluoride didn't give people dementia until they were seventy. But X was on IV antibiotics, so she'd gotten it faster.

"What should I do?" Professor X said. "How can I get it out?"

"You need a good water filter," the nutritionist said.

Professor X looked at the nutritionist's most recent bill, on her desk, and beneath it the letter from the collection company. She asked what kind of filter.

"I can't *recommend* any," the nutritionist said. "They're all faulty. Just don't get the activated-alumina, the coconut shell, or anything with a carbon-based medium . . . none of those work. You'll have to do your own research." The nutritionist didn't know what kind of filter, the nutritionist said, because *she* lived in Reno, one of the last cities in America that didn't fluoridate. The nutritionist spoke with a Western accent, like a cowboy. Professor X imagined her wearing chaps and a wide-brimmed hat, riding a horse into the sunset.

If the nutritionist could just tell her what kind of filter—the cheapest that would be effective—she was low on funds, she said, but she'd do what she—

"You also need to do heavy-metal chelation," the nutritionist said.

Professor X looked out the window. The sky had darkened. In the garden below, the landlord walked between her flower beds.

Ten minutes later, having used the last remaining credit on ten different credit cards to buy the best water filter she could find, Professor X began reading the sixth paragraph of

"Jenn's Day at the Mall." The words did not make sense. But the fault lay with X, not with the manuscript.

A flat blue envelope lay on the table. It was postmarked Boulder, Colorado. Professor X felt a certain trepidation. Professor X opened the envelope. Inside was a jar of Dr. Bronner's Virgin Coconut Oil. Beside the coconut oil was a box of yerba maté tea. A twenty-five-dollar Amazon gift card fell out.

Professor X put the card down. So, she thought. It's come to this. She's written me off with a twenty-five-dollar Amazon gift card. It wasn't the amount that bothered X, but the anonymity. She didn't want to take the time to choose a gift, Professor X thought. This is the gift that says, "Go eff yourself," Professor X thought.

Professor X looked at the enormous box under her desk, full of IV bags of costly Rocephin, bandages, surgical masks, medical tape, PICC line tubing, bandage-change kits, supplies for the home-care nurse to use when she came, as she had every week for the two years of X's use of intravenous antibiotics, $250,000 worth of care, paid for entirely by X's insurance company, coverage that X's sister's letter and documents, sent to the company by X's sister, had almost certainly gotten her.

X's phone rang. She saw that it was the student whose extra story she hadn't read yet. She pulled her wool hat down over her ears.

Dear Sonya,

> *Please forgive the lateness of this gift. I've been mired in hearings, and I also wasn't sure what you can and can't eat right now, or what you'd want, so I'm sending an Amazon Gift Card. I hope you like*

coconut oil. I used to put some in my bathwater, and
when I came out my skin would feel soft. Not greasy
at all! It melts in. It smells good too. It was one of
those things that helped me get through my illness.
Remember, when I was sick, I had days of immense
pain and days of less pain, and sometimes that's a
good way to think about it. You'll get better—you'll
see—I know it.

> *Love,*
> *Yo Sis*

P.S. For the rest of your present, I would like to pay
for you to come to Boulder, and for you to see Dr.
Claroux again, and get whatever supplements you
need from the visit. I know she's helped the most so
far, so maybe she'll help again. The weather here
now is perfect for hiking, and there's some gentle
trails if you're up for it. The girls would love to
see you. They have been asking when Aunt Sonya
will visit.

Professor X put down the letter. A wave of fatigue swept
over her. She lay down joyfully on her bed and went to sleep.

So you see, my future brother-in-law, when you've got a
really stubborn older sister, you've got a good chance of making it through an illness.

It was Leala to whom our mother said, when Leala was seventeen, "Leave this house, if you want; I don't care. I won't
miss you." Weeks later, after Leala's repeated demurrals ("No
no, I love you"), our mother insisted, "Leave. Get out. You are

not a daughter of mine," for I forget what offense, perhaps the
girl returned home ten minutes past curfew, contradicted our
mother, or refused to go to her room. Leala was, of course, an
A student, a student-council member, an athlete who never
smoked a cigarette, etc. etc.; the point being the precarious-
ness of it all fell on one girl, the same girl whose godmother
was a woman who would exist like magic, until one day she
appeared and disappeared back into the stratosphere, and on
that day it was Leala, aged six, who sat still to have her hair
yanked and then said, "Thank you, Haven," eyes glistening.

And it was me who on yank three said, "Stop!" and leaped
up. And ignored our mother, who said, "*You* are going to get
a punishment."

Haven said, "It's okay, it's okay."

And I said, "*Leala* can comb my hair."

The white doll with the china face sat on Leala's bed
through her teenage years, long after the tan sedan had disappeared down our driveway, long after our mother had ven-
tured to say, daring on the front step slowly to raise her head:
"Already? But you've only been here an hour. I thought you
were going to spend the day"; and Haven had sighed, finger-
ing her pearls, her eyes large, not insincere, and said, "It's been
good to see you, let's not let it be so long the next time," and
stepped in brown heels down the flagstone path to her sedan.

Our mother stared at the car as it left. My sister, who stood
in the door of our house as directed, intuited, by a shoulder
spasm, that my mother was crying and flew down the path,
and even though our mother said, "Go inside, I don't want
you"—words I heard while biting a chunk of ice cream I'd
excavated from Haven's cake with a salad fork—my sister
wrapped her arms around our mother from behind and stuck
her face in our mother's rear—a sight I glimpsed from the
doorway while chewing—and said, "I love you," and when

our mother muttered, "Go away," my sister said the finest thing she could think to say: "I love Haven."

This was decades before our mother stopped answering the phone when we called and stopped returning our messages, even if such message should say, "I totaled my car, I'm at the hospital," and started returning the packages we sent with the word REFUSED written on them, which she meant to seem an official postal negation but which was scrawled in her handwriting in blue pen; and, as you know, it was only Leala who sent those packages, birthday presents for our mother, one a keepsake box, hand-painted with roses, encrusted with white shells from Hawaii, which came back to Leala broken because someone stomped on the box; it was only Leala who made the phone calls, Leala who flipped over the guardrail on a high pass in a storm in the Front Range and almost died and called to leave a message. I'd say those precipices are unimaginable but you've seen them.

GOING FOR A BEER

Robert Coover

He finds himself sitting in the neighborhood bar drinking a
beer at about the same time that he began to think about
going there for one. In fact, he has finished it. Perhaps he'll
have a second one, he thinks, as he downs it and asks for a
third. There is a young woman sitting not far from him who
is not exactly good-looking, but good-looking enough, and
probably good in bed, as indeed she is. Did he finish his beer?
Can't remember. What really matters is: Did he enjoy his
orgasm? Or even have one? This he is wondering on his way
home through the foggy night streets from the young woman's apartment. Which was full of Kewpie dolls, the sort won
at carnivals, and they made a date, as he recalls, to go to one.
Where she wins another—she has a knack for it. Whereupon,
they're in her apartment again, taking their clothes off, she
excitedly cuddling her new doll in a bed heaped with them.
He can't remember when he last slept, and he's no longer
sure, as he staggers through the night streets, still foggy, where
his own apartment is, his orgasm, if he had one, already fading from memory. Maybe he should take her back to the carnival, he thinks, where she wins another Kewpie doll (this is
at least their second date, maybe their fourth) and this time
they go for a romantic nightcap at the bar where they first
met. Where a brawny dude starts hassling her. He intervenes
and she turns up at his hospital bed, bringing him one of

her Kewpie dolls to keep him company. Which is her way of expressing the bond between them, or so he supposes, as he leaves the hospital on crutches, uncertain what part of town he is in. Or what part of the year. He decides that it's time to call the affair off—she's driving him crazy—but then the brawny dude turns up at their wedding and apologizes for the pounding he gave him. He didn't realize, he says, how serious they were. The guy's wedding present is a gift certificate for two free drinks at the bar where they met and a pair of white satin ribbons for his crutches. During the ceremony, they both carry Kewpie dolls that probably have some barely hidden significance, and indeed do. The child she bears him, his or another's, reminds him, as if he needed reminding, that time is fast moving on. He has responsibilities now and he decides to check whether he still has the job that he had when he first met her. He does. His absence, if he has been absent, is not remarked on, but he is not congratulated on his marriage, either, no doubt because—it comes back to him now—before he met his wife he was engaged to one of his colleagues and their coworkers had already thrown them an engagement party, so they must resent the money they spent on gifts. It's embarrassing and the atmosphere is somewhat hostile, but he has a child in kindergarten and another on the way, so what can he do? Well, he still hasn't cashed in the gift certificate, so, for one thing, what the hell, he can go for a beer, two, in fact, and he can afford a third. There's a young woman sitting near him who looks like she's probably good in bed, but she's not his wife and he has no desire to commit adultery, or so he tells himself, as he sits on the edge of her bed with his pants around his ankles. Is he taking them off or putting them on? He's not sure, but now he pulls them on and limps home, having left his beribboned crutches somewhere. On arrival, he finds all the Kewpie dolls, which were put on a shelf when the babies started coming, now scattered about the apartment, beheaded and with their limbs amputated. One of the babies is crying, so, while he warms up a bottle of milk on the stove, he goes into its room to give it a pacifier and discovers a note from his wife pinned to its pajamas, which says that she has gone off to the hospital to have another baby and she'd better not find him here when she gets back, because if she does she'll kill him. He believes her, so he's soon out on the streets again, wondering if he ever gave that bottle to the baby, or if it's still boiling away on the stove. He passes the old neighborhood bar and is tempted but decides that he has had enough trouble for one lifetime and is about to walk on when he is stopped by that hulk who beat him up and who now gives him a cigar because he's just become a father and drags him into the bar for a celebratory drink, or, rather, several, he has lost count. The celebrations are already over, however, and the new father, who has married the same woman who threw him out, is crying in his beer about the miseries of married life and congratulating him on being well out of it, a lucky man. But he doesn't feel lucky, especially when he sees a young woman sitting near them who looks like she's probably good in bed and decides to suggest that they go to her place, but too late— she's already out the door with the guy who beat him up and stole his wife. So he has another beer, wondering where he's supposed to live now, and realizing—it's the bartender who so remarks while offering him another on the house—that life is short and brutal and before he knows it he'll be dead. He's right. After a few more beers and orgasms, some vaguely remembered, most not, one of his sons, now a racecar driver and the president of the company he used to work for, comes to visit him on his deathbed and, apologizing for arriving so late (I went for a beer, Dad, things happened), says he's going to miss him but it's probably for the best. For the best what? he asks, but his son is gone, if he was ever there in the first place. Well . . . you know . . . life, he says to the nurse who has come to pull the sheet over his face and wheel him away.

STANDARD LONELINESS PACKAGE

Charles Yu

Root canal is one fifty, give or take, depending on who's doing it to you. A migraine is two hundred.

Not that I get the money. The company gets it. What I get is twelve dollars an hour, plus reimbursement for painkillers. Not that they work.

I feel pain for money. Other people's pain. Physical, emotional, you name it.

Pain is an illusion, I know, and so is time, I know, I know. I know. The shift manager never stops reminding us. Doesn't help, actually. Doesn't help when you are on your third broken leg of the day.

I get to work three minutes late and already there are nine tickets in my inbox. I close my eyes, take a deep breath, open the first ticket of the morning:

I'm at a funeral.

Feeling grief.

Someone else's grief. Like wearing a stranger's coat, still warm with heat from another body.

I'm feeling a mixture of things.

Grief, mostly, but also I detect some guilt in there. There usually is.

I hear crying.

I am seeing crying faces. Pretty faces. Crying, pretty, white faces. Nice clothes.

Our services aren't cheap. As the shift manager is always reminding us. *Need I remind you?* That is his favorite phrase these days. He is always walking up and down the aisle tilting his head into our cubicles and saying it. *Need I remind you*, he says, *of where we are on the spectrum?* In terms of low-end high-end? We are solidly toward the highish end. So the faces are usually pretty, the clothes are usually nice. The people are usually nice, too. Although I imagine it's not such a big deal to be nice when you're that rich and that pretty.

There's a place in Hyderabad doing what we're doing, but a little more toward the budget end of things. Precision Living Solutions, it's called. And of course there are hundreds of emotional engineering firms here in Bangalore, springing up everywhere you look. The other day I read in the paper that a new call center opens once every three weeks. Workers follow the work, and the work is here. All of us ready to feel, to suffer. We're in a growth industry.

Okay. The body is going into the ground now. The crying is getting more serious.

Here it comes.

I am feeling that feeling. The one that these people get a lot, near the end of a funeral service. These sad and pretty people. It's a big feeling. Different operators have different ways to describe it. For me, it feels something like a huge boot. Huge, like it fills up the whole sky, the whole galaxy, all of space. Some kind of infinite foot. And it's stepping on me. The infinite foot is stepping on my chest.

The funeral ends, and the foot is still on me, and it is hard to breathe. People are getting into black town cars. I also appear to have a town car. I get in. The foot, the foot. So heavy. Here we go, yes, this is familiar, the foot, yes, the foot. It doesn't hurt, exactly. It's not what I would call comfortable, but it's not pain, either. More like pressure. Deepak, who used to be in the next cubicle, once told me that this feeling I call the infinite foot—to him it felt more like a knee—is actually the American experience of the Christian God.

"Are you sure it is the Christian God?" I asked him. "I always thought God was Jewish."

"You're an idiot," he said. "It's the same guy. Duh. The Judeo-Christian God."

"Are you sure?" I said.

He just shook his head at me. We'd had this conversation before. I figured he was probably right, but I didn't want to admit it. Deepak was the smartest guy in our cube-cluster, as he would kindly remind me several times a day.

I endure a few more minutes of the foot, and then, right before the hour is up, right when the grief and guilt are almost too much and I wonder if I am going to have to hit the safety button, there it is, it's usually there at the end of a funeral, no matter how awful, no matter how hard I am crying, no matter how much guilt my client has saved up for me to feel. You wouldn't expect it—I didn't—but anyone who has done this job for long enough knows what I'm talking about, and even though you know it's coming, even though you are, in fact, waiting for it, when it comes, it is always still a shock.

Relief.

Death of a cousin is five hundred. Death of a sibling is twelve fifty. Parents are two thousand apiece, but depending on the situation people will pay all kinds of money, for all kinds of reasons, for bad reasons, for no reason at all.

The company started off in run-of-the-mill corporate services, basic stuff: ethical qualm transference, plausible deniability. The sort of things that generated good cash flow, cash flow that was fed right back into R&D, year after year, turning the little shop into a bit player, and then a not-so-bit player, and then, eventually, into a leader in a specialized market. In those early days, this place was known as Conscience Incorporated. The company had cornered the early market in guilt.

Then the technology improved. Some genius in Delhi had figured out a transfer protocol to standardize and packetize all different kinds of experiences. Overnight, everything changed. An industry was born. The business of bad feeling. For the right price, almost any part of life could be avoided.

Across the street from work is a lunch place I go to sometimes. Not much, really, a hot and crowded little room, a bunch of stools in front of a greasy counter. I come here mostly for the small television, up on a shelf, above the cash register. They have a satellite feed.

Today they have it switched to American television, and I am watching a commercial for our company's services.

It shows a rich executive-looking type sitting and rubbing his temples, making the universal television face for I Am an Executive in a Highly Stressful Situation. There are wavy lines on either side of his temples to indicate that the Executive is really stressed! Then he places a call to his broker and in the next scene, the Executive is lying on a beach, drinking golden beer from a bottle and looking at the bluest ocean I have ever seen.

Next to me is a woman and her daughter. The girl, maybe four or five, is scooping rice and peas into her mouth a little at a time. She is watching the commercial in silence. When she sees the water, she turns to her mother and asks her, softly, what the blue liquid is. I am thinking about how sad it is that she has never seen water that color in real life until I realize that I am thirty-nine years old and hey, you know what? Neither have I.

And then the commercial ends with one of our slogans.

Don't feel like having a bad day?

Let someone else have it for you.

That someone else they are talking about in the commercial is me. And the other six hundred terminal operators in Building D, Cubicle Block 4. Don't feel like having a bad day? Let me have it for you.

It's okay for me. It's a good job. I didn't do that well in school, after all. It was tougher for Deep. He did three semesters at technical college. He was always saying he deserved better. Better than this, anyway. I would nod and agree with him, but I never told him what I wanted to tell him, which was, hey, Deepak, when you say that you deserve better, even if I agree with you, you are kind of also implying that I don't deserve better, which, maybe I don't, maybe this is about where I belong in the grand scheme of things, in terms of high-end low-end for me as a person, but I wish you wouldn't say it because whenever you do, it makes me feel a sharp bit of sadness and then, for the rest of the day, a kind of low-grade crumminess.

Whenever Deep and I used to go to lunch, he would try to explain to me how it works.

"Okay, so, the clients," he would say, "they call in to their account reps and book the time."

He liked to start sentences with okay, so. It was a habit he had picked up from the engineers. He thought it made him sound smarter, thought it made him sound like them, those code jockeys, standing by the coffee machine, talking faster than he could think, talking not so much in sentences as in data structures, dense clumps of logic with the occasional inside joke. He liked to stand near them, pretending to stir sugar into his coffee, listening in on them as if they were speaking a different language. A language of knowing something, a language of being an expert at something. A language of being something more than an hourly unit.

Okay, so, Deepak said, so this is how it works. The client, he books the time, and then at the appointed hour, a switch in the implant chip kicks on and starts transferring his consciousness over. Perceptions, sensory data, all of it. It goes first to an intermediate server where it gets bundled with other jobs, and then a huge block of the stuff gets zapped over here, downloaded onto our servers, and then dumped into our queue management system, which parcels out the individual jobs to all of us in the cubicle farm.

Okay, so, it's all based on some kind of efficiency algorithm—our historical performance, our current emotional load. Sensors in our head assembly unit measure our stress levels, sweat composition, to see what we can handle. Okay? he would say, when he was done. Like a professor. He wanted so badly to be an expert at something.

I always appreciated Deepak trying to help me understand. But it's just a job, I would say. I never really understood why Deep thought so much of those programmers, either. In the end, we're all brains for hire. Mental space for rent, moments as a commodity. They have gotten it down to a science. How much a human being can take in a given twelve-hour shift. Grief, embarrassment, humiliation, all different, of course, so they calibrate our schedules, mix it up, the timing and the order, and the end result is you leave work every day right about at your exact breaking point. I used to smoke to take the edge off, but I quit twelve years ago, so sometimes when I get home, I'm still shaking for a little bit. I sit on my couch and drink a beer and let it subside. Then I heat up some bread and lentils and read a newspaper or, if it's too hot to stay in, go down to the street and eat my dinner standing there, watching people walking down the block, wondering where they are headed, wondering if anyone is waiting for them to come home.

When I get to work the next morning, there's a woman sitting in the cubicle across from mine. She's young, at least a couple of years younger than me, looks right out of school. She has the new-employee setup kit laid out in front of her and is reading the trainee handbook. I think about saying hi but who am I kidding, I am still me, so instead I just say nothing.

My first ticket of the day is a deathbed. Deathbeds are not so common. They are hard to schedule—we require at least twenty-four hours' advance booking, and usually clients don't know far enough in advance when the ailing loved one is going to go. But this isn't regular deathbed. It's pull-the-plug.

They are pulling the plug on Grandpa this morning.

I open the ticket.

I am holding Grandpa's hand.

I cry.

He squeezes my hand, one last burst of strength. It hurts. Then his hand goes limp.

I cry, and also, I really cry. Meaning, not just as my client, but I start crying, too. Sometimes it happens. I don't know why, exactly. Maybe because he was somebody's grandpa. And he looked like a nice one, a nice man. Maybe something about the way his arm fell against the guardrail on the hospital bed, nothing dramatic or poignant. Just a part of his body going thunk against metal. Maybe because I could sort of tell, when Grandpa was looking at his grandson for the last time, looking into his eyes, looking around in there trying to find him, he didn't find him, he found me instead, and he knew what had happened, and he didn't even look mad. Just hurt.

I am at a funeral.

I am in a dentist's chair.

I am lying next to someone's husband in a motel bed, feeling guilty.

I am quitting my job. This is a popular one. Clients like to avoid the awkwardness of quitting their jobs, so they set an appointment and walk into their bosses' offices and tell them where they can stick this effing job, and right before the boss starts to reply, the switch kicks in and I get yelled at.

I am in a hospital.

My lungs burn.

My heart aches.

I'm on a bridge.

My heart aches on a bridge.

My heart aches on a cruise ship.

My heart aches on an airplane, taking off at night.

Some people think it's not so great that we can do this. Personally, I don't really see the problem. Press one to clear your conscience. Press two for fear of death. Consciousness is like anything else. I'm sure when someone figures out how to sell time itself, they'll have infomercials for that, too.

I am at a funeral.

I am losing someone to cancer.

I am coping with something vague.

I am at a funeral.

I am at a funeral.

I am at a funeral.

Seventeen tickets today in twelve hours. Ten half hours and seven full.

On my way out, I can hear someone wailing and gnashing his teeth in his cubicle. He is near the edge. Deepak was always like that, too. I always told him, hey, man, you have to let go a little. Just a little. Don't let it get to you so much.

I peek my head to see if I can steal a glance at the new woman, but she is in the middle of a ticket. She appears to be suffering. She catches me looking at her. I look at my feet and keep shuffling past.

It used to be that the job wasn't all pain. Rich American man outsources the nasty bits of his life. He's required to book by the hour or the day or some other time unit, but in almost any crappy day, there are always going to be some parts of it that are not so bad. Maybe just boring. Maybe even more okay than not. Like if a guy books his colonoscopy and he hires us for two hours, but for the first eight minutes, he's just sitting there in the waiting room, reading a magazine, enjoying the air-conditioning, admiring someone's legs. Or something. Anyway, it used to be that we would get the whole thing, so part of my job here could be boring or neutral or even sometimes kind of interesting.

But then the technology improved again and the packeting software was refined to filter out those intervals and collect them. Those bits, the extras, the leftover slices of life were lopped off by the algorithm and smushed all together into a kind of reconstituted life slab, a life-loaf. Lunch meat made out of bits of boredom. They take the slabs and process them and sell them as prepackaged lives.

I've had my eye on one for a while, at a secondhand shop that's on my way home. Not ideal, but it's something to work for.

So now, what's left over is pretty much just pure undiluted badness. The only thing left to look forward to is when, once in a while, in the middle of an awful day, there is something not-so-awful mixed in there. Like the relief in the middle of a funeral, or sometimes when you get someone who is really religious, not just religious, but a person of true faith, then mixed in with the sadness and loss you get something extra, you get to try different flavors, depending on the believer. You get the big foot on your chest, or you get the back of your head on fire, a cold fire, it tickles. You get to know what it is like to know that your dead lover, your dead mother, father, brother, sister, that they are all standing in front of you, tall as the universe, and they have huge, infinite feet, and their heads are all ablaze with this brilliant, frozen fire. You get the feeling of being inside of a room and at the same time, the room being inside of you, and the room is the world, and so are you.

The next day is more of the same. Eleven tickets. The lowlight of the day is when I get to confess to my husband that I have been sleeping with my trainer for the last year. The first year of our marriage. I get to see his face, watch him try to keep it together. Of all the types of tickets, this is the worst. Heartbreak. When I first started at this job, I thought physical pain would be hardest. But it's not. This is the hardest. To be inside here, looking at this man's face, at the lowest moment of his life, watching him try to keep it together. To be inside here, feeling what this woman is feeling, having done this to him. And then the world blinks twice and my field of vision goes blue and I'm a guy sitting in front of a computer screen and the sandwich cart is in front of my cubicle.

So I have lunch.

After lunch, I pass her in the hall. The new woman. Her name badge says Kirthi. She doesn't look at me this time.

On the way home from work, I decide to swing by the secondhand shop and check out my life.

It's not my life, technically. Not yet. It's the life I want, the life I've been saving for. Not a DreamLife®, not top of the line, but a starter model, a good one. Standard possibility. Low volatility. A kindhearted wife with nice hair, 0.35 kids, no actuals, certainties are too expensive, but some potential kids, a solid 35 percent chance of having one. Normal life expectancy, average health, median aggregate amount of happiness. I test-drove it once, and it felt good, it felt right. It fit just fine.

I don't know. I'm trying not to feel sorry for myself. I just thought there might be more to it all than this.

Still, I've got it better than some people. I mean, I'm renting my life out one day at a time, but I haven't sold it yet. And I don't plan to, either. I'm buying in, not selling out. I want to live, not exist, want to have a life, even if it is bits and pieces, even if it isn't the greatest product out there, even if it's more like a life-substitute. I'll take it.

I'm not going to be like my father, who sold his life on a cold, clear afternoon in November. He was thirty. It was the day before my fourth birthday.

We went to the brokerage. It felt like a bank, but friendlier. My father had been carrying me on his shoulders, but he put me down when we got inside. There was dark wood everywhere, and also bright flowers and classical music. We were shown to a desk, and a woman in an immaculate pantsuit asked if we would like anything to drink. My father didn't say anything, just looked off at the far wall. I remember my mother asked for a cup of tea for my father.

I don't want to sell my life. I'm not ready to do that yet. So I sell it bit by bit. Scrape by. Sell it by the hour. Pain, grief, terror, worse. Or just mild discomfort. Social anxiety. Boredom.

I ask around about Kirthi. People are talking. The guys are talking. Especially the married guys. They do the most talking.

I pass her in the hall again, and again she doesn't look at me. No surprise there. Women never look at me. I am not handsome or tall. But I am nice.

I think it is actually that which causes the not-looking at me. The niceness, I mean, not the lack of handsomeness or tallness. They can see the niceness and it is the kind of niceness that, in a man, you instinctively ignore. What is nice? What good is a nice man? No good to women. No good to other men.

She doesn't look at me, but I feel, or maybe I wish or I imagine, that something in the way she does not look at me is not quite the same. She is not-looking at me in a way that feels like she is consciously not-looking at me. And from the way she is not-looking at me, I can tell she knows I am trying to not-look at her. We are both not-looking at each other. And yet, there is something in the way she is not-looking at me. For the first time in a long while, I have hope.

I am at a funeral. Again.

I'm flipped to green.

You can be flipped to green, or flipped to red.

You can be there, or can just feel the feeling.

This is the one improvement they have made that actually benefits us workers. There's a toggle switch on the headset. Flip it to green and you get a rendering of the client's visual field. You see what he sees. Flip it to red and you still feel all of the feelings, but you see what you see.

You can do whatever you want, so long as you don't leave your cubicle. Some people just stare at the cube-divider wall. Some play computer solitaire. Some even chat with neighbors, although that is strongly discouraged.

I was hesitant at first, but more and more these days I am usually flipped to red. Except for funerals. Funerals, I like to be there, just out of some kind of respect thing.

This morning's first ticket: sixtyish rich guy, heart attack in the home office, millions in the bank, five kids from three marriages, all hate him.

Client is one of those kids, trust-fund baby, paid extra for amnesia. No feeling, no pre-feeling, no hangover, no residue, no chance of actually having any part of it, long enough to ensure that he will be halfway in the bag before any of the day's events start nibbling at the corners of his awareness.

I see the fresh, open plot. A little rain falls on the funeral procession as they get out of the cars, but there's a break in the clouds so that it's raining and the sun is shining at the same time.

As usual, everyone is well dressed. A lot of the rich look mildly betrayed in the face of death, as if they are a little bit surprised that good style and a lot of money weren't quite enough to protect them from the unpleasantness of it all. I'm standing next to what I am guessing is widow number two, late thirties, probably, with beautiful sand-colored hair. We make eye contact and she is staring at me and I am trying not to stare at her and then we both realize the same thing at the same time. Raj, I almost say, catching myself before I do, but something in my eyes must give it away anyway, because she smiles, or he smiles. I'm not quite sure which one smiles, Raj, or the person he is hiding inside of.

Rajiv usually works night shift now, so I haven't seen him in a while. He must have picked up a day shift. We used to have a beer or two after work. A friend, I would call him. I want to call him that. One of the few I've had in this line of work.

The pastor talks about a full life lived, and the limits of earthly rewards, and everyone nods affirmatively, and then there is music as the body goes into the ground, I've heard it at a lot of funerals. Mozart, I think, but I am not sure. Sometimes I think that's really what my job is. Nodding and crying and listening to Mozart. And I think, there are worse things. There are.

Death of an aunt is seven hundred. Death of an uncle is six.

Bad day in the markets is a thousand. Kid's recital is one twenty-five an hour. Church is one fifty.

The only category that we will not quote a price on is death of a child. Death of a child is separately negotiated. Hardly anyone can afford it. And not all operators can handle it. We have to be specially trained to be eligible for those tickets. People go on sick leave, disability. Most people just physically cannot do it. There hasn't been one booked the whole time I've been here, so most of us aren't even sure what is true and what isn't. The rumor is that if you do one, you are allowed to take the rest of the month off. Deep was always tempted. It's not worth it, I would tell him. Okay, so, maybe not for you, Deep said. Okay, so, mind your own business, he would say.

The first time I talk to Kirthi is by the water fountain. I tell her we are neighbors, cubicle-wise. She says she knows. I feel a bit stupid.

The second time we talk, we are also by the water fountain, and I try to say something charming, we have to stop meeting like this or something terrible like that. I probably saw it on TV and it just came out. Stupid. She doesn't laugh, but she doesn't frown, either. She just kind of looks at me, as if trying to figure out how I could have thought that was a good idea.

The third time we talk, I kiss her. By the microwave in the snack room. I don't know what got into me. I am not an aggressive person. I am not physically strong. I weigh one hundred and forty-five pounds. She doesn't laugh. She actually makes a face like disgust. But she doesn't push me away, either. Not right away. She accepts the kiss, doesn't kiss back, but after a couple of seconds, breaks it off and leans back and turns her head and says, under her breath, You shouldn't have done that.

Still, I am happy. I've got three more tickets in the bucket before lunch, and then probably eight or nine before I go home, but the whole rest of the day, I am having an out-of-my-body experience. Even when I am in someone else's body, I am still out of my body.

I weep.

I wail.

I gnash my teeth.

Underneath it all, I am smiling.

I am at a funeral. My client's heart aches, and inside of it is my heart, not aching, the opposite, doing that, whatever it is. My heart is doing the opposite of aching.

Kirthi and I start dating. That's what I call it. She calls it letting me walk her to the bus stop. She lets me buy her lunch. She tells me I should stop. She still never smiles at me.

I'm a heartbreak specialist, she says.

When I see her in the hallway, I walk up behind her and slip my arm around her waist.

She has not let me in yet. She won't let me in.

Why won't you let me in? I ask her.

You don't want in, she says. You want around. You want near. You don't want in.

There are two hundred forty-seven ways to have your heart broken, she says, and I have felt them all.

I am in a hospice.

I have been here before. A regular client.

I am holding a pen.

I have just written something on a notepad in front of me.

My husband is gone.

He died years ago.

Today is the tenth anniversary of his death.

I have Alzheimer's, I think.

A memory of my husband surfaces, like a white-hot August afternoon, resurfacing in the cool water of November.

I tear off the sheet of paper.

I read it to myself.

It is a suicide note.

I raise a glass to my mouth, swallow a pill. Catch a glance of my note to the world.

The fail-safe kicks on, the system overrides. I close the ticket. I'm out just in time, but as I leave this dying mind, I feel the consciousness losing its structure. Not closing down. Opening. As it dies, I feel it opening up, like a box whose walls fall away, or a maybe a flowering plant, turning toward the sun.

Kirthi hasn't been to work for the past two days.

It's her father.

That's what Sunil tells me, one day over a beer.

Kirthi's father is still mortgaged, Sunil explains. Locked in. Sold his life. "Just like yours," Sunil says. "Right?"

I nod.

Sunil is in tech support, so he's seen all of the glitches. He knows what can go wrong in the mechanics of feeling transfers. Sunil has seen some strange things.

"There's no upper bound on weird," he says.

"This is going to end badly, man," he says. "You have to trust me on this. Kirthi is damaged. And she knows it."

Sunil means well, but what he doesn't know is that I am fine with damaged. I want damage. I've looked down the road I'm on and I see what's coming. A lot of nothing. No great loves lost. And yet, I feel like I lost something. Better to have loved and lost than never to have loved at all? How about this: I lost without the love. I've lost things I've never even had. A whole life.

But as the weeks go on, I begin to think Sunil might be right.

"Kirthi won't let me in," I tell him. "She tells me to get away from her, to run."

"She is doing you a favor, man. Take her advice."

I ask her about her father.

She doesn't talk to me for a week.

And then, on Friday night, after we walk for an hour in silence, before going into her apartment, she turns to me. "It's awful," she says. "To see him."

"Like that," I say. She nods.

I wrap my hand around hers, but she slides away, escapes.

Why won't you just love me, I ask her.

She says it's not possible to make someone feel something.

Even yourself, she says.

Even if you want to feel it.

I tell her about the life I have my eye on.

"Show it to me," she says.

We walk down to the store where I'd seen it, but it's no longer in the window.

Inside the shop I motion to the clerk, ask about the life I'd been hoping for.

"Someone bought it," he says. "Day before yesterday."

Kirthi looks down at her shoes, feeling my disappointment for me.

I'll find another one just like it, I tell her. A standard happiness package. Decent possibility. The chance of a kid. It wouldn't be enough for us, not quite, but we could share it, take turns living the life. One works while the other one lives, maybe I work weekdays and she gives me a break on weekends.

She looks at me for a few long seconds, seems to be thinking about it, living the whole life out in her head, then without saying anything, she touches my cheek. It's a start.

When Deep was happy, before it got bad and then worse and then even worse, he was always talking about how he knew a guy who knew a guy who knew a guy. He talked like that, he really did. He loved telling stories.

About a week before he cracked up, we were in the coffee room and he told me a story about a guy at Managed Life Solutions, a mental-anguish shop across town, who made arrangements with a prominent banker who wanted to kill his wife. The banker was going to do it, he'd made up his mind, but he didn't want the guilt. Plus, he thought it might help with his alibi if he didn't have any memory.

Bullshit, I said. That would never work.

No, really, Deep says. He tells me all about it, how they arranged it all while talking in public, at work in fact, but they talked in code, etc.

Could never happen, I say. There are twenty reasons why that wouldn't work.

Why not, he said.

It's just too much, I said.

Too much what? There is no upper bound on cruelty, he said.

The next Monday, I came to work, and they were pulling Deep out the door, two paramedics, each one with an arm hooked under Deep, dragging him out, two security guards trailing behind. As they dragged him past me, I tried to make eye contact, but as he turned toward me I got a good look and I saw it: there was no one left. Deepak wasn't inside there anymore. He had gone somewhere else. He just kept saying, okay, so. Okay, so. Like a mantra. Like he was trying to convince himself. Okay. So.

And then the next day, there it was, in the newspaper. The whole story about the banker. Exactly how Deepak told it to me. There were rumors that he was the one the banker hired. He had been inside the body of a monster and the guilt had leaked through. Some things get through. People are not perfectly sealed. The technology of feeling transfer may progress, but something will always get through.

Or maybe not a monster. Maybe that's the point. Not a monster. Just an ordinary man, what a man is capable of.

Deep knew what was out there. There is no upper bound on sadness. There is no lower bound on decency. Deep saw it, he understood it, what was out there, and he let it seep in, and once it gets in, it gets all the way in, and it never comes out.

I open tickets. I do the work. I save up money.

Weeks go by. Kirthi opens up. Just a little.

She still refuses to look me in the eyes when we are kissing.

That's weird, she says. No one does that.

How am I supposed to know? I have not kissed many people. I have seen in American movies that people close their eyes, but I have also seen that sometimes one person or the other will sneak open an eye and take a peek at the other one. I think it makes sense. Otherwise, how would you know what the other person is feeling? That seems to me the only

way to be sure, the only way to understand, through the look
on her face, what she is feeling, to be able to feel what she
feels for you. So we kiss, she with her eyes closed, me looking at her, trying to imagine what she is feeling. I hope she is
feeling something.

I am at a funeral.

I am having a hernia.

I am having a hernia at a funeral.

I am in prison.

I'm at the dentist.

I'm at the prison dentist with a hernia.

I am in love.

I am in withdrawal.

I am in love with someone who doesn't love me back. I
wish I had a hernia.

She takes me to see her father.

He has the look. I remember it. My own father looked
this way.

He is living someone else's life. He's nothing more than a
projection screen, a vessel, a unit of capacity for pain, like an
external hard drive, a peripheral device for someone's convenience, a place to store frustration and guilt and unhappiness.

The thing hanging over us, the thing that's uncomfortable
to talk about is that we could do it. We could get him out.

We stand there in silence for what seems like, for what is,
way too long.

Finally, Kirthi can't take it.

He has only four years left on his mortgage, she tells me.

But, see, the way the market works, sellers like us, we never
get full value on our time. It's like a pawnshop. You hock your
pocket watch to put dinner on the table, you might get fifty

bucks. Go get it a week later and you'll have to pay four times that to get it back.

Same principle here. I love Kirthi, I do. But I don't know if I could give sixteen years of my life to get her father out. I could do it if I knew she loved me, but I don't know it yet. I want to be a better man than this, I want to be more selfless. My life isn't so great as it is, but I just don't know if I could do it.

I am in surgery. For my hernia.

I am bleeding to death.

It doesn't hurt at all.

Things progress. We move in together. We avoid planning for the future. We hint at it. We talk around it.

I am being shot at.

I am being slapped in the face.

I go home.

I rest for a few hours.

I come back and do it again.

When I turned thirteen, my mother told me the story. She sat me down in the kitchen and explained.

"The day your father decided to sell his life," she said, "I wore my best dress, and he wore a suit. He combed his hair. He looked handsome. I remember he was so calm. You wore your only pair of long pants. We walked to the bank. You rode on his back."

"I remember that," I said.

"A man with excellent hair came out from some office in the back and sat down behind the desk."

I remember that, too, I told her.

You get, we got, forty thousand a year, she said.

My dad sold his life for a fixed annuity, indexed to inflation at three percent annually, and a seventy percent pension if he made it full term: forty years, age seventy, and he could stop, he could come back to us.

There were posters everywhere, my mother said, describing that day, the reunion day. The day when you've made it, you've done it, you're done.

There was a video screen showing a short film describing the benefits of mortgage, the glorious day of reunion. We would all drink lemonade in the hot summer air.

Just forty years, it said.

In the meantime, your family will be taken care of. You will have peace of mind.

"Time is money," the video said. "And money is time. Create value out of the most valuable asset you own."

Don't miss out on a chance of a lifetime.

When we went home, I remember, my father went to lie down. He slept for twelve hours, twice as long as normal, and in the morning, while I was still asleep, he rose from bed, washed and shaved his face, combed his hair. By the time I came down the stairs, he was just finishing up his breakfast, a piece of toast and a hard-boiled egg. I walked over to him and tried to hug him back, but I didn't have the strength. My arms were limp. So I just let him hug me, and then he went out the door and that was the last time I saw my father.

Things stop progressing with Kirthi.

Things go backward.

And then, one day, whatever it is we had, it's gone. It won't come back. We both know it.

Whatever it is she let me have, she has taken it away.

Whatever it is when two people agree to briefly occupy the same space, agree to allow their lives to overlap in some small area, some temporary region of the world, a region they create through love or convenience, or for us, something even more meager, whatever that was, it has collapsed, it has closed. She has collapsed our shared space. She has closed herself to me.

A week after Kirthi moves out, her father passes away.

My shift manager will not let me off to go to the funeral. I live through funerals all day, every day. Funerals for strangers, crying for other people, that's more or less what I do for a living. And the one time I want to go to an actual funeral, the one time it would be for someone I care about, I'll be here, in this cubicle, staring at a screen.

Kirthi doesn't even ask if I would like to go anyway.

I should go.

I will be fired if I go.

But I don't have her anymore. If I leave, I won't have a job, either. I'll never get her back if I don't have a job. I'm never getting her back anyway.

I don't even know if I want her back.

But maybe this is why I don't have her, could never, would never have had her. Maybe the problem isn't that I don't have a life. Maybe the problem is that I don't want a life.

I go to work.

I open tickets.

I close tickets.

When I get home my apartment seems empty. It's always empty, but today, more empty. The emptiness is now empty.

I call her. I don't know what to say. I breathe into the phone.

I call her again. I leave a message. I know a guy in the billing department, I say. We could get some extra capacity, no one would know, find an open line. I could feel it for you. Your grief. I could bury your father for you.

Three days later, when I get to work, there is a note on my desk, giving the time of the funeral service. Just the time and, underneath it, she scrawled, okay.

Okay.

I arrange for the hour. At the time, I open the ticket.

I am expecting a funeral.

I am not at a funeral.

I can't tell exactly where I am, but I am far away. In a place I don't recognize. She has moved to a place where I will never find her. Probably where no one will ever find her. A new city. A new life.

She paid for this time herself. She wanted to let me in. For once. Just once. She must have used up everything she had saved. The money was supposed to be for her father but now, no need.

She is walking along a road. The sun devastates, the world is made of dust, but the day is alive, she feels alive, I feel alive for her.

She is looking at a picture we took, the only picture we took together, in a photo booth in the drugstore. Our faces are smashed together and in the picture she is not smiling, as usual, and I am smiling, a genuine smile, or so I have always thought about myself, but now, looking at myself through her eyes, I see that she sees my own smile starting to decompose, like when you say a word over and over again, so many times, over and over, and you begin to feel silly, but you keep saying it, and then after a short while, something happens and the word stops being a word and it resolves into its constituent sounds, and then all of a sudden what used to be a word is not a word at all, it is now the strangest thing you have ever heard.

I am inside of her head.

I am a nice person, she is thinking. I deserve more. She wants to believe it. If only she could see herself through my eyes. If only she could see herself through my eyes looking through her eyes. I deserve to be loved, she thinks. She doesn't believe it. If only I could believe it for her. I want to believe in her, believe inside of her. Believe hard enough inside of her that it somehow seeps through. She turns up the road and the hill gets steeper. The air gets hotter. I feel her weight, the gravity on her grieving body with every step, and then, right near the top of the hill, just the faintest hint of it. She is remembering us. The few happy moments we had. Okay, so. I am standing on a hill. I am looking at a color I have never seen before. Ocean. I am not at a funeral. I am thinking of someone I once loved. I don't know if I am her thinking of me, or if I am me thinking of her, her heart, my heart, aching, or its opposite, or if maybe, right at this moment, there is no difference. Okay, so. Okay, so. Okay.

WAIT TILL YOU
SEE ME DANCE

Deb Olin Unferth

I know when people will die. I meet them, I can look into their faces and see if they have long to last. It's like having a knack for math or a green thumb, both of which I also have. People wear their health on their faces.

There was a time I lived alone in the crappiest neighborhood I would ever live in and had few friends and worked at a place where the people I saw were all quietly abandoning their plans, like I was. I had the faces of dying people all around me. One day the office assistant called me over to her desk and said she was an Indian dancer and how would I like to go to an Indian dance?

This same office assistant had once said to me, "You know what I think every time I look at you? Guess. Guess what I think."

"Here comes the bride," I said.

"Wrong," she said. "I think about that movie where the angel comes to earth and shows a man the future and how bad it's going to be, and the man looks at the future and says, 'But what about Mary? What happens to her?' And the angel says, 'You're not going to like it, George.' And George says, 'Well, I have to know. Tell me, Angel.' And the angel says, 'She's an old maid! She works at the library!' And the man says, 'Nooooooo!'"

"I don't know that movie," I said.

"'She's an old maid! She works at the library!' You should put that on your voicemail."

"I don't work at the library."

"People would know they had the right number."

After that she called me Mary and soon had them all calling me Mary.

This office assistant sat at her desk and handed out notices about forms that people had forgotten to fill out. She wrote down on slips of paper chore lists, reminders, disclosures she'd received from above: Tag your food. Turn in your book orders. You have been chosen for a special assignment. I didn't like her. She was young and hard to talk to and not nice. She wasn't the only office assistant. There were two others who were locked in an eternal battle and fought every single day. A partition had been raised between them in the hope that if they didn't see each other they would each cease to believe in the other's existence. It hadn't worked. All it did was make them think they each had their own office, which they protected fiercely. The entire setup was confusing and inconvenient. If you wanted anything done, you had to depend on the first office assistant, the one who had asked me to the dance.

So this assistant was a lot of things but she certainly was not Indian, and on the day she asked me to the dance I said so. "What kind of an Indian are you supposed to be?" I said.

Then it turned out she meant Native American, or at least American Indian, not Indian. But she wasn't that either.

"You have the cheeks of a cowgirl," I said. "You have the face of a cowboy." It was true. She was both pretty and masculine.

Well, she had learned how to dance some Native American dances and her own mother had sewed her a Native American costume. It was beautiful, the costume, she said, and if you drove out of the city, you could find the land the Native Americans once lived on and still do today and where they dance still. She had a flyer about it, look.

"I never heard of this place," I said.

"Do you want to come or not?"

"I don't know how to dance any Native American dances."

"They'll teach you, everyone will. They're very nice out there."

I didn't know why she wanted me along. Maybe she wanted more friends, which might not be so bad considering the way things were going just then.

"Okay," I said. "I'll go."

"Great," she said. Her eyebrows went up. "You'll drive? I don't have a car."

At this job, four times a day, thirty people assembled before me and it was my duty to tell them some useful fact about the English language, a fact they could then take and go out into the world with and use to better their positions in society. There were no grades in the class. It was a "pass/fail" class and whether they got a "pass" or a "fail" depended on an essay they had to write on the last day, which was read and evaluated by outside sources. These outside sources were supposed to be mysterious, were maybe not even people, were maybe just God, but I happened to know were simply whichever teacher or two the office assistant lined up to do it. It was a probationary class, intended for the students so illiterate that it was almost unseemly to have them there. It was the last-chance class. It went by the number 99. Anyone who passed got to enter college for real, sign up for 101. Anyone who failed had to leave. The students from 99 were all over the hallways. They didn't care about any useful facts to take out into the world. They cared only about the essay graded by outside sources. Thirty percent failed most years and every-body knew this. The students in 99 disliked me with a vigor and a courage that was kind of amazing. I stood at the front of the room on Mondays, Wednesdays, and Fridays, and said, "The test is graded by outside sources." I used this to respond to every complaint, defense, and plea.

The test is graded by outside sources.

The test is graded by outside sources.

The test is graded by outside sources.

That day, after I agreed to bring the assistant to the dance, I went and stood in front of my third class of the day. It was nearly the end of the semester and they had that unstrung look to them—gaunt, spooked, blaming. "Let me remind you," I told them. "I don't grade the tests. And I can tell you this much. Any essay without a proper introduction will not get a 'pass' so let's turn our attention back to the board."

I was what is called an adjunct: a thing attached to another thing in a dependent or subordinate position.

......

The assistant had it a little wrong about the movie, by the way. It wasn't the future that George got to see. The angel's job is to show George what the world would be like if George had never existed. The premise of the movie—because of course I'd seen it, everyone's seen it, if you were born in America you've seen it—is that George is unhappy and has been for many years, his whole life nearly, and he is so full of regret and fear that he wants to die, or even better, to not have been born in the first place.

2.

Some months before the assistant asked me to the dance, the associate chair called me into his office. This was a man whose face held the assurance of the living: he'd hold up a good long while yet.

"Do you have room in any of your classes?" he said.

"No," I said, "I don't have any room. I certainly don't have room two weeks into the semester."

"I'm sorry to hear that, Mary, because we've got this kid here." He pointed to a kid in the corner whom I hadn't noticed yet. A thin boy who clutched several plastic grocery bags to his chest.

"My name's not Mary," I said.

"It's not?"

"He missed two weeks," I said. "Forget it."

"He's here on a visa."

"Does he speak any English?" I said.

We looked at him. He looked back at us as if he might startle himself off his chair.

"Take the kid," the associate chair said.

......

Once a visa student in 99 wrote me a poem about how much I was helping him improve his grammar. One of the lines of the poem went:

Thou laid really strong excellent basement.

The kid was a worse-than-average 99 student. He couldn't write a sentence. He turned in his first jumbled essay and I thought: There is no way this kid is going to pass. And I thought: What a bother for him to fly all the way across the world to sit in my class and then to fly back home. And by the time I finished those two thoughts he was already shifting to the back of my mind, he was already taking a seat amid the blur of other students, whose names I would never know, whose faces I'd forget, and whose passing or failing grades were like changes in the air temperature, were nothing to do with me.

Every semester I went through this. I'd had the job two years. I had local city kids and a few foreign students, all of them ready for certain destruction. Some brought me fruit baskets. Some tried to bribe me into passing them. One threatened me, told me his "alliances" would look me up one day.

By the third week of the semester what this kid was to me was nothing to do with me.

By accident I heard him play. I was walking down the hallway toward another tedious day and a strange sound stopped me. Strands of violin and piano were coming from behind a door. I looked in.

Did I mention that this run-down school, this flat barrel-bottom place was run between the walls of a building designed by a very famous architect? Yes it was. It had been the high point of the architect's career. It was while making this building that the architect had come up with his very best ideas about designing buildings and had summed these ideas up in a short catchy sentence that he said aloud and that was later written into books that were read all over the world and was now familiar even to the layperson. After saying this catchy sentence, the architect succumbed to his drinking problem and never straightened himself out and eventually died bankrupt and alone, but this building still stood, and now somehow these people had gotten their hands on the place and were ruining it as fast as they could. Water damage, broken tiles, missing doorknobs, and worst of all, modern rehab: linoleum floors, drop ceilings, paint over wood. Catastrophe was setting in, but this one room had been preserved—perhaps because the public still encountered it on festive holiday occasions. The architect's one mistake had been to put this room on the seventh floor. The public had to be ushered in past the wreckage to reach it, up the new fake-wood-paneled elevators, over the colorless hallway carpet that had been nailed down there. But once inside, an auditorium opened up overhead and it was perfect. It marked that thin line of one artistic movement shifting into another, one great artist at his best.

On the stage the kid from my class was on the piano. Another student was playing the violin. The kid kept lifting one hand, keeping the left hand going and conducting the violin with his melody hand. Then the violin stopped and the kid continued to play and the sound I was hearing was formal and sad and peculiar. I myself had studied piano for years. I'd wanted to be a concert pianist in high school, which is its own separate bad joke now, but I knew this guy was super good. The piece had a density and a mathematical oddness, an originality. He stopped playing and looked up. I ducked out the door.

I stood in the hallway, thinking. How had such a talented kid wound up at our school? The school was no great music school. There were better music schools up the street, not to mention all over the country and the world.

I felt like I couldn't breathe for a moment, like my lungs were being pressed. I saw the emotional deadness in me and I saw it lift. It was temporarily gone.

Another paper of his landed in the pile. I couldn't understand any of it. Something about cars. The color of cars. Maybe about the color of cars. Something about the advent of America, of bank machines and microwave sandwiches. That afternoon he sat in the back of the class, wrote down whatever was going up on the board. I told him to talk to me at the end of the hour. He came and stood in front of me, his plastic bags in his hands at his sides. He was the same height as me, and he had sharp, dark good looks, though his nervousness shaded them. "Yes, miss?" he said.

"Why don't you explain to me what you're trying to say here," I said. I had his paper in my hand, and he lifted his eyebrows over it.

"Is it not right?" he said.

I dropped the paper on the desk. "This writing is horrendous," I said. "What are you doing at this school? Didn't you apply anywhere else? Proper music schools?"

He said nothing.

Suddenly I was overwhelmed. "Well?" I said. "Well?"

The room was washed out that day. Even the fluorescents were dim.

"You're never going to pass this class," I said.

He turned and walked toward the door.

"I heard you in the auditorium," I said, shaking. "I saw you."

He stopped at the door and looked back at me.

You think it's so easy doing what's right?

Once I had a student from Mexico who'd crossed the Rio Grande over and over and always been caught. At one point he'd been lost for three days and nights, alone in the Texas desert. He'd thought it was the end of him for sure. At last he found a road and thought, My God, I am saved. The first car that came down the road was border patrol. He was back in Mexico in an hour. Another time he had tried to cross and had been sent back and had been so frustrated that he decided to use all his money and fly to Canada that same day, which he did. I don't know why he didn't just stay in Canada. I never asked him that. What's so bad about Canada? But he had that American addiction, I guess. He tried to cross at Niagara Falls, had been caught again, and was sent back again—so two times from two sides of the country in thirty-nine hours. Well, he'd made it to the U.S. at last and the only reason he wanted to be here, he said, was to get an education (what, they don't have schools in Mexico? I'd said, and he'd been annoyed). Here in the U.S. he'd gotten fake papers, he told me. He'd gotten a job with those papers, was working under a fake name. The job paid for him to go to college, so he was getting a degree under a fake name and would have to give up his identity forever, but he didn't care. If he didn't pass the class, the college would make him leave and the job wouldn't pay for school anymore.

He didn't pass.

Frankly I knew it didn't matter if he passed or not, because I knew he wouldn't live for long. I had no idea how he would die but I knew.

I went into the chair's office to find this kid's file. The music kid, not the Mexican kid.

"What are you doing in there?" the office assistant called to me. "You're not supposed to be in there." She followed me in and watched me pull open a cabinet drawer.

"Those are confidential," she said. "That is strictly administrative."

"I need to see something." I took out the kid's file.

"What do you need to see?" she said, coming up behind me and leaning over my shoulder. "You don't get to see."

"Could you shut up for two seconds? For God's sake."

The name of his country was at the top of his file and it surprised me. It happened that his country was in a civil war that year. We'd been bombing them for reasons that had become suspect. It was all over the news. It was a mess.

The file had several notes in it. There was his acceptance date and his refusal letter. He'd received scholarships from several schools. He'd not chosen our school, the letter said. But thank you. Next there was a note from admissions, dated a year later. He wanted to come after all. He'd lost his scholarship from the school of his choice. He hadn't been able to get

out of his country. He was of drafting age. There was a freeze
on his passport. But this year, this *week*, there was a temporary reprieve. He could leave if he had sponsorship. Would
we sponsor him? The date of the note put it two weeks into
the semester, three days before he'd joined my class.

Any other school would have said, Come spring semester,
come next year. But he couldn't come next year. It was leave
then or be drafted and surely die. Probably his second choice
and third choice had refused him. Fourth choice. Who knows
how low on the list we lay. All I know is our school said they
would take him—not out of generosity, it seemed from the
paperwork, but sheer incompetence. If he failed this class,
he'd have to go back, sign up for the war like everybody else.

The odd thing was, I looked at him, and I couldn't get a read
on him. He could live another month, or he could live eighty
more years.

I went to his musical-composition teacher and asked him
what he planned to do about this kid.

"'Do'?" said the composition teacher. "Explain 'do.' Can
you guess how many students I have?" he wanted to know.
"Look, I'm not a blood donor. Do I look like a blood donor?"

"I'm an adjunct too," I said.

"Okay. You know what I'm talking about."

The adjuncts were always tired. Our classes were over-
enrolled. The school didn't give us health insurance. Every
year there was a Christmas party and the adjuncts were never
invited. All the adjuncts shared one big office in a space like

a spaceship, full of desks and boxes and books. We worked
under contract and we were paid nearly nothing. Below minimum wage. People were shocked when they found out how
much I made. I hated the other adjuncts, some younger, some
older, each with their own cowardly reason for being there.
And I hated the associate chair and the smug new-world
music he played with his suburban band on weekends, and
how he assigned me 99 semester after semester, somehow
slotted me in there without even knowing my name. And I
hated myself for hating all these perfectly reasonable citizens
who were just going about their lives.

I needed to just pass him myself. Put a big P on his paper and
move him through.

I guess I was in love with him a little. I didn't want him
to go back.

I wasn't used to being in love, not with anyone and certainly
not with a student, certainly not one eleven years younger
than I, one I barely spoke to. It was horrible. I had to wait
for our class and then hope to see him in the hallway beforehand, maybe walk in at the same moment, and I had to wonder whether he'd be going to some performance at the school
that night and therefore whether I should go too. I had to
puzzle out where he'd be rehearsing and which group he
hung around with (the other foreign musicians: the Chileans,
the Russians, the Japanese) and where they might be and
whether I could sometimes be nearby, watching. I tried to
do an especially good job in his class. I stopped reading aloud
from the textbook. I required the students to visit the writing
center. The papers came back even worse.

I was giving it up, had given it up. He wasn't even going to pass the stupid class.

"That's some lousy job you've got."

This was the office assistant talking. I was stapling sheets of paper together. I was pulling out staples from papers I had incorrectly stapled and restapling the papers to the correct ones. I looked over at her and could suddenly see that she was doomed. I could see it as clearly and abruptly as if I'd reached over and stapled right through her jugular, put six staples in her neck.

"What else do you do," she said, "walk dogs? Clean up their crap? This job's not for you. You should quit."

A staple lodged under my fingernail. "Hey," I said, "do you have anyone lined up to do the essays yet?"

"What essays?"

"99."

"Oh crap. I was going to bribe someone."

"I'll do it."

"No one wants to do it."

"Put me down."

"I can't put you down."

"Go ahead. Put me down."

"Can't do that. You're not an outside source."

She was right about that. The outside sources weren't from outside the school or the country or the planet but from outside 99. The 101 teachers read the 99s. The 205 teachers.

I said, "Who checks? Does anybody check?"

"I check. I'm supposed to check."

"Don't check."

"I'm not putting you down."

I was surprised by this. In previous semesters, I'd been on

the receiving end of mass emails begging someone to volunteer. Anyone not teaching 99 could expect to get asked to come in on the last Saturday of final-exam week. I had thought it would be easy to convince her, that she would be relieved.

I'm not saying it's proper or right to love a student, and I'm not going to pretend I never did anything about it because I did, but I can say I didn't do much.

All I did was to bring the office assistant to the dance and threaten to kill her.

In the movie about George and the angel, the angel shows George what the world would have been like if George had never existed. It turns out that without George the world would be a cold, dark place. Without George people would be poor and lonely. Some people would be dead because he hadn't been there to save them. Others would be older than they would have been if he had lived. Without George a dark force would be in control, and the population would be suppressed and subdued by it. People would walk, bundled against the fierce winds, to their coal stoves to eat their bland Christmas dinners alone.

The moral of the movie is that, well, it's too bad that George is so unhappy and that he never got to do the things he wanted to do, that he never even got to form a clear idea of what he might *want* to do, had instead carried with him in his heart all these years a vague longing, a sense that somehow this was all wrong, that there was a shimmering ship bumping around out there in the dark that he'd wanted to board, not knowing where it was headed but feeling so trapped and helpless where he was that he had to believe the ship would bring him someplace better. It's too bad that's how it was for him, that his life had been so sad, but on the upside, look how much his misery was doing for others. His daily struggles, his failures, his defeats, somehow held in place this delicate system so that while the population wasn't happy exactly, at least they weren't despondent or dead.

3.

It was toward the end of the semester. We were rushing toward winter break, zooming around the hallways. Outside, the city looked as if it had been tacked up and smudged with a thumb. It was the days of early darkness, a few sprigs of tinsel. No snow but somehow we had slush or something slushish and damp on the streets.

"How would you like to go to an Indian dance?" the office assistant said to me.

"What kind of an Indian are you supposed to be?" I said.

On Saturday morning I drove to her neighborhood. It was the first clear bright day we'd had in weeks. Her neighborhood consisted of a set of small streets squeezed between two enormous bridges. She lived at one end of a long brick street that started out luminous, with shiny storefronts and upscale groceries, and smoothed out into pretty little residential three-flats, painted matte colors or made of brown stones. As I drove down it, I could see glimpses of the river between buildings. I pulled up and waited.

......

I had known my brother would die young and he did. I had known my neighbor would die. I had known about a high school friend and about another friend who became a lover and then went back to being a friend and then was dead.

This was the kind of neighborhood where people live long lives.

The office assistant came out of the building. She was carrying a large black case, like for an awkwardly shaped instrument. "What is that?" I said.

"Our costumes," she said.

The dance turned out to be incredibly far. It took hours to get there. We drove on roads leading out of the city and into the vast land of America. It was a hell of a lot of highway out there unreeling beside the median strip, dry fields behind chain-link fences, antennae towers, toll booths, flagpoles, sky. It was the kind of drive where you pass a series of billboards and road signs that promise there will be snow cones, there will be rest in forty-eight miles, God is on the way. There was a sudden insane rainstorm, clear out of a drained day. The rain drummed down so hard on the car it drowned out our voices. All we could see were stars of water on the windshield. We were driving through outer space, through a comet.

"I'm going to pull over," I said.

"No," she said. "Go."

After a while the rain dried up, and we were once again going over the empty land, passing an occasional spray of houses, the lost communities of our citizenry. A line of fat white birds flew by overhead, making it look like real work to get where they were going.

"Is the dance on a reservation?"

No, what did I think, the assistant wondered, that the reservations were just there for anyone to go in and steal out of their wigwams?

"Where then?"

Well, I'd see, for God's sake. Now would I quit asking questions and listen to the story the assistant was trying to tell about her mother, something about the costumes, how her mother had sewed them with her own fingers based on a Native American costume description. Her mother had supported her through everything. When she drew comic books her mother had always been the first to read them. When she had love problems she could always bring them home. She'd had drug troubles, she'd suffered rejection from her father, but her mother had always been there.

I still hadn't told her that no matter how great her mother was I wasn't wearing any fucking Indian costume.

Another note about the movie. The office assistant had not been comparing me to George, the lead, who at the end of the movie cries out that he is grateful for his bad life and enjoins his daughter to get over to that piano and play them all a song. I was being compared to Mary, his wife, who if *she* were not around, nothing would be much different—George would have married a different lady, that's all—and I have to say I do see the connection. Nothing would be different if I weren't around. I haven't caused anything, good or bad. Even if I have done something inadvertently, as, say, in the movies where a man moves a cup and a thousand years later all of humanity explodes, it's likely that if I hadn't been born, my mother would have had a different baby around the same time and that baby would have been somewhat like me or mostly like me and would have made similar choices, probably the very same ones, and she would be here right now instead of me, feeling the things that I feel in my stead. And any ill or beneficial effects that I may have caused would be caused by her, not me. She'd take care of moving or not moving any cup that I would have or not.

"You should quit that job," said the office assistant. "You're no good at it."

"I do all right," I said. "You might let me help you out with those essays."

"What essays?"

"99."

"Not this again."

"Did we talk about this?"

"What makes you think you have any reason to ask me for a favor?"

"Not a favor. I'm doing you a turn. A friendly turn, friend to friend."

"You think we're friends? Why do you think I asked you? You have a car. I asked five other people before you."

"I'll pay you a hundred dollars," I said.

This made her laugh. "You think I'm going to risk my job for a hundred bucks?"

"A thousand."

She looked over at me then, and I could see she knew I had my secret reasons for wanting to do this, reasons that were in some way shameful. And she knew it because she had her own dark shameful secrets, all you had to do was look at her to see them, lurking behind her face, old pains, secrets having to do with the ancient beginnings of her life— with the end of it too.

"Pull over," she said.

"Fine," I said. "Let's go home."

"No way," she said. "I just have to pee."

We were on the blankest, bleakest stretch of road of the whole trip so far. I don't know why she chose that moment and not twenty minutes back at the gas station and not twenty ahead into whatever was up there waiting.

"All right, all right," I said. I eased to the side of the road. "Hurry." She got out and ran over the brown earth.

I stared out the windshield at the flat land. Bits of rain and mud were still coming down. I waited. I considered dumping the costumes on the side of the road where she wouldn't see.

The thing about the kid's music was that you didn't know what was going to happen next. You'd think you knew where it was going but you were wrong. There are very few parts of life like that.

What was she taking so long for? I stretched my neck around, saw nothing. The land around me seemed pressed into the ground, the blades of grass crushed, the few trees bent and barren. I noted the time on the dashboard. She'd been gone twenty minutes. I turned off the engine, put on the flashers. Got out. It was damn cold. Was she playing a trick on me? Had someone picked her up out there? Was I supposed to wait here for hours and then, after dark, drive back lost, run out of gas, wander around on these roads with a gas can, which I didn't even have, only to be made fun of on Monday? I knew there was a game that went something like that, but in the version I knew the person in the field was the one left behind. The one in the car was the one who laughed.

I called to her. I locked the car, took a few steps in the direction I thought she'd gone. I called to her again. It was early afternoon by this time but the sky had turned to a heavy dark gray. I stepped into the field and looked back at my car to be sure she wasn't springing out, breaking a window, hot-wiring the car, and speeding away without me. The wind swayed the antennae. I walked farther into the field. It was when I came to a little block of cement, no higher than my knee, that I finally heard her.

"Hey! Hey!"

"Where are you?" I said. On the other side of the cement was a hole. I leaned in and saw her. "What are you doing in there?" I said.

It was a well that had been partially filled in. The sides were smooth. Her face was turned up to me, and in that moment her death came at me so strongly and vividly I felt dazed. "That's the stupidest question anyone has ever asked me in my life," she said. "Didn't you hear me screaming?"

The fact is, no, I hadn't, until I was almost upon her. The wind, I guess. From the road I hadn't heard a thing. The well was far too deep to climb out of. She could have been out here for days. She could have never been found.

"Are you hurt?" I called down.

"I'm wet. There's mud."

"Did you break anything?"

"I don't think so. Get help."

I hesitated. If I left, went driving down the road, I was pretty sure I'd never find her again.

"Maybe I have something in my car," I said.

"Well, go look."

I ran back to the car, studying the angle so I'd find my way back. I had so much crap in my trunk—crates of books, laundry detergents. I had a board she might be able to grab on to. I found a piece of rope from when I'd tied my mattress to the roof and moved over two blocks. I took the rope and ran back to the well.

"I've got this rope," I said. "Might be long enough." I crouched down on the wet ground.

"Toss me an end."

I almost tossed her an end.

I didn't toss her an end.

I dangled the rope out of her reach. "You'll put me down?"

"Put you down?" She jumped for it, missed.

"99. You'll let me read?"

"For fuck's sake," she shouted.

"Will you?" I waved the rope between us.

She thought about it. "No," she said.

"Suit yourself," I said. I pulled the rope out of sight. So it turned out her death was by my own hand, or lack of, it appeared. I walked away.

I heard her call, "You don't scare me . . ." and then her voice was gone. I went back to the car.

It may seem like I was being heroic here, trying to save this kid, but the truth is I was just grateful to be feeling something.

I started the car. If she was gone, paperwork would jam

up for weeks. There'd be an administrative breakdown. Next week was finals. They'd be grateful to me for volunteering to do the essays.

"Don't worry about 99," I'd say. "I've got it covered on this end."

If, at that moment, someone had been strolling along, they would have thought I was checking my map, not leaving a life in a hole. And if someone were looking in from overhead, she, in her hole, would look completely separate from me. What was really going on was a fact she and I would share and no one else would ever know, because there was no one looking down from the clouds. Civilization settled on that a century ago. It would be her word against mine for all eternity, and who would ever believe a person would do something like that?

I shut off the car. I got out of the car and went back. "You still there?" I said.

"No, I left," she said.

I didn't ask her if she'd changed her mind, if she was ready to beg. I just lowered the rope and she grabbed it.

I had done this for a kid who'd never even looked my way. I grasped the rope with all my might and, inch by inch, I pulled her out.

Something she had on me, this assistant, which I didn't know at the time, was that I had been fired already. Or not hired back. The next semester's class assignments were sitting in our boxes. There was nothing in my box. I just hadn't realized it yet. There'd been complaints about me, poor evaluations. The students in my 99s had the lowest passing rates. For two weeks now she'd been trying to tell me and I'd ignored her. I'd thought she was just being mean.

Me? If I had been her, I would have agreed to anything. I would have let her assist in whatever she wanted if she would have assisted me just then. And assuming she did lift me out, there was no way I would have still gone to the dance with a nut like that, but she was. The fact that she was capable of that, of refusing me and now of brushing off the dirt, hopping into the car, slamming the door, and saying, "We're almost there!" made me a little afraid of her.

We arrived. It was a regular grade school and the dance was held in the gym. And, yes, she had been telling the truth. Regular Native Americans were coming in and going out. And, yes, they had on their regular traditional outfits, just like she had said they would, and some of them had on a piece of a different outfit—from when the British came galloping across the land and the Native Americans knocked them over with a spear and took their jackets and then passed them from hand to hand until today, when one showed up wearing a Benjamin Franklin jacket and another showed up in a white wig, and isn't that interesting? Yes it is.

Everyone started dancing. There were a couple of men on the side with some drums.

"Now look," I told the office assistant, "you don't have to stick to the story. Everybody here knows that we're not Native Americans and that they all are, and what do you think they're thinking about us?"

"But I have our costumes." She patted her box.

"All right, let's see them," I said. "Let's have a look, but even in traditional Native American outfits we are not going to look like Native Americans. Nobody's going to believe it."

"But wait till they see me dance," she said.

She opened the box. Inside were two giant pom-poms, that's what they looked like. Each costume was made out of bright orange yarn, long strings of it, and it covered your whole body and even had a flap for the head. She put it on me. I stood there and let her. Then she put on her own costume. The other dancers had on animal hides, beaded dresses, but no one tried to keep her from dancing. They just stopped and stared as the assistant, in her orange outfit, walked out onto the dance floor. I had never seen anything like it in my life. Of course, I did not dance. Then she came back and got me.

They'd had meetings about me, my name was on the table. There was no way she could have assigned me to do it. So that part I understand. But this is what I wonder: Why had she asked me to drive her to the dance? Was she that nervy? Or was it possible that she meant to warn me, give me advice?

So she got me into the costume, she had me beat on that, but the fact was: she was still going to die. Pulling her out had done nothing. I'd win in the end—not a race I was particularly excited about, a pain-in-the-ass race, one I hadn't asked to be in, one that was far lonelier than I'd expected. But she would be gone and I'd be going on. So we each had something on the other, the office assistant and I, when we went out onto that dance floor.

The kid would not die young. He would live on and on, much longer than the office assistant, much longer than I. He'd live almost forever. I know that because the next semester I had to find out if he'd passed the class and made a life in these United States, or if he'd failed, returned to his war-torn land, fought, and died. I snuck into the school several times after I'd been let go, skulked around the cafeteria looking for him. Finally one day I saw him coming out of the elevator, saw his face, and I hurried back outside.

The office assistant must have slid his paper into the pass pile a week before she died. She'd seen me with his file. It wouldn't have taken a genius to put it together.

Two weeks after the dance she leapt off the building, made the papers.

Okay, so what, so we look crazy in these pom-poms. Leave the poor assistant alone. Imagine what she must have been through to wind up looking like that. Imagine what her life must have been like, having a mother who would make something like these. Imagine what suffering she has had that I will never know. Just clear the floor for her. Everybody get out of the way—can't you see the office assistant wants to dance? Would you give her a little space? Give her a little music too? A little bang on the drum for her to stomp a foot to? Well, the Native Americans were ready to see something like that, so they took seats in the bleachers to watch. And as for me, I may be an old maid, and I may spend my life loving people who never loved me, and loving them in ways that aren't good for me, but I stepped around with her. I danced.

THE LUCKY BODY

Kyle Coma-Thompson

After they shot the body several times, they cut its throat with a scaling knife; after that, they pinched its nostrils and funneled sulfuric acid into its mouth; while some set to yanking the body's toenails out with a set of pliers, others fashioned a noose from a utility cord they had found in the trunk of their car. After murdering it beyond all recognition, they hung it.

Before the bullets had their say, and the knife, the body had been a handsome brown-haired white adult male of lean build, standing at a height of 6'1". From the way it was dressed they could tell it had elegant manners. It might have attended one of the better boarding schools in the upper Northeast, but since then had gained a measure of worldliness, having sprinted through college and burst through the paper target of its diploma into the wilder terrain of the status-mongering world. A series of women had loved the body for its many perfections, but also for the gentleness with which it was inhabited: the warmth coming off its naked length, nights they lay beside it, was a true warmth. Never mind the trickle of some dislodged indiscretion or disagreement had gained in size and force as it plowed down from the heights of their romance to bury them—the avalanche was worth the trouble. The body was kind to them. It had treated them as if they were an extension of itself, and from the openness and understanding with which it explained its feelings they learned just how different men's bodies were from their own; how, though less complex in many ways, with their ridiculous genitals and frank hairiness, they were harder to grasp for the very fact of their exclusivity and foreignness.

But this body had not made them feel any lonelier for not understanding, and this made all the difference.

Now the body was bleeding. Though its heart had stopped hours ago, blood still sprang from its flesh as they hammered a nail into its cheek or drew a razor blade across its nipple. After all the abuse they had invested in it, it was still there—as intact as it was the day it had been born. One of them stood over the rest as they worked and voiced his admiration: here's someone who truly wanted to live; just look at how well he holds together.

At this rate they would have to pry him apart cell by cell with tweezers, under a microscope. It had taken thirty seconds to apply mortal damage to the body, surprising it on its way to work, catching a plastic grocery bag over its head and holding it there as the others pounded the contents with a length of pipe, a tire iron, and a crowbar. Nearly half the objects in a domestic setting could be used to achieve a fatal blow, so, as if determined to exhaust their options, they grabbed anything they could put their hands on—any belongings a lesser criminal would simply steal—and these, they threw at him. It was as if they were testing the reality of the objects by throwing them. The bruises and cuts left by their impact were evidence of the ongoing reliability of the physical world. The body lay there as a witness. As proof, it didn't move.

Soon they were exhausted from the effort involved in the task of killing and rekilling the body. Some had to take a seat while the others kept stabbing and kicking and slashing at it.

Soon they agreed to work in shifts. While some slept, others would pick up where they'd left off and continue to inflict damage. The body, being dead, didn't need to sleep or eat, and in that outstripped their stamina. It had nothing living to keep appeased or alive. Unlike them, who had to break from the act to eat a sandwich or massage the soreness in their arms and lower backs and wrists. Killing was difficult work to extend beyond the normal hours of a workday, but the body, it was still there—they had long ago resolved to remove it from the company of the living. So what could they do but keep to their task despite the irreparable wear and tear it was demanding?

Here was a body unlike the others. They had never beaten one quite like it. Its durability, its unassuming congeniality and composure . . . it lay there without any sign of struggle, more forgiving of its fate and worsening condition than any of them would have been. Surely there must have been parents somewhere far in the depths of its brain matter who had once loved it, raised it with sureness and generosity, without friction of any inner conflict; who had borne it out of their own bodies and fed and clothed it as their own; and borne it brothers and sisters for whom it felt a sense of protectiveness and responsibility; and when it came time to be a grown body, alone in meeting the steep challenges of an adult working life, they sent money when he needed it and always words of encouragement. The body had walked this earth as one of the lucky, and because of that an ineffable glow radiated from every part of it, and it was this they spotted one day and followed for three blocks and admiring it made plans to eventually snatch it off the streets and mine it for what they imagined was its hidden gold.

But opening its guts with a pair of scissors they had found only a mass of bloody brownish entrails. The same grimy mess they would find in any of them. Maybe this was a trick, they thought, maybe the gold wasn't hidden in the body's belly but through a series of internalized deflections had only appeared to glow from beneath its navel. They set about smashing the body's skull open with a hammer. Brains spilled open between their knees like coagulated oatmeal. Tearing it with their fingers they found nothing. In a rage they stamped on the body's sternum until it cracked, then, with bare hands, yanked both halves of the rib cage open. It was the same as with the head and belly, nothing. Handfuls of viscera, heart and lungs, spleen, kidneys, liver, intestines upper and lower flew over their shoulders, but after all that frantic effort they were still left with what they'd begun with—a man, maybe age thirty-five, of average weight and height in the shape of a body.

What else was left? Where else could they search? As before, the body lay at their feet. Barely recognizable, but to whom? To them? Because they could still remember how fresh and frank it was in its youth, days ago, weeks ago, years ago, when they had first accosted it on the street, dragged it behind a dumpster and beaten it into a condition of meekness and carried it from the alley to their car. Was this the body they had first noticed long ago on that bright spring day when they were walking along, looking for something to destroy, and had seen him, this man, this person, this body, relaxed, calm, and boyish, stand from the bench where he'd been sitting, to wave at someone they didn't turn around to see coming? Maybe, maybe not. It seemed so long ago now, they could hardly be held accountable if they couldn't remember.

THE LOST ORDER

Rivka Galchen

I was at home, not making spaghetti. I was trying to eat a little less often, it's true. A yogurt in the morning, a yogurt at lunchtime, ginger candies in between, and a normal dinner. I don't think of myself as someone with a "weight issue," but I had somehow put on a number of pounds just four months into my unemployment, and when I realized that this had happened—I never weigh myself; my brother just said to me, on a visit, "I don't recognize your legs"—I wasn't happy about it. Although maybe I was happy about it. Because at least I had something that I knew it wouldn't be a mistake to really dedicate myself to. I could be like those people who by trying to quit smoking or drinking manage to fit an accomplishment, or at least an attempt at an accomplishment, into every day. Just by aiming to not do something. This particular morning, there was no yogurt left for my breakfast. I could go get some? I could treat myself to maple. Although the maple yogurt was always full cream. But maybe full cream was fine, because it was just a tiny—

My phone was ringing.

The caller ID read "Unavailable."

I tend not to answer calls identified as Unavailable. But sometimes Unavailable shows up because someone is calling from, say, the hospital.

"One garlic chicken," a man's voice is saying. "One side

of salad, with the ginger-miso dressing. Also one white rice. White, not brown. This isn't for pickup," he says. "It's for delivery."

He probably has the wrong number, I figure. I mean, of course he has the wrong—

"Not the lemon chicken," he is going on. "I don't want the lemon. What I want—"

"OK. I know—"

"Last time, you delivered the wrong thing—"

"Lemon chicken—"

"Garlic chicken—"

"OK—"

"I know you," he says.

"What?"

"Don't just say 'OK' and then bring me the wrong order. OK, OK, OK. Don't just say 'OK.'" He starts dictating his address. I have no pencil in hand.

"OK," I say. "I mean: all right." I've lost track of whether it was the lemon chicken or the garlic he wanted. Wanting and not wanting. Which tap is hot and which is cold. I still have trouble with left and right.

"How long?"

"Thirty minutes?"

He hangs up.

Ack. Why couldn't I admit that I wasn't going to be bringing him any chicken at all? Now I'm wronging a hungry man. One tries not to do too many wrong things in life. But I can't call him back—he's Unavailable!

Just forget it.

Forgetting is work, though. I returned to not making spa-ghetti, a task to which I had added not setting out to buy yogurt. Then it struck me that getting dressed would be a good idea. It was 10:40 a.m. Early for chicken. Yes, I should and would get dressed. Unfortunately, on the issue of getting dressed I consistently find myself wishing that I were a man. I don't mean that in an ineluctable gender-disturbance way, it's not that; it's that I think I would have an easier time choosing an outfit. Though having a body is problematic no matter what. Even for our dog. One summer, we thought we would do her a favor by shaving her fur, but then afterward she hung her head and was inconsolable. Poor girl. The key is to not have time to think about your body, and dogs—most dogs, anyhow—have a lot of free time. So do I, I guess. Although, I don't *feel* like I have a lot of time, I feel constantly pressed for time, even though when I had a job I felt like I had plenty of time. But even then getting dressed was difficult. For a while, it was my conviction that pairing tuxedo-like pants with any of several inexpensive white T-shirts would solve the getting-dressed problem for me for at least a decade, maybe for the rest of my life. I bought the tuxedo-like pants! Two pairs. And some men's undershirts. But it turned out that I looked even more sloppy than usual. And by sloppy I mostly just mean female, which can be OK, even great, in many circumstances, sure, but a tidy look for a female body, feminine or not feminine, is elusive and unstable. Dressing as a woman is like working with color instead of with black-and-white. Or like drawing a circle freehand. They say that Giotto got his job painting St. Peter's based solely on the Pope's being shown a red circle he'd painted with a single brushstroke. That's how difficult circles are. In the seven hundred years since Giotto, probably still—

I found myself back in the kitchen, still not making spaghetti, and wearing a T-shirt. Not the one I had woken up in, but still a T-shirt that would be best described as pajamas and that I wasn't feeling too good or masculine or flat-chested in, either. Giotto? It was 11:22 a.m. Making lemon chicken for that man would have been a better way to spend my time, I thought. Or garlic chicken. Whichever. I felt as if there were some important responsibility that I was neglecting so wholly that I couldn't even admit to myself that it was there. Was I really taking that man's delivery order so seriously?

At least I wasn't eating.

I decided to not surf the Internet.

Then to not watch a television show.

Hugging my favorite throw pillow, I lay down on the sofa, and thought, Just count backward from one hundred. This is something I do that calms me down. What's weird is that I don't recall ever having made it to the number one. Sometimes I fall asleep before I reach one—that's not so mysterious—but more often I just get lost. I take some sort of turn away from counting, without realizing it, and only then, far away even from whatever the turn was, do I realize I am elsewhere.

The throw pillow has matryoshka dolls on it. I started counting down. Ninety-six, ninety-five, ninety-four . . .

The phone rings.

It's Unavailable.

I hate my phone. I hate all phones.

Why should I have to deal with this hungry man's problems, these problems that stem from a past to which I don't belong? Not my fucking jurisdiction.

Although, admittedly, the fact that our paths are now entangled—that part kind of is my fault.

"OK?" I say, into the phone.

"I think I know where it is," a familiar male voice says.

"It's not even on its way yet," I confess. "I'm sorry."

"What's not on its way? Are you asleep?"

I locate the voice more precisely. The voice belongs to my husband.

"Sorry, sorry. I'm here now."

"I'm saying I think I know where it is. I think I lost it when I was in the courtyard with Monkey, tossing tennis balls for her." Our dog's name is Monkey. One of the reasons I was lonelier than usual was that Monkey was on a kind of dog holiday in the country, with my in-laws. "My hands were really cold. I had bought an icy water bottle."

"OK," I say.

"You know how it is, when your hand gets cold; your fingers shrink. So maybe that's when the ring fell off. I'm almost sure of it. It's supposed to rain later today and I'm worried the rain will just wash the ring right into a gutter. I'm sorry to put this on you, but would you mind taking a look around for it?"

He is talking about: a couple of weeks earlier, I had very briefly gone away, to my uncle's funeral, and when I returned my husband was no longer wearing his wedding ring. It's such an unimportant thing that, to be honest, I didn't even notice he was no longer wearing it. And he hadn't noticed, either. We're not symbol people. We didn't realize that his ring was gone until we were at dinner with a friend visiting from Chicago and she asked to see both of our rings. Then my husband was a little weird about it. I guess he had simultaneously known and not known. Meaning he had known. A part of him had. And had worried enough about it to pretend that it hadn't happened. Poor guy.

"I'm not going to go look for it," I find myself saying into the phone. It's not really a decision, it's more like a discovery. I'm not going to be a woman hopelessly searching for a wedding ring in a public courtyard. Even if the situation does not in fact carry the metaphorical weight it misleadingly seems to carry. Still no. I had recently seen a photograph of

Susan Sontag wearing a bear costume but still with a serious expression on her face; you could see that she felt uneasy; even a titan is anxious about images that can mislead.

"Just go and even try *not* looking for it," my husband says. "Just give the courtyard a little visit. Please."

"There's no way it's still—"

"You really can't do this one little thing?"

"This is my fault?"

"I'm on hour twenty-nine of my shift here."

"I'm not doing nothing," I say. I find I've neither raised nor lowered my voice, though I feel like I have done both. "You think I'm not capable, but that's not right. You just don't understand my position. You see me all wrong. It's not fair, it's not right—"

"I'm so sorry, my love," he is saying. His voice has hairpin-turned to tender. Which is alarming. "I'm on your side," he says. "I really do love you so much. You know that, right? You know I love you so much."

We hadn't always conversed in a way that sounded like advanced ESL students trying to share emotions, but recently that was happening to us; I think we were just trying to keep a steady course through an inevitable and insignificant strait in our relationship.

"I'm sorry, Boo," I say. "I'm the one who should apologize." I am suddenly missing him very badly, as if I have been woken from one of those dreams where the dead are still with us. Being awake feels awful. I language along, and then at some point in my ramblings he says to me, "I have to go now," and then he is gone.

The daytime hours in this neighborhood belong almost exclusively to deliverymen and nannies. The deliverymen are all men. And the nannies are all women. And the women are all dark-skinned. I had not given much thought to my neighborhood's socioeconomic or gender clustering before I became a daylight ghost. I mean, sure, I knew about it vaguely, but there it was—under cover of day, one saw, or at least it seemed as if one saw, that decades of feminism and civil-rights advances had never happened. This was appalling. Yet there was not no comfort for me in the idea that men had strong calves, and carried things, and that it was each toddler's destiny to fall in love with another woman. Was it my fault that these feelings lived inside me? Maybe.

I had not always—had not even long—been a daylight ghost, a layabout, a *mal-pensant*, a vacancy, a housewife, a person foiled by the challenge of getting dressed and someone who considered eating less a valid primary goal. I had been a fairly busy environmental lawyer, an accidental expert of sorts in toxic-mold litigation—litigation concerning alleged damage to property and persons by reason of exposure to toxic mold. I handled the first toxic-mold case that came into the firm, so when the second case turned up, shortly thereafter, I was the go-to girl. A Texas jury had made an award of thirty-two million dollars in a case in 2001, and that had set a lot of hearts to dreaming. But the Texas case was really an insurance case, and so not a precedent for toxic-mold cases. Most people don't understand that. An insurance company had failed to pay promptly for repairs to leaking pipes in a twenty-two-room mansion that subsequently became moldy; all claims relating to personal injuries from toxic mold were dismissed, and an award was made only for property damage, punitive damages, mental anguish, and to cover plaintiff's legal fees of nearly nine million dollars. But since the case was on the evening news, it was, predictably, radically misrepresented. Hence, toxic-mold-litigation fever. It has been

established that mold, like dust, is environmentally perva-
sive; some of us are allergic to some molds, just as some of
us are allergic to dust, though whether any mold can damage
our health in a lasting or severe way is unlikely, and certainly
not scientifically proven. Also clear is that basic maintenance
is an essential duty of a property owner. But beyond that . . .
I handled quite a large number of mold cases. I filled out
the quiet fields of forms. I dispatched environmental testers.
The job was more satisfying than it sounds, I can tell you. To
have any variety of expertise, and to deploy it, can feel like
a happy dream.

But one day I woke up and heard myself saying, I am a
fork being used to eat cereal. I am not a spoon. I am a fork.
And I can't help people eat cereal any longer.

I judged my sentiment foolish, sure, but it captained me
nevertheless. I laid no plan, but that afternoon I found myself
saying to the managing partner, "I'm afraid I'll need to tender
my resignation." I used that word, "tender."

I could have rescinded all those words, of course.

But that night, after the tender word, I said to Boo, "I
think I'm leaving my job."

He set down his handheld technology.

"Don't worry," I said. "I'll find some other work."

"No, it's really OK," he said. "You don't have to work at
all. If you don't want to. Or you could work at a bakery. Why
not? You'll figure it out. Under no time pressure, OK? I like
my work. We can live from that."

My husband is a pretty understanding guy; nevertheless,
I found myself thinking of an old Japanese movie where the
father gets stomach cancer but the family keep it a secret
from him, and are all just very kind to him. "But you might
wake up one day and not like your work anymore," I said.

"That's not going to happen to me," he said. "I'm just not

like that." Then he added, "I could see you were unhappy. I could see that before you could. Honestly, I feel relieved."

When the phone rings again—Unavailable—I pick it up right away. I had been so childish about not wanting to go look for the ring; I would tell Boo that I would go look for the ring, and then I would do that, I would go and look for it.

"Fifty-five minutes," he says.

"I'm so sorry, I—"

"You said half an hour. It's about expectations and promises. You don't have to make these promises. But you do. You leave people expecting. Which is why you're not just a loser working a shit job but also a really terrible person, the very worst kind, the kind who needs everyone to think she's so nice. I never found you attractive. I never trusted you. You say, Yes, this, and I'm Sorry, that, and Oops, Really Sorry, and We Just Want to Do What Makes You Happy, but who falls for that? I don't fall for it. I'm the one who sees who you really are—"

"I think—"

"Why do you apologize and giggle all the time? To every guy the same thing. Why do you wear that silver leotard and that ridiculous eye shadow? Your breasts look uneven in that leotard. You know what you look like? You look like a whore. Not like an escort or a call girl. You look like a ten-dollar blow job. If you think you're ever going to pass in this city as anything other than just one more whore-cunt—"

I hang up the phone.

I turn off the phone.

I pour myself a glass of water, but first I spill it and then I altogether drop it, and then I clean that up poorly. I don't even own a silver leotard. Yet I had been called out by a small and omniscient god, I felt. I was going to be punished, and swiftly. I put on my husband's boots and his raincoat, unintentionally creating a rubbery analogue of the clean and flat-chested look I have been longing for for years. I left the apartment and headed out for the courtyard, a few blocks away; I wasn't going to come back without that ring.

When I get to the courtyard, I see that it is just some smooth concrete and a few picnic tables at the windy base of the tallest building in the neighborhood. Thinking of it as a courtyard—I guess that was a fantasy on which my husband and I had subconsciously colluded. I do see something glinting in the midday sun; it proves to be a silvery gum wrapper. There's not even a coin on the ground. Bear suit, I'm thinking. It starts to drizzle. And then I remember: doormen are more than just people one feels one has failed to entertain. If I were in a so-called courtyard, and found a band of gold that didn't belong to me—

Between me and the doorman, there at his desk, are two women. The women are dark-skinned; they are both wearing brown; they are wearing, I realize on delay, UPS uniforms. One of them is also wearing a fleecy brown vest. "The guy was totally whacked," the vested one is saying.

I feel somewhat bad because I find I am staring at these women's asses (I think of that word as the most gentle and affectionate of the options) and I feel somewhat good because both of the asses are so attractive, though they are quite different: one is juvenile and undemanding, and the other is unembarrassedly space-occupying and reminiscent somehow of gardening—of bending over and doing things. The pants are tight-fitting. I do know that I—and really everyone—am not supposed to think this way about women, or for that matter about men, because, I guess the argument goes, it reduces people to containers of sexual possibility. But I'm not sure that's quite what is going on. Maybe I just think these women have solved the getting-dressed problem. "I think that was his friend," one of them says, "writing down the license-plate number of the truck."

"Was someone bothering you guys?" I find myself interjecting. "This is a weirdly rough neighborhood. Even as it's kind of a nice neighborhood, it's also sort of a rough one—"

"Every neighborhood is rough today."

"It's iPhone day—"

The UPS women have turned and opened their circle to me.

"They've ordered two million iPhones—"

"Someone in my neighborhood already got stabbed over a delivery."

"I hate phones," I offer. "I really hate them."

"There's no Apple in Russia," the doorman says. "You can sell the phones to a Russian for fourteen hundred dollars. You buy them for six hundred; you sell them for fourteen hundred."

"Delivery must be terrifying," I say to the women. "You never know what's up with the person on the other side of the door. It's like you knock on your own nightmare."

"People love their iPhones," the vested deliverywoman says. "My daughter says it's like they would marry their iPhones."

I keep not asking about Boo's ring. "I've never seen a woman working UPS delivery before," I say. "And now here you are—two of you at once. I feel like I'm seeing a unicorn. Or the Loch Ness monster. Maybe both, I guess."

There's a bit of a quiet then.

"They don't normally travel in twos," the doorman says. "It's only because today is considered dangerous."

"There's at least a hundred of us," the unvested woman says, shrugging.

"Not too many, but some."

"Good luck," the doorman is saying.

The women are walking away.

Now it's just me and the doorman. I am back in the familiar world again. I feel compelled to hope that he finds me attractive, and I feel angry at him, as if he were responsible for that feeling, and I find myself unzipping my husband's raincoat and pushing back the hood, like one of those monkeys whose ovulation is not concealed. I'm looking for, I imagine myself saying to this man, a wedding ring. Oh, he says, You're all looking for rings.

There was no ring there. But you saw a unicorn today, I remind myself. That's something. It's all about keeping busy. We can just buy another ring. Why didn't we think of that earlier? His old ring cost, maybe, three hundred dollars. We could buy a new one, nothing wrong with that, no need to think it means something it doesn't, though it would mean something nice to have it again, I think, as I find an appealing empty table in the back corner of a Peruvian chicken joint, where I order French fries. Some people save their marriages—not that our marriage needs saving, not that it's in danger, one can't be seduced by the semantically empty loss of a ring, I remind myself—by having adventures together. We could pull a heist. Me and Boo. Boo and . . . well, we'd have some Bonnie-and-Clyde-type name, just between ourselves. We could heist a UPS truck full of iPhones. On a rural delivery route. The guns wouldn't need to be real, definitely not. We could then move to another country. An expensive and cold one where no one comes looking and where people leave their doors unlocked because wealth is distributed so equitably. This is not my kind of daydream, I think. This is not my sort of idyll at all. It is someone else's idyll. I may be happy with that. I was never a Walter Mitty, though I always fell in love with and envied that type. But a Walter Mitty can't be married to a Walter Mitty. There is a maximum allowance of one Walter Mitty per household, that's just how it goes.

"Why was your phone off? Where were you?"

I guess hours have passed. Boo is back home. It is dark out.

"I guess I turned off the phone because I got scared," I say. "I was getting scary phone calls. I'm sorry. I'm really sorry."

There's opened mail on the table.

Boo says, "Look, I know there's something important that you haven't told me."

My body seems to switch climates. It must be the unbreathing raincoat.

"I know you're scared," he is saying. "I know you're scared of lots of things. I don't want to catch you out. I'm tired of catching out. I don't want to be a catcher-outer. I just want to be told. Just tell me the thing that you've been hiding from me. This could be a good day for us. You could tell me, and then I will feel like I can begin to trust you more again, because I'll know you can tell me things even when it is scary and difficult to tell."

I see that, along with the mail, there is a shoebox full of my papers on the table. "I was just out," I hear myself saying. Is this something to do with the guy calling for delivery? "I was just lonely in the house, and spooked, and so I went out," I go on. "I had a salad. I guess various things happen in a day.

I guess one can always share more. But I can't think of anything I would call a secret."

There is a long pause now. As if, I'm thinking, I'd made an awkward, outsized observation, like calling *him* the Loch Ness monster, or a unicorn. He is my unicorn, though. I forgot that I used to say that; that's how I felt falling in love with him, as if I'd found a creature of myth. He was less practical then, more dreamy. He had an old belt with a little pony on it; the pony was almost always upside down.

"Please," he says. "I'm asking as nicely as I can. Don't you have something you want to say to me?"

"I went out and looked for the ring," I say. "I wanted to tell you that. I didn't find the ring. But I did look for it. We could just buy another one."

"A severance check arrived for you," he says. "Actually, I've found three of your severance checks."

"That's odd," I am saying.

"None of them are cashed, of course."

The unicorn suddenly has a lot to say. Why couldn't I just tell him that I was fired? he is saying. Or he is saying something like that. I really and truly and genuinely don't know what he is talking about. I am saying that I said I resigned because I did resign. I really do remember using that word, "tender," in offering my resignation. And there's been a lot of misdirected mail lately, I say. Even misdirected calls. I have been meaning to mention that to him.

He is saying that lots of people lie, but why do I tell lies that don't even help me? It's just fucking weird, he is saying. Also something about the rent, and about health insurance. "And I don't even really care that much about any of those things," he says. "I just care that, even when you're in this room with me, you're not here. Even when you're here, you're gone. You're just in some la-la. Go back out the door and it'll be just the same: you're somewhere else and I'm in this room alone—"

I think this goes on for quite a while. Accusations. Analyses. I feel something like a kind of happiness, shy but arrived. A faint fleeting smile, in front of the firing squad. All my vague and shifting self-loathings are streamlining into brightly delineated wrongs. This particular trial—it feels so angular and specific. So lovable. At least lovable by me. Maybe I'm the dreamer in the relationship after all. Maybe I'm the man.

FISH STICKS

Donald Ray Pollock

It was the day before his cousin's funeral and Del ended up at the Suds washing his black jeans at midnight. They were the only pants he owned that were fit for the occasion. Even Randy, the dead man who didn't give a fuck anymore, would look better than Del. The one decent shirt in his trash bag had TROY'S BAIT SHOP stenciled across the back of it.

That wasn't all. Del was with a woman he couldn't get rid of, no matter what he did or said. Every time he dumped her off at the group home, she beat him back to his room with a fresh load in her automatic pill dispenser and another wad of clean underwear. To make matters worse, she kept bugging the shit out of him with these fish sticks she reeled up from the bottomless pond of a plastic purse. They were cold and greasy, feathered with gray lint. And even though she was probably the best woman Del Murray had ever been with—gobs of bare-knuckle sex, the latest psychotropic drugs, a government check—he was still embarrassed to be seen with her in public. Anyone who's ever dated a retard will understand what he was up against.

Del bought a box of soap from a little vending machine that charged exorbitant prices and poured most of it into the washer, then walked over to the bulletin board. Every Laundromat has one, a place on the wall where people can peddle their junk or swap their kids. There was a notice for a big tent revival over on the hopeless side of town, a crudely written flyer promising a better life, something that Del had craved for a long time. In one corner a cartoon Jesus floated on a pink cloud above the earth, in the other a bloody fiend sat in a prison cell snacking on a plate of skulls labeled like home-made preserves: JUNKIE, WINO, HOMO, WHORE, ATHEIST. It was designed to scare the fuck out of the type of people who wash their clothes in a public place. But more than anything, the poster dredged up memories for Del, reminded him of the time he and Randy wasted an entire year attending the Shady Glen Church of Christ in Christian Union just to win a prize, a little red Bible that fell apart the first hot day. They were eight years old.

Several years after they dropped out of Sunday school, Randy and Del enrolled in a mail order Charles Atlas course. This was back in the days when a kid could still change the course of his life by filling out one of the order forms found in the back of a comic book, a long time ago, years before the Fish Stick Girl was even born. A new envelope filled with exer-cises arrived in the mail every week, but Del couldn't get into it, all that work just so you could tear a phone book in half. Instead, he shoplifted a paperback from Gray's Drug-store in Meade called *Reds*. Del wasn't much of a reader, but he needed something to kill time until Randy gave up on building a different body.

Del would never forget *Reds*. He probably read it a dozen times that summer. It had the same powerful effect on him as the public service announcement on the radio about the guy who ripped his arm open with a can opener so he could blow dope in the bloody hole with a plastic straw. In the book, a clean-cut hero named Cole picks up these two run-away girls who shoot sleeping pills in his dad's new Lincoln. For Del, it was like flipping on a light switch, and by the time the crazy bitches dropped acid and torched the hippie's crash pad, he knew exactly how he wanted to live his life.

"Man, you gotta read this," Del said, waving his copy of *Reds* under Randy's nose. They were listening to a Hendrix album while Randy stood in front of the open window and worked out in the nude. Charles Atlas was big on sunshine and fresh air, which probably would have been fine if you lived on the moon, but in their county, the smog from the paper mill made everything smell like rotten eggs. Randy had already scratched the shit out of "Purple Haze," and Jimi kept repeating ". . . while I kiss the sky . . . while I kiss the sky." Glancing out the window over Randy's shoulder, Del saw a dirty brown cloud drifting by, high over Knockemstiff, the holler where they lived.

Randy glanced at the cover of the book, the picture of the four-eyed boy and the two wasted chicks standing by a highway sign with their thumbs in their pockets. He snorted in disgust, then took a big gulp from the jelly glass of raw eggs he kept by the bed. He was up to a dozen a day. Sweat was dripping off the end of his dick. His stomach resembled a car grill. "I could break that sonofabitch like a pencil," he said, flexing his biceps.

"Shoot, this guy gets more pussy than you ever dreamed of," Del said. "He don't need no muscles either."

"Bullshit. Girls love muscles. What about the guy who gets sand kicked in his face down at the beach?" Randy asked.

"You don't even like to swim," Del pointed out. "Look, girls don't care how many push-ups you can do. They just want to get high and wear flowers in their hair. Maybe steal a car."

"Yeah, then we end up in jail like your brothers."

"Hey, I begged them to read this before they broke into that gas station," Del said.

"What the hell are you talking about?" Randy yelled. He'd already started another set of leg lifts. Del reached over and cranked up "I Don't Live Today" past the little piece of tape that Randy's brother, Albert, had stuck on the volume control. The speakers started making a funny noise, like someone was pounding the piss out of them with one of the dumb-bells lying on the floor.

"I say we go to Florida and find these girls," Del said, holding the cover up to Randy's red, pimply face. "It's like hippie heaven down there."

"Damn, Delbert, that little one looks like somebody's sister," Randy grunted, just before the speakers blew.

The Fish Stick Girl took off her army jacket and loosened the belt on her shiny jeans, then got down on the floor in the Laundromat amid the fuzz balls and cigarette butts and started doing stretches. Del figured that somewhere along the way, probably the night he hogged all of her Haldol, he'd confessed that he got a kick out of watching other people work out. It wasn't a kinky sex thing, but more like the pleasure a person gets out of seeing their best friend lose a job or some rich bastard go down in a plane crash. He wondered what other secrets he might have revealed. Del watched his pants slosh around in the window and tried to ignore the sexy sighs the Fish Stick Girl emitted with each slow movement. Though she'd been cursed with certain defects, she could bend into shapes that most people associate only with circus freaks and world-class contortionists. It was, he knew, just another part of her plan to make him a slave.

......

On the bus going to Florida, Del read Randy the juiciest passages in *Reds* over and over, but always avoided the ending. By the time they hit Atlanta, Randy had even memorized the entire chapter about the Spanish fly orgy in the abandoned beach house. He became convinced that the psychotic Dorcie would be waiting for him when they pulled into the station at St. Petersburg. After his cousin nodded off, Del slipped back to the restroom and tore out the last few pages of the novel. He didn't have the heart to tell Randy that Dorcie, his little needle queen, had jumped off a bridge and drowned when the cops started closing in.

"I'm hungry, man," Randy said, the morning they hit the Florida state line. There were rows of orange trees along the highway. Everything smelled like air freshener.

"Look, those oranges are big as basketballs."

"No, I mean I'm losing muscle fast," Randy said. "I got to find some eggs." It was true—Randy was starting to look like a rubber doll that had stepped on a nail. He was deflating before Del's eyes.

"We'll buy a dozen as soon as we get some money."

"How we do that?" Randy asked, his voice cracking. "Does it say in that book how we do that?"

"Don't worry," Del said. "This guy tells you everything."

Three days later in St. Petersburg, they met a hotdog vendor named Leo. He was dumping new meat into a stainless-steel steamer. The smell of snouts and eyeballs wafting from the stand had been driving Del and Randy crazy ever since they'd started sleeping under the pier. "Come by my place this evening, you," Leo said, handing the boys a couple of dogs along with an address scrawled on a matchbook. "Go ahead, eat up, you," he said, winking at Randy.

"Hey, Del," Randy said later, "you think that guy's funny?" Dried mustard was plastered on his chin.

"Who cares? I can't go home, that's all I know. My mom will kill me."

"How much you figure people will pay for something like that?" Randy said.

Leo came to the door wearing a flowered bathrobe and a pair of old tennis shoes with the toes cut out of them. His swollen feet looked like a pair of sea urchins. He lived in a sad motel room, with black tar footprints on the dirty carpet, somebody else's sand in the tub. It was the kind of place that Del would always gravitate toward later on, the kind of dump where something always happens that nobody wants to admit happened.

"He can wait outside," Leo said, nodding over at Del.

"No way," Randy said. "I ain't staying here by myself."

"What? You think I'm going to bite it off? Nibble it like a little fish stick?" Leo said, laughing. "All right. At least have him stand over in the corner so I don't have to look at him, you little fraidy cat, you." Then he handed Randy an old wrinkled *Playboy* to look at while he got ready. The magazine was evidently Leo's idea of foreplay, but some other kid had already drawn pointy beards on all the naked women.

While Leo was in the bathroom gargling mouthwash, Randy instructed Del to smack the bastard in the head if he saw any blood. "You heard what he said," Randy whispered.

"Shit, he might be a cannibal for all we know." He pointed at a lamp by the bed that had blue seagulls flying around a yellow shade. He grabbed Del by the shoulders. "Don't fuck this up," Randy said. Del walked over and pulled the lamp plug out of the wall. Then he stepped into the corner and listened to the ocean just a block away. He could hear little kids squealing in the undertow, happy vacationers laughing in the sand. The whole world seemed louder that day at the Sea Breeze Motel.

"What you thinking?" the Fish Stick Girl asked. She'd finished her workout and was washing her hair in one of the big metal tubs with the last of Del's detergent. She wore her hair parted down the middle, one side dyed jet-black and the other side platinum blond. It made her look like she had two heads.

"Nothing," Del said, staring out the window at the SUDS sign swaying gently back and forth in the wind.

"Jeez, what an answer," she said. "You always say the same thing."

"Well, don't ask then." Somebody had etched WILL WORK FOR DOPE across the grime of the window with a shaky finger. Del turned away satisfied that he would never get *that* bad.

The Fish Stick Girl turned off the spigot and began squeezing the soapy water out of her hair. "Sweetie, I'm telling you," she said, "your best bet is the Henry J. Hamilton Rehabilitation Center. It's a lot of paperwork, but I know some people."

"What makes you say shit like that?" Del asked. He lit a cigarette, ignoring the NO SMOKING signs hanging everywhere.

"Because you're the type that does well in a constructive

environment," she explained, sounding like she was reciting a poem. "I noticed that the first time I saw you. At least you should take the test."

Del decided to ignore her. "I keep thinking about the time Randy and me went to Florida. I ain't never been that hungry. You couldn't buy a job, it was so bad."

"You used to work?" she asked incredulously.

"Well, it was a different world back then."

"I got more fish sticks," she said, reaching for her big purse.

"Put those goddamn things away," Del said. "It was almost thirty years ago."

"You never go hungry at the Henry J. Hamilton Center," she said. "They have special activities. Wanda keeps track of your SSI. Shoot, they even have some old lady do your laundry. We could be snuggled up watching TV right now. I always tip her a fish stick."

"Look, I told you, I ain't moving in that place!" Del yelled.

"Suit yourself. So why did you go to Florida?"

"I don't know," Del said. "I read this book. I guess you could say we were looking for a better life."

"Did you find it?" the Fish Stick Girl asked.

"No, it was just a goddamn book. I ain't read one since."

When Leo finished with Randy, he motioned for Del to help him up. The old man was gasping for air. Del could hear his knees crackle as he stood up. They sounded like a landslide in an old cowboy movie. A white dab of Randy's jizz lay on his bottom lip like a salted slug. Leo's bathrobe came loose, revealing purple stretch marks that crisscrossed his bloated belly. Then he farted and limped over to his Listerine bottle, tipped it up like a wino with a jug. Randy just stood there like a gas station loafer, silent and dazed, waiting for another car to pull in.

Leo scooped some change out of a jar and sprinkled it in Randy's hand like he was pouring gold dust into a little bag. "That's it?" Randy finally said, staring down at the nickels, dimes, and quarters.

"There's quite a bit of money there," Leo said.

"I let you suck my dick!" Randy yelled.

"Quiet down, you," Leo ordered. "That's all I'll pay for something like that. You got a lot to learn, you. I could have had more fun with a slab of bacon." He pulled a sweet roll from the pocket of his robe and chomped the end off it. "Now," he said, "take your ugly friend and get out of here, you. Boys like you are nothing but trouble." Flaky crumbs floated through the air like tiny golden gnats.

Randy looked over at Del and nodded. "I want more," he said, and Del swung the lamp at the fat man's head.

The Fish Stick Girl grabbed hold of one of the metal poles that people hang their clothes on and started twirling like a dancer in a strip club. Del dropped his soggy jeans in the dryer and walked back over to the window. He watched her reflection spin faster and faster in the glass. Her long hair flew behind her like a cape. It seemed to Del that she would surely fly into the wall or bounce off one of the big metal machines. She began emitting a high-pitched squeal that sounded like an ambulance rushing down the highway looking for something to feed upon. Del backed away and waited for the inevitable crash. It was like being at the Atomic Speedway on family night, hoping for someone to fuck up and die so the kids would have a good time.

......

Not long after Randy won the Mr. Ohio contest, Del stopped by to ask a favor. "No way," Randy said. "You never pay back." He was leaned back in a chair behind a gray metal desk in the garage he ran with his brother, Albert. The big trophy sat behind him on a shelf.

"You're famous now," Del said, figuring he'd try a new angle. "What's that feel like?"

"Hell, I don't know," Randy said. "It don't make me no money if that's what you mean. I didn't even get the Bob Evans commercial." He kept squeezing a little rubber ball with his hand. His ears flexed every time he mashed it. Del couldn't imagine him selling sausage patties on TV.

"Look, man, I ain't never said anything about what happened in Florida, you know that."

"Ha! Delbert, that's all you ever talk about," Randy said. "Shit, you even told Sheriff Matthews."

"How about two hundred?" Del asked. "They won't let me back in my room."

"I ain't got it. You realize how much the drugs cost to win a big contest? I got more tied up in these arms than you'll steal in your lifetime," Randy said. "Look, I'm not telling you what to do, but you better get out of here before Albert comes back. He ain't liked you since you fucked up his stereo that time."

Eventually Randy's heart grew too big for his body. He was one of those pincushions who never take a break, the kind that get hooked on size regardless of the consequences. "They won't let me smoke," he wheezed when Del stopped by the rest home to see him. Del looked over at the oxygen tank standing beside the hospital bed. The nurse had told Del that Randy was strapped down because the medication made him hallucinate. He hoped maybe his cousin had some pills stashed away.

"Shit, you don't smoke," Del said. "What would Mr. Charles Atlas say about that?"

"I'm way beyond old Chuck now," Randy said. "Give me a weed."

"Maybe they just want you to get better," Del said weakly.

"Fuck that, I'm a dead man. They say my ticker's big as a football. C'mon, Delbert, gimme a fuckin' cigarette." Del loosened the top restraints, and handed Randy his pack. "Watch that door," Randy said. "That one aide is a real bitch."

Del watched Randy gag on the cigarette in between hits off the oxygen mask. "Hey," Del finally said, "remember that book I used to read all the time? Dorcie and Cole and . . . shit, I can't remember the other one."

"Holly," Randy said. "Her name was Holly. She was practically a virgin."

"Yeah, that's right. Jesus, I can't believe you remember her name."

"Now, that Dorcie was something else," Randy said. "God, I wish I'd met her when I was benching six hundred. I'd have tore that up."

"Christ, Randy, it was just a book. I mean, those people weren't real or anything."

"Oh, no, you're wrong, man," Randy said. "They was real. More real than most shit anyway. I still think about her. What's that tell you?"

"What about the old man then?" Del whispered, leaning in close to the bed. "Do you still think about him?"

"Jesus, Delbert, you act like that's the only thing in your life that ever really happened. Fuck that old bastard. He got what he deserved, the way I see it." Del stood up and began pacing around the room. "Hey, while you're up, hand me that magazine there," Randy said. Del glanced around, saw an old copy of *Ohio Bodybuilder* on the windowsill. There was a picture of Randy on the cover. Del looked at his cousin in the faded photo, the victory smile, veins popping out everywhere. He handed over the magazine just as Randy took another hit off the cigarette and started coughing. It sounded as if someone was busting his chest apart with a jackhammer. He dropped the cigarette on the bed next to the oxygen mask. A small fire erupted in the sheets. When Del grabbed the water pitcher, Randy waved him away. "Get the fuck out of here," he gasped. As Del hurried out the door, he turned back to see Randy ripping up the magazine and feeding photos of his glory days to the flames.

Del had the feeling that he'd go on forever, which is a great feeling really, especially after you've watched your cousin commit suicide with a Marlboro. When the Fish Stick Girl finished her acrobatics and slid down the pole out of breath, he pushed her down on her knees behind the restroom door. "Act like you're doing this for money," he said urgently, unzipping his pants.

"Here?"

"Why not?" Del said. "This place is dead tonight."

"How much money?" she asked, settling back on her heels.

"I don't know. Enough to buy a hot dog."

"A hot dog?"

"Not much, just some change," Del answered, placing his hands on her wet hair. He closed his eyes and began to hear the ocean off the Florida coast in the dryer's muffled rumblings. Inhaling the dank laundry smells, he thought of

Leo's mildewed carpet. He pictured the lamp in his sweaty hands, felt the weight of it, saw the seagulls make another pass around the shade. The Fish Stick Girl kept banging her face into his groin, and for a moment Del was fifteen again. He was on a Greyhound going south and reading that section in *Reds* where Dorcie fires up barbiturates for the first time. Randy was sitting beside him squeezing his pecs together and urging him to jump ahead to the chapter about the black guy named King Coon who knocked the white girls up with his thumb. Then they were laughing, pointing their own thumbs at some blond woman seated across the aisle. When Del realized it was over, he looked down and saw the Fish Stick Girl smiling up at him. He'd forgotten all about her.

After he folded his clean black jeans, Del and the Fish Stick Girl left the Suds and headed up the street. It was one o'clock in the morning and the air was cool and damp with dew. "Boy, you sure get into it," the Fish Stick Girl said. "What was so funny?"

"I think I saw my cousin."

"Nobody ever told me that before," she said. "Have you been taking my meds again?"

"Well, I appreciate it anyway," he said.

"You're welcome. Now you do something for me," she said, opening up her purse.

"What's that?"

"Here," she said, shoving a fish stick in Del's face.

Del hesitated, then grabbed the fish stick and bit a cold chunk off one end. It didn't taste like fish at all, but he imagined it was something else anyway, the way the devout do with the little wafer and the grape juice. "Okay, now close your eyes," she said. Del shut his eyes. "Don't peek," she ordered. As she pulled him down the street, he pretended not to know where they were going. She liked that. Crack-

ing his eyes open, Del saw thick black clouds move across
the sky and cover the moon like a grave blanket. He closed
his eyes again and crammed the rest of the fish stick into his
mouth. Suddenly, he was very tired. He felt like the ragged
ghoul staggering across the screen in an old movie, the peace
he sought always out of reach. They walked on, the Fish Stick
Girl leading him by the hand.

VALLEY OF THE GIRLS

Kelly Link

Once, for about a month or two, I decided I was going to be a different kind of guy. Muscley. Not always thinking so much. My body was going to be a temple, not a dive bar. The kitchen made me smoothies, raw eggs blended with kale and wheat germ and bee pollen. That sort of thing. I stopped drinking, flushed all of Darius's goodies down the toilet. I was civil to my Face. I went running. I read the books, did the homework my tutor assigned. I was a model son, a good brother. The Olds didn't know what to think.

Hero, of course, knew something was up. Hero always knew. Maybe she saw the way I watched her Face when there was an event and we all had to do the public thing.

Meanwhile I could see the way that Hero's Face looked at my Face. There was no way this was going to end well. So I gave up on raw eggs and virtue and love. Fell right back into the old life, the high life, the good, sweet, sour, rotten old life. Was it much of a life? It had its moments.

"Oh, shit," Hero says. "I think I've made a terrible mistake. Help me, ____. Help me, please?"

She drops the snake. I step hard on its head. Nobody here is having a good night.

"You have to give me the code," I say. "Give me the code and I'll go get help."

She bends over and pukes stale champagne on my shoes.

There are two drops of blood on her arm. "It hurts," she says. "It hurts really bad!"

"Give me the code, Hero ."

She cries for a while, and then she stops. She won't say anything. She just sits and rocks. I stroke her hair, and ask her for the code. When she doesn't give it to me, I go over and start trying numbers. I try her birthday, then mine. I try a lot of numbers. None of them work.

I chased the same route every day for that month. Down through the woods at the back of the main guesthouse, into the Valley of the Girls just as the sun was coming up. That's how you ought to see the pyramids, you know. With the sun coming up. I liked to take a piss at the foot of Alicia 's pyramid. Later on I told Alicia I pissed on her pyramid. "Marking your territory,   ?" she said. She ran her fingers through my hair.

I don't love Alicia . I don't hate Alicia . Her Face has this plush, red mouth. Once I put a finger up against her lips, just to see how they felt. You're not supposed to mess with people's Faces, but everybody I know does it. What's the Face going to do? Quit?

But Alicia has better legs. Longer, rounder, the kind you want to die between. I wish she were here right now. The sun is up, but it isn't going to shine on me for a long time. We're down here in the cold, and Hero isn't speaking to me.

What is it with rich girls and pyramids, anyway?

......

In hieroglyphs, you put the names of the important people, kings and queens and gods, in a cartouche. Like this.

Stevie
Preeti
Nishi
Hero
Alicia
Liberty
Vyvienne
Yumiko

"Were you really going to do it?" Hero wants to know. This is before the snake, before I know what she's up to.

"Yeah," I say.

"Why?"

"Why not?" I say. "Lots of reasons. 'Why' is kind of a dumb question, isn't it? I mean, why did God make me so pretty? Why size four jeans?"

There's a walk-in closet in the burial chamber. I went through it looking for something useful. Anything useful. Silk shawls, crushed velvet dresses, black jeans in the wrong size. A stereo system loaded with the kind of music rich goth girls listen to. Extra pillows. Sterling silver. Perfumes, makeup. A mummified cat. Noodles. I remember when Noodles died. We were eight. They were already laying the foundations of Hero's pyramid. The Olds called in the embalmers.

We helped with the natron. I had nightmares for a week.

Hero says, "They're for the afterlife, okay?"

"You're not going to be fat in the afterlife?" At this point,

I still don't know [Hero]'s plan, but I'm starting to worry. [Hero] has a taste for the epic. I suppose it runs in the family.

"My *Ba* is skinny," [Hero] says. "Unlike yours, [   ]. You may be skinny on the outside, but you have a fat-ass heart. Anubis will judge you. Ammit will devour you."

She sounds so serious. I should laugh. You try laughing when you're down in the dark, in your sister's secret burial chamber—not the decoy one where everybody hangs out and drinks, where once—oh, God, how sweet is that memory still—you and your sister's Face did it on the memorial stone—under three hundred thousand limestone blocks, down at the bottom of a shaft behind a door in an antechamber that maybe somebody, in a couple of hundred years, will stumble into.

What kind of afterlife do you get to have as a mummy? If you're [Hero], I guess you believe your *Ba* and *Ka* will reunite in the afterlife. [Hero] thinks she's going to be an *Akh*, an immortal. She and the rest of them go around stockpiling everything they think they need to have an excellent afterlife. The Olds indulge them. The girls plan for the afterlife. The boys play sports, collect race cars or twentieth-century space shuttles, scheme to get laid. I specialize in the latter.

The girls have *ushabti* made of themselves, give them to each other at the pyramid dedication ceremonies, the sweet sixteen parties. They collect *shabti* of their favorite singers, actors, whatever. They read *The Book of the Dead*. In the meantime, their pyramids are where we go to have a good time. When I commissioned the artist who makes my *ushabti*, I had her make two different kinds. One is for people I don't know well. The other *shabti* is for the girls I've slept with. I modeled for that one in the nude. If I'm going to hang out with these girls in the afterlife, I want to have all my working parts.

Me, I've done some reading, too. What happens once you're a mummy? Grave robbers dig you up. Sometimes they grind you up and sell you as medicine, fertilizer, pigment. People used to have these mummy parties. Invite their friends over. Unwrap a mummy. See what's inside.

Maybe nobody ever finds you. Maybe you end up in a display case in a museum. Maybe your curse kills lots of people. I know which one I'm hoping for.

"[   ]," [Yumiko] said, "I don't want this thing to be boring. Fireworks and Faces, celebrities promoting their new thing."

This was earlier.

Once [Yumiko] and I did it in [Angela]'s pyramid, right in front of a false door. Another time she punched me in the side of the face because she caught me and [Preeti] in bed. Gave me a cauliflower ear.

[Yumiko]'s pyramid isn't quite as big as [Stevie]'s, or even [Preeti]'s pyramid. But it's on higher ground. From up on top, you can see down to the ocean.

"So what do you want me to do?" I asked her.

"Just do something," [Yumiko] said.

I had an idea right away.

"Let me out, [Hero]."

We came down here with a bottle of champagne. [Hero] asked me to open it. By the time I had the cork out, she'd shut the door. No handle. Just a keypad.

"Eventually you're going to have to let me out, [Hero]."

"Do you remember the watermelon game?" Hero says. She's lying on a divan. We're reminiscing about the good old times. I think. We were going to have a serious talk. Only it turned out it wasn't about what I thought it was about. It wasn't about the movie I'd made. The *erotic film*. It was about the other thing.

"It's really cold down here," I say. "I'm going to catch a cold."

"Tough," Hero says.

I pace a bit. "The watermelon game. With Vyvienne's unicorn?" Vyvienne's mother is twice as rich as God. Vyvienne's pyramid is three times the size of Hero's. She kisses like a fish, fucks like a fiend, and her hobby is breeding chimeras. Most of the estates around here have a real problem with unicorns now, thanks to Vyvienne. They're territorial. You don't mess with them in mating season.

Anyway, I came up with this variation on French bull-fighting, *Taureau Piscine*, except with unicorns. You got a point every time you and the unicorn were in the swimming pool together. We did *Licorne Pasteque*, too. Brought out a side table and a couple of chairs and set them up on the lawn. Cut up the watermelon and took turns. You can eat the watermelon, but only while you're sitting at the table. Meanwhile the unicorn is getting more and more pissed off that you're in its territory.

It was insanely awesome until the stupid unicorn broke its leg going into the pool, and somebody had to come and put a bullet in its head. Plus, the Olds got mad about one of the chairs. Turned out to be an antique. Priceless. The unicorn broke the back to kindling.

"Do you remember how Vyvienne cried and cried?" Hero says. Even this is part of the happy memory for Hero. She hates Vyvienne. Why? Some boring reason. I forget the specifics. Here's the gist of it: [Hero] is fat. [Vyvienne] is a bitch.

"I felt sorrier for whoever was going to have to clean up the pool," I say.

"Liar," [Hero] says. "You've never felt sorry for anyone in your life. You're a textbook sociopath. You were going to kill all of our friends. I'm doing the world a huge favor."

"They aren't your friends," I say. "None of them even like you. I don't know why you'd want to save a single one of them."

[Hero] says nothing. Her eyes get pink.

I say, "They'll find us eventually." We've both got implants, of course. Implants to keep the girls from getting pregnant, to make us puke if we try drugs or take a drink. There are ways to get around this. Darius is always good for new solutions. The implant—the Entourage—is also a way for our parents' security teams to monitor us. In case of kidnappers. In case we go places that are off-limits, or run away. Rich people don't like to lose their stuff.

"This chamber has some pretty interesting muffling qualities," [Hero] says. "I installed the hardware myself. Top-gear spy stuff. You know, just in case."

"In case of what?" I ask.

She ignores that. "Also, I paid a guy for three hundred thousand microdot trackers. One hundred and fifty have your profile. One hundred and fifty have mine. They're programmed to go on and off-line in random clusters, at irregular intervals, for the next three months, starting about ten minutes ago. You think you're the only one in the world who suffers. Who's unhappy. You don't even see me. You've been so busy obsessing over Tara and Philip, you never notice anything else."

"Who?" I say.

"Your Face and my Face," [Hero] says. "You freak." There are tears in her eyes, but her voice stays calm. "Anyway. The trackers are being distributed to partygoers at raves worldwide tonight. They're glued onto promotional material inside a CD for one of my favorite bands. Nobody you'd know. Oh, and all the guests at [Yumiko]'s party got one, too, and I left a CD at all of the false doors at all of the pyramids, like offerings. Those are all live right now."

I've always been the good-looking one. The popular one. Sometimes I forget that [Hero] is the smart one.

"I love you, [   ]."

[Liberty] falls in love all the time. But I was curious. I said, "You love me? Why do you love me?"

She thought about it for a minute. "Because you're insane," she said. "You don't care about anything."

"That's why you love me?" I said. We were at a gala or something. We'd just come back from the men's room, where everybody was trying out Darius's new drug.

My Face was hanging out with my parents in front of all the cameras. The Olds love my Face. The son they wish they had. Somebody with a tray walked by and [Hero]'s Face took a glass of champagne. She was over by the buffet table. The other buffet table, the one for Faces and the Olds and the celebrities and the publicists and all the other tribes and hangers-on.

My darling. My working girl. My sister's Face. I tried to catch her eye, clowning in my latex leggings, but I was invisible. Every gesture, every word was for them, for him. The cameras. My Face. And me? A speck of nothing. Not even a blot. Negative space.

She'd said we couldn't see each other anymore. She said

she was afraid of getting caught breaking contract. Like that didn't happen all the time. Like with Mr. Amandit. Preeti and Nishi's father. He left his wife. It was Liberty's Face he left his wife for. The Face of his daughters' best friend. I think they're in Iceland now, Mr. Amandit and the nobody girl who used to be a Face.

Then there's Stevie. Everybody knows she's in love with her own Face. It's embarrassing to watch.

Anyway, nobody knew about us. I was always careful. Even if Hero got her nose in, what was she going to say? What was she going to do?

"I love you because you're you, ⬚," Liberty said. "You're the only person I know who's better looking than their own Face."

I was holding a skewer of chicken. I almost stabbed it into Liberty's arm before I knew what I was doing. My mouth was full of chewed chicken. I spat it out at Liberty. It landed on her cheek.

"What the fuck, ⬚!" Liberty said. The piece of chicken plopped down onto the floor. Everybody was staring. Nobody took a picture. I didn't exist. Nobody had done anything wrong.

Aside from that, we all had a good time. Even Liberty says so. That was the time all of us showed up in this gear I found online. Red rubber, plenty of pointy stuff, chains and leather, dildos and codpieces, vampire teeth and plastinated viscera. I had a really nice pair of hand-painted latex tits wobbling around like epaulets on my shoulders. I had an inadequately sedated fruit bat caged up in my pompadour. So how could she not look at me?

Kids today, the Olds say. What can you do?

......

I may be down here for some time. I'm going to try to see it the way they see it, the Olds.

You're an Old. So you think, wouldn't it be easier if your children did what they were told? Like your employees? Wouldn't it be nice, at least when you're out in public with the family? The Olds are rich. They're used to people doing what they're told to do.

When you're as rich as the Olds are, you are your own brand. That's what their people are always telling them. Your children are an extension of your brand. They can improve your Q rating or they can degrade it. Mostly they can degrade it. So there's the device they implant that makes us invisible to cameras. The Entourage.

And then there's the Face. Who is a nobody, a real person, who comes and takes your place at the table. They get an education, the best health care, a salary, all the nice clothes and all the same toys that you get. They get your parents whenever the Olds' team decides there's a need or an opportunity. If you go online, or turn on the TV, there they are, being you. Being better than you will ever be at being you. When you look at yourself in the mirror, you have to be careful, or you'll start to feel very strange. Is that really you?

Most politicians have Faces, too. For safety. Because it shouldn't matter what someone looks like, or how good they are at making a speech, but of course it does. The difference is that politicians choose to have their Faces. They choose.

The Olds like to say it's because we're children. We'll understand when we're older, when we start our adult lives without blemish, without online evidence of our mistakes, our indiscretions. No sexytime videos. No embarrassing photos of ourselves in Nazi regalia or topless in Nice. No footage before the nose job, before the boob job, before the acne clears up.

The Olds get us into good colleges, and then the world tilts just for a moment. Our Faces retire. We get a few years to make our own mistakes, out in the open, and then we settle down, and we come into our millions or billions or whatever. We inherit the earth, like that proverb says. The rich shall inherit the earth.

We get married, merge our money with other money, improve our Q ratings, become Olds, acquire kids, and you bet your ass those kids are going to have Faces, just like we did.

I never got into the Egyptian thing the way the girls did. I always liked the Norse gods better. You know. Loki. The slaying of Baldur. Ragnarök.

None of the other guys showed up for Yumiko 's party. It's just their Faces. The guys all left for the moon about a week ago. They've been partying up there all week. I've never been into the space travel thing. Plenty of ways to have fun without leaving the planet.

It wasn't hard to get hold of the thing I was looking for. Darius couldn't help me, but he knew a guy who knew a guy who knew exactly what I was talking about. We met in Las Vegas, because why not? We saw a show together, and then we went online and watched a video that had been filmed in his lab. Somewhere in Moldova, he said. He said his name was Nikolay.

I showed him my video. The one I'd made for the party for Yumiko 's pyramid dedication thingy.

We were both very drunk. I'd taken Darius's blocker, and

Nikolay was interested in that. I explained about the Entourage, how you had to work around it if you wanted to have fun. He was sympathetic.

He liked the video a lot.

"That's me," I told him. "That's ☐."

"Not you," he said. "You're making joke at me. You have Entourage device. But, girl, she's very nice. Very sexy."

"That's my sister," I said. "She's seventeen."

"Another joke," Nikolay said. "But, if my sister, I would go ahead, fuck her anyway."

"How could you do this to me?" Hero wants to know.

"It had nothing to do with you." I pat her back when she starts to cry. I don't know whether she's talking about the sexy video or the other thing.

"It was bad enough when you slept with her," she says, weeping. "That was practically incest. But I saw the video." So: the video, then. "The one you gave Yumiko. The one she's going to put online. Don't you understand? She's me. He's you. That's us, on that video, that's us having sex."

"It was good enough for the Egyptians," I say, trying to console her. "Besides, it isn't us. Remember? They aren't us."

I try to remember what it was like when it was just us. The Olds say we slept in the same crib. I was a baby, she climbed in. Hero cried when I fell down. Hero has always been the one who cries.

"How did you know what I was planning?"

"Oh, please, ☐," Hero says. "I always know when you're about to go off the deep end. You go around with this smile on your face, like the whole world is sucking you off. Besides, Darius told me you'd been asking about really bad shit. He likes me, you know. He likes me much better than you."

"He's the only one," I say.

"Fuck you," Hero says. "Anyway, it's not like you were the only one with plans for tonight. I'm sick of this place. Sick of these people."

There is a martial line of *shabti* on a stone shelf. Our friends. People who would like to be our friends. Rock stars that the Olds used to hang out with, movie stars. Saudi princes who like fat, gloomy girls with money. She picks up a prince, throws it against the wall.

"Fuck Vyvienne and all her unicorns," Hero says.

She picks up another *shabti*. "Fuck Yumiko."

I take Yumiko from her. "I did," I say. "I give her a three out of five. For enthusiasm." I drop the *shabti* on the floor.

"You are so vile, [   ]," Hero says. "Have you ever been in love? Even once?"

She's fishing. She knows. Of course she knows.

Why did you sleep with him? Are you in love with him? He's me. Why aren't I him? Fuck both of you.

"Fuck our parents," I say. I pick up an oil lamp and throw it at the *shabti* on the shelf.

The room gets brighter for a moment, then darker.

"It's funny," Hero says. "We used to do everything together. And then we didn't. And right now, it's weird. You planning on doing what you were going to do. And me, what I was planning. It's like we were in each other's brains again."

"You went out and bought a biological agent? We should have gone in on it together. Buy two, get one free."

"No," Hero says. She looks shy, like she's afraid I'll laugh at her.

I wait. Eventually she'll tell me what she needs to tell me and then I'll hand over the little metal canister that Nikolay gave me, and she'll unlock the door to the burial chamber. Then we'll go back up into the world and that video won't be the end of the world. It will just be something that people talk about. Something to make the Olds crazy.

"I was going to kill myself," Hero says. "You know, down here. I was going to come down here after the fireworks, and then I decided that I didn't want to be alone when I did it."

Which is just like Hero . Throws a pity party, then realizes she's forgotten to send out invitations.

"And then I found out what you were up to," Hero says. "I thought I ought to stop you. I wouldn't have to be alone. And I would finally live up to my name. I'd save everybody. Even if they never knew it."

"You were going to kill yourself?" I say. "For real? Like with a gun?"

"Like with this," Hero says. She reaches into the jeweled box on her belt. There's a little thing curled up in there, an enameled loop of chain, black and bronze. It uncoils in her hand, becomes a snake.

Alicia was the first one to get a Face. I got mine when I was eight. I didn't really know what was going on. I met all these boys my age, and then the Olds sat down and had a talk with me. They explained what was going on, said that I got to pick which Face I wanted. I picked the one who looked the nicest, the one who looked like he might be fun to hang out with. That's how stupid I was back then.

Hero couldn't choose, so I did it for her. Pick *her*, I said. That's how strange life is. I picked her out of all the others.

Yumiko said she'd already had the conversation with her Face. (We talk to our Faces as little as possible, although sometimes we sleep with each other's. Forbidden fruit is always freakier. Is that why I did what I did? I don't know. How am I supposed to know?) [Yumiko] said her Face agreed to sign a new contract when [Yumiko] turns eighteen. She doesn't see any reason to give up having a Face.

[Nishi] is [Preeti]'s younger sister. They only broke ground on [Nishi]'s pyramid last summer. Upper management teams from her father's company came out to lay the first course of stones. A team-building exercise. Usually it's lifers from the supermax prison out in Pelican Bay. Once they get to work, they mostly look the same, lifers and upper management. It's hard work. We like to go out and watch.

Every once in a while a consulting archaeologist or an architect will come over and try to make conversation. They think we want context.

They talk about grave goods, about how one day future archaeologists will know what life was like because some rich girls decided they wanted to build their own pyramids.

We think that's funny.

They like to complain about the climate. Apparently it isn't ideal. "Of course, they may not be standing give or take a couple of hundred years. Once you factor in geological events. Earthquakes. There's the geopolitical dimension. There's grave robbers."

They go on and on about the cunning of grave robbers.

We get them drunk. We ask them about the curse of the mummies just to see them get worked up. We ask them if they aren't worried about the Olds. We ask what used to happen to the men who built the pyramids in Egypt. Didn't they used to disappear? we ask. Just to make sure nobody knew where the good stuff was buried? We say there are

one or two members of the consulting team who worked on
[Alicia]'s pyramid that we were friendly with. We mention
we haven't been able to get hold of them in a while, not since
the pyramid was finished.

They were up on the unfinished outer wall of [Nishi]'s pyramid. I guess they'd been up there all night. Talking. Making
love. Making plans.

They didn't see me. Invisible, that's what I am. I had my
phone. I filmed them until my phone ran out of memory.
There was a unicorn down in the meadow by a pyramid.
[Alicia]'s pyramid. Two impossible things. Three things that
shouldn't exist. Four.

That was when I gave up on becoming someone new, the
running, the kale, the whole thing. That was when I gave up
on becoming the new me. Somebody already had that job.
Somebody already had the only thing I wanted.

"Give me the code." I say it over and over again. I don't know
how long it's been. [Hero]'s arm is green and black and all
blown up like a party balloon. I tried sucking out the poison.
Maybe that did some good. Maybe I didn't think of it soon
enough. My lips are a little tingly. A little numb.

"[   ]?" [Hero] says. "I don't want to die."

"You aren't going to die," I say. "Give me the code. Let me
save you."

"I don't want them to die," [Hero] says. "If I give you the
code, you'll do it. And I'll die down here by myself."

"You're not going to die," I say. I stroke her cheek. "I'm not
going to kill anyone."

After a while she says, "Okay." Then she tells me the code. Maybe it's a string of numbers that means something to her. More likely it's random. I told you she was smarter than me.

I repeat the code back to her and she nods. I've covered her up with a shawl, because she's so cold. I lay her head down on a pillow, brush her hair back.

She says, "You loved her better than you loved me. It isn't fair. Nobody ever loved me best."

"What makes you think I loved her?" I say. "You think this was all about love? Really, Hero? This was just me being dumb again. And you, saving the day."

She closes her eyes. Gives me a horrible, blind smile. I go over to the door and enter the code.

The door doesn't open. I try again and it still doesn't open. "Hero? Give me the code again?"

She doesn't say anything. I go over and shake her gently. "Tell me the code one more time. Come on. One more time."

Her eyes stay closed. Her mouth falls open. Her tongue sticks out.

"Hero." I pinch her arm. Say her name over and over again. Then I go nuts. I make kind of a mess. It's a good thing Hero isn't around to see.

And now it's a little bit later, and Hero is still dead, and I'm still trapped down here with a dead hero and a dead cat and a bunch of broken *shabti*. No food. No good music. Just a small canister of something nasty cooked up by my good friend Nikolay, and a department store's worth of size four jeans and the dregs of a bottle of very expensive champagne.

......

The Egyptians believed that every night the spirit of the person buried in a pyramid rose up through the false doors to go out into the world. The *Ba*. The *Ba* can't be imprisoned in a small dark room at the bottom of a deep shaft hidden under some pile of stones. Maybe I'll fly out some night, some part of me. The best part. The part of me that was good. I keep trying combinations, but I don't know how many numbers Hero used, what combination. It's a Sisyphean task. It's something to do. There's not much oil left to light the lamps. The lamps that are left. I broke most of them.

Some air comes in through the bottom of the door, but not much. It smells bad in here. I wrapped [Hero] up in her shawls and hid her in the closet. She's in there with [Noodles]. I put [Noodles] in her arms. Every once in a while I fall asleep and when I wake up I realize I don't know which numbers I've tried, which I haven't.

The Olds must wonder what happened. They'll think it had something to do with that video. Their people will be doing damage control. I wonder what will happen to my Face. What will happen to *her*. Maybe one night I'll fly out. My *Ba* will fly right to her, like a bird.

One day someone will open the door that I can't. I'll be alive or else I won't. I can open the canister or I can leave it closed. What would you do? I talk about it with [Hero], down here in the dark. Sometimes I decide one thing, sometimes I decide another.

Dying of thirst is a hard way to die.

I don't really want to drink my own urine.

If I open the canister, I die faster. It will be my curse on you, the one who opens the tomb. Why should you go on living when she and I are dead? When no one remembers our names?

.

Tara.

I don't want you to know my name. It was his name, really.

THE DIGGINGS

Claire Vaye Watkins

★ *for Captain John Sutter* ★

There were stories in the territory, stories that could turn a sane man sour and a sour man worse. Three Frenchmen in Coloma dug up a stump to make way for a road and panned two thousand dollars in flakes from the hole. Above the Feather River a Michigander lawyer staked his mule for the night, and when he pulled it in the morning a vein winked up at him. Down on the Tuolumne a Hoosier survived a gunfight and found his fortune in the hole the bullet drilled in the rock above his shoulder. Near Carson Creek a Massachusetts man died of Isthmus sickness, and mourners shoveled up a seven-pound nugget while digging his grave. In Rough and Ready a man called Bennager Raspberry, aiming to free a ramrod jammed in his musket, fired at random into the exposed roots of a manzanita bush. There he found five thousand dollars in gold, free and pure.

In California gold was what God was in the rest of the country: everything, everywhere. My brother Errol told of a man on a stool beside him who bought a round with a pinch of dust. A child dawdling in a gully found a queerly colored rock and took it to his mother, who, Errol said, boiled it in lye in her teakettle for a day to be sure of its composition. A drunkard Pike told Errol he'd found a lake whose shores sparkled with the stuff but he could not, once sober, retrieve the memory of where it was. There were men drowning in color, men who could not walk into the woods to empty their bladders without shouting *Eureka!*

And there were those who had nothing. There were those who worked like slaves every single day, those who had attended expensive lectures on geology and chemistry back home, those who had absorbed every metallurgy manual on the passage westward, put to memory every map of those sinister foothills, scrutinized every speck of filth the territory offered and in the end were rewarded without so much as a glinting in their pans.

And there was a third category of miner, too, more wretched and volatile than the others: the luckless believer. Here was a Forty-Niner ever-poised on the cusp of the having class, his strike a breath away in his mind. Belief was a dangerous sickness at the diggings—it made a man greedy, violent, and insane. The fever burned hotter within my brother than in any other prospector among the placers. I know, because it was I who lit him.

I. HO FOR CALIFORNIA!

My brother and I came to gold country from Ohio when Errol was twenty and I seventeen. Our father had gone to God in December of 1848, leaving us three hundred dollars each. I had not been especially interested in the activity out west—my eyes looked eastward, in fact, to Harvard Divinity. But my brother was married to the notion. He diverted the considerable energies he usually spent clouting me or bossing me around and put them toward convincing me to join him. I admit I rather enjoyed this process of conversion—it was maybe the first in all our life together that Errol had regarded me with greater interest than that due an old boot. His efforts having roused in me the spirit of adventure, I began to fancy us brother Argonauts, bold and divine.

We left our mother and sisters in Cincinnati in the early spring of 1849, and set out by way of the Ohio and Missouri rivers. In Independence we bought a small freight wagon and spent a week and what was left of our money readying it. We fit iron rims to the wheels, tightened the spokes, greased the axles, secured the bolts, and reinforced the harnesses. We purchased new canvas from an outfitter, coated it with linseed oil and beeswax, and stretched it across the new pine bows. My brother, despite his want of artistic aptitude, painted the canvas with a crude outline of Ohio and a script reading "Ho for California!"

In Independence we took up with a group of men who called themselves the Missouri Overland Mutual Protection Association for California. Errol wrote what was by then surely his hundredth letter to Marjorie Elise Salter, whose family owned and operated Salter Soap & Lye. It was Marjorie for whom Errol was getting rich. That fall and through the winter Errol had developed the habit of slinking off to see her, leaving me to do his chores. I didn't think much of Miss Salter, I'll tell you now. I thought she waltzed rather better than I would want my wife to. But the once I alerted Errol to the infrequency with which Salter girls married into farming families such as ours, he rapped my collarbone with the iron side of a trowel, putting a permanent zag in it.

The day we left Cincinnati, Errol leaned from the steamer, tossed Marjorie a gold coin that had been our father's, and shouted, "Where I am going there are plenty more!"

With the yobs and gamblers of the Missouri Company we followed the Platte then the Sweetwater to South Pass, around the Great Salt Lake then along the course of a river called the Humboldt, whose waters were putrid and whose poisonous grasses killed two of our party's oxen. At the place where that miserable river disappeared into the sand we found a boulder on which an earlier traveler had scraped some words with a nib of charcoal. It read: *Expect to find the worst desert you ever saw and then to find it worse than you expected. Take water. Take water. You cannot carry enough.*

And so we filled canteens, kegs, coffeepots, waterproof sacks and rubberized blankets. Errol removed his gumboots and filled them, then ordered me to do the same. Those we kept secret. We crossed the Hundred Mile Desert only at night, following in the moonlight a trail marked by discarded stoves and trunks and mining equipment and the stinking carcasses of mules and oxen.

II. ABANDONED AT CARSON SINK

At the westernmost edge of the Hundred Mile Desert our leaders unhitched the animals and led them ahead in search of a spring, to recuperate and reconnoiter. Errol and I were assigned, with some others, to stay behind and guard the wagons. The gold fields were close, we knew, and as one day passed and another and we were not retrieved, some of us began to suspect we had been deserted, left to die in that sink, thirsty and scalpless.

After three days without word a young man named Doble, of Shelby County, Indiana, proposed that we remainers set out for the diggings on our own. Errol and I were set to go when I experienced a troubling augury.

Since the time when I was very young I had experienced strange phenomena of the mind in which the visual composition of a scene before me summoned a vivid dream I had

had of the same scenario. I was then able to recall the dream,
including those depictions that had not yet happened in
the waking world. I experienced no tingling, weightlessness,
chills, nor any other of the physical sensations associated
with soothsaying. I felt only a sharpness between my eyes,
which could usually be alleviated by removing my eyeglasses
and pinching firmly the bridge of my nose.

My auguries came at random frequency, and were of random relevance. Sometimes they allowed me to see only the
coming moment, other times I might distinguish the happenings of many months hence. Most events depicted therein
were of little significance: our chickens would squabble over
a scattering of corn, my youngest sister, Mary, would ruin a
pair of our father's stockings while learning to stitch, winter would be cold. Until Carson Sink the most significant
augury I had experienced occurred at the age of eleven,
while I watched two men unload a freight wagon outside
Edward Boynton's store. I saw that a keg of brandied peaches
Boynton had received was tainted, and would make several
people ill. I alerted Boynton of this and he—already suspect-
ing this particular vendor of dishonesty—opened the keg,
found the peaches were indeed spoiled, and lobbied a refund.
I attempted to convey my condition, as I had come to consider it, to my parents, but Errol was the only who believed
me. He was the only who ever believed me.

The visual arrangement which triggered the augury at
Carson Sink was my brother's sack, partially filled, slumped
to the right, and beyond it a bare craggy peak and the white
sun, all in a line. Clear as a sketch I saw Errol and me following Doble and his company into the mountains. I saw the
wagons down in the sink where we would leave them, circled
like the spokes of a wheel. I saw three toes of my brother's

bare right foot black with frostbite. I saw man consuming man in the snow.

"What's that?" Errol said, noticing my affliction. He took me by the arm away from the others. "What have you seen?"

"We cannot go with them." I recounted for him the augury. "We'll die," I finished.

Errol tore off a sliver of fingernail with his teeth and spit it to the ground. "We'll die if we stay," he said finally.

"Likely," I admitted.

"But you say we should stay."

"Yes." I had seen his dead body in those mountains as clearly as I saw his live one before me now.

"Damn you, Joshua. How do you expect we'll get rich without ever setting foot at those diggings?"

I looked at the range, which rose out of the ground as though she knew her peaks were the only thing standing between us and those gold fields. That was the main impression I had during our travels, that the ranges of the West had a way of making you feel watched. "I only know what I've seen," I said, fearing he would strike me.

Errol regarded Doble and the others, who were near ready to depart. He sighed. "Then we stay," he said. "For now." He ordered me to return our things to the wagon. Then he approached Doble and informed him of our intent to remain in the sink. "Storm coming," he said.

Doble looked to the sky, cloudless. "Boy, leave the weather to me."

"This is not the time to cross," said Errol.

Doble scoffed. "It's barely October."

Errol returned to our wagon.

I whispered that we ought not let them go.

"You're welcome to elaborate," he said, "and risk them

shooting you to alleviate you of your madness. Kindly leave me out of it if you do."

We stayed. They went. I did not warn them. I was young and a coward, if you want to know the word. At the time I thought no fate worse than being considered a lunatic.

Errol and I watched from the valley as a tremendous storm took the range. It lasted three days, and the snow remained for ten more. Each night we built a fire and sat shuddering before it, the wagons round ours empty as fresh-built pine boxes. We did not speak of the storm nor the men up in it excepting the first day, when Errol said he would not care for a stroll in those hills right now, and I said I would not, either. That was, I think, his way of thanking me.

The report reached the diggings before we did. It went round and round and still goes round today: an expedition perished under a bad storm. The Missouri Overland Mutual Protection Association. Trapped in the mountains with nothing to eat but their own dead.

III. THE RESCUING SHE-ASS

We survived in the sink on quail which Errol shot and what scant rations the others could not carry. But both supplies and game swiftly dwindled. One night when I lay awake considering starvation and Indian ambush and cougar attack and worse, I saw shadows moving along our canvas. I remained in my ruck, petrified, not even reaching for the knife near my feet nor the musket near my sleeping brother's. The shadows grew monstrous in size until finally a dark shape loomed at the rear of the wagon. When the form emerged through the slit in the canvas, I nearly laughed aloud at my own cowardice.

It was the head of a burro. She stared at me, ears twitching, an almost intelligent expression on her long face. I donned my spectacles and climbed quietly from the wagon. I ran my hand along her coarse mane and dust rose from it. I did not recognize the animal. She likely belonged to another caravan and had been abandoned, like us.

In the dimness I saw that her back bore the black cross of Bethlehem. I traced my fingers along this coloring and felt beneath it each individual knob of her spine. I wished I had an apple to give her, or a pear. I was overcome then by the melancholy that had been accumulating in me since I left Ohio. I wrapped my arms around the beast's soft brown neck and wept. The jenny blinked her long-lashed glassy eye and began to walk. I, trail-weary and homesick and perhaps resigned to death, let her pull me along, stumbling and wetting her mange with my tears.

We walked together through sand and scrub and rock for I knew not how long. We crested a hill and then another. And then the old girl stopped. Before us, quaking in the moonlight, was the giant spherical head of a cottonwood. It was the first tree I had seen in seven hundred miles.

I ran down the hill to the tree, stumbling, and fell finally at its raised roots. Beside the cottonwood was a stream, icy and clear. I drank from it, drank and drank and drank. The water soon returned some of my faculties and I turned to account for the burro. She stood, miraculously, on the hill where I left her.

I retrieved her and we both drank. As the sun rose I rode the old girl back to the wagon, calling *hullo hullo* to Errol. The look on his face suggested he thought us a mirage, and indeed when I drew near he reached up and touched my jaw, lightly. The jenny and I led him to the cottonwood, a warm wind at our three faces. Errol took a bit of the stream in his hand. "It's meltwater," he said.

Errol wanted to set out that day but it was the Sabbath, and he surprised me by agreeing to observe it, which we had not done but once the entire journey. So Errol sat drinking beside the crick and I spoke a service, the first of my life. I knew then that the Word was my calling, but knew as well that it was too late to follow.

At dawn we loaded the jenny with our supplies and those which the others had not been able to carry. That same curiously warm chinook was with us as we followed the stream into the hills, where it branched from a mountain river throbbing with snowmelt. The river led us through the Sierra Nevada, and we spent some threatening cold days in those mountains, our burro growing so weak that we were forced to discard nearly all her load, save for the meagerest provisions and two books—the Bible and *The Odyssey*—which I insisted on keeping with me always.

Finally, she bore us to the diggings. I recall the moment we crested the last ridge on our journey. It was dusk, and lightning bugs blinked among the shrubs. I cleaned my spectacles and saw then that they were no insects but the fires of the gold fields, strung along the foothills below us. We howled in joy and exhaustion. I knelt, and asked Errol to do the same. I spoke a prayer of thanks to God and to the rescuing she-ass He'd sent us. Errol, blasphemer that he was, spoke a prayer of thanks to me.

IV. DECEPTION AT ANGEL'S CAMP

So it was that we arrived at the diggings penniless and without any equipment. Our first stop was the general store in Angel's Camp, which was at that time a log house rudely thrown together with mud. There, we had no choice but to sell our burro to the store's proprietor, a Swede who denied us a fair price, saying she was an Arkansas mule and not of the sturdier Mexican stock.

God had tested my brother with a wicked temper and a walloping hook. It was a test he often failed back home, bloodying Ohio noses and blacking Ohio eyes for no good reason I could see. I was worried he might put his pique to use here, where we had no one. I discreetly reminded my brother that we·were not in the East anymore and that this man was likely the only merchant in the entire county. Inwardly, though, I envied the way my brother could make a man cower.

So, in the first of many injustices in the territory, we sold the jenny to outfit ourselves with a fraction of the very supplies we had dumped in the Sierra: an iron pan for the outrageous sum of sixteen dollars and a shovel at the ungodly price of twenty-nine. We also purchased two red shirts, two pairs of smart-looking tan pantaloons, a tent, a sack of flour, and a shank of dried pork.

Errol sent another letter to Marjorie, which contained many standard fabrications as to our good luck and our promising claim and the clement passage overland, which despite accounts to the contrary was entirely manageable for a lady. I scribbled a postcard to our mother, telling her only the truth: that we had arrived, and that we were alive. Outfitted, we hiked three miles to the American River and established our humble camp at a sand bar where the fat-pocketed Swede had told Errol there was gold for the picking.

I had envisioned the diggings a place of desolation and solitude—such was the portrayal in the literature on the subject—and so I was rather dismayed to find that the American had other Forty-Niners populating her banks. By their accents I made out Southerners and Yanks, Pikes, Limeys,

Canadians, and Keskydees. By sight I identified Mexicans, Negroes, and Indians. A Pike who claimed he had been a riverboat captain in St. Louis informed me that the Negroes were former slaves—fugitives, though he didn't say the word. The Indians, he said, were current slaves.

Whether white or colored, every man wore the same red work shirts which Errol and I had so recently purchased, though most were by now a sort of purple with filth. Their pantaloons had gone a snuffy brown. Some had added sashes about the collar for a touch of the dude, and most of these were all but shredded with wear.

The only deviants from this diggings uniform were two Chinamen who worked the claim adjacent to ours. I had never seen a Chinaman before and I fear I gazed quite rudely at them. The two—a father and his son, whose age I estimated to be around thirteen—wore billowing yellowish frocks gathered in a queer fashion. They panned not with iron but with the same type of pointed bowls of woven straw they wore as hats. Beneath those brims were their curious slit eyes and skin so hairless and smooth as to appear made of wax. But strangest of all were the snake-like black pigtails gathered from a snatch of hair at their napes and falling down their backs. The boy's descended past his shoulders impressively. But it was a sapling compared to his father's, which was so long that when he stooped at the river its tip dipped into the green water and swayed there as he panned.

We staked our ten-by-ten claim and worked it twelve hours a day for two days, Errol at the shovel and me at the pan, then, after Errol called me a duffer, another ten days with me at the shovel and Errol at the pan. Rumor had the territory brimming with gold so handy that men had gouged their wealth from the rock with a pocketblade or a spoon. In truth the work of extracting color was of the spirit-defeating

sort, a labor which combined the various arts of canal digging, ditching, stone laying, plowing, and hoeing potatoes.
The law required us to work our claim every single day,
including the Sabbath, lest we lose our rights to it. Thus we
toiled in the freezing river and under the burning rays of the
sun from dawn to dark, day after miserable day. When finally
we went to bed I could not sleep for the pain coursing along
my back and between my shoulders. Even Errol complained,
the numbness in his hands from rotating the pan all day over-
riding his obstinate nature. When I did sleep, I woke shivering and soaked in heavy dew. Soon I was rousing myself
by scratching my body and scalp bloody where I'd been
munched by fleas and lice, which the Forty-Niners called
quicks and slows. Added to this misery was the constant
terror of those dark mountains looming behind us, shelter-
ing cougars and grizzly bears and other unknown beasts that
I sometimes heard moving through the forest in the night.

During this period we dredged only meager flakes, not
even an eighth of an ounce per day. These I stored in an
empty mustard jar. On the thirteenth day my shovel hit foreign material, making an audible metallic *tink*. Errol and I
both started. I reached into the hole with my hands to dig
but Errol pushed me aside. He scratched at the hole zealously and finally pulled up an empty whiskey bottle, proof
that our spot had already been excavated.

Errol swore and whipped the bottle into the river. He
kicked our iron pan in after it. I plunged into the frigid water
to retrieve the costly tool. I returned ashore intending to
scold my brother, but I was met by a look of such anger and
shame that I could not speak.

"We've been had, Joshua," he said. "We've been taken on
a damned ride."

He set out in the direction of Angel's Camp, cursing and

swinging at every shrub and low-hanging branch along the way. I gathered our shovel and pan and followed him, wet to my waist, goldless California dust making mud on me.

At the Swede's, Errol directed me to follow him inside and not to speak. A hearty fear came over me, and I was glad we had no weapon between us. But my brother removed his hat and greeted the Swede cordially. "Say," Errol said, after trading some pleasantries, "we came up empty at that bar down the way."

"Eh?" said the slippery Swede from beneath a mightily waxed mustache.

Errol asked whether we might have better luck upriver or down, creekside or in the dry hills, in soil yellowish or redder, and the Swede dispensed advice freely.

"One more thing," Errol said to the Swede. "Has the coach been by? With the mail?"

The Swede laughed. "You'll know when it has, boy."

Outside, Errol was visibly glum. "It will come soon," I said.

"Have you _seen_ it?" he asked excitedly.

"No," I admitted. "Only it's bound to."

Errol scowled. "Fetch our things and find me upriver."

"But he said downriver."

Errol took me by the shoulder. "Consider that man our compass, Joshua. He says downriver, we go up. He says hillside and we stay on the banks. Understand?"

V. LUMP FEVER

And so we moved upriver, and upriver further three days after that. From there we were ever on the move. In years hence I have come to believe that the rotten Swede's deception combined with the maddening stories I have described infected Errol with a specific lunacy. Lump fever, it was called at the diggings. It left my brother perpetually convinced that gold was just a claim or two above our own, that the big strike was ever around the bend. He was mad with it.

What agitated him further were the Chinamen, who followed us whenever we moved. We would establish a new camp, and sure as the California sun they would relocate to our old claim. The Chinamen moved in the night, it seemed, for when we woke it was as though they had simply materialized at our abandoned claim. I thought them humorous, with their pointed hats and billowy frocks and pigtails. But they made Errol nasty with agitation. He would emerge from the tent each morning and immediately look downriver to where the tongs were already up and working the patch we'd left. "It's an ignorant strategy," he said often. Indeed, we never saw them pull anything of value from those worked holes.

Errol and I had panned flakes enough only to partially replenish our stock of meat and flour. The rest of what we needed we bought on credit. Each morning and night I fried a hunk of pork in the same skillet we used to pan the river. After, I mixed flour in the grease to make a gray, pork-flecked porridge. I was a lacking cook, I admit, but that pork would have bested the fairest housewife. Pickled, cured or fried, the swine of California was the stinkingest salt junk ever brought around the Horn.

Errol sloughed off weight. One morning I watched him from behind as he rinsed his dish in the river. He had not yet donned his shirt and the way he was bent caused the bones of his hips to rise from his trousers in startling iliac arcs. He reminded me of a bloodhound we had once, with the same scooped-out space where meat ought to have been.

This socket movement was hypnotic, so much so that I felt compelled to run my thumb along one of those bone ridges. When I touched my brother, he jumped.

"You've gone a beanpole," I stuttered.

He held the spoon he'd been washing at my eye level. The reflection was a skeletal version of myself, bug eyes and bony nose. I reached up and touched my whiskers, scraggly thin and clumped with filth. I was unsettled by my reflection and pushed the spoon away. I resolved to shave as soon as we could afford a whetting stone.

Throughout that day and others I considered that reflection. Its most unsettling aspect was not my thinness or my griminess, but my new resemblance to Errol. I'd somehow acquired his nose, his jawline, his seriousness about the eyes. He and I had never looked particularly similar before, but we did there, in the agony of starvation and ceaseless labor. The territory had twinned us.

VI. AUGURY AT AN AGREEABLE SLOUGH

Lump fever took us into November. We would shovel and pan, shovel and pan, shovel and pan. And without fail Errol would get to looking upriver, and we would have to pick up our stakes and start anew. At the rate we were moving, we would retrace our route eastward to Ohio by spring, a notion I would have found more than acceptable, were we not certain to die on the way.

Eventually we came to a sunny slough where the water was shallow and slightly warmer than we were accustomed to. We had barely begun our endeavor when, without a word to me, Errol began to pack our things.

I was crazy with fatigue, perhaps. Instead of packing

I retrieved the mustard jar where I kept our flakes. On it I had pasted a strip of paper which I had marked from the bottom up with the names of foods available in camp: flour, salt pork, pork stew, pork and beans, roast beef and potatoes, plum duff, canned turkey with fixings, and, at the very top, oysters with ale or porter. We had never eaten above pork and beans and I reminded him of it.

"Let's work this bar awhile," I begged him. "A week, say."

Errol stood and looked to me. He made a sad clicking with his tongue. "This is not the place."

"We've been at it less than a day."

He resumed gathering our few things, including that evil keg of salt pork.

"Errol," I said.

"We haven't the time," he shouted. "Men are getting rich around us!"

"A cradle, then." I had read of men using rocking boxes during the rush down in Georgia.

Errol scoffed. "The Swede's asking a hundred dollars for one, you fool."

"We'll build our own. Work twenty times as much rock through it." I held the mustard jar, shaking it like a babe's empty rattle. "This is the place."

Errol hovered over his ruck where he was rolling it. "You're certain?" I knew what he was asking by the way he asked it. He harbored such reverence for my visions that it changed the way he spoke. "You're *certain*?" he repeated.

What I was was homesick and hungry and bone tired. But my brother made no allowances for that. "I'm certain," I said.

Errol dropped his sack and clapped me on the back. "Ho, ho!"

A more decent man would have been troubled to see his own brother go giddy at such a lie. But my conscience was waylaid by his gratitude, which caused a sudden sting in my heart. I had long known my brother had brought me to California not for my strength or my intellect or even for my company. He had brought me so that my auguries could make him rich.

I'd never found the fact troubling; it was in keeping with the way he'd been to me as long as I'd been alive. But what comfort it would have been, I thought now, if but once on this long, torturous journey he had intimated that he wanted me along to help him, because we were brothers. Brotherhood had never been on his mind, and for the first time I hated that it wasn't. I hated that he only considered me of use when the visions overtook me. And in this thinking I saw his cure and mine: I would find our gold. I would tunnel my way to his affections. I would make him love me in the way of brothers.

I removed my spectacles, pinched the bridge of my nose and closed my eyes. "I have seen it," I said. "Oh, I have *seen* it."

VII. A CRADLE AND ITS TROUBLES

Back home we could have built a cradle in two hours for two dollars. But lumber was scarce and expensive so we had no choice but to cut our own. From the Swede I procured a saw, a hammer, and some nails, all on credit. Errol and I worked steadily at the cradle for three days, a lifetime in the gold hills. Once he took a step back to assess our work, the crude box set on rockers. "I must admit," he said, "I never imagined I would be caught a bachelor fashioning a cradle in the womanless wilds." I knew about the branch of juniper he'd notched, a notch for each of the thirty-six days since he'd dispatched his last pitiful letter to Marjorie. But he seemed in good spirits as we worked, and I softened toward him. He had a winning way about him when he chose.

With the cradle finally assembled, we saw that it would indeed move more rock, that neither of us had accounted for just how much rock it was capable of moving. The problem, however, was that the cradle required constant rocking in order for the gold to be captured in the riffles while worthless sediment passed them by. For a day we tested different arrangements. First we had Errol rocking away while I attempted simultaneously to dig the pay dirt, scoop it into the hopper and pour river water over the sediment so that its finer particles might be strained through the canvas apron. Inevitably I would run out of either sediment or water and have to fetch some more, at which point the slurry would stop streaming and our momentum would be lost. The cradle, ingenious a device as it was, depended on a steadier rocking-and-pouring than we two alone could maintain.

Errol, seeing the imperfection of our new method, became frequently agitated, and would often curse me, take the shovel from my hand and push me to the handle. Attempting to man both the shovel and the bucket on his own, Errol would see quickly what I saw: our operation was a man short.

"This won't do," he said finally. "We're just rinsing the soil."

I nodded.

"We need more hands," he said.

I might have made that observation twelve long and fruitless hours earlier, were I not sure he would smash up all our hard work in a fit. "What about the Chinamen?" I said.

Errol shook his head. "I won't split with them."

"And what's our choice? Split nothing fifty-fifty. Fifty-fifty salt pork and gruel? Fifty-fifty sleeping on the ground?" I cast my shovel to the ground. Now I was agitated, and from the corner of my eye I saw the elder Chinaman pause. "Do you know what we owe that Swede?"

Errol returned me the shovel. "You don't become a man of society by keeping quarters with Orientals."

VIII. THE FIRST COACH

When we rose in the morning the diggings were deserted. I trudged sleepily up and down the bank in my long johns. The place had gone a ghost town. Upriver each claim was abandoned, pans half sifted, the wooden handles of shovels jutting like masts from where their heads had been thrust into the soil. Downriver was the same, except for the Chinamen, who worked on same as ever. I approached the father, aware that Errol was following.

"Where's everyone gone?" I said. I pointed to the manless claims. "Where are they?" The Chinaman began to speak in the tong language, which I had never heard. The sound was most bizarre and impenetrable.

Errol interrupted him. "Has there been a strike?" he said loudly.

The Chinaman pressed his lips together, then began to speak again, slowly. And again, the language was entirely incomprehensible.

"A strike! A strike!" shouted Errol, hopping and flailing his arms in the general direction of the mountains. "Has there been a strike, you old fool?"

"No strike," came a clear, effeminate voice beyond the commotion. We turned to see the boy standing on the banks, holding his pan of woven straw. "He say, 'A coach. In the night.'"

We stared like idiots.

"Mail," the boy said.

Errol took off.

"Thank you," I said to the boy. "You know 'thank you'?"

"Yes," he said.

I dressed and followed Errol along the trail to Angel's Camp. Out front of the Swede's a monstrous crowd had gathered around a stagecoach. There were men in numbers I had never seen, hundreds of men not only from our fork of the American but from all of Calaveras County. They were the roughest specimens I have ever seen, and nearly every one of them brandished a revolver or a musket.

The driver of the coach had climbed atop the cab and was arbitrating the rowdy crowd from that position. In his hands he clutched a distressingly small bundle of letters. Errol attempted to pry his way to the heart of the crowd. He pushed between men, struggling to get within shouting distance of the coach. Surely without thinking he shouldered past a ruffian at least half a rod tall with a beard grown down to his chest. The man—a Southerner—informed Errol that he had occupied that spot since before sunup and that he was unlikely to forfeit it to Errol or to anyone. For proof he showed Errol his Bowie knife.

It was then that we noticed that from the mob grew a tail of men. There were too many men to approach the coach at once, and we weaklings had been dispatched to wait in line. We followed this tail through town and out of it, finding its end finally in the woods, behind two Mexicans.

We stood in line for half a day. By the time we came back in view of the coach, emotions had reached the breaking point. Full-grown rough-and-tumbles shouted their names up to the driver and trembled while he searched his bunch. Men who had no letter waiting—and these were the majority—cursed their wives or friends or family for forgetting them. Some desperate fellows offered the coachman flakes in exchange for a missive, as if one might be conjured for the right price. But this was the one place in California where color held no sway.

Very occasionally I watched the coachman pluck a dirty, tattered envelope from his stack and hand it down. The coarse men nearest the coach took the letter as delicately as they might a baby and passed it among them until it reached its rightful owner. As the lucky man opened the letter the others moved away, as if to make room for his reading.

As we neared the coach we spotted the Southern ruffian sitting on a log, holding a letter gingerly between his massive hands. His beard was wet with tears. "Happy devil," Errol said.

By the time Errol and I approached, the deliveryman's bundle had become terribly thin.

"Boyle," Errol shouted, although it was not quite our turn. "Letter for Boyle?"

The coachman, who had by now taken a seat on the edge of the cab roof, searched his skinny bundle. It did not take long. "No letter," he said.

"You're sure?" said Errol. But the man had already solicited the next eager miner.

"Please, sir," I called out. "Check again. The name's Boyle. Errol. Or Joshua."

The coachman did check again, God bless him. "Apologies, my boy. Maybe next time."

I set out in the direction of the river. Errol did not follow me. When I turned, he was standing in the middle of Main Street, which at the time was nothing more than a dirt thoroughfare. His face was blank and he stared at the ground between us. His hands were upturned queerly, as though he carried a burden I could not see.

"Suppose I'll stay in town a bit," he said.

"And do what?" I said. But he was already shuffling toward the tavern.

"Forget her," I called. "She puts on airs."

He came at me swinging to heaven, and struck me once upside the head with a tight, demonic fist. I collapsed, hiding my head beneath my arms. I thought he would strike me again where I lay, but instead he said only, "Don't."

IX. BEASTS OF THE TERRITORY

I panned our claim halfheartedly and alone for what remained of that day, palming secretly the tender knob on my skull. By dusk Errol had not returned. I watched the sunset, gnawing on a rind of salt pork and listening to the heartsick yowls of drunken Forty-Niners. Errol was somewhere among them, I knew, blubbering about Marjorie. I cursed him. How my body complained, how my stomach wanted, how close we had both come to death how many times so he might win the good favor of a girl whose father owned a stinking soap factory!

I found his pitiful notching stick and snapped it, then snapped it again. I threw the pieces into the fire. I learned from the diggings that a love of destruction is in every man's heart, somewhere.

As darkness thickened, my thoughts went to my father. It had been nearly a year since his death and I had nothing of his to touch. I was in a wilderness where he had never set foot, where his spirit would not even know to look for me. I tried to remember everything I could about him. Anything. My freakish mind could conjure up sketches of the future but none of my father's features, not the smell or feel of him. I cried, a little.

I tried to go to bed early but the groans and rustlings of night turned sinister, if not in actuality then in my imagination. I became afraid. I rose and dressed and walked without thinking down the moist bank, to the Chinamen's camp.

The man and boy sat across their fire from each other as I approached, not speaking. Their hats were off and their heads—bald and yellow save for the thick tuft of bound hair at their napes—glowed in the firelight. There was something peaceful in their silence, and their fire was large and warm. The boy saw me first and startled. The man turned slowly, and I saw him reach for a switch at his side.

"I'm unarmed," I said, and raised my empty hands. They spoke in their language for a bit. It seemed they were trying to decipher why I'd come, or perhaps I ascribed those aims to them because I was wondering myself. Eventually the man gestured for me to sit between them.

"Cold out," I said, though it wasn't particularly. They said nothing. "Have you all been hearing those hollers?" I asked. Still, they said nothing. We watched the fire. After some time a pocket of sap popped loudly and I jumped like a Mexican bean. The elder man seemed to find this exceedingly funny. When he was through laughing, he said something to me in his language.

"He say you get a letter," said the boy.

"No," I said. "Not today."

He told his father.

"Sad," said the boy. He was only a child, I saw then, younger than I had originally estimated, but with a sharpness about the eyes that conveyed sure ripsniptiousness.

"Yes," I said.

A man yelped somewhere.

I felt the need to tell him that I didn't care for drink and the boy found this remarkable enough to relay to his father, who nodded what seemed like approval. We were quiet a little longer.

"Say," I said to the boy. "Can I ask you something?"

He nodded.

"Why have you both been following us the way you have? Why not find a claim of your own? Seems a fool's strategy to mine what's already been mined, if you will excuse my saying so."

The child conveyed my question to his father. They exchanged words for what seemed a good long time. I grew nervous. "Tell him never mind," I said.

But the boy waved his thin hand in dismissal. Finally, he turned to me. "He say too many tongs killed that way."

"Which?"

"Like you say. Find own claim."

"I don't follow."

"He say *you* find lode, men happy." He pointed to me and then to the river. "*Tong* find lode men say 'steal.' They say 'hang.'"

The old man spoke again, and the boy's gaze went to the ground.

"What did he say?" I asked.

The boy looked at me. "He say to tell you my father hang that way."

"He's not your papa?" I said, gesturing to the Chinaman. "Your father, I mean."

"He *shu fu*," said the boy. "Uncle."

So we sat, two fatherless boys, two brotherless men. We watched the fire a little longer. I thought it was perhaps time for me to go, and that I should not have come at all.

Just then the elder Chinaman spoke to the boy. In turn the boy fetched a long wooden box from the tent and delivered it to his uncle. The box had been polished up nicely and gleamed in the firelight. The Chinaman removed the carved lid and lifted a long tubular object from the box. Initially I thought the apparatus was a flute or some similar musical instrument of the Orient. The stem of it seemed to be made of a lightwood and the lower portion had been adorned with a saddle of stamped brass. On this saddle was mounted a delicately grooved bulb made of earthenware, the top hemisphere of which the Chinaman presently removed.

From the wooden box he lifted what looked like a lady's perfume bottle and deposited some of its coalish black dust into the bulb's tiny compartment. At that point it occurred to me that the device was a type of smoking pipe.

The Chinaman reattached the bulb's lid, then bent and pulled a branch from the fire by its unburned end. The lit end of the stick flickered wickishly. He held the branch in one hand and the pipe in the other and tilted the pipe so the flame rippled around the bulb. He puffed there for some time before offering it to me.

My father had been a tobacco smoker. He especially liked his pipe late at night, on the back steps. In this way the Chinaman evoked some of the memories I had been longing for. I took the apparatus. The Chinaman held the stick to the bulb and said something.

"He say breathe," said the boy. He tapped his own breastbone. "Breathe here."

The apparatus was heavier than I had imagined, and had a fine, sturdy feel. I wiped the fluted end, put my lips to it and felt that the cylinder was made not of lightwood but of ivory. I puffed as the Chinaman had and he made sounds that I interpreted as encouragement. I took what felt like a chestful and immediately my lungs revolted, setting off a great avalanche of coughs. The Chinaman laughed at this, too.

I returned the pipe and I watched the old man at it. At this proximity I could see the many wrinkles like folds at his small eyes and around his mouth. He finished his puffing and smiled, and when he did I saw that his teeth were brown and soft with rot. I tried the pipe again, with more success. He took his pigtail in his hand and brushed its end on his own palm. The boy did the same. I had a good feeling from them.

"But how do you make a living, working tailings the way you do?" I said.

The nephew smiled a devious little smile. "I find smallest gold," he said. "Smallest and smallest. I see things white men do not."

I sat with them for some time, accepting and passing the ivory instrument and listening to the two talk. Sometimes, the boy would pause to translate some of their conversation for me:

"He say winter no trouble in Gum Shan."

"He say take much care with ball of mud."

"He say tong war coming."

I did not understand what the old man meant by these, but that didn't matter. I was very warm and now pleasantly drowsy, as though I had been submerged slowly into a hot bath. I removed my glasses and held them in my hand, content to watch the blur of the fire and listen. Their language seemed a beautiful thing, something I ought to have understood.

And then the elder Chinaman began to sing.

At first he sang so softly that I wasn't sure his song wasn't something I was imagining, a trick of the fire and the river. But then the boy joined in and they raised their voices together. They sounded like instruments, their voices. I thought nothing of Errol, except to note that I felt more at ease now than I had since setting foot aboard that steamer in Cincinnati. And though the two sang in their Orient language I knew by way of feeling that their song was about fleas and lice and vultures and bluejays and marmots and coons and cougars and grizzly bears, and through their soothing melody all these once frightful and malevolent creatures streamed into my heart as though it were Noah's, and nested there harmoniously.

X. AN OPHIR, AN EDEN

I was awoken by my own sickness. It was morning and though I had no recollection of returning to my camp nor of putting myself to bed, I lay with my torso in the tent, shirtless. I managed to rise and express my queasiness in a nearby manzanita bush. Only after I rose did I see Errol.

He lay face up between the tent and the river, where he'd made a pillow of a stone. He was bare-footed, bare-headed, and bare-legged. His shirt was the only clothes upon his person. A pile of maple leaves had been assembled and arranged to conceal his parts. As I washed myself in the chilly river he woke, groaning.

Errol walked into the woods and emerged sometime later, dressed. "I've misplaced my long johns," he said.

"That is a shame," I said. "Because we've no means to replace them." I felt in no top shape myself but was not about to betray the fact to my brother. He came and looked at the salt pork I was fixing and groaned again. He smelled strongly of tanglelegs.

That morning we two worked at the cradle just as inefficiently as ever. The only difference was that Errol silently took up the harder work at the shovel. We did not speak.

Near noon he paused in his ditching, nodded to my head and said, "See here, Joshua. I apologize for that. I do. Will you just speak to me again?"

"Will you consider taking them on?" My question surprised me.

"They're filthy," he said with a wave of his hand.

"We're filthy," I said. "We've got a city of slows on each our heads. You've got no long johns."

He spit.

"We need them, Errol. All the Negroes are free. All the Indians are owned. This is a new place, Errol. They work hard and they're honest. We are Argonauts. Christians. We needn't bring the prejudices of the East with us."

"Argonauts," Errol said. "You've got a good heart, brother."

"We won't have to pay them as we would a white."

Errol said nothing.

"They work like dogs. They've been pulling dust from our old holes."

This caught my brother's attention. "Have they?"

"The boy has a keen eye."

"And how did you come by all this? Been over there, have you?"

"No." It was easier to lie to him now, after the first. I was thrilled by how easy it was. "I've *seen* it."

"You're sure about this?" said Errol.

I ought to have hesitated from guilt. But it felt good to be heeded, and to be making decisions for once. "They're there, with us." I closed my eyes. "The boy pulls a nugget."

He deliberated a moment then said, "They get fifteen percent of our findings between them. They don't sleep in our camp. They don't socialize with us."

"Agreed." I was relieved, though by logic I shouldn't have been. All I'd done was recruit men enough to better sift through rock that could very well yield nothing. But perhaps I'd come to believe my lies, too. If nothing else, I believed that if only we could stay in one place long enough, California would offer herself to us. And I liked the Chinaman. I liked his boy.

"And they don't eat with us," Errol added. "I'll gut them if they try to eat with us."

"Agreed," I said. I did not ask who in the world would want to join us for our twice-daily pork sludge.

I brokered our new arrangement through the boy. They seemed at first not to understand the proposal, but then I took them over to where Errol stood at the cradle, shoveling a load of river rock into the hopper and then doing his best to pour water over the apron and rock the mud down the riffles at the same time. At such a pathetic sight, apparently, they immediately grasped the proposed cooperation. I was less confident in my ability to explain the proposed financial terms, but they seemed to accept the fifteen percent without comment. I wonder now if they believed they had no choice.

My brother remained silent until the conversation was over. Then he handed the Chinaman the shovel.

The arrangement worked well—the Chinaman on the shovel, me on the bucket, Errol on the rocker, and the boy at the sluice, to spot color. Errol grumbled that the boy was lollygagging there and ought to be hauling pay dirt. I reminded him of the boy's sharp eyes, to which he made a vulgar remark that I will not transcribe. I am sad to say that my brother routinely unleashed the heat in his character on our Chinamen during those days. He forbade them from speaking to each other in their language. He prohibited them from donning their straw hats and insisted their robes be cinched up tightly. It was not uncommon for foreigners or Negroes to be treated so cruelly, even in Ohio. But it seemed a particular injustice in the territory, because it was a place brand new, like nothing we had ever seen, far from the achievements of civilization but also from its ugliness. California was an Ophir, not an Eden.

For two days a pair of old Pikes passing through camped near our claim. With them as audience, Errol strode over to the boy and began tugging at his robes. "Where is it?" he shouted. He turned to me. "He's pocketed a nugget. I saw him. Hand it over, you devil."

The Chinaman stopped his shoveling. The boy, fairly shaken, denied taking anything.

"Turn out your pockets," demanded Errol.

"He has none," I said. It was the truth and Errol knew it was. Still, he pilfered the folds of the boy's robe saying *dirty thief, stinking tong.* The Chinaman moved cautiously closer to Errol and the boy.

Suddenly Errol whirled around, red-faced, and pounced on the Chinaman. He drew his knife and took hold of the man's black pigtail.

I was quite frightened, and the boy was by now frantic. But the Chinaman was still. Errol put the knife to the pigtail and spoke into the man's sun-scarred face. "Are you a citizen of California or not?" he asked.

"He can't understand you," I called, trying to remain calm. "Let him be."

Errol released the Chinaman as quickly as he'd grabbed him. He returned to the sluice as if it had all been a great tease, the Pikes up the bank snarling with laughter. But it was no tease. I had heard rumors out of Hangtown of three tongs hung by their pigtails from a tree, their throats slit.

XI. THE FORTUNE FORETOLD

Despite Errol's occasional volatility, the boy was soon pulling color from the sluice. It was chispa so small and so aggregated that no white man would have ever dug it, and Errol said as much—but it was gold all the same. I directed the boy to deposit his findings in our mustard jar. In this way, little by little, day by day, we did accumulate some dust. Errol went to town whenever he had the chance, where he spent his share on card games and spirit. I spent my share on provisions. One Sabbath I had pork and beans. Another, while Errol was away, the Chinamen and I had secret roast beef and potatoes. That rump could have been the toughest, most befouled muscle ever served a man, but to my starved tongue it was gravy-slopped ambrosia.

Then, the day of the first frost, the boy approached Errol and without celebration presented him a grape-sized yellow nugget, cool with river water.

My brother did not immediately take the nugget, as I'd always imagined he would. Instead, he leapt to embrace me, taking a long, affectionate look into my anomalous, all-seeing eyes.

After some celebration, Errol spirited the nugget into the tent, pounded it carefully to test for softness, distributed a petal of the malleable color to the Chinamen and a larger leaf to me. Immediately I entertained fantasies of ordering sardines, tongue, turtle soup, lobster, cakes, and pies by the cartful, a box of juicy golden peaches. Unsettling, the way even a tiny bead of element could enchant.

Errol instructed us all to continue. "More will come," he called out merrily, barely containing his urge to wink at me. And it seemed more would come, the day we found our nug-

get, the day my brother's infinite faith intersected with coin-
cidence, the day of the first frost.

XII. WAR!

Two days later, Errol appeared by my side late one morning
and said, "There's something I want you to see."

My brother fidgeted with his hands in his pockets excitedly as I followed him to Angel's Camp. "What is it?" I asked
several times. His only reply was, "Something you'll have to
see to believe." We passed the Swede's and continued down
a small hill to where a glade flattened out. Many men were
gathered there and my heart picked up some, with fantasies
of a second mail coach or a bundle of letters lost and now
found. But near the crowd Errol halted and tapped a poster
nailed to the trunk of a pine:

War! War! War!
The celebrated Bull-killing Bear
GENERAL SCOTT
Will fight a Bull on Sunday the 15th at 12 p.m.
at Tuolumne Meadow
The Bull will be perfectly wild, young, of the Spanish breed
the best that can be found in the country
the Bull's horns will be of their natural length
NOT Sawed or Filed
Admission is $6 or one half ounce

I had heard of Spaniards hosting contests of men versus
bulls and the prospect of witnessing this even higher spectacle excited me. Errol and I hustled nearer the arena, which

was composed of tiered seats enclosed by a wood slat fence. We could not see inside. Near the entrance two fiddlers played a lively tune, and a barker lured men by extolling the ferocity of the grizzly General Scott and the virility of the Mexican bull, whom he called Señor Cortez, much to the delight of the Forty-Niners.

But heavy as my pocket was, the entrance fee was pro-hibitive. As Errol continued to the arena I called after him, "That's a costly admission."

"I knew you would say that," he said. "Follow me, cheapskate."

I pursued him to the rear of the corral where a crab-apple stood, its fruit already fallen and rotting in the grass. He climbed near to the top of the tree, then helped me up. From there we were afforded a splendid view of the arena.

"Look there," said Errol, pointing to the clearing at its center. "Your foe." There, tethered by a chain staked into the ground, was a massive grizzly bear. He scratched and scooped at the earth, his great scapulas moving like the machinery of a steam engine. He was carving a burrow for himself, it seemed. Even from our great distance we could see the thick neck shimmering, the monstrous hump at his back swaying, his knifelike claws making shreds of the meadow and the hard-packed soil. I both wished him to roar and feared that he would.

"Now that you've seen one you'll be less afraid," said Errol. I swelled with affection for him then, for I had not thought he'd noticed my fears. This was how I wanted us to be, always.

The barker was riling the crowd, playing on their terror. I scanned the bronzed and bearded faces under hats of many hues, the gay Mexican blankets and the blue and red bonnets of the French. Among all those like mirages were Mexican women in frilly white frocks, puffing on their cigaritas. Until then I had ever conceived that my wife would be a Buckeye, or perhaps a New Englander. But from where I was perched in that crabapple tree it seemed impossible to choose a bony, board-shaped descendant of the Puritans over one of these rosy, full-formed, sprightly Spaniard women.

Errol said, uncannily, "I'll marry Marjorie in a meadow like this. Beneath a tree."

"I expect so," I managed.

"I'll marry her here, then I will build us a great big house on the same spot. Soon, Angel's Camp will be bigger than San Francisco. I'll have more land than Sutter. I'll buy the Swede's store out from under him. Mr. Salter will have to buy a parcel from me. No." Glee flickered across his face. "I'll *give* him one."

Errol's gaze cast out from the tree, across the corral and the meadow and beyond. "Marj and I will have sons enough to line the American River. You'll be there, too. An uncle."

It touched me to be included like this, in both the fight and the fantasy. "And Mother," I said.

"Yes, Mother, too. And Mary and Harriet and Faith and Louisa, too. Everyone."

Then we were quiet, because we knew it would not be everyone.

By now the action below was nearly afoot. The bear General Scott had achieved a burrow several hands deep and presently he lumbered into it and lay there on his back, much in the manner of a happy baby. The crowd hated him for his merriment and screamed for the release of the bull. They stomped an infectious rhythm. Errol and I began to thump the branches of our tree, too.

From the far end of the arena came a large, muscular bull, with horns like none I had ever seen. The crowd went mute.

"Here we go," whispered Errol.

"Are they going to unchain the bear?" I asked. Errol hushed me.

Initially, the bull seemed not even to notice the bear, so one of the vaqueros jabbed the bull in the rump with a prod, sending the beast galloping from the periphery. This was when he locked eyes on the bear. He stomped and snorted a bit, and then charged General Scott where he lay in his den. I gripped my limb as the bull struck the General in his flank, sending a frightful *thunk* through the meadowland. A cheer escaped from the crowd.

The bull retreated and immediately charged again. But this time the bear affixed his powerful jaws to the bull's nose. The bull let out an unsettling cry. But the General would not relent. He latched his forepaws around the bull's thick neck and held on. I whooped, and in so doing discovered my allegiance lay with the bear General Scott.

The bull attempted to free himself by pounding the General's chest with his mighty hooves. In response, the General dug his foreclaws into the meat of the bull's brawny shoulder. Blood spurted, and Errol and I both cheered. The animals separated. Where the bull's nose had been was now only a dark cavity from which dangled stringy bloodpulp. "My," I breathed.

Errol said, "Aren't you a delicate betty?"

The bull paused, then charged again, only to be locked by the General's devastating, trap-like hug. The match went on like this, with the bull trying to hook the General and toss him out of his hole, the General gripping his antagonist and attempting to pull him down to where the bull might be ribboned. The crowd soon grew restless and booed the flagging bull. The impresario emerged, waving his hat, and announced that for $200 in gold he would release another bull. The hat was passed and the flakes raised. I heard some miners accuse the barker of saving his strongest bull to squeeze more color from them, and when the second bull was released I saw that it was likely true, for this bull stood half a rod taller than the first. His horns were twice as girthy and appeared to have been sharpened.

"Oh," said Errol, some trepidation in his voice.

With both bulls in the arena, General Scott was sorely tried. The first and smaller bull continued with his strategy of charging the grizzly and grappling with him, while the second bull attacked from the side. Soon the larger, nameless bull speared the General in his ribs and dragged him from his hole. The grizzly roared then, his long, blood-covered teeth gleaming in the November sun. It was a forlorn, haunting sound, not at all the monstrous bellow I had yearned for at the battle's onset.

Errol had gone quiet. His hand was drawn to his mouth, as was mine.

Exposed in the grassy open, the bear was a pincushion. Horns penetrated his abdomen, his ribs, his haunches and his back. One goring went into his throat and out the other side. Another stabbed his stomach and sliced up and out near the sternum, letting the bear's guts spill onto the grass. A hot fecal smell filled the air, causing the ladies to bring their kerchiefs to their mouths. There seemed no end to the blood that would spurt from this beast. Soon all the meadowland was wet with it.

The crowd had gone quiet and still, transfixed by the carnage. Finally the impresario directed his vaqueros to lasso the bulls and bring them in. He marched to the center of the arena, where General Scott lay grunting and gurgling in the mud made by his own innards, and declared the bulls the victors of the day. Without warning, he shot the General dead.

The mob slowly shuffled from the arena, no uproar or gaiety left in them. The fiddlers held their fiddle cases to their chests. Errol and I stayed unmoving at our branch perch for just a bit, the vinegar smell from the rotten apples rising all around us. When we finally climbed down, the descent reminded me of how high my spirits had been upon climbing into the tree, and how low they were now.

As we walked it began to rain and we went on, letting the rain get us. Somewhere, I thought, those señoritas are running with their lovely white dresses gathered in their hands.

After some time Errol said, "I believe that was a spectacle I would have rather prevented than witnessed."

"Me, too," I told him, and we went on in silence.

It had been easy to succumb to my own deceptions while eating plum duff and roast beef in the sunlight. But now they were suddenly undeniable. We were returning to a ten-by-ten plot of land which I had deceived my brother into believing held his fortune. I was a liar, a manipulator, and a freak. All my brother had accumulated in California was a gambler's thirst and some salty talk.

I said, "You should marry her in a church."

"Don't you know?" Errol said. The rain had stopped now, leaving all the leaves and the soil wet and fragrant and colored vividly. "This is the greatest church there is."

XIII. ORACLE BONES

I had promised that more gold would come but more gold would not come, and after that mournful battle Errol was sick with expectation. He went to town whenever he had the chance, where he spent his share of element on card games and brandy and tarantula juice.

With him gone I spent more time with the Chinamen. The little one was an ace with a stone. It was one of my favorite pastimes to skip stones across the river with him. Sometimes we three whittled miniature boats to race on the water. The elder carved using a small blade with a milky jade handle the exact color of the river at dawn. His ships were the most graceful and well designed. Some of the happiest hours of my life were spent after a whiff of the Chinaman's ivory pipe, watching those moonlit vessels spear along the nighttime water and vanish into the darkness.

Some evenings the tongs took turns shaving each other's heads with the jade knife while I read aloud from the two volumes I had to my name. (The tongs preferred Odysseus to Christ.) One night the boy interrupted my reading to ask if I might teach him. I was a frightful tutor, I fear, but his sharpness hid my inadequacies and soon he had memorized Homer's first song. *Sing to me of the man, Muse, the man of twists and turns.* He orated to his uncle, with the old one smiling dutifully, as though he understood every fine word.

One day the boy snared a deer, and that evening we sat smoking and pulling greasy venison from the spit. Full of roast meat and smoke, I found myself going on and on. I talked mostly of Errol, of the darkness I saw in him and the light I saw in him, too. Of my fear of what would become of him in the territory without me. Then, without thinking, I said to the boy, "I have peculiar vision, too. Like you at the sluice. I can see what's not yet happened. It's a condition I have. A deformity."

He translated this to his uncle, who paused at his venison shank, sifted another thatch of black powder into the bowl, and handed it to me. As I took it, he spoke through the boy.

He said, "There are many people see in all directions. At home, seers set bones in fire, read future in the cracks. These men are . . ." The boy searched for the appropriate word, settling finally for two. "A gift."

Something went through me then: a phantasm that warmed me, physically. The sensation of truly belonging in a place and a moment is a rare one. I have not felt it since.

The Chinaman had contentedly taken up his venison again. I must have gaped at it for some time, because the boy leaned toward me. "Wrong bone."

Errol never asked what I did when he was away, and I never told him. I grew more content, and he became more wretched. Often he would stay in some parlor or another until dawn, then walk the three miles back to the river and take up his post at the rocker, emitting a stench that could have felled a man at sixty rods. By now the silt had given way to orangey clay, then black rock. Each day Errol looked more deranged. This was the state of things when the second stagecoach came.

XIV. THE SECOND COACH

We heard the news from a man who hollered it across the diggings. Errol stopped his rocking, rinsed his soiled hands and face in the river, replaced his hat and said, "I have a letter to retrieve." Then he set off without a word.

The tongs continued their digging and sifting. The old man was wary of large gatherings, and rightfully so. Forty-Niners were a volatile bunch of drunkards and criminals, especially with their sentiments roused. And nothing so roused them as a mail coach.

I had to follow him. I had the sense that my brother stood at a crevasse, that the vellum keeping him on this side was as thin as a sheet of Marjorie Salter's stationery.

The stagecoach had stopped beneath the arms of a giant, leafless valley oak, and men were already gathered around it. Suddenly, I felt a pressing at my brow. The arrangement of the bare branches' veiny shadows along the side and top of the coach and the dusty pool of men's hats beneath it sent forth an augury. I saw from the beginning the wait's disappointing end. I saw Errol approach the coach, and saw him fail to receive the letter he so anxiously wanted. I pressed my hand to my forehead but took it away before my brother should notice.

The mind is a mine. So often we revisit its winding, unsound caverns when we ought to stay out.

At that moment I traveled down a long-forgotten tunnel of memory. At the end of the tunnel I found a cat. When I was nine or so, Errol twelve or thirteen, our mother let us feed a litter of barn cats. There was one for each of us children. Mine was white, with gray boots and gray, eyebrow-like markings. I called her Isabel, because I thought Isabel was the soundest name for a cat that ever there was. Errol called her Eyeballs, probably because she was a touch bulge-eyed. Each time I said *Isabel*—when I fed her or just when I went out to be with her—Errol would be right there, saying *Eyeballs, Eyeballs*. I can still hear him. And lo, the family started calling her Eyeballs, too. People took to Errol like that, even our own parents. He had a way of making you love him even while he was being cruel. I don't know why, but I think we could have been all right, Errol and I, I could have put up with his temper and his beating on me and the way he'd get quiet and mean at the smallest thing bothering him. I think I could have forgiven him all this, could have been on good terms with him come December of 1849, when we rounded the glade and saw the coach spidered with the shadows of oak limbs. I could have warned Errol of the heartbreak I saw at the coach, and maybe he would have been better able to accept it. Maybe not, but maybe so. Maybe we would not have been plunged down the dark path if only I had spoken up, or if only he had let Isabel be Isabel.

And so I stood in line watching Errol worry the brim of his hat and squatting on occasion to sift some dirt through his fingers or toss pebbles. When at last we reached the coachman Errol nudged me to indicate that I should call our name, maybe out of secret superstition or because his voice had gone with nerves. I showed surprise at the gesture, though of course I had none.

"Boyd," I called. The coachman checked his bundle.

"Here," he said, passing down a lovely vanilla-colored envelope. I reached to receive it but Errol snatched it from the driver. His hands trembled as his large fingers carefully negotiated the letter from its paper case. He was smiling. It had been a long time since I had seen him smile. Then, nearly the instant he unfolded the paper, he dropped it to the ground, where our two pairs of boots faced each other. I retrieved the letter as Errol walked away from me. *My dear sons*, it began, as I knew it would.

From there I was back in the realm of the unafflicted, where we cannot know what will come next. I expected Errol to embark on another binge, and I braced myself for it. But he set out in the direction of the river instead and I followed, losing myself in reading our mother's letter as I went. I had never been so delighted to hear of my sisters' schoolwork or the comings and goings of livestock. I read and re-read it all the way back to camp. December had crisped the air pleasantly, and the day was beautiful.

XV. THE DIGGING

That afternoon, Errol resumed his post at the rocker. His working did not soothe me. The Chinamen gave him a wide berth. Come sundown, the hour when we usually retired, Errol stayed at the rocker. I dismissed the tongs and stayed with him, clumsily shoveling and rinsing. I thought hard work might cleanse him of heartbreak and was happy to keep him in ore, if that would do it. But soon it grew so dark that there was no chance that Errol could determine the character of the sediment coming down the sluice. And anyway he was looking not at the sluice but at the stars.

Eventually I stabbed the shovel into the rock and said, "I think I'll heat some beans. Care for some?"

"No. I don't think so," said Errol, taking up the shovel. I fixed dinner and set some on his stump for him. As I ate I watched his futile efforts at the shovel, then the bucket, then the rocker, then the shovel again. He stayed at the shovel then, with his breath puffing into the cold like the stack of a steamboat. I went to bed with him still at it, figuring he would exhaust his frustrations and retire in his own time. I fell asleep to the skeletal scrape of iron against bedrock.

And in the morning I woke to it.

I emerged from our tent but Errol was nowhere in sight. I could hear his work but not see him. There was the cradle, unmanned. In the place where I had last seen him was a large mound of dirt. Beyond it, a pit. I approached. Down at the bottom of the pit was my brother, shoveling earth as steadily as he had been six hours before. The hole was likely five feet deep and vaguely rectangular. The shape of it alone frightened me, but I composed myself and adopted an air of nonchalance.

"Good morning, Errol," I called. "Would you care for some

breakfast?" I peered again into the hole. The sun was not yet very high and so Errol was mostly in shadow. His head alone was illuminated, and it seemed to hover above the darkness of the pit, disembodied. His hat was gone. I later found it buried in the pile.

"I think I'll make some flapjacks," I repeated. "Would you care to take a break for some flapjacks, Errol?" His answer was a shovelful of dark sediment, flashing in the sunlight. It seemed there was nothing to do but what I'd always done. I fixed breakfast, and when I was through I tossed Errol a warm flapjack, only to have it ejected in yet another shovel load.

My brother remained in his mine all morning. The Chinamen arrived ready to work, but I dismissed them. I stood near the lip of the pit, saying his name again and again and again, until his name went meaningless as a tong word. He never acknowledged me, only dug.

I offered him water. He dug.

I read him our sweet mother's letter. He dug.

Noon came. The hole was not so deep that Errol could not climb out—not yet—but it was deep enough now that even when he stood straight, my brother's frame was completely subterranean. I might have lain on my stomach and reached down to touch the top of his head, but I did not. He dug. The ceaseless sound of his shovel on the rock penetrated my every thought.

I flattered him. He dug.

I taunted him. He dug.

I bribed him. He dug.

I told him we could go to San Francisco and nap in feather beds. He dug.

I told him, finally, that we could return to Marjorie. He dug.

By dusk the hole had gone narrower. It was now over seven feet deep. I sat near the lip, dejected and alone. I had no one but Errol here and I suddenly felt it was very important to touch him. I lay my belly against the cool earth, inched my way to the edge of the hole and extended my arm down into it. I called softly for Errol to pause in his task for just one minute, to reach up above his head and stretch his fingers toward mine. So I could test his temperature, I said. He would not turn his face to me.

Night fell, and with it came fury. I cursed him. I stood on the edge of the hole and shouted at him. Men came down to have a look at the commotion, and I ran them off. I shrieked into the pit. I said things I had never said to anyone. Things I have not said since.

I must have slept that night, because I woke before light, shivering with frost, atop the mound he'd made. The scraping went on. The sides of the chasm sparkled with frost, too, and this brought me a strategy. I filled the bucket at the river, returned to the hole, and began trickling water down into it. "Errol," I called. "I think the river's coming in. Hear that? That's the river, old boy." He said nothing but his scraping paused, I thought.

"Don't worry, Errol. I'll get you out." I tied one end of a rope to a tree. I refilled the bucket and poured it in. Then I flung the other end of the rope into the hole and called, "Grab hold, Errol! I'll pull you up!"

The digging persisted, but now there was a watery sound beneath the sound of the shovel.

That night I sat jiggling the rope, touching the notch my brother had left in my collarbone, saying I was sorry and could he please please please please grab hold.

When morning came I gathered the heaviest rocks I could carry and assembled them in a pile near the lip. I was desperate. I intended to brain my brother, climb down the rope, tie it around him, climb up the rope, and then pull him up. Giddy images of his wilted body dangling from the rope passed through my mind at the moment I noticed a strange sound. It was silence. The absence of shovel on bedrock.

I approached the hole, bracing myself for the sight of my brother's dead body at the bottom. Instead, he sat quite alive with his back against the earth wall, as if resting after a morning's work and not three feverish days spent burying himself alive. It was noon and the sun was beaming directly into the hole. I could see his scalp burned pink where his hair had gathered in clumps, and his blistered, bloody hands. He had removed his boots and one was half submerged in the water I'd poured upon him. The rope was well above where he sat now, curled like an animal in a water-logged den.

Then, he began to sing. It was the first I'd heard his voice since he declined the now-crusted beans still awaiting him on the stump. The song was a popular one, and he sang it with an unsettling bounce:

> *Hangtown gals are plump and rosy,*
> *Hair in ringlets, fists of posy,*
> *Painted cheeks and jossy bonnets—*
> *Touch 'em and they'll sting like hornets!*

"That's a fine tune," I said when he was done. I don't know why I said it, except that it was.

Errol looked up at me, finally, squinting against the light. His face had gone gaunt and grimed and socket hollow. He did not look like himself. He said, "There's a good pile coming, Abigail."

That was our mother's name.

"I'm Joshua," I said. "Joshua. Your brother. Say Joshua."

"Sing me 'The Old Oaken Bucket.' You know that one, Abby?"

"Joshua!" I cried.

Errol reached his hand across the shaft and scraped some soil from the wall opposite him. He said, "There's a good pile coming, Abby girl."

I threw myself at the pile of rock and attempted to lift one. I intended to throw my boulders down upon him, smiting him as would the God of that hole. I did not care, at that moment, whether I stoned him to death or buried him alive. But the Lord had taken my strength. I only lay in the dirt and wept.

"Do you know 'The Old Oaken Bucket'?" whispered Errol.

"No," I said through my tears. "How does it go?" And then I passed into darkness.

XVI. A TROUT

A promise unkept will take a man's mind. It does not matter whether the promise is made by a woman or a territory or a future foretold. I know that now. But this was years ago, when I was young and felt the whole world of Errol's collapse was mine to bear. It is strange telling you this, because the boy I was feels so far away from the man I am now. I know I ought to consider that distance a blessing, given the darkness and the difficulty of the time I have described here. But it brings me no comfort to think how far I have traveled nor how much wiser I've become. Because though I was afraid and angry and lonesome much of the time, I was also closer to my own raw heart there in the territory than I have ever been since.

I woke at the China camp. It was dusk. The boy sat near me with a tin cup. Behind him was his uncle, sitting on a stump near the fire, and behind him was the dusky blue Sacramento valley with fires and lanterns burning here and there.

"Where's Errol?" I said. "Where is my brother?"

The boy handed me the tin cup. "Where you think?" He frowned, as if disappointed in himself. "He is in the earth, still."

"Is he digging?"

The boy shook his head.

"Singing?"

"No."

I got up and walked upriver to the hole and looked inside. Errol sat in the muddy water with his legs folded to his chest, alive and shivering. He had removed his shirt and tied it about his head. I jiggled the rope and called to him, but he did not answer. He was apparently through digging, and his hole had not gained any more depth. Yet he felt further from me than when last I saw him.

I returned to the Chinamen's camp and sat looking from the boy to his uncle. The old man was cleaning the blade of his jade-handled knife on his robe and chewing a stalk of grass. I wanted him to say something. I felt if he spoke he would have a way to end this thing. But he said nothing. The yellow stalk of sweetgrass bounced in his mouth.

The Chinaman sheathed his knife and stowed it in the folds of his robe. Then he reached into a bucket beside him and brought up an enormous rainbow trout. It was dead, but freshly dead, shimmering still and with that gruesome pout that dead fish have. Fish were rare on our part of the river, so many were devoured by men upstream. It was a lovely creature, and I knew the tongs must have traveled a long way to catch it.

"For Mister Errol," said the boy.

Then, at the sound of the boy's voice and the gutted shimmer of the trout in the blue dusk, the providence of the thing burst upon my mind. I saw Errol climbing up out of his hole and sitting beside the Chinamen's fire, saw us four scooping soft, steaming handfuls of fish to our mouths. It was no augury, only the visions of my own hopeful heart.

The skin of the fish sizzled wonderfully, emitting a stirring aroma as we cooked it. Surely the meal would return Errol's mind and deliver him the strength and will to reach up and take hold of the rope. I watched it fry, feeling that the rest of my life was lodged in that trout.

With the cooked fish I approached the hole. It was dark now and the moon had risen. The night was clear and the gibbous moon so bright I expected to see its reflection dancing in the water pooled at the bottom of the pit. But there was only darkness. I called to Errol.

"I fixed you dinner," I said, holding the tasty rainbow over the hole. I could not see him but I heard the earth crumble a little as he shifted, heard some stones hitting the water. "Errol, will you come up and have some trout?"

He said nothing. No matter, I thought. I was convinced that all he needed was to see the thing, to lay his hand on its soft fish belly. He would eat it, head and all, and return to me. "Look out below," I said, and dropped the trout into the darkness.

I listened at the hole for some time and heard nothing. I returned to the Chinamen's camp to wait. The boy tossed pebbles into the river and we three sat listening to the sound of them dropping into the water. "He'll die down there," I said, for I had just realized it.

I spent that night in the Chinamen's camp, stretched out on a flat sandy spot near the embers of the fire. Before sleep I resolved that at dawn I would descend into the hole, fight Errol into submission, and bring him up. He would return to me.

No sooner had I fallen off than I was awoken by the mournful roars of a grizzly.

I sat up and saw the bear, standing on its hind legs, staggering toward me. It bellowed and I scrambled along the ground away from the beast. He came at me. I saw in my mind the purple innards of General Scott strung along Tuolumne Meadow. My bowels spasmed.

Through sheer dumb habit I brought my spectacles to my face, and with them saw that the grizzly was no grizzly. It was my brother, naked and covered head to foot with black mud. His arms were raised over his head. He carried something there, as though to an Old Testament altar. He came closer. Moonglow shone upon his lips, blistered and cracked and bloody and trembling. The nail of one of his big toes was missing.

He thrust the trout into my hands. He had not eaten a bite of it. He bellowed again, and this time I understood the word.

"Gold!" he said again, pointing to the fish.

Another man would have identified this as the raving of a lunatic. But I was dazed and accustomed to heeding my brother and did so now. I examined the mangled, mudded fish. I ran my hand along its sides and lifted its fins. Once I saw one I saw them all. Thousands of tiny gold flakes lodged amongst its scales.

The Chinaman and his boy emerged from their tent. The Chinaman was bare-chested, the first I had ever seen him so. Errol pointed a filthy, trembling finger to where he stood.

"You!" he bellowed. Errol charged at the Chinaman, toppling him to the ground. The boy shouted. Up came the sounds of fist on flesh. When the men rose, Errol had the Chinaman by his throat. The Chinaman's eye was cut. He scratched frantically at Errol's hands where they held him.

"You had it all," Errol said.

The Chinaman stomped and kicked at Errol but Errol did not flinch. I stood in horror with the trout in my arms as Errol dragged the Chinaman to the river. The two descended into the slow, dark water. The Chinaman flailed wildly now, sputtering. Errol lifted the Chinaman slightly and then plunged him under the water.

I dropped the trout and ran into the river. Water filled my long johns and pulled at them. A shape moved at my side and then past me. It was the boy, plunging toward the place where his uncle was being drowned.

I did not see it immediately, only saw the boy launch himself at Errol and cling to his backside. Errol screamed and released the Chinaman and the Chinaman surfaced, gasping for air. Errol flung the boy off him. It was then that I saw the jade-handled knife still in the boy's hand where he'd been tossed, and that Errol had a long gash across his bare haunch. Errol twisted to examine the wound and as he did so it opened and out rolled a rivulet of black blood.

The Chinaman and his nephew stood on the bank, checking each other for wounds. The boy was trembling. I approached them. They watched me a moment, then fled.

Errol looked from the gash to me. He motioned for me to come to him, but I could not. "You see," he said, serenely. "They had it all along. It's so clear."

Then I fled. I could not endure the fact of his believing, believing, believing beyond the rotten end. That's all I can say about it.

XVII. EPILOGUE

When I finally came upon San Francisco Bay, it was so dense with abandoned vessels that their masts made a leafless forest atop the water. I found work as a torchboy for the Knickerbocker Five Engine Company, and with them I fought the Christmas Eve fire of 1849 and the Saint Valentine's blaze. When finally I had earned enough money I bought passage aboard a thousand-ton sidewheeler called *Apollo*, where I was the only human cargo among sacks and sacks of gold bullion. Eventually, I disembarked in Boston Harbor. I intended to return to Ohio from there, but it was many years before I was able to meet my mother, the woman whose son I had abandoned in the wilderness. I went to church, and to school. By the time I had the courage to see her I was a grown man.

While I was still in San Francisco, I read in the *California Star* that in Angel's Camp two tongs, father and son, had been captured by a mob of citizens and tried for the crime of robbery and attempted murder. They were hanged, said the report, though I knew that would be their fate the night I sat hiding in the woods above Sacramento, listening to nocturnal beasts moving through the scrub, when the snow ring around the gibbous moon triggered my final augury. The *Star* reported that the tong boy recited a passage of Homer before he was killed.

In the years following the Rush, it became fashionable for Easterners to decorate their parlors with gilt-framed daguerreotypes of Forty-Niners. In these years I've seen many such portraits of Argonauts posed proudly with pan or pick or troy scale, their whiskers cut back in a semblance of civility. Each time I encounter one I hope to see my brother in it, although I know it is unlikely he ever had himself pictured off. It is a false art, I realize. Most of the men used props on

loan from the portraitist. Some were models sitting before
drop cloths in New York City. But a great deal of what I
like about those faddish daguerreotypes is that they show no
trace of the darkness I remember of the diggings, none of the
loneliness or the madness or the hunger. Even the pistols in
the men's belts seem tucked there in jest. I'd very much like
to see my brother there someday, in his red miner's shirt with
his hat tipped back, a fresh sash at his collar, brandishing a
fine new pickaxe and a lump. I'd like to see him poised at the
center of a gleaming gilded frame, as if color was every bit as
bountiful as we'd been told. I'd like to see him posed with his
endless belief and at last surrounded by bright soft gold. And
maybe if I saw him there I might see the Argonaut believer
within myself, too, for we looked so similar in the territory.

What I now know of Errol I know from a postcard he sent
our mother twenty-five years ago, which was postmarked
Virginia City, NT, and said only that the Lode had a hold
of him.

EDITOR ACKNOWLEDGMENTS

Many good people championed the writers in these pages and sent terrific stories my way. I am especially grateful to Matt Bell, Mary Gaitskill, Rivka Galchen, Justin Taylor, Rob Spillman, Kate Zambreno, Blake Butler, Thalia Field, Gary Fisketjon, Joshua Cohen, Heidi Julavits, Sam Lipsyte, Deborah Eisenberg, Rebecca Curtis, Martin Riker, Ethan Nosowsky, Brian Evenson, Halimah Marcus, Ann DeWitt, David McLendon, Calvert Morgan, and Max Porter.

Andrew Eisenman was a sharp and relentless scout from the beginning. He built exhaustive lists, chased down stories, and offered intelligent persuasion when I most needed it.

Thanks to Ryan Smernoff, who helped prepare the manuscript.

To Peter Mendelsund, thank you once again for your stunning work.

Denise Shannon, in a twenty-year streak of generous, smart, and deeply supportive acts, helped me navigate the dark, arid land of permissions, which sometimes seemed conceived solely to prevent anthologies like this one from ever coming into being.

Huge thanks to Tim O'Connell, for inspired editorial guidance and the endless, intelligent determination to get this book right.

Thank you to Kathleen Cook, Aja Pollock, Stephanie Moss, and all the other folks at Vintage who helped me get this book from manuscript to beautifully printed page.

And Jordan Pavlin's fierce belief in the short story as an art form made this book possible in the first place: thank you for everything.

CONTRIBUTOR BIOS

DONALD ANTRIM is the author of the novels *Elect Mr. Robinson for a Better World*, *The Hundred Brothers*, and *The Verificationist*; a memoir, *The Afterlife*; and a collection of stories, *The Emerald Light in the Air*. He contributes fiction and nonfiction to *The New Yorker*, and his work has appeared in *The Paris Review* and *Harper's*. He has had fellowships from the National Endowment for the Arts, the MacArthur Foundation, and the John Simon Guggenheim Memorial Foundation. He lives in Brooklyn, New York.

JESSE BALL is the author of five novels—*Samedi the Deafness*, *The Way Through Doors*, *The Curfew*, *Silence Once Begun*, and *A Cure for Suicide*—as well as several works of verse, bestiaries, and sketchbooks. His prizes include the 2008 *Paris Review* Plimpton Prize for Fiction, and his verse has been included in the *Best American Poetry* series. He is on the faculty at the School of the Art Institute of Chicago's MFA in Writing program.

NOVIOLET BULAWAYO is the author of *We Need New Names*, winner of the Los Angeles Times Book Prize's Art Seidenbaum Award for First Fiction, the PEN/Hemingway Award, and the National Book Foundation 5 Under 35 fiction selection. *We Need New Names* was shortlisted for the Man Booker

Prize and the Guardian First Book Award, and included on the *New York Times* 100 Notable Books of 2013 list and the Barnes & Noble Discover Great New Writers list. Bulawayo attended Cornell University and Stanford University, where she now teaches as a Jones Lecturer in Fiction.

KYLE COMA-THOMPSON is the author of *The Lucky Body*. He lives in Louisville, Kentucky.

ROBERT COOVER has published fourteen novels, three short-story collections, and a collection of plays since *The Origin of the Brunists* received the William Faulkner Foundation Award for notable first novel in 1966. At Brown University, where he has taught for more than thirty years, he established the International Writers Project, a program that provides an annual fellowship and safe haven to endangered international writers who face harassment, imprisonment, and suppression of their work in their home countries. In 1990–91, he launched the world's first hypertext fiction workshop, in 1999 was one of the founders of the Electronic Literature Organization, and in 2002 created Cave Writing, the first writing workshop in immersive virtual reality.

LUCY CORIN is the author of the short-story collections *One Hundred Apocalypses and Other Apocalypses* and *The Entire Predicament* and the novel *Everyday Psychokillers: A History for Girls*. She was the 2012 John Guare Fellow in Literature at the American Academy in Rome. She teaches at the University of California, Davis.

REBECCA CURTIS is the author of *Twenty Grand: And Other Tales of Love and Money* (HarperPerennial) and has been published in *The New Yorker, Harper's, McSweeney's, NOON,* and other magazines. Curtis received her bachelor's degree from Pomona College in California. She also holds a Master's of Fine Arts from Syracuse University and a Master's of English from New York University.

LYDIA DAVIS is the author of *The Collected Stories of Lydia Davis,* a translation of Gustave Flaubert's *Madame Bovary,* a chapbook entitled *The Cows,* and a poem in *Two American Scenes* entitled "Our Village." In 2013, she was awarded the Man Booker International Prize for fiction, and her most recent collection of stories, *Can't and Won't,* was published in 2014 by Farrar, Straus and Giroux.

DON DELILLO is the author of fifteen novels, including *Falling Man, Libra,* and *White Noise,* and three plays. He has won the National Book Award, the PEN/Faulkner Award for Fiction, and the Jerusalem Prize. In 2006, *Underworld* was named one of the three best novels of the last twenty-five years by *The New York Times Book Review,* and in 2000 it won the William Dean Howells Medal of the American Academy of Arts and Letters for the most distinguished work of fiction of the past five years.

ANTHONY DOERR is the author of two story collections: *The Shell Collector,* which won the Rome Prize in 2004, and *Memory Wall,* which won the Story Prize in 2011. His most recent novel, *All the Light We Cannot See*, was a finalist for the National Book Award. He lives in Boise, Idaho, with his wife and sons.

DEBORAH EISENBERG's four collections of short fiction are available in one volume, *The Collected Stories of Deborah Eisenberg*. She is also the author of a play, *Pastorale*. She is a MacArthur Fellow and teaches at Columbia University.

MARY GAITSKILL is the author of four novels: *Two Girls, Fat and Thin*, *Veronica*, and *The Mare*, which is forthcoming from Knopf. She has also written three story collections: *Bad Behavior*, *Because They Wanted To*, and *Don't Cry*. Her work has been translated into more than a dozen languages. She has been a Guggenheim Fellow, a New York Public Library Cullman Center Fellow, and a Civitella Ranieri Fellow. She lives in Brooklyn.

RIVKA GALCHEN is an essayist and fiction writer whose work appears regularly in *Harper's*, *The New Yorker*, and *The New York Times*. She is the author of the award-winning novel *Atmospheric Disturbances* and the short-story collection *American Innovations*.

RACHEL B. GLASER is the author of the story collection *Pee on Water*, the poem book *MOODS*, and the novel *Paulina & Fran*. She lives in Northampton, Massachusetts, and teaches creative writing at Flying Object. She tweets as @Candle_face and @FriendsOnMars.

DENIS JOHNSON is the author of nine novels, one novella, one book of short stories, three collections of poetry, two collections of plays, and one book of reportage. His novel *Tree of Smoke* won the 2007 National Book Award.

REBECCA LEE is the author of *Bobcat*, a collection of stories, and *The City Is a Rising Tide*, a novel. Her fiction has been read on NPR's *Selected Shorts*, and her stories have been published in *The Atlantic Monthly* and *Zoetrope*. She teaches creative writing at the University of North Carolina at Wilmington.

YIYUN LI is the author of *A Thousand Years of Good Prayers*; *The Vagrants*; *Gold Boy, Emerald Girl*; and *Kinder Than Solitude*. She is the recipient of a MacArthur Foundation fellowship, the Frank O'Connor International Short Story Award, the PEN/Hemingway Award, and the Guardian First Book Award, among others. *Granta* named her one of the best American novelists under thirty-five, and *The New Yorker* named her one of twenty American writers under forty to watch. Her work has been translated into more than twenty languages and has appeared in *The New Yorker*, *A Public Space*, *The Best American Short Stories*, *The O. Henry Prize Stories*, and elsewhere. She teaches writing at the University of California, Davis.

TAO LIN is the author of the novels *Taipei*, *Richard Yates*, and *Eeeee Eee Eeee*; the novella *Shoplifting from American Apparel*; the story collection *Bed*; and the poetry collections *Cognitive-Behavioral Therapy* and *you are a little bit happier than i am*.

His most recent book is *Selected Tweets,* a collaboration with Mira Gonzalez. He lives in New York City, and is at taolin.info.

KELLY LINK is the author of the collections *Get in Trouble, Stranger Things Happen, Magic for Beginners,* and *Pretty Monsters.* She and Gavin J. Grant have co-edited a number of anthologies, including multiple volumes of *The Year's Best Fantasy and Horror* and, for young adults, *Monstrous Affections.* She is the cofounder of Small Beer Press. Her short stories have been published in *The Magazine of Fantasy and Science Fiction, The Best American Short Stories,* and *The O. Henry Prize Stories.* She has received a grant from the National Endowment for the Arts. Link was born in Miami, Florida. She currently lives with her husband and daughter in Northampton, Massachusetts.

SAM LIPSYTE is the author of three novels and two short-story collections. His fiction has appeared in *The New Yorker, Harper's, The Paris Review, Tin House, NOON, The Quarterly,* and *The Best American Short Stories.* He won the first annual Believer Book Award and was a Guggenheim fellow. He lives in New York City, where he teaches at Columbia University's School of the Arts.

MAUREEN F. MCHUGH has lived in New York; Shijiazhuang, China; Ohio; Austin, Texas; and now lives in Los Angeles, California. She is the author of two collections of stories— *Mothers & Other Monsters* and *After the Apocalypse*—and four novels, including *China Mountain Zhang* and *Nekropolis.* McHugh has also worked on alternate-reality games for *Halo 2*, the Watchmen, and Nine Inch Nails, among others.

DONALD RAY POLLOCK, recipient of the 2009 PEN/Robert Bingham Fellowship, made his literary debut in 2008 with the critically acclaimed story collection *Knockemstiff*. He worked as a laborer at the Mead Paper Mill in Chillicothe, Ohio, from 1973 to 2005. He holds an MFA from Ohio State University. His work has appeared in, among other publications, *EPOCH*, *Granta*, and *The New York Times*.

GEORGE SAUNDERS's most recent book of fiction, *Tenth of December*, which spent fourteen weeks on the *New York Times* bestseller list, won the inaugural Folio Prize in 2013 (for the best work of fiction in English) and the Story Prize (best short-story collection) and was a finalist for the National Book Award. He has received MacArthur and Guggenheim fellowships and the PEN/Malamud Prize for Excellence in the Short Story, and was recently elected to the American Academy of Arts & Sciences. He teaches in the creative writing program at Syracuse University.

SAÏD SAYRAFIEZADEH was born in Brooklyn and raised in Pittsburgh. He is the author of the story collection *Brief Encounters with the Enemy*, which was a finalist for the PEN/Robert W. Bingham Fiction Prize, and the memoir *When Skateboards Will Be Free*. His short stories and personal essays have appeared in *The New Yorker*, *The Paris Review*, *Granta*, *McSweeney's*, *The New York Times*, and *The Best American Nonrequired Reading*. He is the recipient of a Whiting Writers' Award for nonfiction and a fiction fellowship from the Cullman Center for Scholars and Writers. He lives in New York City.

CHRISTINE SCHUTT is the author of two short-story collections and three novels. Her first novel, *Florida*, was a National Book Award finalist; her second novel, *All Souls*, a finalist for the 2009 Pulitzer Prize. A third novel, *Prosperous Friends*, was noted in *The New Yorker* as one of the best books of 2012. Among other honors, Schutt has twice won the O. Henry Award. She is the recipient of a New York Foundation of the Arts Fellowship and a Guggenheim Fellowship. Schutt lives and teaches in New York.

ZADIE SMITH was born in north-west London in 1975. Her first novel, *White Teeth*, was the winner of the Whitbread Award for First Novel, the Guardian First Book Award, the James Tait Black Memorial Prize for Fiction, and the Commonwealth Writers' First Book Award. Her second novel, *The Autograph Man*, won the Jewish Quarterly–Wingate Literary Prize. Zadie Smith's third novel, *On Beauty*, was shortlisted for the Man Booker Prize and won the Commonwealth Writers' Best Book Award (Eurasian Section) and the Orange Prize for fiction. Her most recent novel, *NW*, was published in 2012 and has been shortlisted for the Royal Society of Literature Ondaatje Prize and the Women's Prize for Fiction.

MATHIAS SVALINA is the author of five books, including *Destruction Myth*, *Wastoid*, and a collaborative book with the photographer Jon Pack, *The Depression*. He lives in Denver, Colorado, where he has taught at universities and in DIY spaces and prisons. He is an editor for the independent poetry press Octopus Books and runs a Dream Delivery Service.

WELLS TOWER is the author of *Everything Ravaged, Everything Burned*, a collection of short fiction. Tower was the recipient of the *Paris Review*'s Plimpton Prize for Fiction, the New York Public Library's Young Lions Fiction Award, a National Magazine Award for fiction, and was included in the *New Yorker*'s list of twenty promising writers under forty. Tower's writing has appeared in *The New Yorker*, *Harper's*, *GQ*, *McSweeney's*, *The Paris Review*, *The Best American Short Stories*, and elsewhere.

DEB OLIN UNFERTH is the author of the memoir *Revolution*, finalist for the National Book Critics Circle Award; the story collection *Minor Robberies*; and the novel *Vacation*, winner of the Cabell First Novelist Award. Her work appears in *Harper's*, *The New York Times*, *McSweeney's*, and *NOON*. She has received three Pushcart Prizes and grants from the Creative Capital Foundation. She is an associate professor at the University of Texas at Austin. Her next collection is forthcoming from Graywolf Press.

CLAIRE VAYE WATKINS is the author of *Battleborn*, winner of the Story Prize, the Rosenthal Family Foundation Award from the American Academy of Arts and Letters, and a Silver Pen Award from the Nevada Writers Hall of Fame. Her stories and essays have appeared in *Granta*, *One Story*, *The Paris Review*, *Ploughshares*, *Glimmer Train*, *Best of the West 2011*, *Best of the Southwest 2013*, and elsewhere. A graduate of the University of Nevada, Reno and the Ohio State University, Claire teaches at Bucknell University. Her first novel, *Gold, Fame, Citrus*, is forthcoming from Riverhead Books.

JOY WILLIAMS's most recent book is *The Visiting Privilege: New and Collected Stories*. She is the author of four novels—the most recent, *The Quick and the Dead*, was a finalist for the Pulitzer Prize in 2001—and three earlier collections of stories, as well as *Ill Nature*, a book of essays that was a finalist for the National Book Critics Circle Award for criticism. Among her many honors are the Rea Award for the Short Story and the Strauss Living Award from the American Academy of Arts and Letters. She was elected to the Academy in 2006.

CHARLES YU is the author of *How to Live Safely in a Science Fictional Universe*, which was a *New York Times* Notable Book and named one of the best books of the year by *Time* magazine, as well as the story collections *Third Class Superhero*, for which he was named one of the National Book Foundation's 5 Under 35, and his most recent collection, *Sorry Please Thank You*. He lives in southern California with his family.

PERMISSIONS ACKNOWLEDGMENTS

Grateful acknowledgment is made to the following for permission to reprint previously published material:

Donald Antrim: "Another Manhattan" from *The Emerald Light in the Air* by Donald Antrim, copyright © 2014 by Donald Antrim. Reprinted by permission of Farrar, Straus and Giroux, LLC.

Jesse Ball: "The Early Deaths of Lubeck, Brennan, Harp, and Carr" by Jesse Ball. Reprinted by permission of Jesse Ball.

NoViolet Bulawayo: "Shhh" from *We Need New Names* by NoViolet Bulawayo, copyright © 2013 by NoViolet Bulawayo. Reprinted by permission of Little, Brown and Company.

Kyle Coma-Thompson: "The Lucky Body" from *The Lucky Body* by Kyle Coma-Thompson (Dock Street Press, 2013). Reprinted by permission of Dock Street Press.

Robert Coover: "Going for a Beer" by Robert Coover, copyright © 2011 by Robert Coover (originally published in *The New Yorker*, March 2011). Reprinted by permission of Robert Coover.

Lucy Corin: "Madmen" by Lucy Corin. Reprinted by permission of Lucy Corin.

Deb Olin Unferth: "Wait Till You See Me Dance" by Deb Olin Unferth (originally published in *Harper's Magazine*, July 2009). Reprinted by permission of Deb Olin Unferth.

Claire Vaye Watkins: "The Diggings" from *Battleborn* by Claire Vaye Watkins, copyright © 2012 by Claire Vaye Watkins. Reprinted by permission of Riverhead Books, an imprint of Penguin Random House LLC.

Joy Williams: "The Country" by Joy Williams, copyright © Joy Williams (originally published in *Tin House*). All rights reserved. Reprinted by permission of Amelia Atlas, agent on behalf of Joy Williams.

Charles Yu: "Standard Loneliness Package" from *Sorry Please Thank You: Stories* by Charles Yu, copyright © 2012 by Charles Yu. All rights reserved. Reprinted by permission of Pantheon Books, an imprint of the Knopf Doubleday Publishing Group, a division of Penguin Random House LLC.

ALSO EDITED BY

BEN MARCUS

THE ANCHOR BOOK OF NEW AMERICAN STORIES

"In twenty-nine separate but ingenious ways, these stories seek permanent residence within a reader. . . . If we are made by what we read, if language truly builds people into what they are, how they think, the depth with which they feel, then these stories are, to me, premium material for that construction project. You could build a civilization with them."   —Ben Marcus, from the Introduction

Award-winning author of *Notable American Women* and *Leaving the Sea* Ben Marcus brings us this engaging and comprehensive collection of short stories that explore the stylistic variety of the medium in America today, featuring stories by George Saunders, A. M. Homes, Jhumpa Lahiri, Mary Gaitskill, David Foster Wallace, and more.

Anthology

ANCHOR BOOKS
Available wherever books are sold.
www.anchorbooks.com